LONE STAR
LITERATURE

LONE STAR LITERATURE

*From the Red River
to the Rio Grande*

Edited by Don Graham

W. W. Norton & Company
New York London

Copyright © 2003 by Don Graham

Since this page cannot legibly accommodate all the copyright notices,
pp. 727–33 constitute an extension of the copyright page.

Manufacturing by the Haddon Craftsmen, Inc.
Book design by Anna Oler

Library of Congress Cataloging-in-Publication Data

Lone Star literature : from the Red River to the Rio Grande /
edited by Don Graham.— 1st ed.
p. cm.
ISBN 0-393-05043-2
1. American literature—Texas. 2. Texas—Literary collections. 3. Texas.
I. Graham, Don, 1940–
PS558.T4L66 2004
810.9'32761—dc22

2003016321

W. W. Norton & Company, Inc., 500 Fifth Avenue, New York, N.Y. 10110
www.wwnorton.com

W. W. Norton & Company Ltd., Castle House, 75/76 Wells Street, London W1T 3QT

1 2 3 4 5 6 7 8 9 0

For Michael Wilding
and
Lyndy Abraham

". . . I must say as to what I have seen of Texas, it is the garden spot of the world."

—*David Crockett, letter, January 9, 1836*

"If I owned Texas and Hell, I would rent out Texas and live in Hell."
—*Philip H. Sheridan, remark,*
Officers' Mess, Fort Clark, Texas, 1855

CONTENTS

———⋆———

Foreword by Larry McMurtry   13

Introduction   15

Acknowledgments   21

THE WEST

———⋆———

ANDY ADAMS   *A Dry Drive*   25

JAMES EMMIT MCCAULEY   *Headed for the Setting Sun*   34

JOHN A. LOMAX   from *Adventures of a Ballad Hunter*   44

O. HENRY   *Art and the Bronco*   52

SALLIE REYNOLDS MATTHEWS   *The Stone Ranch*   65

WALTER PRESCOTT WEBB   *The Texans Touch the Plains*   77

J. EVETTS HALEY   *Graveyard of the Cowman's Hopes*   84

DOROTHY SCARBOROUGH   from *The Wind*   90

HALLIE CRAWFORD STILLWELL   *The Bride*   104

GERTRUDE BEASLEY   from *My First Thirty Years*   115

J. FRANK DOBIE   *Bogged Shadows*   126

A. C. GREENE   *The Girl at Cabe Ranch*   132

JOHN GRAVES   *The Last Running*   143

DAVE HICKEY   *I'm Bound to Follow the Longhorn Cows*   160

THE SOUTH
───── ★ ─────

KATHERINE ANNE PORTER   *The Grave*   177

GEORGE SESSIONS PERRY   *Hold Autumn in Your Hand*   185

ROY BEDICHEK   from *Adventures with a Texas Naturalist*   192

WILLIAM A. OWENS   *Hangerman John*   196

C. C. WHITE   from *No Quittin' Sense*   211

WILLIAM HUMPHREY   *A Voice from the Woods*   219

BILL BRETT   *The Way It Was—Southeast Texas, 1915*   232

ROBERT A. CARO   *The Sad Irons*   235

ROBERT FLYNN   *The Saviour of the Bees*   247

MARY LADD GAVELL   *The School Bus*   255

THE BORDER
───── ★ ─────

JOHN HOUGHTON ALLEN   from *Southwest*   263

AMÉRICO PAREDES   *The Hammon and the Beans*   272

BENJAMIN ALIRE SÁENZ   *Exile*   278

PAT CARR   *An El Paso Idyll*   287

RAY GONZALEZ   *Peace Grove*   308

DAGOBERTO GILB   *The Death Mask of Pancho Villa*   314

ELMER KELTON   *North of the Big River*   324

JIM SANDERSON   *Commerce Street*   335

TOMÁS RIVERA   *The Portrait*   350

✓ ROLANDO HINOJOSA-SMITH   *The Gulf Oil-Can Santa Claus*   355

JAMES CRUMLEY   *Whores*   361

LARRY MCMURTRY   from *The Last Picture Show*   377

PETER LASALLE   *A Guide to Some Small Border Airports*   388

SANDRA CISNEROS   La Fabulosa: *A Texas Operetta*   407

TOWN AND CITY
—————— ✶ ——————

BILLY LEE BRAMMER   from *The Gay Place*   411
EDWIN SHRAKE   from *Strange Peaches*   428
LAWRENCE WRIGHT   *Something Happens*   438
GARY CARTWRIGHT   *Who Was Jack Ruby?*   449
JOE BOB BRIGGS   *How I Solved the Kennedy Assassination*   469
DONALD BARTHELME   *I Bought a Little City*   486
RICK BASS   *Redfish*   493
HARRYETTE MULLEN   *Bad Girls*   502
RAFAEL CASTILLO   *The Battle of the Alamo*   505
SHELBY HEARON   from *A Prince of a Fellow*   515
CAROLYN OSBORN   *My Brother Is a Cowboy*   527
JAMES HOGGARD   *The Scapegoat*   547
CLAY REYNOLDS   *A Train to Catch*   563
NAOMI SHIHAB NYE   *Tomorrow We Smile*   589
BETSY BERRY   *Family and Flood*   596
PAT ELLIS TAYLOR   *Leaping Leo*   615
MARY KARR   from *The Liars' Club*   626
LARRY L. KING   *Playing Cowboy*   631
AARON LATHAM   *The Ballad of the Urban Cowboy*   645
DON WEBB   *Metamorphosis No. 5*   667
STEPHEN HARRIGAN   *What Texas Means to Me*   676
BETTY SUE FLOWERS   *Why Texas Is the Way It Is*   692
MOLLY IVINS   *Texas Women: True Grit and All the Rest*   698
KINKY FRIEDMAN   *Social Studies*   704
WILLIAM C. GRUBEN
    The Last History Ever of Fatigue in Texas   708

Notes on Contributors   713
Credits   727

FOREWORD

———————— ⭐ ————————

T HE MAKING OF ANTHOLOGIES IS NOT A TASK FOR THE
faint-hearted. It always involves reducing an overabundance
of material to something that can fit between the covers of a
normal-sized book, which means leaving out this, that, and the other;
inevitably there will be readers who would like to have seen this, that,
or the other in preference to what has been included.

There's nothing in this collection that I would want to see
excluded: I might just say that I'm particularly glad to see pieces by
three old-timers whose works are far from easy to excerpt: the rather
rambling essayist Roy Bedichek and the distinguished if very different
historians J. Evetts Haley and Walter Prescott Webb. Despite Haley's
controversial politics he wrote some of the best prose of any Texas
writer of the '40s and '50s.

All anthologies, of course, involve compromises on the editor's part.
Even the World Wide Web hasn't rendered editors omniscient
or publishers openhanded. Don Graham is probably as familiar
with Texas literature in all its protean forms as anyone now writing;

he's produced an anthology of the necessary breadth and catholicity to contain at least something from the many cultures and sub-cultures that have contributed to Texas literature during the last century. Grumpy indeed would be the reader who didn't find much to enjoy.

—Larry McMurtry

INTRODUCTION

─────── ⭐ ───────

S TEPHEN F. AUSTIN, DREAMER, IMPRESARIO, FATHER OF Texas, and jailbird, made a most curious remark in a letter he wrote from his cell in Mexico City (February 6, 1835): "I hope that a dead calm will reign over Texas for many years to come—and that there will be no more excitements whatever." His wish could hardly have been farther from the mark, for within a year Texas would be launched upon excitements enough to thrill the ages. In the space of a few months in the spring of 1836, Colonel William B. Travis, Davy Crockett, Jim Bowie, and a hundred and eighty or so other men died in defense of an old mission called the Alamo, in San Antonio; Colonel James W. Fannin's command was wiped out at Goliad; and Sam Houston's ragtag army vanquished Santa Anna at San Jacinto—all are the stuff of legend. The national press celebrated these events, and the mythmaking was off and running. It hasn't stopped since. Here is a brief list of what makes Texas *Texas*, besides the Alamo: (1) the Republic, (2) the Texas Rangers (the law enforcement agency, not the lamentable baseball team), (3) cattle drives, (4) King Ranch, (5) oil, (6) the Kennedy assassination, (7) LBJ, (8) movie/TV imagery, (9) George W. Bush.

The consequences for literature have been formidable mainly because both outsiders and sometimes Texans themselves often seem to expect if not prefer the stereotypes instead of the actual complexity and diversity of Texans. Most states aren't burdened by heavy accretions of myth. There is presumably no Iowa Mystique, for example. But all one has to do is say the word *Texas* and a host of clichés gallop into view: cowboys, vast plains, cattle, six-shooters, oil wells, big hair, etc. It is amazing how many people still derive their views of Texas from *Giant, The Last Picture Show*, and the TV show *Dallas*.

Although Texas is today largely an urban state with a population greater than that of Australia, many outsiders view it as a site of backwardness, yahoo manners, and a source of embarrassment. A commentary in the British magazine *The Economist* (April 4, 1998) is pretty typical of how Texas appears to visitors. A writer—probably British though no name was given—attended the Texas Book Festival, an annual event organized by Laura Bush when George W. was governor. The writer—let us call him/her "Anon"—had this to say about the reading habits of Texans: "Even educated Texans have often preferred insubstantial humour books and western pulp fiction to 'highfalutin' writing." Pass the grits, Ma. In point of fact, even the founding Texans were able to read and write. Astonishing but true. Sam Houston could recite yards of Alexander Pope's translation of *The Iliad*, and Mirabeau B. Lamar, second president of the Republic, wrote poetry. Not very good poetry, but verse nonetheless.

Not to pick too much on Anon, who is woefully uninformed, but less than a mile from the state capitol, where the festival was held, stands the Harry Ransom Humanities Research Center. It houses more British books and manuscripts by authors such as James Joyce, Virginia Woolf, and Samuel Beckett than Anon has doubtless ever seen or read.

Katherine Anne Porter, a Texas author not mentioned by Anon, illustrates a literary dimension of Texas that is sometimes overlooked. A writer of international renown, winner of the Pulitzer Prize and the

National Book Award, and a native of Kyle, Texas, twenty miles south of Austin (her childhood home is now a national historical monument), Porter is not mentioned in Anon's learned account because (A) Anon is unaware of her Texas origins or (B) KAP does not fit the Texas stereotype, being a woman, not a cowgirl, and a Southern-oriented Texan, not a rancher's wife. To take her own interest in literature as one example of Texans' reading tastes, Porter, in 1915, in the sleepy little seacoast town of Corpus Christi, purchased a copy of *Tender Buttons*, Gertrude Stein's path-breaking volume of modernist prose. Books have a way of finding their audiences, even down in Texas.

Texas readers and writers have always read books from other cultures, other places. J. Frank Dobie, once the best known Texas writer, author of many of those books on topics that Anon would like to saddle all Texans as preoccupied with—longhorns, mustangs, rattlesnakes, vaqueros, etc.—read avidly, all his life. Among his constant favorites were the English Romantic poets and Victorian essayists. Larry McMurtry, the state's foremost author and intellectual, deals in fine books with a stock of 250,000 titles and has made his hometown of Archer City into a Texas version of Hay-on-Wye. McMurtry's home itself contains 21,000 volumes, and one room alone is filled with books about rivers. So not everybody in Texas is out in the barn yukking it up with crude humor books or dusty shoot-'em-ups. Not then, not now.

While the power of the mythology has been undoubtedly a problem for some Texas writers, causing them at times to write uncritically, to think in clichés and stereotypes, and to recycle local color for its own sake, a number of Texas writers have tapped into the stirring days of yesteryear to produce works of great quality. To name the most obvious, Larry McMurtry's *Lonesome Dove*, a glorious, gritty epic of the trail-drive era, stands first among Westerns and rivals classics such as *Moby Dick*. And of the hundreds of Alamo novels, Stephen Harrigan's *The Gates of the Alamo* goes a long way toward redeeming the obsession of writers and historians with the story of the old mission where Texas was paradoxically born out of blood and defeat. There are other novelistic appropriations of Texas history worth naming: Edwin Shrake's down-and-dirty recreation of Dallas in November 1963, recorded unflinchingly in *Strange Peaches*; John Graves's much admired narrative of a canoe trip into time, history, and nature, in *Goodbye to a River*; Cormac McCarthy's Melvillian masterpiece of American madness on the frontier in *Blood Meridian, Or the Evening Redness in the West*; James Carlos Blake's ultraviolent novel, *In the Rogue Blood*, which restages the Mexican War of 1846–1848; and Américo Paredes's excavation of the often ignored border troubles of 1914–1915 along the Rio Grande in South Texas, in *George Washington Gómez*. Numerous other titles might be brought forward as instances of writers working with Texas history in a highly inventive literary manner. Texas is a big space and we all have our favorites.

The present collection seeks to provide through fiction, autobiography, and a few discursive essays an overview of the diversity, excellence, and characteristic tropes of Texas writing. I had thought at first to go back to the beginnings, to oral creation myths of indigenous peoples living in what became Texas, and to the first great narrative to be written about the land and its peoples, Cabeza de Vaca's *La Relación*, 1542, and forward into the nineteenth century with firsthand accounts of experiences during the Texas Revolution, the exploits of the Texas Rangers, and so on, but such a collection perhaps remains for another time. Instead I have focused on a century of Texas writing, roughly 1903 to 2002.

I like the year 1903 because it was such a watershed year nationally. It was a year of firsts. The Wright brothers flew the first airplane; Albert Einstein published his first scientific paper; Pavlov began his experiments with conditioned response; the first narrative film, *The Great Train Robbery*, astounded viewers in New York; Henry Ford organized the Ford Motor Company; Gillette marketed the first safety razor with disposable blades, spelling the demise of the Victorian beard; and the first baseball World Series was played.

Word of some of the new scientific marvels even reached far-distant Texas, that vast, rugged, and remote land where, in 1901, at Spindletop, near Beaumont, the first gusher came in, assuring the U.S. that for much of the next century the energy to power the planes and ships and automobiles would come from the Lone Star state.

In American literature the dominant trend for thirty years had been Realism, an attempt to provide with photographic accuracy a true picture of modern life with its cities, railroads, and clash of titans, led by William Dean Howells. In 1903 Henry James, the recognized Master, published *The Ambassadors*, another of his difficult novels about the clash between the Old World and the New, set in Paris.

The literature of Texas, however, was not yet ready to deal with the modern. The state was still too close to the frontier. In 1903 warfare with the Plains Indians had been over for only twenty-nine years, the cattle drives for eighteen years or so; the frontier was very much a part of the present, in 1903, down in Texas. And so the first literary efforts of the new century tended, not surprisingly, to sing of cowboys and cowboy songs, of the long trail, of the excitements and perils of outdoor life lived on the back of a fast horse, and of women, new brides on new frontiers, their lives pitched like a tuning fork to the keenest of divergences and affinities between women and men living in a harsh and challenging land. Texas was hard on women and horses, so the saying went.

I have therefore sought to reflect the early-twentieth-century preoccupation with the frontier in works ranging from O. Henry, the first commercially successful Texas writer to find a national audience, through the obscure but quite astonishing memoirist Gertrude Beasley. But modern writers are drawn to the nineteenth-century frontier as well, and so the frontier motif flickers like a constant flame through the decades.

I have not imposed any kind of thematic grid on the works collected here, although there are some groupings that might appear obvious—a sequence of works, for example, dealing with the Kennedy assassination, another dealing with Hispanic experience on the border,

a cluster of comic pieces, and so on. I have followed chronology generally, from the early years of the twentieth century to the end, though
preferring loose affiliations of subjects and geographical proximity to
dates of publication. To me, this anthology is a kind of archaeological
site, with various soil samples, artifacts, and all the cultural humus
of a field, a ground of literary production. Readers may make their
own discoveries and connections, and they are welcome to whatever
insights may arise.

A word about that most difficult of tasks: the process of selection.
Whenever possible, I have preferred whole works—short stories or
essays—to cuttings from novels and nonfiction books, but in some
cases it was necessary to excerpt a portion of a longer work. Each
selection, however, can stand alone as a coherent entity. All antholo-
gists must at some point experience a sense of anxiety as to what has
not been included that might have been. (At least one major writer is
not included because he does not allow reprints, period.) I can only
allay such unease on my part by telling myself that I looked at a whole
lot of material and that, finally, for a host of reasons—not excluding
personal taste, I admit—I made the decisions that I did. As usual, my
poet friends will be unhappy that I chose not to include poems, but
that is not the way I saw the book. And other friends may be unhappy
because their work is not to be found in these pages. I think most writers are unhappy most of the time, at least when it is a question of their
work in relation to that vast audience who is not reading them at any
given point in time. I do hope, however, that this volume will make a
lot of readers happy and, in doing so, give them a more varied and
memorable picture of writing in the Lone Star State.

ACKNOWLEDGMENTS

———————— ✯ ————————

I must begin by thanking Sean Desmond, formerly of ICM, who first approached me about this project. Second, Jason Baskin, my editor at W. W. Norton, deserves a big round of thanks for his unfailingly helpful and enthusiastic support.

From time to time I sought advice and opinions from old friends who always had plenty of both. These include Jim Lee, Tom Pilkington, Mark Busby, and Dick Holland. Bert Almon of the University of Alberta (Canada) deserves special credit. His excellent book, *This Stubborn Self: Texas Autobiographies*, was published just in time to be of much help in the final stages of selection. In addition, my thanks to Al Lowman, Harwood Hinton, Lou Rodenberger, Francis Abernethy, and Judy Greene for aid in locating hard-to-find authors or heirs.

To the scores of other people who helped me in ways large and small to track down copyright holders, I am grateful, and Sprint is grateful.

As usual, members of the English Department staff provided much needed assistance. Their names are Larry Rone, Allen Graham, Justin Leach, Marshall Maresca, Emil Kresl, and Geneva Walton. I also wish to thank James Garrison, chair of the English Department, for his continued support.

I must also thank The University of Texas at Austin for a Faculty Research Assignment that gave me valuable leave time to complete this project. In addition, I would also like to thank, for additional support, the C. B. Smith, Sr., Nash Phillips, Clyde Copus Centennial Chair Honoring Harry Hunt Ransom. Finally, I also wish to thank Dean Richard W. Lariviere for a Research Proposal Award.

As always, Don Carleton and his staff at the Center for American History, Univerisity of Texas at Austin, are to be commended for their help.

Who else? All the writers living and dead who appear in these pages.

THE WEST

A DRY DRIVE

★

Andy Adams

OUR CATTLE QUIETED DOWN NICELY AFTER THIS RUN, AND the next few weeks brought not an incident worth recording. There was no regular trail through the lower counties, so we simply kept to the open country. Spring had advanced until the prairies were swarded with grass and flowers, while water, though scarcer, was to be had at least once daily. We passed to the west of San Antonio— an outfitting point which all herds touched in passing northward—and Flood and our cook took the wagon and went in for supplies. But the outfit with the herd kept on, now launched on a broad, well-defined trail, in places seventy-five yards wide, where all local trails blent into the one common pathway, known in those days as the Old Western Trail. It is not in the province of this narrative to deal with the cause or origin of this cattle trail, though it marked the passage of many hundred thousand cattle which preceded our Circle Dots, and was destined to afford an outlet to several millions more to follow. The trail proper consisted of many scores of irregular cow paths, united into one broad passageway, narrowing and widening as conditions permitted, yet ever leading northward. After a few years of continued use, it became as well defined as the course of a river.

Several herds which had started farther up country were ahead of ours, and this we considered an advantage, for wherever one herd could go, it was reasonable that others could follow. Flood knew the trail as well as any of the other foremen, but there was one thing he had not taken into consideration: the drouth of the preceding summer. True, there had been local spring showers, sufficient to start the grass nicely, but water in such quantities as we needed was growing daily more difficult to find. The first week after leaving San Antonio, our foreman scouted in quest of water a full day in advance of the herd. One evening he returned to us with the news that we were in for a dry drive, for after passing the next chain of lakes it was sixty miles to the next water, and reports regarding the water supply even after crossing this arid stretch were very conflicting.

"While I know every foot of this trail through here," said the foreman, "there's several things that look scaly. There are only five herds ahead of us, and the first three went through the old route, but the last two, after passing Indian Lakes, for some reason or other turned and went westward. These last herds may be stock cattle, pushing out west to new ranges; but I don't like the outlook. It would take me two days to ride across and back, and by that time we could be two thirds of the way through. I've made this drive before without a drop of water on the way, and wouldn't dread it now, if there was any certainty of water at the other end. I reckon there's nothing to do but tackle her; but isn't this a hell of a country? I've ridden fifty miles today and never saw a soul."

The Indian Lakes, some seven in number, were natural reservoirs with rocky bottoms, and about a mile apart. We watered at ten o'clock the next day, and by night camped fifteen miles on our way. There was plenty of good grazing for the cattle and horses, and no trouble was experienced the first night. McCann had filled an extra twenty gallon keg for this trip. Water was too precious an article to be lavish with, so we shook the dust from our clothing and went unwashed. This was no serious deprivation, and no one could be critical of another, for we were all equally dusty and dirty. The next morning by daybreak the cattle were thrown off the bed ground and started grazing before the sun could dry out what little moisture the grass had absorbed during the night. The heat of the past week had been very oppressive, and in order to avoid it as much as possible, we made late and early drives. Before the wagon passed the herd during the morning drive, what few canteens we had were filled with water for the men. The *remuda* was kept with the herd, and four changes of mounts were made during the day, in order not to exhaust any one horse. Several times for an hour or more, the herd was allowed to lie down and rest; but by the middle of the afternoon thirst made them impatient and restless, and the point men were compelled to ride steadily in the lead in order to hold the cattle to a walk. A number of times during the afternoon we attempted to graze them, but not until the twilight of evening was it possible.

After the fourth change of horses was made, Honeyman pushed on ahead with the saddle stock and overtook the wagon. Under Flood's orders he was to tie up all the night horses, for if the cattle could be induced to graze, we would not bed them down before ten that night, and all hands would be required with the herd. McCann had instructions to make camp on the divide, which was known to be twenty-five miles from our camp of the night before, or forty miles from the Indian Lakes. As we expected, the cattle grazed willingly after nightfall, and with a fair moon, we allowed them to scatter freely while grazing forward. The beacon of McCann's fire on the divide was in sight over an hour before the herd grazed up to camp, all hands remaining to bed the thirsty cattle. The herd was given triple the amount of space usually required for bedding, and even then for nearly an hour scarcely half of them lay down.

We were handling the cattle as humanely as possible under the circumstances. The guards for the night were doubled, six men on the first half and the same on the latter, Bob Blades being detailed to assist Honeyman in night-herding the saddle horses. If any of us got more than an hour's sleep that night, he was lucky. Flood, McCann, and the horse wranglers did not even try to rest. To those of us who could find time to eat, our cook kept open house. Our foreman knew that a well-fed man can stand an incredible amount of hardship, and appreciated the fact that on the trail a good cook is a valuable asset. Our outfit therefore was cheerful to a man, and jokes and songs helped to while away the weary hours of the night.

The second guard, under Flood, pushed the cattle off their beds an hour before dawn, and before they were relieved had urged the herd more than five miles on the third day's drive over this waterless mesa. In spite of our economy of water, after breakfast on this third morning there was scarcely enough left to fill the canteens for the day. In view of this, we could promise ourselves no midday meal—except a can of tomatoes to the man; so the wagon was ordered to drive through to the expected water ahead, while the saddle horses were held available as on the day before for frequent changing of mounts. The day turned out to be one of torrid heat, and before the middle of the forenoon, the cattle lolled their tongues in despair, while their sullen lowing surged through from rear to lead and back again in piteous yet ominous appeal. The only relief we could offer was to travel them slowly, as they spurned every opportunity offered them either to graze or to lie down.

It was nearly noon when we reached the last divide, and sighted the scattering timber of the expected watercourse. The enforced order of the day before—to hold the herd in a walk and prevent exertion and heating—now required four men in the lead, while the rear followed over a mile behind, dogged and sullen. Near the middle of the afternoon, McCann returned on one of his mules with the word that it was a question if there was water enough to water even the horse stock. The preceding outfit, so he reported, had dug a shallow well in the bed of the creek, from which he had filled his kegs, but the stock water was a mere loblolly. On receipt of this news, we changed mounts for the fifth time that day; and Flood, taking Forrest, the cook, and the horse wrangler, pushed on ahead with the *remuda* to the waterless stream.

The outlook was anything but encouraging. Flood and Forrest scouted the creek up and down for ten miles in a fruitless search for water. The outfit held the herd back until the twilight of evening, when Flood returned and confirmed McCann's report. It was twenty miles yet to the next water ahead, and if the horse stock could only be watered thoroughly, Flood was determined to make the attempt to nurse the herd through to water. McCann was digging an extra well, and he expressed the belief that by hollowing out a number of holes, enough water could be secured for the saddle stock. Honeyman had corralled the horses and was letting only a few go to the water at a time, while the night horses were being thoroughly watered as fast as the water rose in the well.

Holding the herd this third night required all hands. Only a few men at a time were allowed to go into camp and eat, for the herd refused even to lie down. What few cattle attempted to rest were prevented by the more restless ones. By spells they would mill, until riders were sent through the herd at a break-neck pace to break up the groups. During these milling efforts of the herd, we drifted over a mile from camp; but by the light of moon and stars and the number of riders, scattering was prevented. As the horses were loose for the night, we could not start them on the trail until daybreak gave us a change of mounts, so we lost the early start of the morning before.

Good cloudy weather would have saved us, but in its stead was a sultry morning without a breath of air, which bespoke another day of sizzling heat. We had not been on the trail over two hours before the heat became almost unbearable to man and beast. Had it not been for the condition of the herd, all might yet have gone well; but over three days had now elapsed without water for the cattle, and they became feverish and ungovernable. The lead cattle, turned back several times, wandering aimlessly in any direction; and it was with considerable difficulty that the herd could be held on the trail. The rear overtook the lead, and the cattle gradually lost all semblance of a trail herd. Our horses were fresh, however, and after about two hours' work, we once more got the herd strung out in trailing fashion; but before a mile had been covered, the leaders again turned, and the cattle congregated into a mass of unmanageable animals, milling and lowing in their fever and thirst. The milling only intensified their sufferings from the heat, and the outfit split and quartered them again and again, in the hope that this unfortunate outbreak might be checked. No sooner was the milling stopped than they would surge hither and yon, sometimes half a mile, as ungovernable as the waves of an ocean. After wasting several hours in this manner, they finally turned back over the trail, and the utmost efforts of every man in the outfit failed to check them. We threw our ropes in their faces, and when this failed, we resorted to shooting; but in defiance of the fusillade and the smoke they walked sullenly through the line of horsemen across their front. Six-shooters were discharged so close to the leaders' faces as to singe their hair, yet, under a noonday sun, they disregarded this and every other device to turn them and passed wholly out of our control. In a number of instances wild steers deliberately walked against our horses, and then for the first time a fact dawned on us that chilled the marrow in our bones—*the herd was going blind.*

The bones of men and animals that lie bleaching along the trails abundantly testify that this was not the first instance in which the plain had baffled the determination of man. It was now evident that nothing short of water would stop the herd, and we rode aside and let them pass. As the outfit turned back to the wagon, our foreman seemed dazed by the sudden and unexpected turn of affairs, but rallied and met the emergency.

"There's but one thing left to do," said he, as we rode along, "and that is to hurry the outfit back to Indian Lakes. The herd will travel day and night, and instinct can be depended on to carry them to the only water they know. It's too late to be of any use now, but it's plain why those last two herds turned off at the lakes; some one had gone back and warned them of the very thing we've met. We must beat them to the lakes, for water is the only thing that will check them now. It's a good thing that they are strong, and five or six days without water will hardly kill any. It was no vague statement of the man who said if he owned hell and Texas, he'd rent Texas and live in hell, for if this isn't Billy hell, I'd like to know what you call it."

We spent an hour watering the horses from the wells of our camp of the night before, and about two o'clock started back over the trail for Indian Lakes. We overtook the abandoned herd during the afternoon. They were strung out nearly five miles in length, and were walking about a three-mile gait. Four men were given two extra horses apiece and left to throw in the stragglers in the rear, with instructions to follow them well into the night, and again in the morning as long as their canteens lasted. The remainder of the outfit pushed on without a halt, except to change mounts, and reached the lakes shortly after midnight. There we secured the first good sleep of any consequence for three clays.

It was fortunate for us that there were no range cattle at these lakes, and we had only to cover a front of about six miles to catch the drifting herd. It was nearly noon the next day before the cattle began to arrive at the water holes in squads of from twenty to fifty. Pitiful objects as they were, it was a novelty to see them reach the water and slack their thirst. Wading out into the lakes until their sides were half covered, they would stand and low in a soft moaning voice, often for half an hour before attempting to drink. Contrary to our expectation, they drank very little at first, but stood in the water for hours. After coming out, they would lie down and rest for hours longer, and then drink again before attempting to graze, their thirst overpowering hunger. That they were blind there was no question, but with the causes that produced it once removed, it was probable their eyesight would gradually return.

By early evening, the rear guard of our outfit returned and reported the tail end of the herd some twenty miles behind when they left them. During the day not over a thousand head reached the lakes, and towards evening we put these under herd and easily held them during the night. All four of the men who constituted the rear guard were sent back the next morning to prod up the rear again, and during the night at least a thousand more came into the lakes, which held them better than a hundred men. With the recovery of the cattle our hopes grew, and with the gradual accessions to the herd, confidence was again completely restored. Our saddle stock, not having suffered as had the cattle, were in a serviceable condition, and while a few men were all that were necessary to hold the herd, the others scoured the country for miles in search of any possible stragglers which might have missed the water.

During the forenoon of the third day at the lakes, Nat Straw, the foreman of Ellison's first herd on the trail, rode up to our camp. He was scouting for water for his herd, and, when our situation was explained and he had been interrogated regarding loose cattle, gave us the good news that no stragglers in our road brand had been met by their outfit. This was welcome news, for we had made no count yet, and feared some of them, in their locoed condition, might have passed the water during the night. Our misfortune was an ill wind by which Straw profited, for he had fully expected to keep on by the old route, but with our disaster staring him in the face, a similar experience was to be avoided. His herd reached the lakes during the middle of the afternoon, and after watering, turned and went westward over the new route taken by the two herds which preceded us. He had a herd of about three thousand steers, and was driving to the Dodge market. After the experience we had just gone through, his herd and outfit were a welcome sight. Flood made inquiries after Lovell's second herd, under my brother Bob as foreman, but Straw had seen or heard nothing of them, having come from Goliad County with his cattle.

After the Ellison herd had passed on and out of sight, our squad which had been working the country to the northward, over the route by which the abandoned herd had returned, came in with the information that that section was clear of cattle, and that they had only found three head dead from thirst. On the fourth morning, as the herd left the bed ground, a count was ordered, and to our surprise we counted out twenty-six head more than we had received on the banks of the Rio Grande a month before. As there had been but one previous occasion to count, the number of strays absorbed into our herd was easily accounted for by Priest: "If a steer herd could increase on the trail, why shouldn't ours, that had over a thousand cows in it?" The observation was hardly borne out when the ages of our herd were taken into consideration. But 1882 in Texas was a liberal day and generation, and "cattle stealing" was too drastic a term to use for the chance gain of a few cattle, when the foundations of princely fortunes were being laid with a rope and a branding iron.

HEADED FOR THE SETTING SUN

———✯———

James Emmit McCauley

O<small>N THE 14TH DAY OF AUGUST, 1873, I CAME PRANCING INTO</small> this world. I was found in Anderson County, Lone Star State, close to Palestine. My mother was also borned in Texas, but my father was from Missouri; so he had to be shown before he would believe. When I was first borned my parents was living at Sherman Mill. My father worked at the mill; that is, he cut saw logs for the company out of the woods. But my first memory was to ride a stick horse and to help hunt for cattle, for every once in a while somebody would go along the big road with a small herd of cattle, drifting them west to grass and the prairie country. Then my first wishes and desires was to be a wild and woolly cowboy. 'Twas all I wanted to do but nevertheless my parents quit the saw-mill and went to farming for a living. So I was reared up to be a plowboy instead of a cowboy.

My parents be poor like Job's turkey. They farmed somebody else's land. The other men furnished the land and the team and the plows and a house for us to live in and we then went cahoots in the crop. But to follow a scooter plow in stumps, bare-footed, all day, didn't suit a would-be cowboy.

So my early life was spent on a farm. Things jogged on this way until I was eight years old and my parents started me to school in the little town of Overton. As I was the oldest boy I went by myself—and a country boy in town at school stands a very poor show. They did me every way they wanted to, as Father had told me when any of them done anything to me to go and tell the teacher. But they would lie out of it and I would be the one punished. So I told Father how they done. So he told me the next one that done anything to me to do everything to him but kill him. So next day I was laying for an opportunity to bust them up in business.

At the schoolhouse overhead was a Mason's hall and on this day by some hook or crook they was repairing the house and was building some brick flues and had some scaffolds built up by the side of the house. And at noon I went out of the house to eat my cornbread and sow-belly. Some of them boys had got up on the scaffold, and when I opened my bucket they throwed a half a brick in my bucket. I upped with the brick and brought the gentleman off there head first and I kept poking the brick until I had three of them down. A doctor was sent for, and while they was attending the sick, lame and lazy, I skeedaddled for home and told Father. So in his company he went back with me. Father told the professor how I had been treated, how the boys lied on me and I bore the blame, and how he had told me to pestle them up some myself. From that day on I bore the name of Bald Hornet, but I was cock of the walk and crowed when I wanted.

It was natural for me, I guess, to be mean. Once an old man (I'll call him Johnson) told Father I had been stealing his apples and he gave me an unmerciful whipping. But I was laying for that old man. A big Methodist camp meeting was in progress, which I was attending with the balance of the family. Father had an uncle of mine living with us and he went on before us and he changed his clothes and I spied his pants. So I sneaked them and he had forgot his knife. That night I watched old man Johnson hang his hat on the brush arbor posts. I slipped up gently and took it down and made for the bushes. I literally cut it all to pieces, and it was laid to me but I lied out of it as I had no knife. But the good old man never said I swiped any more of his apples.

About this time Father had made a raise some way and bought us a horse and occasionally he'd let me ride it to town or some place in the country. I'd ride with one foot out of the stirrup and sit away over on one side as that was the way I had noticed the cowboys riding. The more I saw of them drifting west, the more determined I was to be a cowboy. Then in 1883 my parents moved west out on the Brazos River in Baylor County. That country was then nothing but ranches, only a nester (farmer) now and then. It was the home of the cattle kings, as the buffalo had left and the Indians quit raiding on the settlers. Nothing could have suited me more than to be in a cow country, as farming didn't set well with me. But we moved back a little to the town of Graham and father got work on a ranch close to Graham and they put me to work riding fences. This is getting on a horse and taking a hammer and a steepler and when the fence is loose from the post to fix it up. This was a better job than I had been having, but I wanted to go with the outfit where they didn't do anything but drive cattle.

In 1888 I was going to a little country school and there was a pretty little miss (I'll call her Gussie Thornton) with blue eyes and golden hair that won the admiration of my heart. I built many air castles with her in them, but they all fell through as most air castles do. Another boy quite a lot older and larger than I caused most of my troubles. He undertook to see that I could not talk to her and called me bad names which caused us to fight. In the fight he had me down and was giving me a good, sound thrashing and I was about ready to holler calf rope when his knife fell out of his pocket. When I picked it up he didn't see me, and the blade being loose in the rivet it was not much of a job to open it. I slammed it into him in the hip. I want you to know I did not have to beg him to get off. He got up and yelled he was knifed. This girl was one of the first there to see what was wrong. When she saw the blood all over this boy and my hand bloody she thought I had killed him. I told her that she had caused the trouble. The rest of the children went to inform the teacher; so I bid my first love good-bye and started for home, which I was not long in reaching.

I told my mother what had happened, and after kissing her a fond farewell I started for the setting sun. I felt that if I stayed there that to prison I would go or that else I would be hung or that boy's father would reck vengeance on me. We lived then in Parker County. By nightfall I had walked some twenty miles when I struck a freighter going to Jacksboro. After I had told him what had happened, he said I had done the bully right. After we got to Jacksboro, he kept me at his house some eight or ten days. Next I struck a cow outfit going to the ranch. I struck them for a job and they took me in and in six more days we was at headquarters of the old Figger Eight. They put me to wrangling horses. That job is to herd the horses that the rest of the cowboys ride. Every rider has from six to ten horses and while he is off on the round-up the wrangler herds what they are not riding, and when the chuck wagon moves from one camping place to another he drives the loose horses and keeps with the chuck wagon. I thought this was pretty good. It beat being in jail or being hung. The first thing I done when I had worked out money enough was to send and get me a new Colts 45 six-shooter, so that if anybody come to take me back to Parker County he would meet with a warm reception. I had blood in my eye and didn't mean to be arrested if it could be helped.

I soon got enough of the horse herding, but that was all they would let me do. But when the fall work was over I stayed at the ranch and cut stove wood and done odd jobs around the place until spring. And when spring did come I had a new saddle and a little pony and some $30 in money. About the first of April I struck northwest as I was determined to go up the trail to Montana. I rode to the X I T head-

quarters at Channing, Texas, where five trail outfits was fixing to go to
Montana. After looking the bosses over, I tackled one called Scanlous
John. He looked me over. I was tall enough, but slim was only part of
it. He asked me my name and I told him. "Well," he says, "Slim Jim, I
don't think you would make a cowboy." I told him if I lived I would.
After I hung with him for some two or three days he said, "Well, boy,
I'll take you along if you'll promise to go plumb through."

When I got to the X I Ts, I was broke and I did not have no bed
and not much clothes. So poor old Scanlous John took me over to the
store and bought me some clothes and a new pair of boots and took
me in and let me sleep with him. Cowboys have to furnish their own
bed and saddle blankets, saddle and bridle and spurs, but the company usually furnish rope and the company always boards a man. 'Tis
understood without asking that your board is furnished. I'll never forget poor old John for the kindness he showed me when I was a youth
and in trouble too. We got to be quite chummy before the trail herd
was ready to start for Montana. During the last days of April we got
things together to start. He gave me a gentle mount of horses, for
which I thanked him with all my heart. On the last day of April we
moved out and began to round up to get us a herd. Two herds was put
up before ours come, we being the middle one. But of all the funny
things I had ever saw was the new trail cowboys mounting. Some
could ride them and some would ride about two jumps and then there
was a horse loose with a saddle on. But 'twas fun to me. Beat hoeing
cotton or plowing corn. I wanted to try some of those that pitched but
I was afraid I could not ride them and as I was doing very well I
thought I would let well enough alone.

The first night I stood guard I'll never forget. Standing guard with
cattle is like this: The cattle are driven up as close together as they can
very well stand and have plenty of room, and are held this way. About
dark they will all, or most of them, lay down. And then everybody goes
to the wagon, which is usually camped close, but about two or three.
These cowboys are called the first guard. They will hold the cattle

there part of the night and then they will wake up two or three more and they will stand their part, and so on. I was put on first guard until 10:30 o'clock. I didn't have any trouble with the cattle, as they lay all right, but I didn't think my guard would ever be out, the time dragged so awful slow. But finely the second guard took them and I turned in. The next morning was a fine day and we was moving on towards Montana, slowly.

On the third night, as usual, I was on the first guard, just Scanlous John and me, and about nine o'clock a black cloud from the northwest come up. I had on my slicker, or oil coat. It began to rain in torrents. The vivid lightning began to flash. The thunder began to roar. And all at once the steers got on their feet and in less time than it takes to tell it they was gone. The night was as dark as ink, only for the lightning. My horse was on his job, so he stayed with the cattle. Then I realized that the so much talked of stampeding herd of longhorn steers was now a reality. Every time it would lighten and a loud clap of thunder follow they would change their course, and in a short time I found the herd had split or divided, but into how many bunches I didn't know. After some two hours of storm the rain quit and soon it cleared off and the moon shined out, but I didn't know where my pard was or which way the wagon might be.

I had about three hundred head of steers and after everything was still they lay down and I thought I'd see if I could find the other part of the herd. But to my sorrow I could not, so I thought I'd shoot my six-shooter and see if anybody would come or answer me. Bang she went and away went the bunch I was holding. Now I had more trouble than if I had a let things alone. After chasing them for an hour, I guess, I got them stopped, but I didn't shoot any more. I saw I was in to it for the night and so I made the best of a bad bargain. Well, the moon in all its beauty came at last and as the sun arose across the eastern horizon in all its glory they never was a poor, wore out sleepier boy than I was. But still I was in trouble, for there I was with a bunch of cattle all alone with nobody in sight and I didn't know which way to go to the wagon. I was so hungry and tired I didn't know what to do.

About ten o'clock a man came in sight. They was looking for me but didn't know which way to look. He told me the direction the wagon was. I lit out. I had drifted something like ten miles to the southeast and if any boy ever did enjoy something to eat it was me. If bacon and beans ever tasted good it was then. The boys all told the boss he had lost his tenderfoot, but when they found out I had held a bunch all night they didn't say tenderfoot any more. I thought 'twas the most miserable night I had ever experienced in all my life. They said it was the way they initiated all the down east boys, so I took it for granted and hoped 'twould not happen any more. Things rocked on very well till we struck the Arkansaw River between La Junta and Pueblo, Colorado. It got so stormy up there in the breaks of the Rocky Mountains that we had a storm every night, nearly. Oh, but I did wish I was back in good old Texas plowing corn or hoeing cotton, but alas, I was not, and was made of too good stuff to show the white feather. On we went with a slow but steady gait towards Montana.

My real troubles was yet to come. When we reached the Arkansaw River we went up it three or four days before we crossed. When finely we put into it, it was about level full, as the snow had been melting up in the mountains long enough to swell it until it was a raging torrent. I waited as long as I could before I went in. I didn't get in good until it was swimming. I didn't get far before my horse got tangled in some drift and sank to rise no more. I had taken off my boots and most of my clothes for fear of something like this. The first thing that come handy was a four year old steer. I got him by the tail and away we went for the other side, which we reached after so long a time. I promised myself I'd never swim the Arkansaw any more.

I had lost my saddle, bridle, blankets and spurs and was broke; that is, I didn't have enough money to buy a new outfit. What to do I didn't know, but I kept my troubles to myself, and the boys began to guy me about riding bareback until Scanlous John came to my rescue. He told me to ride on the chuck wagon until he could buy me a saddle. He told me the company would pay for me a new outfit. So I felt some better. In the course of a week he sent to Pueblo and got me a new outfit out and out. Then I was one of the boys—a new $45 saddle. But I promised myself that I'd never go up the trail with a herd any more, that swimming them rivers was just a little bit too dangerous for me.

Finely we came to the last river. It was the worst of them all, and I would not have tried to swim it for all the cattle up there. 'Tis noted for its swiftness and it has two currents. The top current is some two feet deep, and the under current runs twice as fast as the top. 'Twas the noted Yellowstone River. When you go below the top current nothing comes up. 'Tis such a suck to it that to sink in the Yellowstone is a gone fawn skin. When we got there, the other two herds had not crossed. They seemed to be waiting for us. We crossed close to Miles City. There is some islands there. We would put the cattle in and some men there with boats helped us swim them to an island. From it we would swim them for the next island.

After all five of the herds got there about half of the men quit and went to Miles City and blowed in their money. From there on we put all the cattle in one herd and just drifted them on to the ranch, which was not very far. We could not drive so many cattle. All we could do was just drift them through. We was fourteen days crossing the five herds. I helped four days and then went to Miles City and crossed on the bridge, and got on the other side and had a good time herding. It beat working in the melted snow water that seemed colder than any ice water I ever saw. It makes the cold chills run over me now to think of that cold water.

One day I went to town just to see what it was like. I had wrote home to mother from way down the country at Pueblo and I told mother to write to Miles City. A letter from her was waiting me. They had moved to Johnson County close to the little town of Pleasant Point. She said the boy I had the trouble with had got well. She begged me to come home. I drawed $50 of my money and sent it to Mother.

A desire to go back kindly got next to me, but I was determined to go
through or know the reason why. So on August 22nd we landed at the
headquarter ranch of the X I T in Montana.

After staying a few days taking in the sights, Scanlous John and me
prepared to go back to the good old Lone Star State. On the 27th of
August it came a light snow and that made me want to get away worse,
for any place that it snows in the summer don't suit a Texas cowpuncher, or it didn't me. So I asked John when would we start and how
was we going. He told me we would go with a train of beef cattle to
Chicago, and from there to Kansas City and then I'd have to buy my
own ticket from there on. On the 5th of September we left with a train
of beef over the Great Northern Railroad. I have forgot the little town
we shipped from but anyway they jerked them through. We fed and
watered after they was unloaded at St. Paul, Minnesota. That was the
largest city I had ever been in. If I had been by myself I never would
have got out of there, but my boss had been a father to me and I done
just what he said and everything went all right. 'Twas here that I first
saw the great Mississippi River, but I had seen so much water that it
didn't charm me much. But the sight of the steamboats—that took my
eye. I talked to Scanlous John until he agreed to take a ride on one, so
we went up to Minneapolis and back on a steamboat. Next morning
we loaded our cattle and on we went to Chicago—the second sized
city in the United States.

Nothing would do John but that we must each buy us a suit of new
clothes. After visiting the barber shop and having our hair took off
some five inches and a good bath—the first I had had since I crossed
the Yellowstone River—we proceeded to dike up in new clothes from
head to foot. After laying around there two days, I told John I'd have
to go on or I'd have no money. We here got our passes reversed to
Kansas City and from there I had to buy my ticket. It was here that I
had to bid my best friend among cowpunchers good-bye, and from
that day to this I have never seen him any more.

After my ticket was paid for and I was on the train I had just $4.60

in my pocket. I left Kansas City in the afternoon and the next afternoon I reached Fort Worth, Texas, just in time to catch a train for
Mansfield. Mother was there to meet me. Oh, never was I hugged so
much in all my born days and I never was so glad to see anybody as I
was Mother. From back some place Mother dug up stuff after we
reached home—preserves, jelly, jam, eggs, pies and so on until I began
to think I was somebody. We sat up until nearly midnight talking over
the past. Mother said I didn't get out of sight until that boy's father and
the officer was there to take me in; she said they watched the place
for nearly a month before they gave it up. After staying around home
for a few days father asked me if I didn't think I could pick a little cotton. Well, that didn't sound very good, but nevertheless I began to pick
the fleecy staple. I stayed at home until in the spring. I had picked cotton and cut cord wood until I had bought me another pony.

from ADVENTURES OF A BALLAD HUNTER

✯

John A. Lomax

A T THIRTEEN I WAS "CONVERTED" UNDER A BRUSH ARBOR built back of the one-room Grapevine schoolhouse, three miles north of Meridian. Under the camp meeting code my age and experience entitled me to sit on a back seat where the lights were dim. One night Danna Moore, several years older than I, came and sat down close by me during the mourning period and rubbed her cheek against mine. I found the sensation pleasant. Up to that time I cannot recall any other sin I had committed, nor do I think that experience influenced my conversion. Perhaps my mother led me to make my first and only trip to the mourners' bench, together with the emotional appeal of Brother Levi Harris' singing. Anyhow, I remember that between stanzas he kept urging all the unsaved to come up and have their sins forgiven. Somehow, I got up to the altar. When I knelt in the straw and pushed my doubled-up fists into my eyes I felt no twinges of conscience for the sins that were supposed to rest heavily on me. I did not cry or pray, I only felt sorry for myself. When one of the helpers whispered to me to "trust in the Lord, give yourself wholly into His keeping," I was not helped a bit. I simply did not know what she meant. But I did know that I was embarrassed and anxious to put an end to the ordeal. Near me I could hear my mother praying as if she were in deep trouble. I had never heard her pray before, and it hurt me to know that I was the source of her grief. End it I must as soon as I could.

Presently Brother Harris asked all who felt that they had been saved to stand up. Instantly, I rose to my feet. Brother Harris shook my hand; my mother seemed happy. I was greatly relieved that I could get out of such a public place, that I never would have to go to the mourners' bench again. Soon afterward I joined the church and "renounced the vain pomp and glory of the world, and the carnal desires of the flesh, so that I would not follow or be led by them." Again, in an agony of self-consciousness, I had to be the center of many eyes. The strange experience left me in a mental daze. When this ceremony was over and I was at home again, I went out to the lot where my pony was sunning himself, put Selim's head over my shoulder, leaned against him and promised that, since I was a Christian and belonged to the church, I would never again ride him with a curb bit or strike him with a quirt. And that night I fed my favorite pet chicken an extra big supper.

Life in Bosque was hard—both in work and in play. Religion was of the hellfire and damnation brand. "Lost! Lost! Lost!" was the cry which filled hearts and souls with terror.

There is a fountain filled with blood,

Drawn from Immanuel's veins,

And sinners plunged beneath that flood

Lose all their guilty stains,

sang loud and lusty voices. To me it was a gory picture. Often I awoke at night from a nightmare, dreaming that I myself was immersed in a pool of blood, oceans of blood. Against this background of ideas my father and mother must have worked out the rigid rules of conduct they imposed on their children. I cannot remember, however, that I ever felt rebellious. I never flatly disobeyed them on any important issue. We children never played games on Sunday, not even marbles, frog-in-the-middle, mumble peg, roley-holey, antny-over, one-eyed cat, town ball, stink base or bull pen. We could pick up pecans that had fallen to the ground, but we could not climb trees and shake more down. We couldn't pull out a catfish from a set hook that happened to be left out over Sunday, nor could we swim in the silvery Bosque.

Throughout the week we were busy at work on the farm; so our free time for recreation was scant. Sometimes we got Saturday afternoon off for swimming or pecan gathering. But the winter nights were long and on week-ends our friends often came to stay all night, and we could return such visits. The three or four winter months that we went to school gave us our real playtime for outdoor games. But this lack of freedom aroused our inventiveness for indoor amusements. Each family had its stock of riddles and rhymes. Groups musically inclined sang songs and swapped stories with each other.

About the only common meeting place for the country and town folks (and this was only for the men) was the saloon. These "poor man's clubs" were about as numerous in Bosque County as filling stations are today. One of them that I remember bore the brutally frank name of "The Road to Ruin." Over at Eulogy (some of its citizens say it should be called Apology) a saloon had this sign on the wall: "Spit on the ceiling. Anybody can spit on the floor." Through the winters on Saturday the saloons did a big business. Someone said that bartenders were as thick in Bosque County as the proverbial fiddlers in purgatory. The gang of wild buccaroos from the country, led by Bob Hanna, who had been up the trail, habitually rode into town to tighten their belts with a few good drinks. Throughout the day and far into the night they played pool, rattled dice, drank and fought. I used to lie awake as they came past our house, "a-howlin', loose at both ends and goin' somewhere." Bob Hanna and his merry crew, soused to the gills, were riding out of town:

We're the children of the open and we hate the haunts of men,

But we had to come to town to get the mail;

We're the sons of desolation, we're the outlaws of creation,

A-ridin' up the rocky road from town.

The tournaments (everybody called them toonaments) of the Texas cowboys helped crystallize my interest in their songs. The six-foot lances, carried by the riders at top speed, were not pointed at an enemy, but at five small rings hanging from the arms of upright posts strung fifty yards apart along a track two hundred yards in length. Each "knight" rode down the track three times, and a perfect score meant that the rider must thread on his lance all fifteen rings, and take no more than twelve seconds for each ride. The prizes were three wreaths of prairie flowers which would be worn proudly by the chosen ladies. I remember one tournament as if it were yesterday.

At the end of a large glade stood the judges' platform where later in the evening the dance would be held. The rough uprights were wrapped in gayly colored bunting, and flags fluttered overhead. Men and women—the women on sidesaddles with long riding skirts of flashing colors nearly sweeping the ground—rode singly or in pairs across the field. Scattered among them were the contending knights, broad ribbon sashes over one shoulder, fastened with a rosette on the opposite side at the point of the hip, just below the waistline. There the two bands of ribbon crossed, each one ending in streamers tipped with gold or silver fringe. Feather plumes were arched along their hat brims, plumes either snatched from protesting white ganders or peafowls or borrowed from girls. The crowd converged at the grand-stand near where the track began.

The ten contestants on their gayly decorated and prancing horses filed singly before the judges' stand and were introduced by the master of ceremonies, Judge James Gillette, who stood by the Queen of the Jousts and her ladies-in-waiting:

Ladies and gentlemen, I present ten brave and gallant knights who will tilt today each for the favor of a fair lady, not in bloody conflict but with peaceful lances at golden rings in this lovely valley of Bosque County.

May the best man win and may the favor of his lady be granted him.

I present to you Ed Nichols, the Knight of the Silver Cross.

Ed touched his pony's rein. The horse rose on its hind legs, stood for a moment almost perpendicular, dropped to its feet, plunged forward for several bounds, whirled and faced the announcer, then lowered its nose slowly to the ground in a bow as gracefully as Emma Abbott when she took the call after singing "The Last Rose of Summer." Ed rode his horse as if "growed" there.

Each knight as his name was called curvetted his horse or executed some caracole, no two alike, and rode into line with Ed Nichols. They were:

Asa Gary, The Knight of Bosque County

George Scrutchfield, The Knight of the Golden Spur

Johnny Rundell, The Knight of the Lost Cause

Sam Russell, The Knight of the Southern Cross

Jeff Hanna, The Knight of the Lone Star

Ed McCurry, The Knight of the Morning Star

Otto Nelson, The Knight of Green Valley

Frank Hornbuckle, The Knight of Double Mountain

Bob Hanna, The Knight of the Slim Chance

As the last name was called, Ed Nichols swung his horse to the end of the track, leveled his lance, leaned over as he touched his plunging horse with his spurs. He darted forward. By the time he reached the first overhanging ring the lance point was steady and the first ring clicked as it was strung on the lance and struck against the guard just in front of where Ed's hand clasped the shaft.

Click—click—click—click!

In twice as many seconds the five rings were on Ed's lance, now held proudly erect. As he galloped to the judges' stand to have his successful run verified, he shouted to Bob Hanna:

"Oh, you Knight of the Slim Chance, you ain't got no chance against me!"

The crowd clapped approval, the next knight took the rings from Ed's lance and hung them up carefully for his run. The tournament was really under way. Rider followed rider, none getting all five rings, until it was Bob's turn. He strung all five. On Ed's second try his horse "flew the track" and he had no chance at the last two rings. Bob took all five rings again, and repeated on the last run. He was cheered as the champion. Frank Hornbuckle was next, with Ed Nichols having made the best time. When Bob had crowned his lady love he led the dance that started at once on the platform back of the judges' stand. Early the next morning he started out on horseback for the range just south of Abilene.

But Ed Nichols stayed in Morgan, and there are few more interesting men in the world than he. Ed could ride the hardest pitching horse so that daylight couldn't ever be seen between him and his saddle. He made a beautiful figure astride a horse. He never pulled leather; "I never was throwed," he claims. I believe he tells the truth. He once told me about riding a vicious, man-killer horse for two miles with the horse pitching a "fence row high, wide and handsome" and landing stiff-legged at every jump.

"I thought I was a goner," he said. "But at last the horse dropped his head between his legs, his feet spraddled out, and he bawled like a yearling. He was give out and so was I. When I got off, blood was dripping from my nose and ears. Another time, another horse pitched a mile and a half with me and then fell dead."

Ed was full of stories: "Frank Hornbuckle"—the man who won second place in the tournament—"would ride 'em for a drink of whiskey. Harry White had a pretty gray mare that had never been rode. One morning Frank roped her out, put his saddle on her and told Harry to bring him the jug of whiskey and he'd ride her. Harry went to the wagon and found that the jug was empty. He told Frank to pull off his saddle, that the whiskey was all gone. Frank said, 'Bring me the jug.' He took it, pulled out the stopper and smelled. 'Turn her loose,' he said. He rode that mare for a smell of whiskey."

Like many another bullwhacker, muleskinner and cowpuncher, who had little opportunity to read, Ed carried in his memory reams of songs, verses and old ballads. He promised his mother never to drink. But he did not promise her that he would not play cards. In describing one game he told me, "I was so lucky, I could draw to a cow chip and catch a pair of oxen." In describing a room he slept in over in the Cross Timbers, he said it was "so small I had to jump up to get out of my britches."

Tom McCullough over at Kimball's Bend told me this story to show how tender-hearted Ed was: "One night he was riding horseback alone between Hico and Iredell. Passing through a thick wood he heard an old cow mooing. A cow in trouble can sound mighty pitiful. Ed got down, hitched his horse and began to look for her. At last he found her at the bottom of an abandoned windlass well, six feet or more in diameter at the top. The old cow heard Ed and mooed and mooed. Ed had a hard job ahead, but he was full of resources. He looked around until he found a running spring, took off his big, wide-brimmed Stetson, filled it with water, carried it to the old well and poured it in. Again and again he emptied hatfuls of water until finally he filled the well up to the top and the struggling cow swam out."

Men like Bob Hanna and Ed Nichols deepened my love for cowboy songs. I couldn't have been more than four years old when I first heard a cowboy sing and yodel to his cattle. I was sleeping in my father's two-room house in Texas beside a branch of the old Chisholm Trail—twelve of us sometimes in two rooms. Suddenly a cowboy's singing waked me as I slept on my trundle bed. A slow rain fell in the darkness outside. I listened to the patter on the pine shingles above me, and through the open window I could hear the soft musical tinkle of water pouring from the eaves and striking the gravelly earth beneath. These sounds come back to me faintly through the years, a foggy maze of recollections; and my heart leapt even then to the cries of the cowboy trying to quiet, in the deep darkness and sifting rain, a trail herd of restless cattle:

Whoo-oo-oo-ee-oo-oo, Whoo-oo Whoo-whoo-oo

O, slow up, dogies, quit your roving around,
You have wandered and tramped all over the ground;
O graze along, dogies, and feed kinda slow,
And don't forever be on the go—
O move slow, dogies, move slow.

O, say, little dogies, when you goin' to lay down
And quit this forever a-siftin' around?
My legs are weary, my seat is sore;
O, lay down, dogies, like you've laid down before—
Lay down, little dogies, lay down.

Whoo-oo-oo-ee-oo-oo, Whoo-ee-whoo-whoo-whoo-oo
Again came the crooning yodel, most like the wail of the coyote;
only restful and not wild. Over and over and over the fresh young voice
of the cowboy rang out in the long watches of the night, pleading with
the cattle to lie down and sleep and not to worry:
It's your misfortune and none of my own,
For you know Wyoming will be your new home.
There was a stream near our house, a good place to rest the cattle
before they plodded up the trail through the Indian Territory, across
Kansas, Nebraska, and then, finally sometimes to Montana and
Wyoming. During a period of twenty years ten million cattle and a million horses were driven northward from Texas on the Chisholm Trail
and other cattle trails. As the cowboys drove the cattle along they
called and sang and yodeled to them, they made up songs about trail
life. I began to write down these songs when I was a small boy.

ART AND THE BRONCO

★

O. Henry

O UT OF THE WILDERNESS HAD COME A PAINTER. GENIUS, whose coronations alone are democratic, had woven a chaplet of chaparral for the brow of Lonny Briscoe. Art, whose divine expression flows impartially from the fingertips of a cowboy or dilettante emperor, had chosen for a medium the Boy Artist of the San Saba. The outcome, seven feet by twelve of besmeared canvas, stood, gilt-framed, in the lobby of the Capitol.

The legislature was in session; the capital city of that great Western state was enjoying the season of activity and profit that the congregation of the solons bestowed. The boarding houses were corralling the easy dollars of the gamesome lawmakers. The greatest state in the West, an empire in area and resources, had arisen and repudiated the old libel of barbarism, lawbreaking and bloodshed. Order reigned within her borders. Life and property were as safe there, sir, as anywhere among the corrupt cities of the effete East. Pillow shams, churches, strawberry feasts and habeas corpus flourished. With impunity might the tenderfoot ventilate his "stovepipe" or his theories of culture. The arts and sciences received nurture and subsidy. And, therefore, it behooved the legislature of this great state to make appropriation for the purchase of Lonny Briscoe's immortal painting.

Rarely has the San Saba country contributed to the spread of the fine arts. Its sons have excelled in the solider graces, in the throw of the lariat, the manipulation of the esteemed .45, the intrepidity of the one-card draw and the nocturnal stimulation of towns from undue lethargy; but, hitherto, it had not been famed as a stronghold of aesthetics. Lonny Briscoe's brush had removed that disability. Here, among the limestone rocks, the succulent cactus and the drought-parched grass of that arid valley, had been born the Boy Artist. Why he came to woo art is beyond postulation. Beyond doubt, some spore of the afflatus must have sprung up within him in spite of the desert soil of San Saba. The tricksy spirit of creation must have incited him to attempted expression and then have sat hilarious among the white-hot sands of the valley, watching its mischievous work. For Lonny's picture, viewed as a thing of art, was something to have driven away dull care from the bosoms of the critics.

The painting—one might almost say panorama—was designed to portray a typical Western scene, interest culminating in a central animal figure, that of a stampeding steer, life-size, wild-eyed, fiery, breaking away in a mad rush from the herd that, close-ridden by a typical cowpuncher, occupied a position somewhat in the right background of the picture. The landscape presented fitting and faithful accessories. Chaparral, mesquite and pear were distributed in just proportions. A Spanish dagger plant, with its waxen blossoms in a creamy aggregation as large as a water-bucket, contributed floral beauty and variety. The distance was undulating prairie, bisected by stretches of the intermittent stream peculiar to the region lined with the rich green of live-oak and water-elms. A richly mottled rattlesnake lay coiled beneath a pale green clump of prickly pear in the foreground. A third of the canvas

was ultramarine and lake white—the typical Western sky and the flying clouds, rainless and feathery.

Between two plastered pillars in the commodious hallway near the
door of the chamber of representatives stood the painting. Citizens
and lawmakers passed there by twos and groups and sometimes
crowds to gaze upon it. Many—perhaps a majority of them—had lived
the prairie life and recalled easily the familiar scene. Old cattlemen
stood, reminiscent and candidly pleased, chatting with brothers of former camps and trails of the days it brought back to mind. Art critics
were few in the town, and there was heard none of that jargon of color,
perspective and feeling such as the East loves to use as a curb and a
rod to the pretensions of the artist. 'Twas a great picture most of them
agreed, admiring the gilt frame—larger than any they had ever seen.

Senator Kinney was the picture's champion and sponsor. It was he
who so often stepped forward and asserted, with the voice of a bronco-
buster, that it would be a lasting blot, sir, upon the name of this great
state if it should decline to recognize in a proper manner the genius
that had so brilliantly transferred to imperishable canvas a scene so
typical of the great sources of our state's wealth and prosperity, land
and—er—live stock.

Senator Kinney represented a section of the state in the extreme
West—400 miles from the San Saba country—but the true lover of art
is not limited by metes and bounds. Nor was Senator Mullens, repre-
senting the San Saba country, lukewarm in his belief that the state
should purchase the painting of his constituent. He was advised that
the San Saba country was unanimous in its admiration of the great
painting by one of its own denizens. Hundreds of connoisseurs had
straddled their broncos and ridden miles to view it before its removal
to the capital. Senator Mullens desired reelection, and he knew the
importance of the San Saba vote. He also knew that with the help of
Senator Kinney—who was a power in the legislature—the thing could
be put through. Now, Senator Kinney had an irrigation bill that he
wanted passed for the benefit of his own section, and he knew Sena-

tor Mullens could render him valuable aid and information, the San Saba country already enjoying the benefits of similar legislation. With these interests happily dovetailed, wonder at the sudden interest in art at the state Capitol must, necessarily, be small. Few artists have uncovered their first picture to the world under happier auspices than did Lonny Briscoe.

Senators Kinney and Mullens came to an understanding in the matters of irrigation and art while partaking of long drinks in the café of the Empire Hotel.

"H'm!" said Senator Kinney, "I don't know. I'm no art critic, but it seems to me the thing won't work. It looks like the worst kind of a chromo to me. I don't want to cast any reflections upon the artistic talent of your constituent, Senator, but I, myself, wouldn't give six bits for the picture—without the frame. How are you going to cram a thing like that down the throat of a legislature that kicks about a little item in the expense bill of six hundred and eighty-one dollars for rubber erasers for a whole term? It's wasting time. I'd like to help you, Mullens, but they'd guy us out of the Senate chamber if we were to try it."

"But you don't get the point," said Senator Mullens, in his deliberate tones, tapping Kinney's glass with his long forefinger. "I have my own doubts as to what the picture is intended to represent, a bullfight or a Japanese allegory, but I want this legislature to make an appropriation to purchase. Of course, the subject of the picture should have been in the state historical line, but it's too late to have the paint scraped off and changed. The state won't miss the money and the picture can be stowed away in a lumber-room where it won't annoy any one. Now, here's the point to work on, leaving art to look after itself— the chap that painted the picture is the grandson of Lucien Briscoe."

"Say it again," said Kinney, leaning his head thoughtfully. "Of the old, original Lucien Briscoe?"

"Of him. 'The man who,' you know. The man who carved the state out of the wilderness. The man who settled the Indians. The man who cleaned out the horse thieves. The man who refused the crown. The state's favorite son. Do you see the point now?"

"Wrap up the picture," said Kinney. "It's as good as sold. Why didn't you say that at first, instead of philandering along about art. I'll resign my seat in the Senate and go back to chain carrying for the county surveyor the day I can't make this state buy a picture kalsomined by a grandson of Lucien Briscoe. Did you ever hear of a special appropriation for the purchase of a home for the daughter of One-Eyed Smothers? Well, that went through like a motion to adjourn, and old One-Eyed never killed half as many Indians as Briscoe did. About what figure had you and the Kalsominer agreed upon to sandbag the treasury for?"

"I thought," said Mullens, "that may-be five hundred—"

"Five hundred!" interrupted Kinney, as he hammered on his glass for a lead pencil and looked around for a waiter. "Only five hundred for a red steer on the hoof delivered by a grandson of Lucien Briscoe! Where's your state pride, man? Two thousand is what it'll be. You'll introduce the bill and I'll get up on the floor of the Senate and wave the scalp of every Indian old Lucien ever murdered. Let's see, there was something else proud and foolish he did, wasn't there? Oh, yes; he declined all emoluments and benefits he was entitled to. Refused his head-right and veteran donation certificates. Could have been governor, but wouldn't. Declined a pension. Now's the state's chance to pay up. It'll have to take the picture, but then it deserves some punishment for keeping the Briscoe family waiting so long. We'll bring this thing up about the middle of the month, after the tax bill is settled. Now, Mullens, you send over, as soon as you can, and get me the figures on the cost of those irrigation ditches and the statistics about the increased production per acre. I'm going to need you when that bill of mine comes up. I reckon we'll be able to pull along pretty well together this session and maybe others to come, eh, Senator?"

Thus did fortune elect to smile upon the Boy Artist of the San Saba. Fate had already done her share when she arranged his atoms in the cosmogony of creation as the grandson of Lucien Briscoe.

The original Briscoe had been a pioneer both as to territorial occupation and in certain acts prompted by a great and simple heart. He had been one of the first settlers and crusaders against the wild forces of nature, the savage and the shallow politician. His name and memory were revered equally with any upon the list comprising Houston, Boone, Crockett, Clark and Green. He had lived simply, independently and unvexed by ambition, and died likewise. Even a less shrewd man than Senator Kinney could have prophesied that his state would hasten to honor and reward his grandson, come out of the chaparral at even so late a day.

And so, before the great picture by the door of the chamber of representatives at frequent times for many days could be found the breezy, robust form of Senator Kinney and be heard his clarion voice reciting the past deeds of Lucien Briscoe in connection with the handiwork of his grandson. Senator Mullens' work was more subdued in sight and sound, but directed along identical lines.

Then, as the day for the introduction of the bill for appropriation draws nigh, up from the San Saba country rides Lonny Briscoe and a loyal lobby of cowpunchers, bronco-back, to boost the cause of art and glorify the name of friendship, for Lonny is one of them, a knight of stirrup and chaparreras, as handy with the lariat and .45 as he is with brush and palette.

On a March afternoon the lobby dashed, with a whoop, into town. The cowpunchers had adjusted their garb suitably from that prescribed for the range to the more conventional requirements of town. They had conceded their leather chaparreras and transferred their six-shooters and belts from their persons to the horns of their saddles. Among them rode Lonny, a youth of twenty-three, brown, solemn-faced, ingenuous, bowlegged, reticent, bestriding Hot Tamales, the most sagacious cow pony west of the Mississippi. Senator Mullens had informed him of the bright prospects of the situation; had even mentioned—so great was his confidence in the capable Kinney—the price that the state would, in all likelihood, pay. It seemed to Lonny that fame and fortune were in his hands. Certainly, a spark of the divine fire was in the little brown centaur's breast, for he was counting the two thousand dollars as but a means to future development of his talent. Some day he would paint a picture even greater than this—one, say, twelve feet by twenty, full of scope and atmosphere and action.

During the three days that yet intervened before the coming of the date fixed for the introduction of the bill, the centaur lobby did valiant service. Coatless, spurred, weather-tanned, full of enthusiasm expressed in bizarre terms, they loafed in front of the painting with tireless zeal. Reasoning not unshrewdly, they estimated that their comments upon its fidelity to nature would be received as expert evidence. Loudly they praised the skill of the painter whenever there were ears near to which such evidence might be profitably addressed. Lem Perry, the leader of the claque, had a somewhat set speech, being uninventive in the construction of new phrases.

"Look at that two-year old, now," he would say, waving a cinnamon-brown hand toward the salient point of the picture. "Why, dang my hide, the critter's alive. I can jest hear him, 'lumpety-lump,' a-cuttin' away from the herd, pretendin' he's skeered. He's a mean scamp, that there steer. Look at his eyes a'wallin' and his tail a'wavin'. He's true and nat'ral to life. He's jest hankerin' fur a cow pony to round him up and send him scootin' back to the bunch. Dang my hide! jest look at that tail of his'n a-wavin'. Never knowed a steer to wave his tail any other way, dang my hide ef I did."

Jud Shelby, while admitting the excellence of the steer, resolutely confined himself to open admiration of the landscape, to the end that the entire picture receive its meed of praise.

"That piece of range," he declared, "is a dead ringer for Dead Hoss Valley. Same grass, same lay of the land, same old Whipperwill Creek skallyhootin' in and out of them motts of timber. Them buzzards on the left is circlin' 'round over Sam Kildrake's old paint hoss that killed his-self over-drinkin' on a hot day. You can't see the hoss for that mott of ellums on the creek, but he's thar. Anybody that was goin' to look for

Dead Hoss Valley and come across this picture, why, he'd jest light off'n his bronco and hunt a place to camp."

Skinny Rogers, wedded to comedy, conceived a complimentary little piece of acting that never failed to make an impression. Edging quite near to the picture, he would suddenly, at favorable moments, emit a piercing and awful "Yi-yi!" leap high and away, coming down with a great stamp of heels and whirring of rowels upon the stone-flagged floor.

"Jeeming Christopher!"—so ran his lines—"thought that rattler was a gin-u-ine one. Ding baste my skin if I didn't. Seemed to me I heard him rattle. Look at the blamed, unconverted insect a-layin' under that pear. Little more, and somebody would a-been snake-bit."

With these artful dodges, contributed by Lonny's faithful coterie, with the sonorous Kinney perpetually sounding the picture's merits and with the solvent prestige of the pioneer Briscoe covering it like a precious varnish, it seemed that the San Saba country could not fail to add a reputation as an art center to its well-known superiority in steer-roping contests and achievements with the precarious busted flush. Thus was created for the picture an atmosphere, due rather to externals than to the artist's brush, but through it the people seemed to gaze with more of admiration. There was a magic in the name of Briscoe that counted high against faulty technique and crude coloring. The old Indian-fighter and wolf-slayer would have smiled grimly in his happy hunting grounds had he known that his dilettante ghost was thus figuring as an art patron two generations after his uninspired existence.

Came the day when the Senate was expected to pass the bill of Senator Mullens appropriating two thousand dollars for the purchase of the picture. The gallery of the Senate chamber was early preempted by Lonny and the San Saba lobby. In the front row of chairs they sat, wild-haired, self-conscious, jingling, creaking and rattling, subdued by the majesty of the council hall.

The bill was introduced, went to the second reading and then Senator Mullens spoke for it dryly, tediously and at length. Senator Kin-

ney then arose and the welkin seized the bellrope preparatory to ringing. Oratory was at that time a living thing; the world had not quite
come to measure its questions by geometry and the multiplication
table. It was the day of the silver tongue, the sweeping gesture, the
decorative apostrophe, the moving peroration.

The Senator spoke. The San Saba contingent sat, breathing hard,
in the gallery, its disordered hair hanging down to its eyes, its sixteen-
ounce hats shifted restlessly from knee to knee. Below, the distinguished Senators either lounged at their desks with the abandon of
proven statesmanship or maintained correct attitudes indicative of a
first term.

Senator Kinney spoke for half an hour. History was his theme—history mitigated by patriotism and sentiment. He referred casually to the
picture in the outer hall—it was unnecessary, he said, to dilate upon
its merits—the Senators had seen for themselves. The painter of the
picture was the grandson of Lucien Briscoe. Then came the word pictures of Briscoe's life set forth in thrilling colors. His rude and venturesome life, his simple-minded love for the commonwealth he
helped to upbuild, his contempt for rewards and praise, his extreme
and sturdy independence and the great services he had rendered the
state. The subject of the oration was Lucien Briscoe; the painting
stood in the background, serving simply as a means, now happily
brought forward, through which the state might bestow a tardy rec-
ompense upon the descendant of its favorite son. Frequent enthusiastic applause from the Senators testified to the well reception of the
sentiment.

The bill passed without an opposing vote. To-morrow it would be
taken up by the House. Already was it fixed to glide through that body
on rubber tires. Blandford, Grayson and Plummer, all wheel-horses
and orators and provided with plentiful memoranda concerning the
deeds of pioneer Briscoe, had agreed to furnish the motive power.

The San Saba lobby and its protégé stumbled awkwardly down the stairs and out into the Capitol yard. Then they herded closely and gave one yell of triumph. But one of them—Buck-Kneed Summers it was— hit the key with a thoughtful remark.

"She cut the mustard," he said, "all right. I reckon they're goin' to buy Lon's heifer. I ain't right much on the parlyment'ry, but I gather that's what the signs added up. But she seems to me, Lonny, the argyment ran principal to grandfather, instead of paint. It's reasonable calculatin' that you want to be glad you got the Briscoe brand on you, my son."

That remark clinched in Lonny's mind an unpleasant, vague suspicion to the same effect. His reticence increased, and he gathered grass from the ground, chewing it pensively. The picture as a picture had been humiliatingly absent from the Senator's arguments. The painter had been held up as a grandson, pure and simple. While this was gratifying on certain lines it made art look little and slab-sided. The Boy Artist was thinking.

The hotel Lonny stopped at was near the Capitol. It was close to the one o'clock dinner hour when the appropriation had been passed by the Senate. The hotel clerk told Lonny that a famous artist from New York had arrived in town that day and was in the hotel. He was on his way westward to New Mexico to study the effect of sunlight upon the ancient walls of the Zunis. Modern stone reflects light. Those ancient building materials absorb it. The artist wanted this effect in a picture he was painting and was traveling three thousand miles to get it.

Lonny sought this man out after dinner and told his story. The artist was an unhealthy man, kept alive by genius and indifference to life. He went with Lonny to the Capitol and stood there before the picture. The artist pulled his beard and looked unhappy.

"Should like to have your sentiments," said Lonny, "just as they run out of the pen."

"It's the way they'll come," said the painter man. "I took three different kinds of medicine before dinner—by the tablespoonful. The taste still lingers. I am primed for telling the truth. You want to know if the picture is, or if it isn't?"

"Right," said Lonny. "Is it wool or cotton? Should I paint some more or cut it out and ride herd a-plenty?"

"I heard a rumor during pie," said the artist, "that the state is about to pay you two thousand dollars for this picture."

"It's passed the Senate," said Lonny, "and the House rounds it up to-morrow."

"That's lucky," said the pale man. "Do you carry a rabbit's foot?"

"No," said Lonny, "but it seems I had a grandfather. He's considerable mixed up in the color scheme. It took me a year to paint that picture. Is she entirely awful or not? Some says, now, that that steer's tail ain't badly drawed. They think it's proportioned nice. Tell me."

The artist glanced at Lonny's wiry figure and nut-brown skin. Something stirred him to a passing irritation.

"For Art's sake, son," he said, fractiously, "don't spend any more money for paint. It isn't a picture at all. It's a gun. You hold up the state with it, if you like, and get your two thousand, but don't get in front of any more canvas. Live under it. Buy a couple of hundred ponies with the money—I'm told they're that cheap—and ride, ride, ride. Fill your lungs and eat and sleep and be happy. No more pictures. You look healthy. That's genius. Cultivate it." He looked at his watch. "Twenty minutes to three. Four capsules and one tablet at three. That's all you wanted to know, isn't it?"

At three o'clock the cowpunchers rode up for Lonny, bringing Hot Tamales, saddled. Traditions must be observed. To celebrate the passage of the bill by the Senate the gang must ride wildly through the town, creating uproar and excitement. Liquor must be partaken of, the suburbs shot up and the glory of the San Saba country vociferously proclaimed. A part of the programme had been carried out in the saloons on the way up.

Lonny mounted Hot Tamales, the accomplished little beast prancing with fire and intelligence. He was glad to feel Lonny's bowlegged grip against his ribs again. Lonny was his friend, and he was willing to do things for him.

"Come on, boys," said Lonny, guiding Hot Tamales into a gallop with his knees. With a whoop, the inspired lobby tore after him through the dust. Lonny led his cohorts straight for the Capitol. With a wild yell, the gang indorsed his now evident intention of riding into it. Hooray for San Saba!

Up the four broad, limestone steps clattered the broncos of the cowpunchers. Into the resounding hallway they pattered, scattering in dismay those passing on foot. Lonny, in the lead, shoved Hot Tamales direct for the great picture. At that hour a downpouring, soft light from the second-story windows bathed the big canvas. Against the darker background of the hall the painting stood out with valuable effect. In spite of the defects of the art you could almost fancy that you gazed out upon a landscape. You might well flinch a step from the convincing figure of the life-sized steer stampeding across the grass. Perhaps it thus seemed to Hot Tamales. The scene was in his line. Perhaps he only obeyed the will of his rider. His ears pricked up; he snorted. Lonny leaned forward in the saddle and elevated his elbows, winglike. Thus signals the cowpuncher to his steed to launch himself full speed ahead. Did Hot Tamales fancy he saw a steer, red and cavorting, that should be headed off and driven back to herd? There was a fierce clatter of hoofs, a rush, a gathering of steely flank muscles, a leap to the jerk of the bridle rein, and Hot Tamales, with Lonny bending low in the saddle to dodge the top of the frame, ripped through the great canvas like a shell from a mortar, leaving the cloth hanging in ragged shreds about a monstrous hole.

Quickly Lonny pulled up his pony, and rounded the pillars. Spectators came running, too astounded to add speech to the commotion. The sergeant-at-arms of the House came forth, frowned, looked ominous and then grinned. Many of the legislators crowded out to observe the tumult. Lonny's cowpunchers were stricken to silent horror by his mad deed.

Senator Kinney happened to be among the earliest to emerge. Before he could speak Lonny leaned in his saddle as Hot Tamales pranced, pointed his quirt at the Senator, and said calmly:

"That was a fine speech you made to-day, mister, but you might as well let up on that 'propriation business. I ain't askin' the state to give me nothin'. I thought I had a picture to sell to it, but it wasn't one. You said a heap of things about Grandfather Briscoe that makes me kind of proud I'm his grandson. Well, the Briscoes ain't takin' presents from the state yet. Anybody can have the frame that wants it. Hit her up, boys."

Away scuttled the San Saba delegation out of the hall, down the steps, along the dusty street.

Halfway to the San Saba country they camped that night. At bedtime Lonny stole away from the camp-fire and sought Hot Tamales, placidly eating grass at the end of his stake rope. Lonny hung upon his neck, and his art aspirations went forth forever in one long, regretful sigh. But as he thus made renunciation his breath formed a word or two.

"You was the only one, Tamales, what seen anything in it. It *did* look like a steer, didn't it, old hoss?"

THE STONE RANCH

────────── ✴ ──────────

Sallie Reynolds Matthews

II

THE STONE RANCH, SO CALLED BY OUR FAMILY BECAUSE IT was all built of stone, even to the large corrals, lay in an open valley with beautiful hills to the south and, at a farther distance, to the west and northwest. Not far to the northeast there is a little peak which we have always called Buzzard Peak and beneath which flows the Clear Fork whose winding course came to within less than a mile of the ranch house. It was situated in what is now the southwest corner of Throckmorton County and was on the outside border of civilization. The country just northwest of us was occupied solely by Indians and wild animals for hundreds of miles; great herds of buffaloes, deer, antelopes and wild horses roamed the plains. The nearest ranch, Camp Cooper, was five miles east.

It was a bright sunny day when we came to the Stone Ranch, and although the house was not very large, it appeared to be a veritable for-

tified castle with its thick stone walls, and seemed a haven of peace
and quiet to the family after having live in the crowded fort.

The house stood on the north side of a little creek we called Walnut because of the many trees of that species which grew along its
banks. Across the creek on the south was a spring, covered by a stone
house, where we kept milk, butter and meat in the warm weather.

The main building consisted of only two large rooms with fireplace
in each room, and a wide hall between with heavy double doors of oak
opening on both north and south. The hall was made into a bedroom
by closing one side. One room had a plank floor; the other room and
the hall were flagged with stone. On the north was a detached building with two rooms, one with a fireplace. This we called the "bache-
lors' hall" as it was occupied by the young men and boys.

On entering the house, we found it in a state of disorder. Some of
the windows were broken and the glass was lying on the floor. Some
wild animal, a wolf or panther, perhaps, had evidently been in the
house, as one of the inside doors had been badly gnawed on the edge.
The sight of those glaring toothmarks gave me an eerie feeling; I could
imagine many and all kinds of wild animals visiting us at night time.
How such things impress children! I can see that dusty and glass-
strewn floor, and that door deeply marked by animal teeth, in my
mind's eye now. The work of putting things in order was started at
once when Mother began to sweep, and Brother George took the
broom from her, saying, "Let me sweep."

There were a few pieces of furniture in the house when we took
possession, some chairs and a little French bedroom suite in white,
decorated with a spray of flowers on the head and foot boards of the
bed and on the dresser drawers. To my childish eyes this furniture
appeared about the last word in elegance.

One day Glenn was nosing around in the old rock quarry nearby
when he spied a wooden box which on examination proved to be filled
with dishes. I think there was almost a full dinner set of ordinary white
queen's ware, decorated with tiny roses in relief. I remember there

were several covered vegetable dishes. This was a rich find for the family as the supply of china had become so depleted that there was not enough with which to set the table, and tin ware was substituted. With all this new china the table appeared festive indeed.

There were other things found hidden in these rocks, cowbells, staples for ox yokes, and such, for all of which, together with the pieces of furniture, my father paid when the owners came back.

Finding all these articles made the family feel that any pile of rock might contain hidden treasure, so when a small mound of rock was discovered on a hill close by, the men at once proceeded to investigate in order to see what was hidden there. What they found was a tiny coffin. There was no mark of any kind about this mound of rock to indicate that it was a grave. Of course it was immediately replaced as found, and the little mound is still there, but to this day we do not know to whom the child belonged.

The room with the stone floor in the main house was an all-purpose room. Mother's bed was in one corner. At the opposite wall stood a long table at which could be seated twelve or fifteen people, and in some way Mother and Sister managed to set it always with a white cloth, clinging tenaciously to the refinements of life.

The cooking was done on the wide fireplace. On winter evenings after the ovens were set aside, the hearth swept and table pushed against the wall, the family gathered around the fire. Often the boys would be moulding bullets, Mother and Sister sewing, knitting or mending. Many pecans, which had been gathered along the banks of the Clear Fork or Walnut Creek, a short distance away, were cracked and sometimes roasted over the fire. Now and then the cured tongue of a buffalo would be buried in the ashes and roasted; if you have never tasted this special tidbit you have missed something to delight the taste of an epicurean.

Life was never monotonous to me even though there were no other little girls with which to play. I tagged along after my young brothers, Glenn and Phin, as they played. They would make traps and sometimes get a bird, which was always thrilling. They never put them in a cage, but would free them after playing with them a little while.

On the south side of the creek near the spring house, there stood two magnificent elm trees, the interlocking branches of which, like a huge umbrella, made a dense shade. The soil under the elms was moist and alluvial, a contrast to the rocky, arid hillsides.

One day Mother observed Glenn and Phin, very busy with hoe and rake under these trees. She asked them what they meant by all this work; they answered, "We're making a garden."

"Well," Mother replied, "Nothing will grow in that shade."

This was a wet blanket indeed on their spirit of industry. Phin dropped his hoe, saying, "Humph! I'm not going to work in the hot sun." Thus, garden making was over for the time.

Of course, I was too young to realize the seriousness of life, and it seemed a busy, happy time, full of cheerfulness and useful tasks; but as I look back upon it now, I know it was fraught with much anxiety, especially when the boys were out working with the cattle or scouting for Indians. It must have been lonely and rather desolate for my mother and sister with so little contact with other women. There would be an occasional visitor from Camp Cooper and Sister would sometimes ride down there with the men, but I do not believe my mother ever left the ranch except one time during our stay there. There were neither newspapers nor magazines to keep us in touch with the world, no church or Sunday school near.

I wonder how my parents kept track of the days with no calendars. My mother did lose the day once when she did her Saturday cleaning and scrubbing on Sunday, and took a quiet Sabbath rest on Monday. As a rule there was a peaceful calm on Sunday, different from other days, but not always, for at times that was the hardest day in the week, with a crowd of extra men to cook for. Although women were scarce, men were fairly plentiful.

Besides the regular household of fifteen, there were many transient men coming and going. Sometimes they came hunting buffaloes and other game; they did not have to search far for buffaloes as they were seldom out of sight of the house from October to May. At other times they were scouting for Indians who had taken their horses.

The chief recreation for the young men was the hunt and this they thoroughly enjoyed. One noted one while we were at the Stone Ranch was when they went up the river to a place they called Blackjack Thicket, near Fort Phantom Hill, where they had hoped to find some blacktail deer. The common red and whitetail deer were very plentiful where we lived, but there were no blacktail. I do not remember that they got any deer on this expedition, but they did get a white buffalo which was a very great rarity, this being the first we had ever seen or heard of, and among the many thousands of buffaloes that were killed in this country, I never saw but one other white robe; it was owned by Frank E. Conrad.

Two of my brothers, George and Ben, had a shot at this one, but George being the elder, got the skin. It was given to an Army officer at Fort Griffin after the Fort was established, to be placed in the Smithsonian Institution at Washington. In my visits to the Capital I have searched diligently in that and other museums and can find no trace of its ever having been placed there. It was there at one time as some of the family saw it, and it does seem as if there would be some record of it. The officials of these institutions have been most kind in assisting me in my search for it.

When summer came my father made his yearly trip to Weatherford for supplies. On this trip my sister and her baby, my brother, Ben, and I were along. The reason for Sister's and my going was mainly to visit with our relatives, the Barbers, and to have some pictures made, little tintypes they were. While we were away the ranch was raided by Indians.

One Sunday morning after most of the men had ridden off leaving only two as guards and the two younger boys, Glenn and Phin, twelve and nine years of age respectively, fourteen Indians, Kiowas and Comanches, charged about the house and fired a few times. Glenn used a gun as well as the two men and the Indians soon left, taking with them five hundred head of cattle that they had rounded up and all the horses they could lay hands on. In those days it was customary for the cattlemen to put the young calves in the pen in order to keep the mothers from straying away too far and to get them located and gentle. (At one time we also had fifty young buffalo calves nursing the cows with the other calves.) There were sometimes a hundred or so calves in the pen. The Indians turned out the calves and rounded in as many of the mothers as they could find, but not all, as some of them were bawling in deep distress for days afterwards.

As Indians were not accustomed to seizing cattle, their usual quarry being only horses, some people think these raiders were not Indians, but rather white desperadoes. If they were not Indians, they were artfully disguised in Indian dress, war paint and feathers, and their war whoops were well simulated, for the family felt certain they were Indians.

Father knew nothing of this incursion until when nearing home he heard that the ranch had been raided by Indians. After this he thought surely the family would return to the fort. Not my little Scotch mother; she was made of more heroic metal. When someone asked her if she had not been terribly frightened, she said, "No, but I was all-fired mad."

III

The next event of interest happened in April, 1867. Some horses had been stolen from settlers east of us and a party of men, riding in hot haste to overtake the Indian marauders, came to our ranch where they were joined by my brothers, George and William, and Si Hough. They overtook the Indians at the Double Mountain Fork of the Brazos, a distance of thirty-five or forty miles from the Stone Ranch. They were loitering here, taking their ease and shooting buffaloes, thinking they were out of the danger zone. They were taken by surprise and only one escaped to tell the tale. They were outnumbered, there being ten white men to seven Indians. One of our men, John Anderson, was shot through the arm, receiving a flesh wound, and a minie ball passed through William's sleeve. Brother George was the only one seriously hurt. He was shot with an arrow that entered his body just above the navel. He was wearing a United States Army belt buckle which was about two inches wide by three long. This buckle, we think, may have saved his life, as the arrow hit the edge of the buckle, breaking the force of the shot to some extent or it would doubtless have gone through his body. These arrows had great force when shot from strong Indian bows. He pulled the shaft out, but the head was left in his body, where it stayed fifteen years. At first they thought it possibly might have dropped in the loose sand when the shaft was taken out and have been covered, but that was not the case, as was proven in after years.

When Si came up and saw George lying there, he swore he would have the scalp of the Indian who shot him. He was not long in getting it. This particular Indian was marked by his gay trappings; his war bonnet of eagle feathers and bridle covered with disks of hammered silver proclaimed him a chieftain, they thought. The silver-studded bridle was given to Brother by Si Hough and is now treasured by William's sons, Brother George having had none to inherit it.

William and John Anderson rode all night to tell the family what had happened. The night before they came, my father had a dream which so impressed him that he told Mother that one of the boys was wounded, and he was walking the yard in distress and looking for a messenger when the two boys came. This premonition seemed almost psychic.

How to get the wounded boy home was a problem. They tied two horses together, heads and tails, and filled in between with their packs. The packs, called kayaks, were made of cowhide and were on the order of old-fashioned saddlebags, only they were much larger and were used to put across a pack horse for carrying provisions for cow hunts and scouts like this one. These were placed across the horses and filled in with bedding, and the wounded man was laid on this improvised bed. A man on each side led the horses as the slow journey home was begun. You can realize that this mode of travel was anything but comfortable for an injured man; it was almost unbearable, but he endured it until nearing home when he asked to be put upon his horse which had an easy gait. He wanted the family to see him sitting his horse! They, of course, did not know that he was still alive. When the scouting party approached the ranch, the younger boys were on top of the smokehouse watching, and when they counted the full number it was a great relief and joy to those at home.

In the meantime, Sam Newcomb was riding night and day to Weatherford, more than a hundred miles away, for a doctor, only stopping for a bite to eat and a fresh horse at the ranches along the way, and he and Dr. James D. Ray of Weatherford rode day and night on the return trip. When the doctor arrived, he probed the wound a little and that ended his treatment. It was all he could do at that time as he did not have the facilities of modern surgery. Strange to say, the wound healed without infection and soon he was going about as usual. However, he suffered a good deal of pain in his body until the arrow was removed, although no one would have suspected this from the active life he led.

The arrow head either went into the muscles of the back at first, or in some manner gradually worked its way to the back. Years afterward there was a knot pushed out near his spine which he suspected was the arrow head coming to the surface, and he was right about it, for in 1882 he went to Kansas City and had it taken out. The following are excerpts from an account in the *Kansas City Journal* of July 18, 1882.

Yesterday afternoon there was removed from the body of George T. Reynolds, a prominent cattleman of Fort Griffin, Texas, an arrow head, two inches long. Mr. Reynolds had carried this head sixteen years, three months and fifteen days.

On Friday last the gentleman came to this city and registered at the St. James hotel. His coming was for the purpose of having a surgical operation performed.

Then follows an account of the Indian fight which is omitted here. On his back opposite the place where the arrow entered his body, he could feel its head. At last he decided to have it cut out and came to Kansas City as mentioned. Scales of rust were removed from the arrow head when it was taken from his body. The point was blunt as if it had been eaten off with rust.

This operation was performed by Drs. Lewis and Griffith, in the presence of Dr. Powell of New York. The gentleman was resting easy last evening and feeling much relieved.

There was no anaesthetic used and before going into the operation he exacted a promise from the doctor that he would stop when asked. Two friends went into the operating room with him to see him through. One of them ran out as soon as the doctor started work. The other, "Shanghai" Pierce, a well known cattleman of South Texas, became so excited when he saw the deep incision that he yelled, "Stop, doctor, you are cutting that man to the hollow." At this my brother called a halt. The cut had missed the arrow head, and had gone down by the side of it. Brother raised himself to a sitting posture and bent forward. The steel arrow head slipped out into the incision.

In addition to the bridle with the silver discs, there were many other trophies of this battle with Indians, bows and quivers full of arrows, beads, earrings and bracelets by the dozens; and with shame I confess it, there were several scalps, scalps not taken in wanton cruelty, but as a lesson to the Indians. It seemed that by using their own tactics against them, they were more terrified; at least that is what was claimed by the white men.

IV

Before going further, I want to state my sentiments in regard to the Indians. While the pioneers of this country suffered greatly in many ways, not the least being agony of mind as well as body, I do not think

the Indians were by any means altogether to blame. The white people
came to America as Christians. Did not the Pilgrim fathers come primarily that they might worship God according to the dictates of their
own consciences? And they did treat the Indians kindly in the beginning and had a friendly welcome by Massasoit. But this did not continue for long, and as the settling of the country by white people went
on, we know there were many who cheated and exploited the Indians
in every way possible, and in some instances treated them with ruth-
less cruelty.

One such incident came under my parents' knowledge while they
lived in Shelby County. During the rush to the gold fields of California, a party of young men left their neighborhood to go there. In
the party there was one foolhardy fellow who boasted he would shoot
the first Indian he saw. The first Indian he saw happened to be a
squaw, sitting on a log nursing her baby, and in cold blood he shot
her. Could anything have been more dastardly and heartless? They
were immediately surrounded by Indians and the man who did the
deed was demanded, and it was obvious that if he were not surrendered, they would kill the whole party. So they gave him up and he
was deservedly flayed alive. They were merciful not to have killed
the whole company; that is what Mr. White Man would have done
under like circumstances.

Another incident of cold-blooded cruelty on the part of white men
was witnessed by my husband when a young lad. There had been a
band of Indians in the country, and a young man, son of Mr. Browning, a prominent citizen, had been killed. A party of men were out
scouting for these Indians, or any Indians, when they came upon a
lone redskin who apparently was lost. He may have belonged to the
band which had killed young Browning, or he may not, for no one
knew. When found, he was roasting a skunk for his dinner. The scouts
ordered him to march off and he did so, never turning his head. He
was shot in the back, and Browning was given the first shot to appease
his thirst for vengeance. The young lad mentioned above was in the

party and he thought it a shocking display of cowardice on the part of the white men. He says that if they had given the Indian some food and a "plug" of a pony, they would have acted more like Christians and perhaps have served their country better.

Some time during Civil War days, I do not know just what year it was, there was a band of Indians of the Kickapoo tribe passing through this country going across to New Mexico. They were friendly and did not molest anybody or anything. But they were Indians, and that was enough in the minds of some people. When they came to the locality where the city of San Angelo now stands, they saw a body of men and not wanting any trouble they sent one of their men out with a white flag to parley with these white men. The white men wanted no parley, they wanted to fight. They killed this peace messenger and forced an encounter in which the white men were ingloriously whipped. And the Indians went on their way without being further molested.

Now I do not hold any brief for the Indians nor am I posing as a Helen Hunt Jackson, but I do think that our race has much to answer for. How are we going to reconcile that "Trail of Tears" when the Cherokees, a peaceful tribe, were forced to leave their little homes and farms in western Georgia and North Carolina, because, forsooth, the white man wanted the land, therefore the Indian must move on. They were sent into the new country of Oklahoma that the Government had provided, and it is a fine country, a rich and beautiful land. But these people did not want to give up their homes where they had spent their lives among familiar surroundings and which they loved perhaps as we love ours. Many of them were old and feeble, and so many died on the way. It is spoken of by those tribes as the "Trail of Tears" to this day.

I think that if they had been treated more humanely from the beginning, there would have been much less rapine and bloodshed. What could we expect of a people that were gradually being driven from their home and country, their hunting grounds being taken without remuneration? When the United States Government did set aside certain portions for their exclusive use, did not the white man try in every way to get a share of that? If by no other means, he would take unto himself an Indian wife, and in that way acquire land. If there had been more William Penns, this would have been a more peaceful country in pioneer days. I, for one, believe a good bit in the inherent nobility of the Red Man.

THE TEXANS TOUCH THE PLAINS

★

Walter Prescott Webb

THE DIVIDING LINE BETWEEN THE EAST AND THE WEST CUTS the state of Texas into two almost equal parts. As Colonel Marcy pointed out, the Cross Timbers roughly marked the dividing line, which in his time separated civilized man from the savage. Below the Cross Timbers the line veers to the southeast, touching the coast near the old town of Indianola. This brings it about that the country around San Antonio and southward from there partakes of the nature of the Plains. San Antonio was the Plains outpost of Spanish occupation. The Plains Indians raided around San Antonio and on to the coast throughout the open country, or wherever they could ride on horseback. The Mexicans were even less successful than the Spaniards had been.

In 1821 Stephen F. Austin introduced into Texas (then a Mexican province) a colony of immigrants from the United States. He did not, however, attempt to make his settlement near the Plains portion of the state; he chose that portion of the state which is in its nature very similar to the more fertile regions of the Mississippi Valley. Like the people who two decades later went to Oregon, he sought the timbered and well-watered environment, along the Brazos and Colorado rivers, in which the settlers he expected to introduce would feel at home. Austin's biographer has thus described the land that the empresario chose:

> Austin's boundaries included the fairest part of the province then known—land of exhaustless fertility, abundantly watered and accessible to the sea, timber and prairie interspersed in convenient proportions. . . . All who visited Texas and returned to the United States advertised its superior natural advantages, and men who had themselves no intention of emigrating wrote to Austin for reliable information which they might detail to others.

The other American contractors who followed Austin to Texas established themselves as near his colony as circumstances would permit. Although the strength of Austin's colony had something to do with this decision, the nature of the land probably had as much or more. The Americans were appropriating to themselves the agricultural lands lying along the middle courses of the rivers. It is significant that not one of these settlements lay west of the ninety-eighth meridian, and more significant that those which lay north and west of Austin's colony were in continual apprehension of the Indians.

Austin's relations with the Comanches are worth noting here, not because they were important but because they were significant. In March, 1822, he found it necessary to go from San Antonio to Mexico City on business. Between San Antonio and Laredo he came into the barren country, which pushes eastward in this section. He described it as the "poorest I ever saw in my life, it is generally nothing but sand, entirely void of timber, covered with scrubby thorn bushes and prickly pear." He declared Laredo to be "as poor as sand banks, and drought, and indolence can make it." These statements show that the careful and conservative Austin, who became the father of Texas, would have been repelled immediately had he been confronted with the necessity of making a settlement in this, a pure Plains environment. He had no experience that fitted him to live without timber and water.

As Austin went south he found that "between San Antonio and Monterrey the Indians were a continual menace." He was in the southern range of the Apaches and Comanches, and near the Nueces River he and his single companion were surrounded and captured by fifty Comanches, who seized all their belongings. But when the Comanches found that their captives were Americans and not Mexicans, they gave them their freedom and restored all their property except a bridle, four blankets (note that what they kept pertained to horses), and a Spanish grammar! Knowing the Comanches to be horsemen, we can easily understand their keeping the bridle and blankets, but just what they wanted with the Spanish grammar remains a mystery.

In applying for a grant to settle his "Little Colony," on the east bank of the Colorado, north and west of the original settlement, Austin declared that the people of San Antonio requested him to settle there to protect travelers and check Comanche and Tahuacano raids on San Antonio.

That Austin understood the Indian situation in Texas and the difference between a Plains Indian and a timber Indian is perfectly clear from a reading of his biography and letters. In eastern Texas were the generally peaceful Cherokees, Choctaws, and Caddos; among the settlers were the weak Tonkawas, and below them on the coast the ferocious but numerically weak Karankawas. To the west were the Wacos and Tahuacanos, who might be termed a semi-Plains people: they dwelt in the Prairie Plains, and although they cultivated crops they also rode horses and hunted the buffalo. Beyond these were the never-to-be-misunderstood Comanches.

Austin, always keenly alive to the practical policy that he should follow purely in reference to his own colony, did not fail to make good use of the Comanche's partiality for Americans. In connection with this subject Barker says:

> The desperate situation can be inferred from the embarrassing pro-
> posal which Austin made to the political chief for avoiding Comanche
> hostility in 1825. Rumor reported these Indians to be raiding San Anto-
> nio and Goliad, robbing and killing, but the settlers still profited from
> their partiality to Americans and were not disturbed. Though it shamed
> him to the soul, Austin suggested that they take advantage of this cir-
> cumstance until they were strong enough to carry on an effective cam-
> paign. . . . [He] counseled the selfish policy of *sauve qui peut* until the
> settlement was on its feet.

Further light is thrown on the Texas Indian question by two orders which Austin received from the superior military officer in Texas. The first, dated August 21, 1825, ordered him to march at once against the Wacos, Tahuacanos, and Tahuiases; the second, dated five days later, countermanded the order because the Comanches were reported to be at the Waco villages in force. Both orders were received the same day. Austin, foreseeing a repetition of the first order, adroitly began to maneuver the Indian situation into his own hands; that is, he took the initiative and distributed a questionnaire among his people to ascer-tain the consensus of opinion concerning the policy that should be pursued. Should they go to war with the western Indians and leave the colony open to the incursions of the coast tribes? Should they ask the Tonkawas and Lipans (the eastern remnant of the Apaches and undying enemies of the Comanches) to join them? Should they fight or should they make treaties? With unerring skill Austin inserted the suggestion that it would be better to delay. Revenge should wait on the proper time, and that time should be determined by cool judgment and not by passion. In the meantime the colony would grow strong, and, besides, the Leftwich colony was about to be settled between them and the troublesome Indians and would serve as a buffer. Like a skillful parliamentarian Austin kept peace when both his colonists and the Mexican government wanted war. When he wrote a friend that the government was displeased that he had not gone to war, the friend replied that it was better to be driven from the country by the government than by the Indians.

Austin did not hesitate, however, to take strong measures against the Indians. In the winter following the incidents just related his settlement was entered by Choctaws in search of Tonkawas and by Tahuacanos on a horse-stealing expedition. The thieving Indians were attacked, and a number were killed. Austin now made preparations for an Indian campaign in May of 1826, and did exactly what the Spaniards had done in the previous century: he formed an alliance with the Cherokees, Shawnees, and Delawares; but the alliance was vetoed by the Mexican officials, and the campaign was suspended.

In the summer Austin called together the representatives of the various militia districts to adopt a plan by which to guard against the incursions of the Indians. "The result of this conference was an arrangement to keep from twenty to thirty mounted rangers in service all the time."

We do not know whether these rangers were called into service; but it does not matter, for the provision for them is significant. Austin had not settled his colony on the Plains, but he was near enough to the Plains to feel the influence of the Plains Indians, who always came and went on horseback. It is to be noted that the most serious trouble came from the west, and that this trouble had brought into embryo the organization of the Texas Rangers, later to be perfected and developed into a mounted fighting organization whose reputation has spread over the English-speaking world and is intimately known by at least one Latin nation. Just as the explorers who set out from Missouri to cross the Plains had to leave their boats and take to wagons and horses, so the Texans found it necessary to mount their horses in order to meet the mounted Plains Indians. The Texans still had to learn much about horses and horseback fighting, but they had no choice in the matter, if they were to succeed in their contest with the Indians for possession of the Plains.

It is not the purpose here to follow in detail the spread of Austin's colony, the coming of other contractors and immigrants from the United States to Texas. As they came in they found it necessary to push north and west of the original settlements, debouching on the open Plains, where they came into contact and into conflict with the Plains Indians. At first they made no effort at permanent settlement in that direction, but clung almost instinctively to the woodland region. From 1821 to 1836 these venturesome Texans were the outriders of the American frontier. They had thrust a salient into the frontier of Mexico. They were still in a familiar physical environment, but they were so close to the borders of the new environment that its problems confronted them from the first. They could not go northwest, west, or southwest without coming into the range of the Comanches and other mounted Indians. They were also in contact with the Mexicans—not so much with the Mexican population as with the Mexican government, under which they had voluntarily placed themselves but with which they never found themselves in complete accord. Potentially, Texas was a center of three conflicting civilizations—that of the Mexicans, that of the Texans, and that of the Plains Indians. The potential conflict soon became a real one, eventuating in that tempestuous period beginning with the Texas revolution and ending with the Mexican War, between which events the Texans maintained an independent republic.

During the ten years of the republic Texas and the Texans had no peace. Mexico refused to recognize the independence of its lost province and maintained a constant threat of war which expressed itself in occasional partisan raids into Texas. San Antonio was twice captured by Mexican armies. The Texans also made two attacks against Mexico. In 1841 the Santa Fe expedition left Austin with the ostensible purpose of establishing the jurisdiction of Texas over Santa Fe and, if possible, of making good the claim of Texas to the upper Rio Grande valley. In 1842 a party of Texans set out to invade Mexico. Their disastrous venture is known as the Mier expedition, for the reason that when the Texans reached Mier they were captured by a Mexican army. Both the Santa Fe expedition and the Mier expedition ended in disaster, most of the participants being captured and some executed.

Out of their long experience with both Mexicans and Indians the Texans learned that they could never afford to surrender. The memory of what happened at the Alamo in 1836 affected the attitude of those who found themselves in conflict with the Mexicans. But the Mexicans were not the only foes who gave no quarter: the Plains Indians who dwelt in the West did not know the meaning of the word and were past masters in the art of human torture. Thus it came about that the Texans were confronted by two foes to neither of whom they could surrender: *they had to fight*.

It is a military axiom that an enemy imposes on his foe his own military methods, provided they be superior ones. The military methods of both the Plains Indians and the Mexicans had to do with horses. The Texas border war was not a warfare of pitched battles, but of great distances, sudden incursions, and rapid flight on horseback. The attackers always came on horseback, with an organization mobile and fleet and elusive. They had to be met and pursued on horseback with an organization equally mobile. Had Texas been populous and wealthy its task of defense would have been easy; but it had few men to enlist and nothing save land and paper money, equally worthless in Texas, to pay them with. Whatever fighting force Texas devised, therefore, must be small and economical as well as mobile and fleet. From these hard conditions was evolved the organization of the Texas Rangers. What these men had inherited and brought with them to the West was blended with what they acquired after their arrival into a type which was thus set forth by an understanding writer: "A Texas Ranger can ride like a Mexican, trail like an Indian, shoot like a Tennesseean, and fight like a very devil!"

GRAVEYARD OF THE COWMAN'S HOPES

J. Evetts Haley

"KNOWING WE HAD TO PASS THROUGH SOME BROKEN country before camping time," Goodnight said, "I went ahead, as customary, to ascertain whether any Indians were present or not, and to prevent surprise. I went into these breaks two or three hours by sun, at least a mile north of the trail—it being my custom never to follow the trail on such an excursion, knowing the Indians would waylay it first. I saw a man coming into the hills probably three quarters of a mile away, carefully sneaking around from point to point. I felt sure he was an Indian, and knew there would be more not far away. I maneuvered around, aiming to cut him off from the breaks, get him, and return to the herd. I got in behind him all right, but when I got close enough I discovered he was a white man, and rode to him, finding that it was Burleson. He at once inquired about his herd, which I told him was safe and just down the river. Then he commenced to tell me what Loving had said.

"'Loving was killed by Indians, way below on the Pecos!'" I said.

"'Loving is at Fort Sumner,'" he replied.

"'Impossible!'"

"'I tell you, he is in Fort Sumner right now and is very anxious to see you,'" Burleson answered, after which Goodnight heard the complete story. Together they hurried back, met the herds, passed over the hills, and camped. Then Goodnight saddled old Jenny for his long and remarkable ride to Sumner.

Since leaving the Indian-ridden Texas frontier, Goodnight had not unrolled his bed. For thirty-two days and nights his iron will rode whip and spur over his tireless body, and the sleep he got was principally on the back of a horse, snatched in the saddle while around the herd at night and on the trail by day.

On this drive Fate rode hard beside them, and Goodnight, riding too in his prime, was determined not to be outdone. But for a few short naps on a buffalo robe or against a wagon wheel during mealtime, he was with the herd night and day. "It wasn't so hard," he explained, simply; "you got to where you could sleep on a horse without any trouble." This year marked his supreme and unsurpassable effort against all the unfriendly fortune that befell the cattle drive. He and his hands drove relentlessly, hating their own physical limitations, while loving and sparing, so far as possible, only the mounts between their knees.

Goodnight's ride up the Pecos, climaxing a restless month when man and horse were actually one, is worthy of the finest traditions of the riding West. The ride from the resting herd to Bosque Redondo was one hundred and ten weary miles. Old Jenny, the saddle mule, was, he believed, "the second best I ever saw in my life." She was easy-gaited, a good single-footer, and could take a canter and go all day. From experience she knew the trail better than a man, could smell an

Indian as acutely as a bear, and would travel of her own free will. In the middle of the night she carried her rider up the river past the familiar Bosque Grande, where, quitting the cattle trail, Goodnight reined her to the left and took the Navajo trail directly up the river. It was a wild country, looking wilder still by night, but much of the time Goodnight was dozing in the saddle. Several times he waked, the mule steadily swinging along at a canter or a lope, and, viewing the dark country with concern, he thought to himself: "Well, old Jenny is lost, sure as hell." And then a familiar landmark rose from the night to meet him, and again he relaxed and dozed. By early morning the hundred-and-ten-mile ride had dropped with the dusts behind him, and stiffly he stepped to the ground to greet his old partner.

Though the wound in his side had healed, and Loving was up and about, his arm was not doing well. Nevertheless, while confined at the fort, he had learned the whereabouts of their horses and mules stolen the spring before, and after Goodnight rested a couple of days, Loving advised him to go and recover them. Still uncertain as to the wound, Goodnight demurred, saying he did not wish to leave, but Loving insisted for fear the stock would be moved.

For eighty dollars the outlaw had sold Loving's six work mules and Goodnight's fine saddle mule to a priest at San Miguel, and had sold their horses from above Las Vegas through the mountains toward Santa Fé. Goodnight went and took the scattered stock by force, but when he reached San Miguel, he said: "I had to go by law." By chance he met a German lawyer, a partner of Steve Elkins at Santa Fé, who gave him much assistance. The mules were locked in a typically Mexican, walled corral, and as he prepared to resort to legal means, the lawyer advised him that here the law was very uncertain, and if he went to replevy the stock, by the time he got the papers there would be nothing left to serve upon. The German, acting as agent, agreed to forego resort to law and leave the saddle mule upon delivery of the other animals, and soon Goodnight turned down the river for Sumner in possession of all his stock but one.

"When I was within thirty miles of Fort Sumner," he recalled, "I met a courier hunting me, who said that Mr. Loving had sent for me. Gangrene had set in and his arm must be amputated. Loving did not want the operation performed unless I was there, as he feared he might not survive it. I left the stock in charge of the hired man, in a few hours reached Fort Sumner, and the next morning set about to get the operation performed. The old doctor was in Santa Fé, at court-martial, and the young doctor put me off from day to day with various excuses. Loving became fretful, now realizing his serious condition, and said: 'It looks hard to be forced to die in a civilized country, just for want of attention. I have always lived the life of a gentleman, and feel that I am entitled to treatment accordingly.'

"I had not told him about the young doctor putting me off, but I replied that I would now go to him at once and see what could be done. Fortunately, I found him at the hospital alone, and told him briefly and in no uncertain words that I presumed he was putting us off because we were rebels, and that he must now either operate or make wounds on me.

"'All right,' he said, 'I will come and amputate the arm.'"

The doctor and two stewards came to the hotel, administered chloroform, and amputated the arm above the elbow. Loving came from under the anaesthetic and seemed to be doing well. Yet the artery was large and peculiar, and caused the surgeon concern. Goodnight dispatched a runner with relays of horses to Las Vegas for Dr. Shoup, giving the man five hundred dollars to make the trip. On the second night after the operation, Shoup arrived with a companion physician, and as Loving was resting easily, they sat in the hotel yard and talked with the young cowman. Presently the night nurse appeared and said the bandage had commenced to be stained with blood. Upon examination they found that the artery had broken, and it was necessary to chloroform him again and retie it. From the added shock he suffered a relapse and a gradual failing of strength. Yet he was a man of such splendid constitution that, in spite of neglect, starvation, and punishment, he lived for twenty-two days, perfectly rational to the last. He stated simply that he would like to have lived longer on account of his family, and to show his country that he was a man who could overcome difficulties.

For one thing he had in mind his indebtedness.

"The Confederate Government," explained his partner, "owed him a hundred and fifty thousand dollars for cattle he had delivered, which financially ruined him, and he asked me as a Mason to give him my word to continue the partnership for at least two years, until his remaining debts were paid and his family provided for. I told him that while I was willing to do this, his oldest son, who would be executor of his will, knew me only as an illiterate cowboy, and would be certain to object to my going on with the business.

"'I know that, but James does not know you, and I do. Ignore him. Your promise is all I want.' I gave him the promise. Then his mind turned back to Texas, and at last he said: 'I regret to have to be laid away in a foreign country.' I assured him that he need have no fears; that I would see that his remains were laid in the cemetery at home. He felt that this would be impossible, but I told him it would be done. He died September 25, 1867, and was temporarily buried at Sumner."

Goodnight and the doctor who performed the operation became close friends, and one day the latter said:

"I want to tell you how ridiculously you acted. I am a Scotchman and have been in America only about two years, and I don't know a thing about your rebel government. I did not operate on Loving because I had taken a great liking to him, did not think he could stand an anaesthetic, and did not want to kill him. But I found I'd either have to kill you, operate on him, or be killed, and I decided I'd just take my chances on the old gentleman."

After several months on the trail, the establishment of a ranch in southern Colorado, and the location of the herd driven by Joe Loving, at Bosque Grande, Goodnight again returned to Fort Sumner, placed W. D. Reynolds in charge of the outfit, exhumed Loving's body, and prepared to fulfill his promise. From about the fort the cowboys gathered scattered oil cans, beat them out, soldered them together, and made an immense tin casket. They placed the rough wooden one inside, packed several inches of powdered charcoal around it, sealed the tin lid, and crated the whole in lumber. They lifted a wagon bed from its bolsters and carefully loaded the casket in its place. Upon February 8, 1868, with six big mules strung out in the harness, and with rough-hewn but tenderly sympathetic cowmen from Texas riding ahead and behind, the strangest and most touching funeral cavalcade in the history of the cow country took the Goodnight and Loving Trail that led to Loving's home.

Their arrangements were sufficient. Down the relentless Pecos and across the implacable Plains the journey was singularly peaceful. Through miles of grazing buffaloes they approached the Cross Timbers, reached the settlements, and at last delivered the body to the Masonic Lodge at Weatherford, where it was buried with fraternal honors.

In the uncertain scale of human nature, there is no standard for the computation of the influence of one noble soul upon another. Though Goodnight was then thirty-one years of age, until his death, nearly sixty-three years later, he never spoke of Loving except in utmost tenderness, and his vibrant voice mellowed with reverence as he would slowly say, "my old partner," and raise his eyes to the picture that hung on the ranch-house wall.

from THE WIND

★

Dorothy Scarborough

A YOUNG GIRL WAS TRAVELING ALONE ON A WESTBOUND train one day in late December, between Christmas and the new year. Family loyalty had named her Letitia after a great-aunt, but affection had softened that to Letty, so that she had not suffered unduly. Until recently love had smoothed all things in her life. She was a pretty girl, who looked younger than her eighteen years—a slight and almost childish figure in her black dress, with her blonde and wavy hair, her eyes blue as periwinkles in old-fashioned gardens, and her cheeks delicately pink as the petals of peach blooms. She looked tired now, however, for she had come all the distance from Virginia to Texas. She had spent the night at Fort Worth to break her journey, and now she was on the last day of her trip. She would reach Sweetwater that night.

She had never seen Sweetwater, nor heard it described, and she knew of it only as a postmark on a letter. But the name was pleasant-sounding, and so she whispered it to herself from time to time, while her fancy conjured up pictures of what the little town would look like. There would be home-like houses with their dream-inviting open fires in big fireplaces, and their porches overgrown with vines, as in the Virginia villages she knew. There would be lawns and orchards, and gardens with all the flowers one loved, each in its season, a cycle of beauty from early spring to late fall. And trees, of course, whose great, benignant branches sheltered nesting birds in spring, whose leaves in summer laced the sky and rustled softly when the wind blew, and sometimes hung as motionless as pictured leaves when there was no breeze.

Would there be a little river, perhaps, slipping like a silver shadow through the town, where a girl and a boy might row a boat on summer afternoons?—or a creek that showed rainbow minnows in its shallows and ferns along the banks? Or a lake, if only a tiny one, or a pond where water lilies bloomed with creamy petals and hearts of gold, and water hyacinths purple-blue? One thing she was sure of—there would be water, sweet and cool and pure, for wasn't the place named Sweetwater?

As one visions heaven according to his dreams of loved earthly beauty, so Letty Mason pieced together a Sweetwater that was to contain all the things she cared for most. She had to do something to keep from being too bitterly unhappy. When there was nothing to look to but a past that grief and separation had broken up, and a future that held she knew not what, and only so much of a present as a ride on a train, what could a girl do?

She gave a look at her present in an impulse of panic to escape the sorrow of yesterdays and the terror of unknown tomorrows. The day coach with its rows of red plush seats, all turned the same way like people that dared not look behind them, would be all right for any one who was not alone and unhappy and afraid. Until a few months ago Letty could have laughed and had fun in it, while now it seemed ugly and hostile. At one end of the coach there was a big blackened coal

bin and an iron stove as huge and red as a Santa Claus, when the
brakesman had stuffed it with coal. There were not many passengers
in the car—a few men with broad-brimmed Stetson hats, several
mothers with their babies, a few older children, and one grandmoth-
erly grey-haired woman crocheting white-thread lace. A little girl in a
red-plaid dress and hair braided in tight, serious pig-tails, kept pacing
up and down the aisle, touching the tops of the seats as if in some
mysterious game. An urchin of about five, with eyes as round and
expressionless as glass marbles, spilled his plump body half over the
seat in front of Letty and stared at her without winking. She tried to
smile at him, but she could not manage the necessary energy, and in
fact the youngster seemed to expect no response to his scrutiny.

A man across the aisle looked at her now and then over the top of
his *Dallas News*, and smiled tentatively, but she turned away each
time. He was a rather handsome man, with wavy black hair and dark
eyes and a mustache that quirked up at the ends. He was proud of that
mustache, she decided, for he played with it affectionately. He looked
old, over thirty, she felt sure.

There was something faintly familiar about him, suggestive of some
one else she had known, perhaps long ago. As she looked at him sur-
reptitiously, she was sure that she had never seen this man before—
because he was a person that she would have remembered if she had
ever known him—but he was teasingly reminiscent of another. Who
was it? She tried to analyze the impressions he called up—half pleasurable recollections, half fear and repulsion, vaguely commingled as in
the waking remembrance of a dream.

When she had been traveling for several hours, the conductor
came along and stopped to speak to her, as if he thought she might be
lonesome.

"Gettin' on all hunky dory?"

"Yes."

She contrived a smile for him, because he was so kind, and his eyebrows were so funny! They were black and they spurted suddenly out

from above his eyes like mustaches stuck on in the wrong place. They fascinated her, because she had never seen any like them before. But she mustn't let the good man know that she was smiling at his mustaches instead of at him.

"What is Sweetwater like?" she asked. "Do you suppose I'll love it?"

His eyebrows arched themselves jerkily. "Well, h-mm, that depends on the folks you've got there, daughter."

"I don't see why," she contended. "There are lots of places you could like without folks. There are places—you know—where you never could get lonesome, even if you stayed there by yourself for hours and hours. They're so pretty and peaceful they rest you, and happify you, as the darkeys say, so you feel right at home there. And you enjoy being yourself so much that you don't miss other people."

"Yes, that's right." The eye-mustaches twinkled at her cheerily and then the conductor moved off down the aisle without trying to prove his point, as if indeed he preferred not to.

Letty huddled again in the corner of her red plush prison and gazed out of the window. The train was scudding along what seemed to be abandoned peach orchards, where unkempt trees were growing, their leafless branches sprawled and scrawny, instead of being trimmed and tended as in the orchards that she knew at home. And there were no fences round them, no protection at all to keep thieves from stealing the fruit in summer when there was any. Queer!

They were the largest orchards she had ever seen, she reflected, for they stretched along both sides of the track for miles and miles. She hadn't noticed just where they began, and it seemed as if they never would end. The ground was covered with a dead grass that waved in the wind, bent low, as if water were rippling over it. The trees weren't planted in rows, but scattered irregularly in a wild and lawless abandon. She puzzled over the strangeness of it all. She thought illogically of a remark she had heard once from an old man, "All signs fail in Texas."

When the little red-plaid girl came by again, Letty put out a hand to detain her. "Why don't they have fences to their peach orchards?" she asked.

"Where?" the child wished to know.

Letty pointed to the trees on each side of the track.

The little girl stared at her in puzzled fashion for a moment, and then she giggled, with laughter as light and spontaneous as soap-bubbles of mirth.

The *Dallas News* was lowered and Letty saw that the man across the aisle was smiling in amusement somewhat carefully restrained. He had been listening, then, to what she said!

"Those are mesquite trees. Wild," he volunteered.

Letty blushed and drew back. When Letty blushed, the process was one to distract and delight the beholder—as if the pink of peach blooms had suddenly turned into rosy flame. It always scared and upset her when it happened, so that in consequence she blushed more vividly than ever.

As if to reassure her, because sympathetic of her emotions, the man erected the barricade of *Dallas News* again, though with manifest reluctance.

After a moment, when he no doubt thought that she had somewhat recovered, he ventured forth again.

"They do look like old peach trees. I've heard folks often say the same thing."

Letty made no answer.

With a lingering glance, which made her color flare up again, he retired behind his paper and made no effort to prolong the conversation.

As the miles slipped by, Letty noticed that the mesquites tended to grow smaller. At first they had been large, not like forest trees, of course, but good-sized, while now they were dwindling. Why was that? She looked for other trees, but saw none of her old familiar friends—only these stranger mesquites. She felt depressed and forlorn. Would life snatch from her even the trees she loved? But of course it was a long way yet to Sweetwater, and the landscape could change a lot before she got there. She needn't worry. Still, she leaned her cheek against her hand and gave herself up to unhappy premonitions. To go into a country you didn't know about was hard, and to leave the home you had loved all your life was cruel. Life didn't leave you much choice, but just shoved you around as if you hadn't any right to feelings.

Suddenly, when she was wiping away a surreptitious tear, she was roused by a touch on her shoulder. Starting up, she saw that the man from across the aisle had moved over and sat beside her.

He spoke casually. "Like to see some prairie dogs? Maybe you never saw any."

"No," she said, fluttering rosily. "I never have."

He pointed one forefinger toward the ground beside the track and her following gaze saw a stretch of land with small hummocks scattered over it like earthen breastworks thrown up for Lilliputian warfare. Queer little animals were disporting themselves about them, red-brown, dumpy creatures like young puppies that had not yet begun to lengthen into dogs—some sitting on their haunches on top of the mounds, some scampering about on the ground that was bare of vegetation and hard-packed as a floor. Some looked with suspicion at the train, and then dived down into holes in the ground. Some ran clumsily away, while a few held their place with impudent disdain of engines and human beings.

"This is a dog town," the man went on to elaborate.

"They have a colony, you see, and they dig underground homes for themselves, and live down there. I reckon that's where the old settlers got their notion of dugouts. Sometimes rattlers live in the holes with them, or maybe only in holes they've left. And ground squirrels, and hoot owls. They have tunnels running between the mounds all over the place."

"Why, how cunning!" she cried, forgetting her woes and her faint fear of this stranger. To think there were such darling little animals she had never even heard of!

She leaned in excitement against the window and flattened her nose against the glass like a youngster, to watch them in their antics.

"Does a prairie-dog town have a mayor and a city council?" She laughed dimplingly. "I don't see the church, or the school house or the jail."

He grinned. "I reckon they're not much of a religious or educated bunch, any more than the rest of us out here. But they're sociable little cusses and mighty human in some of their ways. The children make pets of 'em."

Her fancy flashed off to the government of a prairie-dog settlement.

"That fat, lazy one there must be the bigwig, the rich man," she hazarded. "His mound is higher than the others, and he didn't duck when he saw the train coming. Some of 'em are silly cowards."

"Like folks," he concurred, as he twisted his mustache with long, browned fingers, and smiled.

He settled back at ease beside her, as if there could be no possibility of his being unwelcome. His air was that of a man who had a lazy energy well controlled, beneath whose apparent indolence a superb strength lay concealed, whose interested indifference was not greatly accustomed to rebuffs. He smilingly looked down at her.

Letty, who had been but momentarily startled out of her shyness in the excitement of seeing prairie dogs for the first time, now gave a quick frown and drew back within her shell of reserve. But the stranger appeared not to notice.

Or was it that he noticed and disregarded?

"Live in Texas?" he asked.

"No," she said coldly. She wouldn't talk with him, and then he would go away and leave her alone. Who was he that he should speak to her like this?

And then, almost without her volition, her sense of truthfulness answered his question. "I—haven't—but I guess I'm going to," she faltered, facing the fact definitely for the first time. The blue eyes filmed with tears, and the scarlet, fluted mouth like a pomegranate flower, quivered.

"Going far?" he probed. Considerately, he made no mention of her emotion.

"I get off at Sweetwater. Do you—know the place?"

"Yes."

Her desire for information, her thirst for facts about this place that was to be her home, struggled with her timidity, and won.

"Tell me about it. Will I like living there?" Her tone had an anxious eagerness that made him slow in his reply, as if he must choose his words with care.

He deliberated with judicial gravity, while she looked her palpitating suspense.

At last he spoke. "What do you say to a bargain? I'll tell you about Sweetwater, if you'll tell me first about the place you come from. Fair enough?"

"I guess so," she stammered. Now she was practically forced to talk to him! Did he really want to hear about Virginia, or was he pretending?

She looked out of the window as if to evoke a picture, and then she turned back to him. "My home is—or was—in Virginia, in a little town you never heard of, I s'pose. It's like the country, but it's a town, too, so you don't get lonesome. There are neighbors, and young people to go about with, but still it's just as green and lovely as the country could be."

She had to pause an instant, struggling with homesickness. Oh, that little loved country town in Virginia! When should she see it again? Would life fling years as well as miles between it and her?

He gave a smile to encourage her. "Sounds nice. Never was in Virginia myself. Tell me how the place looks."

She got a grip on herself. Perhaps he did want to hear about it, and if so she must do justice to Virginia for one who had never been there to see it for himself. She must show it to him in her words, so that he'd know how dear and beautiful it was.

"Our house—" Here she choked an instant, remembering that it was not hers any more. "The house I lived in isn't so very big, but it's homey. It's old, because Grandfather Mason built it for his bride when he was married the first time. It's out in the edge of town, and has a wide porch across the front, so you can sit and watch the sun set through the pine trees at one side. You can see the sun rise on the other side, across a lake that has willows dipping in the water, and alders, and other lovely greeny stuffs."

She closed her eyes a moment, as if blinded with memories.

"There are woodsy roads rambling round, with sumach bright in the sun, and wild honeysuckle trailing everywhere, making the whole place sweet with its smell, and blackberry vines so pretty when the white blossoms are out, and so luscious when the berries are ripe in summer. . . . And Virginia creeper, and the trumpet vine with its wonderful red bugles, climbing up the trees and covering the fence posts and stumps. . . . And a vine we call the cigar plant, with its little, long red bloom like a tiny lighted cigar."

"That's a sensible-sounding plant," he threw in.

"Vines are all beautiful, I think. They're like charity, for they go covering up the ugly things and places, the dead trees, the stumps and rough fence posts, and make everything graceful."

Her tone was dreamily reminiscent now.

"That's right," he agreed, with smiling attention.

"And the flowers. . . . There are all sorts of wild flowers there, too, so many I couldn't name them all, but I love every one. There's the butterfly weed, that the darkeys call 'chigger plant.' How funny to call it that—when it has gay orange blossoms like gorgeous butterflies lighted there for a second. You can almost see them fold and unfold their wings!"

"Yes?"

"Then there are the daisies that bloom everywhere in early summer,

acres on acres of them, white, with golden hearts, nodding at you in the
sun like children telling you to come and play with them. And wild tiger
lilies in the shadowy places, like Indian girls in gay blankets. . . . And
the blue-eyed grass, and Jack-in-the-pulpit, and Bouncing Bet. . . .
And the wild roses are the sweetest things in the world, so pink and
delicate and perfect! And the jewel-weed in shady spots. . . . and wild
violets, and Queen Anne's Lace, with the flowers as fine as cobwebs,
and the little birds' nests of green curled up. And wild morning-glory
running everywhere, and black-eyed Susans. And, oh, I couldn't possibly tell you about all of them!"

She paused breathlessly, after her rush of words. Then she blushed
to think how much she had been talking to this stranger.

"Guess I'll have to go and see them myself some time," he rendered
opinion.

So maybe he was interested, after all, and not pretending.

"And the trees—" she went on, not wishing to slight such dear
friends. "I mustn't forget them. Such wonderful trees as we do have
there! Pines that stand on tiptoe to peek into heaven, so I always feel
like asking them what they see there. And tulip poplars that have such
gorgeous blooms, and dogwood that makes the hills all white in springtime. . . . And holly with its berries for Christmas. . . . There's a big
mimosa on our lawn. Did you ever see a mimosa?"

He shook his head regretfully. His look seemed to hint that he
recognized that not having seen a mimosa tree he had led a wasted
life.

She tried to make it up to him.

"Its leaves are lacy, like ferns, and its blooms are tiny pompons like
flowers of the sensitive plant, pinkish-yellow, soft as soft. There's a big
magnolia there, too. You know a magnolia is such a joy, for you can
write on the leaves while they are glossy and dark, and even after
they've turned brown, you can still read what you've written. . . . And
the flowers! When I see a magnolia blossom, it seems to me it must
have fallen down from heaven in the night."

She caught her breath sharply. "I do hope there'll be magnolias in Sweetwater."

He cherished his mustache without enlightening her on that point. "What else is there?" he asked.

"There's a hedge of crêpe myrtle by the garden. In late summer it has rose-colored blooms like silky, crinkled crêpe, the prettiest thing you ever saw. You want to love it, and make little dance frocks out of it! . . . In the fall the trees in the town and in the woods are all colors, yellow and brown and bronze and red, so that I often wonder which I love best, springtime or autumn."

"What did you do all day?" he questioned.

"Oh, I wasn't idle! I took care of Mother, and made my own clothes, and taught a class in Sunday school, and helped with church suppers. And I read a lot, everything I could get, and I took music lessons, and had a good time with the boys and girls."

She turned to him suddenly, shutting the door on her past. "Now tell me about Sweetwater. And please tell me I'll love it there!"

The blue eyes, the scarlet fluted mouth, the tremulous dimple all entreated him to speak well of Sweetwater.

He uttered but one curt word, "No."

Her eyes widened in dismay and reproach. "Why not?"

He folded his arms and looked at her keenly. "Go back to your Virginia, little girl. This country's not like what you've been used to. Take my advice and vamoose—while the going's good."

Her chin trembled. "But I can't!" she jerked. "I haven't any money—and I haven't got anything to go back to!"

"Why did you ever leave?" he flung at her.

She looked at him with piteous eyes, defending herself against what she felt to be an accusation. "Mother died, and she was all I had left."

She caught her under lip with her teeth to stop its quivering. "And she'd been sick so long that after she was dead, the debts licked up the homestead and everything, just like an earthquake swallowing them."

"What are you doing so far down here?"

"Cousin Beverley owns a ranch in West Texas. I haven't seen him since I was a child, but the pastor wrote to him after Mother died, and asked him if I couldn't come out and live with them. Cousin Beverley said to come on, if I thought it best, that I could teach the children. He was afraid I wouldn't like it much, but the neighbors thought I'd better come. It would be a change for me, they said."

"It'll be a change, all right." His tone was grim. "A hell of a change!"

She felt chill with an indefinable fear of the future, as if some cold, dark wing had fanned her. She tried to ask him a question, but for the moment she could not find her voice to speak. Her blue eyes gazed enthralled at him, as if he could read for her the future, could reveal what lay for her behind the curtains of the coming days.

He turned to face her unsmilingly. "What's your cousin's name?"

"Beverley Mason."

Even the syllables of that dear name sounded unfamiliar to her, as if this strange environment had cast a spell over everything.

"I've seen him. He's a good *hombre*," he answered briefly. "But he don't live in Sweetwater. What made you think he did?"

"His letter was mailed from there."

He gave an unhumorous smile. "Out in this country a man may live a hundred miles from his postmark. He don't go for mail twice a day, y'understand. Bev Mason's ranch is over twenty-five miles from Sweetwater. I've got an outfit farther west myself, but I live in Fort Worth. Couldn't hog-tie me to stay all year round out here. *Savez?*"

The hands that lay loosely in her lap were trembling. "But what is the trouble with the country—that you tell me to go back?"

"It's all right for them that like it. Some do—mostly men, though. It's hard on the women. Folks say the West is good enough for a man or a dog, but no place for a woman or a cat."

"But why, why?"

"The wind is the worst thing."

She drew a relieved sigh. "Oh, wind? That's nothing to be afraid of."

He went on as though she had not spoken. "It's ruination to a woman's looks and nerves pretty often. It dries up her skin till it gets brown and tough as leather. It near 'bout puts her eyes out with the sand it blows in 'em all day. It gets on her nerves with its constant-blowing—makes her irritable and jumpy."

She gave a light, casual gesture with one hand. "It blows every-where, I reckon, even in Virginia. Sometimes in winter we have regu-lar storms of wind and rain. But we don't think anything of them."

He gave her an amused sidelong glance, and twisted his mustache in silence. His air was that of an adult who disdains to attempt to make anything clear to a persistent but silly child.

"What else is there so terrible out here?" she prodded. The man was just teasing her, of course, and she would let him see that she wasn't so easily gulled.

"The work out here is hard on women. Can't get any help, and can't have the conveniences they have in other sections. Plenty o' cowboys to run the ranch, but no women to help in the house. And the chuck department on a regular ranch is no job to sneeze at, let me tell you."

"I won't mind that, either," she affirmed courageously. "I always worked at home, as I told you. I did the dusting."

"You'll have a chore on your hands if you keep up that end of it out here," he said sardonically. His white teeth gleamed in a smile.

She was rather breathless, but would not surrender.

"What else?" she demanded.

"Women get lonesome. No neighbors if you live on a ranch. Just a few cowboys and too damned many cattle and coyotes. It's enough to run a woman loco."

"But the men stand it, don't they?"

"It's a man-sized job. And the cow-punchers can go to town every so often and get on a high lonesome and lose money at poker. That relieves 'em. But the women can't do that, poor calicoes. They got to stay bottled up, and it's liable to bust 'em, sooner or later."

She began to feel that he might be serious. She took a few

moments to study the question, while she looked out of the window in silence.

Then she turned to him. "It's not what I'd choose, but I didn't know what else to do. Oh, why aren't girls taught to make their living and take care of themselves, the same as men?"

Her little black-bordered handkerchief dabbed at her eyes.

The man turned his searching gaze on her and spoke meditatively, with a sort of crisp drawl. "It'd be a pity for that pretty face of yours to be ruined by the wind—like I've seen some women's faces. If you stay out here, 'twon't be long before your skin won't be as pink and white as it is now. In a little while your hair won't be as yellow and soft, after the hot sun has bleached it and the wind has roughed it. Pretty soon your eyes won't be as clear and blue as they are now, after the sand has near 'bout blinded 'em—if you stay out here."

She turned from him in bitter silence and gazed at the telephone poles.

The man beside her whistled softly, a weird, haunting tune. Then he began to sing words to it.

"Oh, bury me not on the lone prai-*rie*,

Where the wild coyotes will howl over me!

In a narrow grave, just six by three,

Oh, bury me not on the lone prai-*rie*!

Tears began to trickle down her cheeks.

THE BRIDE

★

Hallie Crawford Stillwell

I T WAS JULY 29, 1918. I WAS A NERVOUS BRIDE-TO-BE AND twenty years old. I should have been excited and elated that the handsomest and most eligible bachelor around had proposed marriage, but instead I could only think of Papa's words: "He's too old for you and he hasn't led a proper life. That man drinks and gambles too much. He's just not suitable for you, daughter!"

Still, I was a determined woman even at that young age. I chose to marry Roy Stillwell against Mama's and Papa's words of advice. I had too much respect for my parents to blatantly defy them, so Roy and I just climbed into his Hudson Super-6, drove to the Brewster County Court House, got our marriage license, and imposed on my cousin, Sadie Crawford Harrington. After a quick ceremony at her house, we drove to Marathon and boarded the train for San Antonio, where we would spend our honeymoon at the Gunter Hotel.

Four days later we left San Antonio and headed home, where I was to present my new husband to Mama and Papa. I was anxious and apprehensive when we left the train station in Marathon. The drive from Marathon to Alpine was quiet as both of us anticipated the worst reaction from my parents.

We drove up to my home and walked inside. The family was sitting at the dinner table. I stumbled over my words very quickly. "Mama and Papa, Roy and I are married!" Roy and I stood side by side and waited.

After a few moments of tense silence, Papa rose and spoke, "Well, the die is cast! Y'all better sit down and have some supper."

From that day forward, Roy was a member of my family. Mama and Papa never looked back and never treated Roy any worse than any other member of my family. I had anticipated the worst and had gotten what I had really hoped for, acceptance of Roy by my mother and father.

My father did question Roy extensively about our lives together. He asked Roy, "Are you going to be living in your house in Marathon?"

Roy was prompt in his reply. "I own that house in Marathon, but the ranch is my home and Hallie will be living on the ranch with me. We will keep the house in town as a place to come when we need to be in town, which should not be very often."

I knew Papa was not any too happy about my living that far from town, especially in a place so close to the Mexican border. Not only was Pancho Villa a renowned raider but many Mexicans used his name as their scapegoat when they raided isolated ranches along the Rio Grande. Papa frowned, but only warned: "Just take good care of her."

Once we had visited with family and friends for a few days, Roy decided that we had better head for his ranch, a ride some seventy-five miles from Alpine and an all-day drive. As we rode along I could tell that Roy was somewhat apprehensive. He was polite and pointed out many interesting names and places along the way. I absorbed the beautiful surroundings and knew that I would be happy around the mountains and cacti that protected the rough terrain. Once we were within ten miles of the ranch, Roy began to get quiet and looked quite concerned. I finally asked. "Roy is something bothering you?"

"Well, Hallie, there has never been a woman living on my ranch. The cowhands and I have always taken care of everything and never felt we needed a woman. Now, these men are good men but they may need a while to get used to you."

As we drove up to the ranch house, I saw three rough-looking cowboys leaning up against a brush arbor that was attached to a tiny shack that was the ranch headquarters. I really hadn't expected much but I was somewhat surprised at its size, one room about twelve feet by sixteen feet. Still I kept my chin up.

Roy, being quite a gentleman, slid out of the car and came around to open my door. He allowed me to get out and then pointed toward the tiny house. "This is it!"

I started toward the house with Roy right behind me.

"Hell, that woman schoolteacher won't last six months down here in this Godforsaken country" was the remark that I heard from one of the ranch hands as Roy and I made our way toward the arbor. I really did not pay too much attention to this remark because I knew that it was one I was not supposed to hear. Roy either did not hear it or pretended not to hear it, and we walked up to the trio awaiting us.

The men showed respect by removing their hats and extending their hands, but I felt their discontent. They stood quietly under the arbor while Roy ushered me inside. It did not take me long to survey the domain. The room contained a small wood cookstove with a smoke-blackened coffee pot, a huge black iron teakettle, and a few pots and pans. There was a small cabinet (usually referred to as a safe) and on it was a shelf where a water bucket and gourd dipper stood. Also in the room were one table, one chair, two wooden benches, and only one bedroll, a mass of rolled-up quilts wrapped in a tarp in a corner. I then realized that I would have to share that cowboy bedroll with Roy, and that it would be our bed.

"Come on in, boys, let's fix a bite of supper," called Roy to the men waiting impatiently outside, as he immediately began to scrape ashes out of the stove.

I sat in a chair as those clumsy cowboys stomped into the house and began to cook our supper. Little did I know how efficient at camp cooking they were. The more they worked, the more in the way I felt. As those earlier words from the cowboys echoed through my mind, I became more determined to stay. I wanted desperately to make a go of my marriage regardless of the stinging remarks these men had made.

As I sat at the table to have my first meal in my new home, I again felt the coldness of the ranch hands' reception. They were ignoring me, and Roy was bending over backwards to melt the icy atmosphere. I smiled at the hands' crude remarks and complimented the cooks. Not one of the three icebergs thawed that evening.

The only conversation consisted of shallow cutting remarks. "I reckon you'll be a goin' back to town most of the time," Lee said as he gathered the tin plates, three-pronged forks, and case knives to wash.

"No, I expect to live here with Roy, or I wouldn't have married him," I replied.

"It's no fittin' place fer a woman," mumbled Jona as he headed for the door.

"We have work ahead of us tomorrow, boys. See you in the morning," Roy said as he untied the bedroll, spread it on the floor, and prepared our bed for the night.

I watched as the three taciturn men picked up their bedrolls stacked under the arbor and retired to the barn. I was glad to have them out of my sight. They had been acting as if they owned Roy, I thought. I turned to say something to Roy and found him already in the bedroll. I fumbled around for awhile, got myself ready for bed, and rolled in next to him.

"They will never own me," I muttered without thinking.

Roy, already half asleep, asked what I had said.

"Nothing, absolutely nothing," I whispered.

I curled up in the bedroll and thought about the peaceful night, warm with a light stir of a cool breeze. I heard the squeak of the wooden wheel on the windmill as it turned. Once in a while, I heard a coyote yip in the distance or a mother cow bawling for her calf. The hypnotic rhythm of the windmill should have put me to sleep, but it didn't. The remarks I had overheard that evening were still too fresh on my mind. My hipbones ached as I turned from side to side attempting to get comfortable. My mind remained active. I wondered what my role as a pioneer ranch wife would be like. This man lying next to me had had such a different life from mine.

As I mused on the blending of my life and his, my thoughts traveled backwards. I had been born in Waco, Texas, on October 20, 1897, and at the age of one year, my parents, Guy and Nancy Crawford, moved me, my brother Frank, and my sister Mabel to the San Angelo area. As we children grew, my parents became concerned about our education and better opportunities for our family. With these two aims in mind, we made five moves in twelve years, during which time our family had grown to include another brother, Alvin, and another sister, Lovenia. All of our moves were in West Texas except for a three-year period of homesteading in the territory of New Mexico. Alvin had been born in 1900 in Ozona, where we had lived for two years, and Lovenia was born in 1905 in San Angelo, where we had also resided. Included in this family was my father's sister, Lambe, who had made her home with us always. Even though our family was large, my father never hesitated to make a move if he felt that it would be for the betterment of our family.

Moves during this era were hard and we had to move in covered wagons. In preparation for a journey, wagon wheels had to be soaked in hot linseed oil, hubs greased, and wagon beds repaired. We spent several days on the road as we traveled to each new place. And with each new home, we faced a new set of hardships, something Aunt Lambe was always good at predicting. She seemed to have a nose for catastrophe.

The last move I made with my family was in 1910 to Alpine, Brewster County, Texas. It didn't take long for my parents to realize that Alpine met their needs. It offered opportunities to make a good living, the school system was good, and Uncle Jim Crawford (my father's brother) and his family also lived there. Because of the advantages offered in Alpine, particularly in education, my father settled us there and sent all of us children to school except for Frank, who was needed to help with my father's business, a local grocery store.

I started school in Alpine as a sixth grader, and by the time I graduated from Alpine High School in 1916, I not only had my high school diploma but also my teaching certificate. I had completed six weeks of training at the Normal School for Teachers and had taken and passed the state examinations, allowing me certification to teach in the state of Texas.

There were few jobs for women during these years, and teaching was certainly the most respectable job for a woman in the West Texas area. I had heard that there was a vacancy in Presidio, and I quickly wrote a letter to the president of the Board of Trustees of the Presidio Common School. In a short time, I was informed that I had a teaching job.

Presidio was largely populated by Texans of Mexican descent. Most of these people had fled Mexico seeking protection from Pancho Villa and his raiders. Pancho Villa and his army had recently captured Ojinaga, Mexico, just across the Rio Grande from Presidio, and all of Mexico was in a rebellion, causing many hardships within the country and a torn-up government.

My father thought this place was too dangerous for a young lady. He didn't want me to go, and stressed this point often.

"Daughter, I think you're going on a wild goose chase," he said.

I finally replied somewhat flippantly, "Then I'll gather my geese." Even though my father disapproved of my going to Presidio, I armed myself with a six-shooter, my father's favorite and most dependable weapon and one he was very glad to lend me, took my teaching certificate, and headed for Presidio.

When I arrived in Presidio, I found the days hot, the sand deep, the Mexicans strange, and the U.S. soldiers curious about an Anglo girl moving there. There was only one other white girl there, Alice Gourley, who was also a teacher. These soldiers were stationed there to protect the U.S. border and often wondered at our wanting to teach in such a dangerous setting. The lodgings provided for Alice and me were makeshift and not very comfortable. After a short time there, I sent for my sister Mabel to take a teaching position in the school. She, Alice, and I set up housekeeping together, and this made our living there more satisfactory and my stay more pleasant. Although the environment was harsh I was not a quitter, and the dangerous happenings there could not keep me from my school and my sweet little children.

Most of my days in this village were spent working with the children, preparing lessons, or cleaning the schoolhouse. In the evenings, the three of us would often visit with the Texas Rangers and customs agents stationed there. We attended church on Sundays and once a week we were able to watch a silent movie. I never remember being bored or discontented.

Mabel had to walk three miles to her school and I really felt sorry for her. I decided to help her out. I put out word that I wanted to buy a horse, and before long a Mexican approached me. He told me that he had a horse to sell and wanted twenty-two dollars for it. I paid for the horse and led him to our cabin, where I presented him to Mabel. She was excited that she would not have to walk so far any longer.

Mabel got up every morning and rode that horse to and from school for about a month. Then, one day, two customs agents appeared at our door asking about the horse outside and wanting to know who owned it.

Of course, I proudly claimed ownership.

"Lady, you bought a 'wet horse'!" stated the agents, meaning that I had bought a horse that had been brought illegally from Mexico.

I did not understand what he was talking about at first. I was surprised to find out that the horse had been brought from Mexico without proper documents. The agents told me that they would have to seize my animal. We were all depressed about the loss of the horse and Mabel's means of transportation to her school.

I think those agents felt sorry for me and they gave me twenty-five dollars for the horse. They explained that the government was paying for the horse and would return it to Mexico. I knew in my heart that those men created that purse for me, and I will never forget them.

The Mexican people of Presidio were very respectful, as were most of the soldiers. Of course, there can always be one "bad apple in the barrel" and I had to come across that one soldier. One night, around midnight, I was sound asleep. Alice awakened me abruptly, whispering that someone was trying to break into our cabin. I rushed to the front door and called to some passing soldiers who were on patrol. They heard our story, began a search, and found a young soldier boy hiding in a haystack behind our place. That soldier was promptly placed in the guardhouse, and the next day was tried and sentenced to six months in confinement. That soldier's commanding officer came by the next day and apologized for the soldier's bad behavior. He assured us that the soldiers were there to protect us and gave us a strong sense of security. After that we felt much more comfortable.

There was seldom any routine in Presidio, and we were forced to adjust quickly to changes. Many times during that year in Presidio, the Mexicans from Ojinaga heard rumors of Pancho Villa planning a raid on the village. People packed up their families, friends, and belongings and came to Presidio, where they sought refuge. There were nights when we were awakened to the sounds of babies crying, women fussing, and feet rustling along the streets. We knew then that the rumors were flying. Each time the Mexicans moved to Presidio, the three of us had to move to the custom agent's house that was positioned in the center of the fort. We hated to have to move so quickly from our own cabin, but the commanding officer assured us that it was for our own protection.

The times were rough. To get to my school, I had to walk half a mile in deep sand in heat that often soared above a hundred degrees Fahrenheit. I also had to wear my father's gun to school every day. On my way home from school one day, two drunk soldiers began to follow me. I knew that they were not just taking a walk. I quickened my pace and they did too. I took off running and they quickly came after me. I never thought of using my gun; I only thought of getting away. I probably ran faster that day than I ever ran in my whole life, and I did outrun them. When I finally got to our cabin I stormed inside and bolted our door. I knew that the only reason that I got away from them was because they were so drunk. I learned much during that one year, and the experiences prepared me for many hardships I later faced in life.

The following year, 1917, I moved to Marathon, Texas, to teach where the dangers were fewer. This move made my father very happy, but I was not overly excited until I met a tall, handsome cowboy who drove a Hudson Super-6. At this time, I was boarding with the Louie Ritchey family. The Ritcheys were Roy's friends, and they invited him to attend a dance with us at "Punkin Center" (a lone little schoolhouse) just north of town. I danced with Roy until the sun was peeking over the mountains early the next morning. I had the most wonderful time of my life, and Marathon became a much brighter place in which to teach and live.

After that one evening of dancing and fun, Roy invited me for automobile rides (a luxury of that time), picnics, and all social functions held in Marathon. Roy, being old-fashioned, believed that the way to a woman's heart was through a serenade and candy. Roy could not sing or play the guitar, but he found Ira Shely, a fiddler, and a blind Mexican who accompanied Ira with a guitar, to sing to me outside my window. I began to find myself awakening in the middle of the night to melodious love songs. I would be arisen from a deep sleep by the music of my favorite songs, "Listen to the Mockingbird" and "The Reagan Waltz." At that point, I knew that Roy Stillwell was the most dashing, handsome, and romantic man in the country, or at least knew what made my heart do "flip-flops." He was twenty years my senior, but this made no difference and I found myself completely in love. After such fine courting, Roy and I became engaged for a short time: four months.

As I reminisced over these wonderful memories, the hard floor softened and Roy's peaceful breathing began to relax me. As I lay in my new home and listened to the harmonious sounds around the ranch, I knew that I had begun to "gather my geese."

Stillwell Ranch was and is located twenty-two miles north of the Rio Grande as it flows between Texas and Mexico. It is forty-six miles from Marathon, the nearest town. When Roy first brought me to this ranch, it consisted of three hundred sections of open range and small traps (pastures for holding livestock) here and there. This was the last frontier of Texas; it became known as the Big Bend country. I knew that I would come to love the land although it was hot, sandy, and even lonely at times.

As I settled more comfortably in our bedroll I thought of my arrival at the ranch and how I had looked forward to a new life. I thought of the Maravillas Creek and how Roy told me that the creek had water in it only when it rained, which wasn't often. There were rocky mountains, low cactus-covered hills, and dagger flats. This was a land of stark beauty. I knew it was also a land of danger. I began to think about this environment that I knew I loved already. I knew that Roy would protect me from the dangers and teach me how to protect myself. I was ready to accept my responsibilities as his wife and for the ranch. We could and would make Stillwell Ranch what we wanted it to be if we worked together.

I did dwell on the fact that Pancho Villa and his raiders were rampaging the full length of the border. I had heard how they were taking food from ranches, stealing horses, and killing people. I knew that my new home was in a vulnerable position for such raids. Most of the ranchmen in our area had moved their families to town for safety at this time. Our neighbors to the south at Glen Springs in the Chisos Mountains had already suffered bloodshed. I knew that I would have to be very careful in whatever I did, yet I was prepared to face all odds. This final acceptance of my life with Roy eased my mind, and I soon drifted into a restful sleep.

It seemed to me that I had hardly lapsed into sleep when Roy, who had slept the whole night through, woke me with a cup of coffee in his hand. "Drink this, then crawl out and get dressed so the boys can come in for their coffee," he said as he moved me off the pallet, tied up the bed, and stashed it away in the corner of the room.

I was in no mood to greet the boys so early in the morning. With coffee in hand and half awake, I left the kitchen and made my way to a rock at the top of the large sand dune that lay just back of the house to sit and drink my coffee in my own silence. The sun was coming up over Stillwell Mountain as I glanced at the wide expanse of country before me. Not a breath of air was stirring, and the peaceful surroundings of early morning calmed my inner thoughts. I was fully prepared for another day as Jona stuck his head out the back door and called to me, "Biscuits are ready!"

from MY FIRST THIRTY YEARS

Gertrude Beasley

T HIRTY YEARS AGO, I LAY IN THE WOMB OF A WOMAN, CON-
ceived in a sexual act of rape, being carried during the pre-
natal period by an unwilling and rebellious mother, finally
bursting from the womb only to be tormented in a family whose members I despised or pitied, and brought into association with people
whom I should never have chosen. Sometimes I wish that, as I lay in
the womb, a pink soft embryo, I had somehow thought, breathed or
moved and wrought destruction to the woman who bore me, and her
eight miserable children who preceded me, and the four round-faced
mediocrities who came after me, and her husband, a monstrously
cruel, Christ-like, and handsome man with an animal's appetite for
begetting children.

It is perfectly clear to me that life is not worth living, but it is also
equally clear that life is worth talking about. Perhaps talk is the great-

est thing in the world. If I could destroy my bump of curiosity, I would go on this January day to the river at the Kremlin where Russian churchmen are said to be carrying out religious rites (a piece of idiocy which prevents life from being worth while) and throw my body into its icy depths. But I have curiosity, fear, and that potent enemy of death known as hope. Besides I have enough money (U.S.) to keep me going for nearly two years. . . .

The first flood of consciousness in life, the first mile stone of our miserable existence here, stands out, I think, before an intelligent mind. I remember mine. I was lying on my back on the hard, dirt floor of the stalls in my father's horse-lot. My hands were being held by my older brothers and my feet also, I think, and the great weight on my body seemed about to crush me. God, what an awful thing! Would the consciousness, the struggle for breath, which seemed about to be pressed out in case my frame broke in, my ribs stuck into my entrails and heart, ever return! Thus was I first made conscious. The rest was only a dark whirl; perhaps the wind was blowing; and it seems to me now there was laughter. My oldest brother, then about sixteen years old, though he was very small for his age, was trying to have sexual intercourse with me, although I was only about four years old at the time. Of recent years I have been startled at having this picture come into my mind and said, "God, what if I had really been crushed to death!" But I answer now that perhaps it would have been better. I remember distinctly that between the ages of four and about nine, each of my five brothers older than myself tried at one time or another to have sexual intercourse with me. Although I feared and hated my three oldest brothers, the two just older than myself, being nearly my own size, brought me no fear, only shame in case we should be found out. In fact, I think when the three of us were exploring the field of sex together, watching and talking about animals in their sex-acts, and using all the childish expressions concerning sex life, that I was quite as interested in our childish efforts at sexual intercourse as they were.

THERE ARE SOME THINGS WHICH I REMEMBER WITH PLEASURE about the house and surroundings where I was born—pleasurable merely because of the form which the picture takes in my own mind, for I assure you there is nothing in the content of my early life which I should care to remember. I put it down here because I can't forget it, and, because I want to see what forms it will take as I talk about it. . . . It was a two-roomed shack; that is a large boxed house of one room with a small side room, divided into a kitchen and what my mother referred to as a "shed room" for the boys. The stalls, pig-pens, and cow-lots were some distance from the house, as was also the field planted mostly with cotton, cane and corn in the spring. I received my first impression of the beauty of spring here; I remember beauty and light. For although my mother already had ten children to cook for, and all the rest of it, before we left Coleman County, Texas, she had time to cultivate flowers. I think I can honestly say that one of the little flashes of admiration which I early felt for her lay in her ability to give, what appeared to me, such a great number of names of flowers. Then there was song in that age when I was four, impressed upon me in a singular way on the occasion of my mother's catching a dear little humming bird which sang about her potted and tin-canned flowers just without a low door of our house. I remember how she screamed and chattered about it, calling it sweet and dear, as she put her hands over it when finding it in the blossom of one of her flowers. It struck in my soul—here was something lovely, something which the hands of a woman, who so often appeared vulgar, coarse and ignorant to me even when I was a mere baby, put into a fly trap with the tenderest care and assured us, a whole brood of round-faced children, that in a few days it would sing. Here was my first conscious moment of beauty. The sun shone brightly that day. But it was not all delight, for my mother screamed too loudly when she caught the bird, and I felt she was giving us an exhibition, as the saying was she was "putting on"—

there was a note of affectation in her voice. This incident also saddened me, for the bird did not sing and was let out "to be free" by the
same hands. I felt the same strong emotion, this time to weep—and
also wondered if the pretty speech about letting the bird "free" was
quite sincerely stated by this woman, my mother, whom I doubted,
hated, sometimes admired and greatly pitied.

There were many, many emotional experiences which registered
themselves in my consciousness, and were stored away in memory
during this first year of conscious recognition of feelings and events.
For example, I quite understood that my parents did not get on;
indeed, I think I felt their great hatred for one another. In fact, my
mother used to hiss so and pooh, pooh so, with the corners of her
mouth a way down when talking of my father and his family, that I
wondered at him and feared him, so much so that when he came in at
night, sat by the fire, held me on his lap, played and grunted over me,
I wanted to respond rather contemptuously. If he asked me very
ardently, "Hug yer daddy's neck, tight, tight," I would do it very slowly
for I was wondering if it were not true that he was one of the meanest
men who ever lived. My mother had already suggested it in my presence scores of times at this early age and the statement that "the
Beasleys is the sorriest people that God ever made" was not only written in my brain but in my soul. Then, too, I knew that my father beat
his animals unmercifully, a thing which terrified me; and that he
sometimes beat my brothers with as little concern as though they were
cast iron. One day, this same year, I remember, one of the boys ran to
the house from the field and cried out frantically to my mother, "Maw,
he's killing ole Mary." I feel now how it saddened and frightened me.
The old mare which he had been driving at the plough had suddenly
sulked and he had beaten her with chains until her body was full of
welts, and finally with a stray stroke had knocked one of her eyes completely out. My mother ran about with her apron over her arm in a
frenzy and finally disappeared from the house in an effort to stop him.

And then he could swear so loudly and in such ear-splitting tones,

"Hell fire!" "God damn it to hell!" and the like, his god-damning usually rendering me perfectly stiff and dumb. The whole household was
usually silenced with his oaths. Although my brothers swore and all of
us said "God" and "God Amighty" whenever we chose, nobody could
begin to put the cutting swiftness and frightfulness into oaths as the
head of the house did.

Many things crowd into my mind now of the happenings of that
first year of memory, at four or perhaps younger. Going to town was
always a big event for my mother, who went a few times each year to
buy clothing for herself and the family. One of the most humorous
events of her preparation was the putting on of her corsets. Being
inclined to be stout due to excessive child bearing, having been pregnant every second year since she was eighteen, her waist line had naturally disappeared. My three oldest sisters were the instruments for
putting her into this vice. First, the corsets were unlaced as far as the
strings would allow and then the three girls would stand around her as
required, holding her at the waist, while she craned her short neck
over her ample breasts in an effort to put the hooks into the eyes at the
front of the corsets. Then someone pulled the strings at the back until
she called out enough and the corseting was finished; and everybody
was in good humor unless some one of the girls had chanced to laugh,
or to cause her to laugh, to shake her abdomen so as to prevent the
"hooking." Then someone was liable to get a large smack, and she
would turn to nagging and scolding, perhaps saying that everything
went wrong whenever she went to town, besides, "yer Daddy never
wants me to go nowhere." On this occasion I think she was going to
Coleman City, the town where she wanted to put my oldest brother
and oldest sister at school, for she, at least, always considered "ejica-
tion" important. But my father declared that they would only get into
"devilment" and so the plan was never carried out, in spite of the fact
that my mother declared many times after I grew up that there was
money enough to put them to school for several months that year, as
there had been a large cotton crop harvested. I remember sitting near

the fireplace, on one of these occasions, at a very early hour in the morning, watching her dress, and asking her not to forget my tea-set, for it was in the late fall and she was to buy the Christmas things.

THEN, ONE DAY SOMETHING HAPPENED. I STOOD AT MY MOTHER'S bedside early in the morning, and although it was July, I seem to have been cold as I shivered there in my bare feet. A red, soft, little wad lay near her and wriggled a little. I was astonished. Besides my mother looked very ill. An itching desire made me want to stroke its hair, but I was not permitted to touch it. The drawl in my own voice sounds in my ears now, "Maw, where did you git that little baby?" She answered that the doctor had brought it to her during the night in his saddle bags. Nearly everyone in that section of the country rode horseback and usually carried a pair of bags attached at the back of his saddle. I can't recall that it occurred to me to question this baby-in-the-saddle-bag theory. She talked a bit to herself saying that the poor little thing's head was "mashed out of shape" a little but that she would rub it back in place. Perhaps it would not live, and then she enumerated her babies, with the perplexity of a sick woman and with a note of sadness as she spoke. This was the eleventh one.

But the baby proved to be very much alive, growing and requiring a lot of attention, and I was made its nurse maid. A little chair was bought especially for me, in which I used to sit and rock the baby during the long hours when practically everyone older than myself was at work in the field, while my mother prepared the meals and did all the sewing and patching for the family. Fancy what the patching alone amounted to. There were five boys to "patch for" and make over old trousers for, besides my oldest sister never learned to sew at an early age and so my mother had to make all her clothes until she was almost grown, as well as those of the other girls and the babies. Sometimes she would work into the night after the whole household had been snoring for hours.

We stayed here until the second crop was gathered, I think, and my father finding the "grubbing" too difficult and requiring too much time, or the grass too dry, or the summers too hot, or the cotton crop too little, or the water too mineral or "gyp," or that the horses were getting "locoed," or the cows didn't bear calves fast enough—something or other was always wrong with the big central taps of the resources of life—began to talk of "pulling up" and going to look for another place. Although my mother was never what I should call a happy woman, as my earliest remembrances are of how she had been "dragged down" and how hard life had been since she had been in the Beasley family, she became more depressed and almost melancholy at such talk. If there was anything wrong with the farming there was wood to be hauled to the townspeople; there was "freighting" to be done, that is hauling goods from the railway center to the little country town; besides this was a great cattle country, my father having already a small herd of young cows and a number of horses and mules, the young stock and especially the "calf crop" in another year would make farming only as a minor industry, unnecessary. Months passed and the cotton and maize were harvested. I picked my first pounds of cotton at odd times when my mother or some of the others took care of Martha Washington, for that is what my mother called her having about "run out" of names by the time the fifth daughter arrived. One day my father returned from town after selling the cotton; he walked with a slight stagger but seemed in the best of spirits. That is, a smile, if a little bitter, nevertheless curved his lips and radiated his face as he sat by the fireplace and told what his wife considered vulgar (in the sense of obscene) stories. But we children were always a little terrified: whether or not he smiled had no special significance for us, as he was just as likely to turn to storming and swearing the next minute if anything angered him. My mother was angry and pouting, hissing and turning the corners of her mouth down, "I declare to God, there's never been no woman mistreated as I've been." Some of the older children whispered: "Pa's drunk." All talked little or in hushed tones;

and my parents did not speak to one another. I felt that I was thinking and acting just like my mother, at least I would have liked to have assumed her attitude as I walked about the room near the fireplace; and if I registered any other emotions at this time they were fear and sadness.

My second and third sisters whispered together a lot about being thirteen or when one of them would be or was thirteen. One day about this time when I was asleep in a tent or in some house or old wagon yard, as was often the case when we were camped, my second brother, who was then, I think, nearly twenty years old, came and lay by me and tried to wake me for some sexual communication. When I woke and saw his penis which he had laid against my legs, I was frightened, perhaps at the size of it as much as anything, and filled with disgust and shame—shame that almost consumed me with frightfulness and horror. I cried out at first and my brother seemed frightened (although we were alone in the room) and then I turned away from him and feigned sleep; he left me and went to his own bed. I remember that I had a strong sexual desire at this time, a desire which I experienced at the age of five or six when sexual energy was so great in me that I used to press something against myself trying to obtain gratification, but this desire was also accompanied by great shame, and horror that made one's flesh shrivel up or appear to crack as with some dreadful malady. The vow which I made to myself then was similar in seriousness to me to an experience which I had when I was twelve (some three years later) which I afterwards referred to as my "conversion." And that vow was that in spite of my desire, this thing should never happen to me again; in three years I would be twelve and then the next was thirteen; and although I did not know what being "thirteen" meant in any special way, I well understood from my sisters' whisperings and significant glances that something important, perhaps awful, happened to one then; I would keep away from all this. Besides

I had a great deal of contempt for my three oldest brothers; I could spell better than any of them unless it was my second brother and on one occasion I had "spelled down" the whole lot of them. Then my fourth and fifth brothers, a few years older than myself, were no longer of great sexual interest to me as competition had already developed between us not only as to who could read, write and memorize with greatest efficiency, but also as to our physical strength. From the age of seven or eight to about eleven, I used to have from time to time terrible fights—fist-fighting, hair-pulling, and the like—with these two boys, in which bouts I often proved a very good match for them. In fact, I think the intense and consuming sex energy which I felt at my earliest recollections, at four years or perhaps even before, which was far greater, consuming far more of my conscious desires than that of food-hunger, began to diminish as soon as I learned to read at the age of five. At least it appears to me now that, during those first few months of reading, my sex energy was held completely in abeyance.

MANY TERRIBLE THINGS HAPPENED DURING THE FIRST TWO OR three years of my mother's separation from my father—some of them so terrible that I was sometimes quite exhausted for hours or often for several days on account of the nervous strain. One evening about nine o'clock after all the younger members of the family had gone to sleep my mother entered the room where the boys slept with a heavy horse whip in her hand (with my two older sisters standing about the doorway armed in some way, I think) and began beating my fourth brother, a boy about fifteen years old, who had just undressed and gone to bed. He cried out to her at first to stop but she was sufficiently armed and reenforced so that he had to take "what was coming to him." I was poring over some school book when this awful crash came; and the thunder and distress of my mother's voice; the lash and crack of a heavy whip called me to the door where I could see and hear. "Oh, God, I have a notion to take a gun and shoot you," cried my mother in a

frenzy, her face dripping with tears and sweat. At first my brother pretended that he did not know why she was beating him. Then my
mother said she had caught him there in the barnyard with the old
cow. She kept calling out to her God to witness what she was saying
and telling the boy that the most merciful thing she could do would be
to kill him. She kept lashing him as he rolled about on the bed clad
only in his underwear until he cried out half daring, half begging, "Kill
me, I wish you would take the gun and shoot me." Finding herself
exhausted she stood in the room, weeping and explaining to my
brother that if he lived to be a man he would thank her for the lesson
she was trying to teach him. She went on, "I have knowed for years
that some of you older boys was doin' things that no human bein' ought
ever to be guilty of. That's one reason why I left yer ole Daddy because
he would never help me to raise you children right." She became more
quiet and explained to him that such a thing was not only a crime in
the sight of God but it seemed to her, she couldn't quite remember,
that it was a criminal offense punishable by death in the old days. She
had talked this over with my oldest brother who had asked some man
who knew about such things and she was perfectly sure that there was
a law on the criminal statutes of the State of Texas making bestiality a
penitentiary offense. She secured some sort of promise from him that
he would never do such a thing again but she also assured him that
she would never attempt to beat a boy as large and as old as he again.
The next time she would turn him over to the officers and "let the law
take its course." Afterwards she and my two sisters went into the
kitchen to talk; my mother was telling them about having caught my
third brother, who was then about twenty-one years old, at this same
disgusting thing. She added with a deep sigh that she was so glad the
three oldest boys had gone away (during the first two or three years
my three oldest brothers worked or farmed near Abilene, but afterwards they went to quite other sections of the country) for she was
getting afraid of them especially the third one; she had lain awake
nights praying to her God asking what to do. Then she added in a

whisper, "I was just scared nearly to death before that old cow's calf come . . . God, I didn't know." At such times she would sit perfectly dumb for a minute, then jump up from her chair brushing a whole stream of tears from her face with the corner of her apron and start towards the door saying, "Emma, pull that curtain across there; Corrie, see if that other door is locked; I thought I saw a man's face at that window the other night; I declare to God, sometimes I think this will kill me."

The next day we would start off to school and perhaps when we were just ready to go or were just taking the last sop of molasses at breakfast my mother would start up with, "You children, hear me, don't you ever tell ennybody what happened here last night. If ennybody asks you, you tell 'em this or you tell 'em that or you tell 'em you don't know. Don't you ever dare breathe a word about what goes on in this house . . . about yer ole Daddy or about how some of these children has acted. If I ever hear that you have told these little Scott young uns or a child at school enny of the troubles that we have, I'll beat you in an inch of your life." Then she would say in a half whisper to one of the older ones, "My God, I wouldn't have enny respectable person know about this thing for ennything in this world. It's the biggest disgrace that could ever befall enny family." Sometimes threats from my parents rendered me rebellious and angry at heart but this time I was glad of my mother's severe attitude, for I, too, was afraid someone would find out what had happened the night before. I would watch anxiously the expression on the faces of the neighbors' children when we met in the street on the way to school and wonder if they had heard anything or would ask me any questions.

BOGGED SHADOWS

★

J. Frank Dobie

BEFORE FINDLAY SIMPSON DIED IN 1924, HE HAD BECOME A legendary character in the Irish-featured land where he rode and yarned. That was mainly on the O'Connor ranches. He had worked up to be boss under Pat Lambert, and he used to say that Pat Lambert was the most considerate boss he ever knew: he would give every man in his pay eighteen hours to do a day's work in.

They say that one time a cow crowd of O'Connor hands, some white, some black, decided to test out the talking powers of Findlay Simpson. It was early summer and the weather was pleasant. After an easier than usual day's work, the boys got him strung out. They had arranged their pallets so that when a listener became too sleepy to listen longer he could easily awaken the next man, who would egg Findley on. Findlay talked all that night and worked the next day. The second night he kept the relays up, then worked all day. The third night one of the relays went to sleep on him, and then Findlay decided that as nobody was listening he had as well sleep a while himself. He was up with the Morning Star, talking to the cook, when the first hand came to the coffeepot.

He became a kind of court entertainer for parties of young people on the ranch. When the late Tom O'Connor, great-grandson of the Tom O'Connor who founded the ranch, was a young man in camp, he might say at the end of a day's riding, "Findlay, tell me some of those lies. Tell me about the big snow in the northwest the winter you spent up there."

"Yes, it snowed and snowed," Findlay would begin. "The cattle drifted up against the mountains on the south side, and the snow filled up the valleys between the mountains. The cattle were all under it. It held there for six months before it begun to thaw good. Then it melted down so the cattle could walk out. You wouldn't believe they could hibernate that way like bears, but they could. They went into the snow fat, and when they come out they was packing rolls of taller around their tails.

"But I never see anything up in that cold country to what I see here in the big blizzard of 1899. During that die-up hands would take pack horses out from the Melon Creek ranch every morning to bring in the hides skinned off dead cattle. Well, one day I was riding along Copano Creek looking for bogged-up stuff, pulling out cows and skinning as I went. I guess this was maybe a month after the big freeze. Let's see, that was on the twelfth of February.

"Well, over in a little place between some granjeno bushes and a huisache I seen a cow standing. She looked as ga'nt as a gutted snow-bird. I pulled over to make sure she was all right. It was troublesome to get through some bushes right next to her, and I yelled so she'd turn round and show herself better. She didn't budge. Then I started in to her, and when I leaned over to dodge a limb, I seen a calf standing by her side a-sucking. It didn't move neither. When I got slap in on her, she still didn't move and the calf didn't neither. Thinks I to myself, 'This is mighty funny. I've heard of the lockjaw but never heard of the lockfoot.' I quirted her on the back, and still she didn't move. Then I got down and give myself a tap with the quirt to make sure I wasn't paralyzed. That cow was as dead as a doornail just a-standing there, and that calf was as dead as a doornail just a-sucking there. When cattle die standing up, it's hard times.

"That winter of '99 was an awful winter on everything, but I don't know as it was any worse on animals in general than the drouth of '86. The creeks all dried up that year and what waterholes were left got so boggy the buzzards were scared to fly over them for fear their shadders would bog down. The country was full of razorback hogs then, and most of them got such big balls of mud on their tails that the weight would draw back everything on the animal clear up to the snout. When you met a razorback face to face, he'd be grinning at you like a Cheshire cat, 'cause his lips were pulled back. Why, the mudballs on their tails drew their eyelids back so tight the razorbacks couldn't sleep.

"Then the critters drunk so much mud they all got pot-bellied. I've seen one of them just a-rocking and a-teetering and a-seesawing on his belly, unable to get his hindfeet or his forefeet either on the ground. There he'd be up in the air, on top of his own belly, his eyelids pulled back by the weight of mud on his tail, and his eyes bugged out till you could have roped 'em with a grapevine. It was a sight, I tell you.

"But talking about mud and water, one year I went with a train of cattle to Chicago for Dennis O'Connor. We got along all right till we left New Orleans and started across the biggest lake there is, I guess, outside the Gulf of Mexico. We'd no more 'n got out on the bridge when I heard the derndest whistling and screeching from the engine a man ever listened to. The train stopped and still the whistling went on. I was riding in the caboose, and I crawled up in the cupola to look out. Then I seen what the trouble was. It was enough to make a man and an engine both whistle.

"It looked to me like all the alligators in the world had crawled up out of that lake to sun theirselves on the bridge. They were laying acrost the tracks and in between the rails and dangling over the ties and every which way. The cowcatcher had plowed up the first ones, I guess. At least, they was piled up ahead of the engine higher than the smokestack. Now the engine couldn't budge. The engineer kept a-whistling and the trainmen sorter cleared the pile away. Then we went on a few feet, the engine all the time letting out screeches that would have waked up dead Spaniards in the Refugio graveyard. Why, before we got acrost that lake the engineer had wore out his whistle. Then he wore out his bell a-ringing it. After that we didn't have no more trouble and the cattle sold well in Chicago. But them alligators!

"Still, I don't know as they were much thicker on that big lake than I see them oncet in San Jacinto River. I was taking a herd of T H C cattle east, and it was an awful wet year. We'd been having plenty of trouble. We had to pull twenty or thirty out of a bog they got into in a cut at the Colorado River. Then the Brazos was up on a toot, and the herd got into a mill while they were swimming in the middle of it. We'd sweated at some of the little creeks, and I shore was a-dreading the San Jacinto.

"But when we got to it, the sun was right for crossing—back behind us instead of in the cattle's eyes—and I told the boys to pop their leggins and bring 'em a-stringing. I was back a little from the point, and when I got to the bank I never was more surprised in my life. Them cattle was a-walking across dry-shod, like the Children of Israel a-crossing the Red Sea. They was a-stepping on alligators' backs. Seemed like the alligators had all congregated to sun their backs or something like that. They didn't seem to mind the weight. I guess being so thick that way they kinder supported each other.

"When I come to cross, my horse give a snort, but he took the bridge all right. Still, I didn't feel easy. I knowed if one of them alligators give a flip of his tail so's to hit the nose of some snuffy steer, there'd be a stompede would shake their ancestors. But nothing like that happened.

"The biggest alligator I ever see was in the Mission River, right here in Refugio County. I was riding up it one day looking out for bogged animals, and before I knowed it, the bed was practically dry. Thinks I, 'This is mighty peculiar. I was up above here about three miles day before yesterday and the river was bank-full—fuller'n I ever see it except after a big rain. Now down here there ain't no water at all.'

"Well, I kept a-riding on upstream, my curiosity getting more and more het up. Then I come to the answer of all my curiosity. It was an alligator, a regular giant of an alligator, the Goliath of all alligators that ever lived. His tail had got tangled up in a lot of willer roots on one side of the bank and in pawing and struggling he had evidently hung his snout and forelegs in the roots on the opposite bank. There he was stretched out damning the whole river up, so the water was about to make Refugio a deep-sea port up above and the bed drying up down below.

"I could have killed the critter easy, but I wasn't going to destroy a specimen like that. I just took my axe and cut the roots. But when that alligator got loose, danged if he didn't have to crawl out on the prairie to turn around. The river was just too little for him to operate in.

"He really belonged over in the San Jacinto River. People in this country think they have big mosquitoes and big frogs and big cotton-wood trees and all that, but they ought to go over on the San Jacinto. Why, Tom, I remember when you was a boy shaking with a chill one day over on the San Antonio River and getting blue around the gills and imagining you was really having the ague. You'd been tanking up on Grove's Tasteless Chill Tonic. Nobody was heeding my remedy of a glass full of whiskey mixed with the juice of an even one hundred Mexican peppers.

"But I'll tell you again, the chills on the San Antonio River or any-where else in this western country ain't nothing to compare with the chills on the San Jacinto. Ain't nothing, I tell you.

"One time over there I was riding along kinder out from the bottom when I noticed the leaves of a certain cottonwood tree just a-shaking and a-trembling like they was bewitched. I stopped and looked all around and not another leaf in the whole timber was a-moving. It was so dead ca'm I'd been saying to myself how a storm must be brewing. Still, to make certain there wasn't no current of air anywhere, I spit on my finger and held it up to see which direction any little breeze might be blowing. Not a breath from any point.

"Then I rode straight in to that cottonwood to see what in the creation was causing such a commotion, amongst the leaves. If it was squirrels or coons frisking about, the leaves would be shaking just in one place, but they were shaking all over the tree, and it was a big one, high up over all the other trees. Well, sir, when I got there, you'd never guess what I discovered.

"There was the king bullfrog of the San Jacinto bottoms having a chill. He was backed up against that tree and the tears was just a-rolling out of his eyes, he was shaking so hard. And all unbeknownst to him he was shaking so hard against the cottonwood that all its leaves was a-trembling."

About here Findlay Simpson discovered that Tom O'Connor and everybody else had gone to sleep.

THE GIRL AT CABE RANCH

A. C. Greene

THE ROAD TURNED INTO A PUZZLE OF TRAILS GOING OFF
left and right. I asked the boy, Harris, if he knew which was
which and he shook his head, yes.

The woman at the Chamber of Commerce back in Toller said Harris knew the country better than anybody except Uncle Bartlett, whoever that was.

"I don't see how you can tell these ruts apart," I said to the boy as we bounced along in the pickup.

"Just know 'em," he said.

I had picked a bad day in a bad month in a bad season to make the trip. Fifteenth of July. It couldn't have been hotter and it couldn't have been drier. One of the ranchers in Toller said if it rained now all the cows would die from fright. Why had Uncle Sam picked such places for western history, or why had I picked western history as my field when there are so many more timely and relevant disciplines?

After the Chamber of Commerce woman recommended him I found Harris and we made a deal. He said we'd better go in his old pickup truck, the roads might be a little hard on my Chrysler. I thought about the Chrysler now, parked at the courthouse square, its air conditioner doing me no good.

We went north out of Toller on the state highway, across a wide, hot mesquite prairie. The tires on the concrete highway sounded to me like sizzling flesh and went bumpity-bump, bumpity-bump as they hit the tar-filled joints. The sound took the place of the conversation I wasn't having with Harris.

The ranch road turned off the highway ten miles out of town, and now we had driven another five or so over Cabe ranch land.

"I don't see any cattle," I said.

The boy didn't answer but kept glaring down the road like that old picture of the heroic railroad engineer in a storm you used to see.

I hadn't been told the boy's full name. Just Harris. Something Harris or Harris Something; the woman at the Chamber of Commerce didn't say and neither did Harris.

He looked to be about twenty. He might have been a little older. The older I get the less I can tell ages, especially younger ages.

"Any of the Cabes live out here?" I asked.

"Mart Cabe does," he said.

"I don't think I'd want to live out here, even if I owned it all," I said.

"He doesn't own it all. He's got two brothers own part of it."

"Well, I wouldn't want to live on it if I had ten brothers."

"He's just got two."

I told myself I had asked for that comeback, but I knew Harris hadn't meant it as a retort. There was no need for me to be so damned contemptuous of this country. It was mine, too, or I was its. I was born less than fifty miles from the Cabe ranch.

But something had gone different in me, and where boys like Harris whoever-he-was had taken up 4H clubs and horses, I'd taken up history and books. Pretty soon they couldn't understand me and my history books, and I didn't try to understand them and their horses. So I left. That had been a long time ago. Twenty-five years ago, at least. A long time to be away and come back.

The sun was shining from all directions. The ground was red and dusty, the grass was brown and dusty; but then, "brown is the natural condition of the grass," an old emigrants' guide once said of this country.

The land rolled away in hills which fell into breaks and draws. You could see for miles. It was all rocks and grass and red clay dirt and the only trees were mesquite bushes, seldom taller than a man—and the ranchers killed even those because they kept the brown grass from growing.

But I found myself settling into an excited sort of contentment as I rode with the boy, letting him pick out the way from among these twisting, all-alike trails. I breathed deep, feeling the hot, dry air going down into my lungs. The air is the best thing about that country, to me.

The boy was wearing an old Stetson Double X with the wings folded up rodeo style. When I was a boy a rancher wouldn't have been caught dead wearing his Stetson that way. Television even tells the cowboys how to dress. Harris was nice looking, neat around the neck, and his hair clean. He had to have some pride to keep his hair washed, working on the ranches away from everybody like he did.

"Is that the Cabe house over there?" I pointed to a gray, wooden structure, needing paint, with a lone tree beside it.

"That's the Mulkeys'. Mr. Mulkey's the foreman." The boy looked over at the Mulkey house. "The Cabe house is a lot nicer."

We drove around the gray house. A television aerial rose above it and a red Ford was parked in the carport. With a few neighbors and a coat of paint the whole scene would have fit neatly in a suburb. A woman waved at us.

"We going to stop?" I asked as the boy slowed down.

"Not unless you want to," he said.

I laughed. "You're the boss, Harris. You're taking me where we're going."

We didn't stop. The road, if you want to call it that, circled the house and went into a big pasture behind it. We came out of the pasture through a cattle guard, then dropped down the side of a hill and were alone again. Hot it was, but magnificent it was, too. You could turn in any direction and see no trace of the hand of man—except for our pickup truck.

About two miles from the foreman's house the ruts parted like railroad tracks at a switch. One set went right, through a tall gate with a sign on it: Horsetail Ranch. We took that one.

"The name sounds like a dude ranch," I commented as we started down this new branch of the road. Once again my humor failed to reach Harris.

"Horsetail's a big outfit. The Cabes've got land all the way into Young County."

Sometimes I would lose all traces of the road as the entire landscape turned into a brown panorama. Here and there another set of tracks would spill off, disappearing into the grass like a ship's wake. Then we came to a level stretch and I could see tall, green trees about a mile ahead.

"That must be the river," I said, more or less to myself.

"That's the Clear Fork," the boy said. "It runs all year."

"Is it drinkable?"

"Reckon so. I've done it enough. Gets gyppy when it's low. Drains from the gyp beds out on the Plains." He paused, then asked, "You thirsty?"

Before I could answer he said, "We'll stop by the house and get a drink. They've got a good well."

The Cabe ranch house surprised me. I was prepared for something like the foreman's house or possibly something huge and Victorian out of a western movie. It was neither. It had age and dignity and that unexpected beauty one finds now and then left from the frontier. It was tall and stood high off the ground. It was built of rock, old and carefully masoned. A square cupola surmounted the roof, and there were six tall, slender chimneys, three on the east, three on the west, standing in rows. A white, wooden fence was around the yard and four lines of old, big trees outlined the rectangle of land where the house stood.

"That is tremendous," I said in admiration.

Harris drove the pickup to the back door and honked the horn, then got out. "We'll go in," he said.

An old brown hound yelped and barked at us from inside the fence as we walked up to the gate. The boy leaned over and unlatched the gate from the inside and said something to the old hound. He waited to snap the latch on the gate after I went through as though I wouldn't know how.

We walked up to the big, deep porch along the back side of the house. The door opened and a blonde-headed girl came out, looked at me, then at the boy.

"Hello," she said.

"Hello, Sid," he said back. "How about some water?"

She looked at me without answering him.

"Oh. This is Dr. Powell." He made a motion toward me.

"I'm Sidonie Cabe," she said, deciding to hold out her hand. It wasn't hard and dry like some country hands are from work and weather. But then, it wasn't soft and moist either.

She was a good-looking girl. About eighteen, I guessed. She had on shorts, and her long, slim legs were brown. She was barefooted and her toenails were painted bright red. It looked freshly done.

"Come in," she said. "Mother and Sis are over at the Fultons'. I'm here by myself."

"Where's your dad?" the boy asked.

"He's gone to Denver to an auction. He and Zene Mulkey flew."

"It's a little lonesome out here by yourself, isn't it?" I asked.

"She doesn't mind," Harris said to me, then to her, "Dr. Powell's from California. He's come out to see the fort."

"Are you a history teacher?" she asked.

"Sometimes," I said. "Right now I'm writing a book on some of the old outposts in this part of the country. Doing research."

"Oh," she said, and gave a little shrug. "I'll fix some cold water."

We went into a big room that opened off the kitchen. There was a well at one end of the room and the wall of the kitchen was rock.

"This used to be the sleeping porch a long time ago. Before air conditioning," the boy said. "Mr. Cabe says the well was enclosed because of the Indians."

I doubted this but didn't say anything. You learn not to disturb family legends when you're a historian. It looked to me as if the well had been dug close to the house for convenience and whoever added the porch room enclosed it for the same reason.

The girl brought out a big enamel pitcher of ice water with some glasses. Suddenly I felt as if I could drink it all.

"I've lost my hump," I said, over my third glass.

"Your hump?" the girl looked toward me.

"That's what we used to say when I was a kid. Your hump was what kept you from getting thirsty. We thought a camel's hump was full of water."

"Did you live out here?"

"I was born in Taylor county."

"You don't live there now though, do you?"

"No. I left to go to college and never moved back."

"Mr. Cabe says the stone for this house came from the old fort," the boy interjected.

"I was wondering if it didn't," I said.

"There's some frosted glass around the front door that's supposed to be from the fort, too," the girl said.

"How far is the fort from here?" I asked.

"Not far. Just across the river over there," the girl said, pointing out the direction of the back door.

"Can we drive it?" I asked.

The boy answered. "No, you've got to wade the river. Road's been washed out for years."

The girl turned to him coldly. "You can drive there, too. You can go through the Lambert and drive there. You just came the wrong way to get there in an automobile."

The boy grinned. "We're not in an 'auto-mobile.' We're in a pickup."

"All right, or in a pickup either." She reached out a bare, red-toed foot and kicked at a magazine. She must have been reading it when we drove up.

"It's pretty over there," she said, not looking at either of us but concentrating on the movement of the magazine with her toe. "I go there all the time. Ride over. Especially the graveyard. Down where Spring Creek runs into the Clear Fork. Daddy says it's dangerous because of the copperheads but I go there anyway."

"It's too hot," the boy said. "Too hot and muggy." He looked toward me. "The fort's on a flat that backs up against the hill. It's a lot lower than it is here. It doesn't get any breeze."

"Yes," I smiled in historical superiority, "General Pomeroy used to complain in his letters to his wife about how hot it got. 'Sweaty as a well,' he wrote to her."

The girl looked up. "Was General Pomeroy really at this fort . . . the famous one?"

"He was commander here just before the Civil War. Spent nearly two years."

"Well, good," she smiled. "I've lived here all my life and I never have known for sure. I thought it was just a kind of legend."

"I knew it," the boy said, without looking at her.

"General Pomeroy might have spent a lot of his time right where we're sitting," I said. "He wrote his wife that when the nights were too hot, he'd take his gear to what he called 'the Red Bluff beyond the River' and sleep."

"I know where that is," the girl said. 'It's the place around behind the cowsheds. It's real high above the river."

"That may be the spot," I told her. "Of course, in a hundred and some-odd years things can change a lot. The river may have cut the bluff down years ago."

"It doesn't change that much around here," she said. "Nothing does."

"I don't think that's the bluff," the boy said.

"Why?" she turned toward him fiercely. "You don't know anything about it. Dr. Powell said it was. He knows a lot more about it than you do. You're just an . . . an ignorant cowboy," she bit her lower lip, "that's all you are. You don't want to be anything else."

"I still don't think that's the bluff," the boy said, not looking at her. "General Pomeroy would have had to come plumb around to the shallows to get across. He wouldn't have walked that far just for a cool place to sleep."

"He had a horse," she said tautly.

"He wouldn't have saddled up a horse just for that."

"Things were different then. He had aides and servants to saddle his horse. You heard what Dr. Powell said. The river might have been different."

She looked at me as if she were demanding I support her statement.

I ducked out. "All he wrote his wife was that he oftentimes took his bedroll and spent the night on the red bluff beyond the river. I just assumed it might be here, if the fort lies below this land."

The girl looked at the boy sullenly. When she turned back to me I could see tears gathering on the bottom rims of her deep blue eyes.

"Do you write for the movies or TV, Dr. Powell?" she asked.

"No, just history books. I don't even write historical novels."

"And you've come all the way out here just to write a history book?"

"Partly. It's sort of a homecoming for me, coming from near here. I've got to go other places, too."

"If I left here I'd never come back," she said. "I wouldn't come back to write a book or do anything else. I'd go away and I'd stay wherever it was I went."

"Why, this is wonderful country, Miss Cabe," I said. "The old fort over there, just across the river . . . it has a lot of romance connected to it. General Pomeroy's son Catlett brought his beautiful young bride here on their honeymoon. She was daughter of the governor of Virginia."

"He brought her here to live?" the girl asked.

"Yes, and she was just about your age. Cat Pomeroy was a soldier, too. A lieutenant under his father."

"I'd die before I'd let a man bring me to a place like this," she said.

"Well, I'll admit, she didn't stay long. She went back to Virginia."

"Did she divorce him?"

"Oh, no. She just went back there to have a baby and live while her husband was on frontier duty."

"I'd have divorced him," the girl said firmly.

"You wouldn't have done any such thing," the boy said suddenly. "You'd have come out here and lived at that fort with him and liked it, heat and all. And you wouldn't have run back to Virginia just to have a baby, neither."

She shook her head violently. "I would have, and someday when I leave I'll show you. I'll never set foot here again."

The boy watched her. "You couldn't do that. You can't even spend a weekend in Dallas without wanting to come back. Your daddy told me so. He said, 'I can't get a room on the west side of the hotel or old Sid'll spent all her time gazing out the window tryin' to see home.'"

She was crying. "That's a lie you made up. Every word of it. It's daddy wants to come back early. Not me."

"And you wait," the boy continued, "when you go off to that girls' college this fall, you'll be home Christmas and you'll say, 'Oh, Harris, I don't want to go back.' You'll flat hate it, being gone from here."

"I won't!" she was crying hard. "I'll go away and get married to somebody in another place. Anywhere but here."

The boy watched her. They acted as if they were going to do something more, but finally the boy stood up and grinned.

"Well, I guess we better get going."

"I suppose we'd better," I said, standing also. I felt to blame for the little domestic quarrel, as it were. "Thanks again for the water, Miss Cabe," I said. "You saved our lives."

Harris stood there running his tongue over his lips. "All right," he said, then turned to me and motioned, "come on," and walked out the door.

"I'm sorry, Sid," I said. "I didn't mean to start a fuss between you and Harris."

She shook her head, and her hair fell golden around her face. She wiped her tears away with her bare hand, pushing her hair back at the same time.

"You didn't start anything, Dr. Powell. You just got in on something. You better go on before he runs off and leaves you." She tossed her head and looked at me. "He's just a cowboy. All he thinks about is land and cattle. That's all he wants out of life. Just like my daddy. He won't even get any more education. Thinks he knows everything he needs to know." She looked at me sadly. "I'd marry him if he was different."

I took her hand, "Goodbye, Sid."

"Come back again sometime," she said, sniffing.

The boy was seated in the pickup when I walked out. His rodeo hat was pushed down on his forehead.

"Why don't we wade across from here?" I asked.

"Naw. Get in. We'll drive."

"I thought you couldn't get there driving?"

"You can if you go through the Lambert."

"Have we got time?"

"It's not far. It's no further than through the Cabe if you start for there in the first place."

I smiled. "There must not be any cute girls at the Lambert ranch."

My humor failed again. "There isn't anything at the Lambert but cattle and cowmen," he said. "It's a big spread. A genuine ranch, not anything TV dreamed up. I'll guarantee you, I'd like to think I'd ever run something just half as big as the Lambert."

I decided I'd better make my amends to the boy, too.

"Harris," I said, "I apologize for what happened. I didn't realize I would bring up a sore subject, telling about the old fort."

"You didn't. We go through it all the time. In fact, you might have done her some good. That story about the general's son bringing his bride out here . . . she'll go to thinking about it and next time I see her, she'll be telling me how much tougher she is than some Virginia aristocrat." He nodded his head in a strong affirmative. "And, by God, she is."

He wheeled the pickup around and we bounced down another gravelly hill to take up the pursuit of a pair of faint creases in the dry grass. It didn't look like a road to me. But the boy knew where he was going. I leaned back and let him drive.

THE LAST RUNNING

★

John Graves

T HEY CALLED HIM PAJARITO, IN LITERAL TRADER-SPANISH interpretation of his surname, or more often Tom Tejano, since he had been there in those early fighting days before the Texans had flooded up onto the plains in such numbers that it became no longer practical to hate them with specificity.

After the first interview, when he had climbed down from the bed where an aching liver held him and had gone out onto the porch to salute them, only to curse in outrage and clump back into the house when he heard what they wanted, the nine of them sat like grackles about the broad gray-painted steps and talked, in Comanche, about Tom Texan the Little Bird and the antique times before wire fences had partitioned the prairies. At least, old Juan the cook said that was what they were talking about.

Mostly it was the old men who talked, three of them, one so decrepit that he had had to make the trip from Oklahoma in a lopsided carryall drawn by a piebald mare, with an odd long bundle sticking out the back, the rest riding alongside on ponies. Of the other six, two were middle-aged and four were young.

Their clothes ran a disastrous gamut from buckskin to faded calico and blue serge, but under dirty Stetsons they wore their hair long and braided, plains style. Waiting, sucking Durham cigarettes and speaking Comanche, they sat about the steps and under the cottonwoods in the yard and ignored those of us who drifted near to watch them, except the one or two whom they considered to have a right to their attention. Twice a day for two days they built fires and broiled unsymmetrical chunks of the fat calf which, from his bed, furiously, Tom Bird had ordered killed for them. At night—it was early autumn—they rolled up in blankets about the old carryall and slept on the ground.

"They show any signs of leaving?" Tom Bird asked me when I went into his room toward evening of the second day.

I said, "No, sir. They told Juan they thought you could spare one easily enough, since all of them and the land too used to be theirs."

"They didn't used to be nobody's!" he shouted.

"They've eaten half that animal since they got here," I said. "I never saw anybody that could eat meat like that, and nothing but meat."

"No, nor ever saw anything else worth seeing," he said, his somber gray eyes brooding. He was one of the real ones, and none of them are left now. That was in the twenties; he was my great-uncle, and at sixteen he had run away from his father's farm in Mississippi to work his way to the brawling acquisitive Texas frontier. At the age of eighty-five he possessed—more or less by accident, since cattle rather than land had always meant wealth to him—a medium-large ranch in the canyon country where the Cap Rock falls away to rolling prairies, south of the Texas Panhandle. He had buried two wives and had had no children and lived there surrounded by people who worked for him. When I had showed up there, three years before the Comanches' visit, he had merely grunted at me on the porch, staring sharply at my frail physique, and had gone right on arguing with his manager about rock salt in the pastures. But a month later, maybe when he decided I was going to pick up weight and live, we had abruptly become friends. He was given to quick gruff judgments and to painful retractions.

He said in his room that afternoon, "God damn it, I'll see them in hell before they get one, deeper than you can drop an anvil."

"You want me to tell them that?"

"Hell, yes," he said. "No. Listen, have you talked any with that old one? Starlight, they call him."

I said that neither Starlight nor the others had even glanced at any of us.

Tom Bird said, "You tell him you're kin to me. He knows a lot, that one."

"What do you want me to say about the buffalo?"

"Nothing," he said and narrowed his eyes as a jab of pain shot through him from that rebellious organ which was speaking loudly now of long-gone years of drinking at plains mudholes and Kansas saloons. He grunted. "Not a damn thing," he said. "I already told them."

Starlight paid no attention at all when I first spoke to him. I had picked up a poor grade of Spanish from old Juan in three years but was timid about using it, and to my English he showed a weathered and not even disdainful profile.

I stated my kinship to Tom Bird and said that Tom Bird had told me to speak to him.

Starlight stared at the fourteen pampered bison grazing in their double-fenced pasture near the house, where my great-uncle could watch them from his chair in the evenings. He had bred them from seed stock given him in the nineties by Charles Goodnight, and the only time one of them had ever been killed and eaten was when the governor of the state and a historical society had driven out to give the old man some sort of citation. When the Comanches under Starlight had arrived, they had walked down to the pasture fence and had looked at the buffalo for perhaps two hours, hardly speaking,

studying the cows and the one calf and the emasculated males and the
two bulls—old Shakespeare, who had killed a horse once and had put
innumerable men up mesquite trees and over fences, and his lecher-
ous though rarely productive son, John Milton.

Then they had said, matter-of-factly, that they wanted one of the
animals.

Starlight's old-man smell was mixed with something wild, perhaps
wood smoke. His braids were a soiled white. One of the young men
glanced at me after I had spoken and said something to him in
Comanche. Turning then, the old Indian looked at me down his
swollen nose. His face was hexagonal and broad, but sunken where
teeth were gone. He spoke.

The young man said in English with an exact accent, "He wants to
know what's wrong with old Tom Bird, not to talk to friends."

All of them were watching me, the young ones with more affability
than the others. I said Tom Bird was sick in the liver, and patted my
own.

Starlight said in Spanish, "Is he dying?"

I answered in Spanish that I didn't think so but that it was painful.

He snorted much like Tom Bird himself and turned to look again
at the buffalo in the pasture. The conversation appeared to have
ended, but not knowing how to leave I sat there on the top step beside
the old Comanche, the rest of them ranged below us and eyeing me
with what I felt to be humor. I took out cigarettes and offered them to
the young man, who accepted the package and passed it along, and
when it got back to me it was nearly empty. I got the impression that
this gave them amusement, too, though no one had smiled. We all sat
blowing smoke into the crisp evening air.

Then, it seemed, some ritual biding time had passed. Old Starlight
began to talk again. He gazed at the buffalo in the pasture under the
fading light and spoke steadily in bad Spanish with occasional phrases
of worse English. The young Indian who had translated for me in the
beginning lit a small stick fire below the steps. From time to time one

of the other old men would obtrude a question or a correction, and they would drop into the angry Comanche gutturals, and the young man, whose name was John Oak Tree, would tell me what they were saying.

The story went on for an hour or so; when Starlight stopped talking they trooped down to the carryall and got their blankets and rolled up in them on the ground. In the morning I let my work in the ranch office wait and sat down again with the Comanches on the steps, and Starlight talked again. The talk was for me, since I was Tom Bird's kinsman. Starlight did not tell the story as I tell it here. Parts I had to fill in later in conversation with Tom Bird, or even from books. But this was the story.

WITHOUT KNOWING HIS EXACT AGE, HE KNEW THAT HE WAS younger than Tom Bird, about the age of dead Quanah Parker, under whom he had more than once fought. He had come to warrior's age during the big fight the white men had had among themselves over the black men. Born a Penateka or Honey Eater while the subtribal divisions still had meaning, he remembered the surly exodus from the Brazos reservation to Oklahoma in 1859, the expulsion by law of the Comanches from all of Texas.

But white laws had not meant much for another ten years or so. It was a time of blood and confusion, a good time to be a Comanche and fight the most lost of all causes. The whites at the Oklahoma agencies were Northern and not only tolerated but sometimes egged on and armed the parties striking down across the Red, with the full moon, at the line of settlements established by the abominated and tenacious Texans. In those days, Starlight said, Comanches held Texans to be another breed of white men, and even after they were told that peace had smiled again among whites, they did not consider this to apply to that race which had swarmed over the best of their grass and timber.

In the beginning, the raids had ritual formality and purpose; an individual party would go south either to make war, or to steal horses, or to drive off cattle for trading to the New Mexican comancheros at plains rendezvous, or maybe just reminiscently to run deer and buffalo over the old grounds. But the distinctions dimmed. In conservative old age Starlight believed that the Comanches' ultimate destruction was rooted in the loss of the old disciplines. That and smallpox and syphilis and whiskey. And Mackenzie's soldiers. All those things ran in an apocalyptic pack, like wolves in winter.

They had gone horse raiding down into the Brazos country, a dozen of them, all young and all good riders and fighters. They captured thirty horses here and there in the perfect stealth that pride demanded, without clashes, and were headed back north up the Keechi Valley near Palo Pinto when a Texan with a yellow beard caught them in his corral at dawn and killed two of them with a shotgun. They shot the Texan with arrows; Starlight himself peeled off the yellow scalp. Then, with a casualness bred of long cruelty on both sides, they killed his wife and two children in the log house. She did not scream as white women were said to do, but until a hatchet cleaved her skull kept shouting, "Git out! Git, git, git."

And collecting five more horses there, they continued the trek toward the Territory, driving at night and resting at known secret spots during the days.

The leader was a son of old Iron Shirt, Pohebits Quasho, bullet-dead on the Canadian despite his Spanish coat of mail handed down from the old haughty days. Iron Shirt's son said that it was bad to have killed the woman and the children, but Starlight, who with others laughed at him, believed even afterward that it would have been the same if they had let the woman live.

What was certain was that the Texans followed, a big party with men among them who could cut trail as cleanly as Indians. They followed quietly, riding hard and resting little, and on the third evening, when the Comanches were gathering their herd and readying themselves to leave a broad enclosed creek valley where they had spent the day, their sentry on a hill yelled and was dead, and the lean horsemen with the wide hats were pouring down the hillside shouting the long shout that belonged to them.

When it happened, Starlight was riding near the upper end of the valley with the leader. The only weapons with them were their knives and Starlight's lance, with whose butt he had been poking the rumps of the restive stolen horses as they hazed them toward camp below. As they watched, the twenty or more Texans overrode the camp, and in the shooting and confusion the two Comanches heard the end of their five companions who had been there afoot.

"I knew this," the leader said.

"You knew it," Starlight answered him bitterly. "You should have been the sentry, Know-much."

Of the other two horse gatherers, who had been working the lower valley, they could see nothing, but a group of the Texans rode away from the camp in that direction, yelling and firing. Then others broke toward Starlight and the leader a half mile above.

"We can run around them to the plain below," the son of Iron Shirt said. "Up this creek is bad."

Starlight did not know the country up the creek, but he knew what he felt, and feeling for a Comanche was conviction. He turned his pony upstream and spurred it.

"Ragh!" he called to the leader in farewell. "You're dirty luck!" And he was right, for he never saw the son of Iron Shirt again. Or the other two horse gatherers either.

But the son of Iron Shirt had been right, too, because ten minutes later Starlight was forcing his pony among big fallen boulders in a root tangle of small steep canyons, each of which carried a trickle to the stream below. There was no way even to lead a horse up their walls; he had the feeling that any one of them would bring him to a blind place.

Behind him shod hoofs rang; he whipped the pony on, but a big Texan on a bay horse swept fast around a turn in the canyon, jumping the boulders, and with a long lucky shot from a pistol broke Starlight's pony's leg. The Comanche fell with the pony but lit cat-bouncing and turned, and as the Texan came down waited crouched with the lance. The Texan had one of the pistols that shot six times, rare then in that country. Bearing down, he fired three times, missing each shot, and then when it was the moment Starlight feinted forward and watched the Texan lurch aside from the long bright blade, and while he was off balance, Starlight drove it into the Texan's belly until it came out the back. The blade snapped as the big man's weight came onto it, falling.

Starlight sought the pistol for a moment but not finding it ran to the canyon wall and began climbing. He was halfway up the fifty feet of its crumbling face when the other Texan rode around the turn and stopped, and from his unquiet horse, too hastily, fired a rifle shot that blew Starlight's left eye full of powdered sandstone.

He was among swallows' nests. Their molded mud crunched under his hands; the birds flew in long loops, chittering about his head. Climbing, he felt the Texan's absorbed reloading behind and below him as the horse moved closer, and when he knew with certainty that it was time, looked around to see the long caplock rifle rising again. . . . Watched still climbing, and guessing at the instant, wrenched himself hard to the right, seizing the roots of a cedar that grew almost at the top of the cliff.

The bullet smashed through his upper left arm, and he hung only by his right, but with the long wiry strength of trick horsemanship he swung himself up and onto the overhanging turf of the cliff's top. A round rock the size of a buffalo's head lay there. Almost without pausing he tugged it loose from the earth and rolled it back over the cliff. It came close. The Texan grabbed the saddle as his horse reared, and dropped his rifle. They looked at each other. Clutching a blood-greasy, hanging arm, the Comanche stared down at a big nose and a pair of angry gray eyes, and the young Texan stared back.

Wheeling, Starlight set off trotting across the hills. That night before hiding himself he climbed a low tree and quavered for hours like a screech owl, but no one answered. A month later, an infected skeleton, he walked into the Penateka encampment at Fort Sill, the only one of twelve to return.

That had been his first meeting with Tom Bird.

WHEN TELLING OF THE FIGHTS, STARLIGHT STOOD UP AND GES-tured in proud physical representation of what he and others had done. He did not give it as a story with a point; it was the recountal of his acquaintance with a man. In the bug-flecked light of a bulb above the house's screen door the old Indian should have looked absurd—hipshot, ugly, in a greasy black hat and a greasy dark suit with a gold chain across its vest, the dirty braids flying as he creaked through the motions of long-unmeaningful violence.

But I did not feel like smiling. I looked at the younger Indians expecting perhaps to find amusement among them, or boredom, or cynicism. It was not there. They were listening, most of them proba-bly not even understanding the Spanish but knowing the stories, to an ancient man who belonged to a time when their race had been liter-ally terrible.

In the morning Starlight told of the second time. It had been after the end of the white men's war; he was a war chief with bull horns on his head. Thirty well-armed warriors rode behind him when he stopped a trail herd in the Territory for tribute. Although the cowmen were only eight, their leader, a man with a black mustache, said that four whoa-haws were too many. He would give maybe two.

"Four," Starlight said. "Texan."

It was an arraignment, and the white man heard it as such. Look-ing at the thirty Comanches, he said that he and his people were not Texans but Kansas men returning home with bought cattle.

"Four whoa-haws," Starlight said.

The white man made a sullen sign with his hand and spoke to his men, who went to cut out the steers. Starlight watched jealously to make certain they were not culls, and when three of his young men had them and were driving them away, he rode up face to face with the white leader, unfooled even though the mustache was new.

"Tejano," he said. "Stink sonabitch." And reached over and twisted Tom Bird's big nose, hard, enjoying the rage barely held in the gray eyes. He patted his scarred left biceps and saw that the white man knew him, too, and reached over to twist the nose again, Tom Bird too prudent to stop him and too proud to duck his head aside.

"Tobacco, Texan," Starlight said.

Close to snarling, Tom Bird took out a plug. After sampling and examining it and picking a bit of lint from its surface, Starlight tucked it into his waistband. Then he turned his horse and, followed by his thirty warriors, rode away.

In those days revenge had still existed.

He had been, too, with Quanah Parker when the half-white chief had made a separate peace with Tom Bird—Tom Tejano the Pajarito now, looming big on the high plains—as with a government, on the old Bird range up along the Canadian. There had been nearly two hundred with Quanah on a hunt in prohibited territory, and they found few buffalo and many cattle. After the peace with Tom Bird they had not eaten any more wing-branded beef, except later when the Oklahoma agency bought Bird steers to distribute among them.

They had clasped hands there in Quanah's presence, knowing each other well, and in the cowman's tolerant grin and the pressure of his hard fingers Starlight had read more clearly the rout of his people than he had read it anywhere else before.

"Yah, Big-nose," he said, returning the grip and the smile. Tom Bird rode along with them hunting for ten days and led them to a wide valley twenty miles long that the hide hunters had not yet found, and they showed him there how their fathers had run the buffalo in the long good years before the white men. November it had been, with frosted mornings and yellow bright days; their women had followed them to dress the skins and dry the meat. It was the last of the rich hunting years.

After that whenever Tom Bird passed through Oklahoma he would seek out the Indian who had once pulled his nose and would sometimes bring presents.

But Starlight had killed nine white men while the fighting had lasted.

DRESSED, TOM BIRD CAME OUT ONTO THE PORCH AT ELEVEN o'clock, and I knew from the smooth curve of his cheek that the liver had quit hurting. He was affable and shook all their hands again.

"We'll have a big dinner at noon," he told Starlight in the same flowing pidgin Spanish the old Comanche himself used. "Juan's making it especially for my Comanche friends, to send them on their trip full and happy."

Still unfooled, Starlight exhumed the main topic.

"No!" Tom Bird said.

"You have little courtesy," Starlight said. "You had more once."

Tom Bird said, "There were more of you then. Armed."

Starlight's eyes squinted in mirth which his mouth did not let itself reflect. Absently Tom Bird dug out his Days O'Work and bit a chew, then waved the plug apologetically and offered it to the Comanche. Starlight took it and with three remaining front teeth haggled off a chunk, and pretended to put it into his vest pocket.

They both started laughing, phlegmy, hard-earned, old men's laughter, and for the first time—never having seen Tom Bird out-argued before—I knew that it was going to work out.

Tom Bird said, "Son of a coyote, you . . . I've got four fat castrados, and you can have your pick. They're good meat, and I'll eat some of it with you."

Starlight waggled his head mulishly. "Those, no," he said. "The big bull."

Tom Bird stared, started to speak, closed his mouth, threw the returned plug of tobacco down on the porch, and clumped back into the house. The Indians all sat down again. One of the other older men reached over and picked up the plug, had a chew, and stuck it into his denim jacket. Immobility settled.

"Liberty," Starlight said out of nowhere, in Spanish. "They speak much of liberty. Not one of you has ever seen liberty, or smelled it. Liberty was grass, and wind, and a horse, and meat to hunt, and no wire."

From beyond the dark screen door Tom Bird said, "The little bull."

Starlight without looking around shook his head. Tom Bird opened the door so hard that it battered back against the house wall, loosening flakes of paint. He stopped above the old Indian and stood there on bowed legs, looking down. "You rusty old bastard!" he shouted in English. "I ain't got but the two, and the big one's the only good one. And he wouldn't eat worth a damn."

Starlight turned his head and eyed him.

"All right," Tom Bird said, slumping. "All right."

"Thank you, Pajarito," Starlight said.

"Jimmy," the old man said to me in a washed-out voice, "go tell the boys to shoot Shakespeare and hang him up down by the washhouse."

"No," John Oak Tree said.

"What the hell you mean, no?" Tom Bird said, turning to him with enraged pleasure. "That's the one he wants. What you think he's been hollering about for two whole days?"

"Not dead," John Oak Tree said. "My grandfather wants him alive."

"Now ain't that sweet?" the old man said. "Ain't that just beautiful? And I can go around paying for busted fences from here to Oklahoma and maybe to the God damn Arctic Circle, all so a crazy old murdering Comanche can have him a pet bull buffalo."

Starlight spoke in Spanish, having understood most of the English. "Tom Tejano, listen," he said.

"What?"

"Listen," Starlight said. "We're going to kill him, Tom Tejano. We."

"My butt!" said Tom Bird, and sat down.

IN THE AFTERNOON, AFTER THE FRIED CHICKEN AND THE RICE and mashed beans and the tamales and the blistering chili, after the courteous belching and the smoking on the porch, everyone on the ranch who could leave his work was standing in the yard under the cottonwoods as the nine Comanches brought their horses up from the lot, where they had been eating oats for two days, and tied them outside the picket fence, saddled.

After hitching Starlight's mare to the carryall, without paying any attention to their audience they began to strip down, methodically rolling their shed clothes into bundles with hats on top and putting them on the back of the carryall. Starlight reeled painfully among them, pointing a dried-up forefinger and giving orders. When they had finished, all of them but he wore only trousers and shoes or moccasins, with here and there scraps of the old bone and claw and hide and feather paraphernalia. John Oak Tree had slipped off the high-heeled boots he wore and replaced them with tennis sneakers.

A hundred yards away, gargling a bellow from time to time, old Shakespeare stood jammed into a chute where the hands had choused him. Between bellows, his small hating eye peered toward us from beneath a grayed board; there was not much doubt about how *he* felt.

The Indians took the long, blanketed bundle from the carryall and unrolled it.

"For God's sake!" a cowboy said beside me, a man named Abe Reynolds who had worked a good bit with the little buffalo herd. "For God's sake, this is nineteen damn twenty-three?"

I chuckled. Old Tom Bird turned his gray eyes on us and glared, and we shut up. The bundle held short bows, and quivers of arrows, and long, feather-hung, newly reshafted buffalo lances daubed with red and black. Some took bows and others lances, and among the bowmen were the two old men younger than Starlight, who under dry skins still had ridged segmented muscles.

"Those?" I said in protest, forgetting Tom Bird. "Those two couldn't . . ."

"Because they never killed one," he said without looking around. "Because old as they are, they ain't old enough to have hunted the animal that for two whole centuries was the main thing their people ate, and wore, and made tents and ropes and saddles and every other damn thing they had out of. You close your mouth, boy, and watch."

Starlight made John Oak Tree put on a ribboned medal of some kind. Then they sat the restless ponies in a shifting line, motley still but somehow, now, with the feel of that old terribleness coming off of them like a smell, and Starlight walked down the line of them and found them good and turned to raise his hand at Tom Bird.

Tom Bird yelled.

The man at the chute pulled the bars and jumped for the fence, and eight mounted Indians lashed their ponies into a hard run toward the lumpy blackness that had emerged and was standing there swaying its head, bawling-furious.

Starlight screeched. But they were out of his control now and swept in too eagerly, not giving Shakespeare time to decide to run. When the Indian on the fastest pony, one of the middle-aged men, came down on him shooting what looked like a steady jet of arrows from beside the pony's neck, the bull squared at him. The Indian reined aside, but not enough. The big head came up under the pony's belly, and for a moment horse and rider paused reared against the horns and went pin-wheeling backward into the middle of the on-rushing others.

"Them idiots!" Abe Reynolds said. "Them plumb idiots!"

One swarming pile then, one mass with sharp projecting heads and limbs and weapons, all of them yelling and pounding and hacking and stabbing, and when old Shakespeare shot out from under the pile, shrugging them helter-skelter aside, he made a run for the house. Behind him they came yipping, leaving a gut-ripped dead horse on the ground beside the chute and another running riderless toward the northeast. One of the downed hunters sat on the ground against the chute as though indifferently. The other—one of the two oldsters— was hopping about on his left leg with an arrow through the calf of his right.

But I was scrambling for the high porch with the spectators, those who weren't grabbing for limbs, though Tom Bird stood his ground cursing as Shakespeare smashed through the white picket fence like dry sunflower stalks and whirled to make another stand under the cottonwoods. Some of the Indians jumped the fence and others poured through the hole he had made, all howling until it seemed there could be no breath left in them. For a moment, planted, Shakespeare stood with arrows bristling brightly from his hump and his loins and took someone's lance in his shoulder. Then he gave up that stand, too, and whisked out another eight feet of fence as he leveled into a long run down the dirt road past the corrals.

They rode him close, poking and shooting.

And finally, when it was all far enough down the road to have the perspective of a picture, John Oak Tree swung out leftward and running parallel to the others pulled ahead and abruptly slanted in with the long bubbling shriek, loud and cutting above all the other noise, that you can call rebel yell or cowboy holler or whatever you want, but which deadly exultant men on horseback have likely shrieked since the Assyrians and long, long before. Shakespeare ran desperately free from the sharp-pointed furor behind him, and John Oak Tree took his dun pony in a line converging sharply with the bull's course, and was there, and jammed the lance's blade certainly just behind the ribs and pointing forward, and the bull skidded to his knees, coughed, and rolled onto his side.

"You call that fair?" Abe Reynolds said sourly.

Nobody had. It was not fair. Fair did not seem to have much to do with what it was.

Starlight's carryall was headed for the clump of horsemen down the road, but the rest of us were held to the yard by the erect stability of Tom Bird's back as he stood in one of the gaps in his picket fence. Beside the chute, Starlight picked up the two thrown Indians and the saddle from the dead horse, the old hunter disarrowed and bleeding now, and drove on to where the rest sat on their ponies around Shakespeare's carcass.

Getting down, he spoke to John Oak Tree. The young Indian dismounted and handed his lance to Starlight, who hopped around for a time with one foot in the stirrup and got up onto the dun pony and brought it back toward the house at a run, the lance held high. Against his greasy vest the big gold watch chain bounced, and his coattails flew, but his old legs were locked snugly around the pony's barrel. He ran it straight at Tom Bird where he stood in the fence gap, and pulled it cruelly onto its hocks three yards away, and held out the lance butt first.

"I carried it when I pulled your nose," he said. "The iron, anyhow."

Tom Bird took it.

"We were there, Tom Tejano," Starlight said.

"Yes," my great-uncle said. "Yes, we were there."

The old Comanche turned the pony and ran it back to the little group of his people and gave it to John Oak Tree, who helped him get back into the carryall. Someone had caught the loose pony. For a few moments all of them sat, frozen, looking down at the arrow-quilled black bulk that had been Shakespeare.

Then, leaving it there, they rode off down the road toward Oklahoma, past the fences of barbed steel that would flank all the way.

A cowhand, surveying the deadly debris along the route of their run, said dryly, "A neat bunch of scutters, be damn if they ain't."

I was standing beside old Tom Bird, and he was crying. He felt my eyes and turned, the bloody lance upright in his hand, paying no heed to the tears running down the sides of his big nose and into his mustache.

"Damn you, boy," he said. "Damn you for not ever getting to know anything worth knowing. Damn me, too. We had a world, once."

I'M BOUND TO FOLLOW THE LONGHORN COWS

———— ✶ ————

Dave Hickey

"I'm bound to follow the longhorn cows until I get too old;
It's well I work for wages boys, I get my pay in gold.
My girl must cheer up courage and choose some other one,
For I'm bound to follow the longhorn cows til my race is run."

—A Cowboy Song

WHEN THE WHITE SUN HAD SPUN INTO THE PUPIL OF the sky, as it hung at the top of its trajectory between the two horizons and then began to fall into early afternoon, the old man found himself trapped in a bathtub of tepid water on the second floor of his ancient house. He flailed about for a few moments and then he became quiet and listened to the long winds shushing through the empty corridors and rooms of his house, which was Victorian in design, having two stories, an attic, a storm cellar, spires, lightning rods, weather vanes, cupolas, traceries, and an occasional leaded window; it rested on the plain like a child's block dropped on an immense crazy quilt, patched with green and yellow, an old house, but the interior had been completely modernized, and the bathroom in which the old man sat was paneled with cool blue tile.

He had seen ninety summers, as the Comanches, who were gone

now, would say, and he was the only person in the surrounding country who was older than the house. On the old man's first birthday his
father had driven four stakes into a bald ridge on the prairie, and began
to lay the foundation, and the old man had grown up with the house.
It was part of all his memories, the nucleus of his childhood, the point
of departure and the point of return for the many journeys of his youth
and manhood, for, during his first half-century, the old man had been
a rambler and a heller. But unfortunately, unlike his house, the old
man could not be modernized, except by the use of what he called
"contraptions," his false teeth, his electric wheelchair.

He was just a shriveled man with gray eyes whose sight was still
keen, with a yellowish-white mustache drooping below a swollen
pockmarked nose that still smelled well enough. He had only a few
fringes of white hair on his head, and there was more growing out of
his ears than around them, but his hearing was still better than most
since he knew what to listen for. He still had the use of his senses, but
ninety is an age when senses can be a burden, for your body no longer
responds to them. It would have been a blessing if the old man had
been a little deaf, or a little blind: then he could not hear the hooves
clopping beside the stable, or see the Mexican cowboys ride out
toward the pastures where the white-faced cattle dipped their heads
slowly in the heat.

At the age of sixty-five he had lost his teeth and his virility, and
hadn't mourned his teeth for an hour; he put them in a bottle on his
desk. At the age of eighty his right arm was crippled with arthritis, and
at the age of eighty-six his legs gave out. They refused once and forever to clench a horse's side, or even to support his weight, though he
was a small man. When this happened, his son, who was born when
the old man was fifty, bought an electric wheelchair for his father, and,
after several interviews, hired a pretty blonde nurse with heavy breasts
and a slow smile to care for him. For the next four years the old man
spent most of his time resting on a couch in his second-floor bedroom,

watching his land, watching the seasons and the sun change its face. Sometimes the nurse, whose name was Berta May Kuykendall, would read the newspaper to him, and once a week she bathed him. . . .

Berta May had left the old man's face covered with a lather of soap, and it dried into a crust in the first few minutes, while he sat there, immobile, not knowing what to do. Finally he decided to remove the soap by lifting his knees and sliding down into the clear water. His buoyant heels and buttocks leisurely rose and fell as he let the water creep over his chin and climb in a prickly line across his cheeks. He lifted his good arm and freed the dried soap by rubbing his sand-grained face. His skin felt better, but the taste of soap still hung about his gums. Berta May had let one soapy finger slip into the old man's mouth as she fell. He sucked his saliva into a cud and spat vehemently into the bath water.

Berta May lay where she had fallen. She had been scrubbing the old man's neck when her eyes had widened. Her hand jumped, a soapy finger slipped into the old man's mouth, and she had collapsed. She sat for a moment shaking convulsively. She had cried something in surprise and then fallen back, her head striking the tile like a clay jar. And she had died, so quickly it wasn't even sad, sprawled on the blue tile with her blue eyes looking upward, her skirt caught up around her thighs, and one white arm extended so that the hand rested on a crumpled pile of clothes.

The clothes belonged to the old man's son. As Berta May had wheeled him down the hall they had met him coming out of the bath. "I have to fly to Dallas, Pa. I'll see you tomorrow afternoon," he had said and run down the steps three at a time. Now his jeans, his denim work shirt, and his wide-brimmed straw hat lay in a little pile between the toilet and the bathtub, and the girl's hand seemed to be pointing to them. A scrap of a breeze lifted Berta May's skirt, revealing another inch of her thigh.

The bathroom curtains billowed white above the old man's head, and the smell of alfalfa, incredibly sweet, swam into his nostrils, only to be cut by the lingering fumes of the soap. The alfalfa wind died quickly, like a breath sucked in, and becalmed the curtains. The old man heard the starched linen crackle faintly as it collapsed. Then he became aware of grasshoppers clicking in the hot grass of the lawn. Outside the window the lawn sloped down to a barbed-wire fence where the hay fields and pastures began and continued into the horizon, but the sill was two feet above the old man's head. All he could see by looking upward was a rectangle of blue sky.

It irritated him to be able to move with such relative freedom in the buoyancy of the water, and yet not be able to climb out of the tub and into the wheelchair which stood by the bathroom door, but he knew he couldn't. He pulled in his lower lip and clamped it with his gum. Before him the pale image of his body undulated on the surface of the water. His legs were thin and hairless, and the skin on his ankles and thighs had a yellowish cast; his narrow chest was covered with white hair that bristled in patches out of the water, creating little patterns of surface tension. His body (which in its time had mounted many good horses, and many women as good as Berta May) was just a stringy bag of flesh. He glanced at Berta May's nylon-sheathed legs, and then slowly looked away.

Just a few minutes before she died, they had heard the Estansas' Chevrolet clatter by the house, had heard Manuel's special honk which he gave every Saturday when he and Señora Estansa headed for town.

"I can tell you two Mesicans gonna be drunk tonight," the old man said.

"Oh, Mr. Cotton," Berta May said. "Now how do you know that?"

"Well, I'll tell you little girl, I done a little cowboyin' in my time, and whenever *I* got to town, it sure wasn't for no tea party."

"Mr. Cotton, I bet you were a wild one."

"That I was, in my way. I drank a little whiskey, and chased me a few girls might near as pretty as you," he had winked at her. "I ain't gonna tell you if I caught 'em or not."

Berta May had laughed as she bent over and scrubbed the old man's neck. He looked down the V of her blouse and watched her hanging breasts quiver as she laughed. What a sweet hussy you would have been, he thought, and cast a furtive glance down into the water where everything was still. And if the old man had ever cried, which he hadn't, he would have then; he would have clenched his fists and let the hateful tears, squeezed like vinegar from his clenched eyelids, crash down over his cheekbones; he would have dropped his toothless jaws and howled, then or any of a thousand times when Berta May with her soft hands was bathing him or changing his clothes. He would watch her narrowly as she went about her business, as a newly broken horse will watch the wrangler approaching with the bridle dangling from one hand, trailing in the dust. He would decide that she was teasing him, that she was flaunting herself, but closeted in the back of his mind he marked a secret calendar from Saturday to Saturday, when he was bathed by Berta May Kuykendall, who bent forward so casually. Then he would try to convince himself that it was a good thing, nature's law, that old men and young girls could not get together, but never did. And *now* the heart beneath those breasts had stopped, the valves had sucked closed, stopping the surge of blood that flushed her cheeks and made little patterns of red on her neck, and the darkness in her veins, where her blood eddied into stillness, closed around her sight. She had fallen very heavily, not at all as a girl should fall, onto the blue tile, with her blonde hair sprayed around her head. . . .

And so he sat there for a long time, not thinking anything, knowing all along that the day was Saturday, and that the Estansas had gone to town to get drunk, that his son was relaxing in flight somewhere between Sonora and Dallas, in the blue air, and that he, like some goddamned relic, had been left in Berta May's care and that she was stiffening on the chilly tile, but not formulating these thoughts in his mind, not admitting their consequences, until the room began to fill with golden light that poured through the bright window like water from a sluice. It was only then, when he knew the sun was falling, that he accepted the fact that the tub was his prison. Its white slick sides described his boundaries and confined him. He, who owned three hundred sections, who had ridden to Montana and back, might as well have been in a life raft in the middle of a golden ocean, or in a coffin.

But deep in his marrow it was not fear that the old man felt, it was inconvenience; the habits of his last four years, the last fifteen hundred days, plucked at him more urgently than any terror: More than anything on God's green earth he wanted, *desired* even, to be on his couch by the window, dry, in soft pajamas, his knees covered with a Navajo blanket. He wanted Berta May to rise up and read him the newspaper while he watched the prairie change colors, or he wanted his son to come into the room and talk to him, a little dully, about a new cattle deal, or oil deal, or the prospects for the cotton crop. For his warm bedroom was twenty steps away from the bathtub. Behind the blue-tiled wall, one door down the upstairs hall was his couch being warmed by the falling sunlight with the Navajo blanket folded at its foot. He shivered. . . .

It startled him for a moment because he thought he was afraid of dying there, ending his century in the bathtub, but it just irritated him; the whole idea filled him with indignation: to have to spend the night in the *bathtub*! He wasn't afraid, but he was very nearly mad. He lifted his good hand and twisted his mustache, twisting the damp hairs and poking the end into his mouth. "Crap!" he said aloud.

Then, when he dropped his hand, making a little splash, he realized that the water had become chilled. Three hours. With a little effort he lifted his left leg, watched it appear like a continent bursting from the sea, draining, and with his toe he turned on the hot water faucet. The burst of water burned his heel, and so, maneuvering his foot, he turned on the cold faucet and settled back to enjoy the warm surge of water around his feet and up his legs, the tingling when it reached his crotch.

When the edge of the water's surface began to sting like the touch of a hot razor, he turned off the water, and no sooner had the last drop pinged into the tub than a muffling silence settled around him. It pressed against his eardrums and drew sweat from his bald scalp. But the silence, in itself, wouldn't have bothered him, for he had spent a large portion of his life in silence. But it was the noiselessness, the noiselessness of an empty house, and different from the silence of the high plains. Out there, there were distances in the silence, crystalline depths; it had size, magnitude, but it didn't make a man, or a man on a horse anyway, feel small. Somehow the two feet between the stirrup and the ground put a man's head among the stars, if he was young and made the silence right. But in the house where the silence was cut into dusty cubes, divided into a thousand little silences . . .

He grasped the side of the tub, pulled himself into a sitting position, and to the golden room, the dead girl, and the cavernous house he shouted:

"I'm big and I'm bold, boys, and I was big and bold when I was but nine days old. I'm the meanest son of a bitch north, south, east, and west of *Sonora*, Texus. I've rode everything with hair on it and a few things that was too tough to grow any hair. I've rode bull moose on the prod, she-grizzlies, and *long* bolts of lightning. I got nine rows of jaw teeth and holes bored for more, and whenever I get hungry, I eat stick dynamite cut with alkali, and when I get thirsty, I can drink a risin' creek after a goose-drowner plum dry and still have a thirst for a little Texas whiskey cut with cyanide. Why when I'm cold and lonesome, I nestle down in a den of rattlers cause they make me feel so nice and warm!"

He took a long breath and continued at the top of his lungs. "And when I'm tired, I pillow my head on the Big Horn Mountains, and stretch out from the upper Grey Bull River clean over to the Crazy Woman Fork. I set my boots in Montana and my hat in Colorado. My bed tarp covers half of Texus and all of old Mesico. The Grand Canyon ain't nothin' but my bean pole. But boys, there's one thing for sure and certain, and if you want to know, I'll tell ya: that I'm a long way short of being the Daddy of em all. Cause he's full growed. And as any fool can plainly see, why boys, I ain't nothin' but a young un!"

Ho! Drunk in Tascosa or Abilene with your hands behind you holding to the bar, bellied out and hellraisin', stinking of two weeks' sweat, bad whiskey, Bull Durham, and cowdung, with a whole skillet of mountain oysters under your belt. . . . The echoes of his voice wandered for a few moments down the halls and into some of the empty rooms of the old house; then, one after another, like pebbles falling into a stream, they dropped into silence. (Shards and flecks of the yellow light glittered in Berta May's eyes.) There was the silence again, but the old man felt better for having shouted.

He had composed that brag, and a lot more of it he couldn't remember, when he was a boy, seventeen, nineteen, he couldn't remember now, but when he had followed the last of the big herds up the trail through the Indian Territory into Wyoming and Montana. It was something to do while you rode in the drag and chewed on the cloud of dust that billowed from the herd of long-striding cattle who walked steadily with their heads down and their wide horns dipping rhythmically. But most of all it passed the time on night watch after the herd had been thrown off the trail. The old man could remember himself, young Jerry Cotton, sitting in the saddle, there in the tall darkness, feeling his pony breathing, its barrel expanding and con-tracting regularly between his thighs, listening to the sleeping cattle snort and·bluster in their dreams of new grass. There was nothing to do but lean on the saddle horn and compose brags, or rather compile them, adding an occasional flourish of your own, putting them in the order in which the words fell right. It was the kind of thing to do in silence. Or he could count the stars which hung like diamonds on fire around his head. (And he counted the stars so often, and in such detail, that he used to tell his wife: "Judy, I got so I could tell you the date, tomorrow's weather, and who your grandmother was, just by looking at the stars." And she would always say: "What if it was cloudy?" "Then I could only tell you tomorrow's weather and let you worry about the date and your grandmother, which you ought to know anyway.") Or he could sing songs, which he did, in a thin voice that was a little unsteady, but good enough for himself and the cattle. In his prime he had known eighty-five verses to *The Texas Rangers*, some of which he had composed himself.

And so, as the surface of the water grew placid around him, old Jerome Cotton shuttled these memories through his mind, selecting the ones he liked and discarding those he didn't—(and also those dealing with women, in respect for, or at least because of, Berta May, whose feet encased in sandals stood up awkwardly at the ends of her exposed legs). He reflected that he liked these memories, but he was not such a damn fool as to say that there was anything good about those days except that they were the days when he was a young bull and on the prod. He had sold his longhorns and bought white-faced cattle when they produced more beef, and when the railroads came, and hadn't wept one tear for the old rangy cattle who could live on anything and tasted like it. He and his wife had nearly starved when the drought came and the Depression on top of it. He had taken Mr. Roosevelt's money, gladly. When the oil came, he found some, more or less on his property, a good deal of it, and when irrigation was practical he irrigated and planted cotton and alfalfa, but by then George was running the land. But his son didn't get excited about leaving land fallow and taking Mr. Truman's money, or, though he was a Republican, Mr. Eisenhower's, or Mr. Kennedy's.

Whenever some old coot would get to talking about the "good old days" around the table, Jerome Cotton would lean forward out of his wheelchair and say: "I'll tell you what, sir, there is not one good thing about eating dust all day and gettin' rained on at night unless you're young." But by damned if you were young . . .

IT BECAME DARK IN A MOMENT, AS IT ALWAYS DOES WHEN THE AIR is clear, and a square of moonlight appeared on the door opposite the window as if a switch had been snapped. The wreath of white hair around the back of his skull dripped onto his neck, and little droplets traced cold paths down onto his narrow shoulders. He slid again down into the tepid water and, resting his chin on his shoulders, he watched the square of moonlight on the door until he could perceive it moving downward toward Berta May who was stretched in the shadows.

It was an exercise in patience. It kept his mind off his stomach which was tightening painfully, excreting unusable acid, waiting for food, wanting food. He watched the square moving and finally he thought about food: *enchiladas covered with cheese, frijoles, tortillas with steam rising from them, which you picked up gingerly, smeared with butter, salted, poured hot sauce on, folded, bent so the sauce would not run out, and stuffed into your mouth while they were still hot. There was an art to folding tortillas, you had to do it quickly or the thin circles of corn meal would cool, and dextrously or the hot sauce would pour into your lap. And when the sauce burned your throat, when you could feel it burning all the way down to your stomach . . . He could see Señora Estansa silhouetted in the kitchen door holding a big plate of enchiladas and chili con queso . . .* His chin fell forward into the water and awakened him. It frightened him a little that he had fallen asleep, so he reached up with his toe and flipped the handle which let the water out of the tub.

This amused him for a few minutes: listening to the gurgling water and watching his dark body appear like islands growing out of a sea of mercury. But then he felt his weight returning to press him into the bottom of the tub. His head became hard to manage; it seemed to roll erratically on his white shoulders, and his good arm, when he reached up to pull three towels from the rack above his head, was as heavy as a log. But he laboriously dried himself and the inside of the tub as well as possible. His elbows and knees made thumping and clanging noises as they collided awkwardly with the porcelain, sometimes causing little pinches of pain and making red flowers bloom and fade before his eyes. But as he worked in the darkness he was not altogether unhappy;

he enjoyed being without his contraptions, controlling what he did, even if it was only drying a bathtub from which he might never escape, in which he might wake up dead. "This is a hell of a thing for a man ninety years old!" he said to the dark, and a hilarious vision of himself being buried in the tub built itself before his eyes: there he was, arms folded, in a blue suit, resting in the tub. He chuckled.

When the tub was as dry as he could get it, he folded a towel and placed it beneath his head. As he closed his eyes he reflected that the towel was a damn sight softer than some saddles. But it was no good. There is no one in the world, he realized, as naked as a naked man in a damp empty bathtub, and there is no place which is more uncomfortable to sleep in, when you are naked. His shoulder began to ache, as did his arthritic arm. His hip bone was thrust cruelly against the stone-hard bottom of the tub. But worst of all, his manhood (his "gentleman" his Granny had called it). *It ain't no gentleman now*, he thought, *wouldn't stand up for nobody*. It lay damply against his leg. When he rolled over, if it touched the porcelain, he awoke with a start; if he rolled the other way it became uncomfortably wedged between his legs. *If he could only get out!* He grasped one side of the tub with both hands and, with a wrenching movement, began to lift the dead weight of his body. Flares of pain pulsed through his bad arm and the flowers returned whirling before his eyes. But he was almost up, he had almost raised himself high enough to flop forward out of the tub, when he saw dead Berta May Kuykendall, and his bad arm slipped. He fell, striking his chin on the edge of the tub and slithering and squeaking back into its dark maw. He curled in the bottom of the tub with his eyes closed and his breath coming in cries. He knew the side of his chin would be black with a bruise in the morning. *On the other side of the white wall, Berta May rested with her white face framed in the moonlight, lips slightly parted. Her hair flared out to one side, as if windblown, and her eyes flickered in the silver light.*

In an hour he moved; he held his bad arm to his side and rolled over onto his back; then with his toes, he turned on the water full force, and closed the drain. The roar of the water laughed in his ears; it laughed down the halls of the empty house and out into the climbing night. The water was free; it brought heat, buoyancy, freedom, everything a man could want. He arranged a wet towel around his neck so he would not drown himself, turned off the water and relaxed. Involuntarily he glanced at Berta May. The moonlight had moved again and now it fell across her breasts. Only her chin and her half smiling mouth were visible above the V of her blouse. Her brassiere held the breasts upright and they flowed together on her bare neck. But the old man pushed thoughts of the dead girl behind curtains in his ancient mind. Before he went to sleep, he lowered his chin and quenched his thirst, then he leaned his head back comfortably, his "gentleman" floating blessedly free . . .

In his dream the old man was a part of a story which he hadn't believed when he had heard it: Marsh, who had had his nose cut off, squatted just inside the circle of light thrown by the bitter-smelling mesquite fire and spoke with a Colorado twang. "By God it was raining, catfish and nigger babies, and we was so drunk you would have had to sober us up to kill us . . ." They were all drunk and running through the back streets of Tascosa in the rain. Jerome Cotton could feel the deep mud gurgling over the instep of his boot every time he took a step. They ran past bright windows whose light bled in his vision like yellow paint. There were four or two of them running together, and he could see Marsh's noseless profile rising and falling beside him as they ran through the downpour. Finally, after hours it seemed, he realized that they were looking for a special whore.

Suddenly Marsh, without saying a word, dodged into a lighted doorway, and Jerry followed. He burst into dryness and light just in time to see Marsh draw his pistol and shoot a Mexican who was climbing out of a high window. (I don't believe this story, the old man thought, but the Mexican fell with a splash outside the window.) Then Marsh, the two nostrils on his face bubbling because he had a cold, turned the pistols on the whore, who was curled on the bed staring at them. She was a tall black-headed woman, slightly pretty. Marsh lowered the barrel of his pistol, as if he were shooting a bottle off a fence post, and shot her.

"You want her in here or out in the street?"

"Out in the street," Jerome Cotton heard himself say in a young voice.

"Good enough," Marsh said, and slung the whore over his shoulder and carried her into the rain. Jerome Cotton heard the splash as Marsh threw her into the mud, but it seemed to come from down on the river . . .

But then it was daylight, dry beautiful daylight, and they were on the trail. He was sitting on his pony on a grassy slope overlooking the Platte River; its wide sandy bed twined away into green distance. Down on the river the boys were trying to free about ten head of cattle who were being sucked down into a bed of quicksand. He noticed one particular steer who was caught near the bank. A cowboy had waded out and slipped a rope around one of the steer's hind legs. The rope was tied to the saddle horn of another cowboy, who was trying to pull the steer free, and the steer was bawling to the sky. In a moment there was a sucking noise as the leg to which the rope was tied popped up out of the sand and lay at an odd angle in the water. The man on the horse continued to pull but he couldn't free the other three legs. Two men were with the steer in the water now.

Jerry Cotton took off his hat and swatted a fly. There was a nice breeze and it was a pretty day. He seemed to be hearing the shouts of the cowboys and the bawling of the cattle from a great distance. When he looked again down into the river bed, the boys had tied the rope which was attached to the steer to the chuck wagon, and the grub-spoiler was trying to drive the team up the slope, and out of the river bed. There was a clatter of harness and a shout from the cookie as the wagon shot forward. Young Jerry Cotton had to look very closely to see that the steer's hind leg was bouncing behind the wagon, trailing water and blood . . .

The old man was awake during the last few seconds of this dream, but he didn't open his eyes; he let the phantasma play itself out on the back of his eyelids until the team and the driver disappeared behind a melting bluff, but still he did not open his eyes. He knew that the room was lit by the gray gallows-light that crept like smoke before the dawn. He lowered his chin and took some of the bitter water into his mouth and spat it out. He had relieved himself during the night. His face itched with its damp morning bristle which Berta May would— which Berta May used to shave with his electric razor. Still without opening his eyes, he raised his foot and let the polluted water out of the tub; then, feeling with his feet, he turned on the faucets, admitting fresh water. The water crackled like new fire as it spattered on the porcelain. "Just like a goddamn goldfish," he mumbled to himself, but he drank great quantities of the new water.

He opened his eyes, looking straight ahead. His hands were grotesquely shriveled, and his entire floating body was logged and puckered. The old man felt that he could grasp his arthritic arm tightly, and slide the skin right off the bone. All of his joints ached and hunger sent pains sliding up under his ribs. *Ninety years old*, he thought and found the dangling tip of his mustache with his tongue and sucked on it. To avoid looking at the girl he closed his eyes again and waited for the sunlight; Sunday morning.

But even after the light shone dark red through the blood vessels in his eyelids, and an occasional flash fell through his lashes like dawn through a forest, the old man kept his eyes clenched against it. He lifted his hand from the water and pressed two fingers into his eye-sockets until they hurt; but finally he had to; it became, in the darkness of his morning thoughts, a test of courage. He opened his eyes and deliberately looked at the body stretched on the tile. He stared at her for a moment and then, strangely, the vision liquefied. He blinked his eyes fiercely to clear his vision only to discover that there were tears in them. Children, women, cowards, and men in pain may cry, but the old man who had nearly turned a century wept . . .

He wept because during the night some immodest wind had blown her skirt completely up, exposing her legs, her blue garters, and her blue panties; wept for the silliest thing: a heart sewn on the panties just above the left leg, and *Saturday* embroidered just below it. He wept because he had desired her so overtly and called her the names of his frustration. But most of all, and this is why he wept and didn't cry, the tears topped his lower lids and streamed down because she was dead. His own life had only been a furious explosion of days, a mad clock which ran the seasons round, a flash in the eye of time; what a flicker hers must have been, who had touched, and seen, and tasted only one year for his five. And he wept because he was ashamed and brave enough, or old enough, to be.

But he didn't weep for long at all with his forehead pressed to the side of the tub. His sobbing stopped and his throat relaxed. His eyes dried quickly as he stared down into the turquoise water. He was ninety years old, and it seemed to him a little sacrilegious for a man ninety years old to weep for very long, and a little silly for anyone to be weeping in a bathtub where he was preserved like a snake in a fruit jar; too much weeping renounces too many things. And so he raised his head and looked at the girl again, giving her the respect which, perhaps, is due the dead. He looked at her closely and dispassionately, wishing the body could be taken to a funeral home, noticing again her hand which seemed to be pointing to his son's clothing which lay between the toilet and the bathtub. With his good hand the old man reached over . . .

George Cotton arrived from Dallas in the late afternoon. He entered the front door and called, and when he heard the muffled answer he ran up the stairs three at a time. He threw open the bathroom door and saw his father sitting in the bathtub pulling at his mustache, wearing the wide-brimmed hat he had left on the floor.

"You take care of that poor dead girl," his father said.

"Here, Pa, let me get you out of that tub," George Cotton said, and he started to step over Berta May Kuykendall.

"You get that girl," his father said. "I just may never get out."

THE SOUTH

THE GRAVE

✦

Katherine Anne Porter

THE GRANDFATHER, DEAD FOR MORE THAN THIRTY YEARS, had been twice disturbed in his long repose by the constancy and possessiveness of his widow. She removed his bones first to Louisiana and then to Texas as if she had set out to find her own burial place, knowing well she would never return to the places she had left. In Texas she set up a small cemetery in a corner of her first farm, and as the family connection grew, and oddments of relations came over from Kentucky to settle, it contained at last about twenty graves. After the grandmother's death, part of her land was to be sold for the benefit of certain of her children, and the cemetery happened to lie in the part set aside for sale. It was necessary to take up the bodies and bury them again in the family plot in the big new public cemetery, where the grandmother had been buried. At last her husband was to lie beside her for eternity, as she had planned.

The family cemetery had been a pleasant small neglected garden of tangled rose bushes and ragged cedar trees and cypress, the simple flat stones rising out of uncropped sweet-smelling wild grass. The graves were lying open and empty one burning day when Miranda and her brother Paul, who often went together to hunt rabbits and doves, propped their .22 Winchester rifles carefully against the rail fence, climbed over and explored among the graves. She was nine years old and he was twelve.

They peered into the pits all shaped alike with such purposeful accuracy, and looking at each other with pleased adventurous eyes, they said in solemn tones: "These were graves!" trying by words to shape a special, suitable emotion in their minds, but they felt nothing except an agreeable thrill of wonder: they were seeing a new sight, doing something they had not done before. In them both there was also a small disappointment at the entire commonplaceness of the actual spectacle. Even if it had once contained a coffin for years upon years, when the coffin was gone a grave was just a hole in the ground. Miranda leaped into the pit that had held her grandfather's bones. Scratching around aimlessly and pleasurably as any young animal, she scooped up a lump of earth and weighed it in her palm. It had a pleasantly sweet, corrupt smell, being mixed with cedar needles and small leaves, and as the crumbs fell apart, she saw a silver dove no larger than a hazel nut, with spread wings and a neat fan-shaped tail. The breast had a deep round hollow in it. Turning it up to the fierce sunlight, she saw that the inside of the hollow was cut in little whorls. She scrambled out, over the pile of loose earth that had fallen back into one end of the grave, calling to Paul that she had found something, he must guess what . . . His head appeared smiling over the rim of another grave. He waved a closed hand at her. "I've got something too!" They ran to compare treasures, making a game of it, so many guesses each, all wrong, and a final showdown with opened palms. Paul had found a thin wide gold ring carved with intricate flowers and leaves. Miranda was smitten at sight of the ring and wished to have it. Paul seemed more impressed by the dove. They made a trade, with some little bickering. After he had got the dove in his hand, Paul said, "Don't you know what this is? This is a screw head for a *coffin!* . . . I'll bet nobody else in the world has one like this!"

Miranda glanced at it without covetousness. She had the gold ring on her thumb; it fitted perfectly. "Maybe we ought to go now," she said, "maybe one of the niggers 'll see us and tell somebody." They knew the land had been sold, the cemetery was no longer theirs, and they felt like trespassers. They climbed back over the fence, slung their rifles loosely under their arms—they had been shooting at targets with various kinds of firearms since they were seven years old—and set out to look for the rabbits and doves or whatever small game might happen along. On these expeditions Miranda always followed at Paul's heels along the path, obeying instructions about handling her gun when going through fences; learning how to stand it up properly so it would not slip and fire unexpectedly; how to wait her time for a shot and not just bang away in the air without looking, spoiling shots for Paul, who really could hit things if given a chance. Now and then, in her excitement at seeing birds whizz up suddenly before her face, or a rabbit leap across her very toes, she lost her head, and almost without sighting she flung her rifle up and pulled the trigger. She hardly ever hit any sort of mark. She had no proper sense of hunting at all. Her brother would be often completely disgusted with her. "You don't care whether you get your bird or not," he said. "That's no way to hunt." Miranda could not understand his indignation. She had seen him smash his hat and yell with fury when he had missed his aim. "What I like about shooting," said Miranda, with exasperating inconsequence, "is pulling the trigger and hearing the noise."

"Then, by golly," said Paul, "whyn't you go back to the range and shoot at bulls-eyes?"

"I'd just as soon," said Miranda, "only like this, we walk around more."

"Well, you just stay behind and stop spoiling my shots," said Paul, who, when he made a kill, wanted to be certain he had made it.

Miranda, who alone brought down a bird once in twenty rounds, always claimed as her own any game they got when they fired at the same moment. It was tiresome and unfair and her brother was sick of it.

"Now, the first dove we see, or the first rabbit, is mine," he told her. "And the next will be yours. Remember that and don't get smarty."

"What about snakes?" asked Miranda idly. "Can I have the first snake?"

Waving her thumb gently and watching her gold ring glitter, Miranda lost interest in shooting. She was wearing her summer roughing outfit: dark blue overalls, a light blue shirt, a hired-man's straw hat, and thick brown sandals. Her brother had the same outfit except his was a sober hickory-nut color. Ordinarily Miranda preferred her overalls to any other dress, though it was making rather a scandal in the countryside, for the year was 1903, and in the back country the law of female decorum had teeth in it. Her father had been criticized for letting his girls dress like boys and go careering around astride bare-backed horses. Big sister Maria, the really independent and fearless one, in spite of her rather affected ways, rode at a dead run with only a rope knotted around her horse's nose. It was said the motherless family was running down, with the Grandmother no longer there to hold it together. It was known that she had discriminated against her son Harry in her will, and that he was in straits about money. Some of his old neighbors reflected with vicious satisfaction that now he would probably not be so stiffnecked, nor have any more high-stepping horses either. Miranda knew this, though she could not say how. She had met along the road old women of the kind who smoked corn-cob pipes, who had treated her grandmother with most sincere respect. They slanted their gummy old eyes side-ways at the granddaughter and said, "Ain't you ashamed of yoself, Missy? It's aginst the Scriptures to dress like that. Whut yo Pappy thinkin about?" Miranda, with her powerful social sense, which was like a fine set of antennae radiating from every pore of her skin, would feel ashamed because she knew well it was rude and ill-bred to shock anybody, even bad-tempered old crones, though she had faith in her father's judgment and was perfectly comfortable in the clothes. Her father had said. "They're just what you need, and they'll save your dresses for school . . ." This sounded quite simple and natural to her. She had been brought up in rigorous economy. Wastefulness was vulgar. It was also a sin. These were truths; she had heard them repeated many times and never once disputed.

Now the ring, shining with the serene purity of fine gold on her rather grubby thumb, turned her feelings against her overalls and sock-less feet, toes sticking through the thick brown leather straps. She wanted to go back to the farmhouse, take a good cold bath, dust herself with plenty of Maria's violet talcum powder—provided Maria was not present to object, of course—put on the thinnest, most becoming dress she owned, with a big sash, and sit in a wicker chair under the trees . . . These things were not all she wanted, of course; she had vague stirrings of desire for luxury and a grand way of living which could not take precise form in her imagination but were founded on family legend of past wealth and leisure. These immediate comforts were what she could have, and she wanted them at once. She lagged rather far behind Paul, and once she thought of just turning back without a word and going home. She stopped, thinking that Paul would never do that to her, and so she would have to tell him. When a rabbit leaped, she let Paul have it without dispute. He killed it with one shot.

When she came up with him, he was already kneeling, examining the wound, the rabbit trailing from his hands. "Right through the head," he said complacently, as if he had aimed for it. He took out his sharp, competent bowie knife and started to skin the body. He did it very cleanly and quickly. Uncle Jimbilly knew how to prepare the skins so that Miranda always had fur coats for her dolls, for though she never cared much for her dolls she liked seeing them in fur coats. The children knelt facing each other over the dead animal. Miranda watched admiringly while her brother stripped the skin away as if he were taking off a glove. The flayed flesh emerged dark scarlet, sleek, firm; Miranda with thumb and finger felt the long fine muscles with the silvery flat strips binding them to the joints. Brother lifted the oddly bloated belly. "Look," he said, in a low amazed voice. "It was going to have young ones."

Very carefully he slit the thin flesh from the center ribs to the flanks, and a scarlet bag appeared. He slit again and pulled the bag open, and there lay a bundle of tiny rabbits, each wrapped in a thin scarlet veil. The brother pulled these off and there they were, dark gray, their sleek wet down lying in minute even ripples, like a baby's head just washed, their unbelievably small delicate ears folded close, their little blind faces almost featureless.

Miranda said, "Oh, I want to *see*," under her breath. She looked and looked—excited but not frightened, for she was accustomed to the sight of animals killed in hunting—filled with pity and astonishment and a kind of shocked delight in the wonderful little creatures for their own sakes, they were so pretty. She touched one of them ever so carefully, "Ah, there's blood running over them," she said and began to tremble without knowing why. Yet she wanted most deeply to see and to know. Having seen, she felt at once as if she had known all along. The very memory of her former ignorance faded, she had always known just this. No one had ever told her anything outright, she had been rather unobservant of the animal life around her because she was so accustomed to animals. They seemed simply disorderly and unaccountably rude in their habits, but altogether natural and not very interesting. Her brother had spoken as if he had known about everything all along. He may have seen all this before. He had never said a word to her, but she knew now a part at least of what he knew. She understood a little of the secret, formless intuitions in her own mind and body, which had been clearing up, taking form, so gradually and so steadily she had not realized that she was learning what she had to know. Paul said cautiously, as if he were talking about something forbidden: "They were just about ready to be born." His voice dropped on the last word. "I know," said Miranda, "like kittens. I know, like babies." She was quietly and terribly agitated, standing again with her rifle under her arm, looking down at the bloody heap. "I don't want the skin," she said, "I won't have it." Paul buried the young rabbits again in their mother's body, wrapped the skin around her, carried her to a clump of sage bushes, and hid her away. He came out again at once and said to Miranda, with an eager friendliness, a confidential tone quite unusual in him, as if he were taking her into an important secret on equal terms: "Listen now. Now you listen to me, and don't ever forget. Don't you ever tell a living soul that you saw this. Don't tell a soul. Don't tell Dad because I'll get into trouble. He'll say I'm leading you into things you ought not to do. He's always saying that. So now don't you go and forget and blab out sometime the way you're always doing . . . Now, that's a secret. Don't you tell."

Miranda never told, she did not even wish to tell anybody. She thought about the whole worrisome affair with confused unhappiness for a few days. Then it sank quietly into her mind and was heaped over by accumulated thousands of impressions, for nearly twenty years. One day she was picking her path among the puddles and crushed refuse of a market street in a strange city of a strange country, when without warning, plain and clear in its true colors as if she looked through a frame upon a scene that had not stirred nor changed since the moment it happened, the episode of that far-off day leaped from its burial place before her mind's eye. She was so reasonlessly horrified she halted suddenly staring, the scene before her eyes dimmed by the vision back of them. An Indian vendor had held up before her a tray of dyed sugar sweets, in the shapes of all kinds of small creatures: birds, baby chicks, baby rabbits, lambs, baby pigs. They were in gay colors and smelled of vanilla, maybe. . . . It was a very hot day and the smell in the market, with its piles of raw flesh and wilting flowers, was like the mingled sweetness and corruption she had smelled that other day in the empty cemetery at home: the day she had remembered always until now vaguely as the time she and her brother had found treasure in the opened graves. Instantly upon this thought the dreadful vision faded, and she saw clearly her brother, whose childhood face she had forgotten, standing again in the blazing sunshine, again twelve years old, a pleased sober smile in his eyes, turning the silver dove over and over in his hands.

HOLD AUTUMN IN YOUR HAND

★

George Sessions Perry

WHEN SAM TUCKER CAME TO WORK ON THE RISKIN farm it was with a great sense of relief. All he had to do was the mere physical labor, have none of the worry, and draw down seventy-five cents every day he went into the field. When Nona worked, there would be fifty cents additional. All this, mind you, payable every Saturday, eighty per cent in trade at the commissary and twenty per cent in actual cash.

Also, there was no house rent. One wall had fallen off the west room, but he and his wife and the two children could live snugly in the other. That west room made a fine place to pile firewood and hay.

And finally there was the river. In the last few helter-skelter years, Sam had been marooned on dry land, living the partial existence of a river man away from the river. But here it formed the boundary of his lower field, shooting swiftly over the shallow gravel bars and pooling

blue-green and still in the deep holes where catfish waited for darkness and the nocturnal quest for food.

Already Sam had encountered the lord of that domain, had seen
him, a huge yellow catfish, float to the surface near the edge of a drift.
This fish (whom Sam had named Lead Pencil because his antennae
were that thick) was his adversary in that world of mystery, the river at
night.

In his daytime world, Sam's adversaries were weeds and Henry
Devers, who lived on the adjoining farm. The weeds made sense. They
were supposed to plague him. Henry Devers was not.

Henry wanted to rent Riskin's land out from under Sam, since he
could see it, under Sam's care, producing more than his own.

Henry Devers and what Sam thought of as Henry's "hen-house
ways" formed the only major dissonance in Sam's life. Everything else
went swimmingly. The cotton grew tall and was laden with bolls. Jot,
Sam's three-year-old son, had finally got over his spring sickness. Daisy
had started to school and showed every sign of one day learning to
read.

Besides, hardly a week had passed in which there had not been a
mess of fish of some kind. However neither Sam's lines, nor Henry
Devers', had so far been able to catch old Lead Pencil.

One day the school bus had let Daisy off at the crossroads and she
had come running to her father. Sam said, "Hello, honey. What did you
learn today?"

"What's been wrong with Jot and all the rest of us every spring.
What Gran'pappy and Aunt Nettie died of."

Sam had stopped the mules.

"What was it?"

"She said it was pellagra. So did the book."

Daisy told him all the symptoms, how it began by skin sores
brought out by the spring sun, that it was caused by living on cornbread, salt pork, and molasses throughout the winter.

This worried Sam.

"How you gonna eat something you ain't got?" he asked.

"Umph humph. She said raise a garden and put stuff up in jars and when winter came you'd have it."

Sam was impressed.

And as Sam plowed, he made a solemn resolve. This year he would plant an enormous fall garden. And he would make it grow if he had to carry water on his back from the river.

Sam sacrificed his yearly Hallowe'en drunk to buy the finest plants and seeds available.

Rains fell propitiously and Nona spent most of her afternoons in the garden weeding, staking, pruning. Daisy was inexpressibly excited because the teacher had promised a blue ribbon to each child who could persuade its parents to preserve a hundred jars of garden vegetables.

One night however, Henry Devers' three cows got out of their pen and were naturally attracted by this tender greenery. The sight at daybreak, when Sam came outside, was heartbreaking.

He drove the cows home and called Henry.

At the devastated garden, Sam explained why it had been planted in the first place and how much it meant to his family.

Henry was at a loss to know what tone to take.

Finally he said, "There's still plenty of time to re-plant."

"Henry, do you aim to let this happen any more?"

"Oh no."

"I guess my bread and coffee is ready," Sam said and went to the house.

This had happened on Saturday. That night after work, Sam walked to Hackberry for more seed. On Sunday, he re-planted.

Since it was so near the end of the season, Sam's cotton picking money had had to go for the clothing to carry his wife and children through the winter. However he did not despair of getting those glass jars. He inquired for neighborhood odd jobs and tried to get on the "money-relief" but there was nothing for him.

Crossing Riskin's little two-acre mule pasture on his way home, a briar vine caught Sam's trousers and opened an eight-inch rent in the leg.

It gave him an idea.

He started toward the commissary at once. There he said, "Mr. Riskin, that little old mule pasture has got so full of brambles you might as well not have it. How about givin' me a job clearing it?"

"I'm afraid not, Sam. Cost me money and they'd just grow back."

"S'pose it didn't cost you nothing and I kept it cleared for what little ole pecans I could pick up?"

"It'd be a trade."

It was. The job took two weeks.

As the nuts began to ripen Sam sold the crop, while it was still on the trees, to a local buyer for eight dollars.

The next day a voice called him at dawn. It was Henry.

"Come on, Sam. I need you to help me build a pole crib."

Sam went to the door.

"You'll have to get somebody else, Henry. I've got to go to town to get some cannin' jars. Gonna start cannin' up our garden tomorrow."

"All right," Henry said, insulted, angry, "if that's the way you feel about it."

That night his cows ate absolutely all of Sam's garden. Two pigs rooted up the tiny potatoes and carrots that were underground.

When his family stood with him at the back door seeing this devastation, Sam said what he had often said before.

"Try not to fret. We'll make out."

This was Friday. On Wednesday Sam had seen Henry bait his buffalo hole with corn. He knew Henry would go there Sunday morning to fish. That would be time enough.

Sunday, Sam ate his bread and drank his coffee, and, when Nona had finished with the stove, he made a pan of doughbait.

He took down the buffalo pole and approached the creek in a roundabout way. He wanted Henry still to be there.

As he appeared quietly beside Henry, Henry jumped.

"Gee," Henry said nervously. "You scared me, Sam. I didn't hear nobody."

Sam baited his hook, dropped it in the water, and then carefully pushed the butt of his pole into the bank.

He turned to Henry.

"What have you got to say about your stock?"

Henry's tone changed abruptly.

"I'm tired of your naggin' and whinin', Sam Tucker."

"I never came to nag and whine. I came here to whip you, Henry."

From the newspaper beside him Henry snatched a butcher knife. He ran at Sam who scrambled up the bank, straight through a tangle of briar vines.

Henry was fast. Through the openings Sam was making in the vines, Henry was drawing closer.

Sam felt something hot rip across his back. The touch of the blade filled him with terror.

He saw a green elm limb lying in the woods just ahead. Swooping at full speed, he clutched it and got ready to swing.

Then he saw that Henry had caught his leg in a vine and fallen on the ground, ten feet back. Now he was on all fours, pulling the knife blade out of the ground.

Quickly Sam moved in.

Henry was fixed with horror, unable to move. The butcher knife fell.

"Please Sam. I got a family. They need me to work. My kids would starve."

Sam picked up the butcher knife and threw it in the river.

"Get up, Henry," he said. "Now walk out in the middle of that cotton field."

When they got there, Sam threw away his club.

"Henry," he said, "I've tried every peaceable way I know of to get along with you. It hasn't worked." Sam pitched his jumper on the ground. "Me and you are going to do a little boxing."

Cat quick, Henry struck out. His fist caught Sam on the cheek bone. Sam's knees buckled. But they didn't go down, and his long left arm reached through that rain of fists and fastened on Henry's shirt front. Sam's heels dug into the ground. And it began. Sam remembered only the devastated garden; the sound of Daisy's muffled sobs coming from beneath the house.

Soon Henry was lying motionless on the ground. He looked more dead than unconscious. Sam didn't care. Nothing mattered any more since Daisy would not get her ribbon.

At the edge of his field of vision something moved. Turning, he saw it was his fishing pole. Automatically he ran to it, grabbed it, and began pulling.

But the fish must have got away and left the hook caught on a log. It would not budge.

Then that log came to life.

At about the same time so did Henry.

"Damn it all," Henry said, "why couldn't it of been my line?"

It took all of Sam's strength to hold the fish away from a tangle of logs and roots over to the left.

"Be awful if that line broke," Henry said in breathless hopefulness, crawling to his feet. "Lead him over here. I'll land him."

"Never mind," Sam managed to say. "I'll handle him or lose him by myself."

Ten minutes later, with his knees braced against a stump, Sam got his right hand inside the fish's gills and hauled him out on the bank. A few seconds later, panting and weary, Sam was holding Lead Pencil securely pinned to the ground between his knees.

Both men knew he would weigh between forty and fifty pounds. It was the biggest catfish either had ever heard of being caught in the San Pedro river. It was a record, and as such would be remembered and discussed whenever men gathered around a campfire at night.

"I'll take him to the store and weigh him," Sam said. "I'm proud of that monster."

The longer Henry looked at Lead Pencil, the more uneasy he grew. His walk became almost a dance.

When they were halfway to the road, he could endure it no longer. "Sam."

"Yes."

"Listen. If you'll give me that fish and let me say I caught it, you can get anything you want out of my garden. You can have it all."

For a moment Sam stood there.

This fish was the climax of his lifelong association with the river and would never come again.

He thought of the blue ribbon on Daisy's breast. Probably there would be printing on it in gold, like ribbons at the Hackberry poultry show.

Sam held out the fish.

That very afternoon, like locusts, or even the Devers' cows, Sam Tucker and his family began at one end of Henry Devers' garden and came out the other. They could hear Henry in the house trying to quiet his wife, saying it was all right because their cows had eaten Sam's garden.

When Daisy awoke, one hundred and twenty-three jars had been filled. Nona fed the children and sent Daisy to school, then rejoined Sam at the stove.

At noon Daisy ran away from school and walked the four miles home to show her ribbon.

After supper that night, the whole family sat around the fireplace in genuine contentment.

The lamp, near which Daisy sat on sleepy exhibition, shone strongly on the blue and gold ribbon.

In her chair, Nona slept.

from ADVENTURES WITH A TEXAS NATURALIST

★

Roy Bedichek

I N A 1937 NOTEBOOK OF MINE I FIND A PAGE HEADED, "LUFKIN Club—14,000 acres—Good God—dead sweet gum in cut-over pasture." The 14,000-acre tract begins about ten miles west of Lufkin at the Neches, third largest river in Texas. Along the highway it is protected by a high fence on which Game Preserve signs are prominently displayed.

This forest is an island of life in the midst of a weary land devastated by unscientific cultivation which followed in the wake of the insatiable sawmills. Although protection of the wild life here is meant only for the few species which furnish meat for the table and sports afield, thousands of other forms of life profit by it. Things are so arranged in nature that you cannot support one form of life without maintaining others which in turn support it; and, by the same token, one form cannot be destroyed without pulling down the structure upon which it rests, and the superstructure it upholds. Thus the naturalist and the sportsman should be allies and stop their feuding.

There is no profanity in the excerpt from my notebook. I happened to be getting directions from a native when suddenly a pair of pileated woodpeckers near by began their unearthly clamor.

"What bird is that?" I asked.

"A *good* God."

"A what!"

"A *good* God," he replied with more emphasis on the "good," and forthwith explained, "You see, people ain't usta seein' a woodpecker as big as a crow; so when they do see one, they jes' natchally say, 'Good God'!"

Indian hen is another name for this magnificent woodpecker with his brilliant red cap and striking facial pattern—another instance of the folk tendency to attach Indian to any form of life showing striking colors.

But the dead sweet gum is still another matter. Wandering about, that morning, I finally got out of the forest and walked a long time in pastures of cut-over lands where scrawny cattle, principally cows and calves, were managing to stay alive at a bare subsistence level. The big lumber interests had moved out years before and were succeeded here by small ranchers who were mere gleaners, picking up crumbs after the rich and ancient life of the country had been ravished.

The monster sweet gum lay almost prostrate. It had crashed years before and now reclined partially supported by a few of the larger limbs that failed to crumble completely in the shock of its fall. Many of its branches and even twigs remained intact. Not counting its great bole, the top alone covered a space, oval in shape, approximately one hundred feet long and fifty feet wide at the center.

I had found few flowers and fewer birds after getting away from the immediate influence of the forest. There were numbers of rotting stumps here and there, ragged clumps of sprouts, rank frostweed in some of the ravines, scattering trees, and many erosion gullies leading up the gently sloped hillsides.

Presently I heard a humming of rubythroats and I knew that some-where in this waste they must be enjoying a feast of nectar. I moved in the direction from which the sound was coming, and when the dead sweet gum first came into view I thought it was a mound of flowers, so thickly were blooms massed among its branches. Sure enough, buzzing over it were dozens of hummers. As I got nearer I saw around the edges of the mound—tucked in just out of reach of the grazing ani-mal—masses of deep purple tradescantia mingled with red mallow in full bloom. A skinny vine clambered about in the interior dotting in small, white, purple-centered blooms. A mass of sunflowers occupied the central section, while across the top of the fallen tree a morning-glory vine had effectually suppressed all competition. There was also here and there a bell-shaped flower, pale blue with yellow center which I did not identify, and finally, on long, naked stalks, a coneflower called locally queen of the meadow.

The deep bass of the rubythroats, almost too low at times to hear at all, was accompanied by humming in a higher pitch, heard only on nearer approach, coming from numerous honeybees which had also discovered this bonanza. A few highly-colored butterflies associating with many drab ones were about also—some perched on exposed twigs, slowly opening and closing their gorgeous wings, some feeding, some flitting about.

The massive corpse of this tree was disintegrating amid a display of life's most lively and colorful expressions: bees, butterflies, humming-birds, and flowers. Of course, less conspicuous life was thriving therein, but I can't find that I made any note of it. I rarely notice an insect until it is in the bill of a bird, and then I want to know all about it. . . .

This mutual dependence, solidarity, or community of interest is after all and generally nature's most distinctive characteristic. The sin of non-co-operation is severely penalized. "Nature red in tooth and claw" is only a partial view, and expresses incident rather than plot or principle. Those unaccustomed to considering the world in the amplitude of time fail to see this. The hawk rends his prey and the more powerful hawk hovering near robs the killer of his prize; but this is a mere detail or byplay. The whole must be seen not as a still but as a motion picture—as plot, counterplot, and drama of the limitless fecundity of nature, unbelievably clever stratagems and devices, infinite mutations, protean adaptability, all unfolding amid the "dance of materials" in an endless flow of time.

HANGERMAN JOHN

★

William A. Owens

WHEN I WAS A CHILD WE LIVED ON A SMALL SANDYLAND farm about two miles from town. To the front of us was a broad flat field, where we worked the year round plowing, planting, hoeing, or picking cotton. My father being dead, my mother worked the days through with us, putting hand to hoe or plow with all the strength of a man. Beyond the field was the road from town. At the lower corner of our farm it branched. One branch led through sandy hills and flats to the river; the other turned back to the blackland. Mr. Rodgers, the chicken peddler, lived with his family in shouting distance on the river road. They were our nearest neighbors. A Negro family lived on the other side of the woods, but we did not count them as neighbors, though their son George sometimes roamed the woods with us.

These woods lay to the back of our farm. From the road our little house looked like a mound or a haystack against the tall dark trees. My three brothers and I were in the woods as many hours as we could be, hunting rabbits and possums, cutting wood, gathering poke sallet and sheep sorrel for early spring greens. John, the oldest, was a tall slender lad of seventeen, eight years older than I. Herbert and Edward were between us. John led us in work and play. He led us in the game of dare. In the spring, when the tall thin red oaks were full of sap and bent easily, he would swing from the top of one to the next—so fast that his blue overalls and shirt made a blur against the light green of the budding branches. Herbert and Edward followed him from tree to tree, but never with as daring a swing. I followed on the ground, watching him excitedly, waiting for him to come to the last tree in a grove. When he would reach this one he would swing out as far as the branches would bend and then drop lightly to earth. I was always there to help brush the twigs and leaves from his clothes. Then he would roach his yellow hair out of his eyes.

"Next year, Bud," he would say, "you'll be big enough to swing trees. I'll show you how." Then we'd tussle on the earth till Herbert and Edward caught up with us. Sometimes he brought his hand down my face and up again, saying, "Down come a limb, up jumped a rabbit." It was a game I liked. If he was fast enough he tipped the end of my nose with his hand. More often I dodged his hand and sheltered my face under his arm.

When we met George, the Negro boy, in the woods he was glad to join us in play. He was the age of John, but taller and heavier. He could hoist things that John couldn't; but he was not clever at swinging his body through the trees. He was slow at learning our games, but cunning in the ways of woods and animals. Sometimes we went on cold clear nights to the persimmon trees looking for possums. As darkness came on we would leave our house. John would blow a signal on his cupped fists. George would answer, and come running along the path in the forest to meet us. When we found a possum, John climbed the tree and brought him down by the tail, sulled. John held the possum to the ground with an ax handle across his neck, while George pulled him by the tail. There would be a faint sigh and sound of breaking bones. Then the possum was dead. By the light of a fire we would skin him, keeping the hide for ourselves and giving the meat to George.

On warm fall nights we sometimes played "nigger uprising," using stories told us by our mother about times when white men had to go out and "put niggers in their place." Nearly all these stories took place at night. In most of them nigger cabins were burned. We would build up a great bonfire with dry leaves and branches and pretend that it was a nigger cabin on fire. Then we would run about the fire and shout and scream at imaginary niggers. After the niggers were all killed or frightened away we would throw burning sticks at the black sky, laughing with delight at the shower of sparks and arc of falling light. In these games no one would play the part of a nigger. And we never played this game when George was with us.

One night my brothers and I were playing hide-and-seek in the forest. It was a warm moist night the week before Christmas. Being the youngest and smallest, I was nearly always "it" in the game. The other three could outrun me to home base. When I refused to run any more, John took my place.

"I'll count for you this time, Bud," he told me. "I'll count to a hundred by ones . . . you hide good . . . if you hide so good I can't find you, I'll call for you to come in free . . . we'll make Herbert or Edward be it . . ."

He leaned against the trunk of the red oak that was our base and began counting slowly.

"Cover your eyes," I ordered.

When he had covered his eyes I ran into the woods. I was afraid of the blackness among the trees, but I had to go. I had to be able to come in free. John was helping me. He counted to a hundred. His voice was clear in the night air. Then he was giving the warnings he had to give before he could start seeking.

Bushel o' wheat,

Bushel o' cotton,

All ain't hid

Better be a-trottin'.

I found a fallen tree top where we had cut wood in the summer. Dry leaves still clung to the branches. Dead leaves had swirled knee deep on the ground around it. I followed the branches until I found the trunk. I crawled in beside it. The outer leaves were damp. I scooped them away and pressed myself against the log. The smell of wet and dry leaves was about me. I hugged the log and trembled with excitement. I concentrated on lying still. Any move in the dry leaves might betray me. John finished counting.

Bushel o' wheat,

Bushel o' clover,

All ain't hid

Cain't hide over.

As I lay listening to John searching near the base I heard a wagon coming along the dirt road. By the way the wheels knocked on their thimbles I knew it was Mr. Rodgers' wagon. He had gone to town, to the county seat, that morning to sell a load of chickens. I thought of the things he had brought for Christmas: oranges, apples, firecracker . . .

The blast of a shotgun rocked the night and drowned out the sounds of the wagon. I jumped to my feet in fright.

"Oh, my life!"

The voice of a man in agony came from the direction of the wagon. The wagon rattled on for a moment, and then stopped, but the man's voice repeated the terrifying cry over and over. I ran as fast as I could to the house. My brothers were ahead of me. They were standing around Mother on the porch when I got there.

"It's Mr. Rodgers," Mother whispered in horror. "He's been shot."

"I'm going to him," John said. "He needs help."

"You may get in trouble yourself," Mother warned him.

"Cain't help it if I do. He needs a man to help him."

We listened to the bare cotton stalks whipping against his duckings as he ran across the field.

"John ain't scared of nothing, is he?" I boasted.

The wagon started again. Mr. Rodgers repeated "Oh, my life" again and again, growing fainter each time. After a while the wagon stopped. We could tell by the sound that it had stopped at Mr. Rodgers' house. Then there was stillness. We stood on the porch and shivered. It was getting colder. We went in and sat by the fireplace, waiting for John to come back.

Within an hour John was with us again. There was a patch of blood on his knee. Bloodstains were on his hands.

"Mr. Rodgers was shot by a nigger," he said. "I got his blood on my hands and clothes lifting him out of the wagon."

"Is he bad hurt?" Mother asked.

"Awful bad. I'm afraid he'll die. He was shot in cold blood and robbed of forty dollars."

"Who's the nigger?" Mother asked.

"He didn't know. Said it was too dark for him to get a good look. Then he fainted and couldn't talk no more."

John moved over in front of the fire and turned the back of his duckings to the heat. He picked at the blood on his hand with a fingernail.

"They've gone for Ky Johnson and the bloodhounds," he said. "They're going to run that nigger down tonight. I'm going back and help them."

"Will there be a lynching?" Herbert asked.

"Maybe. If we catch him."

"You going to help them?" I asked, frightened.

John looked at Mother, sitting in her chair by the lamp with the Bible in her hands for the evening reading.

"I've got to take Pa's place," he said.

"When your Pa was living," Mother said, looking at the pages of the Bible, "he always took his part in everything that had to be done. Tonight a nigger's got out of his place. It is the duty of white men to put him back. If they don't, white women won't be safe. I'm a widow woman here with you boys. I won't be safe."

The look on her face sobered all of us.

"My son," she said, looking into John's eyes, "you have been taught right and wrong. You will know what to do."

Again John was gone into the night.

Mother went to the organ in the corner and sat down on the stool. She pressed the pedals lightly with her feet. A sound like the hissing part of the Lord's Prayer came from the bellows. Herbert held the lamp for her to read the notes in the hymnbook.

"Come, all you souls by sin oppressed," she sang in her high soprano. We sang with her, ". . . and He will surely give you rest." It was difficult for me to sing. I was thinking about Mr. Rodgers and the bloodhounds and the nigger. Then we sang, "I will arise and go to Jesus." If Mr. Rodgers should die, I thought, he would arise and go to Jesus . . .

We knelt by our chairs while Mother read from the Bible. "O Lord our Lord, how excellent is Thy name . . . What is man that Thou art mindful of him . . . Thou hast made him a little lower than the angels, and hast crowned him with glory and honor . . . O Lord our Lord . . ." Then she prayed—prayed for Mr. Rodgers' recovery, John's safety, protection for widows and orphans, justice and peace on earth, and for heaven "where thieves neither break through nor steal." My face was pressed close against the cowhide chair bottom. Its leathery smell was sharply unpleasant.

Before the last amen was over we heard men and horses on the road from town. We went to the porch to listen. A chill wind blew from the east and I was afraid. I clung to Mother's rough worsted skirt. Its gore seams chafed my cheeks. When the men reached the place of the shooting they dismounted and lighted lanterns. The lanterns were moving balls of fire as the men walked. They were like jack o' lanterns bouncing in some dark swampy place in the woods.

One of the bloodhounds opened up with a clear strong voice.

"There they go," Edward screamed excitedly. "Listen to them yelp."

The second hound had joined the first. Deep tones, light tones. Deep tones, light tones. They seemed to be circling. Then they ran to the southward. The men on horseback followed at a gallop.

"They're heading toward the lake," Herbert said, "and traveling fast."

"Run, nigger, run, paterollers'll catch you," Edward sang. He grabbed my hand and then Herbert's. We danced a circle on the porch singing, "Nigger run, nigger flew, nigger lost his wedding shoe." Herbert changed the words to "Run, nigger, run, Ky Johnson'll catch you." We laughed at the thought of the nigger running through the night with the bloodhounds at his heels. Above our laughing their yelping sounded.

They seemed to be circling again. Their barking was no longer that of hounds hot on the trail. It was the confused howling of hounds that had lost their quarry. Among us was the feeling we had when our own hounds lost the scent on the trail of a raccoon.

"They've lost him," Herbert exclaimed. "Lost him at the lake. What'll they do?"

"Go around the lake till they pick up the scent again," Mother told him. "Bloodhounds can get nigger smell a mile off."

There was silence for a few minutes. We went out in the yard to hear better. We cupped our hands over our ears and leaned on the paling fence. The hounds opened up again. They were in the open and running at breakneck speed. Occasionally we could hear one of the riders, urging his horse along to keep up. When the hounds came to the railroad they turned toward town. We followed the sounds and knew when they reached nigger town. There was a moment of silence, and then they began baying exultantly. They had found their quarry. Then there was silence.

"Wonder what nigger it is?" Edward asked, as we went into the house.

"Must be one of the town niggers," Mother answered. "They're a bad lot."

IT WAS LONG PAST BEDTIME, BUT WE STAYED UP, WAITING FOR John to come home with the news. Mother spread my pallet by the fire, but did not tell me to go to bed. She sat by the lamp and read the Bible. We dug out hollows in the piles of ashes on the hearth and put sweet potatoes in them to roast. Herbert brought out an ear of red corn he'd been saving. We parched the grains on the shovel and cracked them with our teeth, pretending all the time we were redskins.

Herbert raked the ashes away from one of the potatoes on the hearth. A warm, sweet fragrance rose from the ashes. We stopped to listen. A horse was galloping along the road. The rider pulled up long enough for someone to dismount.

"Thanks for the ride," we heard John call. "See you at the shindig. We got to show these niggers—"

I did not know what he meant. Before I could ask the others, he was running up the path through the field.

"Did you catch the nigger?" we all yelled as he came in the door.

"Sure, we got him," he bragged.

"Who was it?"

"George."

"George?" Our voices were sharp, disbelieving.

"Sure. I knew it was him all the time."

"How'd you know?" Herbert challenged.

"From what Mr. Rodgers said. Couldn't a been nobody else."

His voice was assured but unconvincing.

"How'd you catch him?" Mother asked.

"It was easy. Ky Johnson let the bloodhounds get one smell of his tracks. They took out as hard as they could go, like foxhounds with a brush in sight. We had a hard time keeping up. Ky Johnson let me ride behind him on his horse because of Pa. He said I favored Pa most every way."

"Didn't they lose him once?"

"At the lake. He waded it. But as soon as Ky Johnson saw what had happened, he tolled the hounds around the edge till they picked up the scent again. We trailed him up the railroad and into nigger town. The hounds went right into Uncle Wash's cabin. We found George in bed with his muddy clothes on and with the covers pulled up over his head. Ky Johnson had a hard time keeping the dogs from chewing him up when they found him. I nearly died laughing watching how scared George was with the dogs snapping at him and him digging deeper under the covers."

"Did he confess?" Mother asked.

"He had to. He still had Mr. Rodgers' pocketbook in his overalls."

"Why did he do it?"

"He said he wanted money for Christmas—to buy firecrackers and oranges. He said he ain't never had a orange for Christmas."

"He probably hasn't," Mother said, "but that's no reason for him to rob or kill anybody. You cain't tell what a nigger'll do, though. That's why we have to protect ourselves against them."

At the mention of oranges I remembered that George had ventured into our yard the Christmas before to see what we had for presents. When I showed him the two oranges in my stocking he grinned with pleasure and asked me for one. I was unable to part with an orange, but I did give him the peel from one of them. He left with the orange peel wrapped tight around his fingers.

"Where is he now?" Edward asked.

"Ky Johnson locked him up in the calaboose tonight . . . says the high sheriff from the county seat will come and get him tomorrow."

"What if he escapes?"

"He won't. They put a ball and chains on his legs so he cain't walk."

"Will they lynch him?" Herbert asked in a low voice, almost a whisper.

John walked back and forth in front of the fireplace with a boastful swagger I had never seen in him before.

"Maybe so, maybe not," he answered. He and Mother exchanged glances across the room.

"How about a baked potato, John?" Mother asked.

Herbert dug the potatoes from the ashes and handed us each one. Mine was soft and juicy, but I could not eat it. It was like soft warm clay in my throat. Mother spread another quilt on my pallet and I went to bed. After a while Herbert and Edward went off to bed in the shed room. Mother put out the lamp and she and John sat talking by the light of the fire. I could not hear what they were saying. My mind was full of the sound of bloodhounds on the trail . . .

A CROWD OF MEN WAS AROUND THE CALABOOSE THE NEXT MORNING when we went to school. John, who had walked ahead of us, was among them. They were still there when the noon recess came. I went to the calaboose looking for John. Some other boys my size trailed after me. Most of the men in the crowd were silent. A few stayed with the horses tied along the railing. John saw me and caught me by the shoulders. His hard fingers made tears come to my eyes.

"Go back to school," he commanded me. He had never spoken so harshly to me before. I was frightened, but I did not leave at once. I wanted to see George.

The calaboose door was open. I worked my way among the men until I was in front of the door. George was cringing against the back wall. He still had on the overalls and jumper he had worn when he waded the lake. They were crusted with black mud. He was bareheaded. His hair was cut short all over except for the tuft in front that stood up like a spur. His legs were bound with a chain shackle. A heavy ball lay at his feet. When he looked at me I could see that he had been crying. Brine had crusted in white streaks on his black face. He looked at me a moment, but hung his head when I tried to make signs to him.

Last week George had been at our house to help mark hogs. It was a job he enjoyed. I remembered how he laughed and sang as he caught and held hogs for John to mark. "Underbit in the right, crop off the lef'," he called as John cut our mark in the pigs' ears. Then George held their tails for John to snip off with his sharp knife. George took the tails and bits of ears home for a stew. That was last week. Now he was in the calaboose—a robber, maybe a killer. He might be lynched. This was a silent group of men around him. I recalled a song George had sung for us in the woods, "Hangerman, hangerman, slack yo' rope, and slack it for a while . . ."

Ky Johnson closed the calaboose door and hooked the lock in the chain. He did not close the lock.

"You fellers gonna be around for a while?" he asked.

Several nodded at him. I moved out of the way of his rough boots. The pistols on his hips were near enough for me to touch them.

"I'm looking for the high sheriff to come git this coon," Ky Johnson said. "If he comes while I am at the house eating, tell him I'll be back in a few minutes."

He galloped away on his roan stallion.

"Now's the time we been waiting for," one of the men said.

"Johnson's giving us a chance," another man agreed.

"Better git them kids away," a bearded man in a white hat said. 'We cain't do nothing with them around. They'll tell everything."

"You kids git back to school," one of the men ordered. "Recess is over."

John came through the crowd and caught me by the shoulders. He pinched so hard that I cried out. He threatened to beat me if I did not leave. They drove us from the crowd and started us up the main road toward school. As we neared the school we met the high sheriff and two of his deputies on their fine horses. They led another horse behind them. George would ride that horse back to the county jail, where he would be safe from the lynchers' rope.

That afternoon after school I went to the woods to gather sticks for the fireplace. It was gray cold and I shivered in my thin jumper. I put the sticks on a slide John had built for me. Before it was half full John came to the woods calling my name. I ran to meet him, but stopped when I saw the look on his face.

"You little fool," he said bitterly, "you kept us from lynching George today."

"How?" I asked, surprised.

"By hanging around the calaboose when you did. Ky Johnson give us our chance, but you ruined it. If it hadn't been for you George would be swinging from a white oak limb right now. Now he's in the hands of the high sheriff . . . he'll be behind heavy bars at the county jail . . . we cain't do nothing . . ."

He came closer to me. His face was white. His blue eyes looked straight at me.

"Fool," he said, and slapped me across the face with his hand. Then he went back to the house.

I went on picking up sticks until the slide was full. After it was piled high I still lingered in the woods, waiting until I could stop crying.

After dark Ernest, the tiehacker, came by and called John to the front yard. I went to the front window to eavesdrop on them.

"Better come along," Ernest said to John. "There'll be things happening tonight."

"What's up?"

"Mr. Rodgers died this afternoon late. Us vigilantes're getting ready to lynch George. Going to make it a real shindig."

"Ain't he in the county jail?"

"No. He's still in the calaboose. The high sheriff left him there long enough to go out and talk to Mr. Rodgers. Mr. Rodgers died, and the sheriff's still out there. Ky Johnson's with him now. Ain't nobody guarding the calaboose. Seems like they want us to lynch him. You want to go?"

"Sure," John replied.

"Get your stuff."

John went inside for a few minutes, but he did not speak to mother. He came out again with his cap on and a bundle under his jumper.

"Let's go," he said.

I WAS SLEEPING ON MY PALLET NEAR THE FIREPLACE WHEN JOHN came in. He stirred the smoldering chunks of fire and laid some fresh sticks on. They blazed up in yellow-red flames. John stood before the fire to dry the dampness from his clothes. I thought he was sick. From the look of his face and eyes I thought he had come through a malarial chill and the fever was beginning to rise. I sat up on my pallet.

"We lynched George tonight," he boasted in a voice pale as the ashes on the hearth.

"Lynched him?" I asked in horror. "George is dead?"

"Dead as a doornail."

John knelt on the pallet beside me, compelled to talk and glad to have me to talk to. He had forgot striking me in the woods that afternoon.

"Can you keep a secret?" he asked.

"Yes."

"You'd better keep this one. If you tell it, the Ku Kluxers'll get you."

He took a sheet from under his jumper and draped it over his body. He put a pillowcase mask over his head.

"This is the way we looked," he said. "Eight of us looking just like this."

I shivered as if I were looking at a real ghost. It was John under the sheet, but not the John I knew. I drew away from him, fearing he would strike me again. I did not want to hear more of the story, but he made me listen.

"Do you know the big white oak where we get persimmons?" he asked.

I nodded.

"George is hanging from it tonight. It was a tough job."

"Did you do the hanging?"

"Most of it. I nearly got hung myself."

"How?"

"We put a lariat rope over a limb. Then we tied one end around George's neck and the other to the horn of a saddle."

"What did Goerge do?"

"He bellered like a bull calf. They told me to get on the horse and make him run as hard as he would go. They said they would grab the rope and tie it tight when George was pulled up against the limb."

The robe hid all of John except his eyes. I dreaded to look at them as he talked. The fever in them was still rising.

"I got on the horse and spurred him as hard as I could. He started bucking and running. When George was about twenty feet in the air my saddle girt broke. The horse kept going but I swung back. I was swinging from the same limb with George. He was over me and thrashing around hard. I was still clinging to the saddle. I was scared, but I held on till the other men could tie the rope. Then they let me down. They said I was a good man and made me drink some whiskey."

"You left George hanging there?"

"Had to. He's a good example for other niggers. This'll keep them in their place for a while."

"But the buzzards—"

"Let the buzzards have him. He was a bad nigger—a killer. Come here."

John led me to the porch and pointed to the woods. Two great fires were burning. The sky above the forest was red and yellow with their light. Tree tops between us and the sky were like black lace.

"That fire to the west," John said, "is the one we built to hang George by. The other is George's cabin. Ain't nothing like fire and hanging to scare niggers . . ."

John put his arm around my shoulders to lead me into the house, but I moved away from him. He took off the mask and robe. I still did

not recognize him as my brother. There was something in his eyes—
more than whiskey or fever. He smiled a bit and brought his hand
down my face, saying "Down come a limb, up—"

I jerked away from the touch of his hand. I lay down on my pallet
and pulled the quilts over my face. He tucked the covers around me
and stooped over me quietly for a moment. When I did not speak or
move, he went off to bed.

I was warm in my covers but could not sleep. I was thinking of
George . . . and hangerman John.

from NO QUITTIN' SENSE

★

C. C. White

AFTER I LEFT MY FATHER'S FARM I JUST KEPT WALKING. I didn't stop when I got to Nacogdoches. I didn't have no money for food or lodging. I just started walking on towards Center. It was thirty-three miles. About dark I stopped at a white man's farm and asked him if he had any work I could do to pay for something to eat and a place to sleep. He said, "Can you cut sprouts?"

I said, "Yes suh. Mr. Prayter Windham learned me."

The man said he'd pay four bits a day and board and room if I'd stay and work a week. I did. I worked sunup to sundown. I wanted my money, so I give good service. Saturday morning he paid me off at the breakfast table. Said to come back if I ever needed a job.

I started walking along the road again and come to a little place called Swift. Somebody there said, "Man, don't you know they don't allow no niggers here?"

I said, "I'm just passing."

He said, "They don't allow no niggers here at all."

I said, "I'm going through." And I kept on walking.

Out along the road the other side of town I met a man on a horse and he told me the same thing. Said, "They just don't allow colored people in this part of the country. They'll sic dogs on you." He was trying to be nice to me. Said, "If somebody sics dogs on you, you go up a tree. Don't let them dogs catch you, they'll tear you up."

I kept on walking toward Center, but I did stop and get me a stick. It was a strong, green pole about the size of my arm. I carried it like a cane, and I meant to swing it hard at anything that tried to hurt me.

When I walked through Martinsville I saw some men up on a porch roof painting a house. They started laughing and hollering. They said, "Oh-oh, there goes a nigger. Let's go down and paint him." I walked on, with my big stick, acting like I hadn't heard them. And they didn't do nothing.

WHEN I COME TO CENTER I FOUND FRANK STILL WORKING AT the hotel. I got me a job there in Center, too, on the Santa Fe Railroad. It was with a section crew, fixing the tracks. I lived with the other men, in a bunkhouse, and we all ate our meals in another building that was there beside the bunkhouse. Payday was every two weeks, and they took out one day's pay for hospital insurance each time. We worked six days a week, got overtime for Sundays. I never did like to work on Sundays, but I did sometimes. They only fed us on the days we worked. Liza was living in Center then so I generally ate at her house on Sundays.

When I worked for the railroad I worked fast and careful, just like I'd done all my life. The section boss noticed this, and looked like he maybe favored me sometimes. Naturally, the other men didn't like that. But it just wasn't in me to shirk. If I was gonna do a thing I wanted to do it right, I wanted to do it the best I could, that's the only

way I knowed how to do. So I made up my mind to do like I wanted
to, and if the rest of them didn't like it they could lump it.

They said, "Lookit him work. Don't you wish you liked to work like
that? Must be lots of fun." I kept on working, and didn't look up.
Somebody said, "Oh, Charley would rather work than anything. He'd
even rather work than whore."

Another one said, "My goodness gracious man, Charley wouldn't
whore. His mammy told him it wasn't nice."

That evening in the bunkhouse they was still at it. It was Saturday,
and we was all getting washed up. There was a visitor there. He was
the brother of one of the men, and he come in there sometimes to get
cleaned up. He wasn't supposed to, but every once in a while he did.
He was running around without any clothes on, like most of the other
men, and he come over and set down on my bed. I said, "You get away
from here. You got sores all over you. I don't want to catch that stuff."

The other men guffawed. One said, "Somebody better tell our little Charley how you catch the clap, he don't seem to know."

Somebody else said, "Oh, let him go ask his mammy." And he come
over and leaned over in my face and said, "You gonna go see your
mammy this weekend, Charley? You better ask her . . ."

I hit him. I had him pounded up pretty good before they got me off
of him. After that things settled down and everybody got dressed and
got out of there.

I went to see a girl I'd been going with. I wondered about the things
I'd seen and heard in the bunkhouse that evening. I had never gone
around with bad women. I'd only gone with young girls, and I'd always
treated them nice, like I'd want other boys to treat my sister. I didn't
want to mess up no boy's sister, because I figured if a boy messed up
my sister I'd want to kill him. After I left the girl's house, I went and
bought me a bottle of whiskey and went and found Frank and we
drunk it.

Things went pretty good at work the next week. The men had about give up on teasing me. When Saturday come they wanted me to go with them, said they was sorry they'd made me mad, they was only trying to have a little fun. We went over to a place and had a game of craps, then we went and got us some supper. After that we went to what they called Miss Minnie's. It was a red-light house. A couple of fellows I didn't know got into a fight, and one of them got cut up pretty bad. Made me think of the time Albert Jones was trying to cut Dan Kimbrew up in our garden.

After that I generally went with the men on Saturday evenings. I'd follow them around till we'd come to that red-light place. I couldn't take that. Too much going on. Killing folks, and beating up, and slashing with knives. I'd buy me a bottle of whiskey and go back to the bunkhouse.

One evening we went to a place over in "the quarter." I'd been hearing the other men talk about it. There was lots of women there. All kinds. Some old, some young, some half-naked, some dressed nice—just any type you wanted. I guess there must a been twenty-five of them. There was always some of them dancing. Others would be setting at tables with men, drinking. One girl kept teasing me, and teasing me. Finally I bought her a bottle of beer. She said, "Come on, let's go to my room." All these women had rooms close around there. I guess they was hired by the man that owned the place.

When this girl started trying to get me to go to her room, I got up and bought me a bottle of whiskey and went home. I guess I might have gone with her if I wasn't so scared. I was scared of what I might catch. I'd seen that man that hung around our bunkhouse, and he got worse and worse. He was half eat up. Some of the other men had it, too, but they wasn't as bad off as he was. I figured that was one thing I didn't want.

One day after I'd eat Sunday dinner at Liza's I was fixing to leave and she wanted to know was I coming back for supper. I said, "No, I don't expect so."

She moved over between me and the door and said, "Charley, I been hearing things about you."

I'd been expecting her to get around to this, but I tried to turn it off. I said, "What you been hearing, gal? That you got the most handsomest big ole brother there is?"

She didn't tell me what she'd been hearing, but she talked about bad diseases, and how you couldn't get rid of them if you ever got them, and how I'd just be throwing my life away if I caught one. Then she said I ought to watch how I talked. Said, "You sound just like them other men that work on that railroad." She said it was time I was thinking of getting married. Soon as I could get away from her I left and went over where Frank was.

One Saturday night I went to see one of my girls that lived down near Shelbyville, and then I stayed the night with a cousin of Mama's that lived close by. I took my old muzzle-loader with me, so I could go squirrel hunting Sunday.

I hadn't been out in the woods south of Shelbyville since we moved from there to Possum Trot when I was ten. I had about half a bottle of whiskey in my pocket, that was left over from the night before, so I set down on a rock and had a little drink while I loaded my gun. I'd started out without any wadding but it didn't take me long to find a old hornet nest.

I got one squirrel but didn't see no more. I don't think I was looking very hard. I just kept walking, and after while I come out on the path Mama always took when she worked for the George Smith family in Shelbyville, so I decided to go on down and have a look at where we used to live. When I topped the last hill and started down towards the old rail fence I remembered how I set there so many times and waited for Mama, and how tickled I'd be when I seen her come over that hill, and how I'd run to meet her.

The old fence was about rotted down. I punched the bottom rail with my foot and ants piled out, hurrying around, looking for some place to run to. *Like men from a burning whore-house*, I thought. I kicked the rail again. "Run, damn you," I told them.

I walked on down and stood under the big oak tree where I preached to my dolls. I felt silly now, remembering that. "Huh. I sure was a stupid kid," I said out loud.

The old house was still there, but didn't nobody live in it. The door was hanging by just a piece of one old leather hinge. I went in. Had to be careful not to fall through the rotten floor. There was the fireplace where Mama used to cook. And there, still nailed to the wall, was some old shelves she kept meal and syrup and stuff on. I remembered when Dan Kimbrew built the shelves for us, and how he made two doors to shut across them. Part of one door was still there, on the floor. And beside it was one of the old forked-stick hinges he'd used. I picked it up and rubbed the dust off it. I hadn't seen one of them old hinges since we left that place.

I walked over and looked out the window. Wasn't no glass in it. Hadn't been glass in it when we lived there neither. But now even the old wooden shutter was gone, was just a hole in the wall. Out there was the place where we'd had our garden that time when Albert Jones and Dan Kimbrew got into that fight. And there was the chinquapin thicket. And on up on the hill was Albert Jones's house.

I went and set on the steps, where Frank and me had set that day after Albert knocked my teeth out. I started to load my gun, and as I tamped the hornet nest down I begin to hurt just like I hurt that time when Albert beat me. I rubbed my face and finished off the whiskey. Then I got up and started up the hill, kicking chinquapin burrs, hard, every which way with my new shoes.

When I got in Albert's yard I hollered, "Hallo! Anybody home?" Then I raised my gun and waited.

The man that opened the door was a stranger. I said, "Where's Albert?"

The man said, "What you talking about?"

"I'm looking for old Albert Jones. Where is he?"

The man said, "Ain't nobody like that here. And what you doing with that gun? What you up to?"

I lowered the gun. "I been squirrel hunting, and if Albert ain't here where is he?"

The man begin to get mad. "I told you I don't know nothing about no Albert Jones. I never even heered of nobody like that in all the five years I been here. Now you take that gun and git on off away from here, you hear?"

So I left.

The next day the men got to riding me again. We was working there on the track, and I was driving them big spikes that hold the tracks to the cross-ties. One feller said, "Where you reckon Charley was Saturday night? He wasn't at the bunkhouse."

"Well, he weren't at Miss Minnie's," chimed in another one. "Leastwise, I didn't see him. And I was there all night, in one room or another."

Another one said, "Oh, you know Charley only lays around with *nice* girls." He come over to me, "You out with one of them *nice* girls Saturday night, Charley?"

I got me a good grip on the sledge hammer, and I just looked at them, first one and then another. Most of them remembered right away how they had something to do on down the track. The ones that couldn't leave shut up.

FRANK HAD GOT HIMSELF A WIFE BY THAT TIME, AND HIM AND her kept telling me about a girl they thought I ought to meet. I wasn't interested. Frank had introduced me to girls before. "But Charley, this one is different. This is a *nice* girl," he told me.

I said, "Oh, sure. They're all nice." I could see him and his wife thought I was being unreasonable. I said, "Now you just let me tell you something. I ain't looking to find no nice girl. I don't think there is any such a thing. But you want me to find you a bad one? Well you just put a whole bunch of them in a room and blindfold me and turn me loose in there and the first one I put my hands on, that'll be her." So I didn't stay to meet their nice girl.

Liza tried to talk to me every once in a while, but I didn't pay no attention to her. I didn't argue with her. I didn't want to fuss with Liza. But I figured I didn't have to pay her no mind, I was twenty-one years old. I didn't like the way I was living, either. But didn't seem like I knowed anything to do about it. I was mean, and hard to get along with. The men I worked with had stopped teasing me, but I still stayed in a bad humor most of the time.

One morning I kicked all the dishes off the breakfast table. The cook had fried the eggs till they was like shoe leather, and I liked mine cooked soft. It didn't take much to set me off. I was already mad. I'd walked two miles to see a girl the night before, and when I got there I found her with another man. So when I tasted them old rubbery eggs, I just jumped on the end of the big long table and started cussing. I said, "I'm gonna kick every dish off this table. Who thinks I won't?" And I started kicking. The men jumped back. Some of them grabbed their plates, but some didn't have time. I kicked everything off onto the floor and jumped off the other end of the table. They stood there and let me do it. Nobody tried to stop me. Some of them was bigger than me. They could a stopped me. But they didn't.

Them was what I think of as my mean years.

A VOICE FROM THE WOODS

William Humphrey

"Ssh! Listen," says my wife. "You hear? Listen."

"What?" says my mother.

"Hear what?" say I.

"Ssh! There. Hear it? An owl. Hooting in the daytime."

Then I do hear: a soft hollow note, like someone blowing across the lip of a jug: *hoo-oo, hoo-hoo-hoo; hoo-oo, hoo-hoo-hoo* . . .

A ghostly sound, defying location, seeming in successive calls to come out of the woods from all points of the compass. Near at hand one moment, far away and faint the next, barely audible, the echo of an echo. It is not an owl. Yet it cannot be what it is. Not here. So far from home. It comes again, this time seeming to sound not outside me but inside myself, like my own name uttered in a once-familiar, long-dead voice, and my mother says, "Owl? That's no owl. Why, it's a—"

"A mourning dove!" say I.

It is the sound, the solitary sound, save for the occasional buzz, like an unheeded alarm clock, of a locust, of the long hot somnolent summer afternoons of my Texas boyhood, when the cotton fields shimmered white-hot and in the black shade of the pecan trees bordering the fields the Negro pickers lay napping on their sacks and I alone of all the world was astir, out with my air rifle hunting doves I never killed, gray elusive ghosts I never could locate. I would mark one down as it settled in a tree (I remember the finicking way they had of alighting, as if afraid of soiling their feet), and would sneak there and stand listening, looking up into the branches until I grew dizzy and confused. I would give up and move on, and at my back the bird would come crashing out of the branches sounding its other note, a pained squeak, and wobble away in drunken flight and alight in another tree and resume its plaint. They favored cedars, at least in my memory, and cedars in turn favored burial grounds, so that I think of the dove's whispered dirge as the voice of that funereal tree. It would be one of those breathless afternoons when the sun cooked the resin from the trunks of pines and sweet gums and the air was heavy, almost soporific with the scent. Heat waves throbbed behind the eyes. The fields were empty, desolate. High overhead a buzzard wheeled. The world seemed to have died, and in the silence the dove crooned its ceaseless inconsolable lament: *hoo-oo, hoo-hoo-hoo; hoo-oo, hoo-hoo-hoo* . . .

"A what? Mourning dove?" my wife says. "I never knew we had them here." *Here* being among the budding sugar maples and the prim starched white paper birches in the bustle and thaw of a crisp New England spring.

"I never knew you did either," says my mother. "What is a mourning dove doing way off up here?"

"What are you doing way off up here?" I say.

For my mother, too, has left Texas, lives out in Indianapolis. Now she has come on her annual visit to us. We sit on the sun porch, rushing the season a bit. As always, we two have fallen to reminiscing of Blossom Prairie and our life there before my father's death, telling stories by the hour which both of us have heard and told so often now that it is the rhythm which stirs us more than the words, our tongues thickening steadily until the accent is barely intelligible to my Yankee wife, who listens amused, amazed, bewildered, bored, and sometimes appalled.

"Son, do you remember," my mother says, "the time the bank was held up?"

I am still listening to the dove, and I have to ask her what she said. But now she is listening to the dove and does not hear me.

"The time the bank was held up? No, I don't remember that. First time I ever heard of it."

"Hmm? What did you say? First time you ever heard of what?"

"Of the bank being held up. The bank in Blossom Prairie?"

"Really? Oh, you remember such funny things! Old Finus, that used to come around to the house every afternoon selling hot tamales. Why anybody should clutter up their memory with him, I don't know! Lord, I would never have given him another thought this side of the grave. And not remember the great bank robbery! You were old enough. You remember lots of things that happened long before that. I took you with me, and we saw the dead men lying on the sidewalk on the square. You've forgotten that?"

"Dead men? Lying on the sidewalk? On the square? What dead men?"

"The bank robbers. All shot dead as they came out of the bank. You don't remember?"

"What!" says my wife. "You took a child to see a sight like—"

"That's the kind of thing I remember! Not an old boy who used to come around crying, 'Hot tamales!' Why, that was just about the biggest thing that ever happened in Blossom Prairie, I should think."

I open more cans of beer, and she drinks and sets down the can and wipes her lips and says, "Well, it was back in the bad old days. When lots of men were out of work and some of the young ones, who had all cut their teeth on a gun, took to living by it. The age of the great outlaws, when we had Public Enemy Number One, Two, Three. In our parts Pretty Boy Floyd was carrying on. And Clyde Barrow and Bonnie Parker."

"Did Clyde and Bonnie stick up the bank in Blossom Prairie?"

"No, no, it wasn't them. But it was in those days and times. No, the ones that stuck up the bank in Blossom Prairie—"

"Wait. Who was Pretty Boy Floyd?" asks my wife. "Who were Clyde Barrow and Bonnie Parker?"

"You never heard of them?" asks my mother, wiping away her mustache of suds.

"Now we will never get the story of the Blossom Prairie bank robbery," say I.

"Never heard of Clyde Barrow and Bonnie Parker? Never even heard of Pretty Boy Floyd?"

"Pretty Boy!" my wife laughs. "Pretty Boy!"

"Clyde Barrow," I say, "was a notorious outlaw, and Bonnie Parker his gun moll. They came out of West Dallas, the real low-down tough section of the town. They tore around sticking up banks and filling stations and honkey-tonks, and between them shot and killed any number of bank tellers and gas-pump operators and law officers in Texas in the early thirties. We used to follow the exploits of Clyde and Bonnie in the newspapers every day, like keeping up with the baseball scores. We really cannot claim Pretty Boy Floyd. He was an Oklahoma hero."

"You're making fun," says my mother. "Well, no doubt they did a lot of bad things, but let me tell you, hon"—this to her daughter-in-law—"you can go back down there and out in the country and to this day you'll find a many an old farmer will tell you he was proud to give Pretty Boy Floyd a night's lodging when the law was hounding him down like a poor hunted animal, and more than likely they found a twenty-dollar bill under his breakfast plate after he had left the next morning. And he never got that nickname for nothing. Oh, he was a good-looking boy!"

A VOICE FROM THE WOODS

"Well, what about the ones that held up the bank in Blossom Prairie?"

"He was a good-looking boy, too. All three of them were."

"She just never could resist an outlaw," I say.

The dove calls again, and my wife says, "What a sad, lonesome sound. I hope she doesn't come to nest around here. I wouldn't like to listen to that all day."

"As a matter of fact," says my mother, "as a matter of fact, I knew one of them. Travis Winfield, his name was. He was the leader of the gang. You wouldn't remember the Winfields, I don't suppose? Lived in that big old yellow frame house beyond the bridge out on the old McCoy road? A wild bunch, all of those Winfields, the girls as well as the boys, but good-looking, all of them, and Travis was the best looking, and the wildest, of the lot. Well, anyway. One day when you were—oh, let's see, you must have been six or seven, which would make it—how old are you now, hon, thirty-eight?"

"Seven."

"Thirty-seven?"

"Yes'm."

"Are you sure?"

"I *was*. Aren't you?"

"Oh, you! Well, anyway, it was during the summer that you had your tonsils and adenoids out. Remember? We were living at the time in Mr. Early Ellender's little cottage out on College Avenue. I had that little old Model-A Ford coupé that your daddy had bought me."

"Was there a college in Blossom Prairie?" my wife asks.

"No!"

"Well, you were just getting over that operation, and that's how you happened to be at home at the time and not off somewhere or other out of call. I remember I was fixing dinner when the telephone rang. . . . No, honey, there wasn't any college in Blossom Prairie. It was just a little bitty old place—though it was the county seat, and we all thought we were really coming up in the world when we left the farm and moved into town. It was so little that his daddy used to come home for his dinner every day. What you call lunch. . . . Well, the telephone rang and it was Phil. 'Hop in your car and come right down!' he said. 'They've just shot and killed three men robbing the bank!'"

"Then why was it called College Avenue? That doesn't make much sense."

"Don't ask me. I just grew up there."

"Well, but didn't it ever occur to you to wonder why they would call it that when there wasn't any—"

"Now, here is what had happened. These four men—"

"Three, you just a minute ago said."

"I said three were killed. These four men had been camping out down in Red River Bottom and—However, I better start with the woman. There was this woman, see. She had come into town about a month before. A stranger. She took a house, and she gave herself out to be a widow woman interested in maybe settling in the town and opening some kind of business with the money her husband had left her. And she had had a husband, all right, but she was no widow, nor even a grass widow. That came out at the trial. In fact, her husband showed up at the trial. When the judge sentenced her to eighteen years in the penitentiary this man stood up in the courtroom and said, 'Mildred! I'll still be waiting for you!' And she said, 'You'll wait a lot longer than any eighteen years!' And as they were taking her away he yelled, 'Mildred! Darling! I forgive you!' Meaning he forgave her for leaving him and running off with Travis. And that she-devil turned and told him I-can't-tell-you-what that he could do with his such-and-such forgiveness, right there in front of the judge and jury and the whole town and county. And still the poor fool did not give up but went round to the jailhouse and yelled up at the window of her cell until finally she came to the bars. And do you know what she told him was the one thing he could do that might win her back?—and this, you understand, would be after waiting for her to come out of the penitentiary for eighteen years. To get a gun and go shoot the one that had told on them to the law and had got the lover that she had run off with killed. However, it was not him that did it."

"That did what? Wait. I don't—"

"She was a cutter! Well, shortly after coming to town she went to the bank one day and opened an account. The very next day she was back and said she had changed her mind and wanted to draw her money out. They asked her why, and she said she had had her money in a bank once that had been held up, and she seemed to imply that that bank had looked a lot stronger than what she saw of ours. This piqued the manager, and he took her on a tour of the place to convince her that her money was safe with them, showing her all the strong vaults and the time locks and the burglar-alarm system and how it worked and whatnot. Besides, he said, there had never been any bank robberies in Blossom Prairie. So he convinced her, and she said she would let her money stay. After that she would come in every so often and make a deposit or a withdrawal, and she got to know the layout of the bank. She was making a map of it at home, and after each trip she would go and fill it in some more and correct any mistakes she had made in it. That way, too, she came to know when the big deposits were made by the business firms and the big-scale farmers and when there was always the most cash on hand in the bank.

"Meanwhile, she wasn't spending much time in that house in town. She told her neighbors—and of course they told everybody and his dog—that she still hadn't made up her mind to settle in Blossom Prairie and was looking over other spots around the county before deciding. She was seen on the road a lot, and she was a demon at the wheel. I was a pretty hot driver my own self, but—"

"Was! You still are. You scare me half to death."

"Well, that redheaded woman handled a car like no other woman and few men that I ever saw. In town she would spread her shopping over all the grocery stores so it wouldn't look like she was buying more food than a lone woman could eat, and she bought a good deal of bootleg liquor too, it came out later, and she would fill up the car and slip off down to Red River Bottom where Travis and his gang were camped out, though of course nobody knew that at the time. Whenever any squirrel hunter would happen to come up on them Travis kept out of sight, as he was the only local boy among them, and the other three made out that they were a hunting party too.

"Travis had been gone from home for some years, and everybody had pretty well forgotten him, except for maybe a couple of dozen girls who would have liked to but couldn't. Word would get back every now and again of some trouble he had gotten into and gotten himself out of. Now he had rounded up this gang and come back to rob the bank in his old home town. But though he had grown up there, he had to have that woman, or somebody, to draw him a map of the bank, for I don't suppose poor Travis had ever set foot in it in his life."

"All the while that he was holing up down there in the woods lay-ing his plans Travis had living with him in that tent, and eating and drinking with him, one man who was in constant touch with the sher-iff. He had told him all about that woman and about that map she was drawing of the bank and every little detail and switch in their plans. Imagine it? Living with three men for a whole month and letting on to be their friend, listening to them plan how they'll do this and do that to get the money and make their getaway, and knowing all the while that they were walking into a death trap that he himself had set, for pay, and that they were doomed to die as surely as if he himself had pulled the trigger on them? I'm not saying that what they were mean-ing to do was right, you understand. But can you just feature a skunk like that?

"I and Phil must have been just about the only people in town that didn't know the bank was set to be robbed that Monday morning. The sheriff had gone out and hired eight extra deputies, old country boys, good shots, squirrel hunters, and had them waiting, each with a thirty-thirty rifle, on the roofs of the buildings on each corner across the street from the bank, the old Ben Milam Hotel and the other, well, office buildings, stores downstairs on the street and doctors' and lawyers' offices upstairs, four stories high. The tellers in the bank had all been told not to put up any resistance but to give them what they asked for, to fill up their sacks for them, they'd have it all right back. The tip-off man was to wear something special. I seem to recall he wore a sailor straw hat, so they would recognize him and not shoot him.

"You remember, the bank in Blossom Prairie sits on the northwest corner of the square. The street that goes out to the north, Depot Street, goes past the cotton compress and over the tracks and past the ice house and toward the river. That would be the street they would come in on. The one going out to the west went past your daddy's shop and over the creek and on out of town in the direction of Paris. Down this street that morning, headed toward the square, came a wagon loaded high with baled hay. On the wagon seat, dressed up in overalls and a twenty-five-cent hardware-store straw hat, sat Sheriff Ross Shirley, and under the seat lay a sawed-off pump shotgun. At twenty minutes to eleven he set his team in motion with a flick of the reins. A moment later a car came round the corner and pulled up alongside the curb, and four men got out and ducked into the bank. As soon as they were inside, the sheriff says 'Come up' to his team, and up on the rooftops the rifle barrels poke over the walls and point down, followed by the heads of those eight deputies. The woman was driving, and she stayed in the car, keeping the engine idling. The wagon came down the street toward her, rattling over those old *bois-d'arc* paving bricks, until it got to just a little ways in front of the car. There suddenly the left rear wheel flew off the axle, the load of hay came tumbling down, scattering clear across the street, bales bouncing and breaking apart, the street completely blocked. The woman in the car made a sudden change in plans. She threw into reverse and backed around the corner into Depot Street, thinking that now, instead of going out by the Paris road, they would have to cross the square and go out by the southwest. Then she sees ahead of her a man fixing a flat tire on a big delivery van out in the middle of the street halfway down the block. This meant, she thought, that she would have to cut diagonally across the square, through the traffic and around the plaza and out by the southeast corner. She didn't know it, but they had her cut off there, too. In another minute or so the men burst out of the bank carrying the sacks.

"The moment they stepped out the door it began to rain bullets on them. Those that were on the square at the time said it sounded like a thunderclap had broken overhead. You couldn't count the separate shots, they said. The bullets chewed holes in the cement sidewalk. The men must have all died in the first volley, but the deputies poured another round and then another into them as they went down. The fourth man had fallen a step behind, deciding not to trust everything to that sailor straw hat, maybe thinking they would just as soon not pay that reward, and when the noise broke he dove back into the bank. He had cast a quick look up above as he came out, and that woman in the car must have seen it. In any case, when he didn't come out with the rest a thousand things that she must have noticed at the time and shaken off suddenly added up like a column of figures in her mind. She didn't even try to run. She jumped out of the car and up onto the curb, swooped down and pried the pistol from the still-clutching hand of one of the bandits, and stepped over the body into the bank. By then the sheriff was one step behind her. He grabbed her and took the gun away from her and held her until help came. She was more than he could manage alone. They said it was all four big strong men could do to keep her from getting at that one and clawing his eyes out, and then when they dragged her outside she broke away and threw herself on the body in the doorway, crying, 'Travis! Travis! Speak to me, Travis!' They had taken her away, and taken away the informer too and locked him up for his own protection by the time we got there, but the bodies were still lying on the sidewalk where they had fallen."

"Taking a little six-year-old child to see a sight like that!" my wife says, shaking her head.

"It was a terrible sight to see. Three strong young men cut off in the very Maytime of life, shot down like mad dogs before they even knew what was happening to them. I was sorry I had come. I wasn't going to look any closer. I tried to back out of the crowd. Then Phil said, 'My Lord! Why, ain't that one there that Winfield boy, Travis?' Oh, what a funny feeling came over me when I heard Phil say that!"

"Why, had you known him pretty well?"

"Yes. In fact—well, in fact, I had gone with Travis Winfield for a time, before I married your daddy."

"You had!"

"In fact, Travis Winfield had once asked me to marry him. He was not a bad boy then. Wild, yes, but not mean, not any gangster. I—I thought about it awhile before I turned him down. That stung him, and he didn't ask me a second time. I was just as glad. Oh, he was a good-looking boy! I don't know what I might have said a second time. Well, he had quickly forgotten about me and I had gone out with other boys and in time had met and married Phil, your daddy, and wasn't ever sorry that I had. But I want you to know I felt mighty queer standing there looking down at poor Travis—he was still handsome, even there in the dirt and all bloodied—lying on the common sidewalk with people staring at him, and thinking of that wild woman who had loved him so and had shared his wild life and now been dragged off to prison, and I was glad to have you there to hold on to. It was a comfort to me then to have my own child to hold on to his hand."

Silence falls, and in it the dove utters again its dolorous refrain.

"My daddy and my brothers disapproved of Travis Winfield. I think—apart from the fact that I was infatuated with his reputation for wildness, and his good looks—I think I probably went with him mainly just to devil my brothers a bit, let them all worry over me a little maybe, at least give them some reason for all that concern over my reputation. I don't believe I was ever really serious about him, and I never thought he was serious about me, partly because there were already lots of stories of other girls he hadn't been serious over. So I was taken by surprise when he asked me that day to marry him. I told him I would give him my answer next week. I knew then what it would be, but I suppose I wanted a week of thinking of accepting what I knew I was going to turn down.

"You remember, honey, out back of my old home that little family graveyard where all my folks are buried? It was there that Travis Winfield proposed to me. I said to meet me there again next Sunday and I would give him my answer. I remember waiting for him to come. You know how still it can be on a farm on a Sunday afternoon. The only sound for miles around as I sat there waiting for him was the cooing of a dove. I sat there thinking, I'm going to turn him down, of course, but what if I was not to? What if I was to say yes? What would my life be like?

"There are people just born for trouble, you know; Travis Winfield was one of them. It was written all over him in letters like headlines. Wild. Stubborn. Headstrong. Full of resentment against those who had all the things he didn't have. Proud. Vain. Believing the world owed him a living for the sake of his pretty face. No one woman could ever hope to hold him for long. After a while she wouldn't even want to keep on trying, unless she was an utter fool. But certainly life with Travis wouldn't be dull. It would be different from life on the farm, or in Blossom Prairie in a bungalow that had to be swept out and dusted every day.

"But I knew what I was going to say, and I said it. And maybe Travis wasn't sorry to hear it. Maybe during the week he had begun to wish he hadn't asked me. Most likely it was just his pride. He wasn't used to having a girl say no to anything he wanted. In any case, he didn't ask me again, and I was glad he didn't. He just gave me a hot look and turned and left. After he was gone I sat there a long time listening to the mourning dove. I never saw him again until that day on the square. It's years now since I even thought of Travis Winfield. It was hearing that mourning dove that brought it all back to my mind."

We sit listening for some time to its call. Then something alarms it, and though we do not see it, we hear the thrashing of its wings among the branches and its departing cry.

"Who did shoot the one who told?" I ask.

"Oh, yes, him. The trustees of the bank voted him a big reward, but he never got to spend it. They found him a week later floating in the river, though it was a wonder, with all the lead he had in him. It was generally known to be the work of that Winfield tribe, but they could never prove it. Never tried any too hard, I don't suppose."

I make a move to rise, but seeing her face I sit down again. Brushing back a strand of her cotton-white hair, my mother says, "Aren't people funny? There in his blood lay Travis, whom I had forgotten, dead, and deservedly so, I suppose, if any man deserves it. There was I, happy, with a good, loving husband and a decent home and a smooth, even life ahead of me and my own child's hand in mine. And yet, thinking of that redheaded woman—even then on her way to prison—I felt, well, I don't know what else to call it if not jealousy. Isn't that crazy? What did she have? Nothing, less than nothing, and I had everything. It only lasted a moment, you understand, yet it comes back to me even now, and if it wasn't jealousy, then I don't know what else to call it."

THE WAY IT WAS— SOUTHEAST TEXAS, 1915

★

Bill Brett

O H HELL, YES, THERE USED TO BE SOME BAD MEN IN THIS country. Some of 'em meaner than ten miles of blackland road after a three-day rain. But there wasn't many killers here, 'cept some of the law officers. I imagine them old sheriffs and their deputies was one reason there wasn't no more killings than there was. I've seen in the moving pictures law officers go up against some bad man and draw against him out in the street, but them shootouts didn't happen around here. Generally if the sheriff wanted to see a man, he'd just send him word and that man'd have sense enough to come in. If the man didn't, and the sheriff went after him, he'd take a deputy or several to back him up and they'd go with their wherewithal in their hands and get him. Easy or hard, whichever way he wanted.

The way lots of killings happened was accidental during a fight, or two men would have a falling out and start toting guns for each other and when they'd meet one'd kill the other'n. If all things was pretty equal in them cases, they was generally turned loose on a self-defense plea.

I guess, though, the most common killings was just cold-blooded. A feller would decide another'n had done something he couldn't live with, and he'd just go kill him. I've known several men go to the penitentiary for that, but I never knowed one to get the death penalty.

There was a few bad men passed through this country years ago before my time, but I never heard of any that was raised here. My grandmother said one time when she was a small girl she was walking to the store with my Great aunt Ellen and their mother (they lived just west of Walter—that's part of Hardin now), and they met a man on horseback, and their mother seemed to know him and they talked a few minutes. He gave each of the girls a half-dime before he rode off, and later my great-grandmother told them he was John Wesley Hardin. They both kept the coins long as they lived. But John Wesley didn't live here; he just had lots of kinfolk here and was hiding out amongst them for something he'd done elsewhere.

I did know one feller that had killed three men, though, but he was an exception. Bud Knolles, it was. He killed his first one up at Batson during the oil boom, but there was so many killed up there that if it wasn't a plain case of murder, the authorities didn't even arrest them for it. That's what happened to Bud.

The next one he killed was when they was building the Missouri Pacific railroad from Beaumont to Houston. Him and another muleskinner got in a argument, and that evening after they come in and tended to their teams, they each got a singletree and got after each other. Bud got beat up some but finally split the feller's head open and then finished him off on the ground. They took that one to the grand jury, but they no-billed him on self-defense.

The third one was at Liberty. Him and somebody—I can't remember his name right off—had a falling out at a saloon and just fell out in the street with their pocket knives and cut each other down and then laid side by side and kept cutting til they was drug apart. Bud finally got over it, but the other feller died. They no-billed him on that'un, too.

Well, after that lots of folks was skeered of Bud, and he knowed it and got pretty overbearing, 'specially when he'd had a few drinks. People would get out of his way and leave him alone all they could and try to get along any way they could, and he just got worse and worse.

Well, he come to town one day and hit several saloons and was coming out of one just as old Cap'n Nance was going in, and Bud just pushed the old man down on the porch and told him to get the hell out of the way and went on.

Now, if there ever was a mild man, it was the old captain. He'd fought from start to finish in the Civil War, and when he come back, he bought a place a mile or two out of town and settled down to minding his own business and leaving other folks alone, unless he was needed. He'd got too old to farm— he was ever' bit of eighty—but he'd walk into town ever' day, get the mail and one drink, and go back home. That's what he done after Bud pushed him down. Got his drink and went home.

Well, sir, I heard he got some water and cooled awhile and then took a bucket and some other things and went out next to the road and set down on the bucket in a little patch of brush under a big tree. Directly he got up and cut a sprout and set back down and whittled on it while he was waiting.

Just before sundown he heard a horse coming and leaned forward and jobbed the stick in the ground. It was forked, and he laid his old double-barrel on it, and when Bud Knolles got close on the road as he was coming, the captain cut him half in two with one barrel, and when Bud's horse run off and the dust settled, he took his time and walked over and give him the other barrel.

I learnt two things out of that. One is that when they said Colonel Colt made all men equal, they didn't give near enough credit to Mr. Remington's ole double-barrels, and the other'n was that old folks don't like to be pushed around any more than young ones do.

THE SAD IRONS

★

Robert A. Caro

B<small>UT THE HARDNESS OF THE FARMER'S LIFE PALED BESIDE</small>
the hardness of his wife's.

Without electricity, even boiling water was work.

Anything which required the use of water was work. Windmills (which could, acting like a pump, bring water out of a well into a storage tank) were very rare in the Hill Country; their cost—almost $400 in 1937—was out of the reach of most families in that cash-poor region, and the few that had been built proved of little use in a region where winds were always uncertain and, during a drought, non-existent, for days, or weeks, on end. And without electricity to work a pump, there was only one way to obtain water: by hand.

The source of water could be either a stream or a well. If the source was a stream, water had to be carried from it to the house, and since, in a country subject to constant flooding, houses were built well away from the streams, it had to be carried a long way. If the source was a well, it had to be lifted to the surface—a bucket at a time. It had to be lifted quite a long way: while the average depth of a well was about fifty feet in the valleys of the Hill Country, in the hills it was a hundred feet or more.

And so much water was needed! A federal study of nearly half a million farm families even then being conducted would show that, on the average, a person living on a farm used 40 gallons of water every day. Since the average farm family was five persons, the family used 200 gallons, or four-fifths of a ton, of water each day—73,000 gallons, or almost 300 tons, in a year. The study showed that, on the average, the well was located 253 feet from the house—and that to pump by hand and carry to the house 73,000 gallons of water a year would require someone to put in during that year 63 eight-hour days, and walk 1,750 miles.

A farmer would do as much of this pumping and hauling as possible himself, and try to have his sons do as much of the rest as possible (it was Lyndon Johnson's adamant refusal to help his mother with the pumping and hauling that touched off the most bitter of the flare-ups with his father during his youth). As soon as a Hill Country youth got big enough to carry the water buckets (which held about four gallons, or thirty-two pounds, of water apiece), he was assigned the job of filling his mother's wash pots before he left for school or the field. Curtis Cox still recalls today that from the age of nine or ten, he would, every morning throughout the rest of his boyhood, make about seven trips between his house and the well, which were about 300 feet apart, on each of these trips carrying two large buckets, or more than sixty pounds, of water. "I felt tired," he says. "It was a lot of water." But the water the children carried would be used up long before noon, and the children would be away—at school or in the fields—and most of the hauling of water was, therefore, done by women. "I would," recalls Curtis' mother, Mary Cox, "have to get it, too—more than once a day, more than twice; oh, I don't know how many times. I needed water to wash my floors, water to wash my clothes, water to cook. . . . It was hard work. I was always packing [carrying] water." Carrying it—after she had wrestled off the heavy wooden lid which kept the rats and squirrels out of the well; after she had cranked the bucket up to the surface (and cranking—lifting thirty pounds fifty feet or more—was very hard for most women even with a pulley; most would pull the rope hand over hand, as if they were climbing it, to get their body weight into the effort; they couldn't do it with their arms alone). Some Hill Country women make wry jokes about getting water. Says Mrs. Brian Smith of Blanco: "Yes, we had running water. I always said we had running water because I grabbed those two buckets up and ran the two hundred yards to the house with them." But the joking fades away as the memories sharpen. An interviewer from the city is struck by the fact that Hill Country women of the older generation are noticeably stooped, much more so than city women of the same age. Without his asking for an explanation, it is given to him. More than once, and more than twice, a stooped and bent Hill Country farm wife says, "You see how round-shouldered I am? Well, that's from hauling the water." And, she will often add, "I was round-shouldered like this well before my time, when I was still a young woman. My back got bent from hauling the water, and it got bent when I was still young."

The Hill Country farm wife had to haul water, and she had to haul wood.

Because there was no electricity, Hill Country stoves were wood stoves. The spread of the cedar brakes had given the area a plentiful supply of wood, but cedar seared bone-dry by the Hill Country sun burned so fast that the stoves seemed to devour it. A farmer would try to keep a supply of wood in the house, or, if he had sons old enough, would assign the task to them. (Lyndon Johnson's refusal to chop wood for his mother was another source of the tension between him and Sam.) They would cut down the trees, and chop them into four-foot lengths that could be stacked in cords. When wood was needed in the house, they would cut it into shorter lengths and split the pieces so they could fit into the stoves. But as with the water, these chores often fell to the women.

The necessity of hauling the wood was not, however, the principal reason so many farm wives hated their wood stoves. In part, they hated these stoves because they were so hard to "start up." The damper that opened into the firebox created only a small draft even on a breezy day, and on a windless day, there was no draft—because there was no electricity, of course, there was no fan to move the air in the kitchen—and a fire would flicker out time after time. "With an electric stove, you just turn on a switch and you have heat," says Lucille O'Donnell, but with a wood stove, a woman might have to stuff kindling and wood into the firebox over and over again. And even after the fire was lit, the stove "didn't heat up in a minute, you know," Lucille O'Donnell says—it might in fact take an hour. In part, farm wives hated wood stoves because they were so dirty, because the smoke from the wood blackened walls and ceilings, and ashes were always escaping through the grating, and the ash box had to be emptied twice a day—a dirty job and dirtier if, while the ashes were being carried outside, a gust of wind scattered them around inside the house. They hated the stoves because they could not be left unattended. Without devices to regulate the heat and keep the temperature steady, when the stove was being used for baking or some other cooking in which an even temperature was important, a woman would have to keep a constant watch on the fire, thrusting logs—or corncobs, which ignited quickly—into the firebox every time the heat slackened.

Most of all, they hated them because they were so hot.

When the big iron stove was lit, logs blazing in its firebox, flames licking at the gratings that held the pots, the whole huge mass of metal so hot that it was almost glowing, the air in the kitchen shimmered with the heat pouring out of it. In the Winter the heat was welcome, and in Spring and Fall it was bearable, but in the Hill Country, Summer would often last five months. Some time in June the temperature might climb to near ninety degrees, and would stay there, day after day, week after week, through the end of September. Day after day, week after week, the sky would be mostly empty, without a cloud as a shield from the blazing sun that beat down on the Hill Country, and on the sheet-iron or corrugated tin roofs of the boxlike kitchens in the little dog-run homes that dotted its hills and valleys. No matter how hot the day, the stove had to be lit much of the time, because it had to be lit not only for meals but for baking; Hill Country wives, unable to afford store-bought bread, baked their own, an all-day task. (As Mrs. O'Donnell points out, "We didn't have refrigerators, you know, and without refrigerators, you just about have to start every meal from scratch.") In the Hill Country, moreover, Summer was harvest time, when a farm wife would have to cook not just for her family but for a harvesting crew—twenty or thirty men, who, working from sun to sun, expected three meals a day.

Harvest time, and canning time.

In the Hill Country, canning was required for a family's very survival. Too poor to buy food, most Hill Country families lived through the Winter largely on the vegetables and fruit picked in the Summer and preserved in jars.

Since—because there was no electricity—there were no refrigerators in the Hill Country, vegetables or fruit had to be canned the very day they came ripe. And, from June through September, something was coming ripe almost every day, it seemed; on a single peach tree, the fruit on different branches would come ripe on different days. In a single orchard, the peaches might be reaching ripeness over a span as long as two weeks; "You'd be in the kitchen with the peaches for two weeks," Hill Country wives recall. And after the peaches, the strawberries would begin coming ripe, and then the gooseberries, and then the blueberries. The tomatoes would become ripe before the okra, the okra before the zucchini, the zucchini before the corn. So the canning would go on with only brief intervals—all Summer.

Canning required constant attendance on the stove. Since boiling water was essential, the fire in the stove had to be kept roaring hot, so logs had to be continually put into the firebox. At least twice during a day's canning, moreover—probably three or four times—a woman would have to empty the ash container, which meant wrestling the heavy, unwieldy device out from under the firebox. And when the housewife wasn't bending down to the flames, she was standing over them. In canning fruit, for example, first sugar was dropped into the huge iron canning pot, and watched carefully and stirred constantly, so that it would not become lumpy, until it was completely dissolved. Then the fruit—perhaps peaches, which would have been peeled earlier—was put in the pot, and boiled until it turned into a soft and mushy jam that would be packed into jars (which would have been boiling—to sterilize them—in another pot) and sealed with wax. Boiling the peaches would take more than an hour, and during that time they had to be stirred constantly so that they would not stick to the pot. And when one load of peaches was finished, another load would be put in, and another. Canning was an all-day job. So when a woman was canning, she would have to spend all day in a little room with a tin or sheet-iron roof on which a blazing sun was beating down without mercy, standing in front of the iron stove and the wood fire within it. And every time the heat in that stove died down even a bit, she would have to make it hotter again.

"You'd have to can in the Summer when it was hot," says Kitty Clyde Ross Leonard, who had been Johnson's first girlfriend. "You'd have to cook for hours. Oh, that was a terrible thing. You wore as little as you could. I wore loose clothing so that it wouldn't stick to me. But the perspiration would just pour down my face. I remember the perspiration pouring down my mother's face, and when I grew up and had my own family, it poured down mine. That stove was so hot. But you had to stir, especially when you were making jelly. So you had to stand over that stove." Says Bernice Snodgrass of Wimberley: "You got so hot that you couldn't stay in the house. You ran out and sat under the trees. I couldn't stand it to stay in the house. Terrible. Really terrible. But you couldn't stay out of the house long. You had to stir. You had to watch the fire. So you had to go back into the house."

And there was no respite. If a bunch of peaches came ripe a certain day, that was the day they had to be canned—no matter how the housewife might feel that day. Because in that fierce Hill Country heat, fruit and vegetables spoiled very quickly. And once the canning process was begun, it could not stop. "If you peeled six dozen peaches, and then, later that day, you felt sick," you couldn't stop, says Gay Harris. "Because you can't can something if it's rotten. The job has to be done the same day, no matter what." Sick or not, in the Hill Country, when it was time to can, a woman canned, standing hour after hour, trapped between a blazing sun and a blazing wood fire. "We had no choice, you see," Mrs. Harris says.

EVERY WEEK, EVERY WEEK ALL YEAR LONG—EVERY WEEK WITH-out fail—there was washday.

The wash was done outside. A huge vat of boiling water would be suspended over a larger, roaring fire and near it three large "Number Three" zinc washtubs and a dishpan would be placed on a bench.

The clothes would be scrubbed in the first of the zinc tubs, scrubbed on a washboard by a woman bending over the tub. The soap, since she couldn't afford store-bought soap, was soap she had made from lye, soap that was not very effective, and the water was hard. Getting farm dirt out of clothes required hard scrubbing.

Then the farm wife would wring out each piece of clothing to remove from it as much as possible of the dirty water, and put it in the big vat of boiling water. Since the scrubbing would not have removed all of the dirt, she would try to get the rest out by "punching" the clothes in the vat—standing over the boiling water and using a wooden paddle or, more often, a broomstick, to stir the clothes and swish them through the water and press them against the bottom or sides, moving the broom handle up and down and around as hard as she could for

ten or fifteen minutes in a human imitation of the agitator of an automatic—electric—washing machine.

The next step was to transfer the clothes from the boiling water to
the second of the three zinc washtubs: the "rinse tub." The clothes
were lifted out of the big vat on the end of the broomstick, and held
up on the end of the stick for a few minutes while the dirty water
dripped out.

When the clothes were in the rinse tub, the woman bent over the
tub and rinsed them, by swishing each individual item through the
water. Then she wrung out the clothes, to get as much of the dirty
water out as possible, and placed the clothes in the third tub, which
contained bluing, and swished them around in *it*—this time to get the
bluing all through the garment and make it white—and then repeated
the same movements in the dishpan, which was filled with starch.

At this point, one load of wash would be done. A week's wash took
at least four loads: one of sheets, one of shirts and other white clothing, one of colored clothes and one of dish towels. But for the typical,
large, Hill Country farm family, two loads of each of these categories
would be required, so the procedure would have to be repeated eight
times.

For each load, moreover, the water in each of the three washtubs
would have to be changed. A washtub held about eight gallons. Since
the water had to be warm, the woman would fill each tub half with
boiling water from the big pot and half with cold water. She did the
filling with a bucket which held three or four gallons—twenty-five or
thirty pounds. For the first load or two of wash, the water would have
been provided by her husband or her sons. But after this water had
been used up, part of washday was walking—over and over—that long
walk to the spring or well, hauling up the water, hand over laborious
hand, and carrying those heavy buckets back. Another part of washday
was also a physical effort: the "punching" of the clothes in the big vat.
"You had to do it as hard as you could—swish those clothes around
and around and around. They never seemed to get clean. And those

clothes were heavy in the water, and it was hot outside, and you'd be standing over that boiling water and that big fire—you felt like you were being roasted alive." Lifting the clothes out of the vat was an effort, too. A dripping mass of soggy clothes was heavy, and it felt heavier when it had to be lifted out of that vat and held up for minutes at a time so that the dirty water could drip out, and then swung over to the rinsing tub. Soon, if her children weren't around to hear her, a woman would be grunting with the effort. Even the wringing was, after a few hours, an effort. "I mean, wringing clothes might not seem hard," Mrs. Harris says. "But you have to wring every piece so many times— you wring it after you take it out of the scrub tub, and you wring it after you take it out of the rinse tub, and after you take it out of the bluing. Your arms got tired." And her hands—from scrubbing with lye soap and wringing—were raw and swollen. Of course, there was also the bending—hours of bending—over the rub boards. "By the time you got done washing, your back was broke," Ava Cox says. "I'll tell you— of the things of my life that I will never forget, I will never forget how much my back hurt on washdays." Hauling the water, scrubbing, punching, rinsing: a Hill Country farm wife did this for hours on end—while a city wife did it by pressing the button on her electric washing machine.

WASHDAY WAS MONDAY. TODAY WAS FOR IRONING.

Says Mary Cox, in words echoed by all elderly Hill Country farm wives: "Washing was hard work, but ironing was the worst. Nothing could ever be as hard as ironing."

The Department of Agriculture finds that "Young women today are not aware of the origin of the word 'iron,' as they press clothes with lightweight appliances of aluminum or hollow stainless steel." In the Hill Country, in the 1930s an iron was *iron*—a six- or seven-pound wedge of iron. The irons used in the Hill Country had to be heated on the wood stove, and they would retain their heat for only a few minutes—a man's shirt generally required two irons; a farm wife would own three or four of them, so that several could be heating while one was working. An iron with a wooden handle cost two dollars more than one without the handle, so Hill Country wives did their weekly loads of ironing—huge loads because, as Mary Cox puts it, "in those days you were expected to starch and iron almost everything"—with irons without handles. They would either transfer a separate wooden handle from one iron to another, or they would protect their hands with a thick potholder.

Since burning wood generates soot, the irons became dirty as they sat heating on the stove. Or, if any moisture was left on an iron from the sprinkled clothes on which it had just been used, even the thinnest smoke from the stove created a muddy film on the bottom. The irons had to be cleaned frequently, therefore, by scrubbing them with a rag that had been dipped in salt, and if the soot was too thick, they had to be sanded and scraped. And no matter how carefully you checked the bottom of the irons, and sanded and scraped them, there would often remain some little spot of soot—as you would discover when you rubbed it over a clean white shirt or dress. Then you had to wash that item of clothing over again.

Nevertheless, the irons would burn a woman's hand. The wooden handle or the potholder would slip, and she would have searing metal against her flesh; by noon, she might have blister atop blister—on hands that had to handle the rag that had been dipped in salt. Ironing always took a full day—often it went on into Tuesday evening—and a full day of lifting and carrying six- or seven-pound loads was hard on even these hardy Hill Country women. "It would hurt so bad between the shoulders," Elsie Beck remembers. But again the worst aspect of ironing was the heat. On ironing day, a fire would have to be blazing in the wood stove all day, filling the kitchen, hour after hour, with heat and smoke. Ironing had to be done not only in the Winter but in the Summer—when the temperature outside the kitchen might be ninety or ninety-five or one hundred, and inside the kitchen would be con-

siderably higher, and because there was no electricity, there was no fan
to so much as stir the air. In a speech in Congress some years later,
Representative John E. Rankin described the "drudgery" a typical farm
wife endured, "burning up in a hot kitchen and bowing down over the
washtub or boiling the clothes over a flaming fire in the summer heat."
He himself remembered, he said, "seeing his mother lean over that hot
iron hour after hour until it seemed she was tired enough to drop."
Rankin was from Mississippi, but his description would have been
familiar to the mothers of the Edwards Plateau. The women of the Hill
Country never called the instruments they used every Tuesday "irons,"
they called them "sad irons."

Washing, ironing—those were chores that were performed every
week. Then, of course, there were special occasions—harvest time
and threshing time, when a woman had to cook not just for her family
but for a crew of twenty or thirty men; the shearing, when, because
there was no electricity and her husband had to work the shears, she
had to crank the shearing machine, pedaling as if she were pumping a
bicycle up a steep hill, pedaling, with only brief pauses, hour after
hour; "He was always yelling 'Faster, faster,' Mrs. Walter Yett of Blanco
recalls. "I could hardly get up the next morning, I was so tired after
that." Washing, ironing, cooking, canning, shearing, helping with the
plowing and the picking and the sowing, and, every day, carrying the
water and the wood, and because there was no electricity, having to do
everything by hand by the same methods that had been employed by
her mother and grandmother and great-great-great-grandmother
before her—"They wear these farm women out pretty fast," wrote one
observer. In the Hill Country, as many outside observers noted, the
one almost universal characteristic of the women was that they were
worn out before their time, that they were old beyond their years, old
at forty, old at thirty-five, bent and stooped and tired.

A Hill Country farm wife had to do her chores even if she was ill—
no matter how ill. Because Hill Country women were too poor to
afford proper medical care, they often suffered perineal tears in child-

birth. During the 1930s, the federal government sent physicians to examine a sampling of Hill Country women. The doctors found that, out of 275 women, 158 had perineal tears. Many of them, the team of gynecologists reported, were third-degree tears, "tears so bad that it is difficult to see how they stand on their feet." But they *were* standing on their feet, and doing all the chores that Hill Country wives had always done—hauling the water, hauling the wood, canning, washing, ironing, helping with the shearing, the plowing and the picking.

Because there was no electricity.

THE SAVIOUR OF THE BEES

Robert Flynn

T HE SUMMER I WAS THIRTEEN I WAS THE SAVIOUR OF THE bees. At least that's what I called myself. Dad called me his little farmer, especially when he was pleased with the way I did my chores. Mother called me "Granddaddy Longlegs" because I was always hanging around thinking, and because I was all arms and legs and tall like her side of the family. Dad was dark and thick-shouldered and stocky. Mother once bought him a pair of high heeled cowboy boots to make him look taller but Dad wouldn't wear them. Dad had once been a cowboy but said he had outgrown it.

It was the third summer in a row my mother had planned a trip we did not take. The first had been to Fort Worth so I could see the zoo, the second to Carlsbad so I could see the caverns, the third to Corpus Christi because Mother wanted me to see the ocean.

Mother made careful plans and enlisted my support. "Tell your father that the other children have all seen the zoo." "Tell your father that your teacher went to Carlsbad Caverns and said it was something you should see." "Tell your father that you'd do better in Geography if you could see the ocean." I told him but we never got caught up enough with the farm work to be able to go.

It was the summer Dad gave Mother a new pressure cooker for her birthday. Because of the war a lot of things were rationed, but we raised our own beef, pork, chickens, and had an orchard and a garden besides the field crops. The pressure cooker would make it easier for Mother to can fruits and vegetables for the winter. Dad said no matter what fool thing Roosevelt did we were self-sufficient.

Dad and I picked out the cooker and I distracted Mother while Dad hid it, and I placed it in the kitchen the night before her birthday, after he and Mother had gone to bed.

The morning of her birthday, Dad and I sat at the table passing looks, waiting to hear Mother's gasp of surprise when she discovered the cooker. I was trying not to laugh, and then Dad saw something that made his face change. I looked too. Mother was standing at the stove frying our eggs, and she was crying, the tears sizzling when they hit the hot skillet.

I thought Mother must be crying because Dad was sitting at the table in his low quarter shoes with no socks. Dad didn't wear socks in the summer time, not even to town, because they made his ankles hot. Mother said it made him look loose and spiritless. Mother was younger than Dad (she said he had married as an afterthought), and from the city where folks wore socks all year round and were Democrats.

"Why are you crying?" I asked her.

"It does seem to me that sometimes I could be something besides a farmhand," she said, speaking to Dad, not to me.

The wives of Dad's friends talked about how young and pretty Mother was, but Mother didn't feel pretty. "Do you think my face is getting leathery?" she asked me sometimes. "Do you think my hair looks tired?" Now I knew what the words meant. Her eyes were puffy, her dark hair was damp and stringy. I noticed how hot and red her hands were, and the little lines around her mouth, and the way her shoulders sagged making her neck look long. Mother felt old.

"Maybe if I were one of your cows you'd appreciate me," she said to Dad, looking at him now, her eyes hard and angry. "Maybe you'd do nice things for me."

Dad did do nice things for his cows, and he had the look he had when Beulah tried to hook him when he picked up her new calf. Beulah was his favorite cow, the one he bragged on, and he wasn't so much angry, because a man had to expect that kind of thing from a cow, as puzzled and disappointed that it was Beulah, after all he had done for her.

"We got the pressure cooker to make things better for you," Dad said. "The man said it would save you lots of time."

"Time is all I have. All I do is work so what am I saving time for?" Mother asked. "We never go anywhere. We never do anything." Tears were still rolling down her face and her mouth was pinched and ugly. "Did you ever think that I might like something pretty?" She put the plates of bacon and eggs before us and left the room.

I remembered then how carefully she had shown me the rings, bracelets, watches, earrings in the catalog. "When you get married," she said, "these are the kinds of things you should give your wife." But I wasn't even thinking about getting married, and I was impatient to show her the .22 rifle I wanted for my birthday.

After Mother went into her room, closing the door, Dad and I ate quickly, wanting to be out of the house, and knowing there was a lot of work to do before we ate again. "I don't know what she wants," Dad said, taking his hat from the nail beside the door before he left the house. "I gave her the prettiest place in the county."

It was the summer Dad began sleeping in my room because he had to be up early and Mother stayed up late reading books she checked out of the county library. They were romances and mysteries, mostly. She said it was to fill up all the time the pressure cooker saved her.

I thought Dad was trying to make up to Mother because he spent so much time in the fields I was sure we would get caught up with the farm work and go to Corpus Christi. The only time he came in the house was when it was time to eat or go to bed.

He and Mother didn't talk much at the table any more, and when they did I wished they didn't. "Do you think you might get through today in time for me to go to town and get groceries?" Mother asked one morning. Her face had that stiff, tight look that made her eyes and mouth look small. The only time she could get books from the library was when we went to town to get groceries.

"What do we need from town?" Dad asked. His face was swollen. Dad had a short, thick neck, and when he was mad he didn't seem to have any neck at all. Dad didn't like the idea that Mother needed something he couldn't provide.

"Salt and sugar if I'm going to do any canning with the pretty new pressure cooker you bought me."

I stayed away from the house as much as I could. When I finished my chores I went down to the corral and watched the bees trying to get water. I liked to watch the bees. They worked so hard. They had worn the opening to the hive smooth with their coming and going to the honeysuckle and lilac bushes Mother had planted to hide the wire fence that kept the chickens out of the yard. Mother said that people had to be removed from animals. "Decent distance," she called it.

I had never noticed how many bees drowned in the water tank. They scrambled around the sides of the tank, climbing over one another. When the cows stuck their muzzles in the water, the water came up over the bees and they floated around in little circles until they drowned. Wasps floated on top of the water like they thought they were gods.

One morning at the table I asked Dad why wasps floated while bees drowned. Dad knew everything about animals. He could just look at an animal and tell what was wrong with it and what it needed. "Bees have little hairs on their legs," he said. "That's how they gather pollen to make honey. The hairs break the surface tension of the water and they drown. Wasps don't have hairs because they don't make honey, so they can float."

"But that's not fair," I said, appalled that bees were doomed by the very thing that made them valuable, while wasps that did nothing but wound, floated on the water, safe because they didn't make honey or anything else that people could use. "Wasps don't do anything but make nests for themselves."

"Why did you have to tell him that?" Mother demanded. "You have to make everything so ugly."

Dad was not normally a violent man but he appeared about to explode. His neck had disappeared and his head was swollen. "Everything in life is not pretty," he said.

"When you're young it can be," Mother said. "For a little while."

Mother looked at me like she was going to read to me from the Bible. Mother didn't study the Bible the way some folks did, she read it for answers, the way others read the advice columns in the newspaper. And when she read it to me she took on a look that said, you don't have to understand this, you just have to believe that it is for the best.

"Jimmy," she said. Her voice was low and thoughtful, not the way she talked to Dad. "Jimmy, wouldn't you rather be a bee and make something beautiful like honey, even if it made you liable to drowning, than to be a wasp and be hated and feared by everybody?"

"What good is it telling him things like that?" Dad asked. "Bees don't have any choice in the matter, or wasps either."

"People do," Mother said. "We can choose whether we want to do something beautiful with our lives or just think of ourselves."

"Wasps make nests just like bees," Dad said, "and they defend them."

"They don't sacrifice their lives the way a bee does, because when a bee stings you it dies."

They had forgotten all about me and the bees, too. I slipped out of the house with Dad describing the difference between a bald, frayed-wing worker and a sleek and useless drone.

"I thought the drones were all males," Mother said.

I went down to the corral and dipped the bees out of the water. It wasn't fair that bees drowned and wasps floated, and the only thing I knew to do was put myself on the side of the bees.

I started making regular rounds each day, rescuing the bees, placing them on the corral fence to dry their wings, taking care not to be the cause of their self-destruction. It was frustrating saving the bees as they never seemed to learn. I took broken shingles from the barn and made little rafts for them to climb on while I was away at work. Sometimes I splashed water at the wasps trying to make them liable too, but they just flew away.

One day Mother came down to the tank and put her arm around me. She had on her Bible-reading face. "Jimmy, I'm going to leave your father," she said, "and I want you to go with me. Don't you want to go with me?"

She wanted me to look at her but I couldn't. I couldn't look at the house either because I knew Dad was watching. I just looked at the bees, drowning in the water.

"I don't want you to hate your father," she said. "He's a good man, he works hard, he loves this place. He likes plowing and taking care of the cattle. He doesn't want anything else. But there's so much more. Jimmy, if you stay here you'll be buried just like I am. You'll just be a farmhand taking care of his place, feeding his cattle, raising his crops. Come with me."

She waited for me to say something but I didn't. I couldn't. I couldn't get my breath.

"I'm going to the house to get my things," she said. "If you want to go with me, go to the car. Your father won't try to stop you."

I wasn't sure when she started to the house but I was sure when Dad was there beside me. I could feel him standing there, like at night when it was so dark I couldn't see the barn but I could feel it there, towering over me.

"I know your mother talked to you," he said, "but I don't want you to go. I don't want you to have hard feelings about your mother. She is a good woman and she loves you, but she doesn't love this place the way you and I do. She wants things for herself, things she can put back there in that room of hers with the big bed and the fancy dresser, and all her pretty things. I know she wants what she thinks is best for you, but she'll just smother you in prettiness."

They wanted me to choose, but I couldn't help one and hurt the other. After a while, Dad left too, went into the barn I guess. Then I heard Mother come out of the house and get in the car. I don't know what she was taking with her but it seemed like she slammed every door on the car. Then she got in and started it. I could hear the drone of the car for a long time after she left.

I thought about drowning myself in the tank. I thought about running away. I didn't know what to do. After a while Dad told me he had to go to town for a while and took the truck.

It was almost dark when he came back and I had already started the milking. "Your mother and I decided to stay together until you're grown," was all he said. Then I heard Mother drive in and slam all the car doors again, and go into the house and start cooking supper. It wasn't until we sat down at the table that I realized that Dad had put on socks before going to town.

Dad's face wasn't swollen but his head seemed sunk down into his shoulders so that he didn't have a neck. He looked pleased with himself and ashamed at the same time. Mother looked pretty. She looked like she felt pretty, and she kept pushing at her hair to put life in it.

We talked about Corpus Christi, and the ocean, and seeing sharks, and picking up sea shells. Supper seemed to last a long time as they kept talking and talking. Dad said, "Jimmy, go on to bed, you're about to fall out of your chair. I'm going to stay up for a while."

Mother said to Dad, "Why don't you sleep in my room and that way you won't wake Jimmy up when you get up in the morning."

I don't know what happened after that but we didn't go to Corpus Christi that summer. We didn't go to Grand Canyon the next summer either. Mother planned it and talked about it, and I drove a tractor all summer. Mother said I did the work of a man. Dad said he might as well sleep in my room since we both had to get up early, and since Mother stayed up late reading.

I guess the bees took care of themselves. I didn't have any time that summer to save them. And when Dad bought a new cook stove for Mother's birthday I didn't help him pick it out. I didn't help him hide it either.

THE SCHOOL BUS

✶

Mary Ladd Gavell

I T WAS THE YEAR THAT JANE QUIT WALKING THE MILE DOWN
the road to school every day and began riding a school bus
instead. This happened because the school district she lived in
annexed the Rancho Casa Blanca district. The two teachers who had
taught at the Rancho went away, and the little schoolhouse was
boarded up, its windows looking blind the way everybody's windows
did late in August when the radio said that a hurricane was sweeping
up the Gulf of Mexico.

So that fall a great orange school bus went trundling out down the
dusty road every day ten or fifteen miles to the Rancho country and
brought in the children, giggling and squirming and screaming, and yet
already tired when they got to school at eight-forty-five, because most
of them had walked a long way at daybreak to get to the bus line.

"There's no reason," Jane's mother had said, a week or so before
school opened, "why, if there's room enough, Jane shouldn't ride in

with the school bus, too, even if they did get it for the Rancho children." So Jane's father, who was on the school board, asked the superintendent, who was feeling good with the new importance of being
superintendent to two school districts instead of one; and he said sure,
Jane could ride on the school bus if she wanted. Of course she'd have
to be ready in the mornings and out on the right-hand side of the road,
the school bus didn't wait on anyone. He said that if many children
had lived, like Jane, only a mile or so from school in the Rancho direction there wouldn't have been room, but since there was just Jane it
would be all right.

Jane felt a little funny about riding on the school bus. She didn't
know any of the people from the Rancho country, but her father and
her older brother, Edward, sometimes mentioned them, and last year
there had been a shooting out there that had even got into the Corpus
Christi *Caller-Times*. She knew that some of them didn't want to ride
the school bus in to the bigger school; her father said several of the
families had been right ornery about it, but enough of them had finally
come around so that the vote had carried. Her father said that the
Rancho people were mostly pretty trashy and that some of the families
had lice and sore-eyes and things like that, and so it would probably
be best for her not to hang herself around their necks, as he put it.

She had seen where they came from. Sometimes in the early summer her father would say on a Sunday afternoon, "Mom, would you
like to drive out west and look at the crops?" And Jane and her mother
would tie something around their heads, because of the strong wind
that always blew off the gulf, and go driving in the car out to the Rancho country, going slow and staring out at other people's cows and gazing critically down the pivoting rows of other people's cotton, and
craning curiously at the pastures of Rhodes grass, because the seed
had come from Africa, and going faster past the parts that were just
miles and miles of prairie.

Jane had seen the Rancho country then. The great spreadeagle
electric poles stopped when you got out there, and the dirt road got

narrower and more crooked, and the scattered houses got smaller and smaller and were really just little boxes, built with the boards going up and down. Great families of thin noisy children spilled out of them, and gray ragged clothes flapped on the clothesline beside them. Sometimes they passed a ranch boss's house, and it was a little better and might even be painted and have curtains, and sometimes they passed a whole row of Mexican houses, with just open places for doors and banty chickens wandering in and out, and roofs patched with cans spread out and nailed down. Sometimes great pieces of dried goat meat, almost black with flies, and bunches of drying peppers and gourds would be hanging by the door. And in the dirt yards would be fires and pots where the beans were cooking, and old, old Mexican women, bent over and with black shawls over their heads, would be watching and stirring slowly. And the thin hound dogs that stood around by the doorway would be Mexican dogs—you could tell.

Sometimes they drove past smelly, miry corrals, with thin sway-backed cows standing around in them, and the great wind blew the smell right into the car. Sometimes they passed women working in the fields, even though it was Sunday, and sometimes they passed men along the road who were great and hairy and freckled and red-faced and who seemed always to be shouting as they drove by, and who had bowlegs and wore great boots and spurs. And Jane looked, and saw that the thin horses' sides were scarred and cut.

When they got home, her father would say, "Well, Mom, I don't know that I saw any cotton any prettier than ours on the east twenty." And her mother would say yes, she hadn't realized how good it was.

The cotton season was short that summer, and so the beginning of school came early. In the mornings Jane walked down the big front steps and the weedy flagstone walk and through the salt cedar trees to the road to wait for the bus, feeling conscious of her new school shoes and her new tablet and her long pencils. Somehow, it was painful to stand there watching the great orange bus that at first was just a little orange speck far across the flat prairie and then grew bigger and bigger, watching and knowing that it would stop for her and that the big door would open for her and that she would step up into it with dozens of eyes looking just at her.

She noticed, the first days, that the shrill laughing and talking stopped when she got in. At first nobody said anything at all, and then later someone would occasionally say something to her that was neither friendly or unfriendly, some statement that left her uncomfortable and, somehow, apologetic. Once a thin little girl whose name was Bessie looked at Jane's fresh starched dress and said sharply, "Your mama washed that dress yesterday. I seen it on the line yesterday afternoon."

She was afraid of them, and it was days before she looked at them enough to see what they looked like, and then she saw that most of them were freckled fair children with dirt under their fingernails and streaky yellow hair that had been cut at home with jags and dips in it, with bare tough feet and stocky, pasty-fleshed, unclean arms and legs with thick blond hairs on them. Their teeth were like old men's, and sometimes they had great ugly scabs on their faces, and Jane shrank from them a little.

They usually sat toward the front, and in back of them in a little huddled knot sat the Mexican children, small, shrinking, afraid. They looked cold, even though it was still hot in September; Jane would look at them sometimes and be surprised to see that their dark unwashed skins had the look of gooseflesh about them. They sat very still, and their faces never seemed to change, but their black eyes, looking out from the ancient little faces with an intense, opaque, Indian look, followed what the blond children did, watched them talk together, watched them pinch each other and slap each other, watched them shout and scuffle and laugh uproariously.

And then one afternoon, going home, a little girl turned on Jane and said, "I guess you make good grades."

"Of course she does, her father's on the school board," the girl across the aisle said. Jane looked at them and tried to smile, but nobody smiled back, and she saw that their faces were suddenly angry and that their pale mouths were hard.

The thin little girl named Bessie, who was sitting beside her, scornfully flipped the edge of Jane's skirt, bright beside all the faded ones, and cried, "It's a Mexican dress, with them bright checks! I bet your mama got it at Garcia's!"

Jane looked from one to another and saw that more and more of the faces were turning to her. The boys, who were sitting together, were beginning to stop their own intimate laughing and were turning, leaning forward, interested, eager, their pasty faces more alive than usual. And the little knot of strange grave black eyes were looking toward her, too, silently watching. The driver's back was big, solid, blue denim, uninterested.

"Did you ever pick cotton?" someone shouted. "I bet anything you never picked cotton at all." "*I* wouldn't ride a school bus if I lived just a mile from town, I walk that much just to get to the school bus," several of them seemed to be saying. Their voices were louder and louder, they were crowding toward her, and their freckled, scabbed faces were pushing closer and closer to hers, and the smell of them pressed in upon her. The driver's back shifted a little in the seat; skillfully he steered the bus, following the deep ruts in the road worn since the last rain. *"You're no better than anybody else,"* everybody in the bus seemed to be shouting at her. *"Did you ever milk a cow? . . . did you ever pick cotton?"*

The bus was stopping; they were even with her house. She ran, the voices staying in her ears so that she did not know whether they had stopped or not. As she grabbed her lunch basket and books together more firmly, she looked back at the bus and saw, surprised, that the children were not looking at her anymore and that they had stopped shouting. They were looking through the salt cedars up the incline at the big white house, standing in the shady yard where the splashy pink and white oleanders and the ragged fig trees grew, at the bright white washing fluttering on the line and the plump Leghorn hens singing in the backyard, and at the great lawn of Bermuda pasture to the west of the house, where the fat cows were grazing and the calves were playing.

THE BORDER

from SOUTHWEST

★

John Houghton Allen

I N THE FIRST PLACE, YOU HAVE TO SEE THIS LITTLE CANTINA
TO believe it. It stands by the side of the dirt road that goes to
Zapata, on the Tex-Mex Railway, forty miles from the nearest
town in this lost world along the Mexican border. It is forty miles from
anywhere, unless you count the walled town that lies behind it, crumbling picturesquely in ruins a half mile away. It is just a little cantina,
a place of dubious cheer in a hard country.

For this is hard country, brush country, mean country, heartbreak
country. Ugly in summer, drought-stricken, dusty, glaring, but in winter it is hideous. In winter the bare trees, *gran'hena* and mesquite and
huisache that the rest of the seasons have a certain grace, these are
like a dead orchard. The brush lies all around the ruins of this walled
town of San Juan in a graveyard of gloom. The brush is like twisted
debris from a hurricane, it is like a bad dream. The nap is up, the

whole country seems to have been rubbed the wrong way. The brush lies all around like a dry jungle creeping.

The derricks don't add to the beauty of the landscape. This alone is reason enough for the suicides in the oilfields, it is too rank to look at, and the gringos can't take it. They aren't colonizers, anyway, and this is like a foreign country—you can't blame the poor devils, or their lonely wives. There is not a thing to do in this lonely land but drink and fornicate. The roughnecks say it is worse than Venezuela—it is intolerable, they might as well be exiles in this damned country. You agree with them, you drink beer with them, and beer is a melancholy drink, but there is no whiskey in this hypocritical land, only the boot-leg tequila that Margarita serves under the table. They don't even like the smell of it, so they drink the melancholy beer.

They are bilious in this sullen land, with the listless natives looking on without curiosity or intelligence, with the vague air of disappoint-ment, as if they had been waiting a long time, and now they are not bored with anything. The gringos squirm under the implacable stares, but they can't even stare back, because the Mexicans waited a long time to see the gringos, and now the Mexicans are disappointed. So we talk uneasily, self-conscious, of civilization and *white* women and of home with a glint in our eyes, as if this weren't a part of the United States, or some of us just drink morosely while the silent natives stare. It is more elegant to talk, though. The silence can get you down. And there is always that continual eavesdropping, the hollow laughter unuttered.

I know, because I go into the dim dirty cantinas myself, and these suddenly become forlorn places of cheer, I am reluctant to leave these shabby oases in this ragged land, and I want to stay and get drunk. The first thing you want to do when you hit a cantina in this country is to get drunk. There is something in the air. You are homesick with the roughnecks, and sometimes you can forget the hollowness, you can fend off the cry of desolation, the hunger and gripe that eat at your entrails, you can escape the endless purgatory of the southwest. You are in a country that doesn't belong to the gringo, and that the Mexicans don't seem to want after the gringo is through with it. And better men than you have felt this deadlock, the disintegration, and like going to pieces in this hollow dismal land—in fact, the better they are, the faster they go to seed. The only ones who aren't haywire are the morons, they just get louder.

The flies swarm around your beer, and you brush them out of the foam, but it tastes like the best beer you ever drank. It is hot, but it is rare. And a little peace comes as you warm your belly with the hot suds, and you sit and look outside at the twisted whispering debris of a landscape and you know Venezuela cannot be this bad, you wouldn't mind going to Venezuela.

The best way to see the southwest is through the bottom of a glass. You can take it, after half a dozen beers. You hang around the dim cantinas and actually put off going, lulled by the contagious general inertia and the biliousness; you get a glow and things look better after a peculiar fashion, of a sudden even the dull and degenerate natives seem friendly. You had 'em wrong all the time, they are just shy. You cling to them like long-lost friends, and if you were sober you would give them the back of your hand. You buy them a beer, and they smile, they come to life for an instant in this stagnant land, and forget to look sinister. Even these beggars seem to remember they once were people. They can't help it, if they are stupid. God knows what they are waiting for, but even the buzzards lurk in this country.

There is the damned whispering in the air. You feel you are about to be dry-gulched. Exiled, turned out to pasture, cut off from friends and family and whatever you regard as sweet and civilized. This is a cul-de-sac of a country, you look around and you will have something to write home about—even the rest of Texas looks down on it, and that's saying something. You drink the hot beer in the dark cantina, and when you go out to urinate you are blinded by the sun. You sit there and you get drunk, and suddenly you come face to face with somebody else's conscience hovering in the room. Or a lot of old sins you think you have forgotten begin to eat you alive. Maybe it is the staring, the eavesdropping that stirs the dregs, but whatever it is, you are momentarily looking at yourself in the abstract.

Fingers are pointing, and sometimes the nasty voices say *Dirty! Dirty!* And here you are, a pariah in a land of pariahs. The faces of animals remind you of people you know in the hick towns up the road, particularly the pigs and the bilious chickens, and you tell Margarita to shoo them back in the yard, they look too intelligent. And you'd like to have a woman. It is essentially a fearful land, a libidinous land. You can't turn over in bed in the morning, because you're rutting all the time. It is elementary country, raw and primitive, but at the same time, almost perverted—you live naked with it, and eventually, if you have any intelligence, you will be ridden through this hairy kingdom by the furies. And you know it, you take another beer, so the Jabberwock won't get you.

There is no placating the southwest. Every time you attempt to appease this evil land it tortures you, and it will destroy you sooner or later. It is ingrowing, cancerous, dog-eat-dog, mad and cowardly. Principally it is the damned brush, the dry jungle creeping, heart-rotten, that gets you down. You sit here stewing in your own juice, you put another nickel in the greasy juke box and play Mexican music so loud that you cannot think, and you gulp the warm beer and you spit out the door, or perhaps on the earth floor like the Mexicans. The Mexicans always spit eloquently. And while you are sitting thus, digesting the beer and the background, the panic seizes you. The little *frissons* of alarm crawl all over you like vermin, and suddenly you think, there is no going back. You are never going to get out of this hole. And the panic is so expressive that you get up in a hurry and you find yourself stumbling to your car, stinking drunk, heading for Laredo. You might even end up in a *congale*, if you can do any good. Anything, to kill the loneliness.

The secret to living in this inverted half-world is to learn how not to hate everybody in it, and yourself as well. The people actually spoil the landscape, bad as that is, but you can't blame the gringos because they sour and fester on the Mexican border—somebody told them they had a White Man's Burden to carry, that they ought to be ashamed. But they don't put their best foot forward, and they want to be forgiven everything, because they are Americans. They are usually gross Falstaffian fellows, but without humor, about their melting faces a petulant and perennial cast of grievance. They have black hairy noses sticking out of their pumpkin faces like the beaks of manta-rays. Little noses and little mouths, but Christ! they are loud. They are long-winded and loud, and they don't make the loneliness in this country any easier to bear, and the trouble is, they aren't any better than the Mexicans they despise.

The country is intolerable enough without them, but the rub is— they are your kind of people, mine. Salt of the earth, or they were, before they came to the southwest. This is what the southwest does to your kind of people, mine. Or maybe they can't make a living any-where else, and here they can be inconspicuous like the weeds and the cacti. Nothing seems to grow in this wasteland but the weeds and the cacti. And the putty faces, the constipated faces, spiteful faces, ruined faces, crybaby faces, mean faces everywhere, scowling in the sun, looking mad all day, dyspeptic—the housewives behind every screen-door like women in cribs—and these faces grow on you, they give you the creeps. These people would live on the wrong side of the track anywhere else, but here they are the Best People.

This is the habitat of the strong silent men of the west. They ride around in new Fords, even though they live in slummy towns and their children have pellagra. They wear boots with very high heels and never ride horses. They walk like fairies, wiggling their bottoms, strangely effeminate, but they think they are fine figures of men. They stand around on street corners with their hands in their pockets, saying hot-damn. They look vastly superior in the pool-hall or barbershop or the Manhattan Café. They clean their fingernails with a penknife, and pick their teeth elegantly with matches, and they talk like hog-callers, they make such a racket that your heart sinks utterly. As if they were afraid of not being heard in this hollow land, or that someone is about to call their bluff.

They've got you, coming and going. Every mother's son is good as you are, understand. If you don't speak to them you are stuck-up, and if you do, you are no better than they are. If they know you they patronize you with a heavy-handed stupid cunning, and they don't consider they have been treated fairly unless you lose money by trading with them. What it is, to be patronized by pariahs! You bend over backwards not to offend their exquisite sensibilities, but it is no use—you get your nose rubbed in the grievance of their inferiorities, anyway. If you mind your own business, they are amateur Texas Rangers. Every cinema in their towns is a horse-opera. At first you think they are crazy, but after a while you begin to look at them as if they were human—you listen to their incredible slander, their venomous drollery, their implacable spite, and you even try to laugh, but you gag first. It is too bad they didn't absorb some of the natural graces of the Mexicans in this bitter land, but to mention such a thing is enough to bring out the vigilantes. Not that the Mexicans today are any better than the gringos—both races make you want to go out and eat grass. The southwest is no place for an amateur to live, but if you live in this country it serves you right.

And I am bitter against the land and these people because I remember when it was a fine place to live. I sit here in dame Margarita's cantina, with the walled town of San Juan enchanted off in the twisted brush, and I discuss these things with the Mexican proprietor of the only store in that almost deserted village— the store was built of boxboards fifty years ago, and it has always been a curiosity in a town built of *caliche* blocks four feet square—and he is a fine old man; he used to be a friend of my father. He is very gracious and dignified, one of the Old Men, a type of Mexican that existed before the wrong kind of gringo came to this land. And there is real twist-tobacco and chili in garlands and *chorizo* in chains hanging from the rafters of his aromatic store, and for sale articles such as tapers and tinder-wicks and Mexican blankets, horsehair bridles, rawhide *riatas*, metates to grind corn, coffee mills and a complete line of the ancient paregorics. And this fantastic old man complains there is no market for such things, nowadays, we have come upon evil times. It was the same kind of stock his father carried, and it is good enough for him, but his customers are different. He shakes his head, and we sit smoking silently for the most part, peacefully during the siesta hour, the old man and I, sleepless ourselves in the glaring day, and I look out from the cool inside of the cantina and I find myself remembering. . . .

This isn't the country I knew as a boy. For a moment I am carried back, and I sit in this old man's store with my father—it was thirty years ago, but we talked to this same old man; he was just as ancient then, just as friendly. It was in a time before men were afraid to be friendly. He made a little ceremony of selling you anything. You were in his house, and he parted with each article almost reluctantly and for very little profit. Almost as if he were afraid of running out of stock, and not having anything to do. We remember those times together, the old Mexican politely and inaccurately, because he is very old, and it doesn't matter, anyway. And I can see through his eyes and my own memory this country as it used to be. This is like the return of the native, but all the nostalgia I feel is for the land I knew as a boy. Before the land had spoiled the people, and the people had spoiled the land.

It is used to be gentler, quieter, not so ugly. The villages were built of white-washed *caliche* and thatch and the country was open, without a tree for miles and grass up to a horse's belly. The *mogotes* were confined to the foothills, it was before the brush spread like leprosy over the prairies of this land. The rancheros used to ride the finest horses you ever saw, Spanish ponies, small animals with delicate bones and heads fine as sculpture, Arabians in little. You used to be able to buy them cheaper than cattle from the Viscayas and Benavides, and pretty little mules that were gallant and fast. They were very trim mules, and they were used with bells on their harness, and you could hear them coming in over the road to San Juan. The cattle were Chihuahuas, long-horned, all hide and bone. There were herds of antelope on the prairies. Thirty thousand people lived in what is now the ghost-town of Guerrero—it was before the railway came to Rio Grande—but now all that is left of that great town, that was once as important as Laredo, are a few ornate broken doorways and windows in the stone houses, though the poets say of a moonlit night in Guerrero you can still hear the caravans of Spanish mules clattering down the cobbled street enroute to San Antonio de Bexar.

The old man and I talk of these pleasant things that were, and the Texas-Mexican Railway, that runs between Corpus Christi and Laredo, bankrupt and lame and undefeated, in the red but valiantly holding its charter, this shoves a bedraggled freight train into the weird landscape that stalls a minute at the sentry-box station and takes on water and pushes into the wilderness of brush, its cars empty. There are no cattle for market this time of year, and the oil goes by pipeline. Sometimes there are excursion trains to Corpus Christi, and when the *aguadas* are dry, every summer in fact, the tank cars bring in drinking water to San Juan.

And we talk of other things, of fiestas and more of the elegant Spanish ponies, and the gracious people who used to live in such places as Aguilares and Randado and Zapata, and of one village I remember in particular—that has been razed now to provide surface for the county roads—like a dim dream that has never returned, all whitewashed *caliche* and thatch, that stood by a great lake of water in this arid land, smothered in huisache groves, and that belonged to no land and in no time and which is now gone forever. There was never anything so beautiful as this village in a barren land, you rode out of the brush from the foothills and suddenly you were upon it, and it was so beautiful it made your heart ache, it was like something you had been looking for all of your life. And they sold all the *caliche* buildings to surface the county roads.

You came out of the brush upon it, after a long horseback ride, and you asked why nobody had ever told you of such a place. It was a little walled town like San Juan, and it was built on the drybed of the Baluarte, and it left an echo in the senses, though I can't even remember its name.

THE HAMMON AND THE BEANS

────── ✭ ──────

Américo Paredes

ONCE WE LIVED IN ONE OF MY GRANDFATHER'S HOUSES near Fort Jones. It was just a block from the parade grounds, a big frame house painted a dirty yellow. My mother hated it, especially because of the pigeons that cooed all day about the eaves. They had fleas, she said. But it was a quiet neighborhood at least, too far from the center of town for automobiles and too near for musical, night-roaming drunks.

At this time Jonesville-on-the-Grande was not the thriving little city that it is today. We told off our days by the routine on the post. At six sharp the flag was raised on the parade grounds to the cackling of the bugles, and a field piece thundered out a salute. The sound of the shot bounced away through the morning mist until its echoes worked their way into every corner of town. Jonesville-on-the-Grande woke to the cannon's roar, as if to battle, and the day began.

At eight the whistle from the post laundry sent us children off to school. The whole town stopped for lunch with the noon whistle, and after lunch everybody went back to work when the post laundry said that it was one o'clock, except for those who could afford to be old-fashioned and took the siesta. The post was the town's clock, you might have said, or like some insistent elder person who was always there to tell you it was time.

At six the flag came down, and we went to watch through the high wire fence that divided the post from the town. Sometimes we joined in the ceremony, standing at salute until the sound of the cannon made us jump. That must have been when we had just studied about George Washington in school, or recited "The Song of Marion's Men" about Marion the Fox and the British cavalry that chased him up and down the broad Santee. But at other times we stuck out our tongues and jeered at the soldiers. Perhaps the night before we had hung at the edges of a group of old men and listened to tales about Aniceto Pizaña and the "border troubles," as the local paper still called them when it referred to them gingerly in passing.

It was because of the border troubles, ten years or so before, that the soldiers had come back to old Fort Jones. But we did not hate them for that; we admired them even, at least sometimes. But when we were thinking about the border troubles instead of Marion the Fox, we hooted them and the flag they were lowering, which for the moment was theirs alone, just as we would have jeered an opposing ball team, in a friendly sort of way. On these occasions even Chonita would join in the mockery, though she usually ran home at the stroke of six. But whether we taunted or saluted, the distant men in khaki uniforms went about their motions without noticing us at all.

The last word from the post came in the night when a distant bugle blew. At nine it was all right because all the lights were on. But sometimes I heard it at eleven when everything was dark and still, and it made me feel that I was all alone in the world. I would even doubt that I was me, and that put me in such a fright that I felt like yelling out just to make sure I was really there. But next morning the sun shone and life began all over again, with its whistles and cannon shots and bugles blowing. And so we lived, we and the post, side by side with the wire fence in between.

The wandering soldiers whom the bugle called home at night did not wander in our neighborhood, and none of us ever went into Fort Jones. None except Chonita. Every evening when the flag came down she would leave off playing and go down towards what was known as the "lower" gate of the post, the one that opened not on main street but against the poorest part of town. She went into the grounds and to the mess halls and pressed her nose against the screens and watched the soldiers eat. They sat at long tables calling to each other through food-stuffed mouths.

"Hey bud, pass the coffee!"

"Give me the ham!"

"Yeah, give me the beans!"

After the soldiers were through, the cooks came out and scolded Chonita, and then they gave her packages with things to eat.

Chonita's mother did our washing, in gratefulness—as my mother put it—for the use of a vacant lot of my grandfather's which was a couple of blocks down the street. On the lot was an old one-room shack which had been a shed long ago, and this Chonita's father had patched up with flattened-out pieces of tin. He was a laborer. Ever since the end of the border troubles there had been a development boom in the Valley, and Chonita's father was getting his share of the good times. Clearing brush and building irrigation ditches, he sometimes pulled down as much as six dollars a week. He drank a good deal of it up, it was true. But corn was just a few cents a bushel in those days. He was the breadwinner, you might say, while Chonita furnished the luxuries.

Chonita was a poet too. I had just moved into the neighborhood when a boy came up to me and said, "Come on! Let's go hear Chonita make a speech."

She was already on top of the alley fence when we got there, a scrawny little girl of about nine, her bare dirty feet clinging to the fence almost like hands. A dozen other kids were there below her, waiting. Some were boys I knew at school; five or six were her younger brothers and sisters.

"Speech! Speech!" they all cried. "Let Chonita make a speech! Talk in English, Chonita!"

They were grinning and nudging each other except for her brothers and sisters, who looked up at her with proud serious faces. She gazed out beyond us all with a grand, distant air and then she spoke.

"Give me the hammon and the beans!" she yelled. "Give me the hammon and the beans!"

She leaped off the fence and everybody cheered and told her how good it was and how she could talk English better than the teachers at the grammar school.

I thought it was a pretty poor joke. Every evening almost, they would make her get up on the fence and yell, "Give me the hammon and the beans!" And everybody would cheer and make her think she was talking English. As for me, I would wait there until she got it over with so we could play at something else. I wondered how long it would be before they got tired of it all. I never did find out because just about that time I got the chills and fever, and when I got up and around, Chonita wasn't there anymore.

In later years I thought of her a lot, especially during the thirties when I was growing up. Those years would have been just made for her. Many's the time I have seen her in my mind's eye, in the picket lines demanding not bread, not cake, but the hammon and the beans. But it didn't work out that way.

One night Doctor Zapata came into our kitchen through the back door. He set his bag on the table and said to my father, who had opened the door for him, "Well, she is dead."

My father flinched. "What was it?" he asked.

The doctor had gone to the window and he stood with his back to us, looking out toward the lights of Fort Jones. "Pneumonia, flu, malnutrition, worms, the evil eye," he said without turning around. "What the hell difference does it make?"

"I wish I had known how sick she was," my father said in a very mild tone. "Not that it's really my affair, but I wish I had."

The doctor snorted and shook his head.

My mother came in and I asked her who was dead. She told me. It made me feel strange but I did not cry. My mother put her arm around my shoulders. "She is in Heaven now," she said. "She is happy."

I shrugged her arm away and sat down in one of the kitchen chairs.

"They're like animals," the doctor was saying. He turned round suddenly and his eyes glistened in the light. "Do you know what that brute of a father was doing when I left? He was laughing! Drinking and laughing with his friends."

"There's no telling what the poor man feels," my mother said.

My father made a deprecatory gesture. "It wasn't his daughter, anyway."

"No?" the doctor said. He sounded interested.

"This is the woman's second husband," my father explained. "First one died before the girl was born, shot and hanged from a mesquite limb. He was working too close to the tracks the day the Olmito train was derailed."

"You know what?" the doctor said. "In classical times they did things better. Take Troy, for instance. After they stormed the city they grabbed the babies by the heels and dashed them against the wall. That was more humane."

My father smiled. "You sound very radical. You sound just like your relative down there in Morelos."

"No relative of mine," the doctor said. "I'm a conservative, the son of a conservative, and you know that I wouldn't be here except for that little detail."

"Habit," my father said. "Pure habit, pure tradition. You're a radical at heart."

"It depends on how you define radicalism," the doctor answered.

"People tend to use words too loosely. A dentist could be called a radical, I suppose. He pulls up things by the roots."

My father chuckled.

"Any bandit in Mexico nowadays can give himself a political label," the doctor went on, "and that makes him respectable. He's a leader of the people."

"Take Villa, now . . ." my father began.

"Villa was a different type of man," the doctor broke in.

"I don't see any difference."

The doctor came over to the table and sat down. "Now look at it this way," he began, his finger in front of my father's face. My father threw back his head and laughed.

"You'd better go to bed and rest," my mother told me. "You're not completely well, you know."

So I went to bed, but I didn't go to sleep, not right away. I lay there for a long time while behind my darkened eyelids Emiliano Zapata's cavalry charged down to the broad Santee, where there were grave men with hoary hairs. I was still awake at eleven when the cold voice of the bugle went gliding in and out of the dark like something that couldn't find its way back to wherever it had been. I thought of Chonita in Heaven, and I saw her in her torn and dirty dress, with a pair of bright wings attached, flying round and round like a butterfly shouting, "Give me the hammon and the beans!"

Then I cried. And whether it was the bugle, or whether it was Chonita or what, to this day I do not know. But cry I did, and I felt much better after that.

EXILE

―――――― ★ ――――――

Benjamin Alire Sáenz

> Do you know what exile is?
> I'll tell you,
>   exile
> is a long avenue
> where only sadness walks.
> —Roque Dalton

El Paso

THAT MORNING, WHEN THE DAY WAS BEGINNING, I LOOKED out my window and stared at the Juarez Mountains. Mexican purples—they were mine. That was the first time it ever happened, the spring of 1985. It had happened to others, but never to *me*. And when it happened, I didn't like it.

And it will never be over.

As I walked to school, I remember thinking what a perfect place Sunset Heights was. Turn of the century houses intact. Remodeled houses painted pink. The rundown Sunset Grocery store decorated with the protest art of graffitti on one end and a plastic-signed "Circle K" on the other. Bordering the university. Bordering the freeway. Bordering downtown. Bordering the border. People from Juarez knocking on doors and asking for jobs—or money—or food. Small parks filled with people whose English was apparently nonexistent. The upwardly mobile living next to families whose only concern was getting enough money to pay next month's rent. Some had lived here forever, others would live here a few days. A bazaar of colorful people who lived in the shadows of the Juarez Mountains. Sunset Heights: a perfect place with a perfect name, and a perfect view of the river.

After class, I went by my office and drank a cup of coffee, and smoked two or three cigarettes. Lawrence, my office mate, turned on his fan and told me I smoked too much. "Year," I nodded, "I smoke too much—but I'm going to quit." I had no intention of doing so, and he knew it. It was a game we played.

At about three o'clock I put my things together in my torn backpack and started walking home. I made a mental note to sew the damn thing. *One day everything's gonna come tumbling out—better sew it.* I'd made that mental note before.

Walking down Prospect, I thought maybe I'd go for a job. I hoped the spring would not bring too much wind this year. The wind unsettled the desert—upset things—ruined everything. My mind wandered: searched the black asphalt littered with torn papers; the chained dogs in the yards who couldn't hurt me; the even bricks of all the houses I passed. I belonged—the thoughts entered like children running through a park. This year, maybe the winds would not come.

I didn't notice the green car drive up and stop right next to me as I walked. The border patrol interrupted my daydreaming: "Where are you from?"

I didn't answer. I wasn't sure who the agent, a woman, was addressing.

She repeated the question in Spanish, *"¿De donde eres?"*

Without thinking, I almost answered her question—in Spanish. A reflex. I caught myself in midsentence, and stuttered in a nonlanguage.

"¿Donde naciste?" she asked again.

By then I'd regained some composure and quietly spit out, "I'm a U.S. citizen."

"Were you born in the United States?"

She was as brown as I was. I might have asked her the same question. I looked at her for a while—searching for a human being.

"Yes," I answered.

"Where in the United States were you born?"

"In New Mexico."

"Where in New Mexico?"

"Las Cruces."

"What do you do?"

"I'm a student."

"And are you employed?"

"Sort of."

"Sort of?" She didn't like my answer. I looked at her expression and decided it wasn't hurting anyone to answer her questions. It was all very innocent. Just a game we were playing.

"I work at U.T.E.P. as a teaching assistant."

She didn't respond one way or another. I looked at her for a second and decided she was finished with me. I started walking away. "Are you sure you were born in Las Cruces?" she asked again.

I turned around and smiled, "Yes, I'm sure." She didn't smile back. She and the driver sat there for a while and watched me as I continued walking. They drove past me slowly, and then proceeded down the street.

I didn't much care for the color of their cars.

"Sons of bitches," I whispered, "pretty soon I'll have to carry a passport in my own neighborhood." I said it to be flippant. I wasn't angry—not at first. In less than ten minutes I was back in my apartment playing the scene again and again in my mind. It was like a video I played over and over—memorizing the images. Something was wrong. I was embarrassed—ashamed because I'd been so damned compliant, Just like a little kid in the principal's office—in trouble for speaking Spanish. "I should have told that bitch exactly what I thought of her and her job." *Are you sure you were born in Las Cruces?* Piss on her and her green car and her green uniform. I lit a cigarette and told myself I was overreacting. "Breathe in—breathe out—no big deal—you live on a border. These things happen—just one of those things. Just a game. . . ." I changed into my jogging clothes and went for a run. At the top of the hill on Sunbowl Drive, I stopped to stare at the Juarez Mountains. I felt the sweat run down my face. I kept running until I could no longer hear *Are you sure you were born in Las Cruces?* ringing in my ears.

School let out in early May. I spent the last two weeks of that month relaxing and working on some paintings. In June I got back to working on my novel. My working title was *Adagio for Strings: An American Fairytale*. I liked the title more than I liked the story.

From my window I could see the freeway. It was then I realized not a day went by that I didn't see someone running across the freeway or someone walking down the street looking out for someone. They were people who looked not so different from me—except they lived their lives looking over their shoulders.

One Thursday, I saw the border patrol throw a couple of guys into their van. Threw them. Threw them like they were pieces of meat— dead bucks after a deer hunt. The *illegals* didn't even put up a fight. They were aliens, from somewhere else. They just hung their heads— practically scraping the littered asphalt. I sat at my typewriter and tried to pretend I didn't see it. *That's what I get for looking out windows.* I didn't write the rest of the day. I kept seeing the border patrol woman against a blue sky turning green. I thought of rearranging my desk so I wouldn't have to be next to the window. But I thought of the mountains. . . .

Two weeks later I went for a walk. I couldn't stand sitting at my desk for another second. The novel wasn't going well that day. My writing was getting worse instead of better. I needed a break. My characters were getting on my nerves. I hadn't taken a shower—hadn't shaved. I looked in the mirror and talked to the image, "You need a haircut. You need a shave. You need . . ." I threw some water on my face and walked out the door. God, it was hot. I wiped the sweat from my eyelids. Sweat—stinging and blinding. I laughed. It was a hundred degrees, the middle of the afternoon. *I'm crazy—a shower would have been a better idea.* I turned the corner and headed back home. I saw the green van. It was parked right ahead of me.

A man about my height got out of the van and approached me. Another man, taller, followed him. *"¿Tienes tus papeles?"* he asked me. His gringo accent was grating.

"I can speak English," I said. I started to add, "I can probably speak it better than you," but I stopped myself. No need to be aggressive.

"Do you live in this neighborhood?"

"Yes."

"Where?"

"Are you planning on making a social visit?"

He gave me a hard look—cold and blue—then looked at his partner. He didn't like me. I didn't care.

I watched them drive away and felt nothing.

There were other times when I felt watched. Sometimes, when I jogged, the green vans would slow down—eye me. I felt like prey. I pretended not to notice them. I started noting their presence in our neighborhood more and more. I started growing suspicious of my own observations. Of course, they weren't everywhere—I had just been oblivious to their presence—had been oblivious because they had nothing to do with me. The green cars and the green vans were clashing with the purples of the Juarez Mountains. I never talked about their presence to other people. Sometimes, the topic of the *Migra* would come up in conversations. I felt the anger—would control it. I casually referred to them as the Gestapo and everyone would laugh— I was only playing. I hated them.

When school started in the fall, I was stopped again. Again I had been walking home from the university. I heard the familiar question, "Where are you from?"

"Leave me alone," I stared back.

"Are you a citizen of the United States?"

"*Yes.*"

"Can you prove it?"

"No. No, I can't."

He looked at my clothes—jeans, tennis shoes, and a casual California shirt. He noticed my backpack—full of books.

"You a student?"

I nodded and stared at him.

"There isn't any need to be unfriendly. . . ."

"I'd like to be left alone."

"Just trying to do my job," he laughed. I didn't smile back. Terrorists, I thought. Nazis did their jobs, too. Death squads in Guatemala did their jobs, too. An unfair analogy, I knew. I thought it, anyway.

The Juarez Mountains were not as purple that fall.

In early January, I went with Michael to Juarez. Michael was from New York, and had come to work in a home for the homeless in South El Paso. We weren't in Juarez for very long—just looking around and getting gas. On the way back, the customs officer asked us to declare our citizenship. "U.S. citizen," Michael followed. The customs officer lowered his head and poked it in the car, "What are you bringing over?"

"Nothing."

He looked at me. "Where in the United States were you born?"

"In Las Cruces, New Mexico."

He looked at me a while longer. "Go ahead," he signaled.

I noticed he didn't ask Michael where he was from.

THAT WINTER, SUNSET HEIGHTS SEEMED DESERTED TO ME. THE streets were empty like the river. One morning, I was driving up Upson Street towards the university—the wind blowing the limbs of the bare trees. Nothing to shield them—unprotected by green leaves. I noticed two border patrol officers were chasing someone. One of them put his hand out, signaling me to slow down as they ran across the street in front of my car. They were running with their billy clubs in hand. *So it had come to that.*

I wanted the wind to blow them out of existence.

In late January, Michael and I went to Juarez again. A friend of his was in town and we wanted to take him to Juarez to have a look around. We took him to the cathedral and the marketplace, and talked about how markets were a much more civilized way of doing business than going to Safeway. We stopped at the Kentucky Club and had a couple of beers. Walking back over the bridge, we stopped at the top and looked out at the city of El Paso. "It actually looks pretty from here, doesn't it?" I remarked. Michael nodded. It *did* look pretty. We looked off to the side—down the river—and watched the *illegals* looking for a way to cross the Rio Grande. We watched them for a long time. Michael's friend said that this was just like watching the "CBS Evening News."

As we reached the customs building, we noticed that a border patrol van pulled up behind the building where the other green cars were parked. The officers jumped out of the van and threw a hand-cuffed man against one of the parked cars. It looked like they were going to beat him. Two more border patrol officers pulled up in a car and jumped out to join them. One of the officers noticed we were watching. They straightened him out, and walked him inside—like gentlemen. They would have beat him had we not been watching—that's what I thought. But things like that don't happen.

My fingers wanted to reach for the wire fence. To touch it. I felt guilty for living on the freedom side of the fence. That fence—it separated me from myself.

The first day of February I was walking to the Chevron station in downtown El Paso. On the corner of Prospect and Upson a green car was parked—just sitting there. A part of my landscape. I was walking on the opposite side of the street. For some reason I knew they were going to stop me. My heart clenched like a fist. My back tightened up. Maybe they'll leave me alone, I told myself. I wanted to believe it. I should've taken a shower this morning. I should've worn a nicer sweater. I should've put on a pair of socks—worn a nice pair of shoes. . . .

I should've dyed my skin.

The driver of the car rolled down his window. I saw him from the corner of my eyes. He called me over to him—*whistled me over*—much like he'd call a dog. I kept walking. He whistled me over again. *Here, boy.* I stopped for a second—only a second. I kept walking. The border patrol officer and a policeman rushed out of the car and ran toward me. I was sure they were going to tackle me—drag me to the ground—handcuff me. They stopped in front of me.

"Could I see your driver's license?" the policeman asked.

"Since when do you need a driver's license to walk down the street?" Our eyes met. "Did I do something that was against the law?"

The policeman was annoyed. He wanted me to be passive, to say, "Yes, sir,"—to approve of his job.

"Don't you know what we do?"

"I know exactly what you do."

"Don't give me a hard time. I want to see some identification."

"I'd like to know why I was stopped."

"I'm asking you for some identification."

I looked at him. Just looked. He stared back. He hated me as much as I hated him. He saw the bulge of my cigarettes under my sweater and crumpled them.

I backed up a step. "I smoke. It's not good for me, but it's not against the law. Not yet, anyway—and don't touch me. Don't ever touch me. Read me my rights, throw me in the can or leave me alone. Understand?" I smiled.

"No one's charging you with anything."

"Good. Very good." I nodded—and kept nodding.

They walked back to their green car.

My eyes followed them. I'd won. It was an empty victory.

THIS SPRING MORNING I WAKE UP. I SIT AT MY DESK, WAIT FOR the coffee, and look out my window. *This day, like every day, I look out my window.* Across the street a border patrol van stops and an officer gets out. So close I could touch him. On the freeway—this side of the river—a man is running. I put my glasses on. I am afraid he will be run over by the cars. I cheer for him. *Don't get run over. Be careful.* So close to the other side he can touch it. The border patrol officer gets out his walkie-talkie and runs toward the man who has disappeared from my view. I go and get my cup of coffee. I take a drink—slowly it mixes with yesterday's tastes in my mouth. The officer in the green uniform comes back into view. He has the man with him. He puts him in the van. I can't see the color in their eyes. I see only the green. They drive away. There is no trace that says they've been there.

No one knows what I have seen. Except the mountains.

The green van. They are taking something from me. The green vans. This is my home, I tell myself. But I don't know if I want this to be my home, any more. The thought crosses my mind to walk out of my apartment without my wallet. The thought crosses my mind that maybe the *Migra* will stop me again. I will pretend I cannot speak English. I will say nothing. I will bow my head, and let them put me in a detention center for a month or two. I will let them warehouse me. I will let them push me in front of a judge who will look at me like he has looked at the millions before me. I will be sent back to Mexico. I will let them treat me like I am *illegal.* But the thoughts pass. I am not brave enough to let them do that to me. And I never will be.

Today, the spring winds blow outside my window. The reflections I see on the pane have words written on them—graffitti: *Sure you were born? . . . Identification? . . . Do you live? . . .* The winds will unsettle my desert—cover Sunset Heights with green dust. The green vans will stay in my mind forever—I cannot banish them. I cannot banish their questions—*Where are you from?* I no longer know.

AN EL PASO IDYLL

Pat Carr

I

WINTER IS AN ABORTIVE SEASON IN EL PASO WITH THE scant snow barely covering the whitewashed block high school letters cut into the El Paso mountains, lying in horizontal patches like a worn brown and white striped blanket across the Mexican mountains. And even though everyone knows the tiny cubes of adobe houses dropped like careless tinted dice on the hills across the river don't have glass in the windows or more than a single frozen water faucet per dozen, the town is still surprised when the *El Paso Times* reports that two old Mexican women and one ancient grandfather froze in their huts the night of the first snow.

Traffic is slowed along Mesa because people don't remember where they put the snow chains or can't get the links untangled from summer rake tongs if they do remember, but cocktail parties go on as scheduled and after-party suppers at La Corona in Juarez take place no matter how much snow swirls across the International Bridge.

The short and swarthy expressionless maitre d' at La Corona always puts large parties at a single long table and includes every item on a single bill, and that night we sat along the expanse of the white cloth with yet another martini before the arrival of the flautas or the steak tampico submerged in slick green chilies.

I was directly across the table from Willie Oaks.

I'd more or less conceived of the departmental secretary, Barbara, getting her chance at him that evening since he'd come alone to the cocktail party and I knew how she felt about him, but I could see that even with four martinis it wasn't taking.

". . . when you get to be an almost grandmother like I am," she was saying, her cheeks flushed and eager, but dry powdered below her eyes that were looking at him hungrily, and I wanted to tell her to knock it off, that the attempt to give them the commonality of age was a real loser. Anyone should have known that Willie Oaks didn't want to be reminded he was nearing fifty. There'd been too many other times at too many other parties that I'd heard him ask if the beholder could possibly believe his fiancée Carla was less than half his age.

His eyes were resting on me there at the long table and I acknowledged them over my whiskey sour. His eyes were his best feature, dark, a liquid brown that was near black beneath black brows, and they were almost strong enough to make one ignore the twin side curls that curved stiff, wiglike over the balding sheen of his forehead.

The talk flowed on as he turned to answer some direct query from Barbara, and then it paused briefly as he signalled for another round. He was the boss and they would all drink the fresh one.

When the restaurant was almost empty, the food finally came, and by the time we'd finished, only the waiters were left.

"Let me get the tabs for the three of you," he said to Barbara, Joyce and me when the check came. "I've only got a few months to be buying ladies dinners and I want to make the most of it."

"How sweet."

"Three of us in one swell foop is certainly making the most of your temporary bachelorhood, all right," Joyce said, being rather militant about the male-female relationship and not wanting, I could tell, to be indebted even to the boss.

But food at La Corona was always cheap and with the peso spiralling downward just then, it wouldn't be much of a debt. I nodded.

It was still snowing, the wind angling stinging snow pellets against us as we went outside. Barbara got down into Willie's tiny gray convertible, and I remember thinking she might still have a chance if the wait going across the bridge toward customs was long enough for her to get into an intimate conversation.

But the snow and the traffic had cut back by the time we got there, and the customs officials merely bobbed their heads at my nationality, gave a perfunctory "What'reyoubringing?" waved me on, and I knew the others were passed through as easily.

And as soon as my apartment doorbell rang a few minutes after I got in, I knew it was he.

He had on an overcoat and a sort of snarled looking scarf I knew Carla had knitted.

"I thought we might have a nightcap," he said and held out half a bottle of cheap Mexican white rum.

"Of straight rum?" I opened the door wider and he came in, the cold night air surrounding, encasing him.

"I thought you might be able to make a cup of tea. I like it with three spoons of sugar in strong tea." He handed me his coat and the scarf, keeping hold of the neck of the bottle. "You look like the kind who'd drink tea." He said it in a way that reminded me he was a Texan and I was an outsider.

"I think I might have a tea bag."

I went into the kitchen alcove as he went over to the couch and sat down.

"This place furnished?"

"With Victorian antiques?" Sometimes the country boy facade irritated me. "Hardly."

"H-m-m-m-m-m." He reached down and pulled off his cowboy boots. He had on thick blue wool socks.

I poured the water and put the cups and a sugar bowl on a tray.

"Sterling silver?" He looked at it as I set it down on the Queen Anne side table.

"I used to be rich. I took a cut in salary to come down here."

"H-m-m-m-m," he said again.

The snow had dampened his hair and the curls were gone; he no longer looked like something out of the Commedia dell'arte. He carefully took the teabags out of the cups and poured in the rum almost to the brim without measuring. Then he stirred three teaspoons of sugar into each cup and handed me one. "There."

I tasted it and nodded. It was better than I'd expected.

"How come you applied down here?" He leaned back watching me.

"I thought it was a good place to file for a divorce."

He nodded. "That was what I figured when I hired you. Those Women Libbers'd been insisting we get a woman the next assistant professorship that came up." He sipped the rum tea. "And I decided anybody who's getting a divorce can't be all bad."

"I'm actually pretty good."

He looked at me. "Mine was one of the last quickie Juarez divorces before the Mexican government put a stop to them."

"I found out that after I got here. But then I guess I want a good solid divorce anyway."

"You had a bad one?"

I shrugged. "How about yours?"

"A real eighteen karat bitch. I've screwed more in the six months I've been out than I did in the whole twenty-three years I was married."

I wasn't sure there were any overtones in that, but I didn't feel like following them if there were. "I gathered your engagement was a recent thing."

He nodded. "Carla's wonderful and she's all woman."

It was strange hearing him call her a woman when we all knew she was a little younger than his son.

"I didn't come here with any ulterior motives, you know," he said then. "I'm in love with Carla." He drained the cup and held it out to me.

I went out and turned on the tea kettle and watched the electric coils glow orange.

"But somehow it just didn't seem like the party should've been over for you yet there at La Corona." He came around the kitchen alcove. "You had a look that, well . . . I just thought we could have a nightcap together."

His eyes were dark, shadowed beneath his black eyebrows, and he could almost have been Chicano except that I knew he wasn't.

"You know just a . . ."

"I know." I leaned over to kiss him lightly on the mouth.

His arms closed around me in a vise-like grip and he was suddenly kissing me hungrily, passionately.

Then as suddenly he picked me up and we were in the bedroom and were making love on the lace bedspread. It was a desperate, famished sort of lovemaking, almost as if he were a teen-ager, and he came before I was able to fit into his rhythm.

Blue light from the mercury streetlamp came through the windows and the snow-sleet wind clicked against the glass. A thin metallic whistle came from the kitchen.

He rolled over on his back. "I didn't mean for that to happen. I honestly didn't come here to . . ."

"I know." It'd been too sudden, too rushed to have been planned. I touched his arm and he put his hand over mine and pressed it.

I got up and rearranged clothes that we hadn't taken off. His thick wool socks looked very blue in the mercury arc light.

"Do you want another cup of tea? I can hear that the water's hot."

"No. I guess I'd better go." He didn't look at me.

I went out and turned off the burner and he followed me a few seconds later already in his overcoat and scarf.

"It wasn't just because I'm the boss, was it?"

"Don't be silly." I kissed him very briefly on the lips, and he stood very still.

Then he went over and struggled on his cowboy boots, stood up, touched my cheek, and went out.

The sky was a strange yellow green and I saw the snow sift around him as he opened the car door. He glanced back through the chartreuse light for a second and waved, and I noticed he didn't have any gloves.

His little car pulled away from the curb before he turned on the lights, and I watched the taillights disappear.

The phone rang less than half an hour later.

"I just wanted to say again that I didn't mean for that to happen. I want you to understand that it was just an accident and won't be repeated. There was something about the night and the drinks, and . . . ," he trailed off.

"Of course I understand."

"I'm not in love with you. I'm in love with Carla, and what happened had nothing to do with her or us."

"Of course."

"It was just that . . ."

"I do understand."

"Okay."

I could hear him breathing on the clear cold line.

"You ready for bed?"

"Yes."

"I left the rum."

"I found it."

"If you like the tea and rum, it makes a good winter drink."

"I liked it."

"Good." Then, "Well, goodnight. I didn't intend for that to happen."

"I know."

"Goodnight," he said again.

It must have been four by then, but I wasn't sleepy and I went back to the couch and had another cup of tea.

The word was that he got his divorce because he wanted to marry one of his students, the old college cliché of the professor dumping his older model for a younger, later, version, but the first time I'd talked to him at a cocktail party when there were only the two of us at the bar, I remember he'd blurted out, "She thinks I'm going to come crawling back to her. But there's more ass out there than she thinks, and I'm going to let the goddamn divorce go through." Others had come up then, but I remembered thinking at the time that no divorce is as simple as rumor has it.

The next morning as I was getting dressed, the phone rang again.

"I wanted to tell you that I hope we can forget completely about last night. I wouldn't want something like that to get in the way of our working together," he said.

"Of course not."

"And watch out on the freeway on the way to school this morning. These El Paso drivers aren't used to driving on icy streets like you Northerners. Be careful."

2

It was three days later that he called again about midnight and asked if I still had any of the rum left.

"About half of it."

"I'm at school. I just finished up that Ortiz business and since I have to pass by your place, I thought I might stop in for a cup of tea. No ulterior motives."

"One cup of tea and no ulterior motives."

I had a pot of strong tea on the tray by the time he got there and he nodded toward the teapot as he gave me his overcoat. "You got all kinds of silver."

"And you can't afford a pair of gloves."

He looked down at me. "You're probably the most observant woman I've ever met."

"The way you say it, I can't tell if that's good or bad."

"I've been watching you in class." He sat down and took off his boots, a different, more elaborate pair this time, and mixed the rum and sugar into the tea. "You are good."

"How did the Ortiz thing go?"

"Those damned Mexicans." He drank from the teacup as if it were a shot glass. "Not that I'm prejudiced like some of those anglos we've got out there, but by damn, when you get a Mexican that fucks up, they can really fuck up."

I sipped the tea and listened and nodded as he explained what he'd had to do to get it straightened out with the dean, what'd kept him at the university until midnight. He poured another tea for both of us, layered in a generous rum. "Carla told me to come by if I finished up early enough," he said finally, "But she still lives at home, and I thought midnight was too late to disturb her."

"Thanks a lot. You know, one of these days you're going to make me feel unattractive."

He put his cup down. "You're kidding."

"I'm kidding."

He reached out and touched my hair. "You're one of the most . . ." He leaned forward and kissed me gently. And then the same abrupt intensity seemed to take hold of him, and he pulled me off the footstool into him, crushing me against his chest, his mouth opening over mine. He undid the fasteners of my robe in frantic, almost angry, haste, and we were suddenly making love again.

When it was over we lay back on the couch.

"You shouldn't've worn that," he said.

"I had it on when you called."

He kept his arm around me. "There's something about you that . . . I guess you just seem hungry and I . . ."

"H-m-m-m-m-m."

"I won't be coming back even for a cup of tea. I wasn't going to let that happen. I thought we'd just be friends, but . . ."

He waited for me to say something, but I couldn't think of anything.

"Carla's half Mexican, you know," he said then.

"Is she?"

"I look more Mexican than she does, but her mother's from Mexico City, and she was raised like one of the real aristocrats."

"Was she?"

"She's been there for a long time, ever since she was a freshman. Took four classes with me. You'd never know it, but she's as young as my son."

I gave a murmur that would pass for assent or surprise or something non-committal.

"She was there all that time when my wife was doing her damnedest to destroy me and I knew how she felt about me, but I didn't go to her. It was only when she came to me and said she'd be the woman in the casa chica if I wanted, anything I wanted. She didn't have any idea or any hopes that I'd ever get a divorce. She just wanted me. Do you know what the casa chica is?" He moved his arm and looked down at me.

"More or less."

"It's one of those Mexican conventions, for the muy macho, the little house, a sort of bigamy arrangement, where the other woman has another set of kids and keeps another house and family separate from the first wife."

I nodded.

"And I needed that."

He raised himself on his elbows. "How about another cup, the last one we'll have together?"

I got up and heated the water, and when I got back with the tea, he had his boots on again.

"She was a virgin."

I nodded and poured the tea.

"Any bastard who'd deflower a virgin down here . . . not one of your modern anglo girls who go from one bed to another and don't think anything of it, but you know, one of those nice girls who'd be ruined, who couldn't ever marry anyone else afterward . . . that kind of bastard ought to have his balls or his pecker . . ." He paused to slosh rum into the tea. "We killed the bottle."

"I'll get some more next time I go across. That's a good drink."

"You can serve it next time you have somebody over. You dating anybody yet?"

"A couple."

"You are?"

"I don't have anything against men."

"I just thought . . . I hadn't seen you with anybody."

"El Paso feels like a small town, but you probably don't really run into the same people every time you go out."

He took a sharp swallow. "Anybody special?"

"Not yet."

"Anybody I know? I wouldn't want anybody to know about this." He swept his hand toward the bookcase.

"Nobody'll know you were here."

"I'm getting married in less than six months and this was just an accident. It's not going to happen again. I wouldn't want this to get around and . . . You screwing anybody?"

"Nobody special."

His eyebrows jerked downward angrily and his jaw tightened. "I'm sleeping with Carla and I sure as hell wouldn't want to give her anything. If that bastard you're fucking is . . ."

I couldn't help smiling. "Oh, come off it, William. You don't have to be jealous. I haven't gone out with anyone in El Paso as tall, dark, and handsome as you are."

"I don't . . ."

I reached over and brushed the curl back off his forehead.

He started to push my hand away but then he caught it instead. "Am I jealous?"

"Probably all men get possessive just after they've been to bed."

He looked at me. "The kind of understanding you have shouldn't be allowed outside marriage. How the hell did anyone let you get away?"

"That's better."

He stood up, pulled me up and gave me a very long, very gentle kiss. "That's for good-by."

I nodded and watched him put on his coat.

"Buy yourself some gloves one of these days."

He stopped at the door and looked back at me, his almost black eyes liquidly glowing. "Good-by."

I didn't go to the door.

He was one of the finest men I'd run into in a long time.

He was going to marry her no matter what he really wanted, because of a principle, an old fashioned Texan paternalism and machismo that protected the gentle virgin señoritas. I wondered if Carla had known that about him when she made her play.

I was sorrier than I'd thought I'd be to see him go, but the nobility of his going impressed me more than I'd been touched in years.

3

The snow lasted a week. Traffic virtually stopped on Mesa and those who were hardy enough to get out inched along on the very center lanes of the freeway that had been cleared by the snowplow borrowed by El Paso County from the New Mexico highway department and driven down from Ruidoso. The night skies were that eerie green whenever I'd wake at two or three in the morning and glance out the lace curtains.

At the end of the week of snow, a Monday, when the white drifts were beginning to sag into themselves as the undersides melted, soaked into the sandy desert earth, my doorbell rang about eleven. He stood there without saying anything and held out a new bottle of Mexican rum.

"I didn't hear your car."

He shook his head. "I parked it a couple of blocks away and walked over."

I nodded and took the rum to the kitchen.

"I thought you were terribly noble to stay away."

"So did I."

When I brought the tea he added as if he'd waited to say it face to face. "I love Carla and I'm going to marry her. I don't know what this is. I can't figure out what you do to a guy, but I guess it won't hurt anybody as long as Carla doesn't find out. I'm not married yet, your divorce is almost final, and we're old enough to know what we're doing. I don't see why we can't have a drink once a week, and then if somebody special comes along, you can call it off. It's off anyway in May when I get married. I'm not going to start off this marriage on the wrong foot. This is my chance for a new life, and I'm going to take it."

"Did you start the last one off on the wrong foot?"

He shook his head. "Believe it or not, I was virtually a virgin when I got married to the most popular May Queen El Paso High ever had."

I handed him a cup. "Virtually?"

"I'd been to one Juarez whorehouse." He paused remembering. "But I never even looked around for the first twelve years of marriage. I knew something was wrong, but she was really a pretty thing, and I kept telling myself it would get better when I got my Ph.D. and got someplace like this university. I was teaching in high school when I married her, but she didn't want that. She wanted to be married to a college professor." He shrugged a little as if it were cold. "I was a damned good high school teacher."

I nodded. "She sounds a tad shallow if you don't mind my saying so."

"I don't mind. Yeah, she was. That was what finally dawned on me. Shallow and stupid and a real bitch. How about yours?"

"A nice enough fellow I suppose, but an alcoholic, and pretty soon you forget what his personality might have been originally or even if there was one originally."

"I hear that's a rough one."

I shrugged that time. "There probably isn't a good divorce. I think the words may be mutually exclusive."

We drank the tea in silence for a while, then he told me about his two affairs that had started after the twelve years of fidelity, of all the times he'd tried to get something back into the marriage for his one son, but then how at last when the son had gone off to college, he'd finally given up.

"But my wife found out about Carla, so she fought the divorce. She didn't really want me. She just wanted to hit back at me."

"Maybe she realized what she was losing."

He smiled and pulled me over to him. "You know how to get to a guy, don't you?"

"I'd learned by the time I was five years old that males want three things from a female—admiration, admiration, and admiration."

He threw back his head and laughed. It was the first time I'd ever heard him laugh.

He left about two and called back to say he was home.

"I forgot to tell you not to feed that rum to any of your other callers. I'll be about once a week or so to help you drink it up."

But it wasn't once a week. He started dropping by every other night, then sometimes every night for a few minutes with something he'd forgotten to tell me at school. He often stopped in when he knew I had a date to tell me something important that couldn't wait until the next day, and once he parked and waited outside until three a.m. when I'd gone out with a Chicano from the philosophy department whom he particularly disliked.

"Anglo women here don't usually date Mexican men," he said the first thing as I opened the door. "You shouldn't forget you're in Texas."

"I thought that attitude went out with Rock Hudson in the fifties."

"You're not from here," he said stubbornly. Then, "Did you go by his place?"

"We were at a party. Very proper and very anglo."

He picked me up. "You wouldn't've liked him anyway. All the secretaries in Education who've had him say he has the smallest pecker they've ever seen on somebody six feet tall."

"Don't be petty, William. Your jealousy is showing."

He carried me toward the bedroom. "I don't know what it is, but I'm not in love with you. I love Carla."

He continued to say that, but as the months passed and the wedding date got closer, Carla had to spend more time with her mother and her mother's family planning the wedding, fitting the long white dress, sewing the seed pearls on by hand, and he had more time alone, at my apartment.

Often we went to dinner at the Casa Martino in Juarez, his favorite restaurant where he was known by all the waiters, and I sometimes wondered if he subconsciously intended for one of them to blurt something out to Carla when he took her there.

But even if Carla suspected he wasn't completely alone while he was shut out of the wedding plans, there wasn't a breath of it, and engagement parties proliferated in the warming spring.

A week before the wedding, he stopped by with a bottle of champagne.

"It's not for you," he said and put it on the night table where it glowed emerald under the lamp. "The janitors on the third floor gave it to me tonight and said it was for me and "mi corazon." And that's not you. I'm in love with Carla."

"Then what the hell are you doing in my bed?"

He looked at me. "I don't know."

He picked up the bottle of champagne and put it between us. It had an incongruous white satin ribbon pom-pom around its neck. "I tell myself I'm not going to see you, that I'm not being fair to Carla who is my chance for a new life, a new family, the wife I've always wanted. All she wants out of life is to make me happy. And then the first thing I know I'm parked two blocks away and I'm walking over here. I don't know what it is you do to me."

I was tired, too tired to humor him.

"Maybe if you could just get rid of some of that damned stereo-typed thinking. The little woman, the good girl, the dark lady. You're over here because you want to be. We're the same generation, we've got things in common, just plain years of experience you can never have with someone half your age. For Christ sake, Willie, grow up. That *Playboy* ideal of the older man with the sweet young thing is a ludicrous, ridiculous . . ." I couldn't think what it was and I knew I was saying too much, but I hadn't said it in all those months and there it was. "Keeping up with a kid is no big deal; the feat is to satisfy a woman of thirty-five who knows what the hell sex is all about."

He got up slowly, the champagne bottle in his hand, and went out of the bedroom without a word.

I could hear him in the other room and then the front door, but I didn't get up. Goddamned Texans.

But I already had the wedding invitation and I went to the wedding with Joyce, who muttered all the way through the ceremony about how male chauvinistic weddings were and she hadn't noticed before, not hav-ing gone to one since she'd had the female consciousness raising course.

At the reception, Carla beamed and clung to his arm possessively, and in the receiving line I heard her say to Barbara, "Now, I'm the boss."

The coronet of wax orange blossoms was too low on her forehead and made her face look thick, but I pressed her hand and murmured something about what a lovely gown, lovely wedding.

"Good luck, Willie."

He leaned over to kiss my cheek, but I turned my head slightly and he kissed my lips.

"Good-by," he said softly.

4

Spring in El Paso may be even stranger than winter. The sky is so limitless that the stars hang in the darkness, a blue darkness never quite becoming black, like so many stationary plane lights that you have to watch for a while before you decide they're stars.

It was perhaps two weeks after the wedding near the end of the semester that my doorbell rang at eleven. I was grading papers and put them aside with the irritating certainty that some student who'd disappeared weeks before was now bringing me his belated term paper.

"Yes?" I opened the door.

He stood there looking at me and holding a brand new bottle of Mexican rum. "Got any tea?"

"Oh, Willie."

I didn't back away from the door.

"I had to go by school to pick up some exams for tomorrow."

"You don't want to do this, Willie. Remember how you were going to . . ."

"Goddamn you," he said. He jerked me to him with violence and brought his mouth down on mine as he half carried, half pushed me back into the room.

5

Fall is one of the imperceptible seasons, and the only way most El Pasoans are sure that autumn has actually come is to drive the three hours up to Cloudcroft in the New Mexico mountains to see if the aspen leaves have turned gold. But even if they have and the pine cones are dropping, the days stay hot and the great bare classrooms stay air conditioned until suddenly one afternoon the absolutely clear sky is abruptly, between one class bell and the next, spread with a gray cloud cover and the bits of white, more like large dust motes than flakes, begin to waver down as if from the building roofs rather than the sky, and it's winter again.

It was the first snow day that the letter of termination came.

Apologetic, polite, but cold and final, saying that the end of school year would be my last at the university. No additions, no elaborations, signed sincerely by the dean.

I sat looking out the window at the aimless specks of snow, drifting, spiralling white monads, not enough of them to show on the patio stones.

Then I heard his knock and he came in with a bottle of Lancers'.

"Celebrating?"

He came over and bent down to kiss me. "I got a copy of all the letters the dean sent out, and I thought you might like a drink."

"That was sweet of you, Willie."

He got the glasses and opened the bottle.

"I knew this was my year for consideration, but I guess I'd just forgotten, put it out of my head somehow."

He nodded and handed me the glass. "I did all I could, but . . ." The wine looked almost red in the sunset light. "But this way you can look around for something else by next fall."

"Yeah." The wine tasted almost red. It was very cold. "And with the market the way it is, you never can tell, in a couple of years I might even get on at some high school."

"High school's not so bad. In fact, it's pretty damn good. You don't have all this publish or perish shit to put up with."

I poured another glass. "You know that doesn't bug me. I've got enough publications."

"It shouldn't be hard for you to get something better than this podunk university. You always were too good for this place."

"Thanks, Willie."

He looked at his watch. "I've got to run. Carla's folks are coming for supper. I just thought I'd stop by for a second. But if you're not doing anything around midnight, I've got some things to do at the office."

"If I can find enough to drink around here I think I might just sit here and get smashed."

"Don't go out. I'll be back around twelve."

I wasn't sure I wanted him to, but I let him go without saying anything. It hadn't been the same after the wedding somehow, and he was even more possessive, more jealous of whom I was dating, more violent in his lovemaking.

I poured the last of the rosé wine from the bottle and was sipping it when the doorbell rang again and the door opened.

"Hi. Don't you know you ought to lock your damned door. There're two hundred and seventy unsolved rape cases in just El Paso alone for this year and no telling how many in Juarez."

I waved my hand. "Come on in, Joyce. I just poured the last of this one but there's a bottle of sherry in the cupboard."

"For someone who doesn't drink much, you sure have enough of it around." She took off her coat and banged cupboard doors looking for the glasses and the sherry. When she came back in she spotted the extra glass on the coffee table. "Who was here?"

"Just a friend." I finished the rosé and held out my empty for the sherry.

"Boy, you know, you're the most discreet divorcée in town. Everybody in the department is wondering who you go with steady, but it's somebody different at every party."

"Keeps 'em off the scent." The sherry was awful after the rosé. It always surprised me that no one knew. But then he'd been discretion itself. Almost an entire year and . . .

"I just heard," she said then. "I'm sorry." She was looking at me but ready to glance away again in case she saw too much pain.

I shrugged for her. "I can probably find something."

"I'd like to kick that damned Willie Oaks's ass to Dallas and back."

"Willie Oaks?"

"Yeah, he's the one who . . . You didn't know?"

I shook my head.

"He's got the say-so." She looked down and busily poured more sherry in her glass even though she still had some. "Kept that little Harvard pip-squeak instead of you."

"He did?"

"The male chauvinist bastard."

"Rodney doesn't have his degree yet."

"Male chauvinist bastards. Every damned one of them."

"I guess I didn't realize . . ."

"Oh, every time they've got only one slot, it's always some damned man, or almost man, they give it to."

She went on about the prejudice, the anti-feminist sentiment rampant in every department, and I let her talk, making a murmur of assent occasionally, not needing to listen, not needing to pay much attention.

At last she ran out of epithets and seemed to sense my inattention.

"I just wanted to come by, to tell you . . ."

"Thanks, Joyce."

"You want me to lock this?"

"I'll get it in a minute."

But I didn't move, and I was still sitting, watching the vague white snow chips glint in the patio light when he knocked again.

"Come in."

"What're you doing sitting here in the dark?" He leaned across me, kissed my cheek as he snapped on the table light.

The glare was harsh, biting for a second.

"Sitting here not thinking."

"You still feeling bad about . . . Who was here?"

"Joyce."

"Oh." He produced another bottle of wine from his coat pocket. "I thought we'd stick to the same."

"You're a liar, Willie."

"What?"

"You're devious. A fucking liar."

He looked like I'd hit him. I didn't know which word he was reacting to.

"What's the . . ."

"Joyce let me in on the chain of command around here. The choice was yours, not the dean's, and Rodney doesn't even have a degree."

"How should I . . ."

"You're a fake. You've probably always been a fake."

"Don't say that."

"A fucking fake."

"It was for your own good. We can't go on in this . . ."

"For *your* own good."

"No, I . . ."

"Oh, shut up, Willie."

The two stiff curls hung at the sides of his forehead. His face had sagged away from them. He hadn't taken off his coat, and I noticed all of a sudden how big it looked on him.

"Good night, Willie."

"Just let me . . ."

"You don't need to explain. I understand." Strangely enough, as I said it, I realized I did.

He stood looking at me, haggard, the lines deep around his eyes and nose.

"Good-by, Willie."

"I . . ."

"Good-by."

He walked back across the room, his shoulders slumped. He opened the door and turned to look back at me. "The snow will be slick tomorrow. Remember these El Paso drivers . . . Be careful on the free . . . way . . ."

I nodded and he waited a second and then went out.

"Willie."

His eyes jerked back toward me, his hand on the door ready to pull it shut.

"Why don't you buy yourself a pair of gloves this winter?"

PEACE GROVE

★

Ray Gonzalez

THE LAST HOUSE WHERE I LIVED IN EL PASO WAS ONE MILE from the Peace Grove, the cottonwoods Pancho Villa planted on the Mexican side of the Rio Grande near Juarez, where his rebel troops fought government soldiers in 1911. The battle lasted two days and was witnessed by hundreds of El Pasoans who camped along the river to watch. The Peace Grove was Villa's way of showing there could be peace, that the bloody Mexican Revolution could end. But the planting of the trees may have also been a signal to the U.S. and General John Pershing to leave the Mexicans alone to fight their own war. Even though they captured Juarez, Villa's army did not stay long. Two days later, they headed south into Chihuahua to continue the fight.

The idea of a revolutionary planting trees and the fact that the trees are standing today intrigued me when I lived in a tiny adobe house on the border of the two countries. From that house, one hundred yards from the Rio Grande, I saw thousands of illegal aliens, or as some of them preferred to be called, *mojados*, cross into the U.S. I stared every day at the crumbling huts of the Juarez *colonias* across the river.

The area behind my house was a favorite crossing point because the Rio Grande was very shallow west of downtown El Paso. The U.S. Border Patrol could not keep Mexicans out despite their constant patrolling of the area. The Peace Grove stood between the river and the low hills on the west end of Juarez, its neat rows of trees in sharp contrast to the decaying streets and houses, the broken walls painted turquoise, yellow, purple, or pink. The vast poverty and squalor spread for miles, blessed by the enduring limbs of the Peace Grove.

One evening after a sudden thunderstorm had rolled up from the south and swept through El Paso, I went for a walk on the levee road above the irrigation canal. It paralleled the river on the U.S. side. The black clouds moved slowly to the west and their bottom layers turned pink in the setting sun. Despite the heavy rain, the Rio Grande was nearly dry. It flowed in slow, muddy trails. As I walked south, I looked across the river at the cottonwoods and thought about my grandfather, Bonifacio Canales, who fought for Villa in the battle for Juarez. It was the only fighting he did during the revolution. He and my grandmother Julia had just been married. They were both fourteen years old and had fled Chihuahua for the border. When Villa's men entered Juarez, young *campesinos* chose sides, most of them deciding to help Villa take the town. After the victorious rebel army left, my grandparents fled to Arizona, where Bonifacio worked for the railroad in the Yaqui Indian labor camps until too much alcohol brought his early death in 1941.

I wondered what the young boys who fought for Villa thought about planting trees. Did anyone try to destroy the grove after Villa's departure? Did any of the rebels ever return to Juarez to see if the trees had grown? The rebels reminded me of several friends who had gone to Nicaragua in 1985, after the Sandinista Revolution, to show their support by joining local work brigades in planting trees in the war-torn country. They told me how U.S.-backed Contras later destroyed many of the crops in the countryside and burned the young trees the Americans had planted.

My thoughts were interrupted by the sound of tires screeching on gravel. I looked behind me at the Border Patrol car that pulled up in a frantic spin. The officer leaped out of the lime-green car and pointed a finger at me. "Hey, you wetback!" the Anglo officer sneered. "Got you, again!"

"Are you talking to me, Officer?" I smiled and spoke in my clearest Texas drawl. Yes, Chicanos can have good Texas accents when they want to.

"You speak English?" He approached with one hand on his holstered gun. He wore tiny sunglasses and sported a crewcut. He looked like he was in his early twenties.

"Yes. I probably speak it better than you."

He stood in front of me with his hands on his hips, uncertain what to do next. As we stared at each other, I could hear someone speaking Spanish across the river and the busy humming of traffic on Paisano Street to my right.

"You look like a wetback to me. Got any I.D.?"

I looked around to see if there were any potential witnesses nearby, but no one else was in sight. "Yes, I have a driver's license, but I don't think I have to show it to you, since I am an American citizen."

No muscle moved on the stony face behind the sunglasses. "Where do you live?"

I pointed to my house one hundred yards down the road. "Over there."

We both heard the squawking of his car radio and we stared at each other. "Yeah, I've seen you around here. Any wetbacks cross here?" He shook his head toward the river.

I shrugged and didn't answer. He shook his head again and walked briskly to his car. He gave me another look and climbed in. He pulled into reverse, made another loud turn on the narrow road, and screeched away in a thick trail of dust. I watched the car disappear around a bend, and then saw four Mexicans run across the road. They had been crouching behind the tall salt cedars that lined the street. They climbed the embankment and quickly vanished on Paisano toward downtown.

I laughed, but was angry. It was not the first time I had been stopped by the Border Patrol. They probably did have the right to ask for my I.D., but they usually backed down once they discovered that the brown-skinned person they were questioning was an English-speaking U.S. citizen who could report them to their superiors. I had called Border Patrol headquarters once when a patrol car pulled me and a friend over for no reason. The two officers stuck flashlights in our faces, didn't say a word to us, and drove off into the night. I reported them, but of course nothing happened.

I tried to forget this latest confrontation and kept walking to get a better view of the Peace Grove. I stopped another fifty yards down the road and looked across the river. The final light from the setting sun hit the trees and outlined them in orange. The combination of sunset and distant rain clouds cast a dark, burning glow over the western sky and washed over the Juarez colonias, making the houses look like they were on fire. I spotted a few people climbing the dirt streets to disappear over the tops of the hills. Several dogs barked and ran among the garbage that lay in the streets closest to the river.

I sat on the embankment of the levee road and watched the whole area turn darker. The river sparkled but barely moved. Its mud stretched in long layers of smooth sand for hundreds of yards. As I sat on the border of the two countries, watching the still group of full cottonwoods with their huge leaves, I realized that there was no border. Pancho Villa had planted those trees directly across from where I sat because that is where events dictated he should plant them. The two dozen trees, standing tall and healthy along the river, found their spot near the water because the line had been drawn there. It had been

decided decades ago. No Mexican Revolution and no constant prowling of Border Patrol cars, nor the fact that thousands of people crossed
this spot illegally, could affect the way the trees grew. They had no say
in which direction the roots had spread since 1911.

I felt exhilarated and wanted to dig under the river with my bare
hands to find the roots of the trees spreading across the river, covering
this side. I wanted to know that the trees would absorb so much water
that, sooner or later, they would dry the river, making the riverbed disappear. Then there would be no sign of a border! I wanted to see
horses and Villa's troops digging to stick young trees into the mud
across from me. I wanted to find El Pasoans sitting on the bank, having a good time, watching the planting instead of acting like war was
a sporting event to watch, pass judgment on, then interfere with. I
didn't know all the historical details behind the planting of the trees.
My thoughts of roots coming toward me, underground, wiping out the
levee road and the patrol cars, blended with the last light of the
evening.

I heard a splash in the water, but could not see anything in the
river. Smoke from wood stoves and an occasional electric light dotted
the hills of the colonias. I rose and started to walk home, then heard
angry voices across the river. I could barely make out two running figures as they moved through the Peace Grove. One of them shouted
something I couldn't understand, and the angry voice of a woman
replied, "¡Vamonos! ¡Vamonos!"

They stopped under a tree and argued in loud voices. The second
figure was a man who tugged at the woman's dress. She shook him off,
stepped a few feet back, and yelled something at him. He threw up his
hands and joined her. They approached the river and began to wade
across.

I turned away and headed home. When I reached the bend in the
levee, I paused and looked for them. They crouched in the middle of
the low river, two more waiting to enter, watching for *la migra*. I didn't
see any patrol cars. The couple ran the rest of the way and blended

into the darkness on this side. I kept walking, then heard a car engine start. The headlights of a patrol car blinded me and blocked my path. I stopped and waited for the officer, a different one this time, to get out and question me. I knew this meant I was going to take my time getting back to my house along the Rio Grande.

THE DEATH MASK OF PANCHO VILLA

★

Dagoberto Gilb

It's late, very late. I've been in bed since eleven o'clock, for almost four hours, trying to get some sleep. I haven't been going to bed this early, but it's Sunday night and there's nothing on television. Not that I really like to watch television late at night the rest of the days. I do it too much because I don't know what else to do with myself. Probably I could listen to music on the radio. That's not true, I almost forgot. There's nothing on on the radio anymore, and around here, whether it's El Paso tejano or Juárez ranchera, pop from Mexico City, hard or soft American rock, it's all boring, and anyway there's commercial after commercial, just as irritating, maybe even more so, as the ones on late-night television. Okay, so maybe it's me.

Really it's not late, it's early, early morning, and one other reason I need to get some sleep is that I have to be somewhere in the morning.

I've arranged, finally, to see about getting some work. I've been treating it pretty easy for a while, telling myself I was sick of doing physical labor and trying hard to blame my age for feeling that way. Unsuccessfully. So I've been sitting around, not doing as much as I probably should, getting soft. Doing too much television, I'll you the truth. I gotta admit, that isn't what I consider having a great time, but it can't be called suffering either. Our bills might be getting paid, my kids might be running around laughing and breaking things, my wife might finally keep a job for a while, but we're not getting rich. Not that I ever really lived my life trying to get rich. Which is why I've been feeling guilty about my working situation, my lack of it. It's gotten me jumpy and nervous, worried about something really bad happening to us while I'm doing nothing about a paycheck. Which might help explain why I think the worst when I hear that pounding at the door. I don't even realize what it is, and my wife's so asleep I have to shake her awake.

What I do is pick up my son's aluminum baseball bat. I even think of putting on my boots. I guess that's some deal I have, not wanting to get into late night violence barefooted. Why do I think it might be something violent? Good question. I guess it shows how I'm thinking, even if it doesn't make much sense—because obviously violent criminals aren't going to be knocking on the door, ringing the bell to wake me up. I'm just asleep and not reasoning too clearly. Also there's been a lot of talk in the papers about thieves breaking in. Desperate young punks from the other side of the river disobeying all the rules of thief etiquette.

But when I finally get the door open it's just a friend and some other guy I don't know. One of my oldest, best friends in all the world, a guy I started hanging out with in high school, then after that worked a few construction jobs with. We shared a lot of girlfriends, a lot of bottles and cans, and traveled together often when we did . . . well, outlaw business years ago. All to say that I've had some of the best times I've ever had with the guy. We're still friends, but time has passed. We both ended up married—him first!—and we both have kids, and our wives talked to each other more than we did. Which is how I heard he was having some home troubles. First he got suspended from his job at the railroad. Then he got caught, or accused, of being bad with another woman and Dora, his wife, threw him out of the house. In fact she did the whole routine—threw his clothes out onto the driveway with an empty suitcase and locked all the doors and windows.

"You whore," I tell him after I turn on the yellow outdoor light. Gabe's wearing a tight, too-small, white T-shirt and still looks in good shape, particularly for a man in his late-thirties. It makes me feel bad that there he is, like always, a beer in his hand, a glaze in his eyes, somehow being healthier than me, drunk and whatever else. The only thing not like him is that the T-shirt and jeans are a little dirty and wrinkled, and his hair, which when he worked steady he didn't keep so long, looks like it just got off a pillow, the same as mine. Stuff his wife, it would seem, has been taking care of for a long time.

I open the door and go onto the front porch with my socks on. "Everybody in the house is asleep," I say, an explanation for why I'm not offering them the indoor accommodations. We shake hands, then wrap arms around one another for a long-time-no-see abrazo. "I been wondering about you. Hear about you having too much fun."

"Gotta have fun sometimes. You know that." Gabe's grin is almost exuberant.

"I heard about the clothes on the driveway too."

"Which ones?" he asks, still smiling.

"Whadaya mean?"

"There were two sets of them."

I don't understand, and I don't say anything.

"A day or two after the old lady handed me a suitcase, that other bitch came over and threw a pile she had on the driveway too," he tells me, and we laugh pretty good. "You know what I said when Dora called me about that? 'She didn't hit the grease spot, did she?' When she hung up on me my fucking ear hurt."

We're both laughing while Gabe's friend keeps this steady smile throughout. "This is Ortíz," Gabe says, finally introducing us. "Román Ortíz." I shake his friend's hand. Despite the smile, the man's gauntness, for me, translates into something else I can't quite put a name on, and my first impression is that his loose western-style clothes don't seem to suit his character.

It gets too quiet for a moment. Not a dog, not even the shuffle of a breeze. It looks very dark beyond the yellow porch, and cold, though it isn't.

"You wanna beer?" Gabe asks me, plucking a can off from the vine of three he'd carried to the porch.

"No. It's kinda late for me. Or early."

Gabe looks at me disappointed and the other guy looks at Gabe, though still with that smile. Gabe breaks the tab from the can he'd offered me.

I feel bad, immediately, for saying no. Somehow I've done something to spoil the visit, I've brought things down a notch. "So how you been really?" I ask.

"All right," he tells me, uneffusive. He takes a couple swallows of beer.

"What about that job?" I ask. "You gonna get back there?" Working at the railroad, you have to understand, is one of the best paying jobs in the city.

Gabe makes a sour face and leans against the porch railing. "A bunch of suckass culeros. I'll find something better."

Very few people could. Very few people would want to leave that job. Gabe can do both. I know it as well as he does. I used to feel the same way about myself, though not anymore. I try to blame that on El Paso or the times or my age. But I'm only a year older than Gabe. It's another thing I admire about him and dislike about me.

Ortíz hasn't so much as moved except to sip on his beer. "You mind if I piss over there?" he asks, indicating beyond the porch.

"Of course not," I say. "I do it all the time." I don't do it all the time, but once in a while, just to keep in practice.

Gabe and I don't say anything until we hear Ortíz's stream hitting the hard dirt that is my front yard.

"So what's up?" I finally ask.

"This guy has something I thought you'd want to see," Gabe says. "Remember that time we were in Mexico and that old dude said he had pictures of him with Pancho Villa?"

I was into collecting Pancho Villa stuff years ago because he was my hero. More than that really. Anyway, I'd found letters he'd written, bought a holster and pistol that were supposed to be his, and in our front room I still have a framed document Villa'd signed for my great-uncle saying what an honor it'd been to fight together during the revolution. It has been a while since I'd thought about any of this though: I guess because I had children and got married. And worked a lot. And because I got older. I've got all kinds of excuses if I let myself think about it.

"So he has photographs?" I say, trying to sound interested. I'm not at all.

"A mask," says Gabe.

Ortíz is stepping back up onto the porch. "His death mask."

"I never heard of such a thing," I say.

"There were three of them made," Ortíz says. Same smile. "A Hollywood producer has one and a senator has the other." Ortíz opens another can of beer. No change in the smile, but the face around it seems prouder now.

My first impression isn't improving. I'm pretty sure Gabe's just met the guy in a bar, and in my humble opinion . . . well, I'd call it bar talk.

Gabe lights a joint. I'm wishing I were back in bed, the door locked. Which makes me feel bad again. What's happened to me? I don't think anything's wrong with marijuana, and I like smoking it the same as I always have. That's what I say anyway. The only thing is I don't smoke it very often anymore. I even have about two or three joints worth in a bag that was given to me almost a year ago. I guess I never want to smoke it by myself, and I'd be embarrassed now to use it with anyone else because it's so dried out. I should throw it away. I will throw it away.

I go ahead and smoke some because I don't know how to say no to this too, though the truth is that's what I feel like saying. I don't know why we're not talking. I think it has something to do with me, with me standing in my socks, not inviting them in, not saying let's go. Though maybe it's Gabe. He's too quiet, and it can't only be that he's unhappy because I don't feel like drinking beer. Maybe it's something between him and Ortíz. When we used to hang out together a lot, it was Gabe who usually met the guys like this in the first place. Gabe was the one who'd listen and believe, while I was the one who was skeptical. Gabe'd get all the information, I'd put it together, then we'd both come up with a conclusion, a decision—you know, we'd solve another little human-oddball mystery, and sometimes actually do something with the person. Either buy or sell. Was this guy trying to sell Gabe something? Or trade? Or was Gabe thinking of a sale to him? But why would he need me after all these years? And if he did, why doesn't he just say something to me straight out? Then maybe he thinks I'd just want to buy it. But why right now? It's about three a.m., or later, and I can't think.

"So are you selling this thing or what?" I ask Ortíz.

"Absolutely not."

He stares at me with that smile. I look for some kind of indication from Gabe, but there's none. We're finishing off the joint.

"Then what you are you doing with it?"

"He's got it at his place," Gabe says. "Let's go see it."

"You haven't seen it?" I ask him.

"Sure. I want you to see it. All you gotta do is get some shoes." He drops the roach and grinds it out with the sole of his boot. Then he pops another can of beer. He stops leaning on the wrought-iron railing around the porch and stands like he's ready to get going.

Gabe's push isn't out of exuberance now, but it's along the lines of it, some excess of something, and I can't figure it out. I start thinking about the problems he's having. No job, being away from his kids. Except that's not Gabe at all. I know him too well. He'll get back together with Dora whether she thinks she never wants to see him again right now or not, he'll get his job back or a better one, and I know he believes that too, and even if it didn't turn out that way a few years from now, I know he wouldn't think it wouldn't. So it's not that, it's not like he needs me, needs a friend or some TV emotion like that. And somehow it doesn't seem like he really wants me to hang out either. He wants me to go with him, but it doesn't seem personal, it doesn't seem to me like he's asking. It's more like he's telling me to go with them. Like it's for my own good or something.

"I can't go tonight," I say, thinking it's not tonight but this morning.

"How come?" Gabe asks. He's disappointed again.

"I gotta do things. In a few hours, as a matter of fact. Normal shit."

All the sudden a cop car cruises by. Not slow and not fast, just on a routine pass through the neighborhood. Except from behind us, from the dirt alley where we wouldn't have expected that blue-and-white to come from, and a dog starts barking at him because a dispatcher talks over the police radio and the window on the driver's side is down.

"Normal shit?" says Gabe. "Since when did you worry about doing normal shit?"

That stings because he's right. Or used to be. "Why don't I just see it tomorrow? You taking it out of town or something?" I'm feeling a little defensive now. "Somebody buying it?" I look at Gabe. He's not looking back at me.

"I'm giving it away," says Ortíz. "There are only three of them, and I'm sending mine to Moscow." His smile is the same but it's fading.

"Moscow?" I look at Gabe once more and feel stoned. He hits on his beer.

"In Russia," says Ortíz.

"I know where it is," I tell him. "Why there?"

"Because that's where John Reed is buried," Ortíz says. "John Reed wrote about the Mexican Revolution, then went to Russia and wrote about the Russian Revolution."

A smile starts to come on me because now the cop car is cruising by again, only this time in front of us, and it seems so ridiculous especially because we're about to talk about communism or something at three or so in the morning and I don't have shoes on. Then another cop car goes by. We know it has to be another one because it's coming from another street, toward us, too soon after the last one. It turns right, opposite the direction the first one did. And now more dogs are barking in the neighborhood.

"I better turn off the light," I say. I open the screen door, then the other, and reach inside to turn off the yellow porch light. A cop car passes a second later. "You guys better not leave for a while."

"I don't need a DWI," says Ortíz.

Ortíz's car, I notice for the first time, is faded green, or blue, I can't be positive in this dark, with a peeling vinyl roof.

"So how'd you get this mask?" I ask.

"I just did," Ortíz says, finishing his beer.

"How do you know it's Villa?"

"People have seen it. Warren Beatty saw it and wanted it."

Warren Beatty, the actor. Now I am smiling the most. Dogs are barking all over the neighborhood and another cop car passes us. I swear it's a third one. I'm sure we can't be seen without the porch light on though.

"Why not just keep it right here, right here in El Paso?" I suggest. "Probably a lot of people would like to see it. It'd be a great contribution. It seems to me anyway."

Ortíz turns his head away from me and my naiveté. "People here wouldn't respect it enough, and it's fragile. Over there they care about things more than they do here. All of Europe is like that too. They have museums to take care of important cultural things. In Germany there are probably thirty opera houses to every one here." The speech erases

Ortíz's smile, and he steps over and reaches down to get the last can of beer.

"So you've been to Europe, to Germany?" I ask.

"No," Ortíz says, humorless.

It's that I've stolen his smile. I'm looking for cop cars and watching lights go on in the house across the street where a dog is barking the loudest and steadiest. "Moscow, huh?"

Ortíz gathers himself after a big swallow of the beer. "The Mexican Revolution was the first in the century, and the bolsheviks used it as an example of common people rising up. John Reed was there for both revolutions and was buried at the Kremlin as a hero. They'll put the mask near him as a memorial."

I'm still smiling, but not because I'm unconvinced or skeptical. More that the cops have quit driving by and the dog across the street won't stop barking, which is probably why another dog still barks farther down the street. I'm smiling just thinking about how we're having this conversation about Russians and death masks in the dark and quiet right on my El Paso porch with the light out, all while I'm in my socks.

"I'd really like to see it some time," I say.

Neither of them say anything.

"I guess I should probably get a couple hours in," I say.

Gabe looks a little disappointed again. Or maybe apologetic. I don't want him to feel bad for coming by, for banging on my door. I haven't done anything for weeks but watch the stupid television.

"You guys better look around to see if the police are waiting for you to pull away," I say. I wish I knew how to say more.

Gabe just shrugs my worry off. He never did care about things like that, and, maybe because he didn't, never had to.

They both stop and piss before they get into Ortíz's car. It starts with a cheap gas and old motor sound, and finally rolls away without headlights for a few yards.

I lock the door and climb back in bed. I'm thinking that I probably can wait on seeing about this job, and I'm thinking how nice it feels being stoned and sleepy. My wife asks me who it was and I say it was Gabe and wait for her to ask me some more. She doesn't, but in my head I start asking questions for her and answering them. Or asking for myself: He wanted me to go out with him. To go see something this guy he knows had. No, I don't really know why I didn't go. No, I really don't know why he wanted me to. Maybe he thought because of Pancho Villa. Or maybe because he thought I'd have a good time. Which I haven't had in a long time. No, I don't know why I didn't go, I don't know why it didn't seem like I should. I used to not think about it, I used to just go. Gabe and I used to do things together. Things just like this.

I'm on my back in bed and my wife, after I've been lying there all this time, finally asks me what Gabe wanted. Nothing, I tell her, except he wanted me to go look at Pancho Villa's death mask. That makes me smile all over again. At what? she asks. Don't think about it, I say. But what time is it? she asks. What's the difference? I say.

NORTH OF THE BIG RIVER

★

Elmer Kelton

I'D ALWAYS LOOKED DOWN MY NOSE AT RANCHMEN HIRING wetbacks. That's the people who swim over into Texas from the south of the Rio Grande. They generally come in the dark of the moon, looking back over their shoulders for the border patrol.

Folks call me Ike Ballantine. For forty years I've been ranching ten miles north of the river. The way I figured it, cheap wetback labor was unfair to workers on our own side of the river. Besides, hiring wetbacks was breaking the law, just like their swimming over had been. But then Pedro Gonzales came along.

It all commenced one evening when I was sitting in a rawhide chair on my front porch, glancing over the stock news in the San Angelo paper. I happened to look up over my reading glasses and spot this feller slipping up through the brush afoot. I stepped into the house and grabbed my .30-.30. As I levered a cartridge into the breech I watched the man bend low and sprint up to the house. He disappeared under a window.

Little Juanita Chavez was fixing supper in the kitchen. Her eyes got as big as the biscuits she was cutting when I slipped through there with the rifle. I stepped out the door and waited on the back porch.

When the fellow came around the corner, I shoved the gun barrel under his nose. He dropped a little bundle he was carrying. His brownish skin turned a shade lighter, and he licked his lips.

"Please, sir," he said nervously, in good English. "I mean no harm."

I saw then that he was young, not much older than Juanita.

All of a sudden he slumped over onto the porch. I was so surprised I dropped the rifle and grabbed him. That was when I saw the bloodstains on his shirt, and the knife-slit in his sleeve.

I yelled for Juanita to go get her dad, but old Trinidad was already running up from the barn. His soft belly bounced up and down over a low-slung belt. Neither one of us was as young as we used to be, but we managed to carry the boy into the house and lay him down on a couch.

Juanita hustled some hot water. Her pretty face got a little pale as she cleaned up the knife wound. It wasn't too deep, and it hadn't struck an artery. She held a warm, damp cloth on the boy's forehead while I poured rubbing alcohol into the wound. Busy as I was, I couldn't help seeing the way Juanita's dark eyes melted when that boy began to flinch.

I'd known Juanita ever since she was born, and I'd never seen her look that way before. Her dad had been working for me for thirty years. He was nearing middle age when he brought a young wife to share the little house he lived in, out back of mine. The woman had died when Juanita was born. My own wife was gone, too. So between old Trinidad and me, we'd managed to raise Juanita ourselves. Now, watching the way she handled the man, I guess we both felt proud of ourselves.

The young man looked startled as he opened his eyes and saw Juanita bending over him. Waking up and seeing a girl like her would be apt to make any man think of heaven.

We heard the rattling of a pickup truck on the road leading up to the house. The young Mexican's eyes got wide as if it was the hangman coming.

"It's Señor Barfield," he exclaimed. "I must get away!" He jumped up and almost fell to the floor. I helped Juanita put him back on the couch.

"Keep him still," I told her. "I don't know what this is all about, but Barfield won't get him."

I walked out front as Clint Barfield braked his pickup to a stop. Although he was my neighbor on the south, it was the first time he had been on my place since I'd caught him trying to cheat me in a cattle trade a couple of years back.

He crawled out of his pickup like a mad bull coming through a barbed-wire fence. Another man was with him, his dark-skinned segundo named Salazar.

"I'm looking for a damned wetback that left my place this mornin'," Barfield boomed. "If he's come over here, I want him right now!"

Barfield's face had always made me think of a grizzly bear, especially when he was mad.

"What do you want him for?" I asked.

"He stole one of my horses. If you got him here, bring him out."

I could feel a fire kindling up in me. I wished I'd brought my gun along.

"There's nobody here but me and the Chavez family," I told him flatly. "And I'd just as soon you'd git off my place."

Barfield stood glaring as if he wanted to take an ax handle to me. He was big enough to whip me without any help.

Just then Salazar came around the corner of the house. I hadn't noticed him sneak away. He was carrying the bundle of clothes the young Mexican had dropped by the back porch.

"I won't fool with you, Ballantine," Barfield thundered. "Drag that boy out here or I'll tell the border patrol you're harborin' wetbacks!"

I couldn't help snickering. "But you'd have to tell them how you come to know. You probably had him grubbin' prickly pear, then refused to pay him, like you do so many wetbacks. If he took a horse, he'd probably earned it."

Barfield and Salazar began to move toward me. Then they stopped and looked up on the porch. I glanced back. Old Trinidad stood there like a bulldog, the .30-.30 rifle in his hands.

Barfield swallowed hard, and his face got the color of a ripe apple. He raised his fist. "All right, Ballantine, but we'll be back."

They crawled into the pickup and drove off so fast the dust didn't settle for ten minutes.

The boy felt a lot better then. His name was Pedro Gonzales, he told us. He had worked as a vaquero on ranches down in Chihuahua. But the outbreak of foot and mouth disease and the quarantine laid against Mexican cattle by the United States government had been hard on Mexican ranchmen, and Pedro couldn't find work any more. He had decided to swim over and try the Texas side.

He had hit Barfield's ranch, which lay on the river. Barfield and Salazar had offered him a nice chunk of money to help them with a job and keep his mouth shut.

Under the light of the moon Salazar had led Pedro and a couple more vaqueros across the river. They had picked up about forty steer yearlings from a Mexican ranchman and pushed them back across the river. A few hundred yards to the north, on rocky land where tracks wouldn't show, Barfield had a movable sheep-panel corral and a couple of bobtail cattle trucks waiting for the contraband steers. Bought cheap, the cattle would at least triple his money on Texas markets.

By the time Pedro realized what serious trouble he was letting himself in for, it was too late. Next day he bundled up the few clothes he had. He found Salazar in the barn and asked to be paid off.

Salazar knew the boy was pulling up stakes. He slipped out his knife and sprung at Pedro. Pedro grabbed the man's arm and held the knifepoint inches away from his throat. The two pitched and rolled on the barn floor.

Sweat was popping out on Salazar's swarthy face as Pedro held him on the floor and struggled for the knife. Pedro saw a big, rusty gate hinge under a saddle rack. He grabbed it with one hand and slung it at Salazar's head. The knife blade cut into Pedro's arm, but Salazar was stunned.

Holding his wounded arm, Pedro grabbed his bundle and ran out the barn door. A saddled horse stood tied to a fence. It was Salazar's. Pedro swung up and lit out the only open gate.

He should have headed south of the river, he realized later. But the pasture lay to the north, and Pedro's only thought was to get away.

Men came after him, but he stayed clear of them. Finally the tired horse stumbled, and Pedro sprawled on the ground. He was weak, and couldn't get up in time to catch the mount, so he started out afoot.

As he got his strength back, Pedro turned out to be a lot of help to us. At first he worked around the houses and corrals, helping old Trinidad finish up a lot of jobs that there hadn't been time for before. He fixed up the kitchen for Juanita, rearranging shelves and building new ones to save her a lot of steps. He fixed the leaky faucets and cleaned out the stovepipes. I could see Juanita's eyes go soft every time he came around her. It worried me a little.

By the time Pedro had been on the place three weeks, I was ready to let him stay, border patrol or no border patrol. I'd just about forgotten the trouble I'd had with Clint Barfield, and Pedro was a top-notch cowboy.

But then it all came back to me in a hail of hot lead.

Pedro and I were out horseback, looking for wormies in the south pasture which neighbored Barfield's place. I didn't think much about riding across the flat close to the fence. I'd done it ten thousand times before. All of a sudden a bullet zipped between us and whined off into the brush. My horse reared up and like to've spilled me. Another shot came from over past the fence, and a third bullet hit the horse. I sailed out over his shoulder and lit rolling in the sand. The rifleman was really after me now. A bullet thudded into the ground in front of my face as I got up. I started running, and another hit behind me.

Pedro yelled. I turned and saw him spurring after me. He reined up, grabbed me, and helped me swing up behind him. Then we rode for better cover, the rifleman still shooting. Pedro's horse, Snorter, didn't like the double load, but I managed to hold on to Pedro.

We rode straight to the house. I stomped in, grabbed my .30-.30, and got another gun for Pedro.

"From now on this gun is yours," I said, my blood hot enough to melt the watch in my pocket. "If you ever catch any of Barfield's bunch on my place, use it!"

We caught fresh horses and headed back, me ridin' Trinidad's old saddle. Nothing happened when we got to where we'd been shot at. The man was gone. We tied our horses to the fence and crossed over afoot. I was still mad enough to've bit the wires in two.

All we could find was spent cartridge cases, an empty Bull Durham sack, and a penny-size Mexican match box.

"Salazar!" Pedro gritted, half spitting the word out.

"The sheriff'll be interested in this," I said angrily. Then I thought better. He would be *too* interested. I'd have to tell him about Pedro. By this time I knew I sure didn't want to lose that boy.

Juanita didn't want to lose him either. She was waiting by the gate when we rode in. Tears of happiness rolled down her cheeks as she saw that we were both in good shape. She threw her arms around Pedro and clung to him, and I noticed he held on to her pretty tight.

Old Trinidad was standing in the barn door. He shook his gray head. The wrinkles in his face looked deeper than ever. "What do we do when he must go back to Mexico?" he asked me sadly. "Juanita, she has Mexican blood, but she is American. She not happy south of the river."

I felt like there was a heavy rock on top of my heart. "She won't be happy here, either Trinidad—not without him."

That night I began to get some hope. I read in the Angelo paper that Mexico was taking Texas off its labor blacklist and the ranchmen and farmers could make applications to keep any wetbacks that were already on their places.

I didn't tell Pedro or the Chavezes. No use getting their hopes up for something that might not work out.

The next morning I got into the pickup and drove to town. I hunted up a border patrol officer and asked him about the piece in the paper. It was right, he said. I'd have to go to an employment commission office and file application to keep Pedro.

It was mid-afternoon when I finally hit the long road back to the ranch, and not long before sundown when I drove up to the house. Juanita came running out the door when she heard me. Tears were streaming down her face.

"He's gone!" she cried. "He's gone!"

She was so broke up I couldn't get any sense out of her. While she cried on my shoulder, old Trinidad told me about it. Pedro had saddled up Snorter and left a couple of hours before. He had felt he was to blame for me getting shot at. He had told Juanita he loved her, but he knew she couldn't be happy in Mexico. And he didn't want to be torn away from her later, the way he would be if the border patrol got him. So he was going back to Mexico now, before it was too late.

He had taken the rifle I had given him, and a pocketful of shells, on the chance that he might strike some of Barfield's bunch on his way to the river. If we couldn't head him off before he got to the river, there wasn't much chance of ever getting him back. The Mexican government had a habit of throwing Americans in the calaboose for going down there soliciting labor.

I told Trinidad we'd get the pickup and try to overtake him. I took the .30-.30 down off the rack and got my deer-hunting rifle out of the closet for Trinidad.

We took out across country, hoping to beat him to the river. We

NORTH OF THE BIG RIVER

might have, too, if we hadn't hit that rough stretch and got the pickup stuck on high center. We fumed and fussed for an hour before we got the blamed thing loose. It was dark then, but the moon was coming out.

Way ahead of us, and off to the right, we could see car lights moving. We cut our own lights off and felt along in the dark. A mile from the river we heard shots, and I recognized the peculiar sound of that old rifle Pedro had taken.

"Pedro's run onto Barfield's bunch," I said, my heart climbing up in my throat. I gunned the old pickup, and we bounced across that rough country like a matchbox behind a bicycle. I didn't dare turn the lights on now.

A little way from where the shooting was, I pulled to a stop.

"I'm goin' down to haul Pedro out of there, Trinidad," I said. "You better stay here. If somethin' goes wrong, it'll be good to have you out here where you can help us. If we make it, we'll pick you up."

Trinidad protested, but he got out. As I drove off he was still arguing with me, using his hands as much as his mouth.

I stepped on the gas again, heading for that rifle. Soon I saw Pedro.

Jamming on the brakes, I tooted the horn and hollered: "Over here, Pedro! It's me, Ike!"

Pedro fired one more shot and came running. Guns flashed back in the darkness. A bullet slammed through the top of the pickup. Pedro jumped in, and we spun back around.

"Thanks to God you have come," he breathed. "My shells were about gone."

Barfield was bringing cattle across the river again, he told me breathlessly. Pedro had accidentally run into one of Barfield's sentries, stationed down the river a ways to keep a lookout for the border patrol.

When the shooting had started, Pedro had got down behind cover, and his horse had run off.

They were after us on horseback now. Pedro smashed the back window and fired through it with his rifle. Bullets clanged into the pickup. Every time Pedro levered a hot shellcase out of the rifle, I flinched, expecting it to flip down my collar.

That's why I didn't see the ditch ahead till it was too late. A front wheel cut into it. We came to a sudden jolting stop.

By the time our heads had cleared, Barfield, Salazar, and another rider had us covered.

"Crawl out of there with your hands up," Barfield growled. "This is where we even up the score."

There wasn't much else we could do. Salazar and the other rider tied our hands behind our backs.

"What do we do with the pickup, Señor Barfield?" asked Salazar. "Nobody cares about this wetback, but they look for Ike Ballantine."

Barfield grunted. "Nobody'll ever know what happened if they can't find no sign. I know a gully close to here where we can cave a bank in on top of the pickup and cover it up, with them two in it."

Barfield got in the pickup, started racing the motor and rocked back and forth till the pickup came out of the ditch. He left the motor running and jumped out.

"Put them in the back and keep an eye on them, Salazar," he ordered. "We may need them to push if we get in a ditch again." To the rider he said, "Follow along behind us with the horses. We got to have them get away from the gully."

They forced us to get in the bed of the pickup, then Barfield commenced driving slowly across country in the moonlight. Salazar sat there by the endgate, watching us like a cat does a mouse he's playing with.

Behind us, down by the river, we saw three sets of car lights. A few shots rang out, then there was silence.

"The border patrol, Salazar," I said. Any other time I'd have laughed. "The shootin' must've brought them. They'll be roundin' up your friends with the trucks and cattle."

Even at the distance I could see fury cross over Salazar's swarthy face. "They will be too late to help you, señor."

I glanced sideways at Pedro. He was sitting in one corner, his back to the side of the pickup. I noticed he was working his wrists up and down a little. Barfield's bullets had left jagged holes in the pickup. Pedro was sawing his ropes in two on the rim of one of them.

Behind us I could see a rider following along. In the darkness I couldn't tell much about him, but I figured it was Barfield's man.

All of a sudden Pedro shook his ropes loose and sprang up at Salazar like a panther after a horse. The outlaw was too startled to do anything for a second. His gun went flying as Pedro hit him. Then the two plunged over the endgate and sprawled out on the ground.

Barfield braked the pickup to a sudden stop and piled out, a gun in his hand. Pedro wouldn't have a chance, I thought. Although my hands were behind my back, I stood up and jumped out at Barfield, hoping a boot heel in his belly might stop him. He dodged. As I went down on my knees he fetched me a blow with his gun barrel that flattened me out.

My heart seemed to stop beating as I raised up a little and saw Barfield trying to draw down on Pedro. But Pedro and Salazar were rolling on the ground like a couple of mountain lions. For a moment Pedro was on top. Barfield leveled the gun, and I closed my eyes.

But it wasn't a pistol that spoke. It was my deer rifle. I opened my eyes to see Barfield slump to the ground. Old Trinidad was there, the rifle in his hand. He was fighting to keep hold of a boogered horse.

I managed to get to my feet and walk over to him. Pedro and Salazar were still locked together on the ground. I caught the glint of a knife in Salazar's hand, and saw that Pedro was holding the man's wrist like a vise. Inch by inch Pedro forced the knife back around. All of a sudden he shoved it downward.

Salazar stiffened, shuddered, then kind of relaxed. He was dead.

Pedro arose slowly, looking at the knife. He dropped it in the sand and turned to look at us. His face gleamed with sweat.

"I should have killed him on that day at Barfield's," he said bitterly. "The chance was mine."

Car lights moved toward us, and a spotlight played back and forth across the brush. It was the border patrol. Pedro limped over to the pickup and turned on the lights to guide the patrolmen.

Old Trinidad picked up the knife and cut the ropes that my wrists were bound with.

"That was you that was follerin' us on horseback," I said. I still couldn't savvy. "I thought it was Barfield's man."

Trinidad grinned a little. "When you drive into the ditch I run to help. But I see the riders get there before me. I think it is better I wait. As soon as the pickup go, I slip up and take the man's horse away from him."

I began to savvy. "Where's the man now?"

Trinidad broke into a broad grin that reached from one ear to the other. "He's still there, I think. He have one awful headache."

Well sir, to make a long story short, the government was grateful to Pedro. It had suspected that cattle was being pushed across the river. Government riders had secretly searched over Barfield's place, but hadn't found any Mexican stock. That was because Barfield trucked them off.

Old Trinidad moved into the main house with me, putting his gear in the back bedroom. Then we all pitched in and started fixing up the house he and Juanita had been living in.

By the time we got through with it, it was a right pretty little place. Just right for a young couple to start out in.

COMMERCE STREET

★

Jim Sanderson

A s Georgie Chavez set his first foot into Texas mud, he said to himself that *Ignacio* was a Mexican name. His first name would be *George*, after the president. He grabbed weeds and the limb of a mesquite to pull himself on to the dry, hard bank, then looked behind him.

His brother Emilio was stuck in the river. With one hand, Emilio held the wrist of his wife Alicia and, with the other, he pressed the feet of his daughter Delores, who sat on his shoulders, against his chest. The undercurrent was sucking Alicia's feet out from under her. She tried to hold their suitcase out of the water and fought against the current. The bag she had slung around her neck dangled in the river and was pulled by the current. Emilio could do nothing but hold her up.

Georgie threw his pouch and suitcase down and jumped back into the river. He made his way to midstream, toward Alicia. Emilio let go of her wrist, and she took an uneasy step toward Georgie. The suitcase made her lean upriver; the bag around her neck pulled her downriver. Georgie reached toward her as she took another step. The current pulled her under. "No," Emilio said.

Georgie reached into the muddy water but could feel nothing. He saw the suitcase floating farther down river. He dove into the river and felt himself pulled. When he came up, he saw Alicia bob up ahead of him, then go under.

Now, TWELVE YEARS LATER, GEORGIE CHAVEZ WALKED across the Commerce Street bridge. Sweat pasted his T-shirt to his body. His straw hat did not keep the sweat from dripping down his nose and cheeks. He blew at the bead of sweat on the tip of his nose. A bus passed him on the bridge and he smelled its fumes.

Midway across the bridge, he turned east and looked at downtown San Antonio: the Tower of the Americas, the Bell Telephone Building, the Tower Life Building. Downtown posters, signs, the billboards read "Alamo National Bank," "Frost Bros.," "Southwestern Bell," "The San Antonio Folklife Festival," and "Visit the Lone Star Brewery." When he first got to San Antonio, Georgie thought that if he could look hard enough and long enough toward the east, he could see all the way to New York. Now he was satisfied with San Antonio.

He turned and walked west. Here he saw billboards that said "La Cerveza Nacional De Texas: Lone Star," "La Es Mejor: Budweiser," and "Centeno 24 hr. Super Market." Small signs, some hand-painted, said "Davilla's Golden Arcade," "Asar and Solomon: Pecan Shellers," and "Rudy Mendoza's Bail Bonds." Farther down Commerce were the ice houses (not the convenience stores with silly names) where Georgie liked to sit and drink beer with his buddies. Living on the westside made Georgie an American to himself.

Georgie walked four blocks down Commerce and turned south on a side street. He came to Boss's large white house, the finest in the neighborhood. Almost eight years old, it looked new with a manicured lawn, fresh white paint, and well-trimmed hedges. It looked elegant because of the tall pecan trees in the front and back yards. Georgie walked up the long gravel and caliche driveway toward the garage. The pickup truck with the camper over its bed was half out of the garage. A stocky pair of legs stuck out from under the front of the truck; Medina slid out on his back. "Boss wants to see you," he said. Medina stood, stared at Georgie, and wiped his hands on a once-red rag faded to pink. Medina seemed to bounce on his toes and dip his shoulders even when he stood still. He was a real *pachuco*.

Georgie heard a buzz and looked over the hedges and behind him at the front yard. A newly arrived Mexican, smiling broadly, pushed a lawn mower across the lawn. He waved at Georgie. Georgie smiled and waved back, "Who's he?"

"New wetback."

"He got a family?"

"No. You better talk to Boss," Medina said. "Boss wants something." Medina stared at Georgie. Georgie stepped off the gravel and opened the gate that led into the big backyard and immediately felt the temperature drop as he walked under the pecan trees. Even with the lawn mower buzzing, Georgie heard the whir of the cicadas. He took off his hat, pulled his handkerchief out of his pocket, and wiped the sweat off his face. He looked over his shoulder and saw Medina still looking at him.

Boss sat in an iron lawn chair in the shade of a pecan tree. He had a bucket of last fall's pecans sitting beside him, a handkerchief full of bits of pecan shells in his lap, and a box filling with neatly shelled pecans. Georgie heard a pecan crack in Boss's silver nutcracker and watched as Boss gouged the meat out of the shell with a silver nut pry. As usual, Boss had his feet soaking in a plastic tub of cold water.

As Georgie got closer, Boss sloshed his feet in the water and cracked another pecan. He wore a faded and cracked felt hat that had sweat stains along the circle where the crown met the brim, a white short-sleeved shirt, and khaki work pants. Georgie looked around him. "You got another chair, Boss?" he said.

"No, guess not, Georgie," Boss said. Georgie sat in the grass and leaned against the trunk of the pecan tree. He felt cooler. He put his hat in his lap and pressed his head against the pecan tree to look up through the branches at the sky and listen to the cicadas.

"You see J.R. in the last 'Dallas' show?" Boss asked him.

"You bet."

"Mean son of a bitch."

"Wish I had color TV to watch J.R. and the baseball games."

"Don't start that bitching and moaning again about what I pay you. You can afford color TV if you want to."

Georgie shrugged, "Maybe."

Boss smiled, "How's your brother doing?"

"Times are hard."

"See there. And you moan. When's he gonna come up?"

"He don't want to."

Boss shook his head, put a big pecan in his nutcracker, and slowly squeezed until he heard a sharp crack; then he began to pry the shell from the meat.

"Ol' Oscar Benevides still mooching beers at Albert's?"

"Still there."

"Buy him one for me."

"Where's the dollar?"

"I'll owe you." Boss worked at his pecan. "Anyhow, I didn't ask you to come here to talk about your financial condition or your relatives and friends. We have a problem, Georgie boy." Georgie held up his chin, wiped the top of his head with his handkerchief, then put his hat back on.

"Another batch of wetbacks are coming in tomorrow, and I want you to go down with Medina and pick them up."

"Why both of us?"

"I'm a little worried about Medina. I think that coyote fella, that Najereda boy, and Medina have something going on the side. Think maybe they got wetbacks wading across with dope taped to their bellies."

"Medina?" Georgie said, thinking that Medina wouldn't have the guts to cross Boss.

"Mario was raided by immigration last week. They found several wetbacks in his kitchen, but everybody knows there's wetbacks in Mario's kitchen; no news there. Anyway, these wetbacks are being deported, and a friend of a friend says they're glad they are. 'Cause you see, they can come back across with some dope. Somebody has to be paying for the dope, and since most of Mario's help comes across with us . . ." Boss smiles for having figured everything out.

"You really think Medina?" Georgie chuckled to himself.

"I suspect him, and I want this dope smuggling stopped. I run a clean business. I am not about to get tangled up in dope." Boss set his nutcracker and nut pry in his lap. He looked straight at Georgie. "Now I only suspect, you understand, I'd go with him myself, but I'm too old now."

"Sure, Boss," Georgie said. "You got it. No problem."

Boss smiled and picked up his pecan cracker. He wiggled his feet in the water, then rubbed one foot with the sole of the other. "This dope has got young people thinking about nothing but money." He shook his head then looked at Georgie, "You want to help me shell some pecans?"

Georgie stood. "No. I work for you so I don't got to shell pecans." Boss laughed, and Georgie said, "Bye, Boss."

"You come back sometime and help me shell pecans."

"No way," Georgie said over his shoulder as he walked away from Boss and toward the gate. He didn't like the idea of spying on Medina. But spying was best for Boss. When he had gotten to San Antonio, most of the Mexicans he rode with looked out of the open garage door, then walked down the long caliche and gravel driveway to meet a relative or a friend. But Georgie was alone, and Boss had given him a place to sleep.

As he opened the gate and stepped on the gravel, Medina came out of the garage. "What'd he say?" Medina asked.

"Nothing," Georgie said and walked past Medina. As he walked down the driveway, he heard the lawn mower and glanced at the Mexican cutting grass. They waved to each other. The new Mexican was third generation. Like the new Mexican, like Medina, Georgie started by cutting grass, then washed dishes at Mario's, then made the runs. As he walked down the driveway, he heard the gravel crunch under his shoes, and again felt the heat surround him. He remembered finding Alicia's body, a day later, floating face down in the river. She had just her underwear on because some other wetbacks had found her and stolen her clothes.

GEORGIE WALKED TO ALBERT'S ICE HOUSE. HE SAT ON THE curb under the tin awning next to old Oscar Benevides. Oscar was a tiny man whose face looked like a raisin and whose clothes were always too big for him since he found them where he could—in trash-cans, at the Salvation Army thrift store, and in unguarded Kmart aisles. He told Georgie he didn't mind being caught in Kmart. Jail wasn't that bad. They watched a few cars go down Commerce Street. "A *pelado* always does what he got to to get by, don't he, Oscar?"

"No other way. That's why he's a *pelado*," Oscar said.

They had had this discussion before, so Georgie didn't need to go on. He patted Oscar's scrawny knee and said, "*Cerveza?*"

"*Sí,*" Oscar said and smiled at Georgie and patted his back. Georgie walked into Albert's Ice House where there were shelves of can goods, soap, and detergent, and the frosty glass doors to the refrigerated beer, milk, and soda waters. Albert stocked everything; he even had a rack of Mexican magazines. Georgie opened the cool, sweating door to the beers and got two Lone Stars.

He took them to the counter to Joe, who was working today for his brother Albert, and Joe opened the beers when Georgie paid for them. He walked back outside, handed a beer to Oscar, and sat beside him.

Oscar stuck the rim of the can to his lips and held his head back. Georgie watched as he sucked at the can and his adam's apple bobbed in his throat. Oscar put the beer in his lap and said, "This one ain't cold."

"Ah, yi, yi," Georgie said, took Oscar's beer from him, and handed Oscar his beer.

"This one's a lot better."

"You got nothing better than to *chíngale* beer from people all day?"

"I sit in a truck and drive people to San Antonio. That beats working in the sun all day."

Oscar giggled, and they both took a drink. As he brought his can down from his lips, Georgie turned away from Oscar and saw Medina walking up the driveway. He bounced from heel to toe on each foot and dipped a shoulder at each step. Oscar shook his head, clicked his tongue, and said, "That's a worthless *pelado*." Oscar didn't like Medina because he preached *La Raza Unida* and talked other radical shit.

Medina wore a polyester red shirt stained crimson from sweat and unbuttoned so the tails dangled behind him. Georgie could see beads of sweat on his forehead and hairless chest. He acted tough; if he didn't get shot or cut by somebody, he might eventually get as tough as old Oscar. He carried a switchblade in his back pocket, but he didn't scare Georgie.

He walked up to Oscar and Georgie. "You make money, so I ain't going to buy you no *cerveza*," Georgie said to Medina.

"I want a coke." But Medina didn't go to get it. He sat down beside Georgie, brushed his hand through his thick sweaty hair, folded his hands, and looked down at the ground.

"Hell of a place for a young *vato* to hang out," Oscar said and waved his hand in front of his face to shoo away some gnats. "You ought to go downtown and chase some women, huh?" Oscar said, then laughed.

"I like it here," Medina said and looked at Georgie. Georgie sipped his beer.

"Maybe I go downtown and chase the *mujeres*, huh, Oscar?" Georgie said. Medina rested his elbows on his knees.

"And maybe I go too," Oscar said and laughed.

"Shit," Medina said and got up to go inside for his coke. When he came back, a man pulled up in a pickup. Empty paint cans in the truck's bed banged against the sides and rolled across the bed. A man Georgie knew as Bill Howard stepped out of the pickup wearing a yellow baseball cap. He walked toward them smiling broadly.

Bill Howard nodded his head and said, "Fellas. Any of you like a job?"

Oscar laughed and said, "*Sí.*"

Bill Howard laughed, then said, "Either of you other two?" Georgie shook his head. "I've got several contracts for some roofing and some painting."

"We got jobs," Medina said.

Bill Howard smiled at him. "These are legal."

Georgie and Oscar laughed, but Medina only smiled and leaned his head back to drink his coke, and Bill Howard stared at him. When he lowered the coke, Medina stood straight but slumped to his left. "Eat shit, Gringo. *La Migra* know about who you hiring?"

Oscar looked scared and Georgie said, "He don't mean it. We got jobs." Bill Howard took a step back toward his truck, then said, "Your smart mouth might lose you that job." Medina shrugged. Bill Howard turned away from him, got in his pickup and drove off.

Medina smiled, "Kicked his ass."

"Why you want to start shit?" Oscar said.

"Cause he's a *cabrón*. Talking about us being illegal when he don't pay minimum wage."

"So what do you think, you do?" Georgie said.

"I help my people."

Georgie laughed, then Oscar laughed.

"A hell of a lot you know," Medina said.

Georgie patted Oscar's knee and stood. "I got to catch a bus." He set his beer can on the curb and walked away. Medina followed him. "You gonna catch the same bus?" Georgie asked.

"Sure, man."

WHEN GEORGIE GOT ON THE BUS, HE SAID HELLO TO THE DRIVER, walked to the back, and sat down. He liked buses. They were air-conditioned. The light shone in through the green-tinted windows and made the inside shaded yet light. This bus was empty except for him and Medina.

Medina sat across the aisle from him, then sat crossways in the seat to look at him. The bus jerked as it started; then Medina said, "Well, tell me, man, what did Boss say?"

Georgie looked at him, then closed his eyes. He and Emilio had reported the death to the Nuevo Laredo police, and all they got was a free aluminum coffin. Georgie begged Emilio to let the police bury Alicia and go back across the river, but Emilio turned against the whole idea of wading the river. "*Vaya a la Monterrey*," he said.

"You know," Georgie said to Medina, "I was here only three years before I learn all the bus routes."

"So big shit. What did Boss say?"

"You ever take the express bus on the freeways and go to the malls?"

"What you talking about?"

"I like to go to the malls and watch the Anglos dressed in shorts, sandals, and sunglasses. I like to eat the ice cream they have in the malls, real ice cream, you know, not *raspas* like in Mexico. In Mexico you eat *masa harina* until you can never shit. In the U.S.A., you eat peaches and green vegetables. America has air-conditioning, color TV, plastic plants."

"Shit, *loco en la cabeza*. I asked you something."

"My brother Emilio is still in Monterrey."

"Tough shit for him. All he has to do is talk to us; we get him here."

"So why you want to *chíngale* Boss and smuggle dope?"

Medina smiled, "I say fuck him. I say you go in with me. Shit, he ain't no different than that *hoto* in the truck. He don't pay you enough. Gives you a shithook place to live. What you owe him?"

"You remember Mexico?"

"Get some *cojones*, man. No use to tell Boss and get me fired. You shut up and go in with me and Najereda; we all make one hell of a profit."

"How much profit?"

"Hell, eventually we seize the means of production."

Georgie reached up and pulled the cord to stop the bus. He stood even before the bus stopped and walked down the aisle. "Hey, man. Hey," Medina said. "Hey, hey, shit what you say?"

As he walked home, the sun set, the gulf breeze blew in, making the air cooler. After a while fireflies replaced the gnats. . . . So, after they had cruised the river, Emilio, Georgie, and little Delores had gone back to Monterrey. Together Georgie and Emilio made enough at the tin can factory to live on. A year later, Georgie went back to Nuevo Laredo, gave Najereda $350 for a ride to San Antonio, and swam the river himself.

THE WIND CRISSCROSSED BETWEEN THE TWO OPEN WINDOWS of the truck and whipped Georgie's hair around on his head. Medina's long hair flew in front of his face. Georgie glanced out the window of the cab and saw the fields of prickly pear and mesquite trees. In this countryside, everything stung, bit, or stuck. Georgie remembered walking through it to Boss's old shack, his pant-legs were shredded and his forearms were bleeding. Georgie looked back at the road and on to the dirt road that led to the clearing. It had been a quiet ride.

Medina suddenly looked over at Georgie, "So you found your *cojones* yet? Or are you going to tell Boss?"

Georgie spent the night thinking about money. It is important to buy microwaves, color TVs, and air conditioners. But more important was your own good. Georgie would have liked to have stayed with Boss, but he could see that Medina would take Boss's business from him. "You going to have to pay to keep me quiet."

Medina smiled. "Sure, man, we got lots of money."

"And you keep paying for me to be quiet, and you keep me working."

Medina drummed the dash with his forefingers and bounced in his seat. "No problem, Georgie boy."

"Boss calls me Georgie boy, not you."

The brush scratched at the truck as it bounced on the rutted dirt road. Georgie drove into the clearing. Under a mesquite tree were twelve Mexican men hunkered, their butts not touching the ground, the way all poor people learn to rest. They stared at a large woman lying on the ground. A small boy held her head in his lap. Najereda stood to one side. When Georgie stopped the truck, Medina got out, and Najereda waved to him and walked toward him. Georgie opened his door, got out, then slammed the door behind him.

Najereda stopped walking, looked at Georgie, then frowned. He looked at Medina but jerked his chin toward Georgie. "He's cool," Medina said. Najereda was a short, slight man with curly black hair combed off his forehead and a thick black mustache. He limped slightly from an old gunshot wound.

"Our new pardner, *nuestro compadre*," Medina said.

Najereda smiled and stuck out his hand for Georgie to shake. Georgie shook his hand. Both his partners bragged too much.

Three of the wetbacks walked up to them. Najereda looked warily at Georgie. "Okay," Medina said and motioned to the wetbacks. One at a time, the Mexicans lifted their shirts to show plastic bags taped to their stomachs. They winced, one after the other, as Medina yanked the tape off their bellies. He flipped one bag to Najereda.

Georgie walked to the mesquite tree to look at his passengers. As he got close to them, he heard the cicadas buzz and blew from his closed lips at the gnats. He hunkered with the Mexicans and swatted the gnats and flies and watched as the small boy cradled the lady's head. Her teeth were clenched, her face beaded in sweat, one leg swollen. The Mexican men watched as the boy kept the flies from the woman's face. *"Qué pasa?"* Georgie asked. Several men shrugged.

Najereda and Medina and the three dope smugglers walked to the group. Medina went to the front of the truck, lay on his back, and stuck the dope up under the fender. He came back smiling at Georgie, "Nobody gonna find no dope," he said. He stopped when he got to the group and stared at the woman.

Georgie stood and pointed at the woman. "She don't go," he said to Najereda.

Medina kneeled over her and looked at her face. *"Pinche."*

Georgie pointed at Najereda, "You get her out. She's your problem."

"She pays her money," Najereda said, "that makes her your problem." Medina stood and looked from Georgie to Najereda.

"You're pulling some shit," Georgie said to Medina.

"Honest. I don't know. She pays. She goes," Najereda said and held his hands out from his body in a lazy shrug.

Georgie stood and said to the men, "Get on, sit. Don't look out." They lined up at the truck. The boy tried to help the woman up, but Georgie held his hand over her, *"No vaya."*

"You can't just leave her," Medina said.

"I didn't bring her," Georgie said and walked to the truck. He opened the tailgate and the door of the camper; then the Mexicans dutifully with a practiced, orderly rush, loaded themselves on the truck.

He looked over his shoulder to see the small boy crying and jabbering in fast Spanish to the lady. Medina grabbed her under the arms, and Najereda took her knees. With the small boy running in front of them, they carried her to the truck. They got her to the truck and propped her on the tailgate. Two of the dope smugglers helped pull her inside as Najereda and Medina pushed. "*Ella putrido,*" one of the men said and cupped his hand over his mouth and nose.

"What's wrong with her?" Georgie asked Najereda again.

"Who knows."

"We goddamn can't leave her here," Medina said.

"She better not cause no trouble," Georgie said to Medina, then pointed at Najereda.

"Take it easy, man," Najereda said.

When Georgie climbed into the driver's side of the cab, he gave Medina a hard glance. As he pulled the truck out, he looked in the side mirror to see Najereda waving good-bye with both hands.

As THEY DROVE OVER THE BLACK RANCH ROAD, THE TEMPERATURE neared 100 degrees. Georgie's back stuck to the vinyl seat. Medina cussed Boss for being so cheap and not buying an air conditioner or radio for the truck. Every so often, Georgie heard a low groan from the back of the truck. The Mexican woman, the men, and the boy would be hot; the bed of the truck would burn into their butts; but they would see that the ride, the trip across the river, the walk through the brush was worth it.

Boss would understand about his deal with Medina. He knew about doing what you had to. Emilio didn't. The U.S.A. is the only way, Georgie remembered telling Emilio when the tin can factory closed down. Neighborhood fiestas, Mass, a *cura* who came by and prayed couldn't keep you alive, he told Emilio. But Emilio stayed with Delores in Monterrey. Now, Georgie sent him money-stuffed Christmas cards with no return address.

A man banged on the back window of the truck. "What the hell," Medina said. Georgie pushed up with the toe of his left foot and slid his back up the slick, sweat-soaked vinyl seat to look through the back window. The large woman was sprawled across several of the men. Puke was on her shoulder.

"She's sick," Medina said to Georgie.

"Yeah."

"She needs to go to a hospital."

"We need for her to shut up."

"But she's sick."

"You don't think too good. How the hell we going to go to a hospital?" Georgie turned to look at Medina.

"What's with you, man? We ain't got a choice. She's got to go."

"We take her to a hospital, we lose all these guys and have to guarantee them another trip back."

"So what? It's Boss's money."

The man banged against the window. Medina turned and looked through the window. They both heard the man shout, "*Cabrones.*"

A loud scream that hurt to hear came from inside the truck. Georgie, without thinking, hit the brakes and the back of the truck swerved. "*Chinga,*" Georgie said and pulled the truck off the road. The woman screamed again, and two men banged on the window. Georgie turned to see the woman; her head was in the boy's lap and jerking from side to side. He looked toward Medina to see him jump out of the cab and slam the door behind him.

Georgie got out and ran to the back of the truck. Medina opened the tailgate. The stink and the heat and the buzz from the flies rolled out from the bed in a wave. Georgie and Medina pulled their heads back. "*Qué pasa?*" Medina asked the boy, who held the woman's hand and babbled in Spanish. The woman was his aunt; they were making the trip alone. A snake bit her early in the morning when she wandered off to pee in the brush. The boy begged them to take her to a hospital. One of the men who banged against the window demanded they take her to a hospital.

Medina slammed the tailgate shut, stepped around Georgie, and walked to the driver's side of the cab. Georgie grabbed his shoulder and pulled him around. Medina reached in his back pocket and spun around with his knife in his hand. He flipped his wrist and the blade locked into place. He held the knife close to his body as Georgie had been told you should hold a knife.

"*Pendejo*," Georgie said and took a step back and saw a man's face pressed against the side window of the camper.

"We got to go to a hospital."

"*Eh, stúpido*. Tough *vato*. Think. We go to a hospital, we're both arrested and sent back to Mexico. Then we do time in Mexico cause you got dope under the fender."

"You want her to die?"

"They knew their chances."

"We'll drive fast for San Antonio."

Medina took another step toward the cab. "Have some *cojones*," Georgie said. "No other way." Medina folded the blade back into the handle and put the knife in his pocket. "Now let's go and don't try no more shit," Georgie said to him. Georgie walked past him to the driver's side of the cab, got in, and looked in the rearview mirror to see Medina shut the tailgate.

When he came back into the cab, Medina looked like he would cry. Georgie heard one of the Mexicans in back say, "*Cabrón*."

He started the truck and looked at Medina. "It don't matter what those *pendejo* wetbacks say," he said to Medina. Then looking straight ahead, he said for his own good as well as for Medina's, "They gotta learn. You gotta learn. You got to have *cojones* in America."

THE PORTRAIT

★

Tomás Rivera

S SOON AS THE PEOPLE RETURNED FROM UP NORTH THE portrait salesmen began arriving from San Antonio. They would come to rake in. They knew that the workers had money and that was why, as Dad used to say, they would flock in. They carried suitcases packed with samples and always wore white shirts and ties. That way they looked more important and the people believed everything they would tell them and invite them into their homes without giving it much thought. I think that down deep they even longed for their children to one day be like them. In any event, they would arrive and make their way down the dusty streets, going house to house carrying suitcases full of samples.

I remember once I was at the house of one of my father's friends when one of these salesmen arrived. I also remember that that particular one seemed a little frightened and timid. Don Mateo asked him to come in because he wanted to do business.

"Good afternoon, traveler. I would like to tell you about something new that we're offering this year."

"Well, let's see, let's see . . ."

"Well, sir, see, you give us a picture, any picture you may have, and we will not only enlarge it for you but we'll also set it in a wooden frame like this one and with inlays, like this—three dimensional, as they say."

"And what for?"

"So that it will look real. That way . . . look, let me show you . . . see? Doesn't he look real, like he's alive?"

"Man, he sure does. Look, vieja. This looks great. Well, you know, we wanted to send some pictures to be enlarged . . . but now, this must cost a lot, right?"

"No, I'll tell you, it costs about the same. Of course, it takes more time."

"Well, tell me, how much?"

"For as little as thirty dollars we'll deliver it to you done with inlays just like this, one this size."

"Boy, that's expensive! Didn't you say it didn't cost a lot more? Do you take installments?"

"Well, I'll tell you, we have a new manager and he wants everything in cash. It's very fine work. We'll make it look like real. Done like that, with inlays . . . take a look. What do you think? Some fine work, wouldn't you say? We can have it all finished for you in a month. You just tell us what color you want the clothes to be and we'll come by with it all finished one day when you least expect, framed and all. Yes, sir, a month at the longest. But like I say, this man who's the new manager, he wants the full payment in cash. He's very demanding, even with us."

"Yes, but it's much too expensive."

"Well, yes. But the thing is, this is very fine work. You can't say you've ever seen portraits done like this, with wood inlays."

"No, well, that's true. What do you think, vieja?"

"Well, I like it a lot. Why don't we order one? And if it turns out good . . . my Chuy . . . may he rest in peace. It's the only picture we have of him. We took it right before he left for Korea. Poor m'ijo, we never saw him again. See . . . this is his picture. Do you think you can make it like that, make it look like he's alive?"

"Sure, we can. You know, we've done a lot of them in soldier's uniforms and shaped it, like you see in this sample, with inlays. Why, it's more than just a portrait. Sure. You just tell me what size you want and whether you want a round or square frame. What do you say? How should I write it down?"

"What do you say, vieja, should we have it done like this one?"

"Well, I've already told you what I think. I would like to have m'ijo's picture fixed up like that and in color."

"All right, go ahead and write it down. But you take good care of that picture for us because it's the only one we have of our son grown up. He was going to send us one all dressed up in uniform with the American and Mexican flags crossed over his head, but he no sooner got there when a letter arrived telling us that he was lost in action. So you take good care of it."

"Don't you worry. We're responsible people. And we understand the sacrifices that you people make. Don't worry. And you just wait and see. When we bring it to you'll see how pretty it's gonna look. What do you say, should we make the uniform navy blue?"

"But he's not wearing a uniform in that picture."

"No, but that's just a matter of fixing it up with some wood fiber overlays. Look at these. This one, he didn't have a uniform on but we put one on him. So what do you say? Should we make it navy blue?"

"All right."

"Don't you worry about the picture."

AND THAT WAS HOW THEY SPENT THE ENTIRE DAY GOING HOUSE to house, street by street, their suitcases stuffed with pictures. As it turned out, a whole lot of people had ordered enlargements of that kind.

"THEY SHOULD BE DELIVERING THOSE PORTRAITS SOON, DON'T you think?"

"I think so, it's delicate work and takes more time. That's some fine work those people do. Did you see how real those pictures looked?"

"Yeah, sure. They do some fine work. You can't deny that. But it's already been over a month since they passed by here."

"Yes, but from here they went on through all the towns picking up pictures . . . all the way to San Antonio for sure. So it'll probably take a little longer."

"That's true, that's true."

AND TWO MORE WEEKS HAD PASSED BY THE TIME THEY MADE the discovery. Some very heavy rains had come and some children who were playing in one of the tunnels leading to the dump found a sack full of pictures, all worm-eaten and soaking wet. The only reason they could tell that these were pictures was because there were a lot of them and most of them the same size and with faces that could just barely be made out. Everybody caught on right away. Don Mateo was so angry that he took off to San Antonio to find the so and so who had swindled them.

"WELL, YOU KNOW, I STAYED AT ESTEBAN'S HOUSE. AND EVERY day I went with him to the market to sell produce. I helped him with everything. I had faith that I would run into that son of a gun some day soon. Then, after I'd been there for a few days, I started going out to the different barrios and I found out a lot that way. It wasn't so much the money that upset me. It was my poor vieja, crying and all because we'd lost the only picture we had of Chuy. We found it in the sack with all the other pictures but it was already ruined, you know."

"I see, but tell me, how did you find him?"

"Well, you see, to make a long story short, he came by the stand at the market one day. He stood right in front of us and bought some vegetables. It was like he was trying to remember who I was. Of course, I recognized him right off. Because when you're angry enough, you don't forget a face. I just grabbed him right then and there. Poor guy couldn't even talk. He was all scared. And I told him that I wanted that portrait of my son and that I wanted it three dimensional and that he'd best get it for me or I'd let him have it. And I went with him to where he lived. And I put him to work right then and there. The poor guy didn't know where to begin. He had to do it all from memory."

"And how did he do it?"

"I don't know. I suppose if you're scared enough, you're capable of doing anything. Three days later he brought me the portrait all finished, just like you see it there on that table by the Virgin Mary. Now tell me, how do you like the way my boy looks?"

"Well, to be honest, I don't remember too well how Chuy looked. But he was beginning to look more and more like you, isn't that so?"

"Yes, I would say so. That's what everybody tells me now. That Chuy's a chip off the old block and that he was already looking like me. There's the portrait. Like they say, one and the same."

THE GULF OIL-CAN SANTA CLAUS

★

Rolando Hinojosa-Smith

B Y THE TIME THE JAPANESE IMPERIAL FORCES WERE DEEP into the mopping-up operations in the Bataan Peninsula, preparations for the siege and fall of Corregidor were also under way. One of the defenders was Clemente García, a 23-year-old youngster from Mercedes, down in the Valley.

He was born not in Mercedes but in northern Mexico; his mother, two brothers and a sister crossed the Rio Grande at Rio Rico, Tamaulipas, Mexico, and settled in Mercedes some two or three years after the death of don Clemente senior, a victim of the Spanish influenza epidemic in the twenties.

Don Clemente had been a veteran of the Mexican Revolution; upon his death, as he was an enlisted career man, his widow began to receive a smallish pension from the Mexican government.

Mrs. García's decision to cross the Rio Grande was an economic one and thus no different from that made by hundreds of thousands of European and other immigrants who settled in the United States. The choice of Mercedes was no accident, however; many newly arrived Mexican nationals made it a type of halfway house before they spread out all over Texas, the midwestern United States and beyond.

Of the many Garcías, these settled in Mercedes. Aurora, an only daughter, did needlepoint and also constructed some remarkably intricate paper designs used as cemetery decorations. Two of the youngsters, Arturo and Medardo, were apprenticed off to neighborhood *panaderías*—bakeries. Clemente, clearly the brightest, according to the family, enrolled at the all-Texas-Mexican neighborhood school, North Ward Elementary.

He logged in the mandatory six years there and, at age sixteen, had learned to read and write enough English to hire on as a sackboy for a local grocery store. Later on he became the deliveryman as well as the driver.

On his twenty-first birthday, he came to our home and knocked on the east porch door. I was the only one home at the time and invited him in. He thanked me but said he was in the middle of a delivery; he had stopped, he said, to ask my father's advice on some matter, but that he would call again.

Our people came to the Valley, as had his, with the Escandón expedition and colonists of 1749. Our family happened to live on the northern bank of the Rio Grande when it became part of the American Union; his ancestors had lived on the southern bank, and thus, with the proclamation of the Treaty of Guadalupe Hidalgo, they became Mexican nationals, and we, American citizens.

Since Clemente had no father, he called on mine for advice; this was in the late '30s, and there were still strong remnants of the old patriarchal system established in 1750. "It's a serious matter, don Manuel," he said to my father. This was the obligatory phrase, and it could encompass almost anything, from a request for my father, as a sponsor, to ask for a girl's hand in marriage to putting in a good word—

dar una recomendación—for whatever was needed. In short, almost anything, but certainly something of importance to the petitioner. The Great Depression was still hanging on in the Valley and elsewhere, and steady jobs were hard to come by. In Clemente's case, though, it was something different. During one of his deliveries in the Anglo-Texan side of town, he had met a man named Claude Rodgers. According to Clemente, Rodgers was going to own and operate a Gulf Oil gas station in the Texas-Mexican part of town. And Rodgers had asked Clemente if he wanted to work there, full-time. Clemente had not known what to say to this, but Rodgers solved that when he said, "Think it over. Come by in a week or so."

My father listened to Clemente, nodded, and then pointed to a chair. Clemente sat down, and one of my sisters brought him a tall glass of limeade. I was about to leave, but my father said I could stay, and I did so.

The upshot was that he took the job, the gas station was directly across the street from our house and I would see him every day on my way to and from North Ward Elementary.

In November 1940, a week before Thanksgiving, as I was crossing North Texas Avenue on my way home, I heard a series of shrill whistles; it was Clemente.

"*Acá*," he said. "Over here." He grinned and yelled out, "*Andale*. Come on, hurry it up." He was standing under the car wash and surrounded by Gulf Oil cans.

"What's up?" I asked.

"Look." And he pointed.

"At what? The oil cans?"

"Yeah; I've been saving them."

"Can you sell 'em, like milk bottles?"

He laughed then and said, "No. I'm going to weld them, all of them. I'm going to weld them and make us a Santa Claus for Christmas."

"Really? Out of cans?"

"Yeah, you just wait."

"Can I help?"

"You better; it's my Christmas present for you."

"For me?"

"Sure. We'll begin by rinsing them and drying them out. What's your dad going to give you?"

"A pair of khaki pants. And a leather belt, from Matamoros."

"And this will be your third Christmas present; everybody's entitled to three, you know. Like *los magos*, the Magi."

Thanksgiving came and went, and every afternoon, after running errands and doing the daily chores, I'd run over to Rodgers's Gulf, rinse some more cans and watch Clemente weld them for the Santa Claus.

"We're going to put it up there, on top of the car wash. I'll get us some good, strong wire, and nothing'll blow it down, not even the Gulf wind."

Clemente finished it a week before Christmas, and then in January, on the Day of the Magi, he received a notice from the local Selective Service Board.

He took and passed his physical in San Antonio in March 1941, and he was on his way to the Philippines by October of the same year. What letters he wrote to his mother were brought to my father to read. My father also translated the fateful telegram sent by the War Department in the summer of 1942.

The Santa Claus stayed on top of the car wash for some 10 years after World War II. Rusted out, finally, but I remember it was big and red and white and held there by big black boots. Perfect.

In the way of the world of the living, I forgot about it, and I had almost forgotten Clemente García, "*La Nortenita.*" It was an affectionate name and feminine, but he was called that, in the singular, in honor of his favorite song, "*Las Nortenitas*—Those Oh-so-sweet Northern Girls."

Then, one December day, I went down to Mercedes on some now-forgotten family business. Urban renewal had taken care of the house in which I was born and turned it into a parking lot, but across the street, Rodgers's station had been replaced by a tire store; it was owned by a man named Leopoldo Martínez.

As I crossed the street to see Martínez, I thought I saw the Gulf Oil-Can Santa Claus. I walked on, and I was sure I had seen it again. Somewhere.

I ran inside the store and then almost knocked down a clerk taking inventory.

"Oh, it's you, Doctor. How are you?"

I stopped and looked at him for some sign of recognition but found none.

"I'm sorry," I said. "Who's your father?"

"Leocadio Gavira, the truck driver; he knows you."

I nodded and apologized again. He couldn't help noticing my searching for something and asked, "Can I help you?"

I didn't know what to say, where to begin. Images of the '30s, '40s and '50s flicked on and off again as in a slide show, until finally I said, "No . . . thanks; I thought I'd seen something . . . it's nothing." He nodded, and as I turned to go, the image flashed on again, as a reflection somewhere.

Why, it was nothing more than a blown-up Michelin Man waving and smiling at me. Someone had painted him up as Santa Claus.

THE GAVIRA YOUNGSTER LOOKED AT ME AND SAID, "OH, THAT. It's a new line. You know, some of the older people come in and stare at it for the longest time. You know why they do that?"

I nodded slightly, and on an impulse asked, "Did you ever hear of the widow García on Hidalgo and First?"

"Sure, she must be close to 90, 95, a hundred, maybe. She's still alive, you know, lives with a daughter, I think."

And with her silent memories, I added silently.

"Thanks. . . . What's your name?"

"John, sir,"

"John! Well, thanks again."

"Yes sir." And he went back to his inventory.

The Michelin Tire Man. It looked grotesque, somehow, but—and again somehow—it looked like my third Christmas present, my Gulf Oil-can Santa Claus, the one I got the year before the war.

WHORES

★

James Crumley

I

ON LONG SUMMER AFTERNOONS WHEN OUR IDLE TIME LAY as heavily upon our minds and lives as the torpid South Texas air, often my friend and colleague, Lacy Harris, and I would happen to glance across our narrow office into each other's eyes. Usually we simply stared at each other, like two strangers who have wandered into an empty room at a party, ashamed of solitude among mirth, then we turned back to the disorderly stacks of freshman themes, heaped uncorrected upon our desks. Occasionally, though, the stares held; one would shrug, the other suggest a beer, and in silence we would rise and go out, seeking a dark and calm beer joint.

Sometimes French's, a place south of town, where a cool high-yellow bartender, Raoul, let us bask in the breeze of his chatter, as ceaseless and pleasant as the damp draft roaring from the old-fashioned water-cooled window fan. Sometimes the Tropicana to joust with an obtuse pinball machine called the Merry Widow, while off-shift roughnecks slept drunk at the various tables scattered among the fake tropical greenery. Easy afternoons, more pleasant and possible than hiding in the air-conditioned cage of our office, where the silences had no meaning. Dusty air, dark bars. Outside, the sun, white hot upon the caliche or shell parking lots, reminding us how pleasant the idle afternoon. Dim bars, cold beers, our mutual silence for company. Harmless.

Or so they'd seem until I'd catch Lacy's hooded blue eyes slipping toward the heated doorway. His wife, Marsha, was already prowling the town like a lost tourist, looking for him in the bars. Almost always she found us. One moment the doorway would be empty, the next a slim shade stood quietly just inside, perhaps a glint of afternoon sunlight off her long blonde hair. Somehow I always saw her first. When I said "Lacy," he never moved, so I would walk to Marsha, welcome her with the frightened ebullience of a guilty drunk. She seldom spoke; when she did, in a hushed murmur, too quiet for words. She moved around me to Lacy's side, slipped her hand into the sweaty bend of his elbow, led him away. At the doorway, framed in heated light, his face would turn back to me, an apologetically arched eyebrow raised.

On those rare occasions when she didn't find us, we drank until midnight, but without frenzy or drunkenness, as if the evening were merely the shank of the afternoon. Then I drove Lacy home, let him out in the bright yellow glare of his porch light. As he sauntered up the front walk, his hands cocked in his pockets, his head tilted gently back, his tall frame seemed relaxed, easy. A tuneless whistle, like the repeated fragment of a birdsong, warbled around his head as he approached that yellow light. At the steps he'd stop, wave once as if to signal his safe arrival, then go inside the screened porch. Sometimes, glancing over my shoulders as I drove away, I'd see him sitting on the flowered pillows of the porch swing, head down, hands clasped before him, waiting.

On the mornings after, he never spoke of the evenings before, no hangover jokes shared, never hinted of those moments before sleep alone with Marsha in their marriage bed. And on the odd chance that I saw Marsha later, no matter how carefully I searched that lovely, composed face, no matter how hard I peered beneath her careful makeup, I caught no glimpse of anger. Unlike most of my married friends, the Harrises kept their marriage closed from view, as if secrecy were a vow. Aside from her sudden intrusions into our afternoons, his too-casual saunter toward the bug light, as casual as a man mounting a gallows, and a single generality he let slip one night—"Never marry a woman you love"—I knew nothing about their marriage.

On rare and infrequent summer afternoons, when the immense boredom that rules my life stroked me like a cat and the heavy stir of desire rose like a sleepy beast within me, when our eyes met, I would say *Mexico*, as if it were a charmed word, and Lacy would grin instead of greeting me with a wry smile, a boy's grin, and I could see his boy's face, damp and red after a basketball game, expectant. On those afternoons, we'd fill a thermos with gin and tonics, climb into my restored 1949 Cadillac, and head for the border, bordertown whorehouses, the afternoon promenade of Nuevo Laredo whores coming to work at the Rumba Casino or the Miramar or the Malibu, the Diamond Azul or Papagayo's.

Perhaps it was the gin, or the memory of his single trip to Nuevo Laredo after a state basketball tournament, whatever, he maintained that grin, as he did his silences, all the way across the dry brush country of South Texas, my old Caddy as smooth as a barge. Or perhaps it was the thought of Marsha driving from bar to bar, circling Knight until full dark, then going home without him. He never went intending to partake of the pleasures, just for the parade.

Sometimes it seemed the saddest part, sometimes the most pathetic, sometimes the most exciting: the dreadful normalcy of the giggling girls. Dressed in jeans and men's shirts knotted above their brown dimpled bellies, they carried their working clothes, ruffled froth or slimy satin, draped over their young and tender shoulders. Although they chattered in Spanish, they had the voices of Texas high school girls, the concerns of high school girls. Dreadfully normal, god love them, untouched by their work, innocent until dark.

Occasionally, because I knew the girls more intimately than Lacy—unlike him, I'd never married either the loved or unloved—I could convince one or two to sit with us a moment before they changed clothes. But not too often. They seemed shy, unprotected out of their whore dresses, like virgins caught naked. If the mood seemed right, the shyness touching instead of posed, I'd have one then, slaking my studied boredom on an afternoon whore as the sun slanted into the empty room. Afterward, Lacy often said, "I'll have to try that again. Someday." I always answered, as if wives were the antithesis of whores, "You've no need. You've a lovely wife at home." To which he replied, "Yes, that's true. But someday, some summer afternoon, I'll join you . . ." His soft East Texas accent would quaver like a mournful birdcall, and a longing so immense that even I felt it would move over him. Even then I knew he'd want more than money could buy.

Most whores in Nuevo Laredo are carefully cloistered in a section of the city called, appropriately, Boys Town, a shabby place with raucous bars spaced among the sidewalk cribs, but the better-class whores worked in the clubs we frequented, outside Boys Town. By better-class I don't mean more practiced. I mean more expensive, less sullied by the hard life. More often than not, they're just good old working girls, pleasant and unhurried in bed, not greedy, and sometimes willing to have fun, to talk seriously. Many were sold into the business as young girls, many are married, making the most of a bad life. And then there are the rare ones, girls a man can fall in love with, though I never did, never will. Whores help me avoid the complexities of love, for which I am justly grateful. But even I have been tempted by the rare ones. Tempted.

One afternoon in Papagayo's in the blessed stillness after the parade—the waterfall silent, the jukebox dead—Lacy and I sipped our Tecates. A moist heat had beaten the old air conditioners. Behind the bar one bartender sliced limes so slowly that he seemed hardly to move; the other slept at the end of the bar, his head propped on his upright arm. Lacy's whistle seemed to hover about us like a swarm of gnats. All of us composed, it seemed, for a tropical still life, or the opening act of a Tennessee Williams play. Absolute stasis. And when Elena came in, moving so slowly that she seemed not even to stir the hot air with her passing, she seemed to hold that moment with her lush body. As I turned my head, like some ancient sleepy turtle, she too turned hers toward me. A slack indifferent beauty, eyes always on the verge of sleep, the sort of soft full body over which frenzy would never leap. Otiosity sublime. Surely for a man to come in her would be to come already asleep.

I clicked my Tecate can lightly on the tile bar as she eased past us. The sleeping bartender, knowing my habits, looked up. I nodded, he asked her if she would join us for a drink. Halting like a tanker coming into dock, she nodded too, her eyes closing as she lowered her head. A life of indolence is really a search, I thought, a quest for that perfect place to place one's head, to sleep, to dream . . . but behind me, Lacy whispered, "This one, Walter." So I let her go. Walter Savage, perfect languor. Habits can be restrained; passions should not.

After the preliminaries, an overpriced weak brandy, an unbargained price—local airmen had ruined the tradition—Lacy left with his prize ship, walking away as casually as he wandered into the force of that yellow porch light, hands pocketed, loafers shuffling, head back, his aimless whistle. But as he held the door for Elena with one hand, the other cradled itself against her ample waist. I meant to warn him, but in the languorous moment all I could think was, "You've a lovely wife at home," and that seemed silly, the effort too much.

They were gone quite a time, longer than his money had purchased, so I knew it had to be an amazing passion, impotence, or death. Afternoon slipped into evening, the waterfall began flushing. Two students from the college came timidly in, then left when they recognized me. The girls returned in bright plumage. I took the gaud-

iest one, ruffled her as best I could, but when I came back, Lacy
hadn't returned. The bartender cast me a slimy smile. I drank.

When Lacy finally came back, Papagayo's hummed with all the
efficiency of a well-tuned engine, and I would have stayed to watch
the dance, but Lacy said, "Let's go."

"Why?" Though I could guess.

Hesitating, unable to meet my eyes, he shook himself as if with
anger, a flush troubling his pale face. Then he answered, "I don't want
to see her working."

Not just impotence, but love, I thought, wanting to laugh.

More silent than usual on the trip back, he drank beer after beer,
staring at the gray asphalt unwinding before us. Outside Falfurias, I
ventured, "Impotent?" To which he answered, with hesitation, "Yes."

"It happens," I said. "Guilt before the deed. With whores and wives
and random pieces . . ."

"Don't," he said, almost pleading.

"Hey, it doesn't matter."

"Yes," he whispered, "I know."

When I dropped him at his house, he said good-night, then walked
into that yellow haze quickly, as if he had unfinished business.

During the twenty years or so I've been beating love with bordertown whoring, I've had it happen to me—drink or boredom or simple
grief—and I knew most of the techniques with which whores handled
the problem. Those who took simple pride in their work, those honest
tradeswomen of the flesh, usually gave the customer his best chance,
along with motherly comfort and no advice except to relax. Then they
would try to laugh it off. Others, working just for the money and those
few natively cruel, would pointedly ignore or even scoff at the flaccid
gringo member. Or, as happened to me once, they would act terribly
frightened, whimpering as if caged with a snake or a scorpion instead
of a useless man, occasionally peeking out of the corners of their sly
brown eyes to see if you'd left yet. Whatever the act was meant to do,
it did. Perhaps because of my youth, when it happened to me, it kept

me away from the whores for months, nearly caused me the grief of marriage with a rather chubby woman who taught Shakespeare very badly.

But Elena did none of those things. She was after all only a child, in spite of that woman's body, so she just started talking aimlessly, in her child's voice, winding her black hair with her fingers. What she did was, of course, more cruel: she talked to him, told him about her life. The dusty adobe on the Sonoran desert, the clutch of too many children, both alive and dead, the vast empty spaces of desert and poverty. When their time was up, he asked if he might pay for more, to which she shrugged, lifted a shoulder, cocked an eye at his member. And she answered, *why not*, she covered her breasts with a dingy sheet and smiled at him. God knows what she had in mind. When I told her, months later, of his death, she also shrugged at me, slipping into her dress.

Although Lacy and I were both in our thirties and both knew that, except for a miracle, we were going to ease out the rest of our academic careers at South Texas State trying to make them as painless as possible, I accepted my failure more gracefully than he. I'd been born in Knight, still lived in a converted garage behind my parents' house, and I taught because it was a respectable way to waste one's life. Unlike my mother's attachment to morphine and my father's to the American Conservative Party, teaching is respectable. The salary may be insulting, the intellectual rewards negligible, but when I tried doing nothing at all, the boredom drove me to drink. So I teach, my U.T. Ph.D. a ticket to a peaceful life.

But Lacy, like so many bright, energetic young men, once had a future. Articles published in proper journals, one short story in a prestigious quarterly, an eastern degree, that sort of thing. And he came to South Texas State for the money, just for the money. When he came, he thought that, like a boulder tumbling down a hillside, he had only lodged for a moment, a winter's rest perhaps, and when spring came with heavy rains, he would be on his way once again. By the time he realized that no more showers were going to fall, he had been captured by the stillness, the heavy subtropical heat, the endless unchanging days of sun and dust. He hadn't accepted his defeat, but it didn't matter. By the time of this last summer, he had stopped writing letters of inquiry, had ditched his current Blake article, replacing somehow his fiery vision with Elena.

II

They say the second acts of all boring plays take place at parties, where truth looms out of the drunkenness with all the relentless force of a tidal wave. But in Knight the parties were dull, deadly dull, and whatever shouted insults rose above the crowd like clenched fists, whatever wives were hotly fondled by whomever in dark closets or under the fluorescent glare of kitchen lights, was beside the point. The truth lay in the burnished dullness, not in the desperate cries of hands clutching at strangely familiar bodies. The last party at the Harrises' seemed no different, perhaps was no different, despite the death of our chairman.

Even Lacy had risen from his torpor long enough to become a bore. Each time he found me near enough to Marsha for her to overhear him, he would remind me loudly of our golf game the next day, suggesting earlier and earlier tee-offs. But he had El Papagayo's in mind, not golf. We had been back three or four times in less than a month, more often than was my habit, and his love remained unconsummated. He had passed through acceptance to sorrow to rage, and on quiet midnights in my apartment I had begun to think of Lacy and Marsha abed, he cursing his errant virility, she pliant upon their bed. His untoward passion had begun also to disturb the tranquility of my life, and when he reminded me about our golf game the fifth or sixth time I answered querulously, "I don't think I'll play tomorrow, I think

I'll go to Mexico and get fucked." Then I left him, his stricken face like a painted balloon above the crowd.

It was then I noticed our chairman, a pleasant old gentlemanly widower who asked no more of life than I did, leaving the party. He wore a tweed jacket, as if fall in South Texas were autumn in Ithaca, that smelled lightly of pipe smoke, paper, and burning leaves. We chatted a moment, the usual graceful nothing, then bid each other good-night. He suffered a coronary thrombosis just off the porch and crawled under the oleander bush at the corner of the Harrises' house; slipped away to die, I like to think, without disturbing anyone. The party continued, somewhat relieved by his absence, until those wee dumb hours of the morning. Shortly before noon the next day, Marsha found him as she worked in the flower beds. On his side, his head cradled upon his clenched hands, his knees lifted toward his chest, the rictus of a smile delicate across his stubbled face, the faint stink of decomposition already ripe among the dusty oleander leaves. She brushed bits of grass and dirt from his face as she knelt beside him; she began crying and did not stop.

In an ideal, orderly world, on this day Lacy would have performed his necessary act, a final act of passion before we went home to his mad wife, but the world is neither ideal nor orderly, as the life we forge from the chaos must be. Elena, who was I can attest a very dull girl despite her interesting beauty, decided that day to become interested in Lacy's failure. She no longer babbled about her past but promised to cure his problem, if not with her antics, then surely with a *curanderas* potion. Of course, neither worked, and Lacy's life was complicated for the next month with an infernal dose of diarrhea. Even now, even in my grief, I know he deserved no better.

When he returned that night, we both noticed the absence of the porch light. He took it as a favorable omen, I thought it an oversight. Even as I unlocked my apartment door—unlike most folk in Knight, I lock my door; I have a small fortune in medieval tapestries and Chinese porcelain, two original Orozco's—the telephone's shrill cry shattered the night. Lacy.

After the bodies had been disposed of, our chairman's beside his wife, Marsha into a Galveston hospital, instead of driving Lacy back to Knight, I made him stop with me in Houston, not so much to cheer him up as to hold him away from the scene of disaster for a few days. We stayed at the Warwick, drank at the nicest private clubs, where my father's money and name bought us privacy. Finally, on our third night, as we were sipping scotch at the Coronado Club, our nerves uneasy in their sheaths from seventy-two hours of waking and sleeping drunk, Lacy began to talk, to fill in the gaps, as if by breaking his silence he could restore his shattered life.

His mother, as she often said, had made only one mistake in her life, she'd fallen in love with a Texas man and followed him out of Georgia and into exile in East Texas. In exile her native gentility grew aggressive, proud. No girls in Tyler met her standards, none quite good enough for Lacy, so except for one wild trip after a basketball tournament his senior year, a single fling to the border, Lacy knew nothing of girls. Where he found the courage to remove his clothes before a strange dark woman in a dank cubicle behind the 1-2-3 Club, and how he overcame his disgust long enough to place his anointed body upon hers, I'll never know. What guilt he suffered, those days he carried himself carefully around Tyler as if a sudden knock would unman him, he never said. I like to think of that first time, Lacy's body lean and as glossily hard as a basketball court, yet tender, vulnerable with innocence, a T-shirt as white as his buttocks, flapping as he humped, his wool athletic socks crumpled about his ankles, his soul focused on the dark, puffy belly of a middle-aged whore with an old-fashioned appendix scar like a gully upon the center of her stomach.

In college, his career as young-man-about-campus kept him so busy that girls were just another necessary accessory, like his diamond-chip KA pin, scuffed bucks, and chinos with a belt in the back, and it wasn't until he began graduate school at Duke, where all the other teaching assistants seemed to have thin, reposed women at their elbows, that he discovered the absence of women in his life. Then too he looked over a freshman composition class and mistook that dark quietness in Marsha Long's wide eyes for intelligence, mistook her silence for repose.

The brief courtship could only be described as whirlwind, the wind of his stifled passion whirling around her pliant young body. Surprised that she wasn't virgin, he forgave her nonetheless, then confessed his single transgression in Mexico. Marsha nodded wisely, just as she did when he suggested marriage, expecting her to hold out for magnolia blossoms and fourteen bridesmaids. But she didn't. They were married by a crossroads justice of the peace on the way to South Carolina to tell her parents.

They lived on the old family plantation on the Black River in a columned house right off a postcard, and as he drove up the circular way, Lacy thought how pleased his mother would be. But inside the house he found an old woman, perfumed and painted like a crinolined doll, who called him by any name but his own and confused Marsha with her long-dead sister. In Marsha's father's regal face he saw her beauty, larded with bourbon fat. Everywhere he turned, each face— black, white, or whitetrash—every face on the place had the same long straight nose, the broad mouth, the wide dark eyes. Only the blacks still carried enough viable intelligence in their genes to maintain some semblance of order. Marsha cried ten solid hours their first night, only shaking her head when he inquired as to why. By dawn he expected a black mammy to waddle in from the wings and comfort the both of them, but none came. At breakfast, Marsha had redrawn her face, and stare as he might through his own haggard eyes, he could see neither hint nor sign of whatever endless grief lay beneath her silence.

They left later that morning, since nobody seemed to mind. Mr. Long ran wildly out of the house, spilling whiskey, and Lacy, fearing now for both sanity and life, just drove on. But he heard the shouted, "Congratulations, son." He looked at this mad child, now his wife, seeing her now, dumb, painted, pliant. Perverse marriage vows followed; he made her silence his, vowed to love her.

"They were so old, old enough to be her grandparents, they didn't have her until they were in their forties. God knows what her childhood must have been like, locked on a movie set with those mad people, and every face she saw for ten miles in any direction, every club-foot, hump-back, cross-eyed genetic disaster, was her face. She thought she was ugly. You know that, ugly. In all the years we were married I saw her without make-up just twice. Once, when she had the flu so badly that she couldn't even crawl to the mirror. I found her like that, on her goddamned hands and knees, mewling and crying and holding back the vomit with clenched teeth. When I tried to carry her back to bed, she fought me like a madwo . . . fought like a wildcat, hiding her face from me as if she'd die if I saw her . . . Listen, I shouldn't be here, I should be back in that room, room, shit, cage with her. She needs me, she needed me and I wasn't there . . . And all those niggers in that house, so goddamned servile, so smug butter wouldn't melt in their assholes. Listen, drive me back to Galveston, will you? This isn't helping."

I led him out of the club, holding his elbow as if he were an elderly uncle. And it had helped. In the car he slept, quiet, not mumbling or twisting or springing awake. Slept really for the first time in days. I checked us out of the Warwick, drove us back to Knight on benzedrine—bordertown whorehouses are filled with more vices than those of the flesh. When I woke him in front of his house, dawn flushed the unclouded sky as birds chittered in the mimosa trees of his yard. He mumbled a simple thanks, grabbed his grip, and went into this empty house, his toneless whistle faint among birdsong. I thought he'd be all right.

III

He seemed all right for the next few months, more silent perhaps, uninterested in afternoons at French's or jousting with the Merry

Widow, but accepting his life on its own terms. I hadn't the heart to suggest a trip to Nuevo Laredo, and Lacy didn't invite me to accompany him on the frequent weekends he spent in Galveston. So we began to see less of each other. He had his grief, I had a spurt of ambition and energy that threatened to destroy my wasted life. I handled it, as usual, by spending a great deal of my father's ill-gotten money. Christmas in Puerto Vallarta. An antique Edwardian sofa. Two Ung Cheng saucers in famille rose that made my father take notice of me and suggest that I was worse than worthless, expensively worthless. I even gave a party, a Sunday morning champagne breakfast, fresh strawberries, caviar, an excellent brie, and, although Lacy didn't come, those good folk who did, didn't make church services that morning, not even that night. For reasons beyond me, I made the mistake of resuming my affair with my chubby Shakespearian, an affair it took me until spring to resign.

Spring in South Texas lacks the verdant burst of those parts of the world that experience winter, lacks even the blatant flowering of the desert, but it has its moments. A gentle mist of yellow falls upon the thorned huisache; tiny blossoms, smaller than the hooked thorns of the catclaws, appear briefly; and the ripe flowers of the prickly pear, like bloody wounds, begin to emerge. And the bluebonnets, sown by a grim and greedy highway department, fill the flat roadside ditches.

On a Sunday when he hadn't gone to visit Marsha, I took Lacy out into the brush country north and east of Alice to show him the small clues of our slight season. But it only works for those who take pride in the narrowness of their vision, who stubbornly resist boredom, whatever the cost. By one o'clock we were drunk in the poolhall in Concepcion, by three, drinking margaritas at Dutch's across the border in Reynosa, at seven, stumbling into the waterfall hush of Papagayo's in Nuevo Laredo, giggling like schoolboys.

Lacy, standing straight, asked loudly for Elena, but she wasn't working that night, so he collapsed into his chair, morose and silent for the first time that day. I, ever-present nurse and shade, bought him the

two most expensive girls in the place, sent him with them to find
Elena's room. *Dos mujeres de la noche*. Where love had failed, some
grand perversion might work.

And of course it did. When we met at the dry fountain in the courtyard afterward, Lacy had a bottle of Carta Blanca in each hand, a
whore under each arm, his shirt open to the waist, and a wild grin
smack on his face. "Hey, you old son-of-a-bitch, you set this whole
fuckin' thing up, didn't you?"

I smiled in return, trying to look sly, but failing. My eyes wouldn't
focus. "I'm responsible," I said. "How was it?"

"Ohhh, shit, wonderful," he said, stumbling sideways, his two
ladies holding him up with a patient grace that my father's money
hadn't purchased. "Listen," he said to them, "I want you to meet
my best friend in the whole damned world, he's a good old boy." He
lifted his arm from the right one's red satin shoulders, gathered me
into his fierce grasp. "Stood by me, held me up, laid me down, introduced me to the woman I love . . ."

"We've met," I said, putting my arm around the abandoned whore.
Her skin, warm and sweaty from the bed, smelled like all those things
that men seek from whores: almonds and limes, dusty nights, cheap
gin, anonymous love. I buried my face in her neck, had a moment's
vision in which I bought both girls and fled south across the desert
toward some other pleasantly idle life, a Yucatán beach, a mountain
village, Egypt. But even as it came, it passed like a night wind. Lacy
began to shout and shuffle our circle around.

"Ohhh, what a great fucking night." The girls slipped out of the circle, whores again, leaving the two of us. Lacy hugged me until my
breath faltered, repeating, as if it were a litany, "Ol' buddy, Ol' buddy,
little ol' buddy."

It had been years since I'd been frightened by a man's embrace, or
ashamed, or, I must add in all honesty, aroused, but Lacy held me with
such a fierce love, so much drunken power and love, that I clutched
him, hugged him back, and for a few seconds we whirled, stumbling

about the dark courtyard. Then—perhaps he thought it a disgusting revelation, perhaps he responded, I'll never know—he flung me from him as if I were a sack of dirty laundry. My knees hit the fountain wall, my head the fountain.

IV

The next morning I woke in the back seat of my car, not a great deal worse for the night. A bit stiff and sore, but no more. Because I am terribly responsible about the way I exhaust my life, I cleaned up, made a thermos of Bloody Mary's, and went to my office. Lacy was already there.

"Listen," he said as I sat down, "I'm sorry."

"Hey, it doesn't matter."

"I know, I know."

He smiled once, nearly grinned, then raised his hand and left the office, walking with a bounce and energy that I'd never seen, striding as he must have onto the hardwood courts of his youth. I never saw him again. Elena says he was drunk, but I doubt it. She thinks he was drunk because of the wad of bills he offered her to flee across the border with him, because of the wonderful grin on his face.

"Did he make it?" I asked.

She shrugged again, not knowing what I meant until I showed her. Then her whore's face brightened, like a cheerleader's welcoming home a winner. "*Bueno*," she said. "*Muy bueno*."

I tried to excuse her, telling myself that the craft of whoredom is lying; I tried to excuse myself, blaming my grief. But it didn't work. I paid her for another time, and as she slipped out of her yellow dress, she shrugged once again, as if to say *who knows about these gringo men*. Inside her, I slapped her dull face until she cried, until I came.

I don't go back to Nuevo Laredo anymore: I satisfy my needs up or down the border. Of late my needs are fewer. I visit Marsha occasionally. We sit in her room, I talk, she nods over the doll they've given her. Her parents would rather have her back than pay for her keep, so I pay; that is, my father pays. Even in her gray hospital robe, without a trace of makeup left on her face, she is still lovely, so lovely I know why men speak of the face of an angel. She neither ages nor speaks; she rocks, she nods, she clutches her painted doll. I believe she's happy. When I told her about Lacy, just about the accident, not the cause, she smiled, as if she knew he were happy too. I didn't tell her that it took a cutting torch to remove his body from the car.

As they say, the living must live. I don't know. From my parents' house I can hear them living: my mother's television tuned to an afternoon soap opera, the volume all the way up to penetrate her morphine haze; in the kitchen my father is shouting at a congressman over the telephone. I don't know.

I'll marry my chubby Shakespearean, or somebody so much like her that the slight differences won't matter. I'll still go bordertown whoring, and it will never occur to her to complain. And we'll avoid children like the plague.

from THE LAST PICTURE SHOW

――――――― ✦ ―――――――

Larry McMurtry

ALL DAY THE BOYS ALTERNATED, ONE DRIVING THE OTHER sleeping, and by late evening they were in the Valley, driving between the green orange groves. It was amazing how different the world was, once the plains were left behind. In the Valley there were even palm trees. The sky was violet, and dusk lingered until they were almost to Matamoros. Every few miles they passed roadside groceries, lit with yellow light bulbs and crowded with tables piled high with corn and squash, cabbages and tomatoes.

"This is a crazy place," Duane said. "Who you reckon eats all that squash?"

They drove straight on through Brownsville and paid a fat, bored tollhouse keeper twenty cents so they could drive across the bridge. Below them was the Rio Grande, a river they had heard about all their lives. Its waters were mostly dark, touched only here and there by the yellow bridge lights. Several Mexican boys in ragged shirts were sitting on one of the guardrails, spitting into the water and chattering to one another.

A few blocks from the bridge they came to a stoplight on a pole, with four or five boys squatting by it. Apparently someone had run into the light pole because it was leaning away from the street at a forty-five degree angle. As soon as Sonny stopped one of the boys ran out and jumped lightly onto the running board.

"Girl?" he said. "Boy's Town? Dirty movie?"

"Well, I guess," Sonny said. "I guess," Sonny said. "I guess that's what we came for."

The boy quickly got in the cab and began to chatter directions in Tex-Mex—Sonny followed them as best he could. They soon left the boulevard and got into some of the narrowest streets the boys had ever seen. Barefooted kids and cats and dogs were playing in the street, night or no night, and they moved aside for the pickup very reluctantly. A smell of onions seemed to pervade the whole town, and the streets went every which direction. There were lots of intersections but no stop signs—apparently the right of way belonged to the driver with the most nerve. Sonny kept stopping at the intersections, but that was a reversal of local custom: most drivers beeped their horns and speeded up, hoping to dart through before anyone could hit them.

Mexico was more different from Thalia than either of the boys would have believed. The number of people who went about at night was amazing to them. In Thalia three or four boys on the courthouse square constituted a lively crowd, but the streets of Matamoros teemed with people. Groups of men stood on what, in Thalia, would have been sidewalks, children rushed about in the dust, and old men sat against buildings.

Their guide finally ordered them to stop in front of a dark lump that was apparently some sort of dwelling.

"This couldn't be no whorehouse," Duane said. "It ain't big enough to have a whore in it."

Not knowing what else to do, they got out and followed their guide to the door. A paunchy Mexican in his undershirt and khakis opened it and grunted at the guide. "Ees got movies," the boy said.

They all went inside, into a bedroom. Through an open doorway the boys could see an old woman stirring something in a pot, onions and tomatoes it smelled like. An old man with no shirt on and white hair on his chest sat at a table staring at some dominoes. Neither the old man nor old woman so much as glanced at the boys. There were two beds in the bedroom and on one of them three little Mexican boys were curled up, asleep. Sonny felt strange when he saw them. They looked very helpless, and he could not feel it was very polite for Duane and him to barge into their room. The paunchy man immediately brought up the subject of movies. "Ten dollars," he said. "Got all kinds."

He knelt and drew a tiny little projector out from under the bed and took several rolls of eight-millimeter film out of a little bureau. The boys looked uncomfortably at one another. They either had to pay and watch the movies or else refuse and leave, and since they had driven five hundred miles to see some wickedness it was pointless to refuse. Duane handed over a ten dollar bill and the man stuffed it in his pocket and calmly began to clear one of the beds. He picked the sleeping boys up one at a time, carried them into the kitchen, and deposited them under the table where the old man sat. The little boys moaned a little and stirred in their sleep, but they didn't wake up. The paunchy man then put the projector on their bed and prepared to show the movies on a sheet hung against the opposite wall.

"I don't like this," Sonny said, appalled. "I never come all this way just to get some kids out of bed. If he ain't got a better place than this to show them I'd just as soon go on."

Duane was of the same mind, but when they tried to explain themselves, the guide and the projectionist both seemed puzzled.

"Ees okay," the guide said. "Sleepin' away." He gestured at the three little boys, all of whom were sound asleep on the dirt floor.

Sonny and Duane were stubborn. Even though the little boys were asleep, it wouldn't do: they couldn't enjoy a dirty movie so long as they were in sight of the displaced kids. Finally the projectionist shrugged, picked up the projector, and led them back through the hot kitchen and across an alley. The guide followed, carrying the film. Above them the sky was dark and the stars very bright.

They came to what seemed to be a sort of long outhouse, and when the guide knocked a thin, middle-aged man opened the door. He had only one leg, but no crutch, the room being so small that he could easily hop from one resting place to the next. As soon as they were all inside the guide informed the boys that it would cost them five dollars more because of the change of rooms: the one-legged man could not be put to the trouble of sitting through a pornographic movie for nothing. Sonny paid it and the projectionist plugged the projector into a light socket. An old American calendar hung on the door, a picture of a girl in mechanic's overalls on the front of it. The one-legged man simply turned the calendar around and they had a screen.

"You mean they're going to show it on the back of a calendar," Duane said. "For fifteen dollars?"

The light was turned off and the projector began to buzz—the title of the picture was *Man's Best Friend*. It was clearly an old picture, because the lady who came on the screen was dressed like ladies in Laurel and Hardy movies. The similarity was so strong that for a moment the boys expected Laurel and Hardy to come on the screen and do dirty things to her. As the plot unfolded the print became more and more scratchy and more and more faded; soon it was barely possible to tell that the figures on the screen were human. The boys leaned forward to get a better look and were amazed to discover that the figures on the screen *weren't* all human. One of the actors was a German shepherd dog.

"My God," Duane said.

They both immediately felt the trip was worthwhile, if only for the gossip value. Nobody in Thalia had ever seen a dog and a lady behaving that way: clearly it was the ultimate depravity, even more depraved than having congress with Negro whores. They were speechless. A man came on and replaced the dog, and then the dog came back on and he and the man teamed up. The projectionist and the guide chuckled with delight at this development, but the boys were too surprised to do anything but watch. The ugliness of it all held them spellbound. When it was over they walked to the pickup in silence, followed by the guide and the projectionist. The latter was making a sales pitch.

"Lots more reels," he said. "Got French, Gypsy, Chinese lesbian, all kinds. Five dollars a reel from now on."

The boys shook their heads. They wanted to get away and think. The guide shrugged and climbed in beside them and they drove away, leaving the fat man in the middle of the road.

"I hope he puts them kids back in bed," Sonny commented.

"Boy's Town now," the guide said happily. "Five hundred girls there. Clean, too."

They soon left the downtown area and bumped off toward the outskirts of Matamoros. A red Chevrolet with Texas license plates was just in front of them, throwing the white dust of the dirt road up into their headlights. Soon they saw Boy's Town, the neon lights from the larger cabarets winking red and green against the night. At first it looked like there were a hundred clubs, but after they drove around a while they saw that there were only fifteen or twenty big places, one on every corner. Between the corners were dark, unlit rows of cribs. The guide gestured contemptuously at the cribs and took them to a place called the Cabaret ZeeZee. When the boys parked, a fat policeman in khakis walked up and offered to open the door for them, but the guide chattered insultingly to him and he shrugged lazily and turned away.

The boys entered the cabaret timidly, expecting to be mobbed at once by whores or else slugged by Mexican gangsters, but neither thing happened. They were simply ignored. There was a large jukebox and a few couples dancing, but most of the people in the club were American boys, sitting around tables.

"The competition's gonna be worse here than it is in Thalia," Duane said. "We might as well get some beer."

They sat down at one of the tile-topped tables and waited several minutes before a waitress came over and got their order. She brought them the first Mexican beer they had ever tasted, and they drank the first bottles thirstily. In their tired, excited state the beer quickly took effect—before they knew it they had had five bottles apiece, and the fatigue of the trip seemed to be dropping away. A fat-faced girl in a green blouse came over, introduced herself as Juanita, and with no further preamble squeezed Sonny intimately through his blue jeans. He was amazed. Though responsive, he felt the evening would bring better things than Juanita, so he politely demurred. Juanita went around and squeezed Duane the same way, but got the same reply.

"Texas ees full of queers," she said, swishing her buttocks derogatorily as she walked away. The boys contemplated themselves over the beer bottles, wondering if they had been seriously insulted.

As the night wore on Sonny gradually set his mind on a slim, black-headed girl who spent most of her time on the dance floor, dancing with boys from Texas A & M. There were a good many boys from Texas A & M in the cabaret.

"I thought Aggies was all irresistible cocksmen," Duane said. "What's so many of them doing in a whorehouse?"

In time Sonny approached the girl, whose name was Maria. She cheerfully came to the table with him and downed three whiskeys while he was having a final beer. Between drinks she blew her warm, slightly sticky breath in his ear and squeezed him the way Juanita had.

"All night party?" she asked. "Jus' twenty-five dollars. We can leef right now."

It seemed ungallant to haggle with such a confident girl, so Sonny agreed. It turned out he owed eight dollars for the drinks, but it didn't seem gallant to haggle about that either. He paid, and Maria led him out the back door of the Cabaret ZeeZee into a very dark alley, where the only light was from the bright stars far above. The place she took him didn't even have a door, just a blue curtain with a light behind it. The room was extremely tiny. The one light bulb was in a socket on the wall and the bed was an old iron cot with a small mattress and a thin green bedspread.

In the room, Maria seemed less perky than she had in the club. She looked younger than she had inside. Sonny watched her unzip her dress—her back was brown and smooth, but when she turned to face him he was really surprised. Her breasts were heavy, her nipples large and purplish, and she was clearly pregnant. He had never seen a pregnant woman naked before, but he knew from the heavy bulge of her abdomen that she must be carrying a child. She tried to look at him with whorish gaiety, but somehow it didn't work: the smile was without life, and showed her gums. When he was undressed she splashed him with coolish water from a brown pitcher, and scrutinized him with such care that an old worry popped into his mind. Perhaps his equipment was too small? He had worried about that when he first began to go with Ruth, and had even tried to find out how large one's equipment was supposed to be, but the only two reference works in the high-school library were the *World Book* and the *Texas Almanac*, neither of which had anything helpful on penises. Gradually it had ceased to worry him, but with Maria he had begun to feel generally hesitant.

"But aren't you going to have a baby?" he asked, not sure that the question was proper.

Maria nodded. "Two already," she said, meaning to reassure him. Her heavy breasts and large grape-colored nipples were not at all congruous with her thin calves and girlish shoulders.

Sonny lay down with her on the cot, but he knew even before he began that somehow twenty-five dollars had been lost. He didn't want to stay in the room all night, or even very much of it.

Two minutes later it came home to him why Ruth had insisted they make love on the floor: the cot springs wailed and screamed, and the sound made him feel as though every move he made was sinful. He had driven five hundred miles to get away from Thalia, and the springs took him right back, made him feel exposed. Everyone in town would know that he had done it with a pregnant whore. Suddenly he ceased to care about the twenty-five dollars, or about anything; the fatigues of the long trip, down from the plains, through the hill country and the brush country, through Austin and San Antone, five hundred miles of it all pressed against the backs of his legs and up his body, too heavy to support. To Maria's amazement he simply stopped and went to sleep.

WHEN HE AWOKE, HE WAS VERY HOT. THE GREEN COUNTERPANE was soaked with his sweat. It was not until he had been awake a minute or two that he realized the sun was shining in his face. He was still in the room where Maria had brought him, but the room had no roof—the night before he had not even noticed. It was just an open crib.

He hurriedly got up and put on his clothes, his head aching. While he was tying his shoes he suddenly had to vomit, and barely made it past the blue curtain into the street. When he had finished vomiting and was kneeling in the white dust waiting for his strength to come back he heard a slow clop-clop and looked up to see a strange wagon rounding the corner into his part of the street. It was a water wagon, drawn by a decrepit brown mule and driven by an old man. The wagon was entirely filled by a large rubber water tank wrapped in ragged canvas; as the wagon moved the water sloshed out of the open tank and dripped down the sides of the wagon into the white dust. The old man wore a straw hat so old that it had turned brown. His grizzled whiskers were as white as Sam the Lion's hair. As he stopped the mule, three or four whores stepped out of their cribs with water pitchers in their hands. One passed right by Sonny, a heavy woman with a relaxed face and large white breasts that almost spilled out of her green robe. The whores were barefooted and seemed much happier than they had seemed the night before. They chattered like high-school girls and came lightly to the wagon to get their water. The old man spoke to them cheerfully, and when the first group had filled their pitchers he popped the mule lightly with the rein and proceeded up the street, the slow clop-clop of the mule's feet very loud in the still morning. When he passed where Sonny was kneeling the old man nodded to him kindly and gestured with a tin dipper he had in his hand. Sonny gratefully took a dipper of water from him, using it to wash the sour taste out of his mouth. The old man smiled at him sympathetically and said something in a philosophic tone, something which Sonny took to mean that life was a matter of ups and downs. He stayed where he was and watched the wagon until it rounded the next corner. As it moved slowly up the street the whores of Matamoros came out of their cribs, some of them combing their black hair, some with white bosoms uncovered, all with brown pitchers in their hands and coins for the old waterman.

Sonny found Duane asleep in the front seat of the pickup, his legs sticking out the window. Three little boys were playing in the road, trying to lead a dusty white goat across into a pasture of scraggly mesquite. The goat apparently wanted to go into the Cabaret ZeeZee. A depressed looking spotted dog followed behind the boys and occasionally yapped discouragedly at the goat.

Duane was too bleary and sick to do more than grunt. His hair was plastered to his temples with sweat. "You drive," he said.

By some miracle Sonny managed to wind his way through Matamoros to the Rio Grande—in daylight the water in the river was green. The boys stood groggily under the custom's shed for a few minutes, wondering why in the world they had been so foolish as to come all the way to Mexico. Thalia seemed an impossible distance away.

"I don't know if I can make it," Sonny said. "How much money we got?"

They found, to their dismay, that their money had somehow evap-

orated. They had four dollars between them. There was the money
that Sam and Genevieve had given them, hidden in the seat springs,
but they had not planned to use that.

"I guess we can pay them back in a week or two," Sonny said. "We'll
have to use it."

When the customs men were through the boys got back in the
pickup and drove slowly out of Brownsville, along the Valley highway.
Heat waves shimmered above the green cabbage fields. Despite the
sun and heat Duane soon went to sleep again and slept heavily, wal-
lowing in his own sweat. Sonny drove automatically; he was
depressed, but not exactly sleepy, and he paced himself from town to
town, not daring to think any farther ahead than the next city limits
sign.

Soon the thought of Ruth began to bother him. In retrospect it
seemed incredibly foolish that he should drive a thousand miles to go
to sleep on a pregnant girl's stomach, when any afternoon he could
have a much better time with Ruth. The thought of her slim, familiar
body and cool hands suddenly made him very horny and even more
depressed with himself. It occurred to him that he might even be dis-
eased, and he stopped in a filling station in Alice to inspect himself.
Duane woke up and exhibited similar anxieties. For the rest of the day
they stopped and peed every fifty miles, just to be sure they could.

There was money enough for gas, but not much for food, so they
managed on Cokes, peanuts, and a couple of candy bars. Evening
finally came, coolness with it, and the boys got a second wind. The trip
ceased to seem like such a fiasco: after all, they had been to Mexico,
visited whorehouses, seen dirty movies. In Thalia it would be regarded
as a great adventure, and they could hardly wait to tell about it. The
country around Thalia had never looked so good to them as it did when
they came back into it, at four in the morning. The dark pastures, the
farmhouses, the oil derricks and even the jackrabbits that went dashing
across the road in front of them, all seemed comfortable, familiar, private even, part of what was theirs and no one else's. After the strange-

ness of Matamoros the lights of Thalia were especially reassuring.

Duane was driving when they pulled in. He whipped through the red light and turned toward the café. Genevieve would be glad to see they were safely back.

To their astonishment, the café was dark. No one at all was there. The café had never been closed, not even on Christmas, and the boys were stunned. Inside, one little light behind the counter shone on the aspirin, the cough-drops, the chewing gum, and cheap cigars.

"It ain't a holiday, is it?" Sonny said.

There was nothing to do but go over to the courthouse and wake up Andy Fanner—he would know what had happened.

Andy woke up hard, but they kept at him and he finally got out of the car and rubbed his stubbly jaw, trying to figure out what the boys wanted.

"Oh yeah, you all been gone, ain't you," he said. "Gone to Mexico. You don't know about it. Sam the Lion died yesterday mornin'."

"Died?" Sonny said. After a moment he walked over to the curb in front of the courthouse and sat down. The traffic light blinked red and green over the empty street. Andy came over to the curb too, yawning and rubbing the back of his neck.

"Yep," he said. "Quite a blow. Keeled over on one of the snooker tables. Had a stroke."

Soon it was dawn, a cool, dewy spring dawn that wet the courthouse grass and left a low white mist on the pastures for the sun to burn away. Andy sat on the fender of his Nash and told all about the death and how everybody had taken it, who had cried and who hadn't. "Good thing you all got back today, you'd 'a missed the funeral," he said. "How'd you find Mexico?" Sonny could not have told him; he had lost track of things and just wanted to sit on the curb and watch the traffic light change.

A GUIDE TO SOME SMALL BORDER AIRPORTS

Peter LaSalle

"Here we go round the prickly pear."
—T. S. Eliot

1. EAGLE PASS, TEXAS.

BE CAREFUL OF THIS ONE. IF THERE ARE A HALF DOZEN legitimate airports along the border in West Texas, clear out to El Paso, this is the first and the one I learned to trust the least.

When I fly down from Austin I stop there only because at the end of the cracked airstrip one of the stubby red-and-white Phillips pumps serves up automotive gas, "mo-gas." My Cessna 182 is old enough to run well on the stuff. Plus, going west after Eagle Pass everything turns to blond desert, peppered with aqua scrub, restricted military property for thousands and thousands of square acres. It is a stretch where you don't want to run short and have to put down if you are circling for time.

I was there last month and something strange happened.

It is really not much of a setup, just that strip and those pumps, and a decrepit galvanized hangar shed with an office for an enterprise called Bravo Flying Service. I have never been to the town of Eagle

Pass, or to the gritty Mexican town across the weeded-over Rio Grande, Piedras Negras. But last month this guy was at the airport again, supposedly waiting to have some work done on his Skywagon. It was one of those single-engine six-seaters that is basically nothing more than a flying bus. I remembered him from my previous trip, and I remembered that then he was also supposedly waiting to have some work done.

He was slim and tall, about my build, in his forties and a bit older than me. He had curly gray hair, a leathery face, squinting too-blue eyes. We were alone there, except for the Mexican guy now up on the aluminum ladder and pumping my mo-gas. There is a camaraderie in these small airports. You talk about the winds and the weather, which was a steely low ceiling that afternoon, a late February blow of blue cold in a place you never think of as being cold. He had his hands jammed in the pockets of a cloth bomber jacket, the wind blew that hair. It wasn't as if he was trying to pump me for information, because he just nodded a lot. When he did talk the words came with some smiling, a cowboy's squint, though this guy wasn't from Texas at all. In fact, though he didn't remember me, or let on that he did, I remembered that he had told me the last time that he was living out there, doing general aviation stuff like flying geologists and rich ranchers, and glad to be away from city life. So many people out there tell you they are glad to have escaped the rush of city life—what else can they say?

"You like that power of the 182," he said.

"Six cylinders is better than four," I said. The Cessna I have is a single-engine overhead wing, built in sixty-seven, and it does pack a load of power. I was looking at his Skywagon, painted a yellow-and-red combo. I was noticing what I had also noticed the last time, how he had removed the fenders to allow for the oversized balloon tires on the landing gear and how the undersides of the wings were crusted with thrown-up cinnamon mud. He had been putting that thing down in some far-out places, places even geologists and rich ranchers didn't go.

"Lets you get right in there for your picture taking," he said.

"Yeah, I guess it does at that," I told him. "Lets me get in and then pull right out for my picture taking."

He nodded. But I hadn't given him my stock line about aerial photography being my trade this time, and that was something that must have come up before. And all the while I had been thinking that he didn't remember me, and now it was obvious to me that he had been playing along, letting me pretend that I didn't remember him. In short, each of us remembered the other, neither admitted it.

In a way, I later thought, we were ghosts, acting out a dream that neither was quite sure of. But I was there and he was there, with his same story about waiting for repairs and with a plane that had obviously been places that a for-hire didn't go.

Like I said, be careful of Eagle Pass.

2. DEL RIO, TEXAS.

This is two hundred miles west of Eagle Pass. Believe me, there is nothing much in between.

It is small, but you can lose yourself in an operation like the one they have. Out in that dust, on the very edge of the town that is principally known for the fact that six-gun-shooting Judge Roy Bean himself is buried there, the little airport is Chamber of Commerce neat. A slate-blue humpbacked hangar with a new lounge wing attached: tinted glass; red wall-to-wall and red Naugahyde sofas and chairs right out of a dentist's waiting room; copies of *Flying* and *USA Today* on glass-topped coffee tables; an alcove with the usual sandwich and chip machines and the more-than-usual Dr. Pepper, rather than Coke, machine, because, after all, you are in West Texas. Nothing really distinguishes it, except for a classic old wall chart of the region, dulled to watercolors, and the bulletin board with maybe an extraordinarily large number of Polaroid shots of planes up for sale. As I said, nobody pays much attention to you, even if you are the only plane stopping to

refuel. You get the feeling that those who check in and out are probably Del Rio doctors who took up flying as a hobby, the way local doctors are always taking it up as a hobby.

There was a time. Back in that other world when I myself had actually used the phys ed degree I never thought I would use, and when I
had a job teaching gym and coaching track at the junior high serving
one of those new Austin subdivisions. I was out of the so-called business then, and though I didn't want to think of the border, think of all
that time flying "low and slow" in the swallowing desert without lights,
think of putting down sometimes on those rough strips in the mountains that you dropped onto just about elevator-straight, I came out to
Del Rio with Lizanne.

She had gotten her sister to take care of her kid, Rosie. Which I
thought was a start. The Rosie thing with her had become an obsession by that point, and I was glad that she had at last agreed to leave
town with me for a weekend. She was from Corpus, had married while
at a j.c. there. Her husband, Billy, owned two galleries in Corpus, and
they had met when she found herself at some of the parties of that
crowd, seeing she was a beauty and had been modeling clothes since
she was in junior high for local department stores, even local TV. But
when Rosie was born with the defect of that left leg being slightly
shorter than the right, Billy wasn't ready for the responsibility of that.
He was gone before long, either Tampa or Jacksonville, Lizanne was
never sure which. She eventually moved to Austin where her married
sister lived, and by the time I began seeing her, Rosie was ten and had
already been through a half-dozen operations to try to get that one leg
to match the other. The last had been a substantial bone graft, unsuc-
cessful and in truth only emphasizing that the situation was worse—
what had started as a fractional difference at birth was now, sadly, a
full two inches. Lizanne had begun taking night courses at the University of Texas for a B.A. and she held down a full-time job typing at
the state comptroller's office.

It was true. At that stage I finally thought that the craziness of my

life flying in the business was over. I was teaching and the last place I
wanted to think about was the Texas border. But Acuna, across from
Del Rio, had always been special to me. I liked to rest there a few days.
I told Lizanne so much about the spot that we decided to head to it
for a weekend, using the little four-cylinder Piper I had borrowed from
a pal. (I have always flown, crop-dusting in Pennsylvania as a teenager,
later a pilot in the Army.) We set out, stowing ten-speed bicycles in the
back. And after touching down at that Del Rio strip, we put what we
needed in nylon daypacks and planned to use the bikes for the few
miles into town, then across the border. It was this same time of year,
true spring. We sped by the squat little bungalows on the dusty cross
streets of Del Rio, looped around the central square with its proudly
pillared 1930s bank buildings and neat red brick storefronts, all the
cascading purple wisteria in full bloom, and continued right down that
long final empty stretch of slick asphalt two-lane and the occasional
souvenir and money-changing shack, toward Customs and the international bridge. We were well outside Del Rio, a couple of miles from
Acuna too. But the day was so warm and so ever-blue. Beyond the arc
of the narrow span of the bridge, painted silver, rose the dry yellow
hills, the little town with its bone-white cathedral bell tower above the
puffs of lime-green trees. Still as slim as she was when she modeled,
Lizanne had full lips and dark doe eyes now fringed with incipient
lines that made her womanly and maybe more handsome still. She
stopped halfway across the bridge. She was wearing white camp shorts
and a white T-shirt, and she looked back, straddling her ten-speed
while I caught up.

"What?" I asked her.

"Look at it," she said smiling. "I can tell from here it's special. I just
wanted to make sure that you knew I knew. Everything you said about
it will be true. It will." She smiled some more, and the sun sheened
her dark hair blown stringy from riding.

In Acuna we stayed in what was the only real hotel. A place called
Mrs. Crosby's, it was on a corner of the main street right after the

bridge, a Spanish setup around a central courtyard of gaudy ceramic tiles and well-groomed garden. We must have bought the begging little kids out of their supply of Chiclets when we strolled the streets. We ate at cheap restaurants good enough to make you take an oath you would never even bother with Mexican food outside of Mexico again. In the bruised blue evenings we sat in the park across from the cathedral. The teenage girls in frilled dresses giggled among themselves, and the leathery old men wearing straw cowboy hats played dominoes under the big live oaks that had trunks whitewashed lower down, and the dignified statues of all those blessed heroes of the republic just nonchalantly looked on. At night we drank cool Carta Blanca in the hotel bar with its hypnotizing ceiling fans, the only Americans, and later we made love, moonlight gently washing the floors of that admittedly seedy room, whining mariachi music crackling from the little transistor I had set up on the dresser. Afterward we talked.

On the second night there, the last, we lay silent for a while.

"You're thinking of Rosie, aren't you," I said.

"I was thinking that I hadn't really thought much of her at all," she said. "That scares me."

I kissed her on the forehead.

Rosie suffered brain damage after the next operation. It was the result of an infection, then a fever that the doctors originally claimed they had under control. I had stopped seeing Lizanne before that, but she called to tell me about Rosie. My older brother in Pennsylvania died around the same time. And I was drinking, and I knew I wasn't long for that job at the junior high. I first went back to what I told myself would be just one trip flying in and out of Mexico. Then it was half a dozen. But I promised myself that would be all. Nevertheless, I bought the Cessna, made still more runs, and spent the money fast. And here I am on the border again.

Enough about Del Rio, and Acuna across the long-ago way.

3. LAJITAS, TEXAS.

The story about this trip really starts in Presidio, still further west toward El Paso. But before that is an airport so small that it usually is unmanned, Lajitas.

It is at the far end of Big Bend. That is the national park as large as a couple of small states combined. True badlands of erosion-clawed chocolate mountains, and such heat even in spring that every thermal updraft becomes a jarring speed bump to a small plane like mine. You have to fly with the side windows flapping open against the wings above, just for air. A rich man named Cooke Thompson III came out from Houston not long after the oil embargo, in that time of fast and then faster money in that glass-spired supposed city of the future that was swelling with two thousand newcomers a week by 1980. Cooke Thompson was oil money, Beaumont old, and he saw this patch of land, a literal stone's throw from the Rio Grande, as his chance to develop what Californians had a long time before and what rich Texans finally needed themselves—another Palm Springs. It is all tucked in by orange mesas, and the sole natural vegetation is the starred yucca and the paddles of prickly pear. Cooke Thompson has built a huge luxury hotel, a rustic takeoff on something in a B-Western, with a gray planked sidewalk out front and inside red silk wallpaper for the lobby and the dozens of rooms upstairs that must go for an easy two-fifty a night. Some sprawling modern houses have gone up on the higher plateaus. There are tennis courts where the play sounds like corn popping in the heat, and an eighteen-hole golf course even more emerald than the composition courts, studded with mop-headed palms. From the air, the ponds and the sandtraps are pieces from a spilled puzzle, tiny carts chug along under candy-striped awning tops.

The strip is isolated, but long enough to handle Learjets. Cooke Thompson's social set from Houston whisks out there for the weekends. They import name singers and famous dance bands to entertain themselves and their blueblood wives in the starry nights, at get-

togethers after all the sport and all the booze and all the talk, talk, talk
of more real estate and more oil, how they are really going to strike it
even bigger than before as soon as OPEC reorganizes and eventual
prices make anything seen during the gas-line days seem like only a
pittance.

It is a good place to land if you miss the strip in the desert where
you were supposed to touch down for your ten-minute drop. Nobody
notices you in Lajitas, and they do have fuel pumps, though you have
to walk a ways to that new hotel there to find the guy who handles
them. In twenty-five years this could all be luxury homes and even
freeways, I told myself when I stopped there on this trip. Cooke
Thompson surely knows what the rest of us only suspect: money *can*
do anything.

4. PRESIDIO, TEXAS.

Yes, this is where the madness of this trip genuinely started, and
where I had my suspicions confirmed that I was being watched, ever
since the month before and that strange exchange with the pilot of the
Skywagon. Be very careful of Eagle Pass.

Presidio is my base of sorts. You can't go much further out on the
Texas border, except for El Paso, where the state ends halfway across
the bottom of New Mexico. It is as simple as this. Alvarez, a Mexican,
supplies and arranges. I simply fly to Chihuahua, a pretty big city in
northern Mexico, filing my flight plan with the Mexican authorities. I
then fly back to Presidio, filing my estimated time of arrival there with
the U.S. Flight Service, who arrange to have a Customs man out at the
desolate Presidio airport when I land. All my real work is done in
between. I bill myself as an aerial photographer. The plane is overflowing with cameras and lenses, all carefully registered with U.S.
Customs right down to the twelve-digit or more serial numbers. I am
so up front about everything that openness has become my cover, and

who the hell would register a peach basket full of Canons and Nikons to prove he wasn't smuggling them, and then actually be involved in smuggling—dope? It is all marijuana, just ninety-pound bales, and my theory is that because it isn't the big money, the risk is less. I make wages and not much more from Alvarez. His leg men who give me my load on one side and his leg men who pick it up on the other aren't all that hardcore. The surveillance for this kind of operation on both sides has to be lighter, you tell yourself; and so, you tell yourself too, it doesn't seem to be true that if you're bringing something across illegally you might as well make it something with as much value as possible. Once I am in Chihuahua, it is easy to fly out to a desert strip for a pick-up from Alvarez's crew, because nobody makes you file a plan after you are inside the country. And when I announce what time I will be landing in Presidio, I always make it a good six hours ahead of time, which allows me to circle and circle, even put down in a place like Lajitas, if the basic look of the desert strip agreed on for the drop in Texas doesn't seem right.

I worked it smoother than usual this run. I made the delivery, then looped above Presidio a couple of times, taking a roll of full-focus camera shots of the way they have used irrigation to nurture some fragile green agriculture. At least some proof of my pretended trade. I radioed down to Charlie at the little airport operation below, and he said that the Customs man was already there. I slid in easy to the velvety black runway, which is off to one side of the new yellow-enameled metal trailer and the new yellow-enameled metal hangar that Charlie wrangled through some bank refinancing. He has one corner of the hangar set up with a small Astroturf carpet on the fresh concrete, four cheap easy chairs, and a cooler that offers a pool of icy water and only, of course, that cherry-syrupped Dr. Pepper. But Presidio is my base. And I had a few Budweisers with Charlie in his dim trailer, while the Customs man wearing his heavy blue uniform stooped into the Cessna with his clipboard and started his thorough inspection. He was new, the way Customs men here are always new. Border Patrol men are always older, tougher, headquartered in their pale-green buildings closer to town, beside that lot ringed with chainlink and filled with confiscated "vehicles," bullet holes riddling some of them; it is a detail you don't like to think about.

If I owned a small airport, I think it would be like Charlie's. It is far enough outside of the town that you see only more desert and the low purplish mountains all around you. Charlie is my age, with a gut and sideburns of the ilk that really haven't been spotted much outside of a place like Presidio, Texas, since lying Nixon stalked the Oval Office. Ruddy-faced from too much beer, he has massive hands and wrists the size of fireplace logs. He smiles a lot too, not so much out of dumbness but maybe out of loneliness, which Charlie seems to savor. He has a Mexican wife who has two kids, with hair as black as crow's feathers, by another marriage. But the trio of them seem to show up only on Sundays. Since that last time I had been there Charlie had gotten a new satellite rig for television reception, and with the doors wide open on that mobile home and the desert sky even more neon blue than when you had last noticed it above the mountains' jagged silhouette, we sat in the front room. The furniture was new, reddish-brown stuff; the carpet was new, reddish-brown stuff. He demonstrated how to use the dial that rotated the dish, and at one point he found what he was sure was a baseball game direct from Boston.

"That's up in your neck of the woods, isn't it?"

"Pennsylvania," I said.

"That's close. Or, I guess it's close if you think about it all from down here. It all seems so far away."

"It all seems so far away," I repeated.

We drank for a while without saying anything, the television off. A couple of hours passed, but I don't think we ever really noticed them. Time that was lost, probably before it was even ours to spend. I borrowed Charlie's pick-up truck, had a meal at the one attempt at a restaurant (really just a barbecue place) in Presidio proper, which can't be more than a thousand in population, and booked into the one motel, new, at the edge of town.

I wasn't tired. I lay on the bed with its yellow nubbed spread. I stared at the thermo-insulated plastic pitcher and the two glasses in clear wrap on the dresser. What was it Charlie had said, it all seems so far away. And it did. Pennsylvania was part of that other world too, and it wasn't a part I could manage to get even a slight grip on, like that whole business with Lizanne and Rosie. In Pennsylvania my father had worked in the coal mines. This was in Wilkes-Barre, up in the northeastern corner of the state. There as a kid in the fifties you actually learned to put your butch-cut head flat on your desk for civil defense drills, and as a teenager in the sixties the Polish and Czech girls you were nervous about and looked at from a distance argued over who among them was really first to own a Beatles album. But all that aside, football was everything. And my older brother, Al, was about everything in football in our city. It was a place of soot and orange trolleys still sparking their blue, because ordinary buses just couldn't muster the climb into the neighborhoods.

Al was a natural, a running back. Low-browed and heavy in the shoulders. He was maybe a little awkward in some ways, my father's oafishness, but he wasn't bragging. My father surely made up for that, but who could blame him? Here was a son who had not only been wooed by Dartmouth and the University of South Carolina, but, most importantly, Penn State itself. Though the handsome campus where the Nittany Lions played in their massive bowl (showing so much assurance and class that they didn't need anything more than numeral markings on their navy-and-white uniforms) was in a way local, that made it only more impressive. Our heroes went to Penn State, and USC and even Notre Dame were nothing to compare to it, let alone some place totally unheard of like South Carolina. And then *Life* magazine did a piece on Pennsylvania schoolboy football. Ten glossy pages of action photographs and the usual journalese on "tough" kids from "tough" coal and steel backgrounds. My brother's picture wasn't there along with some of the state's true stars, but there was a mention of him and also our high school, where I ran track, somewhat relieved that with a brother as "famous" as mine I felt no need to even try to compete for stardom. One fall afternoon it happened; the school was on its way to the state divisional championship.

Actually, this was the quarter-final in Pittsburgh. The stadium was an old poured-concrete affair, and the day stretched milky, November dim. Even if the stands were just half full, the crowd seemed enormous, when you remembered this was only a high school game. Our school was indeed one from a supposedly tough coal town, and the opposition's was one from a supposedly tough steel town. Their players were huge, including the backfield. They had on ancient uniforms with black-and-yellow-striped sleeves, bees' markings, and the helmets weren't even plastic, but museum-piece, leather-covered jobs that had been repainted so often that the gloss cracked in spiderwebbing. It was in the fourth quarter, a grinding game of slams and bruises as the score stood stalled at a three-all tie on field goals, and I was right down at the bench with my father. My father, a solid man from those years of mining, shouted himself hoarse, while the band's pep song blaringly repeated itself over and over, off-key horns and machine-gun drums, and the cheerleaders chanted like lost children in the diluted cold. Al finally took the ball on a quarterback hand-off, and I had seen him zig-zag so often, maybe even in my dreams, that I knew from his acceleration alone that this was going to be it for him. He dodged twin tackles near the line, then jetted loose of the whole crowd, springing into the clear of that frost-lumped field. One of their men was waiting for him, however, the safety, poised and low, and Al really turned it on. . . .

But we would never know if Al could have avoided that last snag. Because just then my father in his bulky Army surplus parka and porkpie hat was already crazed and out on the field tackling that last man himself. The crowd was stunned. The referees called the entire play invalid. Escorted to the sidelines, my father looked dazed, my brother looked dazed.

My brother did break away again. Our team won, but lost in the semi-finals. Al went to Penn State, though never made it much beyond the taxi squad. He went to work in the mines when he dropped out of college, married. For a while in our family the story of my father's mad running onto the field was something we all awkwardly tried to laugh about, but later, after I had left home, my father and brother argued bitterly, about everything. And years later my brother told me, "I think I would have stood a chance at Penn State, if it hadn't been for that. The way the papers reported it and all, and the way it got even worse when it was picked up on TV. But the story of it followed me, and somehow nobody ever remembered that I went on to score again, legitimately winning that game. They just remembered me as a clown, a joke. I truly hate him for doing it."

By the time the knock on the door came there in Presidio, I was half asleep. It was Alvarez's runner, the teenage kid in his hipster's getup. A baggy silver shirt, baggy gray trousers with pleats, fringed loafers. I needed some time to calm down after I heard from him that he didn't have the money, that Alvarez himself was up from Chihuahua and in Ojinaga, across the international bridge. He wanted to see me.

"See me about what?"

"Just see you, man," the kid said.

"Yeah, and I want to see some money. Money for the work I did, paid here, as agreed to."

"You'll get your money, man." Did this kid's acquired English require him to nail "man" on everything? "I'll drive you, man."

"No, I'll drive myself. Where is he, the Estrella?"

"I have a car, a fucking big Monte Carlo." Where was the "man?"

"And I have a pickup, with Texas plates, which makes me feel a lot safer. You know, *man?*"

"I like the Monte Carlo, man. Eet's turbo-charged."

I crossed the new international bridge. The sleepy Mexican guards with their droopy mustaches and fascist-brown uniforms must have recognized Charlie's truck. They waved me through. No problem. Ojinaga certainly isn't an Acuna, where I had spent time so often, and then that weekend with Lizanne. Ojinaga is too far out in the desert, and the old rail line that used to go directly from the town down to Chihuahua has been abandoned, and with it has gone the town's lifeline. Ojinaga is gritty and rough, and in the inky blue of that night I could almost taste its dead-end something in the rotting stink of diesel fumes and bad corn-oil cooking. The junker cars never seem to have mufflers in Ojinaga. The dark men in the usual straw cowboy hats stumble staggeringly out of the bars in Ojinaga. I saw the kid's black Monte Carlo in front of what had formerly been the Estrella. It was now painted glossy orange and glossy yellow on its crumbling stucco outside, and it had been renamed Bikini Bar.

The Bikini Bar still offered a long bar proper, running parallel to the front and stretching maybe a block. The redecorating squad had used more of that glossy orange and yellow inside the dive, which could have been frequented by Pancho Villa when he lived here. Two new posters, framed, on the wall: one of Cheryl Tiegs in a white bikini, maybe a blown-up shot from one of those sports magazine swimsuit issues; the other of the short girl, buxom and spilling long blonde hair, who used to play the wild younger sister on "Dallas" and whose name I probably never knew to begin with, in a black bikini. A couple of old men drank at one end of the bar. At the other end, sitting at a table, were middle-aged Alvarez, and two more teenage lieutenants who certainly had learned everything they knew about haberdashery from overdosing on a lot of MTV along the line—*and* the silver-haired guy I had run into that time a month before in Eagle Pass. That didn't surprise me. I had to admit I knew all along that I would eventually see him. Because on one level, that charade he waltzed through that afternoon in Eagle Pass indeed had the texture of a dream, and as all my life turned less and less tangible lately—marbleized memory as interrupted occasionally by the physical solidity of the booze—it had to get dreamier still.

"Ah, Rafferty," Alvarez said to me. Balding and overweight, he wore a light-blue guayabera and could have been simply another meek Mexican shopkeeper.

I looked around. I didn't want to look yet at the tall guy and his squinting blue eyes.

"What's this Bikini Bar stuff?" I said.

"You like that, man," the kid who had relayed the message said. "Just looking at those pictures, that leetel broad, and I feel strong, man." He had his fist clenched; he jabbed it upward for a power signal. I nodded, without laughing.

"You like the little one, huh," I said.

"Sit down, sit down, Rafferty," Alvarez said.

"Yeah," I said, and sat.

"You know Mr. McCord?" Alvarez asked.

"I'm not sure that I do."

"And I'm sure that you do," the guy said. "And I'm sure that you know that I'm DEA, a bird-dogger. And I know that you've been spreading that aerial photography bullshit like it was Betty Crock-of-It's cake frosting for too long a time now, pal, and the only thing that it took a while for me to figure out was who you were taxiing for. That gets our life stories out of the way."

It was so direct, such a turnabout, that if I had been dreaming that earlier scene with him, I could in fact have been dreaming this as well. He leaned back. He smiled that sleepy smile, back to the treatment I had gotten in Eagle Pass.

"What is this?" I asked Alvarez.

"Relax, Rafferty. What this is, is business. Hey"—he poked one of the other teenage hipsters, the sallow specimen sitting right next to him—"play some shit."

The waiter brought more Carta Blancas, the jukebox blared some song about a man wanting his heart to fly like a dove to his faraway love, like a paloma. The junk cars and trucks were loud outside, back-firing in rifle shots, and sweat beaded on the brown bottles with their red-and-white labels. The silver-haired guy said no more. Alvarez explained.

It was as simple as this. A particularly troublesome DEA man had gone too far. He had been operating out of Mexico, Chihuahua specifically—Alvarez described it in his decent English—and there had been no reasoning with him. He had been shot by Mexican *federales* sympathetic to the "business," but now the problem was transporting the body back across the border, to the States. The DEA didn't like to let its men just disappear, and they would put pressure on everybody in Chihuahua until they extracted some answers. This could degenerate to an international incident, and with the two DEA men being gunned down in Guadalajara a couple of years before, nobody wanted another international incident, to put the heat on everybody. If found in the States, the body would be evidence of just another sad killing in the line of duty here. Open and easily shut.

"You've got a problem," I told him.

"*Nosotros* got a problem," Alvarez said, using the pronoun to stress his point. The silver-haired guy said nothing. He could have been watching it on television, stupid entertainment.

"*Nosotros* got a problem," the teenager with the Monte Carlo laughed. "That's funny, man."

"Shut up," Alvarez told him. "Rafferty, my friend, let me tell you this again."

This time he tightened his case: this is what McCord needed done, and we should listen to his "wishes"—the word seemed formal, not faring well in translation from the Spanish—seeing that he, McCord, was Alvarez's most important new "associate" in the business—that "associate" seemed formal too. Next, without my saying anything, he anticipated my complaints, that I shouldn't tell him that I was just a taxi for a few marijuana bales, not bigtime shipments, or worse, bodies, and something like this wasn't my problem.

"It's not my problem," I said.

"You know about it now, Rafferty, and it is your problem. Mr. McCord, he knows about you, and he is DEA. He is an American agent, you are an American. Listen, it is as simple as a run with marijuana, but the money is not simple." He named the figure; I didn't hesitate.

"No problem," I told him. I flashed to Lajitas for some reason, how a man not much older than me was turning a desert into a city, and what did I have to show for anything?

"No problem," I said again.

"*Nosotros* got no problem now, man," the kid said, liking that too. His teeth shone like shells.

The sweat was running in genuine rivulets down Alvarez's brownish pate. It was almost as if his fingernail had worn the white enamel off the cheap Carta Blanca table that you find in every one of these cantinas, as if his clawing nervousness had gouged right through to the black underneath, though the nick must have been there for years. Wet soaked under the arms of the light-blue guayabera. I realized now how scared he was himself about this.

"No problem at all," I told him.

The silver-haired McCord, Alvarez's associate, smiled, nodded some more.

5. THE FOREVER COMMONLY CALLED NEW MEXICO.

Let me tell you how beautiful this is.

There is a central valley that runs right up the middle of New Mexico. I am deep in it now, well out of Texas, following the Rio Grande north, truly toward its source. The 182 seems to like the tailwind, and flying like this is easy and special, the needles on the black-faced dials and gauges as steady as stone and nothing much to do except adjust the big elevator wheel now and then for trim. The river below winds silvery; flat orange sands, patterned with huge patches of aqua prickly pear, spread out on either side, for the plain of it. The mountains rise beyond on both sides, hazily blue now that I am this far north, whiter-than-white snow-capped peaks starting to show. The sunlight is a soft presence snagging on the scratches in my Plexiglas windshield, a little warm on my face. I am too far beyond any strip to pick up anything on the radio, which dished out only scratchy static the last time I tried a frequency I got from my sectional chart. I like the hum of the engine, entirely smooth, and the way that olive clouds are starting to pile up, gilded, straight ahead. Beautiful clouds. The corpse is sealed tight in a few layers of black trash bags bound with white nylon line. A lump beside me. But now I have gotten used to having it—no, *him*, here.

I made the pick-up on one of the strips near Chihuahua where I had made my marijuana pick-ups in the past. But I wasn't so stupid as to land again on the strip on the Texas side, as agreed to at the meeting with Alvarez and the DEA man. They just wanted the evidence back in the States, and after that was handled I was obviously expendable. Plus, I was the witness that nobody would want around. If nothing else I knew that I had to avoid any small place, those border airports, where they could close in on me. El Paso was the nearest city of any size, after more desert west of Presidio. (At Presidio Charlie appeared to turn strange around me too when I flew out to begin my errand this morning. Was he working with them? Did he know, and does everybody know what there is to know about everything except for me?) But at El Paso, with its futuristic new international terminal so neat out in that stretch of suburban malls and fast-food places, none of it was quite making sense. I filled both tanks with mo-gas and simply headed up into this big valley, where I am now.

And where I know what I am going to do. Or would that be the thing to do? Because I could still loop and retreat, even though these clouds look like real trouble now. They are closing in from three sides, and there is some chop. And if there is one place you don't want to be in an overhead job like this 182, despite all the power of those six tiger-purring cylinders, it is where one of these mountain storms can swallow you whole.

Money isn't the answer to anything after all. Yet here is what I am wondering. What if you go into a cloud build-up like this, a glare of blowing ice and snow that is already rainbowing a hundred times over up ahead, and what if you and this dead man, all the dead from this world, find that by venturing to that place you have never gone before, all the sadness, all the loneliness, doesn't mean a thing any more. And in that land of quiet and sunny stillness is maybe Lizanne's kid, Rosie, sitting on the edge of a puffy cloud, both her legs fine at last, her mind a cheery whole. And on another cloud you see your brother Al waving, so maybe he wasn't killed in the cave-in in the reopened mine that had supposedly been checked out by company inspectors only two weeks before the crushing collapse, and he calls over to you echoingly that he understood all along that a father once ran onto a football field on a dim day in Pittsburgh because of love and love alone, tells you if you can just find love in your own heart, you—

Damn, is this chop ever bad now. I must have dropped three hundred feet in the last hit, and the windscreen is icing in layers now. I give it more gargling throttle, straight ahead, too rich at first so I nearly stall out, then I have it right, the semblance of a hum once more. I come out of the next drop better. Then straight in again.

"When I get to Albuquerque," I whisper to him beside me, "nobody will believe we got through this, nobody will believe the wonderful things we have seen." And already I realize that I really do want to make it through this, for once in who knows how long I really do want to live. "This is starting to get interesting," I tell him, my hands tight on the twin grips of the black plastic yoke, bracing myself for that next slam of it all.

The dead and me.

LA FABULOSA: A TEXAS OPERETTA

— ★ —

Sandra Cisneros

SHE LIKES TO SAY SHE'S "SPANISH," BUT SHE'S FROM LAREDO like the rest of us—or "Lardo," as we call it. Her name is Berriozábal. Carmen. Worked as a secretary for a San Antonio law firm.

Big *chichis*. I mean big. Men couldn't take their eyes off them. She couldn't help it, really. Anytime they talked to her they never looked her in the eye. It was kind of sad.

She kept this corporal at Fort Sam Houston. Young. A looker. José Arrambide. He had a high school honey back home who sold nachos at the mall, still waiting for him to come back to Harlingen, marry her, and buy that three-piece bedroom set on layaway. Dream on, right?

Well, this José wasn't Carmen's LUH-uv of her life. Just her San Antonio "thang," so to speak. But you know how men are. Unless you're washing their feet and drying them with your hair, they just can't take it. I mean it. And Carmen was a take-it-or-leave-it type of woman. If you don't like it, there's the door. Like that. She was something.

Not smart. I mean, she didn't know enough to get her teeth cleaned every year, or to buy herself a duplex. But the corporal was hooked. Her genuine guaranteed love slave. I don't know why, but when you treat men bad, they love it.

Yeah, sure, he was her sometime sweetheart, but what's that to a woman who's twenty and got the world by the eggs. First chance, she took up with a famous Texas senator who was paving his way to the big house. Set her up in a fancy condo in north Austin. Camilo Escamilla. You maybe might've heard of him.

When José found out, it was a big *escándalo*, as they say. Tried to kill her. Tried to kill himself. But this Camilo kept it out of the papers. He was that important. And besides, he had a wife and kids who posed with him every year for the calendar he gave away at Christmas. He wasn't about to throw his career out the window for no *fulanita*.

According to who you talk to, you hear different. José's friends say he left his initials across those famous *chichis* with a knife, but that sure sounds like talk, don't it?

I heard he went AWOL. Became a bullfighter in Matamoros, just so he could die like a man. Somebody else said *she's* the one who wants to die.

Don't you believe it. She ran off with King Kong Cárdenas, a professional wrestler from Crystal City and a sweetie. I know her cousin Lerma, and we saw her just last week at the Floore Country Store in Helotes. Hell, she bought us a beer, two-stepped and twirled away to "Hey Baby Qué Pasó."

TOWN AND CITY

from THE GAY PLACE

✦

Billy Lee Brammer

THE COUNTRY IS MOST BARBAROUSLY LARGE AND FINAL. IT is too much country—boondock country—alternately drab and dazzling, spectral and remote. It is so wrongfully muddled and various that it is difficult to conceive of it as all of a piece. Though it begins simply enough, as a part of the other.

It begins, very like the other, in an ancient backwash of old dead seas and lambent estuaries, around which rise cypress and cedar and pine thickets hung with spiked vines and the cheerless festoons of Spanish moss. Farther on, the earth firms: stagnant pools are stirred by the rumble of living river, and the mild ferment of bottom land dissolves as the country begins to reveal itself in the vast hallucination of salt dome and cotton row, tree farm and rice field and irrigated pasture and the flawed dream of the cities. And away and beyond, even farther, the land continues to rise, as on a counterbalance with the water tables, and then the first faint range of the West comes into view: a great serpentine escarpment, changing colors with the hours, with the seasons, hummocky and soft-shaped at one end, rude and wind-blasted at the other, blue and green, green and gray and dune-colored, a staggered faultline extending hundreds of miles north and south.

This range is not so high as it is sudden and aberrant, a disorder in the even westerly roll of the land. One could not call it mountain, but it is a considerable hill, or set of hills, and here again the country is transformed. The land rises steeply beyond the first escarpment and everything is changed: texture, configuration, blistered facade, all of it warped and ruptured and bruise-colored. The few rivers run deep, like old wounds, boiling round the fractures and revealing folds of slate and shell and glittering blue limestone, spilling back and across and out of the hills toward the lower country.

The city lies against and below two short spiny ribs of hill. One of the little rivers runs round and about, and from the hills it is possible to view the city overall and draw therefrom an impression of sweet curving streets and graceful sweeping lawns and the unequivocally happy sound of children always at play. Closer on, the feeling is only partly confirmed, though it should seem enough to have even a part. It is a pleasant city, clean and quiet, with wide rambling walks and elaborate public gardens and elegant old homes faintly ruined in the shadow of arching poplars. Occasionally through the trees, and always from a point of higher ground, one can see the college tower and the capitol building. On brilliant mornings the white sandstone of the tower and the capitol's granite dome are joined for an instant, all pink and cream, catching the first light.

On a midsummer morning not very long ago the sun advanced on the city and lit the topmost spines of hill, painting the olive drab slopes in crazy new colors, like the drawing of a spangled veil. Then the light came closer, touching the tall buildings and the fresh-washed streets. The nearly full-blown heat came with it, quick and palpitant. It was close to being desert heat: sudden, emphatic, dissolving chill and out-distancing rain . . .

It was neither first light nor early heat that caused the two politicians to come struggling up from sleep at that hour, but an old truck carrying migratory cotton pickers.

The younger of the two politicians was named Roy Sherwood, and he lay twisted sideways in the front seat of an automobile that was parked out front of an all-night supermarket. Arthur Fenstemaker, the other one, the older one, floundered in his bedcovers a few blocks distant in the governor's mansion.

The old truck banged along the streets, past dazzling store fronts and the Juicy Pig Stand and the marble facades of small banks in which deposits were insured to ten thousand dollars. The dozen children in the back of the truck had been first to come awake. They pulled aside the canvas flaps and peered out at the city, talking excitedly, whooping and hee-hawing as the old truck rolled north, straining, toward the capitol grounds and the governor's mansion, where Arthur Fenstemaker slept, and the supermarket where Roy Sherwood's car was parked.

The truck came to a sudden stop and began, with a terrible moaning of gears and transmission, to back into a parking space next to Roy Sherwood's car.

Roy heard the commotion and blinked his sore eyes in the early light. He struggled to untangle his long legs from between the steering wheel and seat cushion, and he was able, finally, to sit up and examine the truck. He unrolled a window and leaned his head out, taking deep breaths, blinking his eyes. The children in the truck watched him gravely for a moment and then began to giggle. Their laughter subsided abruptly when Roy called out to them: "*Buena día* . . ."

There was silence and then a small voice answered back: ". . . *día* . . ."

Roy smiled and opened the car door. He stood on the cool pavement for a moment, weaving slightly, trying to hold his balance. He was dizzy with fatigue and an hour's poor sleep and possibly a hangover. "One hell of an awful *día*," he muttered under his breath. The children were laughing again, and fairly soon he began to feel better. The driver of the truck climbed down and came round to Roy's side to stare at him. The fellow had a murderous look—a bandit's look. He was wearing a wrinkled double-breasted suit coat over what appeared to be a polo shirt and uncommonly dirty and outsized denim slacks. He stared at Roy with his bandit's eyes until Roy lifted his hand in a vague salute. Then the Mexican smiled, showing hilarious buck teeth, lifted his arm in the same indecisive gesture and almost immediately turned and walked toward the supermarket, flapping his feet in gray tennis shoes.

The children attempted to engage Roy in conversation. Roy came closer to the back of the truck, trying to understand some of it, cocking his head and listening carefully and interrupting now and then: "*Qué?* . . . *Cómo?* . . . *Despacio*, for chrissake, *despacio* . . ." The children giggled hysterically; two or three adults in the front cab stared at him, looking uneasy, and finally Roy gave it up and waved good-bye and wandered into the supermarket.

The inside of the store was aglow with yellow light. Everything was gorgeous and brightly packaged. Only the people—the cashier and the Mexican gathering breakfast staples and Roy himself—seemed out of phase with the predominating illusion. Roy looked all around, examining the market with as much wonder and concentration as might have been demonstrated in viewing Indian cave mosaics or a thousand-year-old cathedral. He stared all around and then he uncapped a bottle of milk and tore open a bag of cinnamon buns. He wandered over the market eating and drinking, pausing occasionally to stare enraptured at a prime cut of beef or a phonograph album or a frozen pizza or a stack of small redwood picnic tables. There seemed no limit to what the market might conceivably have in stock. Roy decided the pussy willow cuttings were his favorite; they were a little fantastic: out of season, out of habitat . . . He wondered if the pussy willow had been shipped fresh-frozen from the East, like oysters or cheese blintzes. He moved on; he had something else in mind.

He located this other without difficulty—a tall pasteboard box containing twenty-four ice cream cones, maple flavored. The box of cones was part of it; the plastic scoop stapled to the outside of the box solved the next most immediate problem. He carried the cones and the scoop to the cashier and then went back to pick up two half-gallon cartons of ice cream.

Outside again, at the back end of the truck, the children and two or three of the older Mexicans crowded round to watch. Roy left off serving after a while, letting one of the older girls take his place. There were a few accented whoops of *Ize-Cream . . . Aze Creeem*, but the children were unusually quiet for the most part, sweetly, deliriously happy waiting in line to be served. Presently, he returned to his car and sat in the driver's seat to watch. One hell of a crazy *día*, he reminded himself. Not to mention the *día* before and the night or the goddam *noche* in between.

He turned now and looked in the back seat. It was all there . . . All of it . . . All his art objects purchased during his twelve hours travel on the day before: the button-on shoes, the iron stewpot, the corset model, the portrait of President Coolidge, the Orange Crush dispenser with its rusted spigot, part of an old upright piano. Everything except . . . But he remembered now. The television set, one of the earliest models, big as a draft animal, with a seven-inch picture tube . . . He'd left it in knee-high Johnsongrass fifty miles outside town. He grunted to himself, thinking of the television set: it was a terrible loss; he'd been blinded by the wine on the day before and thoughtlessly left the television behind. He grunted again and reexamined his treasure in the back seat.

The Mexican children were finished with their ice cream, and he could hear their singsong voices rising in volume. The elder, the old bandit in gray tennis shoes, came out of the supermarket carrying his grocery sack. He moved past Roy, nodding, showing his wonderful teeth.

"You need a stewpot?" Roy said suddenly.

The Mexican was jerked back as if suspended by a coil spring. His face twitched, but he managed to smile and mumble an incomprehensible something in Spanish.

"Stew pot," Roy repeated. "Fine piece of workmanship . . . You need one? For free . . . *por nada* . . . *Tiene usted una stew pot-to?*"

The old Mexican gasped in alarm, altogether mystified. Roy climbed out of the car and opened the back door, pointing to the soot-covered vessel. It was very much like the ones in which neighborhood washerwomen had boiled clothes during his childhood. He loved the stewpot. But now he knew he must *make the gesture*. It was part of being a public figure. He addressed the Mexican: "Here . . . You want it? Desire you the stew pot?"

Roy struggled with the pot; it was big as a washtub. The old man accepted it on faith, smiling as if vastly pleased. He bowed politely and turned toward the truck, carrying the stewpot with great dignity. The children in back greeted him with strident questions. Roy sat in the front seat of the car and watched, wondering if he ought to make a speech. They'd never understand a word, but he could make pleasant sounds. It was no matter. His Mexicans back home never understood anything, either. You just paid their poll taxes and showed them where to mark ballots when election time came round. He'd made a speech the night before. One of his best. Parked alongside a narrow river, he and the girl had lain on a picnic blanket and finished the last of the wine and the chicken. Then he had climbed a huge magnolia tree and plucked a great white bloom from the top, before descending to one of the lower limbs to make the presentation speech. He'd never been in better form. Though there had been some difficulty about addressing the girl. Using her name seemed to take all the fire out of the occasion. "Ladies . . ." he had said in the beginning, but it wasn't quite right. Nor "Fellow ladies . . ." He'd made a number of attempts: "Dear Lady" and "Most High and Mighty Ouida, Bride of My Youth, My Rock, My Fortress, My Deliverance, Horn of My Salvation and My High Tower . . ." But that had been too excessive for what, basically, was meant to be a ceremony of some dignity and restraint. He'd finally called her "My Dear Miss Lady Love . . ."

He thought he might step outside the car and possibly stand on the Orange Crush dispenser, addressing the Mexican children briefly, but after a moment the truck started up with a great thrashing sound and began backing out of the driveway. Roy sat for a moment, rubbing his eyes, and then he got his own car started and proceeded slowly down the main street of the city behind the truck carrying the cotton pickers. After a block or so, he grew impatient with the business of waving at the children, and nodding, and blinking his lights, and waving again; and finally he raced the car's engine and passed them by. A noisy, high-pitched cry came from the children; their flapping arms caught his vision briefly through the side windows. He grinned oafishly, studying his face in the mirror. "I have a way with crowds," he said aloud to himself. "I have gifts of rare personal magnetism . . ." He listened to the dying cheers from in back, and he thought he detected a clanging in the midst of it, a series of bell tones, deep and dull and flattish, metal on metal. My old iron stewpot, he thought . . .

ARTHUR FENSTEMAKER HEARD THE CHEERS AND THE CHILDREN'S laughter and the groan of the truck's motor blended with the blows struck on the stewpot. He lay in his bed on the second floor of the governor's mansion and listened thoughtfully. He was reminded for a moment of an old International he'd driven in the oilfields years before. The Mexicans were blocks away now, and he opened his eyes, still wondering over the sound from the street below. He reached for cigarettes and matches. After a moment he lay back in the bed, gasping for breath. He left the cigarette burning in a tray and pulled himself closer to Sweet Mama Fenstemaker. His right arm was pressed under his own huge weight, but he did not want to turn away just yet. Sweet Mama smelled goddam good; she nearly always perfumed herself at bedtime.

The governor lay like that for several minutes, listening for sounds in the house or from the street, pressing his big nose against his wife's skin, until the kitchen help began to arrive downstairs. Then he rolled off the bed and went to the bathroom. He brushed his teeth and smoked another cigarette; he swallowed pills and massaged his scalp and began to stalk about the second floor of the mansion. He looked in on his brother: Hoot Gibson Fenstemaker lay sleeping quietly, knotted in bedclothes. The governor turned back to his dressing room and stared at himself in a full-length mirror, sucking in his stomach, shifting from side to side. He slipped on gartered hose and shoes and a robe, and again stood listening, leaning over a stairwell and cocking his head. Soon he could hear the limousine being eased into position on the concrete drive. Fenstemaker strode down to the end of the hall and opened a casement window. A highway patrolman circled the car, examining tires, polishing chrome. The governor put his head through the window and yelled: "Hidy!"

The patrolman looked up, squinting against the sun, trying to smile.

"Hah'r yew, Mist' Fenstemaker," he said.

"Nice mornin'," the governor said, looking around.

"Hassah!" the patrolman said.

The patrolman stood on the concrete apron, gazing up at the governor. He kicked a tire with the heel of his shoe; he patted a fender of the car. He stared at the governor, and finally added, ". . . Sure nice one . . ."

Fenstemaker turned his head, looking over the city from the second-story window. The mansion was constructed along Georgian lines and was situated on a small rise that placed it nearly level with the capitol dome and some of the office buildings downtown. Mist blurred the hilltops to the west, and occasionally, a mile or more away, lake water flashed in the sun. The smell of flowers, blooming in profusion in the backyard garden, was fused with the harsh bouquet of compost heaps and kitchen coffee. Fenstemaker pinched his big nose and took deep breaths. The patrolman continued to gawk at him.

"I'm not goin' anywhere right off," Fenstemaker said.

He pulled his head back inside and rang for his coffee. He sat at a desk in his study and shuffled through papers. The butler arrived with a small coffeepot, dry toast, juice, and a half dozen newspapers.

"You had your breakfast?" Fenstemaker said. "You had your coffee?"

"Yessir," the butler said.

Fenstemaker sipped his coffee and shuffled papers.

"I hope it was better than this," he said. "Siddown and have some more."

The butler poured himself a cup and stood blowing on it, waiting.

"Siddown for Christ's sake," Fenstemaker said.

"Yes sir."

"Goddam."

"Sir?"

"I'm just goddammin'."

"Yes sir."

"Let's get a new brand of coffee," Fenstemaker said. He made a face.

"I'll tell the cook."

"Nothin' tastes like it used to," Fenstemaker said. "Not even vegetables."

"Sweet potatoes especially," the butler said.

"Not even goddam sweet potatoes," Fenstemaker said.

The two of them sipped coffee. The governor turned through the newspapers, talking but not looking up. "You think it's gettin' better?"

"What's that?"

"Bein' a colored man. You think it's any better?"

The butler looked at him desperately. "I got a good job," he said.

The governor did not seem to pay attention. He went on talking and turning pages. "Maybe little better, I guess . . . Discussions goin' on . . . Least *that's* not like it used to be. Hell! I remember old Pitchfork Ben Tillman—the things he said . . ." Fenstemaker broke off momentarily, peering at the newsprint, then went on: "Of course bein' better still don't make it very good. I was thinkin' yesterday, signin' my mail, how I'd feel if I wrote a public official about, you know, my rights? I was lookin' over what I'd been sayin'. 'Well now this sure is a problem, involvin' grave emotional questions, and we can't tolerate havin' second-class citizens in this free country and I'm sure gonna do what I can . . . Try to make reasonable progress toward a solution . . . Sure keep your views in mind . . .' Why *God damn!* Some cornpone Buddha say that to *me*, I'd set a bomb off under him."

The butler grinned. "I think most colored people vote for you," he said. "Even when you don't say things exact . . ." He began gathering cups and saucers.

"I'm a damned good politician," Fenstemaker said. "I know how good I am and I ain't doin' much, so what about the others not so good? Goddam and hell!"

"You want another pot?" the butler said.

"Yes," the governor said. "Switch to that ersatz stuff—I think it's probably better than this . . . And some fruit. They got any watermelon down there?"

"I'll see," the butler said. "They don't, we get you some."

The governor's brother, Hoot Gibson Fenstemaker, appeared at the door. He rubbed his eyes and smiled, looking deranged. "You get me some coffee, Jimmy?" he said. The butler nodded, carrying the tray. Hoot Gibson stepped inside.

"Mornin' Arthur."

"You enjoy that party last night?" the governor said.

"Sure did. I like parties here."

"I think you danced with every lady."

"I think I did," Hoot Gibson said, "I liked that orchestra, too. It was like Wayne King."

"I remember at college you had some Wayne King records," the governor said, looking up from the papers. "And Henry Busse. What in hell ever happened to Henry Busse?"

"He dead?" Hoot Gibson said. He thought a moment. "*Hot Lips!* I booked old Henry Busse once for the gymnasium. A dance. Made two hundred dollars promoting old Henry Busse . . ." Hoot Gibson's eyes went cloudy, thinking about Henry Busse. He sipped from his brother's coffee cup.

Fenstemaker looked up patiently. "Don't make that noise," he said. Hoot Gibson gripped the cup with both hands and stared at the coffee. The governor read the papers. Hoot Gibson picked up one of the sheets and glanced over the headlines. "I think I got a hangover," he said.

The governor cleared his throat but did not comment.

"I might go back to bed a while," Hoot Gibson said.

"Take some aspirin and sleep another hour," the governor said.

Hoot Gibson stood and stretched and scratched himself. He loosened the drawstring on his pajamas and retied it. "I think I'll do that," he said ". . . You got anything for me today?"

The governor looked up and said: "You remember that fellow talkin' to me and Jay last night? Up here—out on the screen porch?"

"That new lobbyist?"

"That's the one."

"I know him. He's workin' the capitol nearly every day now."

"Well suppose you keep an eye on him," the governor said. "Follow him around. Or get someone to do it for you. Find out where he goes, who he's seein'. Do that today and tonight. Maybe tomorrow. Don't for God's sake let him know he's bein' watched. Give me a report—and don't come around *tellin'* me about it. Write it up."

Hoot Gibson looked vastly pleased. He vanished down the hall, humming to himself.

The governor signed some papers. He looked at the clock—it was nearly seven; nearly nine in the East. He reached for the phone and got the long distance operator, making notes of persons he could call in the Eastern time zone. He talked with an economist in New York. They discussed investments; Fenstemaker asked questions about the stock market; he complained that none of the big investors seemed interested in municipal bonds. "I got some mayors in trouble," he said. "They need help. You got any ideas?" He listened to the economist's ideas. They complained to each other about the goddam Republican high interest rates.

Fenstemaker rang off and placed more calls; he talked with his two senators, a union official in Philadelphia, a college professor in Boston. The professor was a nephew whom he'd put through college a half-dozen years before. "Listen," the governor said, "those are wonderful speeches you been sendin' down—especially if I was runnin' in Oyster Bay or Newport. But I'm not, happily. Try to remember I'm way the hell down here in coonass country . . . You forget your beginnin's? You need a little trip home? Might do you good . . . I need some ideas . . . You got good ideas . . . But I want 'em in speeches that sound like Arthur Fenstemaker and not some New goddam England squire . . ."

He completed the calls and turned back to the papers on his desk. An assistant had left him a note attached to a handwritten letter: *"This may interest you, though I advise against reading it when you're trying to shake off a low mood. It is very sad."*

He read the letter attached:

Sirs:

We the people of the 9th grade Civics class at Hopkinsville feel that you the people of the Government should try to conquer the world here before you try to conquer outer space. We feel that there may be some kind of gas on the moon that is under the surface and if a rocket hit it, it may open the surface of the moon and these gases may escape and get into our own environment and kill us. So we feel that you should leave well-enough alone. We feel that if the Good Lord had wanted us to conquer outer space he would have put here on earth instruments instead of people. We would like to know what you think about this issue.

Sincerely,
The 9th Grade Class

Fenstemaker rubbed the back of his neck and pulled on his nose and sat staring at the names of the ninth grade class at Hopkinsville. He put the letter down and reached for the phone.

"Jay . . ."

Jay McGown's voice came to him feebly; then it got stronger. There was music being played on the radio in Jay's room. The music ended and an announcer talked about a cure for piles.

"Sir?" Jay was saying. ". . . Sir?"

"What in hell's goin' on there?"

"Sir?"

"You think we got a chance on that school bill?"

"School bill? Sure we got a chance," Jay said.

"I got your note and that letter," the governor said.

"Ah."

"Let's take a run with that bill this week," Fenstemaker said.

"You think this week's really the best time?" Jay said. "Old Hoffman's still in the hospital. We'd need him. He wrote the damn thing. At least his name's on it."

"Who's that? Who wrote it, then?"

"A lobbyist for the schoolteachers. A lawyer from the education agency."

"Who else?"

"Me."

"Well let's take a run with it," Fenstemaker said.

"Who'll we get to floor-manage?"

"Who's on the committee?" the governor said.

"You know that committee better than I do," Jay said.

"Name some," Fenstemaker said. "I forget."

"Who you want me to name?"

"Name some."

Jay named some of the members.

"They don't sound so good to me," the governor said.

"They aren't," Jay said. "We'd probably end up with half a bill. Old

Hoffman's not much, but he won't lose us any votes. He knows how to manage a bill."

"How 'bout Roy Sherwood?" Fenstemaker said.

"Roy's a good friend of mine," Jay said.

"So?"

"But he's not exactly one of our boys."

"Maybe he just never got invited in," the governor said.

"He's pretty damned independent," Jay said. "And lazy. That's a bad combination."

Chimes from the college signaled the half hour. The highway patrolman polished the limousine on the side drive. The butler came into the room with an enormous slice of watermelon. Fenstemaker broke off a piece with his hand and began to eat. There was a silence on the phone while the governor ate watermelon. Then he said: "He help write that bill? He do anything at all?"

There was another silence before Jay began to answer: "That's right. He helped a lot. Fact is, he was the only one on that lousy committee who gave a damn. With Hoffman gone."

"Well old Hoff got it reported out for us before he went to the hospital," Fenstemaker said.

"How'd you know about Roy?"

"It just sort of came to me in the night," the governor said.

"Well I thought you might disapprove. My getting him to help us. He's a friend of mine, like I said, and we needed some help from someone on the committee. Desperately."

"All right," the governor said. "That's just fine. I'm delighted. You think he could carry it?"

"I don't know. I really don't. He's never worked a bill in three terms here. I'm not even sure he'd accept the job."

"Well I'll just ask him and see."

"You think he could hold the votes we've got? He might scare some off."

"See about that, too," the governor said. He paused, and then added: "He ain't worn himself out on Earle Fielding's wife, has he?"

There was a pause before Jay answered: "That piece of information just come to you in the night, too?"

"Everything does," the governor said, his voice warm with pleasure. "Borne on the wind. Like a cherub. It do fly . . . Listen . . . We'll just see how old Roy reacts. Okay? Take a little run. Pull out all the stops and try to get this thing through. Maybe tomorrow. We can't afford to wait much longer. They'll be building up opposition soon's it appears Hoffman's well. We put off any time, we lose votes and we lose hard cash in that bill . . . You want some cash for Hopkinsville, don't you? We'll just have to get that goddam thing through in a hurry. Can't afford to have any great debates . . ."

Jay was silent on the other end of the line while Fenstemaker talked. Then the governor rang off without formality. He dialed another number on the phone and waited during the six or seven rings. He pressed the disconnect and dialed again. After another interval, Roy Sherwood answered.

"What're you doin'?" Fenstemaker boomed.

"Sleeping," Roy Sherwood said. "Real good, too."

"Hell of a note," Fenstemaker said. "World's cavin' in all round us; rocket ships blastin' off to the moon; poisonous gas in our environment . . . Sinful goddam nation . . . laden with iniquity, offspring of evildoers. My princes are rebels and companions of thieves . . ."

"What?"

". . . A horror and a hissing . . ."

"Who the hell is this?"

"Isaiah," Fenstemaker said. "The Prophet Isaiah."

"I'm going to hang up in just about three seconds," Roy said, "but first I'd really like to know who the hell this is?"

"Arthur goddam Fenstemaker. Hah yew?"

"I think it really is," Roy said after a moment. "Governor? That you?"

"Come over the mansion and see," Fenstemaker said. "You like watermelon? I got some damn good watermelon. You come over here and we'll break watermelon together."

Roy's response was plaintive but respectful: "It's awful early in the morning for breakfast."

"Nearly eight."

"I know," Roy said. "That gives me nearly three hours sleep."

"Well, you're a young man. I needed five."

Roy was silent.

"You come over and talk to me about this bill?" Fenstemaker said.

"What bill's that?"

"That school thing you did for Jay. Damn good job."

"Thanks. I appreciate it. But what do you want to talk about?"

"About when you're gonna get off your ass and pass it for me."

"*Pass* it. Hell, I'm just the ghost writer. Passin' it is your—"

"I mean take charge in that madhouse."

"Hah?"

"I mean floor-manage for me."

"You sure you got the right man, Governor? I never in my life—"

"I got you, all right," the governor said. "Roy Emerson Sherwood. Nonpracticin' lawyer. Family's got cattle, little cotton. Never struck no oil, though. Elected Sixty-third Legislature. Reelected without opposition to Sixty-fourth, Sixty-fifth. Never did a goddam thing here till you wrote that bill the other day . . ."

"You got the right man, I guess," Roy said.

"You help me with that bill on the floor?"

"When you plan to bring it up?"

"Tomorrow."

"*Tomorrow!* Godalmighty—"

"Day after, maybe. Come on over here."

"Governor, I couldn't learn the *number* that bill, condition I'm in right now. Let me sleep a little. Just a little. Let me think about it."

"*Sinful* goddam nation . . . Laden with iniquity . . . My princes are—"

"All right," Roy said wearily.

"How you like your goddam eggs?" the governor said.

from STRANGE PEACHES

——————— ✦ ———————

Edwin Shrake

I SAT DOWN ON THE COUCH AND STARTED PULLING OFF A BOOT, but it would not come off, and the effort made me dizzy. I stamped my foot back down into the boot and put on my hat and ran for the car with the Bolex. I had trouble starting the Morris Minor and feared I might miss the motorcade, but the engine finally caught and the radio came on. Because of the cleared weather that caused me to stop and roll up my sleeves, the bubble-top had been removed from the President's black Lincoln, the radio said. Plenty of Dallas cops had been at the airport, where the President had touched hands with admirers, and hundreds more were spotted along the route—a map of which had been printed in the newspapers—where three hundred thousand people were waiting to see the Kennedys ride past in the open car with Governor Connally and his wife, and Lyndon Johnson riding a few cars behind. I drove fast and parked the Morris Minor by the Texas & Pacific Railroad tracks on Pacific Street in a brown-brick warren of warehouses. As I stepped over railroad tracks and around boxcars, I saw a few people sitting on loading platforms eating sandwiches out of paper bags, but most of the workers had gone over a couple of blocks to Dealey Plaza to watch the President. The sidewalks at Elm and Houston beside the School Book Depository Building were crowded, and I didn't immediately see an opening in the crowd across Elm in Dealey Plaza, so I trotted on along Houston to Main Street, going past the Criminal Courts Building, looking for a view for the Bolex. At the corner where the cars were to turn north off Main onto Houston, I squeezed among people at the curb as I heard cheering and the motorcycles coming amid a roar that boomed toward me along Main like the roar of a football crowd. People flinched back from me, but it didn't matter. I leaned out and saw the motorcade approaching very close, first the motorcycles and then a pilot car of cops, then six more motorcycles and the white lead car with the Sheriff and the Police Chief and the Secret Service boss, and finally four or five lengths back came the black Lincoln. Through the viewfinder I saw Connally's wavy blue-silver hair. Mrs. Connally was in the other jump seat, hidden from me. Now I found John F. Kennedy. He was on the side of the car nearest the curb, his eyes crinkled and puffy underneath, an arm on the rim of the open car, shirt cuff showing, wearing a dotted necktie, looking at the people along the curb as they applauded and called out to him. Kennedy was smiling a very good smile with very white teeth, and his wife was smiling almost the same way but without as much heart in it. His hair looked thick and healthy, and his face was tanned, and his eyes were clear and seemed to be enjoying what they saw. I was struck by how much like a movie star he looked, what an air of ultimate celebrity there was about him, everything put together exactly right and a good heart showing from that smile and the eyes, with his wife sitting there beside him trying to smile in the same manner. She had the look of celebrity, too, but more distant from the people and from life, a movie star's smile that was like a fence between her and the crowd; where her smile said *keep away*

I'm doing all right, his said *we've got it going and I love it all*. They both looked as if they had been made up for the cameras, whites of the eyes sparkling, teeth polished, skin tinted copper, grander than the rest of us, but his face shone with intelligence and humor that broke through the celebrity mask without apology for the mask itself.

As the car pulled abreast, I didn't want to see him through the viewfinder, but the movie might require this vision. I lifted the camera and the President's gray eyes looked directly at me leaning out from the curb, took me all in with an instant's deep gaze, and looked squarely into my lens, and his lips moved a bit, the smile broadening, and he raised a finger and pointed at me, and I took my eye away from the viewfinder and looked straight into his eyes, and a communication flashed from him to me that said *there you are you freak what a time you must have among these people I like you for it don't give up*. At the same second he was sending me that message I was receiving it and thinking as well, with surprise and embarrassment that I would have such a thought, that if I'd wanted to hurt the man, I was so close I could crack his skull with a five-iron or couldn't conceivably miss with a pistol. But I could tell this perverted thought never reached him. He had trained himself to tune out small paranoias. I smiled at him as he looked at me, and his right eye squinted very slightly as if it occurred to him that he had seen me before but could not recall where. Then his eyes left me and held their place in the crowd that was moving past the car, and he said something to his wife, and she looked back, smiling with the flowers in her arms, but our eyes never met, and then the black limousine was going on down the road and I was looking at the back of the President's head.

I didn't wait to film Lyndon Johnson or any of the others. To me they were just politicians, not great men, just part of the crowd the same as me, and I still didn't care for all this big-ass politics, but I knew a great man when I saw one. Reflecting on the sensation of having connected in a mental relay with the President, and repeating to myself *there you are you freak*, I ran and caught up with the car as it turned onto Houston Street. I flipped on the long lens and got the Lincoln in my magnified sight again as the motorcade turned once more onto Elm at the red-brick Depository Building and started down toward the triple underpass and the railroad trestle.

POP

I knew it was a rifle shot. The sound is so common as to be quite distinctive. Later, many said they thought it was a firecracker, or the popping of a paper bag, or a backfire, but I knew at once that it was a rifle shot and I heard myself moan as I looked through the viewfinder and saw Kennedy raise his hands toward his throat and Connally starting to turn back toward him.

Pigeons flew up from the Depository Building. The car kept moving slowly. I was expecting the car to leap ahead and disappear through the underpass, but it moved so very slowly.

POP

The car had passed an oak tree, and now people were screaming and had begun running around in Dealey Plaza, and the pigeons were circling in the sky, and cops in helmets on motorcycles were looking back and forth, wondering where the shots were coming from. Through the viewfinder I saw Connally sliding down, and Kennedy leaning to the left toward his wife, and the black Lincoln almost seemed to be stopping, edging down from slow motion into stop-frame.

"Go on!" I cried. "Goddamn you, go on before they kill him!"

Someone shouted into my ear. I kept my finger on the button. I was waiting for another shot. The first two shots echoed through the Plaza, bounced off the county jail and the Depository, caroming around the Plaza, and people were running, falling, dodging, throwing themselves onto the ground as in war movies. On the grassy knoll I saw figures scattering, and Kennedy continued to lean in the creeping Lincoln.

POP

Pieces of skull sailed out of Kennedy's head. A red spray flew out, as if a stone had been thrown into a pot of tomato soup.

"No! They've got him now!" I yelled.

At last the car moved. As the President's wife began scrambling out the back of the car, out of this blood and madness, at last the car moved forward, carrying its passengers too late down into the underpass.

I knew he was dead.

For a moment I kept the camera on the tumult around the Plaza, on the stunned and frantic crowd, and then I took the camera away from my eye and began trotting toward the Depository Building for no special reason other than that my car was over in that direction.

"He's shot! He's shot!" a voice cried.

Beside me a woman was screaming.

A man with a transistor radio at his ear said, "Well, I'll be damned, they've shot them all."

By then the Plaza and the sidewalk in front of the Criminal Courts Building were blurred with people running and milling, and voices rose in wails and sobs, and police with riot guns and helmets scurried in the smell of motor oil and exhaust fumes and human breath, and many people were shouting. I didn't look at the rest of the motorcade now passing, at the press buses or the cars of the functionaries. I jogged toward my car, my mouth open, staring straight ahead.

He's shot!

I jogged on.

"Grab that long-haired guy! Get him!"

He's shot! Who did it? Where are they now? Jogging along, I looked at the underpass, at the banks of green grass sloping down to the street. I looked up at the windows of the Depository and at the big Hertz sign on top. A weeping woman in a flowered hat looked at me and said, "I didn't want him to die." Jogging, I felt possessed by anger and terror, and the old dread was coming back, the knowledge of the presence of madness and murder as the forces that ruled us. Our truth was lunacy and our destination oblivion, and I had it in the Bolex.

He should not have tuned me out.

"Officer, get that long-haired fellow!"

"What's your name, Buddy?"

"Wallace."

"What's your business here?"

"I came to see the President."

"What kind of work you do?"

"I'm a cowboy."

"Okay, move along."

"Who shot him?"

"How the fuck do I know? Get moving."

I went across the street and passed beside the School Book Depository Building. A man came out of the building carrying a Coke, and we looked at each other, and I went on down the narrow street among the warehouses and boxcars and railroad tracks, and the Morris Minor started at once. I put the Bolex on the seat. I didn't want to touch it any more right now. I turned on the radio. There was a report that the President, his wife, John Connally and Lyndon Johnson had all been shot. They were all in Parkland Hospital, the radio said. My God, all of them rolling on slabs down the hall where Ina Mae Leclaire had sat looking at the concrete with foolish attention. Listening to the radio, shivering, with a hot knot in my stomach, I drove out Cedar Springs to the Villa Lopez. Shot!

Hector, his wife, a busboy and two waiters were sitting with the two club waitresses of Buster's morning bed. They were at a big table, with bottles of beer around a radio.

"He won't die," Hector said.

But I knew he was dead already. I saw his brains fly out.

I got myself a beer and sat down. By now the radio had explained that the President and Connally had been shot, but not the others. We kept sitting there, with our elbows on the table, listening to the radio. No customers came in, and nobody made a move toward the kitchen. Each of us recounted where we had seen the President that noon and how he had looked, as a sort of liturgy to reestablish his presence, a juju against death. In their minds the broken head was healing, the bullets becoming part of a myth, but I knew better. I told them the President had sent me a message, and what he had said, and they smiled, not understanding. Then the radio said Kennedy was dead. One of the club waitresses began to moan, and tears spurted from Hector's eyes. Everybody in the room was crying. We knew we were helpless. We knew what was waiting for us.

And we had a new king.

"That man can't be dead," Hector said with tears pouring down his face.

A new king in the land of death. A new Caesar from the provinces.

"God, he was pretty," said one of the girls.

"He was a good son of a gun," Hector said.

The new king was out there now at Love Field on that airplane waiting for the coffin, to take it back to Rome.

Sunlight burst in as the front door banged open.

"Kennedy is dead!" a boy shouted.

The door shut again. Hector went into his small office behind the cash register and came back with a bottle of tequila. He put the bottle in the middle of the table and then brought more beer.

"We can't do nothing else about it," he said.

That was the truth. Things go away.

We had been drinking tequila a few minutes when Buster came in. His khaki shirt was smeared with sweat. He drank from the tequila bottle and picked up a beer.

"Were you at Dealey Plaza?" he said.

I nodded.

"You got it?"

I nodded.

"Christ in heaven, I wish we didn't have it," he said.

"I'll rip it out of the camera," I said.

"It happened," Buster said. "We've got it. It's real now."

He swigged down the beer and picked up another.

"At the Trade Mart they had yellow roses and organ music and everybody was eating steak," he said. "Annabel and Charlie Withers were at a table. They didn't have a banner. Then I went to Parkland and shot the reporters and the cops. Now I'm going to the police station. But first I'm going over to Turtle Creek and beat the hell out of the first right-wing bastard I see."

"I'll go with you," I said.

"You're crazy," said a waitress.

"It was those right-wing bastards that did this," Buster said.

"I'll fight the son of a bitch, you show me who!" shouted Hector.

"Let's go," I said, needing to do it.

"I'll get my pistol," said Hector.

"No guns," Buster said.

"They'll shoot us down right off," said Hector.

"We'll fight, though," Buster said.

Murder was loosed, and lunacy was unburied, and there was no other way.

In the Plymouth station wagon with the bottle of tequila, we started driving down Cedar Springs toward Turtle Creek. The day had a strange dreamy quality, cars moving silently, people frozen on sidewalks in yellow sunlight, the dusty beery smell in the station wagon, our senses loaded beyond capacity to reason as we had been trained to do.

"There's two son of a bitches," Hector said.

In front of a tall gray mansion at the back of a green lawn, two men in business suits were talking. As we looked at them, they started laughing. I wanted to kill them.

"I'll get these guys myself," said Hector.

"We'll stomp their grinning fascist butts," Buster said.

Then the radio announced that the Dallas police had information that the suspect in the Kennedy murder was a Communist who had recently returned from Russia. More details were forthcoming.

We sat in the car and looked at the two men in business suits.

"The government is saying this to stop people like us. They know it's all about to come apart," said Buster.

One of the men on the green lawn went to the porch of a big gray house, and the other walked across the driveway toward the house next door.

"So let's get them," I said.

A police car slowed as it cruised past. The cops looked at us. Seeing my cowboy hat, one of the cops smiled. The police car went on. Both men had gone inside their houses, where, in Dallas in that neighborhood, they presumed themselves safe.

"So much for frontier justice," Buster said. "We don't even hit back. What the hell has happened to us?"

Not being working reporters any longer, and unable as yet to face what might await at the police station, we drove to the End Zone. Someone had strung up an old parachute as an awning out front. We sat at a wooden table under the awning and the light bulbs. People wandered in and out, getting very drunk, and always the portable radios and televisions, and the large television inside, were turned on until you could finally feel the city trembling with electricity, and all the minds in the city connected into the circuits, and the minds and electric machines connecting in expanding networks with broader webs of mind and machine until the entire world was linked into us sitting there in Dallas, and then those outside feelings of hate and fear began to overwhelm our own feelings of shock and anger and disgust with ourselves, and we became the receptacle for the guilt of all the world. We didn't want it, we couldn't stand it, and we couldn't refuse it. After that burst of motion and fury, that moment when we might have acted without regard for opinion and worked off our rage with blind violence against those we knew deserved it, after that moment we retreated into stunned revulsion at ourselves. The world was grieving—the television showed us so, the weeping faces in Europe, the people asking why we had done it. The country was outraged. We were becoming paralyzed. A man sat on the grass in front of the End Zone and wept and then stood up and said he was selling his jewelry store and moving to New York, and an advertising executive hit him on the jaw. "This is my town, this couldn't have happened," the executive said, crying. We cursed ourselves and defended ourselves. What did I do? How am I to blame? There were rumors of the city in flames. The new king spoke to us, and we knew from his voice that it was all different now, the old government overthrown. His hound's eyes gazed out at paranoia worse than his own. One move would have torn the society apart, but the move never came. The tissues were stronger than we realized, holding back the move. Conspiracies crept among us, phantom gunmen and mysterious airplanes, threats from all sides as we huddled together. The death was our failure.

By now we had heard of the murder of the policeman, Tippitt, and the arrest of Lee Harvey Oswald, who had hidden—where else?—in a movie theater.

At last Buster and I got up to drive down to the police station. Buster locked my film of Dealey Plaza in a metal box in the rear of the station wagon.

"I don't like this movie, John Lee, but we've got to see the end of it," he said. "It's the movie we've been making."

SOMETHING HAPPENS

★

Lawrence Wright

I N THE MORNING I WENT OUT TO GET THE *News* AND FOUND
on our doorstep a flier that looked like a wanted poster in the post
office. It was John Kennedy, full face and profile, and the flier said
he was wanted for treason. Below that his crimes were listed:

1. Betraying the Constitution (which he swore to uphold): He is turning the sovereignty of the U.S. over to the Communist controlled
United Nations.

    He is betraying our friends (Cuba, Katanga, Portugal) and befriend-
ing our enemies (Russia, Yugoslavia, Poland).

2. He has been WRONG on innumerable issues affecting the security
of the U.S. (United Nations—Berlin Wall—Missile Removal—
Cuba—Wheat Deals—Test Ban Treaty, etc.).

3. He has been lax in enforcing Communist registration laws.

4. He has given support and encouragement to the Communist
inspired racial riots.

5. He has illegally invaded a sovereign state with Federal troops.

6. He has consistently appointed anti-Christians to Federal office;
   Upholds the Supreme Court in its anti-Christian rulings.
   Aliens and known Communists abound in Federal offices.

7. He has been caught in fantastic LIES to the American people
   (including personal ones, like his previous marriage and divorce).

I brought the flier in with the paper and read it on the way to the breakfast table. I had heard most of it before—who hadn't? It was the same old right-wing tirade, except for the charge of Kennedy's "previous marriage and divorce," which was new to me. I was already running late to school, so I didn't read the *News* that morning, but later in the day one of my first instincts would be to save the paper (as did many other people in Dallas, including eight-year-old John Hinckley, Jr.). It was November 22, 1963.

My sister Kathleen recalls seeing that date written on a blackboard several days before—she had a school assignment due that day—and feeling an instantaneous surge of horror, a buzz, almost an electrical shock. There were other premonitory currents in the city. Later, the guilt we felt for Kennedy's death would have less to do with his assassination by a man only slightly associated with our city than it would have to do with our own feelings of anticipation. Something would happen—*something*. We expected to be disgraced. It had happened with Lyndon Johnson, it had happened with Stevenson, it would happen again. There was a low-grade thrill in the city such as there might be in a movie audience when a gunfight is about to occur—it was that kind of secondary excitement, not the fear that someone would really die, but an expectation that something dramatic would appear to happen, that we would see it or hear about it, certainly talk about it later, but that it would pass with no harm done. Political theater, in other words.

My father was one of the city leaders invited to the Trade Mart for Kennedy's luncheon speech. He had gone there with his friend Jack Evans, who would later serve as mayor. As they were driving down Irving Boulevard they saw *Air Force One* just above them, approaching Love Field. It was 11:40 A.M. They remarked on the close timing of these presidential occasions, and how brief they were; Kennedy would be here and gone in a couple of hours.

Although schools were let out in Houston and San Antonio when the President's motorcade passed through, in Dallas we could be excused only in the custody of a parent. So like most of my classmates I was in school when it happened. It was right after lunch. I was in Algebra. Mr. Irvin Hill was describing a parabola on the blackboard when the three tones came over the public-address system and the principal started to speak. We knew something was wrong before he said a word. There was a choked pause. We could hear a radio playing in the background.

"The President has been shot."

It was only a fraction of a moment before he gave us details and then played the radio commentary into the PA for the remainder of the hour. But in that instant the world we knew shattered and collapsed. *It happened*—the something we had been waiting for. *It happened!* We were dazed and excited. We turned in our chairs and looked into each other's faces, finding grins of astonishment. Later, when reports appeared about Dallas schoolchildren laughing at the news, I wondered if I hadn't laughed myself. It was such a release of anxiety. At that point in my life I knew no more about the nature of tragedy than a blind man knows about the color blue. All I knew was that life could change, it had changed at last. Hadn't we known? Hadn't we been scared of exactly this? We asked ourselves these questions with our eyes, looking for some fixed response to this new flood of circumstance. We were giddy and frightened, and as for me I was grateful for the loss of innocence.

Meanwhile, in the Trade Mart, my father and the other guests waited and waited and began to grow impatient. Finally the first course was served. Then Eric Jonsson, president of the Citizens Council, arose and said in a quavering voice that there had been an "accident"—he wasn't more specific. "The President has been hit," someone reported. My father supposed there had been a rowdy demonstration of some sort. Another friend of mine stayed in the Trade Mart until the nature of the tragedy was revealed. Kennedy was his hero, but in the fumbling moments that followed the announcement, my friend, aged fifteen, went boldly to the dais and stole the salt and pepper shakers from Kennedy's place setting.

". . . shot in the head, Governor Connally wounded . . ."

My father overheard these words on a police radio as he passed by a motorcycle outside the Trade Mart. It was the first time he ever heard the term "grassy knoll." Shocked, confused, he drove back to the bank and watched television with his tellers.

Some of the details were off base. We heard that Vice President Johnson was shot too, that he was seen entering Parkland Hospital holding his arm. Who else? Were they killing everybody? I never paused to think who *they* were. It was Dallas, of course—faceless assassins but essentially Dallas pulling the many triggers. I supposed we were in the middle of a right-wing coup.

As we sat there, gazing crazily at each other and at the PA box on the wall, I finally noticed Mr. Hill and saw tears streaming down his wrinkled cheeks. His chest began to heave, then he sobbed in great barks. Everyone was watching him now, studying him as if he had some simple formula for this new hypothesis, but his grief was a private thing, and he picked it up like the greatest burden he had ever lifted and carried it out of the room. As he left, I felt the first prodding overture of shame.

"The President is dead."

IT WAS A SHOCK HOW MUCH THE WORLD HATED US—AND WHY? Oswald was only dimly a Dallasite—he was a Marxist and an atheist— you could scarcely call him a product of the city. He was, if anything, the Anti-Dallas, the summation of all we hated and feared. How could we be held responsible for him? And yet the world decided that Kennedy had died in enemy territory, that no matter who had killed him, we had *willed* him dead.

The truth is we had drawn closer to Kennedy even as the rest of the country grew disenchanted. The disgrace of the Bay of Pigs actually helped Kennedy in Dallas. My father admired the way the President shouldered the blame. The missile crisis in Cuba showed Dallas that Kennedy had learned the use of power; it also showed us the danger of Ted Dealey's bluster. Kennedy was tough after all. We liked him. We wanted him to like us. When he came to Dallas we gave him the warmest reception he received in Texas. It was the perfect confrontation between Kennedy's vaunted courage (walking into crowds, stopping the motorcade to shake hands) and our new willingness to make friends with him.

The crowds and the cheering were real responses. In fact the last words Kennedy heard in life were spoken by Nellie Connally, the governor's wife, who turned and said, "Mr. President, you can't say Dallas doesn't love you." It was a true observation, but also history's damnedest irony, for an instant later Jacqueline Kennedy had to respond, "They've killed my husband. I have his brains in my hand."

She said *they*—meaning Dallas, an assumption the whole world shared.

Dallas killed Kennedy; we heard it again and again. Dallas was "a city of hate, the only city in which the President could have been shot"—this from our own Judge Sarah Hughes, who swore in Lyndon Johnson as president aboard *Air Force One*.

But Dallas had nothing to do with Kennedy's death. The hatred directed at our city was retaliation for many previous grievances. The East hated us because we were part of the usurping West, liberals hated us because we were conservative, labor because we were anti-union, intellectuals because we were raw, minorities because we were predominantly and conspicuously white, atheists and agnostics because we were strident believers, the poor because we were rich,

the old because we were new. There were few of the world's con-
stituencies we had failed to offend before the President came to our
city, and hadn't we compounded the offense again and again by
boasting of these very qualities? In any case we were well silenced
now.

Oh, we felt sorry for ourselves, all right. The city's display of self-
pity was another reason to hate us. The impression we gave was that
Oswald's real crime was not murder but libel—of our reputation, our
good name. We were not penitent, we were outraged. We were the
victims.

The final words of the speech the President would have delivered
in the Trade Mart were the Psalmist's injunction: "Except that the
Lord keep the city, the watchman waketh but in vain." He had meant
to be speaking of his generation of Americans, who were charged with
keeping peace in the world. But, as my father thought, Kennedy might
have been speaking of Dallas as well, because all the watchmen of our
city had not been able to protect him from one fey killer. It seemed an
awful prophecy for Dallas that, despite our piety, God had let it happen here.

In church that Sunday, November 24, my father, Kathy, and I heard
our minister preach a sermon entitled "Let's Change the Climate."
The word "climate" already had acquired a supercharged meaning in
Dallas. Where it once had been used only to describe the abundant
opportunities for business growth, now it was appropriated by the
newscasters and magazine writers as a sort of net that could be tossed
over the entire city, implicating everyone in the crime. Yes, there were
fanatics in Dallas, but weren't we all responsible for creating a climate
in which fanaticism could take root? a climate of hate? a climate of
intolerance? a climate of bigotry? It was an unanswerable charge. My
father's jaw set as we heard the minister accepting the blame on behalf
of the city—his sermon was being broadcast nationally on ABC
radio—the blame for the climate that was responsible for Kennedy's
death. At the end of the sermon, when we had sung the doxology and

were standing to leave, someone walked to the pulpit and handed the minister a message.

"Oswald's been shot!"

The congregation slumped back into the pews. The police were telling us to leave downtown, to evacuate the area. What now? What was going on?

It was simply too much—a psychological breaking point for many of us, who, like my father, had held out against the insinuations of the press, who had refused to accept blame for the climate in Dallas. But the more we learned about the circumstances of Oswald's death and the background of his killer, the more we had to acknowledge our responsibility. A local nightclub operator named Jack Ruby had wandered upon Oswald being transferred from the city jail, and shot him down in front of the whole world. Unlike Oswald, Jack Ruby was one of ours, he did his deed in the very bowels of our own city hall, and he did it in a spirit of horrified civic-mindedness. Our incompetent police force let him do it. The defense we had established for our city in the death of the President didn't apply in the death of the President's killer. Dallas didn't kill Kennedy, but in an awful, undeniable fashion it did kill Oswald.

A PHENOMENON REMARKED ON BY PSYCHIATRISTS AFTER THE assassination was the dearth of dreams. The normal functions of the unconscious mind seemed to have been displaced by unending hours of television viewing. Commercials disappeared— that was itself a weird and ominous phenomenon. From the moment of the President's death at noon on Friday until after midnight the following Tuesday, the broadcasts virtually never stopped, and as they are played back in my mind now—the death march, the half-stepping troops, the riderless horse, John-John's salute—they have the quality of a remembered dream, haunting, full of meaning, experienced but unlived.

Americans have always had a secret love of pageantry, unfulfilled because of the absence of royalty, and this massive grandeur was new to us and thrilling. I remember being struck by the vocabulary of the occasion, words like "bier" and "caisson" and "catafalque," which had a sound of such solemn importance that they could be used only a few times in one's life—like rare china dishes one sets out only for the king.

My mother and Rosalind stayed home on Sunday morning to watch the Mass for the dead President. Cardinal Spellman called him "the martyr of this century," a designation we accepted without questioning what cause he had died for. Kennedy was lying in the East Room of the White House, where Lincoln had lain nearly a hundred years before. This was a parallel, Lincoln and Kennedy, we would never quite shake off, although the assassination of President McKinley might have drawn a closer analogy. McKinley had been a popular president, but he was not a martyr like Lincoln—except perhaps to the cause of laissez-faire capitalism. Kennedy's claim to martyrdom was based on the belief that Dallas had killed him. But even I wanted to believe that his death had meaning, and so I allowed myself to think that he was a martyr to something—perhaps to my own evil desire for something to happen.

After Mass, the procession to the Capitol began to form, and the networks switched their coverage to the Dallas City Hall. It was a scene of confusion and anticipation. Before now we had had only a brief glimpse of the accused assassin. He had spoken briefly to the press in a wild, impromptu press conference. He didn't sound like a Dallasite; despite his years in Russia he retained his gumbo New Orleans accent—he said "axed" instead of "asked." He had a spooky composure about him, although according to our district attorney he was as good as convicted, so few of us doubted his guilt.

Finally Oswald appeared in the doorway, dwarfed by the beefy detectives on either side of him but still looking cool and at peace, while all around him chaos raged. I suppose this was the supreme moment in Oswald's unhappy life. He had always been the outsider, unaccepted, unloved, but he had turned the tables on us. He was suddenly the man with the answers, his secrets were locked in his skull, and we were all outsiders now.

And as he entered the basement of the city hall, Oswald's defiant glare fell directly on Jack Ruby. Was it an illusion, or was there the surprised look of recognition between conspirators at that moment, replayed a million times by now, when Ruby stepped into Oswald's path and gunned him down?

Since Oswald's death we have learned very little more about that or the event of the assassination, but we have learned unimaginable things about our country. The assassination sent a shaft through our society, throwing unexpected light on creatures used to the dark—spies, mobsters, informers, mistresses, all of them surprised in strange alliances. It was not the assassination itself but this vivid exposure that would forever change our understanding of how our country worked. We would become ashamed of our naïveté. Simple explanations would never satisfy us again.

It is odd that a single moment of reality—Oswald's assassination of John Kennedy—can be folded and refolded into infinite origami constructions. Was it a plot on the part of H. L. Hunt to protect the oil-depletion allowance? Was Oswald a secret agent for the Russians? for the Cubans? for us? Was he a part of a larger conspiracy? Was there really only one Oswald? Some theories suppose there were three, perhaps even five. Not a single assumption goes unchallenged; perhaps Kennedy is not even dead. (For years we heard the rumor that he was still alive in some vegetable state in Parkland Hospital, that another body had been smuggled out and buried at Arlington.) It is a way of explaining everything, of giving meaning to events. Reality is twisted into art. Is there such a thing finally as truth? (If there is not, there must be a God.)

I think what each of us believes about the assassination says something about the kind of person we are, what we are willing to believe about our country and ourselves. I believe Oswald acted alone. Perhaps it is easier for me to locate evil inside the single human heart than it is to believe in broad conspiracies. Also, killing has come easy for me. I once took a potshot at a red-tailed hawk that was circling below the clouds, and to my astonishment he folded his wings and fell out of the sky like a sack of mail. The year of the President's death I went hunting with my father and some of his business friends on a South Texas deer lease. I had experienced, I thought, enough of killing by then, but as I was walking across an open field carrying one of the hunters' guns, a stag broke out of the brush, nearly 175 yards away. I knelt and fired, then watched him cartwheel and fall on his side, his feet pointed at me. I've always had good luck in killing.

Why did I shoot the deer when I told myself I wouldn't? For one thing, I was licensed to kill (my father had taken that precaution). My action had been approved in advance. At the heart of the Dallas-killed-Kennedy argument is a similar presumption about Oswald: the community hated Kennedy so much that Oswald felt licensed to act out our fantasy.

There is another reason I killed the deer. I was there, I had a gun, the deer appeared. *He came to me.* It sounds mindless, I suppose, but I don't believe that thinking has very much to do with instinctive responses. Oswald must have felt something like this when he read in the newspaper that Kennedy's motorcade would pass directly in front of the School Book Depository, where Oswald was a warehouseman. *He's coming to me.* "He" who? Did it matter—any more than the identity of the deer in the field? Oswald had already tried to shoot General Walker. On another occasion he told Marina that Richard Nixon was in town, and he was "going to have a look" at him; Marina locked her husband in the bathroom and hid his pistol until she was certain Nixon was safe. However, Oswald never stalked Kennedy; Kennedy came to him. He said on several occasions how much he admired the President. After his arrest he told police "My wife and I like the President's family. They are interesting people" and "I am not a malcontent; nothing irritated me about the President." I don't think Oswald would have chosen to shoot Kennedy if the President had made different arrangements, if he had not come to Dallas, if he had not ridden in an open limousine, if he had not passed by the School Book Depository. In a similar way I don't think Jack Ruby would have shot Oswald if he had not been carrying a gun anyway (because he had gone to the Western Union with a wad of money to wire to one of his strippers), if he had not been downtown at that moment and seen a commotion at city hall, if he had not wandered down into the basement to see what was going on ("Curiosity got the best of me"), if he had not stumbled at that very moment into the presence of Lee Harvey Oswald. Conspiracists sneer at coincidences such as these, but I think coincidence can be a powerful, irrational spur to violent response. One opportunity— *act now or else!*

WHO WAS JACK RUBY?

★

Gary Cartwright

ALL I KNOW ABOUT THE BEST MAN IN MY WEDDING IS HE didn't exist.

Five days before John F. Kennedy was assassinated in Dallas, I got married for the second time. It was a Sunday, the day after I'd covered the SMU-Arkansas game at the Cotton Bowl, and Jo and I—who had known each other a good three weeks—were convinced by this romantic con man who called himself Richard Noble that we should drive to Durant, Oklahoma, and get married. Richard Noble personally drove us in his air-conditioned convertible. He paid for the blood tests and license. We used his 1949 Stanford class ring in the ceremony, and we drank a quart of his scotch and sang "Hey, Look Me Over" ("Remember when you're down and out, the only way is up!") on the way back to Dallas.

There was no such person as Richard Noble, and the Stanford class ring was bought in a hock shop. Whoever the man was who called himself Richard Noble had set up a bogus sales office in a North Dallas apartment complex inhabited mainly by airline stews and indomitable seekers and had managed to ingratiate himself with his personality, credit cards, liquor supply, and national WATS line. A month or so after the assassination, which I assume he had nothing to do with, Richard Noble vanished in the night. The FBI came around asking questions, and that was the last I heard.

A lot of bizarre people were doing some very strange things in Dallas in the fall of 1963, and Richard Noble was only one of them. Madame Nhu bought a dozen shower caps at Neiman-Marcus and tried to drum up support for the Diem regime in Saigon, even while her host in the U.S., the CIA, laid plans to assassinate Diem himself. Members of the American Nazi party danced around a man in an ape suit in front of the *Times Herald* building. Congressman Bruce Alger, who had once carried a sign accusing Lyndon Johnson of being a traitor, went on television to denounce the Peace Corps as "welfare socialism and godless materialism, all at the expense of capitalism and basic U.S. spiritual and moral values." Zealots from the National Indignation Committee picketed a UN Day speech by Ambassador Adlai Stevenson; they called him Addle-Eye and booed and spat on him and hit him on the head with a picket sign. When a hundred civic leaders wired strong and sincere apologies to the ambassador, General Edwin Walker, who had been cashiered by the Pentagon for force-feeding his troops right-wing propaganda, flew the American flag upside down in front of his military-gray mansion on Turtle Creek. There were pro-Castro cabals and anti-Castro cabals that overlapped and enough clandestine commerce to fill a dozen Bogart movies. Drugs, arms, muscle, propaganda: the piety of the Dallas business climate was the perfect cover. A friend of mine in banking operated a fleet of trucks in Bogotá as a sideline. Airline stewardesses brought in sugarcoated cookies of black Turkish hash without having the slightest notion of what they were carrying.

Jack Ruby was having one of his customary feuds with an employee of his Carousel Club, but this one was serious. His star attraction, Jada, claimed that she feared for her life and placed Ruby under peace bond. Newspaper ads for the Carousel Club during the week of November 22 featured Bill Demar, a comic ventriloquist—hardly Ruby's style, but the best he could do.

And someone took a potshot at General Walker in his own home. People said later it was Lee Harvey Oswald.

IF THERE IS A TEAR LEFT, SHED IT FOR JACK RUBY. HE DIDN'T make history; he only stepped in front of it. When he emerged from obscurity into that inextricable freeze-frame that joins all of our minds to Dallas, Jack Ruby, a bald-headed little man who wanted above all else to make it big, had his back to the camera.

I can tell you about Jack Ruby, and about Dallas, and if necessary remind you that human life is sweetly fragile and the holy litany of ambition and success takes as many people to hell as it does to heaven. But someone else will have to tell you about Oswald, and what he was doing in Dallas that November, when Jack Ruby took the play away from Oswald, and from all of us.

Dallas, Oswald, Ruby, Watts, Whitman, Manson, Ray, Sirhan, Bremer, Vietnam, Nixon, Watergate, FBI, CIA, Squeaky Fromme, Sara Moore—the list goes on and on. Who the hell wrote this script, and where will it end? A dozen years of violence, shock, treachery, and paranoia, and I date it all back to that insane weekend in Dallas and Jack Ruby—the one essential link in the chain, the man who changed an isolated act into a trend.

Jack Ruby had come a long way from the ghettos of Chicago, or so he liked to think. He described the Carousel Club as a "fucking classy joint" and patrons who challenged his opinion sometimes got thrown down the stairs. The Carousel was a dingy, cramped walk-up in the 1300 block of Commerce, right next to Abe Weinstein's Colony Club and close to the hotels, restaurants, and night spots that made downtown Dallas lively and respectably sinister in those times of official innocence. You can see more flesh in a high school biology class now than you could at any of the joints on the Strip in 1963, but that wasn't the point. Jack Ruby ran what he considered a "decent" place, a "high-class" place, a place that Dallas could view with pride. "Punks" and "characters" who wandered in by mistake were as likely as not to leave with an impression of Jack Ruby's fist where their nose used to be.

Cops and newspapermen, that's who Ruby wanted in his place. Dallas cops drank there regularly, and none of them ever paid for a drink. Any girl caught hooking in his joint would get manhandled and fired on the spot, but Ruby leaned on his girls to provide sexual pleasures for favored clients.

Jack Ruby was a foulmouthed, mean-tempered prude who loved children and hated ethnic jokes. He didn't drink or smoke. He was violently opposed to drugs, though he maintained his own high energy level by popping Preludin—an upper—and it was rumored that he operated a personal clearinghouse for mob drug-runners. He was involved in shady financial schemes, and the IRS was on his back. A swindler who called himself Harry Sinclair, Jr., told Secret Service agents that Ruby backed him in a bet-and-run operation. Ruby supplied cash and introduced Sinclair to likely victims. (H. L. Hunt was supposed to have been one.) If Sinclair won, he'd collect; if he lost, he'd write a hot check and split. Ruby got forty percent of the action.

Sex shocked and disturbed him, and that's how Ruby had his falling-out with Jada, who had been imported from the 500 Club in New Orleans so that the Carousel could compete with the much classier Colony Club (where Chris Colt was stripping) or Barney Weinstein's Theatre Lounge around the corner, where you could catch Nikki Joy. Ruby was childishly jealous of the Weinsteins, who drove Cadillacs and Jaguars and took frequent trips to Las Vegas; and he assuaged his envy by drafting complaints to the strippers' union, the Liquor Control Board, and the IRS, accusing the Weinsteins of whatever. Even the FBI, to its sorrow, knew of Ruby's antipathy for the Weinsteins. Of all the Ruby rumors that have flourished and died through the years—that Ruby fired at Kennedy from the railroad overpass, that Oswald visited the Carousel Club a few days before the assassination—only the most current one, that Ruby was an informant for the FBI, seems to have much truth to it. Hugh Aynesworth, a *Times Herald* reporter who knew Ruby well, verified it: "In 1959 the FBI tried eight times to recruit Jack Ruby. They wanted him as an informer on drugs, gambling, and organized crime, but every time they contacted him, Ruby tried to get his competitors in trouble. 'Ol' Abe over at the Colony Club is cheating on his income tax. . . . Ol' Barney at the Theatre Lounge is selling booze after hours.' After a while the FBI gave up on the idea." The Weinsteins, not surprisingly, considered Ruby a creep.

I first met Jada about a month before the assasination. Bud Shrake and I shared an apartment on Cole Avenue that autumn, and since we were both sportswriters, Ruby considered us favored customers. He invited us to the Carousel one night, and Shrake came home with Jada. We all became good friends, and when Jo and I got married a few weeks later, Jada gave us our first wedding gift—a two-pound Girl Scout cookie tin full of illegal weed she had smuggled across the border in her gold Cadillac with the letters JADA embossed on the door. Jada cleared customs with one hundred of the two-pound tins in the trunk of her car. She was accompanied by a state politician (who knew nothing about the load) and wore a mink coat, high-heel shoes, and nothing else. The first thing she did at customs was open the door and fall out, revealing more than the customs official expected. That was one of Jada's great pleasures, driving around Dallas in her mink coat and high heels, her orange hair piled high and the coat flaring open. It was a better act than the one Ruby paid for.

Ruby planted the story that Jada was trained in ballet, had a college degree in psychology, was a descendant of John Quincy Adams, and a granddaughter of Pavlova. Jada's name was Adams, Janet Adams Conforto, but she hadn't been inside a classroom since she ran away from a Catholic girls school in New York at age fifteen, and she couldn't dance her way out of a doughnut. Her act consisted mainly of hunching a tiger-skin rug and making wild orgasmic sounds with her throat. As a grand climax Jada would spread her legs and pop her G-string, and that's when Ruby would turn off the lights and the hell would start.

The other strippers and champagne girls hated Jada. She was a star and acted the part. The bus-station girls from Sherman and Tyler came and went—Ruby automatically fired any girl who agreed to have sex with him—but Jada treated Ruby like a dog. She called him a pansy and worse, and she spread word among the customers that the hamburgers served out of the Carousel's tiny kitchen were contaminated with dog shit.

One night while Jada was ravaging her tiger skin, a tourist stepped up and popped a flashbulb in her face. Ruby threw the startled cameraman down the stairs. Jada popped her G-string about a foot, and Ruby threw her off the stage. All this took a few seconds, but for those few seconds Ruby was an absolute madman. Then he walked over to our table and said in this very weary, clear, huckster voice, "How's it going, boys? Need anything?" I don't think he remembered what had just happened.

On the morning of the assassination, Ruby called our apartment and asked if we'd seen Jada. Shrake said we hadn't. "I'm warning you for your own good," Ruby said. "Stay away from that woman." "Is that intended as a threat?" Shrake inquired. "No, no," Ruby apologized. "No, it's just that she's an evil woman."

Unlike the other clubs on the Strip, the Carousel was strictly a clip joint where Ruby's girls hustled $1.98 bottles of champagne for whatever they could get.

"We kept the labels covered with a bar towel," a onetime Ruby champagne girl told me. The woman, who is now married to a well-known musician, went to work for Ruby when she was seventeen.

"Jack would tell us to come on to the customers, promise them any-thing—of course he didn't mean for us to deliver, but sometimes we did on our own time. The price for a bottle of cheap champagne was anywhere from fifteen to seventy-five dollars. We'd sit with the cus-tomer as long as the bottle lasted, drinking out of what we called spit glasses—frosted glasses of ice water. We worked for tips or whatever we could steal.

"Actually, Jack had a soft heart. He was always loaning us money and knocking the snot out of anyone who gave us a bad time. He liked that image of himself—big bad protector. He'd fire you, then ten min-utes later break in on you in the john and demand to know why you weren't on the floor pushing drinks. One girl there got fired about three hundred times."

The only "decent" woman in Jack Ruby's life was Alice Nichols, a shy widow who worked for an insurance company. He dated her on and off for eleven years. The reason Ruby couldn't marry Alice, he told many of his friends, was that he had made his mother a deathbed promise that he wouldn't marry a gentile. Ruby's mother had died in an insane asylum in Chicago.

Ruby had the carriage of a bantam cock and the energy of a steam engine as he churned through the streets of downtown Dallas, glad-handing, passing out cards, speaking rapidly, compulsively, about his new line of pizza ovens, about the twistboards he was promoting, about the important people he knew, cornering friends and grabbing strangers, relating amazing details of his private life and how any day now he would make it big. He once spotted actress Rhonda Fleming having a club sandwich at Love Field and joined her for lunch. You could always spot him at the boxing matches. He'd wait until just before the main event, when they turned up the lights, and he'd prance down the center aisle in a badly dated hat and double-breasted suit, shaking hands and handing out free passes to the Carousel.

He was always on his way to some very important meeting, saying he was going to see the mayor, the police chief, some judge, Stanley

Marcus, Clint Murchison. And every day he'd make his rounds—the bank, the Statler Hilton, the police station, the courthouse, the bail-bond office, the Doubleday Book Store (Ruby was a compulsive reader of new diet books), the delicatessen, the shoeshine parlor, radio station KLIF.

KLIF was owned by Gordon McLendon, whom Ruby once identified as "the world's greatest American." McLendon, who billed himself as "the Old Scotchman," made his reputation recreating baseball games on the old Liberty Broadcasting System until organized baseball conspired to shut him down. The Old Scotchman would sit in a soundproof studio a thousand miles from the action he was describing, reading the play-by-play from the ticker, his voice shrill and disbelieving, while his sound man (Dallas' current mayor Wes Wise was one of them) beat on a grapefruit with a bat and faked PA announcements requesting that the owner of a blue 1947 Buick please move his car out of the fire lane. Later McLendon pioneered the Top Forty music/news format, introduced a series of right-wing radio editorials, ran unsuccessfully for Ralph Yarborough's Senate seat, and launched a one-man campaign against dirty and suggestive songs like "Yellow Submarine" and "Puff, the Magic Dragon." The Old Scotchman, Jack Ruby liked to say, was his idea of "a intellectual."

Ruby wasn't a big man—five foot nine, 175 pounds—but he had thick shoulders and arms, and he was fast. He swam and exercised regularly at the YMCA, and was a compulsive consumer of health foods. He had an expression that dated from his street-fighting days in Chicago: "Take the play away." It meant to strike first. He usually carried a big roll of money, and when he carried money he also carried a gun.

Hugh Aynesworth saw the many personalities of Jack Ruby as clearly as anyone. Aynesworth recalled a night at Ruby's second club, the Vegas, when a drunk came in after hours with a bottle bulging from his inside coat pocket. Ruby took the man's two dollars, showed him to a table, then smashed the bottle against the man's rib cage.

Another time Aynesworth encountered a dazed, bleeding wino stag-gering near the Adolphus Hotel. The wino had tried to bum a quarter from Ruby, who smashed him in the head with a full whiskey bottle. Yet at times Ruby could be embarrassingly sentimental.

"Ruby was a crier," Aynesworth recalls. "I mean, he could go to a fire and break out crying."

Aynesworth has been investigating the events of that week for twelve years and has concluded that the Warren Report is mostly accurate. Two nuts, two killings. "In Ruby's case the conspiracy theory is totally ridiculous," he told me. "Ruby would have told everyone on the streets of downtown Dallas. *Ho, ho, ho, they asked me to help kill the President. Of course I'm not gonna do it.*"

Joe Cavagnaro, one of Jack Ruby's best friends, made the same observation. "Nobody would have trusted Jack with a secret," he said. "He talked too much."

Cavagnaro is the sales manager of the Statler Hilton, a neat, man-icured, gregarious man who exudes the personality of downtown Dal-las, but he was just a man in need of a friend when he arrived in 1955. Cavagnaro was eating at the Lucas B&B Restaurant next to the Vegas Club one night when Ruby sauntered in, said hello, and picked up the check.

"He was a fine person," Cavagnaro said. "Much different than the picture you read. He had a big heart. He was good to people. Anyone down on his luck, he'd help them to the point of excess. There was a policeman whose wife and kid were in an accident, he took over a sack of groceries. He'd read something in the paper about some poor fam-ily and he'd go to the rescue. Sure, he had a short fuse, but remember, he had to police his own business; otherwise they'd close him up. The vice squad was always hanging around his place. Some drunk would act up and Jack would remove him without the vice squad being aware it ever happened."

Cavagnaro and Ruby had coffee at the Statler a few hours after the assassination. Ruby was extremely upset, and blamed the *Morning News*.

"He said it would be a cold day in hell before he placed another ad with the *News*," Cavagnaro told me. "Jack was a true patriot. He was also a Democrat. He thought Kennedy had done a lot for the minorities. Just from a business standpoint, he said, something like that could kill a city."

Did he say anything about killing Oswald?

"I think everyone in Dallas said something to the effect that 'I'd like to kill that S.O.B.'"

But Ruby *did* it; that is the difference. What did Cavagnaro think when he heard the news?

"I thought, yes, Jack *could* do that. I'd seen him hit a guy once for insulting a girl. The guy practically left his feet and flew across the street."

In the same block as the Statler Hilton and the Dallas police station, in a spot called the Purple Orchid, Ruby's ex-champagne girl joined eighty million viewers of Ruby's astounding crime on television. The girl turned to the bartender, who had also worked for Ruby, and she said: "Well, Jack's finally gonna get recognized."

Times Herald editorial page editor A. C. Greene and his wife had just driven home from church. Betty Greene ran ahead to answer the telephone, and when A. C. walked in the kitchen door she told him that someone had just killed the man who killed the President. He was someone who owned a downtown nightclub, Betty Greene said, bewildered. *Oh, God*, A. C. thought: *Jack Ruby!*

While Ruby was shooting Oswald, Jo and I were driving from Columbus, Ohio, where I had just met my new in-laws, to Cleveland, where the Cowboys were playing the Browns. The NFL was the only shop that stayed open that weekend. They claimed that it was a public service, and in retrospect I think they were right. Shrake met me at the press box entrance and told me what had happened.

"Jack Ruby!" I said. "Why not."

"Why not," Shrake said, shaking his head.

If you believe that Jack Ruby was part of a conspiracy, a "double

cutout" as they say in the spy trade, then you must also conclude that
the conspiracy involved dozens or even hundreds of plotters, including
Captain Will Fritz of the Dallas police department. Time and events
make Ruby's role in a conspiracy almost impossible. Oswald was to
have been transferred from the city jail to the county jail at 10 A.M.—
that was a solid commitment Chief Jesse Curry made to his intimates
among the press corps. If Ruby had been gunning for Oswald, if he
had premeditated the crime that eighty million witnesses saw him
commit, he would have been at the police station at 10 A.M. But he
wasn't. There were several reasons for the delay in transferring
Oswald, but the main one was Will Fritz's insistence on interrogating
the suspect one more time in city jail.

Ruby knew when the transfer was scheduled. He had covered the
event like a reporter on a beat: Parkland Hospital, the assassination
site, the press conferences. He was always at the center of the action,
passing out sandwiches, giving directions to out-of-town correspon-
dents, acting as unofficial press agent for District Attorney Henry
Wade—who, like everyone else on the scene, simply regarded Jack
Ruby as part of the furniture. Twice during a press conference Wade
mistakenly identified Oswald as a member of the violently anti-Castro
Free Cuba Committee. The second time a friendly voice at the back
of the room corrected the DA. "No, sir, Mister District Attorney,
Oswald was a member of the Fair Play for Cuba Committee." The
voice was Jack Ruby's. How did he know that? Well, it was in all the
news reports, but there is a more intriguing theory: an FBI report overlooked by the Warren Commission suggests that one of Ruby's many
sidelines was the role of bagman for a nonpartisan group of profiteers
who stole arms from the U.S. military and ran them for anti-Castro
Cubans.

Ten o'clock came and went, and still Oswald hadn't been transferred. It was after ten when Ruby received a telephone call from one
of his strippers who lived in Fort Worth. The girl needed money; she
needed it right then. Ruby dressed and drove to the Western Union

office in the same block as the police station. He couldn't have missed the crowd lingering outside on Commerce and on Elm. At 11:17 A.M. Ruby wired the money. He walked up an alley, passed through the crowd, and entered the ramp of the police station, a distance of about 350 feet. He was carrying better than two thousand dollars in cash (he couldn't bank the money because the IRS might grab it) and his gun was in its customary place in his right coat pocket.

Three minutes after Ruby posted the Western Union money order, he shot Oswald.

If the world at large was shocked at that precise minute, consider the bewilderment of Jack Ruby as the Dallas cops pounced on him. What was wrong? Had *he* done something he wasn't supposed to do? Didn't *everyone* want him to kill Oswald? What the hell was this?

"You all know me," he said pathetically. "I'm Jack Ruby."

Jack Ruby had to believe that he was guilty of a premeditated, calculated murder. The alternative—to admit he was crazy—was too awful to contemplate.

During the trial he told his chief attorney, Melvin Belli, "What are we doing, Mel, kidding ourselves? We know what happened. We know I did it for Jackie and the [Kennedy] kids. I just went in and shot him. They've got us anyway. Maybe I ought to forget this silly story that I'm telling and get on the stand and tell the truth."

The silly story that Belli, Joe Tonahill, and other members of the defense team were attempting to pass along to the jury was that Ruby killed Oswald during a seizure of psychomotor epilepsy. Belli and Tonahill still subscribe to this contention.

"The autopsy confirmed it. Ruby had fifteen brain tumors," Joe Tonahill told me. Tonahill, a huge, deliberate, friendly man, maintains that the Ruby trial "was the unfairest trial in the history of Texas." Judge Joe Brown, exhibiting a classic downtown Dallas mentality, appointed Dallas advertising executive Sam Bloom to handle "public relations" and overruled the defense on almost every motion. Ruby himself considered hiring a public relations man—or that's what he wrote in a letter to his intellectual hero, Gordon McLendon.

"Jack Ruby needed help long before Kennedy came to Dallas," Tonahill said. He was seated at the desk of his law office in Jasper, in front of a four-by-eight-foot blowup of Bob Jackson's Pulitzer prize-winning photograph of the Oswald murder. "He was a big baby at birth—almost fifteen pounds. That could have had something to do with it. His mother died in an insane asylum in Chicago. His father was a drunk and was treated for psychiatric disorders. A brother and a sister had psychiatric treatment. Ruby tried to commit suicide a couple of years earlier. His finger was once bitten off in a fight. He had a long history of violent, antisocial behavior, and when it was over he wouldn't remember what he had done. What provoked him? Maybe the flashbulbs—that's a common cause in cases of psychomotor epilepsy—or the TV cameras, or the smirk on Oswald's face."

I asked Tonahill what he thought of Ruby as a person.

"He was a real object of pity," Tonahill said. "Anytime you see a person overflowing with ambition to be someone, that person is admitting to you and the world that he's a nobody. Ruby was like a Damon Runyon character—a total inconsistency."

If Jack Ruby was not crazy when he gunned down Oswald, it's a safe bet the trial drove him that way. Day after day in the circus atmosphere of Judge Brown's courtroom, Ruby was forced to sit as a silent exhibit while psychiatrists called him a latent homosexual with a compulsive desire to be liked and respected, and his own attorneys described him as a village clown. He didn't even get to tell his own story, and by the time the Warren Commission found time to interview him months later, Ruby was convinced that there was a conspiracy to slaughter all the Jews of the world.

"In the beginning," Tonahill told me, "Ruby considered himself a hero. He thought he had done a great service for the community. When the mayor, Earle Cabell, testified that the act brought disgrace to Dallas, Jack started going downhill very fast. He got more nervous by the day. When they brought in the death penalty, he cracked. Ten days later he rammed his head into a cell wall. Then he tried to kill himself with an electric light socket. Then he tried to hang himself with sheets."

Ruby wrote a letter to Gordon McLendon claiming he was being poisoned by his jailers. Many Warren Report critics take this as additional evidence of a conspiracy. If someone did poison Ruby, it was a waste of good poison. An autopsy confirmed the brain tumors, massive spread of cancer, and a blood clot in his leg, which finally killed him.

The trial of Jack Ruby may have been one of the fastest on record. The crime was committed in November and the trial began in February. "The climate never cooled off," Tonahill said. "He was tried as it was peaking. There was this massive guilt in Dallas at the time. The only thing that could save Dallas was sending Ruby to the electric chair."

Though there are unanswered questions in his mind, Tonahill supports the conclusions of the Warren Report.

"If there was a conspiracy, and it was suppressed, it had to involve maybe a million people. That's a bunch of crap.

"The worse mistake the Warren Commission made was yielding to Rose Kennedy and suppressing the autopsy report. There was something about Kennedy's physical condition the family didn't want made public. I don't know what it was. Possibly a vasectomy—there was a story he had a vasectomy after the death of his baby. Being good Catholics, the Kennedy family wouldn't have wanted that out."

One close participant in the bizarre happenings of Dallas who isn't satisfied with the Warren Commission investigation is Bill Alexander, the salty, acid-tongued prosecutor who did most of the talking for Henry Wade at the Ruby trial. Alexander and former state Attorney General Waggoner Carr both urged the commission to investigate FBI and CIA personnel for information linking the agencies to Lee Harvey Oswald. There is no indication that such an investigation took place.

"I'm in Washington telling the commission to check out this address I found in Oswald's notebook, in his apartment, the day of the killing," Alexander recently told the Houston *Chronicle*. "None of those Yankee hot dogs are paying any attention to me.

"So I say, 'Waggoner, c'mon, let's get a cab.' We jump in and tell the driver to take us to this address. We get there and what do you think it is? The god-damn Russian Embassy. Now, what does that tell you?

"To this day, I don't think anybody from the commission followed that up."

Although Alexander, known to members of the press as "Old Snake-Eyes," was the main reason Henry Wade got the death penalties that the leaders of Dallas were convinced would deter crime, he is no longer on the DA's staff. Shortly after his infamous declaration that Chief Justice Earl Warren didn't need impeaching, he needed hanging, Alexander resigned to enter private practice.

When I telephoned Alexander for an interview, he told me he didn't want to talk about the assassination.

"I'd like to kick the dog shit out of every Yankee newspaperman, club the fuckers to the ground," he said. "You can still see them, right up to this day, hanging around the Book Depository," Alexander went on. "Fat-ass Yankees in shorts and cameras getting the roofs of their mouths sunburned. A carload of Yankees pulled up to my friend Miller Tucker and said [Alexander slipped into an Eastern accent], 'Officer, where did Kennedy get shot?' Ol' Miller taps the back of his head and says, 'Right here, friend, right here.'"

That afternoon I met Alexander in his law office and he told me about his Manchurian Candidate theory. "I worked a solid two years on this," he began. "I read the entire twenty-six volumes of the Warren Report just to protect myself, and tracked down every lead I could get my hands on, and I don't have any evidence that anyone acted with Oswald.

"Now," he said, raising a finger and slipping into third person singular so that it would be clearly understood he was speaking hypothetically, "who knows how a person has been brainwashed—motivated—hypnotized?

"A man is cashiered out of the Marine Corps—he moves to Russia—he marries the niece of the head of the OGPU spy school—he stays a certain amount of months, then turns up at the American Embassy and says, 'King's X, fellows, I want to go home. Do you think you people might could pay my way back to New York?' Wouldn't somebody debrief that man? Hell, the FBI knew he was in New Orleans. They sent his folder to Dallas before the assassination."

On the other hand, Alexander has not the slightest doubt that Ruby acted alone in a legally sane, premeditated manner. Alexander and Dr. John T. Holbrook were among the first to question Ruby after the shooting.

"I'm paraphrasing now," Alexander said, "but it was like he wanted to open the Jack Ruby Show on Broadway, get a TV show, write a book. He asked me if I thought he needed an agent."

Alexander spat tobacco juice in a can and said, "Jack Ruby was about as handicapped as you can get in Dallas. First, he was a Yankee. Second, he was a Jew. Third, he was in the nightclub business.

"That's horseshit about him being a police buff. He didn't think any more of a policeman than he did a pissant. It was just good business. The vice squad kept plus and minus charts on the joints 'cause the licenses came up for renewal each year. The vice squad can kill a joint if they get in the wrong mood. Who wants to drink beer with a harness bull looking over his shoulder?

"Quit kidding me about how much Ruby loved people. Or how much he loved the Kennedys. Hell, where was he while the motorcade was passing through downtown? In the goddamn *Dallas News*, placing an ad for his club."

The ex-prosecutor sat back and sighed.

"It's a real experience to see how real, factual history can be distorted in ten years so that people who lived it can't recognize it."

And the end of all our exploring

Will be to arrive where we started

And know the place for the first time.

    —T. S. Eliot, from *Little Gidding*

On a warm day twelve years removed from that time of Ruby and Oswald, my son Mark and I walk the streets of downtown Dallas and know the place for the first time.

The Blue Front where you could eat the world's best oxtail soup and watch Willie sweat in the potato salad is gone. The Star Bar is gone. Hodges, Joe Banks, the Oyster Bar, the musty little bookstores with their dark volumes, the mom and dad shops, the smell of pizza, of chili rice, of peanut oil, of stale beer, of perfume, lost now in the tomb of our memory. What you smell twelve years later is concrete. What you see are the walls of a glass canyon.

The corner of Commerce and Akard, which used to bustle with beautiful women in short skirts and quick men with briefcases, is nearly deserted, except for a few Hare Krishnas and some delegates to the Fraternal Order of the Eagles. The Carousel, the Colony, the Theatre Lounge, the Horseshoe Bar, the whole Strip has been leveled and turned into a gigantic parking lot for the invisible occupants of the glass skyscrapers. The big department stores and the theaters and the good restaurants have gone to the suburbs. Twelve years ago you could have dropped a net sixteen blocks square from the Republic National Bank tower and been fairly sure that you had caught a quorum of the Dallas oligarchy. There is still a feeling of affluence, but the vortex of power has moved to the suburbs, out Stemmons, out Greenville, out Northwest Highway, out to Old Town—whatever Old Town is.

There are blacks on the city council, and the mayor is a former grapefruit hitter for the Old Scotchman. The Old Scotchman long ago sold KLIF and is seldom seen anymore; he is a Howard Hughes figure, dabbling, so it is said, in multinationals and worldwide real estate. When the sun disappears behind the canyon walls, what you see in downtown Dallas is blacks with mops and brooms, waiting for an elevator. Slack-faced office workers wait for a bus in front of the old Majestic theater, and black hookers with beehives appear to show the Fraternal Order of Eagles the sights.

I wonder: could there be a Jack Ruby in 1975? Where would he go? What would he do? The Dallas Jack Ruby knew is gone.

That Dallas was a city of shame, but it wasn't a city of hate. Its vision was genuine and sincere, but it had the heart of a rodent. In the subterranean tunnels of those proud spires of capitalism and free enterprise crawled armies of con men and hustlers, cheap-shot artists and money changers, profiteers and ideologues, grubbers, grabbers, fireflies, eccentrics, and cuckoos. Dallas was just like everyplace else, except it couldn't admit it. It was not Lee Harvey Oswald and the murder of John F. Kennedy that proved what Dallas was really like, but Jack Ruby and the murder of Lee Harvey Oswald.

We drive out Turtle Creek past General Walker's prim gray fortress. On the front lawn, a crude, hand-lettered marquee says Dump Estes, a reference, I suppose, to the Dallas superintendent of schools who apparently isn't resisting integration fast enough. Like downtown Dallas, the general is quieter these days. Ken Latimer, a resident actor at the Dallas Theater Center (DTC), tells us, "General Walker and his people used to picket us fairly regularly, but they've been quiet for some time now." Latimer played the lead in the DTC production of *Jack Ruby, All-American Boy*, a drama that attempted without much success to answer the question: Was Jack Ruby a typical American?

"Ruby wanted to be liked, to be respected, to be successful according to the value system of our society," Latimer says. "He was a cheap success, but in his own mind he had class. Violence was admissible to his system—toughness—let no one push you around.

"You asked me was it the climate of the times that made Ruby do what he did? No, Jack Ruby would do the same thing today."

We talk to stripper Chastity Fox, who played the role of Jada. Chastity had never met Ruby or Jada; she was a junior in an all-girls

Catholic school in Los Angeles when Kennedy was assassinated. She is fascinated that I knew them and asks me four questions for every one I ask her. Chastity looks something like Jada, except better.

She refused to do Jada's tiger-rug hunch in the play. "Her show was nasty," Chastity says. "I'm more of a dancer." Chastity's best act is belly dancing, a subject she teaches at the University of Texas at Arlington. But like Jada she's come through some tough places—she remembers stripping in the Lariat Bar in Wyoming while a three-piece Western band played "Won't You Ride in My Little Red Wagon?"

"The club action in Dallas is different now than it was in Ruby's time," Chastity says. "There are still a few clip joints like Ruby ran, and there are three, maybe four, traditional strip places where you can go watch a show and not get hustled. The big thing now is topless. The traditional strip show—we call it parading—is dying out. It's sort of sad. It is an American tradition, but it dates back to the forties and fifties when you couldn't see ass or boobs walking down the street."

Although she never knew Jack Ruby, Chastity had heard of him for years from her agent, Pappy Dolsen. Pappy was one of Ruby's contemporaries, an old-time club owner and booking agent, a gentleman tough from a truly tough time. Pappy had told the story many times how Ruby telephoned him the day before Oswald was killed and said: "I know I did you wrong, Pappy, but I'll make it up to you. I'm going places in show business, and when I do, you're going with me."

Pappy has had a heart attack and is in the intensive care ward at Baylor Medical Hospital, but Chastity shows us a letter that Ruby had written to Pappy years ago. It said:

We regret, at this time, we are unable to book the "act" you have for us—I'm sure its as wonderful as you mention but the price is to fucking high. Hoping to confront you on a more senseable base in the future. I remain.

Jack Ruby

There is one more thing to do. Mark was six years old, a Dallas first-grader when Kennedy was murdered. He doesn't remember much of it. But there was an article in *Look*, written by a Fina Oil Company executive named Jack Shea, which mentioned that at one public school in Dallas, children cheered the news of the assassination. Jack Shea was a good Catholic and a top-level businessman, but his gut feeling that Dallas was big enough to hear the truth from one of its own was a serious miscalculation. Shea was fired. He is now a partner in a Los Angeles ad agency.

Jo and I named our son Shea after the Fina executive, and I was curious to read the article one more time. Funny, I had never told Mark or his sister Lea how Shea got his name. I hadn't thought about it for a long time. Too many things had happened.

Twelve years ago, when the first announcement that the President had been shot was broadcast over the PA system at Richardson Junior High School, Gertrude Hutter, an eighth-grade teacher, began crying. Bob Dudney, who is now a reporter for the *Times Herald*, recalled the moment. She turned her back long enough to compose herself, then addressed her class with these prophetic words:

"Children, we are entering into an age of violence. There is nothing we can do about it, but all of us must stay calm, and above all, civilized."

HOW I SOLVED THE KENNEDY ASSASSINATION

★

Joe Bob Briggs

IT WAS WHILE I WAS IN THE CORPUS CHRISTI JAIL THAT I solved the Kennedy Assassination. I know it's a familiar story, so I'll just go over the outlines here. A lot of people don't realize that solving the Kennedy Assassination wasn't my first choice when I got to prison. For the first six months I was there, I pressed license plates by hand. Then I got a year added on to my sentence cause it's illegal to make license plates at that prison. While I was workin off my solitary, I learned to play blues guitar, harmonica, and tuba. Sometimes I would play blues tuba, but I had to stop cause all the black inmates were getting p.o.ed at me. After that I started collecting Fudgsicle sticks and building an Egyptian pyramid, but the warden put a stop to that. He said, in the future, if I wanted to build Egyptian pyramids in my cell, I would have to take the Fudgsicles off the sticks first. You can see the kind of constant persecution I had here, just like Burt Lancaster in

The Birdman of Alcatraz, where he spends his whole life fighting the tweeter-haters.

I guess I'll always remember where I was when they told me President Kennedy was dead. I was in the Corpus Christi Jail and it was August 17, 1969. I guess I'd been doing about nine months worth of "time" (that's what we called it on the inside) before it hit me one day and I said, "Hey, I'm in prison. This is kind of interesting."

And my hard-boiled cellmate, a guy named "The Rock" cause his head looked exactly like a piece of crumbly shale with graffiti all over it, said, kinda sarcastic, "Yeah, they killed Kennedy, too."

"They did?"

Six years since it happened and *nobody told me*.

"What'll happen to Jackie?" I said.

And The Rock said something totally disgusting about Jackie's pill-box hat, and I had to attack his brass knuckles with my face in order to teach him a lesson.

It was while I was in the prison infirmary that I first started piecing the facts together. Here's what I was able to find out from newspaper accounts, library books, the complete report of the Warren Commission, and stuff I heard in the men's bathroom:

1. Kennedy and Jackie go to Dallas.

2. Kennedy gets sick on the plane, but nobody thinks much about it.

3. On final approach, Kennedy turns to Jackie and says, "Do you realize there are seven letters in 'Kennedy' *and* seven letters in 'Lincoln,' that Lincoln was killed on a Friday by a lone gunman shooting at the back of his head, and that Lincoln was succeeded by a Vice President named 'Johnson'?"

4. Jackie replies, "Oh, honey, don't be silly. A lot of names have seven letters. Like, oh, 'Onassis.'"

5. At 9:45 A.M., Lee Harvey Oswald reports to his job at the Texas School Book Depository and starts mouthing off about the "Fair Play for Aruba Committee," an extremist political group dedicated to the violent overthrow of tourist casinos in Venezuela. His co-workers

ignore him. One of them says, "Fuck Aruba." No one notices that Oswald is carrying a 32-millimeter semi-automatic Czechoslovakian-made shoulder cannon.

6. At 11:47 A.M., JFK says, "Hey, let's take the convertible, what do you think?"

7. At 12:07 P.M., Secret Service Agent-in-Charge Ivan Vladimirovich Kunyetsov leans over to JFK and says, "Mr. President, John Connally says he wants to ride in the front seat." The President gets a pained expression on his face, but finally says, "Okay, but I get the front seat on the way back." (This part always brings a tear to my eye, because, of course, as we all know, there would be no "way back" that fateful day.)

8. At 12:14 P.M., the President tells his driver to stop so he can get out of the car, walk over to a young boy holding a "We Love You, Jack" sign, and give him a quarter. The boy stares up into the President's eyes, takes the quarter, and gives the President a plastic bag containing one-fourth ounce of marijuana.

9. At 12:19, as the motorcade rolls past the gaily decorated buildings on Main Street, Lee Harvey Oswald shoves nine crates of *Dick and Jane* readers and two crates of *This Wonderful World!* seventh-grade science books into position next to an unopened bag of French fries, left on the windowsill that will serve as his grisly lunch table. A co-worker happens by, notices Oswald erecting a telescopic sight for a laser-guided hand-held missile, and says, "Are you gonna eat those greasy fries? Yecccch!" Little did he know that Oswald would have no time for more than six or seven fries on this day.

10. As the President's limo approaches Dealey Plaza from the east, a right-wing photographer for the *Dallas Morning News* takes up his position atop the Triple Underpass, where he opens a camera case and starts carefully unloading his venom.

11. At 12:31, the motorcade makes a complicated zig-zag motion through Dealey Plaza, and at that moment Jackie looks up at the Texas School Book Depository and says, "Oh, look, isn't that a pretty

Czechoslovakian shoulder cannon?" In the front seat, Governor John Connally turns to his left so that he can speak over his shoulder to the President and says, "You *always* get to ride in the front."

12. At 12:32, Secret Service Agent Yuri Jakov jumps onto the running board of the President's limousine, jumps off again, and says, "Gee, this is fun."

13. At 12:33, an overweight man carrying an umbrella stands at the corner of Elm and Houston, absentmindedly massaging the crotch of his trousers. Several people notice, but say nothing.

14. At 12:34, in suburban Irving, Marina Oswald flips through a yellowed copy of *Life* magazine, comes across a photograph of Connie Francis, and feels a sudden sensation of horror and dread.

15. At 12:35, a manhole cover in the middle of Elm Street, just 20 yards from the Grassy Knoll, goes unnoticed by everyone.

16. At 12:36, Abraham Zapruder presses the button on his Bell & Howell home-movie camera and says, "I hope Jackie has one of them strapless numbers on."

17. At 12:37, with the presidential limousine moving forward at 11.2 miles an hour and approaching the Triple Underpass, Lyndon Baines Johnson, two cars behind the President, notices the unmistakable sound of a Czechoslovakian shoulder cannon being fired rapidly. He says, "They must be some good squirrel-huntin around here."

18. At 12:38, it's all over. The Prez disappears off the map of human history.

19. At 12:41, Lee Harvey Oswald walks downstairs, gathers together eight or nine of his co-workers, and says, "I was just up there shootin off my shoulder cannon and I accidentally killed the President." No one thinks this is odd.

20. At 12:49, Oswald decides to ride the bus to the Texas Theater and take in an Abbott and Costello double feature. He takes his pistol with him, in case they show the one where they land on Venus and start playing footsie with Anita Ekberg.

21. At 1:01 p.m., emergency-room doctors at Parkland Hospital diag-

nose the President as suffering from three gigantic shoulder-cannon wounds to the head and neck.

22. At 1:20, the opening titles roll for *Abbott and Costello Meet the Mummy*. Enraged, Oswald starts firing his pistol at the screen, killing a Dallas police officer in the process.

23. At 2:05, Jack Ruby, a Dallas nightclub owner, walks into the entertainment department of the *Dallas Times Herald* and says, "Wait till you see the titties on this one."

24. Two days later, Jack Ruby says, "Don't scrunch up the side of your face like that if you know what's good for you," and pumps three bullets into the abdomen of Lee Harvey Oswald. Oswald says, "I did it for Aruba." Nobody thinks this is odd.

25. Two weeks later, three casinos in Aruba close forever.

26. Four years later, the Warren Commission enters its final report. "One man, acting alone." Who that man was, we'll probly never know.

And that's basically the story we all know, the one we grew up with, the one they teach in school.

But is it the *whole* story?

No way, José.

No way, José Napoleon Duarte.

As I say, I had six months solitary to consider the facts of this case, then another two, three months in the infirmary, so I think I can say with authority that I'm the world's leading prison authority on the Kennedy Assassination, except for the people directly involved in the conspiracy, of course.

And I won't go into all my sources, except to say I read the following books in their entirety:

The President Is Dead! The President Is Dead! by Kurt Withers, former special assistant to the assistant district attorney, Dallas County, Texas.

The Assassination Please Almanac, edited by Tom Miller, the master himself.

Jack You Devil: My Life With Jack Ruby by Heather "Hooters" Lee.

How the Dirty Commies Did It by John Wayne, as told to Irving Reinfeld.

Conspiracy? Murder? Just a Guy With a Cannon? and Other Misleading Information About November 21, 1963 by Bob Woodward, as told to his wife, Babs.

Please Forgive My Bullet: What Really Happened Out There by Marina Oswald, as told to Mikhail Stepanovich Grigorin.

El Presidente Morte by de Manuel Olivares, Washington bureau chief for the respected *Diario Castro de Havana.*

Rush to Judgment by Mark Lane.

Highlights from Rush to Judgment by Mark Lane.

Another Rush to Judgment Book He Put Out Right After That One by Mark Lane.

The Warren Commission Report: Boy, Did Those Guys Blow It! by Stan Silver, Earl Warren's brother-in-law from Milwaukee.

Who Is Dealey Anyway? The Story of Dealey Plaza by Joe B. Dealey.

Who Screwed Up? by Jack "Dogface" Strindberg, special agent-in-charge, Dallas FBI assigned to the "Oswald, Lee Harvey" section.

He's Not Really Dead by Sister Mary Ignatius Candelaria, deceased.

It Sounded Like Squirrel Huntin to Me by Lyndon Baines Johnson.

And, of course, I went back and read all the back issues of *What Will They Dig Up Next?* the official journal of the assassination conspiracy binness, and based on all my research, I decided we had *quite a few* unanswered questions out there. Like:

Numero Uno: Who was really the President in 1963? They say Kennedy now, but it's been a long time and who can remember dates like that? Try this trick on yourself. Was Warren G. Harding President in 1914 or 1924? See? You don't know, do you? And it could mean a difference of *ten years* in our understanding of history. So take Kennedy, he could of been President in '53, '63, '73. Who the heck remembers now?

Numero Two-o: It's well known that many people keep Czechoslovakian-made shoulder cannons in the back of their pickups for routine weasel hunting. Why did Lee Harvey Oswald buy his in Russia?

Numero Three-o: Did Jackie really expect to get away with those shoes?

Course, I had to wait until my parole to actually go check out the Conspiracy situation up in Dallas, but once I did I made a beeline for the Oswald rooming house on Beckley Avenue, which is where I started my investigation. When I got there—and we're talking May 21, 1970, for all the historians in the audience—there were quite a few hippies living upstairs, throwing fairy dust on each other and watching Peter Fonda movies. As far as I know, these hippies have never been explained. But I questioned several of them extensively, researched all their astrological signs, and discovered that, of the 14 hippies living upstairs in the Oswald rooming house, 13 had never heard of Lee Harvey Oswald. The 14th, a pale and sickly woman named Lucille "Aqualung" Pisces, told me that on the afternoon of November 22, 1963, she was attending fourth-period classes at Vince Lombardi Junior High School in Mason, Georgia. I subsequently traveled to the aforementioned junior high and verified that the woman's story was, in fact, correct. Lucille Pisces also entrusted me with the information that one night, while rooting around on the floor listening to Grateful Dead music and doing "The Gator," she noticed one of those trick fountain pens that have nekkid ladies inside the glass part, resting against a windowsill, coated with cobwebs. On one side of the pen, stamped in gold, it read:

MANNY'S WEAPON PHOTOGRAPHY
WE MAKE YOUR GUN LOOK LIKE A MEMBER OF "THE FAMILY"
403 W. JEFFERSON
"DON'T SHOOT, JUST TOOT"

At first glance it looked like just a plain old ordinary ad for a gun-photo studio. They're all over that part of Dallas. But then I remembered: Lee Harvey liked to have his picture made with *all* his guns. It was kind of a hobby with him. If this place was still there, then maybe, just maybe . . .

"Sure I remember him," said Floyce Viridiana, a robust woman who looked like she just loaned out her lower body for trampoline practice. "He was the skinny kid that always came in here mumbling about howitzer ammunition."

"What caliber?"

"Forty-sevens. What else?"

"That's him. And what did he want from you?"

"Just the usual. Pictures of him with his Mannlicher pump-action with telescopic. Him with his .38 Smith & Wesson. Him with his Czechoslovakian shoulder cannon."

"Did you say Czechoslovakian shoulder cannon?"

"Right. You know, the kind they use for weasels."

"What did it have on it?"

"If I remember right, he had a laser-guided telescopic sight with a little engraving on top of it."

"An engraving?"

"Yeah. Something like 'This one's for you, Jack.'"

"'This one's for you, Jack'?"

"Yeah. 'This one's for you, Jack.' We never could figure out what it meant."

"Probly something personal."

"I wouldn't know about that, Mr. Briggs."

So there I had my first clue. Evidently Oswald had traveled to the gun-photo shop on Jefferson Street with the *express* intention of having himself photographed with a Czechoslovakian shoulder cannon. We didn't know it was the *same* cannon yet. But we knew it had a distinctive marking on the telescopic sight. Now all we had to do was find this *Jack* guy.

"Thank you very much, Floyce. By the way, did you happen to keep the negatives of this picture of the Czech shoulder cannon?"

"Yes, sir, I always do."

"Would you mind if I took a look at those?"

"I'm sorry, sir, but that would be an ethics violation for those of us in the gun-pitcher binness. You know, sometimes people like to get *comfortable* with their gun, if you know what I mean, before we snap the picture."

"I suppose you're speaking of *in flagrante torpedo?*"

"That's right. I wouldn't wanta be responsible for somebody getting caught with their pump-loader exposed."

"No, ma'am, we wouldn't want that."

"Sorry."

"I don't guess you'd show it to me if I exposed my pump-loader, would you?"

After I had all the buckshot surgically removed from my hiney, I went on to the next phase of the investigation, which was to trace the origins of the slogan "'This one's for you, Jack.'"

To do this I went directly to the Dallas Public Library and read the complete works of A. C. Greene, because A. C. Greene wrote all the books in the Dallas Public Library, beginning with *Famous Drunk Indians That Visited Dallas in the 1860's and Got Killed With Muskets*, continuing right on through *Dallas in the Eighties: Gimme Some Money*. What I was searching for was any book with a reference to this mysterious "Jack." I suppose I read books for durn near two weeks before I finally came to one solitary entry:

Jack Brangus, also known as "Jack" and "Hatrack Jack," Women's Clothing Department, Neiman-Marcus; accused in 1964 of physically attacking a boutique customer with a Masonite hatrack; cleared by the Dallas County Grand Jury after seven weeks of testimony; previously known as the designer of a white-satin rose-petal headdress once worn by Mae West; originated the slogan "Don't crochet with lamé."

That was it—all that was known about the man. But somehow, I don't know, I just had a hunch about Hatrack Jack, and so I set out to find him. I tried Neiman-Marcus, but nobody wanted to talk.

"Listen, buddy," said Sylvia Swanson, head of costume jewelry, "you ask too many questions about Hatrack Jack and you're gonna wish you hadn't."

"Oh yeah?" I said.

"Listen, I don't know if you've ever heard of black egret feathers fitted on a black velvet gown that flares at the knees and squeezes the bodice, but I saw that done to somebody one time and it's not a pretty sight."

"I think I heard about that case."

"Sure you did. Everybody did. Those egret feathers were famous. They knew a dress designer did it, or at least somebody *posing* as a dress designer. And I would say about 99 point 9 per cent of us thought it was Hatrack Jack."

"Is that right?"

"Not that we could ever prove anything, mind you."

"Sure."

"So you see what you're dealing with here?"

"Satin Lastex on an Esther Williams bathing suit?"

"Right. That kind of thing. Killer fabrics."

"I'll remember that."

But not all the Neiman's employees were so cautious. Finally, an assistant cashier in the Ridiculous Belts Department pulled me aside and said, "Hey, did I hear you asking about Hatrack Jack?"

"Maybe. What's it to you?"

"I know where you can find him."

"And it's gonna cost me, right?"

"That depends on you."

"Oh, yeah. Depends on me what?"

"Depends on whether you'll expose your pump-loader or not."

Three days later, I had the address I needed. It was a run-down tenement in East Dallas with a sign out front that said "Rooms for Free." As soon as I stepped inside, I felt like I was stepping into a run-down tenement in East Dallas.

"Anybody home?" I said.

Three rats convened a rodent convention under the stairwell and elected me the social director.

"Yoohoo! Anybody here?"

Upstairs I heard the unmistakable sound of pro basketball, as though ten massive bodies were jostling for a rebound. I made a few tentative steps up the stairs, then stopped with a jolt.

Suddenly the door at the top of the stairs swung open and a high-pitched, nasal voice said, "Somebody down there?"

"Yes, I'm looking for Mr. Hatrack Jack Brangus. Does he live here?"

There was a moment of silence, and then, "Wait just a minute."

I waited maybe ten minutes, and finally Mr. Brangus emerged from his room. He looked like he'd been making French toast.

"Sorry it took so long," he said. "I had a professional basketball team in my room."

"So I noticed."

"Soooooooooooooo. What can I do for you?"

I immediately noticed that Mr. Hatrack Jack Brangus put twelve extra o's in the word "so."

I said, "Depends on you."

"Well, I'm not exposing my pump-loader, if *that's* what you're after."

"No, no, nothing like that. All I need is a little information."

"Yeah."

"On Lee Harvey."

Suddenly Hatrack Jack's face turned the color of a three-day-old Hostess Twinkie.

"Not . . . not . . ."

"*That's right, Brangus—Lee Harvey Oswald!*"

Suddenly Hatrack Jack's arms turned the color of an engorged walrus.

"How did you find me?"

His voice sounded pathetic, like the sound of a baby hamster being forced into a Vienna Sausage can.

"So you know something, do you?" I said.

"Did they already tell you about the ostrich neck-ruffs and draped oversleeves?"

"Ostrich? I heard about some *egret* feathers."

"*Not the ones on the lace Medici collars and seed-pearl arabesques!*"

The man was crumbling into a little pile of catalogue copy, right before my very eyes, so I grabbed him by the collar and shook him and said, "Okay, Hatrack, get ahold of yourself. Whatever you got to say, you can say it to me. But I'm not leaving till I find out what's going on here."

He looked frightened by my manly brusqueness.

"Okay," I said, "let's start with these ostrich neck-ruffs."

He swallowed the lump in his throat, stared up at me with trembling eyes, and spilled his guts.

Before he started to confess, I made him go get a mop and pail and clean up his guts.

"The neck-ruffs were nothing really," he said. "It started innocently enough. One day I was hanging around Women's Jewelry and I picked up this set of pigeon-egg pearls. They were darling—you should of seen them. It was *nothing*. I mean who cares, right?"

"And what did you do with aforesaid pigeon-egg pearls?"

"I'm getting to that. I'm *getting* to it. Don't you see how hard this is for me? Don't you have just a *little* compassion for a man in my position?"

"Okay, okay."

"So what happens? The woman behind the counter, a dear dear woman, Aubrey Bohannon Davies, she says to me, 'Have you seen the white lacquered wig we have to go with those?' You know, just kidding around. She didn't mean anything by it. And then . . . and then . . . I don't know if I can do this."

"Brangus, you're gonna tell me what you did with those pigeon-egg pearls and that white lacquered wig or else we're gonna march over to Stanley Marcus's house and you're gonna have to tell *him*."

"No, no, not that. Okay, okay, I'll talk. . . . So I put on the pearls."

"You *what*?"

"It was just *one* little string of pigeon eggs. At least at first."

"And what about later?"

"Do we have to go into all of it?" he whined.

"All of it."

"Then I put on the white lacquered wig and did the Dance of the Seven Veils."

"Right there in the store?"

"Right there in the store. You know, just horsing around."

"Without any *music*?"

"Right. No music. No warning. I just put on the wig and started doing the Dance of the Seven Veils."

"You expect me to believe that?"

"I don't care if you believe it or not. It happens to be true."

"What did you use for veils?"

"Peacock feathers."

"Not *real* peacock feathers."

"No, no, of course not. That was much later. Imitation peacock feathers."

"And what happened when you did the Dance of the Seven Veils?"

"Nothing at first. That's why it was so *seductive*. Nobody seemed to mind. Aubrey didn't mind. Phil *certainly* didn't mind."

"Who's Phil?"

"He used to get the peacock feathers for me."

"Oh."

"But then it started to become a sickness. I don't know how it happens. One day it's pigeon-egg pearls and peacock feathers, the next day it's embroidered chiffon and ruby-stone berry beads. You don't know what's happening to you. I used to excuse myself three or four times a day, go into the private dressing rooms, and get a taffeta fix. I remember one time I was so deep into 'dressing-up' that I wrapped a red velvet evening gown, with white ermine collar and cuffs, in a gold-foil package so we could go in the back and 'play Santa Claus.'"

"That's *disgusting*."

"But you must understand. It's a disease. It's beyond your control.

You get to a point where you have to sniff the chinchilla twice a day or else you get the shakes. Have you ever seen a silk-brocade junkie with Joan Crawford shoulders?"

"No, can't say that I have."

"The shoulders get that way from constant exposure to laurel-leaf epaulets. Some people get permanent spinal injuries. I've seen two cases of paraplegia."

"And this really happened to you? You were that far gone?"

"Are you kidding? I used to go over to Cosmetics and *beg* for porcelain makeup on my eyelids. That was after I got into the heavy stuff—Harlow white-satin halter necks, marabou stoles, bugle-bead skullcaps. And, of course, so much chiffon I can't even remember. Chiffon is the worst. There's no way to stop once you get started. You either run out of money or you run out of chiffon. That's the only way you'll get off the stuff."

"So you were drowning in chiffon?"

"Honey, I was *swathed* in it."

"So how did it all end?"

"It ended"—and he looked at me with fear and dread, like I was a used wool pants suit on the discount rack at Kmart—"with the Assassination."

Could I have a little hokey Jack Webb music here please?

"Just as I thought," I said.

"I had this customer. 'Dorothy Lamour.' That wasn't her real name, of course, it's just what we called her. She'd come in two, three times a week, usually wrapped in sarongs. A beautiful woman. A real dear. Ostrich fronds out the kazoo. Anyway, Dorothy would come in and model spangled organdy for the children on Saturdays. That's the kind of person she was. But she was a strange person in other ways. She had a temper. She could get bent out of shape over little things, like whether it's okay to put pleated ruffles on butterfly sleeves."

"I wouldn't exactly call that a *little* thing."

"Well, no, that's not a very good example. But one time she was looking at a leopard-print crepe and considering it for the accessories that go with a black-satin ensemble, and I said, 'Honey, we're talking beauty disaster,' and she flew into an absolute rage over it. But I ask you, was I wrong? Leopard-print crepe with black satin. Of course I was right."

"It does sound like she was a little cockeyed."

"Okay, so you see what I was dealing with. But there was one subject we could never, never, *ever* mention around Dorothy."

"Yeah?"

"And that was Jacqueline Kennedy."

"Jackie?"

"Dorothy thought she was a fashion reptile."

"You're speaking figuratively, of course?"

"No, Dorothy was of the opinion that Jackie hunted flies with her tongue when it came to dressing for dinner."

"I see."

"It first started with the whole Oleg Cassini thing. Jackie would go to Paris and come back with these aquamarine frocky things, and Dorothy would be *hysterical* for a week. We'd have to use ermine to get her revived. Then, you probably remember what happened next."

"The pillbox hat?"

"Right. Dorothy started hyperventilating, and we had to tickle her soles with a feather boa. But even *that* wasn't the thing that did it. It was the shoes."

"I knew it."

"Jackie Shoes were too much for her. The first time I saw those pink pumps, I knew Dorothy would be coming in, ready to blow. But the strange thing about it, this time she just kind of sailed in and didn't say a word. She wandered over to Accessories, fingered a few alligator handbags, and then let out a big sigh. I knew what was on her mind, and so I said, 'Dorothy, I wouldn't get too upset. The woman is entitled to wear . . .' But Dorothy put her finger over my lips and said, 'Don't worry, dear, I've already handled it.' That was the last day I saw her."

"What? That's all?"

"The President came to Dallas three weeks later, and I guess you know the rest."

Hatrack started to sob. "*I could have stopped her. I could of done something.*"

"Now, now, it's not your fault," I told him. "Besides, we don't *know* that it has any connection."

"Oh, she wanted to kill her all right. She *despised* those square bodices. She would of done anything to get rid of that woman."

"Are you saying the woman known as 'Dorothy Lamour' actually pulled the trigger?"

"Pulled it, hired somebody to pull it, paid Castro to pull it—what difference does it make? Our President is dead."

"Hatrack?"

"Yes."

"Do you know where Dorothy Lamour is today?"

"Runs a weapon-photo studio down on West Jefferson."

"*What?!*"

"Why, you know the place?"

"Does she look like she rents out the lower half of her body for trampoline practice?"

"Sure, that's the woman. Floyce something."

"Floyce Viridiana. She's *Aruban*. She has ready access to photographs of guns. And do you know what she carved on Lee Harvey Oswald's Czechoslovakian shoulder cannon?"

"What?"

"'This one's for you, Jack.'"

"*Oh my God!*" cried Hatrack Jack, and apparently it was all the heart of this sad little man could handle. At that exact moment, he suffered a massive heart attack and collapsed into my arms. He would never live to dangle another bangle.

I don't know why I never turned Floyce in. By that time I guess I'd fallen in love with her. I drove back out to Jefferson Street, parked my car, tried to summon up the courage to go inside and tell her I knew about Hatrack Jack, but something about the guy's story had pierced through me. There was a sadness about it, something that said, "Okay, okay, the lady was right. Everybody *hated* those shoes." There was a certain justice to the whole deal, especially since the wishes of Floyce Viridiana had been frustrated by God. He took our President, but he freed Jackie to shop again. What the heck, I thought. It's no skin off my nose. And until now, I never told a soul what I found out in the little East Dallas tenement that day. But I would always remember the great lesson of the Kennedy Assassination:

Never mix textured fabrics with paisley.

I BOUGHT A LITTLE CITY

★

Donald Barthelme

S O I BOUGHT A LITTLE CITY (IT WAS GALVESTON, TEXAS) AND told everybody that nobody had to move, we were going to do it just gradually, very relaxed, no big changes overnight. They were pleased and suspicious. I walked down to the harbor where there were cotton warehouses and fish markets and all sorts of installations having to do with the spread of petroleum throughout the Free World, and I thought, A few apple trees here might be nice. Then I walked out this broad boulevard which has all these tall thick palm trees maybe forty feet high in the center and oleanders on both sides, it runs for blocks and blocks and ends up opening up to the broad Gulf of Mexico— stately homes on both sides and a big Catholic church that looks more like a mosque and the Bishop's Palace and a handsome red brick affair where the Shriners meet. I thought, What a nice little city, it suits me fine.

It suited me fine so I started to change it. But softly, softly. I asked some folks to move out of a whole city block on I Street, and then I tore down their houses. I put the people into the Galvez Hotel, which is the nicest hotel in town, right on the seawall, and I made sure that every room had a beautiful view. Those people had wanted to stay at the Galvez Hotel all their lives and never had a chance before because they didn't have the money. They were delighted. I tore down their houses and made that empty block a park. We planted it all to hell and put some nice green iron benches in it and a little fountain—all standard stuff, we didn't try to be imaginative.

I was pleased. All the people who lived in the four blocks surrounding the empty block had something they hadn't had before, a park. They could sit in it, and like that. I went and watched them sitting in it. There was already a black man there playing bongo drums. I hate bongo drums. I started to tell him to stop playing those goddamn bongo drums but then I said to myself, No, that's not right. You got to let him play his goddamn bongo drums if he feels like it, it's part of the misery of democracy, to which I subscribe. Then I started thinking about new housing for the people I had displaced, they couldn't stay in that fancy hotel forever.

But I didn't have any ideas about new housing, except that it shouldn't be too imaginative. So I got to talking to one of these people, one of the ones we had moved out, guy by the name of Bill Caulfield who worked in a wholesale-tobacco place down on Mechanic Street.

"So what kind of a place would you like to live in?" I asked him.

"Well," he said, "not too big."

"Uh-huh."

"Maybe with a veranda around three sides," he said, "so we could sit on it and look out. A screened porch, maybe."

"Whatcha going to look out at?"

"Maybe some trees and, you know, the lawn."

"So you want some ground around the house."

"That would be nice, yeah."

"'Bout how much ground are you thinking of?"

"Well, not too much."

"You see, the problem is, there's only x amount of ground and everybody's going to want to have it to look at and at the same time they don't want to be staring at the neighbors. Private looking, that's the thing."

"Well, yes," he said. "I'd like it to be kind of private."

"Well," I said, "get a pencil and let's see what we can work out."

We started with what there was going to be to look at, which was damned difficult. Because when you look you don't want to be able to look at just one thing, you want to be able to shift your gaze. You need to be able to look at at least three things, maybe four. Bill Caulfield solved the problem. He showed me a box. I opened it up and inside was a jigsaw puzzle with a picture of the Mona Lisa on it.

"Lookee here," he said. "If each piece of ground was like a piece of this-here puzzle, and the tree line on each piece of property followed the outline of a piece of the puzzle—well, there you have it, Q.E.D. and that's all she wrote."

"Fine," I said. "Where are the folk going to park their cars?"

"In the vast underground parking facility," he said.

"O.K., but how does each householder gain access to his household?"

"The tree lines are double and shade beautifully paved walkways possibly bordered with begonias," he said.

"A lurkway for potential muggists and rapers," I pointed out.

"There won't be any such," Caulfield said, "because you've bought our whole city and won't allow that class of person to hang out here no more."

That was right. I had bought the whole city and could probably do that. I had forgotten.

"Well," I said finally, "let's give 'er a try. The only thing I don't like about it is that it seems a little imaginative."

We did and it didn't work out badly. There was only one complaint. A man named A. G. Bartie came to see me.

"Listen," he said, his eyes either gleaming or burning, I couldn't tell which, it was a cloudy day, "I feel like I'm living in this gigantic jiveass jigsaw puzzle."

He was right. Seen from the air, he was living in the middle of a titanic reproduction of the Mona Lisa, too, but I thought it best not to mention that. We allowed him to square off his property into a standard 60 x 100 foot lot and later some other people did that too—some people just like rectangles, I guess. I must say it improved the concept. You run across an occasional rectangle in Shady Oaks (we didn't want to call the development anything too imaginative) and it surprises you. That's nice.

I said to myself:

Got a little city

Ain't it pretty

By now I had exercised my proprietorship so lightly and if I do say so myself tactfully that I wondered if I was enjoying myself enough (and I had paid a heavy penny too—near to half my fortune). So I went out on the streets then and shot six thousand dogs. This gave me great satisfaction and you have no idea how wonderfully it improved the city for the better. This left us with a dog population of 165,000, as opposed to a human population of something like 89,000. Then I went down to the Galveston *News*, the morning paper, and wrote an editorial denouncing myself as the vilest creature the good God had ever placed upon the earth, and were we, the citizens of this fine community, who were after all free Americans of whatever race or creed, going to sit still while one man, *one man*, if indeed so vile a critter could be so called, etc. etc.? I gave it to the city desk and told them I wanted it on the front page in fourteen-point type, boxed. I did this just in case they might have hesitated to do it themselves, and because I'd seen that Orson Welles picture where the guy writes a nasty notice about his own wife's terrible singing, which I always thought was pretty decent of him, from some points of view.

A man whose dog I'd shot came to see me.

"You shot Butch," he said.

"Butch? Which one was Butch?"

"One brown ear and one white ear," he said. "Very friendly."

"Mister," I said, "I've just shot six thousand dogs, and you expect me to remember Butch?"

"Butch was all Nancy and me had," he said. "We never had no children."

"Well, I'm sorry about that," I said, "but I own this city."

"I know that," he said.

"I am the sole owner and I make all the rules."

"They told me," he said.

"I'm sorry about Butch but he got in the way of the big campaign. You ought to have had him on a leash."

"I don't deny it," he said.

"You ought to have had him inside the house."

"He was just a poor animal that had to go out sometimes."

"And mess up the streets something awful?"

"Well," he said, "it's a problem. I just wanted to tell you how I feel."

"You didn't tell me," I said. "How do you feel?"

"I feel like bustin' your head," he said, and showed me a short length of pipe he had brought along for the purpose.

"But of course if you do that you're going to get your ass in a lot of trouble," I said.

"I realize that."

"It would make you feel better, but then I own the jail and the judge and the police and the local chapter of the American Civil Liberties Union. All mine. I could hit you with a writ of mandamus."

"You wouldn't do that."

"I've been known to do worse."

"You're a black-hearted man," he said. "I guess that's it. You'll roast in Hell in the eternal flames and there will be no mercy or cooling drafts from any quarter."

He went away happy with this explanation. I was happy to be a black-hearted man in his mind if that would satisfy the issue between us because that was a bad-looking piece of pipe he had there and I was still six thousand dogs ahead of the game, in a sense. So I owned this little city which was very, very pretty and I couldn't think of any more new innovations just then or none that wouldn't get me punctuated like the late Huey P. Long, former governor of Louisiana. The thing is, I had fallen in love with Sam Hong's wife. I had wandered into this store on Tremont Street where they sold Oriental novelties, paper lanterns, and cheap china and bamboo birdcages and wicker footstools and all that kind of thing. She was smaller than I was and I thought I had never seen that much goodness in a woman's face before. It was hard to credit. It was the best face I'd ever seen.

"I can't do that," she said, "because I am married to Sam."

"Sam?"

She pointed over to the cash register where there was a Chinese man, young and intelligent-looking and pouring that intelligent look at me with considered unfriendliness.

"Well, that's dismal news," I said. "Tell me, do you love me?"

"A little bit," she said, "but Sam is wise and kind and we have one and one-third lovely children."

She didn't look pregnant but I congratulated her anyhow, and then went out on the street and found a cop and sent him down to H Street to get me a bucket of Colonel Sanders' Kentucky Fried Chicken, extra crispy. I did that just out of meanness. He was humiliated but he had no choice. I thought:

I own a little city

Awful pretty

Can't help people

Can hurt them though

Shoot their dogs

Mess 'em up

Be imaginative

Plant trees

Best to leave 'em alone?

Who decides?

Sam's wife is Sam's wife and coveting

Is not nice.

So I ate the Colonel Sanders' Kentucky Fried Chicken, extra crispy, and sold Galveston, Texas, back to the interests. I took a bath on that deal, there's no denying it, but I learned something—don't play God. A lot of other people already knew that, but I have never doubted for a minute that a lot of other people are smarter than me, and figure things out quicker, and have grace and statistical norms on their side. Probably I went wrong by being too imaginative, although really I was guarding against that. I did very little, I was fairly restrained. God does a lot worse things, every day, in one little family, any family, than I did in that whole little city. But He's got a better imagination than I do. For instance, I still covet Sam Hong's wife. That's torment. Still covet Sam Hong's wife, and probably always will. It's like having a tooth pulled. For a year. The same tooth. That's a sample of His imagination. It's powerful.

So what happened? What happened was that I took the other half of my fortune and went to Galena Park, Texas, and lived inconspicuously there, and when they asked me to run for the school board I said No, I don't have any children.

REDFISH

★

Rick Bass

CUBA LIBRES ARE MADE WITH RUM, DIET COKE, AND LIME juice. Kirby showed them to me, and someone, I am sure, showed them to him. They've probably been around forever, the way everything has. But the first time we really drank them was late at night on the beach in Galveston. There was a high wind coming off the water, and we had a fire roaring. I think that it felt good for Kirby to be away from Tricia for a while and I know that it felt good to be away from Houston.

We were fishing for red drum—redfish—and somewhere, out in the darkness, beyond where we could see, we had hurled our hooks and sinkers, baited with live shrimp. There was a big moon and the waves blew spray into our faces and we wore heavy coats, and our faces were orange, to one another, from the light of the big driftwood fire.

It is amazing, what washes in from the ocean. Everything in the

world ends up, I think, on a beach. Whales, palm trees, television sets.
. . . Kirby and I were sitting on a couch in the sand drinking the Cuba
Libres and watching our lines, waiting for the big redfish to hit. When
he did, or she, we were going to reel it in and then clean it there on
the beach, rinse it off in the waves, and then we were going to grill it,
on the big driftwood fire.

It was our first time to drink Cuba Libres, and we liked them even
better than margaritas. We had never caught redfish before, either, but
had read about it in a book. We had bought the couch for ten dollars
at a garage sale earlier in the day. We sank down deep into it and it was
easy, comfortable fishing. In the morning, when the tide started to go
out, we were going to wade-fish for speckled trout. We had read about
that, too, and that was the way you were supposed to do it. You were
supposed to go out into the waves after them. It sounded exciting. We
had bought waders and saltwater fishing licenses and saltwater
stamps, as well as the couch and the rum. We were going to get into a
run of speckled trout and catch our limit, and load the ice chest with
them, and take them back to Tricia, because Kirby had made her mad.

But first we were going to catch a big redfish. We wouldn't tell her
about the redfish, we decided. We would grill it and drink more Cuba
Libres and maybe take a short nap, before the tide changed, and we
had our sleeping bags laid out on the sand for that purpose. They
looked as if they had been washed ashore, too. It was December, and
about thirty degrees. We were on the southeast end of the bay and the
wind was strong. The flames from the fire were ten or twelve feet high,
but we couldn't get warm.

There was all the wood in the world, huge beams from ships and
who-knows-what, and we could make the fire as large as we wanted.
We kept waiting for the big redfish to seize our shrimp and run, to
scoot back down into the depths. The book said they were bottom
feeders.

It seemed, drinking the Cuba Libres, that it would happen at any
second. Kirby and Trish had gotten in a fight because Kirby had for-

gotten to feed the dogs that Saturday, while Trish was at work. Kirby said, drinking the Cuba Libres, that he had told her that what she was really mad about was the fact that she had to work that Saturday, while he had had the day off. (They both work in a bank, different banks, and handle money, and own sports cars.) Tricia had gotten really mad at that and had refused to feed the dogs.

So Kirby fed his dog but did not feed Tricia's. That was when Tricia got the maddest. Then they got into a fight about how Kirby's dog, a German Shepherd, ate so much more, about ten times more, than did Tricky Woodles, a Cocker spaniel, Tricia's dog. Good old Tricky Woo.

On the beach, Kirby had a pocketbook that identified fishes of the Gulf Coast, and after each drink we would look at it, turning to the page with the picture of the red drum. We would study it, sitting there on the couch, as if we were in high school again, and were studying for some silly exam, instead of being out in the real world, braving the elements, tackling nature, fishing for the mighty red drum. The book said they could go as much as thirty pounds.

"The elusive red drum!" Kirby shouted into the wind. We were only sipping the Cuba Libres, because they were so good, but they were adding up. They were new, and we had just discovered them, and we wanted as many of them as we could get.

"Elusive *and* wily!" I shouted. "Red E. Fish!"

Kirby's eyes darted and shifted like a cartoon character's, the way they did when he was really drunk, which meant he would be passing out soon.

"We could dynamite the ocean," he said. "We could throw grenades into the waves, and stun the fish. They would come rolling in with the waves then, all the fish in the world."

He stood up, fell in the sand, and still on his knees, poured another drink. "I really want to see one," he said.

We left our poles and wandered down the beach: jumping and stamping, it was so cold. The wind tried to blow us over. We found an ancient, upright lifeguard's tower, about twenty feet tall, and tried, in our drunkenness, to pull it down, to drag it over to our fire. It was as sturdy as iron, and had barnacles on it, from where it had spent some time in the sea. We cut our hands badly, but it was dark and cold, and we did not find that out until later.

We were a long way from our fire, and it looked a lot smaller, from where we were. The couch looked wrong, without us in it, sitting there by the fire, empty like that. Kirby started crying and said he was going home to Tricia but I told him to buck up and be a man. I didn't know what that meant or even what I meant by saying that, but I knew that I did not want him to leave. We had come in his car, the kind everyone our age in Houston drove, if they had a job, if they had even a little money—a white BMW—and I wanted to stay, and see what a red drum looked like in the flesh.

"I've an idea," I said. "Let's pull the tower down, and drag it over to the fire with the car."

"Yeah!" said Kirby. "Yeah!" Clouds were hurrying past the moon, something was blowing in quickly, but I could see that Kirby had straightened up some, and that he was not going to pass out.

It's been ten years since we were in high school. Some days, when I am with him, it seems that eternity still lies out in front of us; and other days, it seems that we've already died, somehow, and everything is over. Tricia is beautiful. She reminds me of that white sports car.

WE KICKED MOST OF THE SAND OFF OF OUR SHOES, AND GOT IN the car, and it started right up, the way it always did. It was a nice car, all right, and Kirby drove it to work every day—though work was only one-point-eight miles away—and he kept his briefcase in the back seat; but in the trunk, just thrown in, were all of the things he had always kept in his trunk in high school, things he thought he might need in an emergency.

There was a bow and arrows, a .22 rifle, a tomahawk, binoculars, a tire inflator, a billy club, some extra fishing poles, a tool box, some barbed wire, a bull riding rope, cowboy boots, a wrinkled, oily tuxedo which he had rented and never bothered to return, and there were other things, too—but it was the bull riding rope, which we attached to the tower, and to the back bumper of the little sports car, that came in handy this time.

Sand flew as the tires spun, and like some shy animal, the BMW quickly buried itself, up to the doors.

To the very end, I think Kirby believed that at any moment he was going to pull free, and break out of the sand, and pull the tower over: the engine screaming, the car shuddering and bucking . . . but it was sunk deep, when he gave up, and he had to crawl out through the window.

The Cuba Libres, and the roar of the wind, made it seem funny; we howled, as if it was something the car had done by itself, on its own.

"Let's take a picture and send it to Tricia," he said. I laughed, and winced too, a little, because I thought it was a bad sign that he was talking about her again, so much, so often, but he was happy, so we got the camera from the trunk, and because he did not have a flash attachment, we built another fire, stacked wood there by the tower, which is what we should have done in the first place.

We went back to get the couch, and our poles and sleeping bags, and the ice chest. I had worked, for a while, for a moving company, and I knew a trick so that I could carry on my back a couch, a refrigerator, or almost anything, and I showed it to Kirby, and he screamed, laughing, as I ran down the beach with the couch on my back, not able to see where I was going, carrying the couch like an ant with a leaf, coming dangerously close to the water. Kirby ran along behind me, screaming, carrying the other things, and when we had set up a new camp, we ran back and forth, carrying the larger pieces of burning logs, transferring the fire, too. We took a picture of the car by firelight.

Our hands and arms had dried blood on them almost all the way up to the elbows, from the barnacles, and we rinsed them off in the sea, which was not as cold as we had expected.

"I wish Tricia was here to see this," he said, more than once. The wind was blowing still harder, and the moon was gone entirely.

We got a new fire started, and were exhausted from all the effort; we fixed more drinks and slumped into the couch and raised our poles to cast out again, but stopped, realizing that the shrimp were gone; that something had stolen them.

The other shrimp were in a live well, in the trunk, so we re-baited. It was fun, reaching in the dark into the warm bubbling water of the bait bucket, and feeling the wild tiny shrimp leap about, fishtailing, trying to escape. It didn't matter which shrimp you got; you didn't even need to look. You just reached in, and caught whichever one leapt into your hand.

We baited the hooks, and cast out again. We were thirsty, so we fixed more drinks. We nodded off on the couch, and were awakened by the fire going down, and by snow, which was landing gently on our faces. It was just starting. It was beautiful, and we sat up, and then stood up, but didn't say anything. We reeled in and checked our hooks, and found that the shrimp were gone again.

Kirby looked out at the darkness, where surely the snowflakes were landing on the water, and he looked up at the sky, and could not stand the beauty.

"I'm going to try to hitchhike back to Houston," he said. He did not say her name but I know he was thinking of waking up with Tricia, and looking out the window, and seeing the snow, and everything being warm, inside the house, under the roof.

"No," I said. "Wait." Then I was cruel. "You'll just get in a fight again," I told him, though I knew it wasn't true: they were always wild to see each other after any kind of separation, even a day or two. I had to admit I was somewhat jealous of this.

"Wait a little longer, and we'll go out into the waves," I said.

"Yes," said Kirby. "Okay." Because we'd been thinking that would be the best part, the most fun: wade-fishing. We'd read about that, too, and Kirby had brought a throw net, with which to catch mullets for bait.

We'd read about wade-fishermen with long stringers of fish—the really successful fishermen—being followed by sharks and attacked, and so we were pretty terrified of the sharks, knowing that they could be down there among our legs, in the darkness and under water, where we could not see, following us: or that we could even walk right into the sharks. That idea of them being hidden, just beneath us—we didn't like it a bit, not knowing for sure if they were out there or not.

We fixed a new batch of Cuba Libres, using a lot of lime. We stood at the shore in our waders, the snow and wind coming hard into our faces, and drank them quickly, strongly, and poured some more, raced them down. It wasn't ocean any more, but snowdrift prairie, the Missouri breaks, or the Dakotas and beyond, and we waded out, men searching for game, holding the heavy poles high over our heads, dragging the great Bible cast-nets behind us.

The water was not very deep for a long time; for fifteen minutes it was only knee-deep, getting no deeper, and not yet time to think about sharks.

"I wish Tricia was here," said Kirby. The Cuba Libres were warm in our bellies; we'd used a lot of rum in the last ones. "I wish she was riding on my shoulders, piggy-back," he said.

"Nekkid," I said.

"Yes," said Kirby, picturing it, and he was happy, and even though I didn't really like Tricia, I thought how nice it would have been if she could have seen him then, sort of looking off and dreaming about it. I wished I had a girlfriend or wife on my back, too, then, to go along with all the other equipment I was carrying. I was thinking that she could hold the pole, and cast out, waiting for a bite, waiting for the big fight; and I could work the throw net, trying to catch fresh mullet, which we'd cut up into cubes, right there in the water, and use for fresh bait: because the bait had to be fresh.

It was like a murder or a sin, cutting the live mullet's head off, slicing the entrails out, filleting out a piece of still-barely-living meat and putting it on the hook, and then throwing the rest of the mullet away; throwing it behind you for the sharks, or whatever—head, fins, entrails, and left-over meat—casting your hook then far out into the waves and dark and snow, with that warm very fresh piece of flesh on the hook—it was like a sin, the worst of the animal kingdom, I thought, but if you caught what you were after, if you got the big redfish, then it was all right, it was possible that you were forgiven.

I wanted to catch the largest redfish in the world. I wanted to catch one so large that I'd have to wrestle it, maybe even stab it with the fillet knife, like Tarzan with the crocodiles.

Kirby looked tired. He had put on about twenty pounds since high school, and it was hard work, walking with the poles over our heads.

"Wait," I said. We stopped and caught our breath. It was hard to hear each other, with only the wind and waves around us; and except for the direction of the waves, splashing into our faces from the Gulf, we couldn't tell where shore was, or in which direction the ocean lay.

"I've an idea," said Kirby, still breathing heavily, looking back to where we were pretty sure the shore was. If our fire was still burning, we couldn't see it. "There's a place back up the beach that rents horses in the daytime. Some stables."

"They shoot horse thieves," I said. But I thought it was a wonderful idea. I was tired, too; I wasn't in as good a shape as I'd once been either.

"I'll go get them," I said, since I wasn't breathing quite as hard as he was. It was a tremendous picture: both of us on white horses, riding out into the waves, chest-deep, neck-deep, then the magic lift and float of the horse as it began to swim, the light feeling of nothing, no resistance.

Mares, they would be, noble and strong, capable of carrying foolish, drunken men out to sea on their journey, if they so desired, and
capable of bringing them back again, too.

"Yes," I said. "You stay here. I'll go find the horses."

Back on shore, walking up the beach to the stables, I stopped at a
pay phone, and dialed Tricia's number. The cold wind was rocking the
little phone booth, and there was much static on the line.

"Tricia," I said, disguising my voice, mumbling. "This is Kirby. I love
you." Then I hung up, and thought about how I really liked her after
all, and I went to look for the horses. It would be perfect.

We could ride around out in the gulf on the swimming horses until
they tired, casting and drinking, searching for what we were after,
pausing sometimes to lean forward and whisper kind things, encouragement, into the horses' ears, as they labored through the waves,
blowing hard through their nostrils, legs kicking and churning, swimming around in wide circles out in the gulf, in the darkness, the snow;
no doubt full of their own fears of sharks, of drowning, of going down
under too heavy of a load, and of all the things unseen, all the things
below.

BAD GIRLS

★

Harryette Mullen

T HERE WERE ALWAYS BAD GIRLS. FAST GIRLS. GIRLS WHO were "developed" at thirteen. Who surprised everyone with their sudden lovely breasts when other girls their age were still wearing undershirts. Who learned early how to take what God gave them and use it in devilish ways. They noticed how men would look at them, and they thought it gave them power they could use for themselves. They were hot enough to set a man on fire. They were the girls who most often got into trouble. Whose mamas never taught them better or who were just wild and fast and wouldn't listen.

The bad girls wore tight clothes and high-heeled shoes and smeared bright lipstick on their little girl faces. They streaked and tinted their hair and grew their fingernails long and pointed. Wore a different color of nail polish on each finger. They smoked cigarettes. They went to dances and stayed out late. Even in church they were giving some boy the eye. They had stiff bras that pointed and pushed out. Made you think about what was inside their clothes. The bad girls always sat with a boy in the balcony of the theater. When the movie was over, they would have to smooth their rumpled and disheveled clothing, pat down the mussed-up hairdo. They let the boys feel on their ass when they slowdanced. They were like bitch dogs, letting the boys sniff between their legs.

The fast-tailed girls were the bad examples that mothers preached against. The ones who broke their mamas' hearts. Who ran off and were never mentioned by their families anymore. They were the bad crowd it didn't do no good to run with. They were girls with a bad reputation. Girls no decent boy would be seen with. Girls who sneaked around at night doing sinful and nasty things. And it was going to ruin their lives. No one would want them after all the boys had "run through" them. They were girls who had cheapened themselves. Young Jezebels. Sluts, strumpets, whores, trollops, low-down dirty gals. Girls who would lie down anywhere, any time, for anybody. Who left their scent in the grass. Who were fucked behind bushes and in the backseat of cars. Who would just as soon hike their dresses up in an alley or a dark hallway 'cause they wore no drawers, and so they were always ready. They were young tramps. Girls who could be had "for a fish sandwich and a bottle of orange soda water."

Some of them had big legs and creamy skin. Brown, wavy hair tied back in a long ponytail with a red ribbon. Gray-green cat-colored eyes. Others were smooth, deep-black satin and thin as knifeblades. Their smiles cut a slice of flashing white in their nighttime faces. The whites of their eyes, rolling sad and slow in the dark face, could, without warning, slash at you suddenly with a cutting glance. Some were chubby brown girls with dimples or charming gaps in their teeth, who already looked maternal as hens. Who soon would have babies their mamas would raise.

The bad girls would go on welfare, or they might get involved with a pimp or with drugs, or both. They would make some more babies for their mamas to raise. Some of them would end up dead. Shot in the head by a crazy-jealous man or some man's jealous wife or stabbed in some free-for-all in some low-life dive. They might get picked up for shoplifting or hustling or writing bad checks. Some would go from man to man, collecting scars as they once had collected high school class rings from boyfriends, chunky, oversized rings strung on a chain around their neck.

They might shack up with a man who was as beat down and desperate as they were. They might live in alcoholic squalor in some low-rent, one-room apartment, or run-down, evil-smelling shotgun house. But no one expected that they would ever marry or prosper. It was agreed they would live lives of sin and shame. It was assumed they would never be happy. Certainly they had no respect—from others or for themselves.

And if one of them, grown up now, was seen walking down the street, shaking her behind and looking good in a tight purple dress, walking like she knew she was the finest-looking thing on the sidewalk, it was, "Well, it just ain't caught up with her yet." Or if she was heard laughing with a man, her gold tooth flashing as she held on to her drink in the Green Parrot Lounge or the China Doll Club, laughing a clean laugh with no sharp edges and fully enjoying the sound of her laughter, then it was, "Well, she's laughing now, but wait and see, there will come a time . . ." If somehow she got her hands on some money and opened her own club or beauty shop or steam table cafeteria, it was, "Where she get the money from to go into business for herself? Couldn't be any kind of honest money behind that."

Even if she finally settled down and married some man who didn't know or didn't care what she had been—some hard-working man who took in all her bastard children and brought his paycheck home every week. And even if she started going back to church again regular and joined the choir and tithed every Sunday, still the matrons, wearing pastel hats covered with chiffon flowers, would circle the preacher after the service and see to it she never hovered too close to the Reverend. Never shook his hand too long after a sermon on the wages of sin.

THE BATTLE OF THE ALAMO

Rafael Castillo

A T OUR TWENTY-YEAR CLASS REUNION, I FOUND OUT JULIO Berlanga had died in Viet Nam. They said Julio had been shot somewhere in the Quang Ngai Province. He hated people calling him Julio, said it reminded him of some relative he despised. So the guys in the barrio started calling him Berga. It had a funny ring to it. El Berga. Short for Berlanga.

I remember Berga. Who could honestly forget him. A big, burly guy with a skull-and-crossbones tattoo on his left arm, El Berga was a pachuco who didn't take shit from nobody. Tough as nails. I wouldn't doubt it if the big guy didn't take a couple of the bastards down before they took him out. They say he knew he was gonna die 'cause he had written a letter to his mother telling her to go ahead and give away the stereo and his Temptations albums. He even stopped writing home. They even said he had stopped writing to his girlfriend Sylvia. The moment old Berga left San Antonio in his Marine dress blues, she had a string of guys waiting to make the move. She was a looker, that Sylvia, a tall, slender girl with a big red mane and a slutty strut.

And do you think Berga didn't know?

Knowing Berga, the guy was just too smart, probably why he stopped writing to her. He had other girls, anyway.

I met Berga at Cooper Junior High, back then a feeder-school for the Voc-Tech misery that awaited our fates. I was a skinny kid weighing about a hundred and ten, with acne. But hey, who didn't have pimples. For most kids, Saturday nights were for cruising and Sundays for studying. In the '60s, street gangs were our problem.

The city was parcelled into neat little territories, turfs, and safe zones. Everything was buried in ritual and culture. Even fashion trends had a snail-like quality arriving to the fringes of the West Side because we were always about ten years behind the times. When the world had the Rolling Stones, we were still dancing the Twist—except for a few progressives.

I lived in the valley of El Con, between Calaveras and Sabinas streets, a tough neighborhood where crazy batos who ruled our barrio hung out around an old grocery store with a battered sign of a Big Ice Cream Cone. It was downright stupid, really. Then again, every generation does stupid things. "Con" was colloquial Spanish for Cone. No one knows why it was dubbed El Con, only that some candy-ass decided to call it, "El Con." And so, history began.

I guess, back then, everyone wanted to belong to a family. Even if it was just a bunch of guys.

Berga was from El Ghosttown, thirteen miles west of El Con and bad ass. Lots of toughs. Knives. Zip Guns. Souped-up Chevys. Heavy stuff. The ten o'clock news always carried something about the Ghosttown and how many kids had been arrested for gang fights and illegal possession of knives and beer. It didn't matter, anyway. No matter how many were arrested, a fresh crop of recruits was there to take over the turf. Everyone needed some sort of protection.

Our school was divided by groups: Pachucos, jocks, bookworms, and rejects. Now and then—and it was rare—some hippies with long hair and bell-bottoms would come down from Michigan or Wisconsin, and they'd soon assimilate into the culture and become homogenized like the rest of us.

As for me, I made friends with all the groups, especially the jocks and the pachucos. I wanted to survive whatever onslaught came my way. But Berga had many friends. Lots of them. He always wore his Stacy Adams mirror-shined, starched khaki pants, and three-quarter sleeve shirts that he'd bought at Penner's, the downtown haberdashery of pachuco garb. It was sort of an unofficial Pachuco uniform. Almost all chucos wore the typical apparel with bravado and pride. And Berga was a dresser.

In the early mornings, when he'd swagger down the halls, waves parted. He commanded respect. Smelling of Old Spice with his hair slicked back and his shirt buttoned to the neck-collar, Berga pretended he wasn't afraid of nothin'. *Nada es nada,* he would say in an existential hip sort of way. I knew otherwise. Berga was afraid all right, scared the world was going to swallow him up. We were all afraid, there was a war going on somewhere in Southeast Asia.

It was kinda strange how we met. Almost eerie, I suppose. Back then, I was a budding reporter. It was my fantasy to become another Clark Kent or something. I enjoyed writing. And since our school didn't have a school paper, Old Man Wilson, the Math teacher, assigned me the dubious task of becoming the first student editor.

"You're kiddin'," I said.

"Nope, can you do it?" Wilson asked.

"Does a bear shit in the woods, ooophs."

He guffawed and handed me the keys to the closet that secured the mimeograph machine. I was given the responsibility of assembling Cooper's first newspaper, The Hawkeye. I had a skeleton staff of two flat-chested dorky girls, named Mylinda and JoAnna, who'd transferred from Guadalupe Catholic School and who didn't speak Spanish, even though they looked more Mexican than me.

The school basement served as the office until our advisor could find us other lodgings. There wasn't much news to cover, except sports. The girls started by writing down the class advisories while I covered sports and everybody did the song dedication bit. That proved our best seller. We sold ten-cent dedications. What were they you ask? It worked like this: we'd list a song, say, "Stop in the Name of Love" by the Supremes, and you got to dedicate it to someone. Simple. Before long, we had pages and pages of dedications, plus enough money to start a real fledgling newspaper. Hey, we weren't competing with *Teen* magazine, but it was still pretty serious. It was something, and I was on top of the mountain.

Little did I know that my mountain was about to be climbed.

On my way home one day, lugging my books, I stopped by Gutierrez's Dry Goods to buy a Coke and a bag of chips when some guys from La Tripa were waiting outside for me. Tripa meant intestine in Spanish, and La Tripa was the name of the barrio from where these guys originated. They had inherited the title because some toughs from an uptown gang had been found massacred with their tripas strewn everywhere—a new gang had been formed and christened. It wasn't long before a rival gang poked fun at La Tripa, saying that the story had been a hoax; La Tripa had been actually named after the Roegelein Slaughterhouse, where blood and tripas (cow's intestines) were discarded. Either way, I didn't care. It still sounded pretty bad.

When I came out, these two guys were waiting for me outside. A tall, lanky guy with crooked teeth and a dark, fat guy with a pork belly. I didn't look in their direction and moved toward an opposite path.

"Hey, you ese."

Just the sound of the word made me cringe; I pretended I hadn't heard them. I turned and gave them a bewildered, you-talking-to-me? expression. "He's talking to you, ese," the fat one repeated. The one with the crooked teeth grabbed my arm, while Porky took my Coke. The books fell and my notebook opened, scattering paper like fleeting doves. This is it, I said to myself, initiation time. Two against one wasn't quite sportsmanlike, but these guys were playing by the Queensberry rules anyway.

"Hey, pendejo!" Crooked Teeth snarled.

"I don't speak Spanish," I said. That ploy had saved my ass many times. But this time I knew it was wrong immediately because I felt a swift kick to the pants. I was just beginning to understand their dialect. Pachucos spoke an idiom of their own, complete with code words and dirty terms, not found in the *Random House Dictionary*. One way to really get the wrath from these guys was to pretend you were something else, or deny your culture.

Crooked Teeth felt I was pulling his leg, because he repeated, *"Orale, este pinche bato no habla Español*. What's your name Lucas McCain?" Oh bother, I thought, how corny. I didn't say a word. My legs weren't obeying my brain.

"What's wrong, pussy? Cat got your tongue," Porky taunted, taking a swig from my Coke. Well, when you gotta do it, I guess you have to, I thought to myself, as I prepared to kick Porky in the balls. Just about that time, Berga arrived at the scene. There was nothing that happened that Berga didn't know about.

"Hey! What the fuck you guys doing? That's the main man. That dude's El Profe!" he shouted. Crooked Teeth and Porky were dumbfounded. Everyone had nicknames in the barrio; it was an easy way of codifying people for name recognition, perhaps, peer identification.

"What's happening, Berga?" the lean one said. They began dusting me off as though they had just been playing with me. That was the first time anyone had ever called me "El Profe"—The Professor.

"Berga, we didn't know, man. You know this guy?" Crooked Teeth asked.

"Yea, I know him."

They looked at one another and shrugged.

"Well, we got a score to settle. *Este pinche bato* didn't run our dedications," Crooked Teeth hissed.

Run their dedication.

The phrase flashed like grease on a hot skillet. So that's what all this was about. Now, I remembered. One of the nerdy girls had asked me if I would run some dedications on credit.

"Credit! Are you crazy!" I remember yelling, "What the hell! We're not running a welfare agency."

She scowled.

I even gave her a smartass closing remark, shouting: "Tell 'em this isn't Christmas and I ain't Santa Claus!" I never thought she was dumb enough to give them the message.

Berga inched closer, and shook his forehead.

"Not this dude. You gotta go through me."

The guys were aghast. They couldn't believe their ears. Was I hearing right? I thought to myself. Crooked Teeth let go of my arm and eased away. Porky got the hiccups. Embarrassed. They both started walking away slowly until I motioned to Porky to hand back my Coke. Porky took a swallow and I could see bubbles of saliva drooling down the bottleneck and then I told him he could keep it. Porky gave me a smug, self-assured smile and they both wandered off.

Berga and I stood there looking at one another. Sizing each other up. There really wasn't anything to size up. He was taller than me, heftier. He grinned and gave me the Pachuco clenched fist. The you're-okay-sign.

"Thanks guy," I said, grabbing my books. He stood there looking at all my books.

"Hey, man. What you gonna do when you finish reading all them books?"

I was always reading. Good stuff. Edgar Allan Poe, H. G. Wells, and even Albert Camus. Books like that.

"I guess read some more," I said.

Berga picked up a copy of Steinbeck's *Tortilla Flat* and cracked wryly, "Reading a cookbook?" We both laughed, and then Berga walked away. News spread fast the next day that I had friends in high places.

People began respecting me. I owed him one. The following day, Berga came to collect. He wanted some dedications. I told him I'd pay for the dedications out of my pocket, but he refused.

"Ese, no problem. Just sit tight my man. I've got money." He flipped a crisp five-dollar bill from his bulgy wallet, while I just stared in complete amazement at the thick wad of greenbacks. I didn't even have change for a five.

"Don't worry. Just pay me whenever you can. I trust you." From that day, Berga had a running account with the monthly Hawkeye, and his dedications ran on the front page with a fancy etching of the hawkeye, its talons grabbing a gopher. Right below it was the month's eggheads and Spanish-language violators who'd been fined a penny-a-word. Dedications and fast money weren't what impressed me about Berga because at the time there were many hoods in my barrio with hard cash and a slick tongue. Berga was different. Berga had principles.

I learned later he had been destined to rewrite history. That's where Berga's contributions stand out in my life. We do things in life that never stand out until much later, past our adolescence, when we can reflect and weigh the consequences of our actions. This is why I sought him out at the reunion because I wanted to tell him that I had learned a valuable lesson in history that day when he stood up against Mrs. Lancaster.

You see, I forgot to tell you that Texas history was taught quite differently when I was growing up. We were supposed to feel ashamed of ourselves. We were a colonized people. But pachucos weren't ashamed. They were the few, the proud, Los chucos. They were rebels way before James Dean larded his hair with that greasy kid stuff and even before Marlon Brando donned a leather jacket. I was neither a pachuco nor rebel. I was a conformist. I followed the rules, dressed properly, cropped my hair closely to the skull, didn't wear khakis, did my homework. In short, I was your average American striving to assimilate into the larger society, shredding the carcass of the old culture.

But secretly I harbored a deep respect for these guys, especially Berga.

Why, you ask? Because Berga was the conscience, the wound that didn't heal. The voice denied.

Mrs. Lancaster was a towering woman built like an old battleship. Lards of fat surrounded her waist and she had enough jewelry to decorate a Christmas tree. She wore teardrop glasses with diamond studded tips and a beehive hairdo. Her Texas history class had been one boring semester until Berga and some of his chuco friends transferred into our class.

"The name is Mrs. Lancaster," she said. "And I don't expect any problems from you boys. Is that understood?"

Chino, one of the chucos, smiled and said, "You got it, Burt Lancaster." Everyone chuckled. I let out a chuckle.

"Now you stop that young man!" Mrs. Lancaster snapped.

Berga looked around at the mayhem and snapped his fingers and the laughing stopped. Berga had pulled the plug. Mrs. Lancaster probably thought her looks had frightened Chino. But it was Berga they were afraid of.

We had just gotten on the chapter of the dreaded Alamo. The heavy, quite busty Mrs. Lancaster, swaying down the hall like an old vessel, got her kicks by putting kids in their place. Everybody knew she had a thing for teaching her favorite chapter, "The Battle of the Alamo." She even had posters of John Wayne and Fess Parker in her classroom. It was like digging the knife into us and twisting off the handle.

"Turn to chapter seven," she said. She took pleasure in it, wetting her lips as though she had manifest destiny on her tongue. "Those brave heroes of the Alamo were about to be massacred. The gutless Santa Anna had ordered that no prisoners were to be taken."

I looked around and saw faces buried in textbooks; they were hiding their shame. Berga sat in the rear, almost aloof, nodding his head, thinking, sizing up the situation. On his left flank, the chucos were whispering.

A hand lifted from the rear of the class.

But the old lady continued reading aloud until the boy coughed so loudly that old Battle-Ax finally looked up.

"Yes, Felipe," Mrs. Lancaster asked.

"Can I go to the bathroom?"

"No! You may not!"

A few muffled giggles.

She continued: "And then, thousands upon thousands of Mexicans lined up. They had the best weapons, cannons, artillery while the poor defenders of the Alamo had their rusty muskets. Suddenly, the bugle was heard."

Someone cut a fart. There was an uproar. I strained to keep my composure, but the whole thing was kinda funny. Mrs. Lancaster frowned and raised her voice: "Stop that nonsense! Stop it, now!" Rising from her desk, her hand quivering, and holding a small ruler, Lancaster the blaster, said: "Next one who gets out of line is going to Brewington's office. Is that understood!"

It got so quiet you could hear Lancaster's wheezing.

She resumed her seat and fixed her glasses and ritualistically wet her lips and returned: "And then the assault occurred. Thousands upon thousands of dirty Mexicans stormed the Alamo. Davy Crockett and Jim Bowie were killed, but not before a hundred or so sneaky Mexicans met their maker."

The "Mexican" part didn't annoy us. It was the "dirty" and "sneaky" adjectives that Mrs. Lancaster adroitly snuck into her lectures. Some kids had complained to the school principal, but the old codger had laughed it off, saying, "You people are Americans, not Mexicans. And remember, don't speak Spanish." Berga sat in the back, not amused at all. All the while, he was thinking, thinking. Berga climbing the walls of Lancaster's Alamo. Berga planning the assault. Berga about to blow the bugle.

He hadn't liked her tone nor the way she emphasized those dirty Mexicans. He wasn't going to take any of this crap, and so he raised his hand.

Irritated by all the interruptions, Mrs. Lancaster chose to ignore him. That was a mistake. Suddenly, Berga asked, quite jokingly, "But who won at the Alamo?"

"The Mexicans," Mrs. Lancaster muttered.

Berga snapped his fingers and his friends yelled triumphantly, "Hip-hip, hoorah! Yeaaaaa!!!!! The Mexicans!!!" like a booming cheer-leading squad at a football pep rally. It was pandemonium.

"Quiet! Quiet!!!!" Mrs. Lancaster shouted, beating her ruler on the large oak desk. But the momentum couldn't be stopped; they kept stomping their feet, yelling, "But who won??? Whoo wonnnn!!"

Later that day, we found out Mrs. Lancaster had reported Berga to the school principal and the rabble-rousing pachucos had been expelled for unruly behavior and conduct unbecoming students.

After school, I sat with Berga at Gutierrez's Dry Goods drinking a Big Red and sharing a moonpie.

"It ain't fair, man," I said.

"Nothin's fair. You just work harder, okay. Keep reading those books. It's the only way out," Berga said.

"What about your plans?"

"Don't know. Probably join the Marines or something."

Luckily, Berga came back. Finished school. He was older than a lot of us. Seventeen but looked twenty. We never forgot him, El Pachuco. Berga in his tough-guy humor had stood up to one of the meanest teachers at school and we would never see the likes of him again.

That evening, I met Chino, El Louie, Pato, Juan the John, all Viet Nam vets, all graying chucos, who had gone to war to serve our country and protect the American way of life. Somewhere out there, in the horizon, was a voice yelling, "Who won?"

from A PRINCE OF A FELLOW

★

Shelby Hearon

I LOVE TO INTERVIEW WRITERS, AS THEY ARE NOT FETTERED BY facts. Thrusting characters and parrying plots spin from their fingers onto the yellow pad as slickly as spider webs. Silently inside their heads herds thunder and doors slam with a reverberation that we in the world of sound can only envy. Each time I coax a writer to open his vocal cords on my show I expect sudden magic; expect verbal rabbits snatched from the top hat of his subconscious.

Of course, I am habitually disappointed. Last year's Dobie Fellow, hungrily surfacing from under Los Angeles' thick sky, had spent six months staring through the barbwire fence at the milling livestock, his vocabulary locked in constipation. On the air, so full of his oneness with the land and its manure, he had had the opposite problem. I purposely omitted mention of his work in progress, lest it never progress.

I had high hopes that this year's visiting writer would be better. For one thing he possessed the irresistibly German name of Gruene

Albrech; for another, his brooding voice, accepting my invitation to appear on my interview show, had suggested a prodigal son come home to confront an archetypal father—to kill or to forgive him (depending on the size of the Dobie grant).

Now, considering him through the pane of glass, he didn't look as I expected. He was not brooding at all; in fact, he seemed eager as a kid on his first day of school all decked out in new clothes, which he was—board-stiff jeans, creased Western pearl-snapped shirt, hand-tooled glossy leather boots. Even, sticking from his back pocket, a red bandana with the price tag still on it.

Right off I could see he was no German. Looking closer at his wide face whose skin stretched across high cheekbones tight as a drum, I decided he must be Slavic. His deep almost golden tan gave him a general yellow wash that appeared to color even the whites of his eyes and his teeth, and darkened to copper his bow-shaped mouth. In the manner of symmetrical faces, his chin was cleft in the center, Czech, there was no question.

That charade was all right with me; I was used to that. Things are seldom what they seem. None of us are as we present ourselves.

The old men in this fenced-in town in Central Texas, named for Prince Solms, the nobleman who brought their ancestors from the old country inland from the coast to this rolling edge of a ring of weathered hills, purport to live in a German-speaking hamlet.

In fact, they dream of a remembered past; today they make up less than half the town. Beer-bellied, polka-dancing Mexicans, heirs of the original land-grant holders, now outnumber the beer-bellied, polka-dancing German descendants of the prince's immigrants. Nor is this the lush verdant farmland they claim to their grandsons, hoping to keep them close at hand; only the thinnest veneer of grass and scrubby shrubs cover the rocky soil of this insular place whose factions shut themselves off from their neighbors as surely as its rivers cut apart its three hills.

We aren't what we claim either, here on my beloved Mole in the

Tunnel. Our very show pretends one thing as it delivers another. KPAC, a remote broadcast station, sells itself as Pasture Radio, down home sound brought to you from the land of the Aberdeen Angus and Poland Chinas. Actually, although we pipe our audience the picking sounds of country and western's finest, we sit ten miles out of town on a rise so that we can beam our advertisers to the Porsche drivers and politicians in both San Antonio and Austin. We are no more authentically rural than Neiman-Marcus custom-cut bluejeans.

Otto, my sidekick, who gives the news and weather in a heavy German accent, is really a forty-five-year-old Mexican, with Pancho Villa mustache, who works afternoons (out of his lederhosen and into his stiff black suit) as the cemetery sexton.

Nor am I, Avery Krause, the cowgirl my faded jeans and blue work shirts would imply. I am, rather, as my mama is, a Swede sitting like a burr in the saddle of a large German family. A corn on the sole of the old grandfather's foot.

For twenty years in the coal-burning state, as Papa in his German way called the black, gutted mountains of eastern Kentucky, Mama and I were mistaken for any other Appalachian towheads. Which angered Papa into deep silences over his journals and ledgers. I, so like the other schoolgirls with blue eyes pale as watercolor—all of us blanched, bleached, with peaked faces—made faint impression on the eye. We were Polaroid shots not yet developed. Now, come back here last year to bury Papa and replant ourselves, Mama and I are set apart from the Germans we married or were born into by our near-white curls, our wide thighs, even our sweet Swedish smiles.

If my appearance was the same in Kentucky, so was my manner of dealing with the world. I was a drama teacher, which, if you think about it, is not too different from what I'm doing now. In both settings I present illusions as real. In both theater and radio the audience is let in on the hoax; together we share the thrill of belief suspended. Here, by consent, coconut shells pound into horses hoofs and squeaking doors signal mysterious entries and ominous departures. There, small white faces grew bold with greasepaint and eager hands slew dragons with broom handles.

So it was fine with me if today's prince was after all a golden impostor, faking his German birthright; I too make my living by delusion.

As I stared at his large dark head and wide palms which seemed designed to compensate for lack of height, he flashed a hesitant grin of greeting.

Wanting to get the feel of him before we went on the air, I put on the easy sounds of Willie Nelson's "Remember Me" and left the control booth to Otto, who was assembling the good tidings of local news and the usual bad tidings of local weather.

"Good morning, I'm Avery Krause. We talked on the phone."

"I'm here early." Gruene Albrech rose, short in the leg as I had perceived.

I shook his firm hand, deciding that the touch was worth coming out for. "Would you like a cup of coffee?"

"If it's no trouble. I left in a hurry. It looked farther on the map. I thought it would take me longer to get here."

"You were good to drive out at eight o'clock in the morning."

"I've never been on radio."

Which must explain the scrubbed look. People always forget we on radio see only with our movie-making minds.

"We're very informal," I tried to put him at his ease. "I'll ask a few questions, play some music. We'll let the listeners call in their comments. They like to feel they're taking part in the show."

Which in fact they did. The weekday interview hour was now the station's most popular feature, and the high point of Otto's and my shift. This was satisfying to me as last year, returned home and job hunting, I had sold KPAC's managers on the idea that visiting dignitaries and celebrities from San Antonio and Austin, and even stammering ordinary citizens from Prince Solms, telling their versions of daily events, would create a wider advertising market than followed their existing mix of country sounds, news, and weather.

"You can ask me about my book," the writer told me. "That's why I'm here."

I was more interested in him than in his proposed translation of himself into fiction, but, guessing he wanted a dress rehearsal, I asked, "What is your novel about?"

He cast about as if he hadn't thought of it before. "It's about these people."

Clearly he needed to warm up. Some writers obviously grew tongue-tied in the morning. Leaving his work, I moved to him, a matter of more concern to me anyway. "How long have you been away from Texas?"

He studied his cup. "Uh—since I left high school. Several years."

"Do you have family back here?" The Dobie grant as I recalled had to be bestowed on a native Texan.

"Uh—that's right. My mom's folks are from Veramendi."

"Czech?"

He looked relieved, as if the business of disguises bothered him. "How could you tell?"

"Long practice at observing dissembling."

"I guess I do that. Writing, I mean."

"Is Albrech your real name?"

"Actually it's Billy Wayne Williams." He looked sheepish at this admission.

"Why did you change it?"

"Who reads books by Billy Wayne Williams? If your name is Gruene Albrech they take you seriously. They give you a grant to the Dobie Ranch." He grinned. "They ask you to appear on radio shows."

"So they do." I smiled my blondest smile.

"Besides, I thought the German name would prepare me to tell my story."

"About these people—"I chided him.

"I'll tell about it when we're on the air. I don't want to waste myself now. I'm saving up for when it counts."

"Is that the way you write?"

"What?"

"Keeping it all inside until it goes down on paper?"

"I guess so. I never thought about it."

His crisp just-purchased clothes must also be a way to get into his tale and into this part of the country again. They did not look like the tweeds and Shetland sweaters I imagined for Connecticut. "How do you like being back here?" I asked.

"That's part of what we'll talk about." With that, he went back to the guest chair and turned his attention to waiting. Moving his knees apart and planting his feet squarely as a peasant, he simply sat.

It came to me I was observing an actor, off stage, getting into his role. A fine development, and one that I had missed.

Most people did not know that when the first sounds gave the cue that the curtain had gone up, we were on our invisible stage. Most people played to me, thinking me their audience. Most gestured to me, looked to me for confirmation, took my silent nods as answers. Most people did not believe that anyone was Out There; it would be grand to work with an actor again.

It took me back to another actor who had seemed, for a time, to be a prince of a fellow. An actor with a fine hairy belly against which I slept for five years of weekends. Remembering that earlier tale (or perhaps a later one) made me wonder about the writer before me—did he make love as the Czech rodeo rider or as the moody German?

However, I knew that such thinking was unproductive. After all, I had only taken one guest to bed, and he was no prince. Still, you had to consider it again each time; otherwise you ceased to take the risk that goes with looking.

Otto wrapped up his good tidings of local news with, "It vill be a goot day, as ve shall see." Popping his alpine suspenders, he plugged in a public service cartridge and signaled for me to take over.

"Pronounce my name *Green*." My guest spoke up suddenly. "That is the German way."

Then back in the booth the sorcery began again; we were crackling out over the air waves into the waiting ears. "Hello out there, this is Avery Krause on KPAC, Keep Peace, the station which brings you morning. Our guest today is that distinguished novelist Gruene Albrech, returned to the land of his forefathers in search of an ancient tale. You at home refill your freeze-dried and you in your economy cars move closer to your FM while we listen to his story. It isn't every day we get a real live word wizard on our show, so stay tuned and be sure to call in your own questions for him." At home in my eyeless world, I beamed myself to my unknown intimates.

"Tell us, Gruene, how does it feel to be back here in your homeland coming to terms with your past?" I fed him the cue.

With the first answer he was before the floodlights. His hands led him; his planted stance anchored him. He was Everyman, struggling to find himself and, in the process, each of us. As he talked he brushed his brown hair continually away, as if brushing aside deception or falsehood.

In the heavy tones of a Günter Grass he shared the anguish of going home again. He was the tortured expatriate, returned to wring the truth from the meager lives of his ancestors.

"And what is your novel about?"

"My book is a fable of a grandfather blinded by his villagers. It is a parable; for we are all that grandfather, the world is that village. Do you know the works of——?" He plunged into a comparison of himself and a little known but powerful German writer, exiled from his home soil, writing of alienation.

Now I was not thinking of him in bed, but with his pencil and pad. Wondering if he wrote as this fine actor, the tormented Albrech, or as the golden cowboy. Most of all wondering did he write well?

"Do you write from your own experience?"

"I am everyone I invent, but they each transcend me."

"How do you know when your writing is good?" This was something I had never understood, as the actor is dependent on immediate response. The kids would put on a tablecloth, a bandit's cape, and ride their chairs backwards, and it was a good performance if their watchers shouted and clapped. And if they didn't, it wasn't. But for a writer the lapse from entrance to applause required a far vaster attention span to approval.

"Not until it's read. And then, if it comes from your deepest level of consciousness, you can only hope it will speak a truth to the deepest level of the reader."

He spoke then not of theater but of a message in a bottle, of himself stolidly gathering clams until the tide went out and came in again. Nodding my admiration of such patience, as well as such fine answers, I gave us both time to catch our breath and myself time to answer the blinking red phone that flashed a listener's call. Putting on John Prine's bittersweet ballad of "Donald and Lydia," I spoke into the off-air receiver. "Good morning, Keep Peace."

"How would you like to interview me tonight?" It was the all too familiar voice of the mayor of San Antonio. I felt a flush rise to my face. Wasn't it enough that I was still engaged in a shabby affair with this burgher in white socks; did he have to intrude himself into my ear as well on that ultimate invasion of privacy, the, telephone?

"I can't talk now, Sterling, I have a guest."

He drew in his breath. It excited him to call when I was on the air, knowing he couldn't be heard by the audience but knowing it rattled me. He liked getting a reaction from me whenever it appealed to him—the usual attitude of a man to his mistress. "I can be at the cabin at a quarter to seven." Breathless, aroused by his call, he proffered the weekly rendezvous.

"How long will you have?" I did not relish the drive to our hideaway, a trip that took me more than an hour.

"I don't have to be at the reception until nine. Plenty of time for what I have in mind."

"I'll try to come."

"See that you do." He laughed, titillated by the double meaning. He knew I would appear; after a year it had become a foregone conclusion.

After a year he knew that he could count on my weekly treks to hear how things were going with his boys. He had surmised that whatever thrill the clandestine provided him, I was willing to settle for the feel of a man again.

As the music faded and Otto stroked his mustache in disapproval of the call, I invented a final question for our writer. "How long have you had this story in your mind?"

Through the pane of glass he acknowledged my invention, meeting my eyes above my flushed cheeks. "The blind old man surrounded by others," he concluded, "represents the primal scene in my life. I have never been without it."

If he writes badly, I admitted, I cannot bear it.

"Thank you for being with us, Gruene Albrech, and now stay tuned while Otto brings you news of the outside world from our fertile field among the mooing Angus."

Out in the front, I shook the writer's hand in thanks.

"Otto is Mexican, isn't he?" He studied the newscaster through the glass.

"His name is Ramirez. He's the cemetery sexton."

"He does a good imitation of the language."

"None of us is really German, are we?" I looked about the studio where we had each performed in costume. "Not to the grandfathers, anyway."

"I guess not." He looked away.

I studied his face, not knowing how to proceed. I had never known how to make overtures to men. If they wanted you then you either said yes or you said no, but it was their question before it was your answer. I had never learned how to move things along with the ones who didn't ask.

In Kentucky where I taught drama there had been a school principal who supported me in my attempts to get the mountain children to loosen their bodies, to wrestle a smile to the floor, or to pretend to be a caterpillar crawling in the dirt. He was one of those rumpled, dedicated men you always mean to end up with, conscientious and underpaid. Educated but with some flaw visible as a rip in his jacket which meant he had settled for a poor rural school in a backwater. In three years we never got past his encouragement and my redoubled efforts in the classroom. We never got past ending up at the same lunch table with our sacks of sandwiches and apples.

The one who finally did ask, the extravagant actor, had also, as Gruene had, rechristened himself. He had given himself, as he liked to pun, three *given* names. Called himself Charles Henry David in a take-off on the famous men whose parents give them three surnames at birth (Custer Lincoln Grant). To his delight, people could never remember whether he was Charles David or David Charles. I called him Henry; I never knew his real name. At least this time, with the writer, I had got that far.

"Do you have time for another cup of coffee?" I asked, finally. "We could go watch the cows eat grass."

"Sure. I set the morning aside from my work."

We took our refills outside and leaned against the fence.

There were no Angus in sight, nothing in the rolling green fields but air waves whispering messages.

"What did Billy Wayne do to eat in Connecticut?"

"How do you mean?"

"Nothing deep. English faculty?"

"Uh—yeah. The usual stuff. Teaching. Writers' workshops."

"Does Texas seem changed to you?"

"Everything stays pretty much the same down here."

I tried another tack. "When we were on the air, who were you talking to?"

He cast his eyes about, as if trying to visualize. "Just someone out there, I guess. Someone I don't know."

"I beam myself to a woman who is clearing the table, grabbing her things, getting into her sports car to go to work, taking me along with a fresh cup."

He considered. "I couldn't imagine anyone specific like that. If I did I would get involved in where he was going to work and what kind of car he had and then I would get into his wife and kids and their fights and that personal business and then I couldn't talk to him. I guess I was talking to the same person I write to: just someone out there."

"How long do you have at Dobie?"

"Six months. Isn't that standard?"

"Sometimes they give the grant for a year—"

"I figure if I can't get my book started in six months then I can't do it anyway."

"Do you write every day?"

"The research is what slows me down. I thought I knew my people but it is taking me longer than I planned."

It couldn't be going slower than my research on him. I could only guess that he had put on the new country clothes in order to leave behind the world of the teacher and method act his fictional villagers. "You made your tale very convincing to our listeners."

"I have never been on radio before."

Which was where we came in. Stymied, I watched as his hazel eyes focused on some scene out there past the fields.

Unexpectedly, he asked a sudden question of his own. "Who were you talking to?"

"I told you. Just a woman in her car—"

"I mean on the phone. When you made up that question for me."

"Oh." I felt the red come back again. "The mayor of San Antonio. A friend of mine." Which I guess spelled out the whole thing for him. But I didn't know what else to do but tell the truth; I did not bill myself as what I was not.

"You got opaque."

"How do you mean?"

"You closed up."

"I may do that a lot."

"That's not good for you."

I shrugged. Some things it was better not to stay open to. "It's self-defense."

"I know about that," he said.

"Around here you have to—" But he must remember all that.

"—Well," he said.

I asked one parting query. "Do you write in those clothes?"

"I never wore these before."

I didn't press further. Maybe he wrote in turtlenecks and corduroys, or, emulating the grandfather, in an old man's nightshirt. Maybe he got up every day and sharpened all the pencils in his cigar box, in the nude. Maybe I would never know.

We emptied our cups and scanned the horizon—toward Prince Solms and the lavender hills to the north, toward Veramendi and distant Mexico to the south. I had run out of inquiries. If not out of all I wanted to know, at least what it was possible to ask. Holding out my hand one last time, I called it a morning. "Thank you for coming. Otto will have to move on to ag news and polkas if I don't rescue him."

"Here—" He tugged the bandana from his back pocket and stuck it in my hand. "I don't need this."

I tried to leave things open. "Stop by on your way back to see the folks in Veramendi."

He left them closed. "Right now I'm working out the village in my head." Getting into a car as new as his name, his Levis, and his performance on my show, he backed out onto the unpaved access road.

I tied the bandana on my tow head. Sometimes you had to make do with souvenirs.

MY BROTHER IS A COWBOY

———————— ✯ ————————

Carolyn Osborn

M Y DADDY USED TO ADVISE MY BROTHER AND ME, "DON'T tell everything you know." This was his golden rule. I keep it in mind as I constantly disregard it. I've been busy most of my life telling everything I know. My brother Kenyon took it to heart. He tells nothing, not even the most ordinary answers to questions about his everyday existence. If my mother asks when he'll be home for supper, he says, "I don't know." The nearest he'll come to giving the hour for when he'll come in or go out is "Early" or "Late." His common movements, the smallest events of his day, are secret.

Mother follows these like a female detective. "Kenyon left the bread out this morning and the pimento cheese. I wonder if he had pimento cheese for breakfast, or took sandwiches for lunch, or both?" If, after she counts the remaining bread slices, sandwiches seem a possibility, she wonders where he has to go that's so distant he needs to take lunch with him. The names of surrounding towns come to her mind. "He won't be going anywhere near Lampasas because they have good barbeque there and he wouldn't take pimento cheese if he could get barbeque." She has advantage over Daddy; at least she's observed Kenyon's eating habits through the years and can spend hours happily trying to guess what he's going to do about lunch and whether or not he's going to turn up for supper.

Daddy doesn't care about where Kenyon eats lunch. What he wants to know is how many ranches Kenyon is leasing, how his sheep, goats, and cattle are doing, if he's making money or not.

We all want to know if he's ever going to get married. Does he have a girl? Does he want to marry? He is almost thirty, taller than my father's six feet, though how much we don't know for he won't stand and be measured. He has dark hair that curls when he forgets to get it cut, which is most of the time. The curls come over his forehead and disgust him so much he is forever jamming his hat down low to cover his hair. When we were children he made me cut the front curls off. I was spanked for doing it. His nose is long and straight. There is a small slanting scar just missing his eye running over his left eyebrow. His eyes are brown. His mouth is wide and generally closed.

When we ask if he's ever going to marry, and nothing will stop us from asking, he says, "Find me a girl who'll live out in the country, cook beans, and wash all day." He runs his hands over the creases in his clean blue jeans, sticks the shirttail of his clean shirt in, and laughs. Mother gets angry then. She's responsible for all his clean clothes and feels sometimes this is the only reason he shows up at the house. Often she says, "He doesn't need a wife! He needs a washerwoman!" Not once, however, has she ever said this to him, fearing he'll put on his boots and walk out the door to some unknown cafe one last time.

She isn't curious about where I'm going to eat. Everybody in town knows I each lunch every day at the Leon High School cafeteria. I'm the singing teacher. Wouldn't you know it! Since I've already told you Kenyon's almost thirty, you might as well know I'm almost twenty-six. At least nobody asks me when I'm going to get married, not to my face anyway. Being related and having practically no heart at all, Kenyon has the gall to wonder out loud if I'm ever going to catch a man. When he does this, I tell him I have as much right to uphold the long tradition of old-maidhood as he has to represent the last of the old west. My brother is a cowboy.

I tell him, "You're the last of a vanishing breed, the tail end of the roundup of the longhorn steers, the last great auk alive, a prairie rooster without a hen!"

All he replies to this is, "Sister, there ain't no substitute for beef on the hoof." He gets out real quick before I can go on about helicopters substituting for horses and feed lots replacing the open range.

Since the wires have been cut between Kenyon and his family, we have to depend on other sources of information, the weekly newspaper for instance. That's where we found out he'd been riding bulls in rodeos the summer after he flunked out of college. He got his picture on the front page for falling off a Brahma bull headfirst. The photographer caught the bull still doubled up and Kenyon in midair, his hands out in front of him right before he hit the dirt. My daddy strictly forbade any more bull-riding on the grounds he wasn't going to have his son associating with a bunch of rodeo bums.

Kenyon said, "These bums are the best friends I got and I'll associate with whoever I want."

"You are going to kill yourself and me too." Daddy put his hand over his heart like he was going to have an attack that minute. "And, furthermore, I'm going to cut you out of my will if you keep up this fool riding." Then he laid down on the bed and made me take his blood pressure. I was home on vacation from nursing school in Galveston.

Kenyon smiled, showing he still had all his teeth, and the next thing we read in the newspaper was he'd gone off and joined the paratroopers, joined of his own free will, mind you, for three years. Daddy, who'd been in the infantry in WW II, was half proud and half wild. "He doesn't have enough sense to keep his feet on the ground! If he isn't being thrown from a bull, he's throwing himself out of airplanes!"

He wrote an old army buddy of his who'd retired, like he did, near his last post—except the post was up in Tennessee where Kenyon was stationed instead of Texas where we are. This old buddy wrote back saying:

Dear Willie,

Your boy is doing fine. I talked to his C.O. yesterday. He told me Pvt. Kenyon K. Lane is making a good soldier.

Yours truly,

Henry C. Worth, Lt. Col., Ret.

P.S. He told me Kenyon inspires good morale because he jumps out of planes with a wad of tobacco in his mouth and spits all the way down.

Your friend,

Lt. Col. Henry C. Worth, Ret.

I think Daddy was happy for a while. He showed the letter to me before he went downtown to show it to some of his friends at the drugstore where they all meet for coffee. By the time he came home, Mother was back from the grocery.

"William, how can you go around showing everybody that letter when I haven't read it!" She read it and was crying before she finished. "Who taught him how to chew tobacco? He'll ruin his teeth. He was such a nice clean boy."

"Ruin his teeth!" Daddy shouted. "You've got to worry about his teeth when he's falling out of airplanes every day!"

"He's not falling," I said. "He's jumping and he's doing it of his own free will."

"Free will nothing!" Daddy turned on me. "Don't you be telling me about free will in the U.S. Army. I know about the army. I spent twenty years in the army."

I had to take his blood pressure after that. He spent the next three years writing to his army buddies near whatever post my brother happened to be on, and getting news of Kenyon from them. All his letters were signed Col. William K. Lane, Ret.

I spent those years finishing my education, they thought. In the daytime I was. I wore a white uniform and low white shoes and went to nursing school in Galveston. Friday and Saturday nights I put on a red sequined dress and a pair of red high heels and went to sing at one of the nightclubs. My stage name was Gabriella and I wore so much makeup nobody from Leon would have known it was me. I had learned something from Kenyon, not to tell everything I knew and to follow my own free will. It worked too. When I was home I took Daddy's blood pressure and Mother's temperature; when I was in Galveston I was singing two nights a week.

Don't get any ideas either—singing and wearing a red dress was all I was doing. The men in the combo I sang with were more strict with me than they would have been with their own daughters if they had had any. I could drink soda pop only, and I had to sit with one of them while I was drinking. Except for the sequins I might as well have been in a convent. I sang songs like "I Cain't Say No" without ever having a chance to not say it. Still, I was satisfied. Singing was what I wanted. I thought if I could support myself by nursing, I could gradually work my way into show biz and up to New York. So I was down in Galveston nursing and singing while my brother was on some army post jumping out of airplanes, I supposed.

One Friday night I was giving out with "Zip-Pah-De-Do-Dah" trying to cheer up a few barflies when in walks Kenyon. He knows me right away, red sequins, makeup, and all. He is wearing a tight-fitting paratrooper's uniform, his pants tied up in his boots, which laced to the knee practically. Very spiffy and clean. Mother would have been happy to see him.

"My, oh, my, what a wonderful day!" I finish. The barflies applaud. My brother just stands quietly while I slink off the platform. It's time for the break, so Tiny the drummer, who is actually a big fat man, married with a wife and baby he calls every night in Dallas, takes me by the arm to a table. Kenyon comes right over. I can see immediately he has gotten himself all shined up for one reason—to get roaring drunk—to the disgrace of family and country. He's just off the reservation and ready to howl. Obviously, I'm in his way.

I smile at him and say, "Hi. What are you doing down here? Are you AWOL?"

"No," he grins, "I'm on leave. You're the one that's AWOL."

Tiny says, "Scram, soldier boy."

"It's my brother, Tiny. He's in the paratroopers. He jumps out of airplanes."

"Gay Baby, don't pull the brother bit on me."

"But he is," I insist. "Show him your birthmark or something, Kenyon."

"Jump on out of here, fly boy," says Tiny.

"If I go, you go too, Gay Baby," says Kenyon with a merciless smirk.

"I'm not going anywhere till I finish here tonight. You sit down and behave yourself. Have a beer."

"You're leaving right now. My sister isn't going to hang around no honky-tonk." With this he grabs me by the arm and I scream at him, "Let go!" But he doesn't and by this time I'm furious. "You auk! You dodo! You idiot!"

Tiny rises like a giant blimp slowly filling with air. Before he can signal to the other fellows though, Kenyon pulls me to my feet. The other four members of the combo—Louie, the piano player; Max, the bass; Joe, the sax; and Evans, the trumpet—run to assist us.

Kenyon turns the table on its side. "She's going with me," he says.

I peek between the fingers of my free hand to see if he's got a six-shooter in his free hand. He's got nothing, nothing but swagger. Pretty soon he has a cut over his left eye—Tiny did it with a chair—and I have not one red cent left of all my savings from singing nights. My going-to-New York money has gone to bail Dangerous Dan Kenyon McGrew out of the Galveston jail.

"Listen, Kenyon," I tell him, "this is not Leon and this is not the nineteenth century. It's the second half of the twentieth in case you haven't noticed it from your airplane riding! There is nothing wrong with me singing in a quiet respectable bar."

"No sister of mine—"

"You just pretend I'm not any sister of yours. We're so different one of us must have been left on the doorstep."

"You think I'm a bastard?"

"Well, you're the one calling the cards," I said and flounced out of the jail. I was mad and in a hurry to get home to bed. All I cared about right then was sleep. That particular Saturday I had to work the 7:00 A.M. shift at the hospital. Kenyon being such a zipper-lip type, I certainly wasn't worrying about him telling anybody I was working in a nightclub and him spending some time in jail. I should have let him stay in jail. He got in his car that very same night and drove straight to Leon. And, when he got there early the next morning, he told. He told everything he knew.

They didn't give me any warning, not a phone call—nothing. Daddy appeared in full uniform, the old army pinks and greens with eagles flapping on both shoulders. He had been getting ready to leave for a battalion reunion at Ft. Sam Houston when Kenyon showed up, and he didn't waste time changing clothes. He should have. His stomach had expanded some since WW II so his trousers were lifted an inch too high over his socks.

The first thing I said when I saw him was, "Daddy, what on earth are you doing down here in your uniform? It's non-reg. They don't wear that kind anymore."

"Sister, don't you tell me about the U.S. Army regulations. I gave twenty years of my life to them."

"Well, they are likely to slap you in the loony bin here for walking around dressed up like that."

"If I was you, I wouldn't be talking about how other people are dressed."

"Daddy, there is nothing wrong with my uniform," I said. I'd been wearing it for eight hours and hadn't spilt a thing on it. There was nothing wrong with the way I looked at all except for the circles under my eyes from staying up till 2:00 A.M. getting a certain person out of jail. I was just about dead from exhaustion.

"I hear you've got another dress, a red one."

We were talking in the lobby of the hospital and when he said that I wanted to call for a stretcher.

"No daughter of mine is going to hang around with gangsters at nightclubs."

I don't know where he got the gangsters, probably from the last time he was in a nightclub.

"This isn't 1920 and I don't know any gangsters. The fellows Kenyon got in a fight with are musicians. They were trying to protect me." He wasn't listening. He didn't want to hear my side. His mind was already made up.

"You go and get your things," he told me. "No daughter of mine is going to be corrupted by jazz and booze."

What could I do? I'd spent all my savings getting Kenyon out of jail. I went with Daddy back to Leon thinking it would all blow over after a while. Mother, at least, would be on my side since she knew what it was to live with a husband who still thought he was in the first half of the twentieth century and a son who hadn't progressed past 1900. When we got to Leon though, I found out different. The very first thing Mother did was to show me mine and Kenyon's birth certificates.

"Look here, young lady, neither you nor your brother was left on anybody's doorstep. I hope this is proof enough for you." She shoved the yellowed pages with their loopy-de-loop handwriting in my face and started crying before I could say I never really meant it.

I stayed home that weekend and the rest of that semester. Good-bye nursing. I wasn't so crazy about it anyway. I guess what happened to me could happen to anybody, but I wonder how many girls end up teaching a bunch of high school kids to sing "Sweet Adeline" after they started out with a great career in show biz. Daddy took me completely out of school. In January he let me enroll in a Baptist church college only forty miles from Leon. I got my teacher's certificate there in music education and that's all I got. They had a short rope on me.

When I finished I was twenty-three, due to the interruption in my education. Daddy had a heart attack that year and I went home to help Mother nurse him and to teach singing in Leon High School.

My brother, when he was through with the paratroopers, came home too. He started working on ranches and slowly saved enough to lease places of his own. He hadn't paid me back the bail money yet. I hadn't paid him back either, but I was planning on how I was going to. Someday, I thought, he is going to find some girl who wants to quit riding the barrel races in rodeos and get married. When he brings this cutie home in her embroidered blouse and her buckskin fringes, I am going to tell everything I know, not about him being in jail. The fact he spent a few hours in the Galveston jail wouldn't bother her. Galveston's a long way from Leon.

I wasn't going to tell this rodeo queen Kenyon was bound to drag home about his past; I was going to predict her future. I was going to let this little girl know she might as well throw away her western breeches and get into a skirt that hit the floor. And, I was going to tell her she'd better wave good-bye forever to the bright lights, the crowd, the band, and the Grand Entry Parade because all that was in store for her was a pot of beans to stir and blue jeans to wash at home on the range. She wasn't to expect any modern appliances to help her out either, because I knew Kenyon. He wouldn't buy her a single machine, not even a radio. If she wanted to hear any music she'd have to invite me out to sit on the front porch and sing "Zip-Pah-De-Do-Dah" as the sun sank slowly in the west.

I had it all planned out, a feeble sort of revenge, but at least I'd have my say—me, the Cassandra of Leon, prophesying a terrible future for a fun-loving cowboy's sweetheart. Of course, like a lot of too well planned revenges, it didn't turn out that way. I got restless sitting around in the teacher's lounge, going to the movie every Saturday night

with a man I'd known since we were both in high school, Alvin Neeley, the band director. We weren't anything to each other but companions in boredom, chained together by what everyone thought was our
common interest, music. We were supposed to be a perfect couple
because we could both read notes. Everyone imagined we were sitting
on the piano bench warbling duets, but we weren't.

Alvin was a marcher. He kept in step even when we were walking
a few blocks down the street, and believe me, he wasn't marching to
the sound of any distant drum. Alvin had his own drum in his head,
and when he puckered his lips, I knew he wasn't puckering up for me;
he was puckering up for Sousa. Sometimes, just for diversion, I'd
refuse to march in step with him. If he put his left foot forward, I'd
start out on my right, but he'd always notice and with a quick little skip
in the air, he'd be in step with me. Off we'd go marching to the movie
to the tune of "The Stars and Stripes Forever" every Saturday. And all
this time Kenyon was stomping in and out of the house bird-free,
intent on his own secret purposes.

Mother would come and sit on the foot of my bed after I got home
from a date with Alvin. "Did you have a good time?" she'd say.

"All right." I wasn't going to tell her I'd had a bad time. She had
enough troubles as it was. Since his heart attack my daddy spent most
of his time sitting around the house with his right hand on the left side
of his chest the way actors used to indicate great pain in the old silent
films.

She'd ask me what movie we saw and I'd tell her, *Monsters of the
Slimy Green Deep* or whatever it was. Nothing but Grade B movies
ever made it to Leon, and Alvin and I went regularly no matter what
was showing—like taking a pill on schedule.

"Well, how is Alvin getting along?"

She wasn't interested in Alvin's health. What she wanted to know
was how Alvin and I were getting along. I'd say all right to that too. I
kept on saying the same thing till one night she said, "I sure would like
to have some grandchildren."

"Mother, you better get Kenyon to work on that because you're not going to get any grandchildren out of me and Alvin Neeley."

"Why not?"

"I'd have to marry him—that's why, and I'm not going to even if he asks, and he's not going to ask. He can barely hold a conversation anyway. All he can do is whistle—and march." I was sitting across the room from her rubbing my aching legs.

"Why do you keep on going out with him then?"

"I don't see anybody else bashing the door down to ask me to a movie. I go out with Alvin because he takes me. It's one way of getting away from this house, a way of getting out of Leon even if it's to go to the *Slimy Green Deep*."

"You worry me," said Mother.

"I worry myself," I told her and I did. I was stuck with Alvin Neeley in Leon. I'd done what they all wanted me to do and now they were stuck with me. They had me on their hands.

Mother evidently spoke to Kenyon about my miserable unwed existence and insisted he find somebody for me. I say Mother did it, put the idea in Kenyon's head that he find somebody for me, because, left to himself, Kenyon was not at all bothered by an old-maid sister. He thought he'd saved me from the gutter. From there on I was supposed to be continually thankful and permanently respectable.

When I got home early one Saturday night I was told, before I had time to say anything, that he'd "fixed up" a date for me the following Saturday.

"Who with?"

"Fellow named Frank Harwell from Lampasas. He ranches out west of town. He's going to take you dancing."

"He's from a big family. I know some of them. Harwells are spread all over Lampasas," Mother said happily.

"He served in Korea, in the infantry," said Daddy as if he'd just pinned the Distinguished Conduct Medal on somebody.

They all knew what they wanted to know about Frank Harwell and

I didn't know a thing. "How old is he? Is he short or tall, skinny or fat, intelligent or ignorant, handsome or ugly?" I could have gone on all night throwing questions at them, but I quit. They were all sitting there looking so smug.

"He's the best I could do," said Kenyon. "You'll like him. All the girls do."

"Where are we going dancing?" Since Leon's in a dry county there's not a real nightclub within twenty miles.

"We'll go out to the VFW Club," Kenyon said.

"We? Are you going too? Who do you have a date with?"

"Nobody. I'm just going along for the ride."

"Kenyon, I'm twenty-five years old going on twenty-six, and I'll be damned if you're going anywhere as my chaperone."

"Sister, watch your language," said Daddy. "Is he a good dancer, Kenyon?"

"Daddy, what do you care if he's a good dancer or not? You're not the one who's going to be dancing with him."

"I don't want my daughter marrying some Valentino. Good dancers make bad husbands."

"Daddy! You are hopelessly behind times! If you'd turn on your TV set you'd see people dancing without even touching each other. The Valentinos are all gone. Anyway, I'm not going to my wedding Saturday night. I'm going to the VFW Club!"

They had me. I was trapped into having a date with Frank Harwell just to prove to Daddy he wasn't a Valentino. I didn't mind so much. After all, I'd endured a long dry march in the desert with Alvin Neeley. And, I wanted to know what Kenyon did with himself when he wasn't riding the range.

On Saturday night I pranced into the living room in my best and fullest skirt. You have to have plenty of leg room for country dances. Kenyon was standing talking to Frank Harwell, who looked like a cowboy straight out of a cigarette advertisement, lean, tanned, and terribly sure of himself. He was every young girl's dream, and old girl's too. My knees were shaking a little when he looked me over. For a minute I wished I hadn't worn a sensible dress. I wished I was all togged out in my red sequins and red high heels again.

We all three got in Frank's pickup. He and Kenyon did most of the talking. We hadn't gone two blocks before Kenyon insisted he had to stop and look at some stock at the auction barn on the way to the VFW.

"Fine," said Frank in a grand, easygoing way. He was the most totally relaxed man I'd ever seen. He drove his pickup through town with one hand on the wheel, guiding it to the right and left as if he were reining a horse.

When we got to the auction barn Kenyon shot out of the truck, leaving the door open behind him.

"Always in a hurry," said Frank and leaned over me to pull the door shut. I felt like a huge old cat had fallen in my lap.

"You don't seem to be."

"Naw." He eased himself up, pulled out a package of cigarettes, lit one, then leaned back and blew smoke out. I kept expecting to hear an announcer's voice saying something about how good cigarettes were so I waited a minute before saying anything myself. Finally, I asked him about his ranch. He told me about his spring round-up, how much mohair had been clipped from his goats, how many cows had calved, the number of rattlesnakes he'd killed, how much a good rain would help, and other interesting things like that. We sat there, with Frank worrying about his wells running dry and the miles of fence he needed to repair; I was worrying about whether we'd ever get to the dance. The VFW Club was on top of a hill behind the auction barn. We could have walked up there, but it could have been in the next county as far as Frank was concerned. He got a bottle of bourbon out of the glove compartment and took a long swallow from it. When Kenyon came back he passed the bottle to him. Neither one of them offered me a swallow and I knew I'd have to be seventy and taking whiskey for medicinal purposes before either one of those two would dream of offering a girl a drink.

Kenyon was excited about a bull he'd seen. "He's that same old Brahma that throwed me. I'd know him anywhere. Gentle as he can be outside the ring, but let somebody get on his back and he goes wild. Wonder why they're selling him. He's a good rodeo bull."

"Getting old maybe," Frank drawled. They both laughed as if he'd said the most hilarious thing in the world. Then they both took another drink so *they* were in a good mood when we got to the VFW at 9:30 P.M. The hall was an old WW II army surplus barracks the veterans had bought and painted white. Judging from the noise coming out of the place, the men standing around cars outside talking and sneaking drinks, and the two cops at the doorway, it was wilder than any Galveston club on a Saturday night. The cops nodded at us as we went in. The girl who was selling tickets to the dance warned Frank and Kenyon to hold on to them because nobody was allowed to come back in without one.

Frank swung me out on the dance floor and that was the last I saw of Kenyon for a while except for a glimpse of him out of the corner of my eye. He was dancing with one of my ex-students, a not so bright one, who'd somehow managed to graduate the year before. Every once in a while Frank would excuse himself to go out and take a swig from his bottle. I sat at a table by myself drinking soda pop and thinking about my Galveston days when I at least had the company of some grown men when I was drinking. The musicians at the VFW that night, by the way, hardly deserved the name. They sawed and wheezed through their whole repertory which consisted of about fifteen songs, all sounding alike. It's fashionable now to like what everyone calls "country music," but if you had to sit out in the VFW and listen to it, you'd get pretty tired of the music and the country.

After a while I caught sight of Frank strolling in the front door. He stopped by another table for a minute to pat a girl on the top of her frizzy blonde head, then he ambled on over to me.

"Where's Kenyon?" I was tired of listening to the whining songs, tired of being flung around the dance floor. The new dances I'd told Daddy about hadn't gotten to Leon yet—they probably never will get to Frank Harwell. The more he drank the harder he danced, not on my toes, but stomping hard on the floor taking great wide steps and swinging me around in circles. It was 1:00 A.M., time to go home. Nobody else seemed to think so though. The hall was even more packed than when we first came in.

"Last time I saw him Kenyon was outside arguing with the cops. He's lost his ticket and they won't let him back in."

"Why doesn't he buy another one?"

"He thinks they ought to take his word he already bought one. You know he's got high principles and—"

"I know about his principles all right. He's got high principles and no scruples!!"

"Aw, don't be too hard on your brother."

I was getting ready to tell him that Kenyon had been hard on me when we both turned our heads to see what was causing all the shouting down by the door. It was my brother leading that gentle old Brahma bull by a rope around his neck. The crowd was parting before him. Some of them were jumping out the windows and everybody else was headed for the back door. The blonde Frank had patted on the head was standing on top of a table screaming, "Help! Somebody do something!" Nobody was doing anything but getting out. Kenyon staggered through the hall with a mean grin on his face, drunk as the lord of the wild frontier and cool as a walking ice cube. Behind the bandstand the musicians were crawling out the windows. The bass fiddler tried to throw his fiddle out first, but it got stuck. He left it there, half in, half out, and wriggled through another window. A man following him didn't watch where he was going and caught his foot in the middle of a drum.

Behind Kenyon the bull, uncertain of his footing on the slippery floor, was trying to adjust himself. He slid along, his tail lashing frantically, his hooves skidding in all directions. When Kenyon slowed down a little to get past some tables the Brahma snorted and jumped—like Alvin Neeley doing his little skip in mid-air to keep in step.

"Come on. We can't stand here gawking. Somebody's going to get hurt if Kenyon lets that old bull go." Frank grabbed my hand and we headed for the back door. By the time we got out Kenyon and the bull had the VFW Club to themselves.

We waited out back. The cops waited too. Kenyon appeared in the doorway. The bull nudged up behind him. He turned and scratched the bull's head.

"I told you," Kenyon hollered at the cops, "I already bought one ticket." Then he walked down the steps carefully leading the bull, talking to him all the way. "Watch your step, old buddy. That's right. Easy now."

The cops let Kenyon put the bull back in the auction pen, and when he was finished, they put him in their car. He was laughing so hard he couldn't fight very well, but he tried.

"Oh Lord!" Frank sighed lazily from the safety of his pickup. "If he wouldn't fight, they'd let him go. Those boys were ready for that dance to break up anyway."

"Aren't you going to help him?"

"Naw. He took this on hisself. You want us both in jail?"

"In jail?"

"Yeah," Frank drawled and hoisted his big handsome self across the seat toward me.

"Shouldn't we follow them?"

"Look at that moon."

There wasn't a moon in sight, not a sliver of one. Gorgeous Frank Harwell was so sleepy drunk he mistook somebody's headlights for the moon. All the excitement on top of all the dancing we'd done was too much for him I guess, because the next thing I knew he'd passed out. I lifted his head off my shoulder, propped it up against the window, and climbed into the driver's seat.

I got to the jail in time to hear them book Kenyon for being drunk and disorderly and disturbing the peace. He paid his own way out this time, but the only reason they didn't lock him up for the night was I was there to take him home. Of course, I couldn't take him home in his condition. Daddy would have had an attack and Mother would have probably fainted at the sight of him. Her clean-cut, hard-working, tight-lipped boy was a living mess. He looked like he'd been riding the bull rather than leading him. I managed to brush most of the dust off of him. The cops gave him back his hat. We stopped at Leon's one open-all-night cafe, where I went in and got a quart of black coffee. When he'd finished this he was sober enough to go in the men's room and wash his face. Frank slept through the whole rehabilitation.

Kenyon wanted to park the pickup on the square across from the jail and walk home, leaving Frank there snoring. "Maybe the cops will come out and get him," he said.

"It's not any use to get mad at Frank. It was your idea to bring that animal into the dance hall."

"You taking up for him?"

"I got you out of jail, didn't I?"

Kenyon nodded. I went in the cafe to get some more coffee for Frank. When I came back out Kenyon started shaking him, but before he got him awake he turned to me and said, "Sister, don't tell everything you know."

"Why not? Mother and Daddy are going to find out anyway. By church time tomorrow everybody in town will be talking—"

"I'd rather they get it second-hand."

By this time I was so mad I jabbed Frank with my elbow, handed him the coffee, and lit into Kenyon. "You'd rather everybody get everything second-hand. Nobody is supposed to do anything but you."

"What are you talking about?"

"Never mind! You wouldn't understand if I kept talking till sunup, but I'll tell you this, Kenyon—I'm not going to devote the rest of my life to keeping you out of jail. From now on you are on your own."

"Sister, I've always been on my own."

How contrary can a person be? Here I'd just saved him from a night in the Leon County jail, not to mention the time I got him out of the Galveston jail. I didn't argue with him though. I knew if I told him he wasn't on his own till he left home, he wouldn't wait a minute before telling me the same thing—with Frank Harwell sitting right next to me taking in every word.

"You want me to drive?" Kenyon asked him.

"Naw, you have got in enough trouble tonight, you and that dancing bull. I'll make it."

They both laughed. Frank even tried to slap my knee, but I dodged him.

"I want to go home," I said.

"Gal, that's where we're going."

It was 2:30 A.M. I could imagine Daddy sitting on the front porch wrapped in his overcoat with his M-1 stretched across his knees. For once, we were lucky. Mother and Daddy were both in bed asleep. Kenyon and I tiptoed to our rooms without waking either one of them. When they asked us the next morning where we'd been so late, Kenyon said, "Dancing." Since they were used to short answers from him he didn't have to say anything else. Of course Mother came and sat on the foot of my bed and asked me all about Frank Harwell.

"Mother, Frank is a very handsome man and no doubt all the other girls like him, but he is a cowboy and I think one cowboy is enough in the family."

Then I told her. "In June I'm going down to San Antonio and look for a job in one of the schools there."

"You can't—"

"Yes, I can. If I don't leave home now, I'll be right here the rest of my days."

"She might as well," Kenyon said. He was leaning in the doorway, eavesdropping to see whether I was going to tell on him. "She's too uppity for anybody in Leon." With that he turned around and left. He didn't know it, but it was the best thing he could have said. Daddy blamed himself for giving me too much education and Mother was so anxious to be a grandmother I think she'd have been happy to see me off to New York.

In June I went to San Antonio and found a job at one of the high schools. I found a husband, too, a fine doctor who sings in the chorus during opera season. That's where I met him—in the chorus. We were rehearsing for *La Traviata*. His name is Edward Greenlee. Dr. Edward Greenlee.

"Can he rope?" Kenyon asked.

"Can you tie a suture?"

"What branch of the army was he in?"

"He was in the navy, Daddy."

"Is he from a large family?"

"Mother, there are Greenlees all over San Antonio."

We had a June wedding in the First Methodist in Leon. Daddy gave me away. Kenyon was an usher. He looked handsome in his white tux jacket, the only one he'd ever worn in his life. I told him so when I got to the church in my bridal finery. He said thanks and grinned his tight-lipped grin. I looked down. The black pants covered all of the stitching decorating the tops, but I could plainly see, and so could everybody else at my wedding, that Kenyon had his boots on.

I guess he'll go on being true to the code and die with them on. He's living out on one of his ranches now, fifteen miles from the nearest town and ninety miles from San Antonio. Sometimes on Sunday afternoons Edward and I take the children and drive up to see him. There's no way of letting him know we're coming because he doesn't have a telephone. We don't have to worry about inconveniencing anybody though; Kenyon lives by himself.

The last time we were there we missed him. My five-year-old boy, William, walked around on the bare floors and said, "Doesn't he have any rugs?"

When we were checking the cupboards in the almost bare kitchen Cynthia, our three-year-old, wailed, "Doesn't he have any cookies?"

"No, he doesn't have any rugs and he doesn't have any cookies. But he does have a bathtub, hot and cold running water, a bed, a fire, three cans of chili, a sack of flour, two horses, a sheep dog, and a whole lot of sheep, goats, and cattle."

"Why doesn't he have any cookies?"

"This sure is a lumpy old chair," said William. He should have known. He was sitting in the only one in the room. "Is Uncle Kenyon poor?"

"All of your Uncle Kenyon's money is tied up in stock, the sheep, and goats and cattle," said Edward, who always tries to explain things.

"Uncle Kenyon is a cowboy," I said, which was really the only explanation.

THE SCAPEGOAT

★

James Hoggard

I HEARD THEM.

"How long you gonna keep on doin' it?" Cravens asked.

"Till it by god gets right," Elwood told him.

They were standing outside the cafe where a lot of us stay when the weather's right. It's often not.

"You're just a goddurn nuisance," Cravens said.

"Can't help it," Elwood told him. The sun was in my eyes, and I think Elwood also flickered out a little smile, the kind that makes serious people angry.

"You better help it," Cravens insisted, not sounding like the lay preacher he acted like he was on Sundays.

"Why?"

"We're gonna run ya off if you don't quieten down. We might even hang ya."

"I never had thought of it that way."

"You might start. I'm not the only one thinking such."

"How come you to tell me all this?"

"Cause I don't wanta hang ya," Cravens said, winding back down. "So please. Just be quieter."

"Can't. My project demands noise."

"Then quit your damn—just give us some peace for awhile."

"Can't. Pipe and hammers make noise. Sound of it might even be good for you."

"Damnit—"

It bothered me to hear them talk like that. My folks, the old couple took me in and brought me up, always said I was short on spine, but Cravens' belligerence and Elwood's taunting him back were making me feel raw. I knew that Cravens wasn't joking about their getting Elwood. I just didn't think they were actually going to hang him. Sadder than that is the fact that the poor devil almost got away; at least one person around here, for a time, even said he did. That was Amarilla, and for awhile she was right, too. Her enterprise around here was pleasure: mine included.

Cravens hadn't been bluffing. In fact, the time they got Elwood I'd just left Amarilla's place—it's just outside town—and was smiling and laughing all through my flesh from what me and her had been doing. It was dark and I heard a commotion out in the field. There was all sorts of yelling and carrying on. Someone had a torch and had set what looked like a big cottonwood afire. The light from the blaze looked like glory. The tall grass in the meadow even quivered, like it was thrilled or frightened by the hot light. At least four men were out there carrying on and maybe even fighting each other. Also a coondog I couldn't see was barking itself hoarse. Then a rifle, then a shotgun went off. That stopped some of my curiosity. I got the hell out of there and didn't hear what else happened till the next day, and some of that was contradictory.

"OLE ELWOOD GOT WHAT WAS BY GOD COMIN TO HIM."

"For a fact. Moment that rope jerked taut he let out a smell stronger'n—"

"Heard some even fainted."

"I heard the same, though we weren't exactly there, directly there, when it all occurred."

"This mornin over coffee I heard you were."

"My heart was out there with'm. So was Szczepinski's."

Theo Szczepinski had the most hatchet-like face in town and passed for Will Cravens' best friend. I never liked either one of them.

"I be dog, Cy. You mean you weren't out there among'm either?"

"Was for awhile, but I had to get back. My nephew's been having some fever."

"Then who the hell was out there?"

"There was at least several."

"Who?"

"Too sonofabitchin dark for me to see, but ole Elwood got it. Popped his head clean off his neck."

"Then he didn't have to suffer."

"Hell, have to suffer! He got what he by god had comin. Keepin everybody up like he was. Project he called it. But we got him. Things're gonna be different, too—just us'n God'n the scenery now. No noise."

"Then I don't guess either one of y'all heard."

"Heard what?"

"That rumor sayin' Elwood weren't even there. Somebody at the grocer's told somebody he got away."

"Hell he did."

"Some others've been talkin about it, too, down at the cafe."

"That's a by god lie."

"It ain't either, Szczepinski. I've heard more'n one say the same."

"Then they weren't there. How the lord could they know? We got him, I saw it."

"While ago you said you didn't."

"You just ask the ones there the whole time. We got him. And there ain't gonna be any more racket durin the night either. Elwood's project is *through!*—gone! Just flat out *done!*"

One of our town's problems—anybody should've known this—was that nobody here knew exactly what Elwood's project was. They just knew it made noise. The second problem was that a couple nights later, the racket all began again. It sounded like a locomotive running over a mess of broken, warped track—that and the wind howling like God or somebody big had the asthma. The pounding, too—irregular like all the other noises. It had no rhythm you could adjust yourself to. But I didn't think the racket was all that bad. I will admit, though, I was away during most of it. I'd gone down to Austin to get myself checked. Doctor here said I had heartworms, but the two I saw in Austin said only dogs have that malady (as a rule). They thought, though, they ought to check over my liver. So they poked around my belly and said I was all right, except for gas; but that's from goobers. I ain't giving them up either, even if they do cause wind. Nor am I giving up pitching washers for wagers. I don't care if Cravens does say gambling's a sin.

It was when I come back I heard about Elwood which I've never been close to, him or his project either. That night when the racket started again, after his apparent passing, a lot of the men got riled. Some of the kids spooked, too, but the women didn't react to the hoorah. When I asked, my sweet friend Amarilla said she would not comment on the project. The women and the men, neither one, she said, understood it. She indicated she was probably the only one in town knew what Elwood was trying to do, and how come he wouldn't tell anybody was because he intended on getting rich and didn't want anybody, he'd say, stealing his bygod damn idea. That's what she told me, and also that they might get married—a fact I disliked, but I didn't let on. I kept my simmering to myself.

"What was he trying to do?" I asked. "And did they get'm or not?"

"Which one you want to know?"

She was trying to be teasy with me, but I wouldn't bite.

"Both," I answered.

"They did and they didn't. And he may or may not recover."

"You mean you know where he is?"

She didn't even look at me. She just stayed lying there on her bare back with her ankle on her knee. I couldn't even tell if she was avoiding my question. But she did mention what Elwood had been about: trying to make some kind of cattle-screwing machine. Seems he'd heard somewhere about the possibility of breeding being increased. He was trying to make a machine to help the bull out, and I guess the cow, too. But mostly his own pocketbook.

Notions like that plumb amaze me. I wouldn't even know how to start. Apparently Elwood didn't either, but he kept on banging his hammer on the pipe all night trying to adjust what hadn't even been put together right in the first place.

"Then how come all that racket after they hung him or whatever?"

"It wasn't Elwood," she said. "What it was was someone trying to finish up what he'd been trying to get started."

"But you said nobody knew."

"Somebody might've seen him. Probably all it was, though, was somebody finding his stuff and trying to figure out what it was he'd been after. I imagine it'll be awhile before we hear anything else from his gear. But what I'm curious about is if you plan on sleeping over."

"Indeed I do," I told her. She needn't never asked, her knowing how partial I was to waking up in the breeze of the morning and hearing them yellow-bellied freckle-breasted meadowlarks singing and me feeling all blowsy with them, like I'm swimming up out of some crazy dream to find my sweet lady slow-loping my mule.

We had another drink before sleep, but when I woke up in the night she was gone. She wasn't anywhere in the house. The back door was wide open. I couldn't find her out back either, so I figured she must be tending to Elwood, wherever she had him hid. I found out later I was wrong. Someone had threw her down the well.

It's just extraordinary how a mind'll pull your ninners. Here I was half in love with her and grateful she hadn't suffered pain from her fall, her death having occurred before. Some bastard had planted an ax in the middle of her back, right near the spot where my fingertips used to meet when I clutched her and we got so lathery neither one of us cared about the poop-noises our bellies made against one another.

But she was gone and I swore I was going to get revenge. I didn't care who I had to hurt. I was so angry pissants were crawling all inside my craw. She hadn't ever done anything but help poor people feel better. I swore I'd get whoever hurt her. And I did, too. Got both of them, and quicker than I thought, too, me not even ever having pretended to be swift in the head.

What I did was find me that contraption Elwood had been working on. They did hang him and he did die, but not at the same time. I staked his outfit out for two nights, but no one showed up. Fact, the only one came near it was a scrap-buyer in the middle of the day, and he didn't know what to do with it any more than anybody else here in this curly dogtail place did. Nobody came around the well either, except maybe a pig or two from over Szczepinski's farm. I asked around the cafe and saloon, but nobody said anything more'n what a shame it was all this carrying on and disaster. But you can't tell with folks around here whether they're telling the truth or not. I don't think it's because they're so clever. I think it's because they ain't figured out themselves what the truth is. I have heard outsiders come in and call them sly like a snake, but those are the suckers coming through town and buying the trinkets kids make out of sticks and nails and ribbon when they're playing hooky. The kids tell those sports the doodads were made by Indians living over by the bluff. It was a pig, though, broke the ice and let me undrown the crime's awful secret.

Szczepinski didn't help either—or that jackass Cravens who I myself heard threaten Elwood with hanging. It was that young sissy dude, Heinz Fretlinger, who hadn't never done anything fit to talk about other than try to gamahuche a goat. I caught him attempting the same thing with the pig, only he didn't notice I was around. He didn't have any luck either—the pig kept biting him—young Fretlinger cussing and crying and swearing he'd get an ax. That's when I started taking notice. Folks around here don't use axes except to chop wood; they don't even have any ax-throwing contests the way they do in some places, like Austin and San Antone. Swinging an ax is just damn hard work—except apparently for Fretlinger who's always been a sissy. He lives in a shack back of Cravens' wheatfield. I followed him home and early that evening found on the handle of the ax at his place all the evidence I thought I needed.

When he went out that night I slipped in his shack and found a yellow ribbon tied on a nail in his wall. I knew where it came from: way up high on Amarilla's thigh—garter you call them. I lifted it off but when I put it in my pocket I started feeling sad all over and missing her.

There wasn't any place to hide so I went outside in the dark till Fretlinger came back. I figured he'd be drunk, but he wasn't anywhere close to it. He just walked in and lit a lamp. I stayed outside watching through a window, then noticed a coil of rope on a pile of clothes in the corner. The end of the rope was a noose. Somehow, I realized, Elwood was involved in all this, but I wasn't sure how. Fretlinger couldn't've done the hanging himself, or firing the shot either. He was too weak for the first and too lily for the second. Still, something told me everything was tied together, that I was just too damn crazed with grief to know how, only that's not the way I felt. When Fretlinger finally let the secret out, everything was all taken care of—only not in the way I'd planned.

Thinking he'd get scared, I chunked pebbles at his window, but all he did was raise the window and ask if anybody out here wanted him. Like a fool, I said yes.

"Who ith that?"

"Somebody knows what you did, Fretlinger."

"What ith it I thupposed to do?"

"I know—a bunch of us know. We're gonna get you for it, too."

"You juth come on in. We'll talk about it."

Thank god I stayed hid and he didn't have an ear worth a damn. He poked a shotgun out and pulled the damn trigger, only I was in the other direction from where the blast went. I admit it, I was scared and must've lost control and yelled because he whoopeed and came running out of his shack. I kept hugging shadow. When he finally gave up looking I'd snuck around the other side and would've give anything for a couple rattlesnakes to toss up on that little pecker of a porch leading into his place. He went on back inside and blew out the lamp, I don't even think scared. And rattled as I was, I wasn't even sure any more he was guilty. I thought about the ax handle again, saw it up close in my mind. What I thought had been blood was just paint. I'd put it there myself a couple years back, about a month before it had disappeared from Amarilla's tool shed. Fretlinger might've been a thief, but I don't think a killer.

Next day the story circled, the story about Fretlinger shooting me, only they didn't know who I was, just that there had been commotion. I was delivering groceries back to the cafe's kitchen when I heard Sally Cravens say, "Husband told me something like this'd happen."

She was standing outside the dry goods store between me and the woman she was talking to so I didn't know who it was. I could just hear their voices.

"You ask me, it all goes back to Elwood," the other woman said and I agreed. "I think he got away and killed her." But I disagreed with that. "He's the one had the ax," she said. "They didn't hang him. He got away."

She was right. Nobody but me now knew what happened to his body.

"Got away? How?"

"Someone helped him."

"Who? Young Mr. Fretlinger?"

"No. At least not directly. I think it had to be the woman herself—maybe Fretlinger with her."

"Fiddle! Heinz Fretlinger never had anything to do with that woman, or any woman. Just Elwood and all the other damn men. But they sure didn't hang or kill anybody."

"How do you know?"

"The atmosphere around here'd be tighter than it is."

"But Cy was upset—and so was your husband Will."

"They're always upset. The noise ever bother *you?*"

"No. I heard it but I didn't think it was that bad. I don't ever lose sleep less a baby's crying sick or such."

"That's what I mean. I don't know a woman in town that that noise bothered."

"Then why the men?"

"I told you—that woman. Oh, they were upset with Elwood all right—but not about his noise. Not mainly."

"About her then?"

"Her and him both. Him hogging her. And someone else, too, but I'm not sure who it'd be. Just mark my word—Heinz Fretlinger's a victim. He's no more guilty than we are."

I'd better back up. Long about then I drifted out of earshot and couldn't be sure if she'd really said Fretlinger *was a victim* or if she'd said Fretlinger *was gonna get'm*. The sun was in my eyes and if I can't see good I have trouble hearing.

Confused, I started feeling sick in my stomach and somehow guilty, too, and cheap for what I'd been ready to do to Fretlinger, titty that he was. Then it struck me: I didn't have a damn friend left, and maybe never did, at least the way I'd thought. For awhile I even wondered if

I might not've invented about that ax and Amarilla doubled up at the bottom of the well. And even all the things me and her used to do—did I just dream that? And if I did then how come everything fell smack-dab in their sonofabitchin places?

So there I was: one moment convinced Fretlinger was a rotten damn killer then the next minute realizing he didn't have anything to do with it. And what's worse: even ready to give up memories I wasn't even sure any more me and her had ever had. And them women to blame. They'd messed up my notions, and not only that: for the first damn time it upset me to realize how spineless I was. Talking to themselves and not even shining my way—face or butt either—they threw the truth on me. It was hotter'n a brand stuck up in my face. There was only one person I hadn't even considered might've did all the trouble, and that unlucky bastard was me.

I had a reason, too: hatred of Elwood and hatred of her: that grief I hardly even told about, or faced myself either, till then. And Heinz Fretlinger didn't even own an ax, except the one he'd stole a good while back—stole or just hadn't returned. I had put it there on his place as evidence—but just in my head. I threw the real one in the salt cedars down by the river, which was dishonest. The ax wasn't even mine. It was hers and I was mixed up. Then it happened—her getting killed—that last night I was with her, when I woke up and found her gone.

I'd gone outside, gone out to the barn where I heard hay or such rustling and a loud cranky squealing. She'd been hiding Elwood up in the loft. But it must've been just a short while before that she'd found he'd passed. I say that. I don't know. The noise was coming from his weight putting a strain on the rope that pressed against a pulley as she lowered him in jerks back down on the ground. I stayed back and watched. She drug him out in the clearing. She piled down on him hay and the wood I'd chopped. She slopped kerosene on the stack then struck it all up in a big damn fire. All she had on was her nightclothes. I watched her through the shadows and glare. I watched them toys on her body I sometimes played with—me and ever damn sonofabitch man around here. Even Elwood, dead and dumb as he was now, popped his eyes open at her when the wind blew a flip up under her gown and pressed it fast against her.

It wasn't just jealousy stirring me. It was the fact she was burning him with a look on her face showing a lot more agitation than sorrow. That's when I knew that if something similar had happened to me, she'd've set me on fire, too, and not even broke a sweat digging a hole. That was the kind she was, and I hadn't known that. That was just damn hard to take, and an awful lot worse than being thought spineless. She didn't think I was anything, except something to piddle around with so I'd do her damn hard work. I wasn't anything to her, and Elwood wasn't either, except a chance to get rich. It wasn't even pleasure we'd had together. All it was was convenience, and something like that rips deeper than anything can ever scab over. That's the way I felt then, and I didn't get over it till I put the pain—thought I'd put it—plumb out of my squirrelly damn mind.

After she stoked the fire a lot more than I ever thought was necessary, Elwood wasn't no more than ashes. You couldn't tell what was him from what the wood used to be: everything mixed together, except for charred staves that could've been bones.

But pretty and nasty and unruffled as ever, she went to the well to wash her damn hands. And that's when I started thinking myself into fits. I thought that if I was still asleep she'd have done the same thing she just did and come on back to bed, acting like nothing had happened. I couldn't stand that. I knew what she'd been fiddling with, and I don't mind saying it either: I ain't enough man to be casual about being played with by a hand that's just been messing with a corpse. So I gritted my teeth and went back to bed, but not before first I allowed myself to set that ax down deep in her back

When I woke up I felt like I'd been having another one of my squirrel-headed dreams. I went outside to find her but couldn't. I didn't know where she'd gone and hoped I hadn't really done what I'd just dreamed I'd done. I was sure I hadn't. So I went over to the cafe for coffee, which for a month or so I'd been having in the morning instead of beer. That was near the time when I heard those damn two women chattering. I still don't know why but somehow they made me start facing what it was I'd done. In spite of their cussing their men, they were part of a good world I'd never known, and that made me feel small and to blame—and separate from everything, even myself, because those people, tidy as they think they are, hadn't cared any more about Amarilla than she'd cared about me. I wasn't even sure any more they cared about each other. Life felt cold and I felt to blame, like a damn blue norther had crawled in like worms and crickets under my skin. That was the misery I was going to have to face: nobody around here cared shit, not about me or anybody else. Only I was the one who'd used the damn ax—they hadn't—and on somebody I once considered sweet and still even love in my drizzle-headed way.

I COULD'VE ESCAPED. I COULD'VE JUST LEFT AND NOBODY CARED, everybody used to me lighting a shuck, and they sure not going to go to any trouble or grief either over a lady like Amarilla. Even if the men had been inclined, the women wouldn't've let them do anything open about it. So I could've got away. But I didn't. I went back in there at the cafe and confessed. Only nobody believed me, except in his own crooked way Will Cravens, who like I said's a lay preacher; and here that's bigger than sheriff, which we don't even have.

"Well, if you really did it," Cravens said, "we oughta hang ya."

I stood stout like a man and admitted I deserved that.

He said he wasn't one to judge but if it would make me happy he'd be glad to get the boys and some rope and pop my neck off my shoulders for me. He hollered them all over, but, laughing, they said they were going to buy me a drink first, and a fresh hot plate of fried eggs. They made me sit down at a table, and old skinny Cy Szczepinski held the fork and fed me faster than I could even swallow. I think he was trying to strangle me.

"When you want us to string you?" Cravens asked.

My mouth was so full I couldn't answer so just shook my head to tell him I didn't know.

"You want it later on this afternoon or just wait till morning?"

Scrunching my chin down to force some gas out, I indicated I didn't care, and they commenced laughing, one of them even suggesting they pull my pants off and run me out in the street. Everbody thought that was a fine idea, except Szczepinski who said that when I saw the women if I got a bone on he'd cut it off with his big case knife. Finally able to swallow my throat free, I told him not to worry, that even if that snake-like joke in my drawers tried to rise I wouldn't ever let it do damage. Then someone poured a pitcher of beer over my head, and all of them piled on me, stripped my britches off and chased me out the door—hitting and kicking and throwing onions and ever damn thing they could find. Even the picture of the naked lady on the wall which looked a little like my friend, deceased now, and theirs, too.

Outside, like I feared, was a cadre of women, but except for showing a bit of disgust they didn't pay much attention to us. The men chased me down the street and pushed me down in mud puddles by the watering troughs. They knocked me up against horses, which got skittery, and ripped my shirt off and even some of them rubbed hockey in my hair. They didn't hang me, though. They just run me out of town.

And Cravens, who's got breath smells like corn that's been pissed on, shoved his stout belly up against me and knocked me stumbling over a big fanning spread of prickly pear. He told me I was a liar, that Amarilla hadn't died in any well, she'd just moved because her place was going broke and there wasn't anything or anybody here to hold her.

What they were doing to me hurt. If I could've cried I'd've leaked tears all over the dirt, but I didn't. Worthless and spineless, I just sputtered and choked and heard Cravens saying again how much a liar I was and how they couldn't stand or put up with such trash. And everbody hurrahed him, or maybe they were all now just hurrahing me.

Finally getting a hold on myself, I knew there wasn't any point arguing with them. They don't listen. People like Amarilla don't either. They just take what they want and go, and no feelings of loyalty or staying still with someone ever hit them. She pulled some good work out of me, and pulled a chance at a fortune out of Elwood, too. She pulled some life out of everbody here except Fretlinger who'd rather court a damn animal and Cravens who's rank and stove up with talk. But they were all kicking me now and beating on me and yelling at me to hurry up and leave, which I did, in spite of them being all over me and grabbing me back down. Naked and bruised as I was, I scrimmaged out from under them, and spineless or not, I ran.

"Catch!" one of them called. I turned around and jumped but it wasn't a snake Cy was throwing at me, just a piece of rope. He hollered at me to hang myself, that they didn't want to take the trouble, then they all started after me again. I ran. They yelled at me to stop and come get my rope, but I kept running, and feeling as gutsick as I'd ever been. I wasn't going to slow down or go back. I was quit of them and free—free of them and free of everything. All I wanted was a cliff to jump off of, and I would have, too, if I'd found one.

There was only one thing left: keep going and, first chance I got, steal some clothes.

When I did look back they'd all gotten small. A few of them were chunking rocks at me, but the distance between us was smart; and before the day was over I'd swiped a pair of overalls off a clothesline.

What I'm doing now is living out in the woods near the river. I don't mind it either, being cut off. I don't mind it damnit at all. My dreams have started coming back and, silly as some of them are, they do me good. When it's dark I don't even have too much trouble hearing the sounds of Elwood pounding on his pipe: things back the way they were. I do, though, miss my sweet friend. Most people like her live only near town, and I can't go back there any more. I can't ever just plop myself down near where she is. I'm to blame, too. I feel bad about what I think I probably did with that ax. It would've been more mature to have planted something else in her. Sometimes she let me do that.

It seems funny now. Afterward she'd start carrying on about how stout Will Cravens' preaching was—she did go to church now and then—and how, though most of the people where we lived didn't know what sin was, she said, there really was such a thing, and women knew about it better than men, which didn't mean, she said, that women sinned more; it meant they had a more practical sense of what it was, they being less prone to hoorah and such, and having more practice with forgiveness because of the men.

I never did understand what she was talking about those times— which is another reason I miss her and why, as time ripples past, I get the notion more and more that I really wasn't the one who stuck that ax in her back. Sometimes I'm certain I didn't. But I don't believe she just moved. I wouldn't've invented about her being dropped down that well. I couldn't've come up with something like that any more than I could've ever come up with that idea and that contraption Elwood was making everybody miserable with. But somebody got her, and the more I think about it, the more I don't have any idea who did it. I don't even know if she knew. But I still feel to blame, and I can still feel that ax's oak handle solid and hard in my hands. I don't care whether Cravens believes me or not, the blade would belong to him: wedged right between his eyes.

But I do remember one time her saying when I was cleaning up her place, her saying how come most people don't pay attention to me is because I'm so much like them, only me and they don't notice it. She always did have a way of talking and thinking funny. And I wasn't one to ask her to explain herself either. The reason for that being the questions never occurred to me till a long time later. One time I even told her such, but she just laughed and wiggled her body which somehow reminded me of clouds. We have a lot of them around here—all kinds. We just don't have much rain. And the songs those freckle-breasted meadowlarks sing beneath them in the morning, when the clouds are red and purple or even just grey and blue, always seem to me sweet but sassy enough that you don't even mind how ridiculous they are, and how different they are from what they sometimes look like: them birds I mean —all puffed up soft in front like my friend and making you want to dive on in and just lose yourself blind in their feathers.

A TRAIN TO CATCH

★

Clay Reynolds

MATTIE CUMMINGS SWUNG HER LEGS OVER THE SIDE OF her bed and sat up. She stretched away the mustiness of sleep, ran mental fingers all over her body, searched for anything wrong. She was a bit stiff, but that was natural, given the weather. She had an aching in her fingers. Her fingers always annoyed her when it was about to snow. She rose, turning automatically to make the bed. Tight corners, nice tuck of the heavy comforter under her pillow. The mattress was too hard. She knew that hard mattresses were supposed to be better, but she liked to sink deep into a bed, feel it all around her.

In the bathroom, she completed her morning toilet, brushed her thick gray hair in the small mirror over the sink. Like everything in her life, the bathroom was cold, sterile. It defied her attempts to personalize it with a small basket of perfumed soap. There was no tub, only a hospital-type shower with an overlarge stall for a handicapped user.

She thought of them as "cripples." She was a long way from being crippled. Her hair was unruly this morning, wiry and full of static electricity. She tried dampening the brush, but that only seemed to make it worse. She'd have to clip it to hold it down.

Back in her small room, she slipped off her nightgown and stood naked before the bureau mirror. Her body was sturdy. Age and hard work hadn't bothered it much. There was a little fat around her hips, a slight bulge across her belly, but her shoulders were level, her breasts still firm, still had some bounce left in them. Once, she went for a week without wearing a bra just to see if anyone noticed. No one said a word, but she detected envious disapproval in House Manager Yvonne Garrett's glances. Though she was thirty years younger than Mattie, Yvonne's breasts sagged to her paunch with gravity no brassiere could arrest.

Outside, the wind was up. A chill seeped into the room, and she shivered. She pulled out a housedress and put it on. She found a pair of cotton socks in the bureau, then her lace-up rubber-soled shoes. She refused to wear house shoes, never had. She saw them as a sign of laziness.

Rising, she walked over to the window. Brittle cold swirled on a bitter north wind. The trees were bare, stark fingers grasping uselessly at the sky, grass yellow and dead, clouds the color of gunmetal, darker around the edges of the morning horizon. "Snow before dark," she said aloud, rubbing her sore knuckles. Her breath formed a pear-shaped cloud on the window. She ran a crooked finger through the liquid fog.

She broke the finger when she was a girl trying to catch a chicken for Christmas Eve dinner. When the fat hen dodged away from her, she slipped on the ice, fell against the porch, and the digit snapped backwards. She tried to remember the pain, but she could only remember her daddy setting it with string and a clothespin while she sat at the kitchen table and smelled her mother's cooking. It mended with a bending twist. "Christmas," she said softly. The childhood anticipation of the holiday took root deep in her and grew.

She smiled and allowed her crooked finger to continue its wet design, turning the pear into a tree-shaped triangle, then adding small circles for balls, ornaments. She'd always loved Christmas.

Across the norther-swept street a movement caught her eye. It was a young Spanish boy helping a girl into a battered old open bed bobtail truck. "*Mestizos*," Mattie frowned and whispered the old term. Migrant workers, she mentally corrected, and not Spanish, but *Mexican*. Too late in the season for them to be here, whatever they were. Work was long gone. They looked dirt poor. The girl was fat—for a Mexican, Mattie thought. She absolutely waddled. People that poor shouldn't be well fed enough to be so heavy at so young an age, or at any age. The girl had trouble getting up into the cab. She had long, dark hair spilling out of a stocking cap over a threadbare denim jumper. Even from a distance, her hands and bare legs looked raw with the cold. Fat or not, she was pretty when she turned and flashed a bright smile at the boy, who was short, chunky. He jogged around to the other side and banged into the vehicle. Frost from their breaths covered the windows as the old truck lurched away.

She estimated they were heading out to the old boxcars by the Short Road where the migrants generally lived. No running water or electricity. Just shelter, and not much of that. They were poor and ignorant, Mattie thought. But they looked happy. She envied them and was angry at herself for admitting it.

It was time to go to breakfast. She hated breakfast. For more than six decades, she had arisen every morning and made biscuits, hard-fried eggs, bacon, gravy, and set the whole ensemble out with a half gallon of strong coffee on an oilcloth-covered table for Dutch. He liked a good breakfast. She loved making it. Now, though, she knew that the dining room table of the Willow Oaks would be laden with nothing more substantial than lukewarm oatmeal. There would be some yogurt, low-cal jellies to go on bagels or some other rubbery excuse for bread, some decaffeinated coffee and weak tea, a couple of pitchers of juice, and skim milk for those who wanted cold cereal with overripe bananas.

That wasn't breakfast, Mattie thought. That was just stupid.

She glanced around her room. The bed was against one wall, her bureau—the only piece of furniture she was able to bring with her other than a rocker—against the other. A rubber-backed, washable cotton throw rug occupied the middle of the area, covering green and white tile, gone black in the corners from years of wax and dirt build-up. She had put a few small mementos on the wall, but they seemed out of place, temporary, as, truly, they were intended to be. She had photos of her mother and father, and one of her and Dutch. It was a picture they took the day they paid off the farm. Ten years ago, she remembered. It seemed a lifetime ago. In a way, it was.

With a sigh, she left the room. There was little choice. It was nearly eight, and Yvonne would be coming down to check on her if she didn't appear. It made her feel helpless, at Yvonne's mercy.

The hallway smelled of camphor and antiseptic, human waste and the sickly sweet odor of age. Indefinable, it permeated the house, even the residents' clothing. No matter how hard people cleaned their surroundings, themselves, it remained, overcame everything. It had no source, it was just part of the stink of Willow Oaks.

What kind of stupid name was "Willow Oaks," anyway? Mattie wondered as she padded down the sterile hall. A willow was a willow. An oak was an oak. There was no such thing as a "willow oak." In north-central Texas, there wasn't much of either one, anyway.

The dining room opened before her gaze. Maria Chivington, the girl Yvonne worked like her personal slave, scurried around helping the half dozen residents seated at the table with various needs. Yvonne herself breezed through, gave Mattie an acidic smile, inspected the table, departed. Yvonne had been an ugly girl, Mattie thought as she sat down and reached for a piece of cold whole-wheat toast. Now, she was an ugly woman. Too lazy to get a husband when she was young, she gave up on herself and decided if she couldn't be happy, she'd make it her mission in life to see to the perpetual unhappiness of others. So far, she'd been successful. As house manager of an old folks' home, she'd found the perfect calling.

Yvonne forbade anyone to call Willow Oaks an "old folks' home," Mattie reminded herself with a wry smile. This was a "benevolent care center." She thought it more closely resembled the death house of a prison. Yvonne was the perfect warden.

Mattie's fellow tenants didn't talk much at breakfast. At first, this distressed her. But after a few weeks, she realized that it wasn't that they were unfriendly. They just had little to say. Beyond complaining about their most recent surgeries or comparing medications, their lives had been reduced to dim memories. There were plenty of those. Enough to fill each eight-by-twelve room with a combination of misery and regret, laced only occasionally with the joyful recollection of something wonderful. No one needed to share another's. It hurt too much to drag the past out and dust it off for the indifferent inspection of someone whose life was just as disappointing as everyone else's.

The average age in the house was seventy-five. Mattie knew this because Yvonne kept a large chart on a wall in the kitchen, a running count. If someone died or moved in, she made the adjustment. At eighty-two, Mattie was the oldest ambulatory resident on the premises. This vexed Yvonne, who thought anyone as old as Mattie should have to rely on a walker or at least a cane.

Mattie reached for coffee, sniffed it, and asked Maria if there was any fresh made. Maria gave the kitchen door a brief glance, then winked and slipped through. Mattie's conspiracy with Maria was another satisfying element in her life. She slipped the girl five dollars a week to keep a thermos of regular coffee handy. She made it at home and brought it in. If Yvonne knew, she'd probably fire her. Mattie worried about that. But she needed and wanted her coffee, regular, strong, and black as Yvonne's heart.

BREAKFAST OVER, AND TWO CUPS OF MARIA'S STOUT COFFEE consumed on the sly, Mattie retired to the "rec room." It really was just a living room, doubled in size from the original house's design when it was converted from a private residence to Willow Oaks. Four hard sofas were placed here and there, with some easy chairs—no recliners, as Yvonne explained she was afraid of lawsuits in case someone hurt something getting into or out of one. A few end tables held ugly lamps with low-wattage bulbs and stacks of outdated magazines that offered advice on cooking, home decorating, child-rearing, and for some reason, sexual gratification. There were some old *Texas Monthlys*, advertising restaurants, boutiques, and luxury vacations no resident of Willow Oaks could even imagine. A handful of business magazines were for the investment-minded reader who might want to plan a prosperous future. Willow Oaks residents were in the middle of their future, Mattie thought, and it was far from prosperous.

The room was cheerless and as impersonal as a hospital waiting area. A 19-inch color TV on a wobbly stand was parked against one wall. There was no cable or satellite dish, only a rickety antenna that struggled to pull in three—sometimes four—stations from distant towers. Four wheelchairs were aligned in front of the snowy screen that morning, their occupants waiting for the news programs to end and game or talk shows to begin. The volume was perpetually too loud to talk or concentrate on reading. Christmas music spilled out from commercials and network greetings. Mattie picked up a stack of *Southern Living* and *Better Homes and Gardens*, took a seat. She'd never developed an interest in television, as they never could get any reception on the farm. She had a radio in her room, but farm market reports and implement ads depressed her. She never learned to like modern music.

She glanced out the window. The weather was deteriorating. No walk today. She had nothing to do until dinner, which Yvonne called "lunch," and which like everything else at Willow Oaks was served on a strict timetable. Today, it would be a real thrill, Mattie thought. Maria told her that cream of broccoli soup and pasta salad were on the menu. "Just as soon have peanut butter on a stale soda cracker," Mattie told her.

Mattie came to Willow Oaks three months before. It wasn't a choice she enjoyed making. Dutch's death caught her by surprise. It probably caught him a little by surprise, too. He had always been a strong man, brought eagerly to hard work. At eighty-four, he often bragged that he never saw a doctor, "took no tonic nor pills" and "had every tooth he was born with." But against a brain tumor, none of that mitigated. He could have handled the pain, the discomfort. What he couldn't handle was the wasting away. She saw the change in him when he returned from the first chemo treatment: He was frail, required help just to get into bed. He might have gotten past that, too, she thought. Might have survived the indignity of peeing all over himself, of vomiting down his shirtfront every fifteen minutes. But what he couldn't get past was the fact that the tumor was inoperable. He'd never get better. All he could do was suffer the humiliation of watching the farm fall apart around him because he was too sick and weak to do the work. But his death wasn't exactly a well-planned departure from sixty-two years of marriage and a lifetime of building something. Just a quick jerk of the trigger and a mess to clean up in the barn. That was a year ago. It was a horror, at first. Now, it was just a galling memory.

She and Dutch never had children, had no siblings left alive, and never were close to their nieces or nephews. She'd survived all their friends who were her age. For a suicide widow, there is no insurance, only heartache and embarrassment. The farm was hers, but so were the expenses, and the taxes. A farm has to pay for itself to keep going. That meant work, more work than a woman her age could do or could afford to hire done. Each month since Dutch got sick, their reserves went down. Finally, after burying Dutch, there was little left, so she had no choice. She put the place up for sale and followed her banker's advice, moved to Willow Oaks, hoped her funds would hold out until the place sold. Given the market these days, that wasn't likely.

Willow Oaks was the only old folks' home in the county. Yvonne's daddy, who operated the town's funeral home, owned it, let her run it as she saw fit. She had a degree in something or other from Texas A&M, and she made the place her own private hell on earth with herself as chief devil. Mattie figured there was some kind of kickback for anyone Yvonne hurried along to her daddy's main business. There was a lot of profit in death, she thought.

Mattie had enough money left to pay for a year in advance. If and when the farm sold, she could move to another town, maybe a better place. But for the time being, she was stuck. Willow Oaks was worse than jail, she thought as she flipped the pages of the old magazines. At least prisoners had some hope of parole. The only hope Mattie had was for transfer to a nicer prison. That, or death. Lately, she'd been thinking more and more about Dutch's final choice. She had thought it was the wrong thing to do, but maybe he'd known something she didn't.

She flung the magazines aside and looked around the room. Five or six more of the tenants had drifted in, found seats where they would wait out the morning. Most seemed to be waiting merely to die. There were twenty-four tenants at Willow Oaks, but ten were bedridden and virtually comatose, eight more confined to wheelchairs, and a solid majority were virtually deaf or blind. The medicine tray Yvonne carted around twice a day looked like a portable pharmacy.

Mattie stood and went out onto the porch, patting her pocket to make sure she had her cigarettes. Yvonne forbade smoking, but Mattie didn't care. She never smoked more than four or five cigarettes a day, but the habit was a hard one to break. She took it up the night she met David "Dutch" Cummings at a Christmas USO Canteen next to the Fort Worth and Denver Depot. Handsome in his sailor's uniform and on his way to "Somewhere in the South Pacific," as the newsreels said, he shouldered aside a G.I. to get to the spot in front of the doughnut table where she sat, then offered her a wide grin.

"Want to step outside for a smoke?" he asked.

Her heart fluttered. "It's cold out there," she replied through a smile so big it hurt.

"I've got something to keep us warm." He winked, patted his bag, then extended his hand. "C'mon. It's Christmas, and I've got a train to catch." She stood, held out her hand. He spun gallantly and took her arm, and together, they stepped outside into the breathless cold.

They sat on wooden benches out in the frozen night of a depot platform and sipped Cokes laced with bootleg rum and smoked Lucky Strike Greens until his train left at daybreak. She wanted to go with him so bad, she ached. He wrote to her every week, and when he came home, they married, bought the farm, made a life.

It was blistering cold outside, and Mattie wished she'd brought a coat. As she pushed the door against mild protests from those caught in the icy gust, her visible breath disappeared on wisps of wind rushing by her face. She cupped her hands and lit her smoke, drawing the heat deep and holding it before letting it escape into the frigid atmosphere. These days, having a smoke was about all she could do to connect her to Dutch, to his memory.

WHEN SHE RETURNED TO THE PARLOR, HUGGING HERSELF against the cold, her attention was arrested by a large white box in the center of the room. Lettering on the side announced that it contained a "Full-sized, Life-Like Christmas Tree." Mattie walked over and nudged the box with her toe. Closer inspection announced that a six-foot Douglas fir was inside the box. All that was required was assembly.

"A plastic tree?" she muttered. "They're going to put up a plastic tree?"

"*We're* going to put up a plastic tree!" Yvonne announced from the doorway. Her arms were full of tinsel, ornaments. All were in boxes boasting a Kmart sale price sticker. "We'll start right after dinner while the Perry Como special is on."

"I don't want a plastic tree," Mattie said. "I—*we* want a real tree."

Yvonne was already on her way out. She spoke over her shoulder. "People are allergic to real trees."

Mattie continued to stand in the middle of the room. A plastic tree. Not in all her life had she even considered such a thing. She remembered Dutch coming in with a fresh cut cedar in tow. The smell of it, so fresh, crisp and green filled the house, excited her out of common sense. Plastic had no odor. None. She looked around the room. A full majority of the ambulatory residents were now present.

"Who's allergic to real trees?" she asked. No one paid her any attention, so she stepped to the center of the room, spoke louder. "I asked who here is allergic to real trees?"

A few heads shook in denial, and several sets of rheumy eyes turned toward her. Finally, Leanda McGillicutty spoke up. "Yvonne doesn't like real trees. They make a mess, she says. And cause fires. You be quiet, now. *Oprah*'s coming on."

Mattie stared at the dying forms surrounding her. Their total attention was fixed on the screen. Their entire lives had been reduced to sitting here, day after day, watching some silly box. They couldn't even have a real tree for Christmas.

"I think we should take a vote," she said. "We're *paying* tenants here. I think if we want a real tree, we should have one." Again, only a few gave her attention, so she stepped over in front of the set. "I said I want to vote on this. We have a quorum here. Let's have a vote!"

Herbert Bugerman, a one-time robust rancher and former All American, now a humpbacked, bald man with claw-like fingers and perpetual urine stains on his pants, raised his hand, palm out. "This ain't a lodge meeting, Mattie," he said. "Yvonne runs this outfit. She says no real tree, that's what she means. Ain't no telling what she might do, we take a vote against her."

Several heads bobbed in agreement. "He's right," Clara Florentine, once the town's librarian, said in a quaking voice. "We buck Yvonne, she's liable to take away the television."

That caused a stir. Everyone in the room began muttering, and one or two stood and started wagging fingers, lecturing Mattie. "You're new here," Bernie Cartwright, one-time high school principal, shouted. "You don't know Yvonne. She's too mean to live."

"That's right," Faye Newsome, who once ran for Congress on a populist platform, added, putting on her oversized glasses for a better view of Mattie. Her sparse hair was dyed pink and curled close to her head, giving her the appearance of a giant, mangy poodle with owl eyes. "She's took away the television before. Missed a whole week of my soap!"

"Fine!" Mattie yelled. "Watch your damn television!" She threw up her hands and left the room. Yvonne was there to meet her, her chubby cheeks red with annoyance.

"Do you see what happens when you get them all worked up? We have a way of doing things here, and everything's done for a *reason*."

"A plastic tree is *not* Christmas," Mattie said, feeling suddenly childish, hating herself for it. "Christmas is smells and sounds and tastes—"

"Christmas is just what we make it," Yvonne cut her off. "And it will be the same here as it is every year. A very nice time. They're rebroadcasting the Perry Como special tonight, and I plan to have the tree all up and ready for the ornaments. We'll have punch."

"With rum, or maybe some brandy in it, I expect." Mattie said with a sneer.

Yvonne ignored Mattie, brushed past her, and went into the dining room. Mattie stood for a moment, the odor of camphor and sickness swirling around her. She suddenly felt ill.

SHE SKIPPED THE NOON MEAL, STAYED IN HER ROOM. THE AFTERnoon began to darken as clouds thickened overhead. She could hear the wind against the building, felt the cold through her window. This room, she thought, was like a coffin, a coffin in a grave. Christmas was here, and everything was dead, dying. She didn't expect gifts, not even a card. But she had expected that for a few moments there might be something, some recollection of years gone by. That's what Christmas was for, she thought. That's what it was supposed to be: memories.

From the window, she observed the gray street beneath the winter day. She and Dutch were Baptists, but they mostly went to church for weddings and funerals—especially funerals, it seemed. Farmers didn't take Sunday off when there was work to be done, so they weren't regular. Besides, Dutch told her, he lost his religion on Guadalcanal.

"You spend about a week burying several thousand rotten pieces of what used to be healthy kids, and you come to the notion that there ain't no God. And if there is, he's not worth much of a damn." He said he was glad they never had children. "Kills you to bury a child," he said. "Kills your soul." He'd stop, then get a faraway look in his eyes. "I never want to bury a child again."

Mattie kept her faith, but she didn't much care for the new brand of ministers. Most of them she saw as glad-handing fools with expensive haircuts and capped teeth, eager to squeeze money out of the faithful, but unable to deliver the kind of spiritual strength that preachers should offer. She knew what the meaning of Christmas was, and she acknowledged it in her prayers. But she also knew that it was so much more. It meant thinking of her brothers and sisters, her parents—all gone now—and of Dutch. And he was gone as well. Burying a husband isn't particularly good for a person's soul either, Mattie thought.

Disappointment welled in her heart, and tears filled her eyes. It seemed that without thinking about it she'd been looking forward to nothing more than Christmas, to putting up the tree, singing carols, eating rich foods tasty with bad-for-you ingredients and enticing with holiday aroma. She could almost smell the chicken cooking on Christmas Eve. More than any other, that scent was always Christmas to her. If Yvonne had her way, she thought with a sudden surge of bitterness, Christmas dinner would be a turkey sandwich and a fruit cup. "It's healthy," she could hear the home manager saying in her whiny, fat-girl voice. "We have to do things a certain way around here. There's a *reason* for everything we do."

Mattie wiped her eyes and looked out again. Parked off to one side of Willow Oaks was her old Dodge pickup. She remembered the day Dutch bought it. Bobby Kennedy was shot that very afternoon. She had no idea how many miles it had traveled—or how many rebuilt engines and transmissions and clutches Dutch had put in it—since that dark day. Held together as much by faith as by bailing wire and spot welds, the old vehicle had bounced its way over the crusted ruts of field roads for three decades. Its seats were worn out, windshield cracked, tires nearly bald. Its only virtue was that it was hers. She refused to include it in the inventory of things to sell.

She now remembered that she had excluded other things from the sale of the place and all its furnishings. A whole room full of personal possessions. They were all boxed up back at the house, in the spare bedroom, awaiting some solution as to storage: her mother's china and silver, some old clothing, her wedding veil. There were most of Dutch's personal things: his hunting knives, his wallet and watch, his Navy Cross and Purple Heart, and that old flask from the night they met.

And among those boxes and bags, she now recalled with growing excitement, was something else: a large, green box tied with ribbon: her collection of Christmas tree ornaments. Gathered for decades, no two were alike. They came from all over, sent by friends and distant relatives, handed down from their families. She could see them dangling from the evergreen branches, glistening, sparkling in the excitement that, for her, always was Christmas. Her breath went short with the memory.

Those people, she pictured the somnambulant group in the parlor, had given up. Something like Christmas was what they needed to keep them moving, keep them hoping, make them remember something good in their lives. If they couldn't have a real tree, why couldn't they at least have real ornaments? Why not have something that would in some small way at least remind them of a real Christmas? There was no reason. No reason in the world, she thought. They would love it!

She turned suddenly and looked at the door. She half expected Yvonne to be standing there, shaking her fat face, insisting on putting up her cheap Kmart decorations on the plastic tree, telling her why her ornaments wouldn't fit in with the way things were done at Willow Oaks. But the doorway was empty. Mattie's eyes trailed to the bureau, to the jewelry box where she knew were the keys to the truck, the house. She hadn't driven it in months, wasn't even sure it would start. But if it would, what could it hurt?

It was already after three. Supper, which Yvonne called "dinner," was at five. The farm was five miles out, but if she took the Short Road, she could get there, find the box, and return in an hour. Almost breathless with daring, she raced to the closet, pulled on a heavy coat, grabbed some gloves from the bureau, tied a wool scarf around her head, and slipped down the hall, out the fire exit, and bent her body against the icy pellets now peppering the town in front of a strong north wind. She trudged toward the ancient pickup.

When the old Dodge cranked on the first try, she began singing "Jingle Bells" as loud as she could. She slammed it into gear, and sped around the corner trailing a cloud of blue exhaust. For the first time since Dutch died, she was truly happy. For the first time in a long time, she thought, she was acting, not merely reacting to something she couldn't control. "In a one-horse open sleigh," she shouted at the web of cracks in the frosty windshield.

WHEN SHE REACHED THE FARMHOUSE THE STORM WAS WORSENING. Wind tore at the Dodge when it lumbered past the "For Sale 600 Acres and House" sign, crossed the cattle guard and ground up the rutted drive to the dooryard. For a moment, Mattie peered at the old house through the cracked windshield. Stark, empty against the wintry blast, the house looked colder than even the weather could make it. The chimney was void of smoke, something that would never have been the case in weather like this. She saw the henhouse door was open, and she was sure she could see some birds inside. Percy Walker was supposed to have taken them, but some of the flock probably wandered off before he came, then returned later. She wondered why varmints hadn't gotten them. The garden was overgrown with onions and wild asparagus, and a piece of tin roof was peeled back on the tool shed, slapping in the icy gale. To her faded eyes, the whole farm seemed to be sulking because it had been abandoned at such a time.

She shook off somber thoughts and stepped out into the icy wind that now scythed unimpeded across the prairie. The sleet had lessened, but snow now mixed in with it. The ground was soft, warm, not yet frozen hard, so that meant mud soon. She needed to hurry or the Short Road would be an impassable loblolly. It wasn't really a road, just a trail for irrigation workers cut along the edges of fields near shelterbreaks and deep drainage ditches.

The wind nearly blinded her, forced her to duck her head as she mounted the old steps, held the door key in her hand like a lance. Slippery ice covered the porch. All she needed was to fall, she thought, to break a hip or a wrist. Wouldn't *that* give Yvonne a thrill? She reached the door, ripped open the screen, jabbed in the key, remembering to give it a slight push on the right side to swing it wide.

Inside, she was halted by a gloom that haunted the raw emptiness of the house. Motes and cobwebs swirled in drafts lit by the blue-gray light from the sash windows. The house sagged, moaned in the wind. Cold covered everything. The furniture, draped with bed sheets, squatted in a dusty room that had never been less than perfectly clean with hardwood floors polished to a mirrored sheen. Sadness welled inside her, but she pushed it back, took a deep breath. She had a purpose here, she reminded herself.

She moved quickly down the hall, wishing she'd remembered to bring a flashlight, and wondering if the oil lamps in the pantry were filled. But her memory provided a sufficient beacon. In the bedroom, the bright green box was on top of a stack of other containers. It wasn't heavy, and she shook it lightly to hear the tingle of a small, glass bell she remembered was packed in cotton down toward the bottom, cushioned by thick coils of wide red satin ribbon.

Holding the box made her feel whole. Warmth built inside her like a newly stoked fire. She moved slowly out of the room, then back down the hall and to the door. She had trouble pulling it to, relocking it, but she finally made her way back to the pickup and nestled the box securely in the seat. This was a victory, she knew. A small one, but a victory nonetheless. And that's what Christmas was about, she thought to herself: victory.

EAGER TO RETURN BEFORE SHE WAS MISSED, SHE TOOK THE Short Road. That was a mistake. The storm was now fully arrived and coated the land with white powder that rapidly deepened. No mere snowfall, this was a blizzard that blotted out natural light, and Mattie's visibility was soon reduced to a few feet in front of the old Dodge's hood. The ineffective defroster wheezed uselessly against the thick vapor in the windows while the wipers clanked against the thickening snow.

The one-lane trace was sandy and uncertain in the best of weather. It took two miles off the same trip by the highway, but it was liable to washouts in heavy rains. The steering wheel seemed to have a life of its own as the truck's tires fought to find reliable ruts to guide it. More than once when rounding a curve beside a plum thicket or copse of overgrown mesquite, she felt the rear wheels lose purchase, skid onto the edge of one of the deep ditches alongside, as if some monster was trying to pull her into its icy maw below.

She fought fear and cold away, concentrated on steering the truck around the winding curves, longed to see the highway emerge after each. How long *was* this road? It only seemed to take minutes when she used to drive it. Today, it was more like hours. The clouds were lower, darker than ever. Her headlights shot a yellow beam into a white curtain that billowed almost parallel to the ground. It felt like midnight, though it couldn't be later than four. She slid around one more curve, certain that this time she would see the highway ahead, then she spotted the old bobtail truck blocking the road immediately in front of her.

She jammed both her feet onto the brake, stood up on it, and was sure she was screaming when her head struck the windshield and, after a brilliant flash of light, everything went from stormy white to utterly black.

SHE WAS HAVING A DREAM ABOUT THE TIME SHE HAD THE FLU. That, too, had been at Christmas. Her body was racked with fever, but she shivered with chills. Her head ached, and Dutch was wiping her forehead with a cool cloth, talking to her in soothing, low tones. Through a haze, she could see the lights of the tree reflecting off her ornaments.

Then, her eyes fluttered open, and all she saw was a circle of darkness floating in a sea of white specks, like alabaster moths encircling an ebony flame. Dutch's face slowly transformed into the swarthy features of an Hispanic youth only inches away, his chocolate eyes wide with fear. He was applying a dirty rag to her forehead. As she came more to herself, she realized he was speaking to her, but his words made no sense. At last, she understood he was speaking in Spanish.

"I don't—" She choked, swallowed, continued, "I don't habla the lingo," she finished gruffly. She pushed his hand away, tried to sit up. Dizziness spun her head, forced her to lie back. He held the rag over her like a charm, but no longer touching her, merely staring at her, wide-eyed. She was now aware that she was out of the pickup, down on the ground. Snow swirled overhead, but he had pulled her around behind the vehicle, out of the wind. "I'll be all right," she said. "Just let me get my breath."

It took a few minutes, but she sat up. There was a momentary swimming behind her eyes, but the pain settled into a dull throb in the center of her forehead. She touched the spot. Bright blood stained her gloves. The youngster was jabbering at her in rapid Spanish.

"I don't speak it," she said. "You might as well talk Greek to me."

He nodded as if he understood, then sat back on his hams and stared at her. He looked familiar, but she discarded the thought, started again to rise. He tried to stop her—or maybe help her—but she pushed his hands away. "I'm all right. Hell, I've been hurt worse than this slopping hogs." She made it to her feet, but her head gyrated and the ground beneath her wanted to tilt. It seemed very dark, and the blizzard blasted by her like a train. She took a deep breath, steadied herself.

Her mind flew to the box of ornaments. She stumbled over to the pickup and jerked open the passenger door. The box was shoved against the dash, and there was a large tear in one corner, exposing the red satin ribbon, but the container was otherwise intact. She wondered if any of her precious treasures were ruined. Angry now, she spun on the boy, "What're you doing out here? Blocking the road like that? Are you crazy?"

He stepped back and spoke in Spanish.

"¿*Loco?* Are you *loco?*" she demanded.

He gave her a bewildered look, then grinned nervously, spoke again in Spanish.

"Fine," Mattie said, pointing at the box. "If even one of those are broken, I'll have the sheriff on you!" He stared incomprehensively at the box, but she ignored him, braced herself against the truck and walked down to inspect the damage. When she went around front, she saw what had happened. The larger vehicle had slid off the road, clipped a utility pole. The truck was hopelessly stuck across the narrow passage.

She limped around to the front of the Dodge. It was wedged into the bobtail, and the windshield over the steering wheel was webbed where her forehead shattered it. "Damn it," she said. "Yvonne'll sling a litter of green cats!"

Over the howl of the wind, she became aware that the boy was still talking to her, more rapidly now, mixing heavily accented English words with Spanish. He pulled frantically at the sleeve of her coat and gestured for her to follow. She resisted, but he kept waving toward the bobtail. She now remembered where she knew him from. The Spanish couple, the *mestizos*. She had seen him earlier that morning. Where was the girl? Maybe he took her home—back to the boxcars that passed for homes among these people. He kept tugging, blabbering, and finally she shrugged, followed him. If he was bent on doing her harm, she thought, he already would have.

They skirted the narrow margin of sandy ledge around the bobtail. Mattie looked up into the cab's window where he was pointing, jabbering constantly and with increasing anxiety, pointing. Finally, she grabbed the handle and stepped onto the running board. Her head spun once more, but she found her footing and looked inside the cab.

Now, she understood what he was saying, what he was trying so hard to make her understand. Now, she knew why he had taken chances and was speeding along this road in such weather. She looked down at him. He was no more than twenty. The beginnings of a mustache formed on his upper lip, but his cheeks were smooth under dark eyes that showed more fear than concern as he babbled. He was practically dancing under her gaze, but she couldn't tell if it was from the cold or from panic. Should be both, she thought. And she peered again into the cab.

There lying across the spring-scarred front seat was the girl, wrapped in the old denim jumper and shivering in pain as well as cold.

She was alive, and she was well, and, Mattie saw, she wasn't fat at all. She was, however, in imminent danger of having a baby.

IT TOOK MORE THAN HALF AN HOUR TO LOOSEN THE PICKUP from the smashed side of the bobtail, get it started, and turn it around on the narrow trail. Eventually, they had the old Dodge on its way. Mattie let Julio—a name she learned through gestures and mimes—drive, and she sat in the bed, her coat and two ratty blankets wrapped around the girl—Mariana, she determined—who was now having regular and more frequent contractions and kept Mattie in a panic that warmed her more than any covering could have. There was no question that the baby was coming, and soon.

Mattie had delivered calves, colts, piglets, puppies and kitties when their mothers were unable or unwilling to do it alone. But she had no experience with a human baby or with a terrified teenaged mother. Mattie's teeth clenched against the fear that jumped in her heart with every bump. She frequently pounded on the back glass, flattening her hand to try to make Julio slow the vehicle over the rougher spots. She didn't know if he saw her. Because the windshield was smashed, he was driving with the window cranked down, leaning outside, trying to penetrate the blinding white storm that raged around them. Next to him, the box of ornaments bounced high with every bump. Mattie yelled about that, too.

The pickup was not as "okay" as Julio assured her when they backed it up and got it going, either. She could hear the engine coughing, the gears grinding roughly when he downshifted. It would take a miracle to get them back to town, to the hospital, even to a telephone. Almost every house in this part of the county was either for sale or abandoned, she knew, recalling what the banker told her when he convinced her to sell out. Those that weren't, were probably empty, their residents in town at church or off visiting relatives for the biggest family holiday of the year. The only two homes they passed along the way exhibited nothing but cold, dark windows and snarling, barking dogs against the approach of the old truck out of the blowing snow. Each time, Julio slowed, but Mattie shook her head, pointed down the road. They drove on.

Mariana cried out with every bump, every turn that caused her to move. Her knees kept bunching, and Mattie pressed down on her bulging stomach, unsure of what to do for her.

It was full dark when they finally made the highway turn-off—five miles back to town or at least a telephone—but Julio stopped, jumped out, yelling in a panic. Mattie stared over the top of the cab. A bright geyser of steam whiter than the swirling snow around it was spewing from the hood. Mattie's resolve sank. If the Dodge died, they were done for. Even if someone came along, who would stop on a night like this to help two Mexicans and an old woman in a beat-up pickup? She peered into the snow dancing across the blacktop highway. Who but a bunch of fools would *be* out on a night like this?

She peered across the highway to the pasture gate. The house was just over a mile away. She pointed toward the gate. "Go," she yelled at Julio who was staring at her finger. He stood looking dumbly at her. Panic swelled her voice. "Vamoose! We got to move, *now*, or this child's going to drop her calf right here beside the road! Go!"

With no more assurance than his faith in her voice, he leaped back inside, gunned the ailing pickup across the highway, bounced through a barbed wire gate and onto the pasture road. He was moving too fast, the truck bounced and veered, careened dangerously near fence posts and mesquite stumps. Over the wind, she could hear the engine whining high and loud. She held Mariana to her own body, tried to soften the bounces, heard the girl cry out with every bump. Mattie gritted her teeth and turned her eyes up where the snow blotted out the night sky, the flakes iridescent in the reflected headlights of the old pickup as it made its familiar way back home.

WHEN THEY SKATED UP ON ICY MUD TO THE DOORYARD GATE, THE truck whined, coughed, then died with a hissing expulsion of steam. Mattie leaped down, pulled the bewildered boy out and grabbed the keyring. "Inside!" she screamed over the howling wind. "Get the girl." She stumbled across the yard and up onto the slick porch. She stopped, saw him still standing by the pickup, gaping at her.

"*Inside!* You stupid—" She stopped herself, took a breath, searched her memory for the right words. "In *el casa!*" she yelled, pointing to the house. "*Mi casa. ¡Mi casa!*" She spun, slipped on the slick porch and went down on one knee. Pain, sudden and sharp shot up her thigh, into her hip. She tried to rise, couldn't. Her eyes shut against the agony. "Oh, Dutch," she hissed through gritted teeth, her eyes wet with tears of panic and pain. "Give me strength." She saw Julio's form lumbering through the snow toward the porch, Mariana in his arms. "Don't you dare let me bury a child, tonight."

She took a cleansing breath, pulled her feet under her, then staggered toward the door, keyed the lock, and shoved the door open. Once inside, she limped around, jerking sheets off furniture and carrying them to the front bedroom—their bedroom. Julio, Mariana in his arms, stumbled through the door. He was, the fleeting thought passed through Mattie's mind, the first Mexican ever to cross their threshold. As if he read her thought, he stopped in the entryway, staring at the dark, empty room.

"Don't just stand there, you idiot," Mattie snapped. "We've got work to do."

There was no power. No heat. Julio, though, proved adept at building a fire in the old wood stove in the kitchen, pumped water from the cistern and set it to boil while Mattie found an oil lamp and brought it to the bedroom. She spread the sheets on the mattress, then stripped the girl's threadbare dress off of her while she screamed in the agony of almost constant contractions. Mattie went to the bathroom and located enough pieces of soap to cleanse her hands in a bowl of hot water Julio, jabbering constantly, finally brought in. Unable to abide him any longer, she shoved him from the room, shouting "go make yourself useful" into his frightened face.

"Go on!" she insisted, pointing out the front door. "Get the blankets, at least."

"¿*Que?*" he asked.

"Blankets, you idiot!" She shouted, pointing again. "In the truck!" And she slammed the door. She was panicked enough for both of them, she thought, and she wanted him out of the way.

She turned to Mariana, writhing on the soft mattress, her knees spread, her face twisted in pain. "Damn it, Dutch," she whispered. "What do I do, now?" Then she went to the girl. "It'll be all right, honey," she said. "You're not the first one to go through this, and I'm sure you won't be the last."

IT WAS OVER QUICKLY, ALMOST BEFORE SHE KNEW IT. MATTIE barely had time to reach the bedside before the screaming girl's pretty face scrunched once more, then she delivered into Mattie's waiting hands a suddenly squalling baby boy.

For a moment she stood there in the dark room, the tiny, bloody infant writhing in her arms, his eyes squinting against the faint light of an old oil lamp, his fists opening and closing in reflexive samplings of the frozen air around him. Mattie traced his perfect chin with her crooked finger and something warm touched her heart. "Merry Christmas," she whispered. "You're right on time."

She handed the baby to Mariana, whose eyes in the yellow lamp's reflection were as large and black and beautiful as anything Mattie had ever seen, then talked softly to the girl as she finished the business of the birthing. She took her time and washed the baby and mother, found a box of quilts in a closet and made a decent bed on the bare mattress, then stood back for a moment, admiring the scene. It was frigid in the room, but the mother and babe lay snug and peaceful in the bed Mattie and Dutch had shared for so many years. She felt her eyes moisten, but then shook away the sentiment. "Time to meet your daddy, I guess," she said and went out to fetch Julio.

He sprang to his feet when she came through the door and stared his question. But she could offer him no attention. Her shock when she came into the old living room stunned her speechless, motionless. Julio had found candles. Dozens of them. The entire room was ablaze with golden light. He asked something, but she could only nod, too amazed to say anything. He leaped past her into the bedroom, but she never saw him. Instead, she stepped forward into the candle light, overcome. The old wallpaper, faded and torn over the years, outlined with the shadows of frames and hangings now packed away, seemed brilliant, almost new. The floor was freshly swept, the reflected candles dancing in its shine. But what captured her eye, what amazed her was something else entirely, something utterly astonishing. "Oh, my," was all she could say. "Oh, my."

Draped across the walls, strung from window sill to window sill, doorjamb to doorjamb, was a rope of wide red satin ribbon, and hanging from it, spaced carefully against the wall were all her ornaments, each sparkling and twinkling in the candle light. The tiny glass bell was over the front door.

Her hand went to her throat, she turned round and round. Her eyes wide and glistening in the reflected beauty of the room. "Oh my," she repeated and turned to see Julio standing in the doorway. He put his hands together and laid them to the side of his inclined face. Mariana and the baby were asleep.

She swallowed, then stepped toward him. "How?" she started, but had no words to finish.

He shrugged, then smiled timidly. "¿Le gusta?" He asked. "¿Bonita, verdad?" She continued to stare, and he shrugged again. "Es navidad," he said, bowing his head slightly.

All at once, to her nostrils came a wonderful, familiar aroma. She looked down the hall toward the kitchen, then back at the stocky boy, who grinned self-consciously.

"*Pollo*," he said. He made a gesture of wringing a chicken's neck, shrugged again. "*Para las tamales navidad*. Is okay?"

Her smile began slowly, then widened. "It's okay," she whispered. "It's very okay." Then she said aloud, "Very, very okay."

Weariness suddenly swam up from her feet like a wave. Pain from her forehead returned with a spinning throb. She also felt a lurching jab from her knee. Standing was too much. Julio rushed to her as her legs buckled and she slumped into Dutch's old chair and sighed deeply. Julio fluttered around, speaking quickly, concern wrinkling his brow.

"Just leave me be for a minute," she said, waving him away. "I need to rest." He looked at her, a wide smile on his face. "You're grinning now," she said. "That won't last."

She looked once more at the stunning decorations of the room, savored the scent of chicken boiling, basked in the warm gold light of the candles, and sighed. This, she thought, was Christmas. Then her eyes fell to her hands, folded on her lap. A large scarlet drop had fallen onto her crooked finger. Another soon joined it. She thought to reach up, touch her injured brow, but somehow, her hand lacked the strength. She looked at Julio. His dark face, black eyes shone in the soft lights of the candles, the sparkle of her ornaments. What would become of him? Of them? They had nothing but each other. But, then, she thought, that was more than most had, more by a long shot. It was more than she had, but not more than she remembered having.

She smiled and settled into the soft warmth of Dutch's chair, utterly satisfied with the comfortable inner peace she felt. Willow Oaks and Yvonne were far from her mind, from her life. For the moment, it seemed enough to sit quietly in her house, to look at her ornaments, to smell Christmas, and to remember.

She looked up once more at Julio, but he wasn't there. Instead, there was Dutch. He wore his sailor's uniform and looked as tall and handsome as the night they met, his grin stretching wide.

"Want to step outside for a smoke?" he asked.

Pain and weariness fled before a fluttering heartbeat. "It's cold out there," she replied through a smile so big it hurt.

"I've got something to keep us warm." He winked, patted his bag, then extended his hand. "C'mon. It's Christmas, and I've got a train to catch."

She stood, held out her hand. He spun gallantly and took her arm, and together, they stepped outside into the breathless cold.

TOMORROW WE SMILE

★

Naomi Shihab Nye

I USED TO SAY TO MY FRIEND JUAN FELIPE THAT I LIKE MEX-ico because Mexico still has a sense of the miraculous and he would slap me on the back and say, "You just like the peppers, come on, be honest," but I saw how he had *milagros*, little silver arms and legs, pinned up by his bed too. So I would tell him what happened in my neighborhood, like when José Palomo's father died, a big eagle came to light in his patio and stayed for days, just sitting there. José said it stared at him with a meaningful look and then one morning it was gone. When I tell Juan, he says we don't have eagles in the city. Maybe it was a lost bird that got thirsty from flying too long. But I see how a candle deep in his eyes is suddenly glowing and I don't mention it again.

Then there are things that happen to us personally, what about them? We first met Domingo Flores when we ran out of gas on the highway south of Uvalde, Texas. Juan, his mother, and I were headed for the border that day—to eat fragrant soup with cilantro, buy woolly ponchos and bottles of vanilla, and walk the streets of Piedras, fat with joy. We used to go to Mexico like that in those days, for soup and joy. It was before they said the vanilla had arsenic in it. Juan's mother wanted to find a set of blue tin plates and Juan just wanted to drink the air. We always came home before midnight on those trips, unless we were driving in farther, to Rosita or Múzquiz or one of those buttonlike villages that is nothing but a dusty plaza and a bar.

In the back seat Juan's mother was snoring into the Lifestyle section of the newspaper. Juan had the radio turned to *conjunto*. His eyes kept darting over the landscape like goats. Naturally no one else had checked the gas gauge. Thirty miles this side of Mexico, on the thorny stretch that somehow manages to link our lands, the engine sputtered and died.

Juan got out and poked his head under the hood. He still hadn't noticed the gas gauge. His mother sat up, startled, and touched her hair. If you've never been there, picture a drab two-lane sided by brush and cactus, no billboards, no restrooms or telephones, and very few cars. We hadn't seen another car since we left La Pryor, thirty miles back. "This could be bad," said Juan, trying to start the car again. Then he noticed the little arrow sagging below the empty slash. He was embarrassed. He sat there silently, staring into the sky.

That day there weren't even any clouds to thumb a ride on. You can imagine people drowning in a sky like that.

For awhile we all sat, gazing at various items. I gazed at the dashboard and later, the pebbles in the ditch. Juan's mother stared at the *TV Guide*. Then the three of us walked in different circles, bugs trapped inside a window, hoping for a crack.

After an hour, we heard the unmistakable buzz of a car. It was strange how we couldn't tell which direction it was coming from. Gradually a 1965 Chevrolet chugged into view, from the south. It had strips of pom-pom balls pinned up around the inside and a pair of dice mingling with the Virgin on the mirror. I like how people fix up their cars. I used to decorate mine with Arabic donkey beads and feathers, hoping some positive vehicular voodoo might occur. The pom-pom car was traveling very slowly. It stopped, engine still running, and a young man with a wide, clear face got out.

"¿Qué está pasando?" he asked, grinning.

He knew what was *pasando* as well as we did.

The back seat of his car was loaded with boxes, beat-up suitcases, a lamp without a head. Juan talked to him in Spanish and learned he was Domingo Flores, moving to Austin, Texas, to find his wife, who had preceded him there. He would locate work and eat white bread and buy a little TV with an antenna. Gas? Sure he would help us, *no problema*.

Juan said, "I am a man with a donkey's head."

Domingo said, "I travel slower than the donkey."

They climbed into the front seat of Domingo's portable shrine and chugged off, heading north.

His mother and I stayed with the car and fell asleep with all the windows open. She said she dreamed about when the boys were little, how they used to wear capes and underpants and jump from the dresser to the bed, shrieking. I dreamed about my mother pulling me in a wagon on the day a milk carton broke in her hands. Under a sky like that you could go backward forever.

A long time later the car of Domingo Flores chugged toward us again, a green dot getting larger.

We had wondered how Juan would return. Only one truck had roared past since his departure and the driver had a hard face.

Juan and Domingo climbed out comfortably, friends from the journey, and reported: yes, they had found gas, they had rousted the sleepy attendant from his bed, after stopping at three farms to find him, and no, there was no unleaded gas in the whole town of La Pryor, so they toted three gallons of regular and had to devise a funnel out of Prime Minister Thatcher's front-page head.

Domingo stayed around to see the job finished, his car running all the while. When Juan's mother suggested he turn it off, he said, "I can't." If he turned it off, it wouldn't start again. I'd known cars like that. Domingo smiled when our engine coughed awake and opened his palm up to heaven, as if saying, "You see?" Juan offered him money for his own gas. Back-and-forth meant he was going out of the way for us over sixty miles.

His face changed. He looked stunned and said, "No one gives me anything I don't earn."

"But he earned it!" I poked Juan. "Tell him he earned it!"

Juan went on in delicate Spanish as he counted out dollar bills from his wallet.

I thought Domingo was going to cry. He jumped back into his car and rolled the window up fast so Juan couldn't stick the money in. When he threw it into gear, the engine nearly quit. Now wouldn't that have been something? We could have driven him the other direction for a tow truck and gone on and on like that for days. But it caught, and he was off. He raised one hand, didn't look back, and swayed into the distance, like a camel.

"I think he was too sensitive," said Juan's mother, as our own car pulled forward. "A lot of those people with old *frontera* traditions still act like money and dignity can never go together."

We drove to Mexico and arrived as the shopkeepers were sweeping out the aisles at the *mercado*. "You're late," they said.

Months later, in the middle of a conversation about B. Traven and the Chiapas jungles, Juan said, "I wonder if what's-his-name made it to his wife. That car was a bomb!"

"Who's that?"

"The guy on the highway—Domingo Flores."

"I hope so." It was hard to picture Domingo in Austin among glossy governmental buildings and health-food pubs.

Juan said college towns were unnatural. "We need to live in a town where at least half the population feels like fading paint. It is important, this sensation."

THE SEASONS SLID INTO ONE ANOTHER. DALLAS RESIDENTS WERE wearing short sleeves on the day a devastating ice storm struck down their trees. The Valley grapefruit growers wept on the news. One man held out his hands and said, "My orchard was all I had and now I don't have it either." At home in San Antonio pipes were bursting like fountains on every block.

Juan was off along the border somewhere, interviewing Tex-Mex accordionists for a project he said would be "the greatest tribute since *Chulas Fronteras.*"

I was in Central Texas compiling an anthology of local memoirs for an arts council. Though the job paid decently, other factors kept me sobered: bank tellers asking if I were "born again" before they would cash my checks, and the general terrifying sense that all the best things—porches, grandmothers, independent cafés—were swiftly vanishing from the earth.

I called Juan's mother, who told me where he was. "S.O.S., can you come up here?" He said I sounded wistful. Two nights later I was sitting at the desk when he knocked. "Listen to this!" I yelled in greeting. "How much do you know about rounding up snakes? Today I met a man from West Texas who used to . . ."

Then I noticed he looked pale. "What's wrong?"

He sat down gingerly, holding himself forward on the chair.

He wiped his hand across his forehead.

"What's the matter?"

"There was fog on the road tonight, hanging low," he said. "About ten miles north of Austin I saw a hitchhiker and glancing over automatically—it was Domingo Flores! I slammed on the brakes and he came strolling toward me at a normal pace, not rushing like hitchhikers usually do. I yelled, "Domingo, is that you?"

He nodded and extended his hand. Casually. "You have gas tonight?" he said in Spanish, so I knew he recognized me, but the strangest part was, he didn't act surprised. Can you figure it? It's five months later, hundreds of miles from where we first met, we meet again in the fog, and he's acting nonchalant! He had a pillowcase with him that he held on his lap very closely.

I asked where he was going and he said, "Dallas." I asked where his car was and he said, "They stole it." Then he proceeded, in the most carefully measured voice, to tell me he'd arrived in Austin to find his wife living with another man. Nacho, he called him. She was living with Nacho. My heart split, he said. But he moved into an apartment near them and got a job clipping bushes or something. I asked him a stupid question, "Do you have a work visa?" and he nodded. Here he is telling me the Tale of the Splitting Heart and I'm thinking of visas.

He said he was praying she'd change her mind, leave this other guy and come back to him, her true and rightful husband in the eyes of God. But he said everything in the same flat voice. He said it like he was reading out of a book.

"I made myself a small and hopeful life." He repeated that twice. And then one night the wife, he never used her name, showed up at his door. She announced that she was coming back to him, she and Nacho had parted, she'd made a mistake. "I opened my arms," he said. That's it. "I opened my arms."

For a week they lived together, he was working, she had some job, and he "bought the television." Do you remember last summer when he mentioned the television? I guess that's the one he bought.

The next day she asked to drive him to work and said she wanted to use the car for a "surprise." It was her day off. When five o'clock came, she didn't pick him up, so he waited awhile and started walking. When he got home the apartment was stripped, television gone, everything gone, even the plates were gone.

I asked him if he'd called the police and he said no. "My shame."

"Your shame!" I yelled. "What about your anger?" Domingo acted blank. "She was my wife," he said. "I opened my arms."

I asked if he had any money, but he shook his head. "I used to," he said, "but I showed her where I was hiding it under a cactus."

For a moment I slowed the car to see if there was a place to turn around, and he almost jumped out. "I'm going that way," he pointed north. He was very stubborn about it. "I'm going to Dallas."

I asked him why Dallas and he said he had a cousin in Dallas. Did he know his address? Of course not. I said, "Domingo, go back to Mexico," and he shook his head. "My shame."

So I asked if I could put him on a bus to Dallas and he nodded. We drove into Belton to an ice-house Trailways station where they said a bus was due in ten minutes. Domingo nodded gravely. "It's luck," he said. Luck? His wife just robbed him of everything he had and he's talking about luck?

I said, "*This* time you take the money." I gave him every cent I had. He said, "You'll get it back." And when the bus came, he shook my hand and said a weird expression I never heard in Spanish before, "*Mañana sonreíremos.*"

"What does it mean?"

"Tomorrow we smile."

Now Juan sat back in his chair and covered his eyes. It was a black night, no stars. My friend had come to save me.

"Did you give him your address?"

He shook his head.

"Do you know how many highways there are in Texas?" I said.

"How many people named Flores?"

"How many people named Juan?"

That's it. That's what happened. I look for Domingo sometimes, on roads out of Dallas, on any old road.

FAMILY AND FLOOD

——————★——————

Betsy Berry

N ONE OF THEM KNEW THE COLOR OF THE WATER.

Because they were not there when the water entered their home. Neither time.

Two floods were markers on either end of twenty-five years of the family. Time and water and a quarter of a century to sand edges smooth and cut new indentations. And the family—a son, a daughter, and their parents—hung on. There had been no claim filed for the first flood; they had no insurance. For the second they did. In both they lost everything.

Worldly goods, part of their spirit. Much confidence, in so very many ways. The triangle paper points that pinned their lives, the progression of their lives in photos in a heavy book, survived. The photos did not. All their earlier memories, once and then from that point on again, would not be seen but revisited in such words and stories and images as they were able to retain.

What the water didn't take the first time it got the second. People who do not know the water, who have not known the rise and roil of a flood, never imagine what comes after the receding. They think it is a matter of some fixing, putting back—a drying-out period. The sun to soothe and heal, freshening breezes to assuage. As if nature is in the business of making reparations. All this the family had learned.

In the very beginning, for the daughter, there was an island. Giant palm trees with hoary trunks and glossed fringe, which did a slow kind of hula in the breeze, beckoning to the incoming waves. A tropical bulge of land rising out of the water, it was American soil, where the father, an air force officer, had been sent for service. Stationed, they called it, a good term because he was often away. The couple already had a little boy, born in a Midwest "Yankee" state—the mother had no truck with the Midwest and linked its inhabitants with easterners—and they were glad that here on the island, in the heat of a southern sun was born to them a little girl. The father, a pilot and somewhere above Cuba when his daughter arrived, raced toward home through the blue of skyscapes and time zones.

Flying in low over the pink washed house where now a family of four would live, his plane carried thick aromatic cigars and strong rum and hand-painted wooden animals for his wife and the new baby. All the pilots brought in such contraband, for these were days when parties were happy ones, full of laughter and the wonder of the exotic— the lovely mixture of tastes that a cocktail could be.

Their lives were uncluttered, a dream they lived in this protected little cove of paradise, plucking fresh mangoes off the trees in their backyard. On the base there was the constant sound of plane engines droning, having just landed or warming up, always the vague threat of a war on the horizon—though the paradise setting made children at least think nothing bad could ever happen. This was a family who was to make mistakes, to know deep rifts and heartache, to be worried or frightened, to grow older with the earth's rotations. But in the beginning there were the four of them tightly together, surrounded by the beauty of an island.

And one day the father came home from the beach with a sheet of printed music and the song he would maintain for his life had been written for his little girl. A group of men, native to the island, gathered on the beach to play alongside the rhythm of the sea and the flap of palm fronds in the wind. The men knew the daughter, the tiny girl whose parents carried like a fragile sea creature to the beach and plopped gingerly down at the edge of warm turquoise water. Her backdrop was the safety of land and a calypso croon.

Miss Maryanne, sweet Maryanne

Beside the deep blue sea

When she was able to understand the words to the song the daughter took them to heart and like many other girls vowed to marry her father, the man she already loved more than any other. When she was almost six the family moved, leaving behind their tropical island in a wake of jet fuel from a plane the father flew in as a passenger. Following them was another plane, a transport in which the mother had smuggled a dozen tiny banana trees to graft in her new garden, wherever that garden might be. She had left her mark on paradise, coaxing the flora and fauna to grow in chosen shapes and chosen places, like trained pets. The son left behind a group of playmates and a large iguana named Willy, which he had kept in an open-air cage in a corner of the yard. After he would walk Willy, using a short rope he tied around the lizard's neck, he would rope him to a palm tree. It made the boy's sister sad. In the eyes of the creature, there or missing from them, was something she took with her when she left the island where she was born. The last she saw of that island was from the plane, looking down at the soft foam lapping the west shore and, beyond the sunlit stucco houses that dotted the scalp of land that was the air force base, the dark green undulations of the jungle.

WHEN THE FATHER RETIRED FROM HIS SERVICE, THE FAMILY lived in a house they designed and had built on a small, man-made island on a small lake created from a dam off the Guadalupe River. The place looked less like Texas than it did Florida, where weekend fishermen had to contend with the whine of jetskis and wide wakes from passing speedboats. The three of them lived there, the mother and father and daughter, who attended high school in the city thirty miles away. The son had finished college and was starting a new life in another city a few hours' drive east.

Early in the first hours of a morning that had been preceded by almost a month of soft but steady rain, the daughter was awakened by the phone, by what she sensed were the final two rings of a prolonged attempt to waken the family. She thought of her brother first, and that an insistent call so late could only mean trouble. But after some moments the familiar lull of the falling rain was like a sleeping tablet, and when she heard the pounding on the door from her bedroom at the front of the house it took her some time to thread her hands through the sleeves of her robe and stumble into the hall. Outside the door as she opened it stood three men, in long, wet slickers and various kinds of hats. One stepped close to her, his foot partially inside the door, out of breath in his urgency.

"Get your parents up and dressed now, honey! There's a thirty-foot wall of water coming down from Placid!"

Lake Placid was north by a few miles, and the notion of how fast such a sheet of water the man was describing, like a tidal wave, could reach the island terrified her. She ran back to her parents' bedroom, shouting.

"Mim! Dad! Get up! Get up now! Don't stop to get anything—we have to leave at once!" The men had told her this over their shoulder as they backed away and turned to run to the next house on the street. As the father scrambled into pants and reached in the back of his closet for his metal lockbox of records and documents, the mother switched on the TV. When no station came on, she mistook the noise of the static for the water arriving.

"Is that it?" she cried. "Has the water come?"

In the frenzied moments of what they later remembered happening in slow, sharp detail, they got in the car and—water coming through the bottom of the door and over the floorboard—they made it across the only bridge to the island.

That was in 1973. They called it a hundred-year flood plain, here where the parents had chosen to live out their lives, although they had not heard or talked much about floods. Four years ago, when they had first come there to the lake to visit friends, they gathered at a recreation ground for servicemen and women and their families. People were talking and laughing and eating picnic foods; there were shouts and shrieks from a volleyball game of girls against guys.

And dark clouds had suddenly eclipsed the sun and a cool, stiff wind frothed the calm water into white peaks, and then the sky had opened up and let loose a gush of cold, grey water. A young couple with their three-year-old son and infant daughter were in a rowboat between the shore and the island, not fifty yards away. Only three of them, the couple and their son, soaked to the bone and in shock, returned to land, where the other picnickers had turned from revelers to rescue party. The rowboat had capsized in the storm and the mother held on to the little boy. The baby girl, a man in the crowd had said, "sunk like a rock." The daughter of the family, who would later live in the middle of this body of water which had claimed the baby, covered her ears to stop the voices of the frantic searchers. Her brother was one of the divers, but not in the group that hours later found the baby on the lakebed and still covered in the blanket that had been tucked tightly around her. "Just laying there like a rock," the man said.

The numbing shroud of the mother's shock had been warmed by a blanket and a cup of hot tea, and it was then she began to sob. A keening it was really, an animal wail, thought the daughter of the family. Years later she could hear the sound in dreams.

"It's such a beautiful place here," someone had said that day. "But with water, you never know. You just never know."

AFTER THE WATERS OF THE FAMILY'S FIRST FLOOD FLOWED BACK to their rightful place again, the National Guard kept watch for a few days and then opened the island to its residents, who were at last allowed to see what the river's fury had done to their homes. The water had come not in the form of a wall but a great swell, a bursting upward and outward that crested to five feet inside those homes, like the family's, nearest the lake's edge. A sponge cake the mother had baked and left on the stove at the back of the house had floated up front to greet them in the entrance hall. Helicopters flew in pairs overhead, their blades beating time with each new picture of devastation and destruction. In the family's driveway people gathered, comparing their fates.

"Didn't get the mud they did on the other side," said one neighbor who lived across the street. "Hell of a lucky thing." But the fury unleashed had left its mark on the family.

The son came in from out of town and with a terrible sense of timing had brought a new girlfriend with him. "I've been dying to meet ya'll," she chirped to the mother. "Not under such conditions, of course."

The mother looked at her blankly, holding her husband's ruined oil portrait by a corner of the busted frame.

"I have some friends in Houston who've had some water in the house," the girlfriend said. "The way I'd look at it is that you're okay. And you still have some stuff, right?"

"Yes, well," said the mother after a moment. "Wet stuff." And she turned to go back into her moldy, ruined home.

"What a time to bring her here, really," said the sister privately to her brother.

"Thanks for the big brain, midget. In fact it may be the best time. Something like this, families stick tight. Lori may be family someday."

"And your mother," he added—this is what he always said to his sister, *your mother, your father*—will just have to deal with it."

Together, with the help of good friends and neighbors and workers and a baking summer sun, the family rebuilt their house, slowly replacing their possessions as they could. Twenty-five years later, two failed marriages between the son and daughter and two new ones begun, the family would still point out to visitors the spot where the water had crested and just as quickly flowed back out of their lives.

"We've loved it here, living by the water," the mother would tell people. "But nature will have its moments."

The daughter remembered something from a book she'd read, a line she didn't share with the family. "Nothing brings violence and death closer than an abundance of life and beauty."

IN OCTOBER OF THE YEAR WHEN THE MOTHER AND FATHER turned seventy-five a serious rain began. This time a week's worth fell in a day's time, a dense blanket of rain. For days it came down. The heavy drops sounded like hail as they hammered the roof and splashed down the outside walls of the house. The river rushed so fast into the lake that it rose inches at a time. So quick was the rise it was hard to remember where the lake's level had been a half hour before.

The daughter, in the Texas city where she now lived, an hour's drive north of her parents, was on the phone with her mother. From their kitchen windows both watched the rain sluice down. The daughter had slept the night without the trouble of dreams, what her husband called her "sleep of the dead." That morning she awoke groggy and slow, to putter away a dark, rainy day with small chores to restore some order to her home. She and her husband had planned to leave early for their frequent weekend drive to her parents' house, where they would spend a night.

But the delicious late morning she had anticipated, surrounded by soaking, cleansing rain, was to become something else. She had awakened to the image in her mind of the baby tomato plants she and her husband had recently planted, imagining them opening themselves to the weather, swelling outward. She wanted to stay at home today, go later to her parents in the afternoon where there would still be ample time for a visit, maybe a video or a game of Trivial Pursuit.

In the cocoon of her floodlit kitchen she sipped from a mid-morning cup of coffee and phoned her mother to let her know when to expect them. In the house on the lake, in the same band of rain, her mother had finished her daily cup and almost resented the intrusion as the telephone jangled. Since the rain had begun the mother had stopped her husband from turning on the television for a weather report. "That TV's on too much as it is. Think of how long it's been since we've heard that beautiful sound on the roof."

And down the rain came, making up for its long absence. As the mother passed the bay living room window to answer the phone, she noticed how close the level of the water was to the top of the dock. There had been other times since the last time the water flowed into the house that a flood had threatened. Her children had dismissed her fears so many times that now it was like crying wolf.

"Yes?" she answered.

"Mim?"

"Pete!" she said, the daughter's childhood nickname.

"How's the weather down there? It's raining so hard here we'd like to wait 'til later this afternoon to drive down."

"Well, we've had it all day and night," her mother told her. "Harder than you could imagine. I can hardly see the other side of the lake. I just don't know, Pete . . ."

Twenty-five years. Twenty-five it had been since the daughter had opened the front door to the men in wet slickers.

"Now don't start, Mim. Just try to enjoy your day. I'll call you as we're leaving, okay?"

She did not see it as a duty spending time with the family—nor did her husband, as far as she could tell anyway. In a John Updike novel she liked, "Rabbit" Angstrom describes a childhood memory of a little girl in a schoolyard playground, "so full of life her nose would start to bleed for no reason." The daughter imagined her mother and father

much like that, their possession of all the sights and sounds and pleasure and disappointment, the run-off from a full life lived and relived.
Her father was still—next to her husband—the funniest man she had
ever known or would know. She was sure she'd had boyfriends who
hung around her solely to be in her mother's company. Watching her
sing and dance. Laughing at the corniest of jokes she told as if they
found them not only charming but funny besides. Age had grayed her
mother and father; time had slowed them down. The dropping off of
a few feathers here and there, but still a gleam peeking from under the
surface. They seemed very much in love.

After an hour or two more and no let-up of weather, she dialed her
mother again.

"Yeah, still coming down," her mother said. "A bit ago we heard
someone on a loudspeaker from across the island, somewhere on the
mainland. I think it might have been coming from the old campground. Probably a party." The campground. Where the baby girl had
gone down.

And again the daughter reassured her mother. She didn't believe it
herself anyway, that the water might rise again to drive the family a
second time from home. After they had recovered from the last flood
her father had said to them, his son and daughter, "Well, the next time
it'll be up to the two of you to deal with it if you keep the house after
we're gone." They had all smiled as he said it.

No, not now. Not again. Not for another seventy-five years at least,
when the children, too, would be gone.

The small TV in the kitchen was on, sound muted, and as the
daughter hung up from the call a readout from the Weather Channel
inched its way across the bottom of the picture. *Front stalled over central Texas, inches fallen presently exceeds earlier predictions by 8 to 12
inches in some low-lying areas. Local creeks and rivers rising rapidly,
expected to crest above flood level in the following counties: Hays,
Milam, Travis . . .*

No, not this time. The family's county hadn't appeared in the alphabetical list. She began putting a day and night's worth of clothes in a bag for her and her husband. Books, vitamins, coffee—far better than the kind her parents made—she threw in a paper sack.

It was when she made the final call, to say they would soon be on the road that she began to waver from the conviction that was supposed to last the rest of their lives. But there it was, on the tube, the authority of the written word, irrefutable, crawling across the screen. *Comal, Gonzales, Guadalupe* . . .

The fixed print appearing the above the scroll read *EVACUATIONS PRESENTLY UNDERWAY. Stay tuned for more details regarding your area.*

Guadalupe.

She grabbed the remote control and jabbed it with her thumb, racing the volume upwards and switching to a local channel. It showed a remote feed from above the banks of an overflowing creek in her city. The reporter was wearing a slicker and a cowboy hat.

"A special thanks to our weather watchers who've called in," he said into the camera. "Took us all a little by surprise, but as you can see behind me, it has made its presence known. A real crazy scene out here. Back to you, Troy."

The meteorologist, safe and dry behind his desk at the station, updated his audience with a stack of incoming weather bulletins. "Comal, Gonzales, Guadalupe . . . ," he read, intoning like a priest.

Our Lady of Guadalupe. Guadalupe, the same name of the river that for twenty-five summers and falls of the family's lives had remained obediently within its banks.

Setting the bulletins down on his desk, the weatherman removed his glasses and faced the camera. "For those of you who have just tuned in, let me repeat. We have a dangerous, potentially deadly situation and will continue to review safety procedures on this station. Crests on some waterways have been predicted to reach from thirty-five to possibly fifty feet. That is a level significantly higher, I repeat, higher than the devastating central Texas flooding in 1973."

The daughter stood frozen to the spot as the weatherman put his glasses back on and began reading emergency safety procedures. *People in the following areas should immediately seek higher ground. Do not attempt to cross low water areas by any means. Park well away from rising water and, if feasible, remain in the safety of your automobile until the water has receded. The force of cresting water presents hazards for the heaviest cars and the strongest swimmers.*

This time when she telephoned her mother she did not tell her to be calm, did not tell her she was being silly. The tide was rising. Nor did she speak of the report she had seen. As her mother was pleading with her not to set out on the road right now the truck with the loudspeaker the mother had apparently heard before passed slowly down the family's street.

"Here we go I guess," said the mother." There was a long pause, and the daughter breathed slowly into the phone. "Evacuate the island immediately, they're telling us. I've got to run, got to try to get some things together." She sounded almost calm.

"Where will you go? What will you do?" asked her daughter, her thoughts gathering together to a greatness in panic that traveled a path from her head to her stomach, down her legs and back again. Now all three local stations were on continual emergency weather watch, all the warnings blurring together as she flipped forward and backward through the channels.

"We have to leave the island, Pete. We'll drive to higher ground, as nearby as we can—wait it out in the car, just until they let us back on."

"But we're on our way, Mim! Get as many things together as you can and we'll load them in the attic."

"No, sweetie. No. Not possible. When we talked to your brother a few minutes ago he told us parts of the highway have already been closed down."

The daughter knew just how fast it could happen. One moment, a quiet lull; the next, swimming furniture.

"Promise me you'll call us the very second you're safe. The very minute you can get to a phone. Promise."

An hour north, she waited, stalking about the house. Fifteen minutes seemed like an hour, and she dialed her parents again. This time it was her father who answered, sounding exactly like her mother had so many years ago when the daughter had awakened them with the news.

Is that it? Has the water come?

It was rising, over the backyard and inching upward as if the house were a magnet. Her father spoke rapidly over the phone; they had loaded the car and were leaving. Things outside were quiet except for the steady rain. They had been told that Placid and Canyon were releasing water and surrounding areas had pretty much been told that flooding would be a certainty. The warning truck had already left the island.

And the rain fell over the daughter's city, rain that brought the island closer and bound them together. When the lamps blinked the daughter lit candles and sat at the kitchen table with her husband, where the two of them waited. Her brother had called her, from his city, where also it rained and he waited.

A dozen times she picked up the phone just to hear the hum of the dial tone, some connection. Hours passed before it rang again. Her mother and father, some of the last off the island and with less than forty minutes before the water would be over the high bridge. They had driven to the convenience store four miles away and planned to camp there until the water crested. But a store employee, leaving after her shift, had checked on them in their car and insisted they follow her to her home on even higher ground. Even still, where she lived turned out to be near enough to the river that in the middle of that night there was talk of escape, using a rowboat she had tethered to a wall in the garage. The father had not slept a minute, not thinking so much about the lake swallowing his house as wondering how he, sev-

enty-five years old and getting around with a cane, could get himself
and his wife in a tiny boat on rushing water.

As with the other flood, people would later ask them what it was
like to imagine their home actually in the lake, the island a hill in the
bed of the lake, its houses a suburban Atlantis. Again all the many
things they had collected, accumulated in their long lives, succumbed
to a putrid gray-brown foam. One of course did not imagine that, could
not imagine that. It happened outside of imagining, apart from the
prediction or fact.

Sometime during the night the phone line to the woman's house
went dead. Now there was nothing to do but listen to the endless bulletins, more waiting. By early morning the rain had slowed to a soft
mist, and still they waited. The daughter was finally able to again get
through by phone to the house that had sheltered her parents, and she
was told by the woman there that her parents had gone. As the water
began retreating, about five in the morning she was told, her parents
had tried to drive back toward the island, but a deep stream of water
over the road ahead had forced them to turn back. Around 9 A.M. they
had told their hosts they intended to set out again, this time to drive
north, to their daughter's home.

WHEN HER DOORBELL RANG, SHE OPENED THE DOOR TO THE
mother and father, mud-streaked and forlorn. This day they wore the
full uniform of their considerable age, a watermark of its own kind.
The mother and daughter clung together, weeping, while the father
told his son-in-law the ridiculous things he'd discovered had been
grabbed and put in the car—a black notebook, the wrong pillows,
some frozen lobster tails they had brought to cook for the daughter's
visit. Most of the medicine, documents, records, and other items that
would be hard or impossible to replace, these had been left behind to
fend with the flood.

The four together held out hope. There were no news reports of how much the lake had overflowed its banks, nor was there confirmation that it had flooded, period. They would have to see for themselves what had happened, and until then it was easier to believe they had been spared. To believe that nature had considered them this time, had withdrawn its claim at the last moment.

Later in the day, her parents in their soiled clothes, the only ones they had, went with the daughter and her husband to eat Mexican food. They laughed and talked, ate enchiladas, drank margaritas and beer, and every once in awhile the mother grew quiet, shaking her head slightly. "We have lived too long," she would say. And the daughter would look into her mother's eyes and almost believe her.

They spent the night, and initially they thought they would stay one more day in peace and then the four of them together would drive back to the island the following morning. But by that night much of their natural self-defense and the cloak that distance insists upon when something has happened some place else had fallen away. Her mother's mood swung wildly from one extreme to another. She needed to witness the damage at once. She would leave all as it was and never go back at all.

"I've told your father," she said. "I say this time we just walk away from that house and everything in it. I don't care if I never see it again."

"That's your home, Mim," the son-in-law said quietly.

She looked at him a moment with eyes ablaze. "That's the home of that goddamn Guadalupe," she said. And they burst into laughter. "The temptation is irresistible never to move from this spot where we are."

This from the woman who had loved nothing more than travel, unless it was to be tucked in warmly at home—when she had had somewhere to come home to.

THEY WERE ON THE HIGHWAY, A FINE MIST FALLING, A WEAK SUN showing through from time to time. The daughter drove her car, her

mother with her, and her husband drove his father-in-law in the parents' car. The mother would wring her hands at times; at others she sat
rigidly. There was much traffic and a wet road to negotiate, so that the
hour's trip took far longer, worsening as they neared the county. A mile
from the island police were directing long lanes of traffic and National
Guard trucks were parked in muddy ditches on the sides of the road.
The family knew the worst then, that there had been a flood, that they
had paid for their human intrusion, land-dwellers flirting on the edge,
and that a price had been exacted.

Still a couple of miles from the house, flooded fields far from the
river spread out on both sides of them.

On the island they made their way slowly to the white house eleven
houses down. Everything was covered with debris washed in from the
lake and out of the houses. When they drove into their driveway they
saw the thin, telltale line of moist mud marking the height of the crest,
just a few inches below the top of the gray slate roof. The mist had
turned back into a light rain, and the quiet around them was the thick
silence that might follow a deep snow. They didn't need to use a key
for the front door; warped and bowed it pushed open against the slime
that coated the entrance hallway, such slippery footing the father had
to go back to wait in the car.

Better, really. The house's interior could not be described to those
unable to see the fullness of it for themselves. The idea that water simply rises by degrees and then retreats to let things dry is more com-
forting than the reality of a flood, the oozing slime and funky smell, the
gray-brown coat of plants collapsed under the weight of the same sub-
stance that sustained their lives. They had drowned.

Lifeless silver minnows lined the floors and cabinets and drawers
by the thousands. The sheet rock of walls and ceilings had given way,
spilling out thick chunks of sodden gray insulation over everything, so
that everything conspired together to leach all color from the view. The
son-in-law was reminded of a trip he had taken with his wife, an elevator's ride a mile below ground to the caverns beneath Carlsbad, New

Mexico. The inverted, upside down world of a nature probably meant to remain hidden, a planet's inner depths submerged in the grayish tones of the womb, the texture of nightmare.

Furniture from one room was now in another or missing entirely, carried out a door and who knows where. The basin in what had been the daughter's bathroom had been ripped from the cabinet and was overturned in the mud on the floor. The oven in the kitchen lay on its side. The lovely stacks of books that were one day to have gone to the daughter and son-in-law were ravaged, even on the highest shelf in the bookcase, over nine feet. One portion had been rearranged in macabre trick, spines up, still neatly stuck together in a row.

And all around were constant reminders that nature made its own capricious decisions. A pencil had risen with the water and was impossibly balanced in the shallow mortar between bricks near the top of the wall where the fireplace was, a magic trick the family left there for others to see, defying every physical law of the force and pull of water retreating. Mattresses were no longer on their bed frames but strewn across the rooms; the boat in back was on its end, bow stuck in the shallow mud under the boathouse. A Queen Anne silver chest, long a favorite of the mother's, stood on the brown lawn. When they used a screwdriver to pry open its drawers glued shut by the water, plump minnows shimmered alongside stacks of silver cutlery. A few were still alive, gasping for breath in tiny pools of droplets.

Too much water it had been and now not enough. Even then it took away.

THE DAUGHTER REALIZED THE EXTENT OF THE LOSS WHEN HER mother and father began visiting "assisted care" facilities as they looked for a place to live. "A bunker," her father said—when he was in the mood to say anything, not so often now. The mother's hearing, which had been failing, was swifter now; she perceived everything as an attack. There was continuous talk of what few items had dried and warped but still held their place and what would be done with them. "For the time we have left," said the mother, whose photographic record of slim, unending legs and a smile like a lamp switched on in the room, was forever gone. She talked about her loss often enough, not as if there if there was work to be done or a new beginning to launch, but as if the final fraction of their lives was a test of will and to be endured.

"They weren't hurt, though, your parents?" asked a younger friend of the daughter's. Her mother had died the past year of cancer at age fifty-three. "The rest of it, all of that—it's just stuff, right?"

As sympathetic as the daughter was to her friend's loss, she still saw this as what she called see-through talk; it sounded enormously logical but hollow at the center, a kind of box of emotions with constricted boundaries. How the family presented their lives to themselves had been formed in one way, and had been changed a great deal. The paper records of their lives had not disappeared as in a fire but reduced to faint sworls by nature's heavy hand. In the murky, moldy aftermath of disbelief and the gray otherworld of uncertainty and inertia, something positive began to grow.

When the sister was still a young girl just entering her teens her brother was beginning a new career in a new city, creating a life apart from the family. He talked with his sister infrequently, and when he did it was about the weather, or a good restaurant he'd found, a golf tournament he'd played in, or how the Oilers' season looked that year. When she learned that he married Lori, whom she had met in the ruin of the flood, the news came from their mother. Her father had been the one to tell her when her brother's business—he sold the mud that packed oilrigs—went bust when the industry tanked. He was a gregarious sort, with many friends—someone who told a story well and enjoyed a good party or a night out on the town. His sister felt that she knew him like it feels, on the surface of things, to know someone.

A few days after the flood he had piled his Suburban full of the silver his mother had collected during her marriage. His sister watched him drive away, sunlight catching the glint of bowls and soup tureens and trays and wine goblets like jewels through the vehicle's windows.

"This is hard to say," she told him later, long-distance. "All of that which is so dear to Mim and Dad, these things that are to be passed on to us later—I have watched so much of this heading east with you. And something about this makes me feel uneasy—and even worse that I feel uneasy. Do you see? Because I don't know how to explain it. It's the distance between us that's the issue, I think, that always has been at issue." The terrible creep of finance and value, the gouge that drives a rent through families—or any relationship.

"I brought it to my house so it could be polished," he said. He knew he and his sister had been close, and he thought about wasted years during which they had lived separate lives even when they were together.

When next he came to her city, they got together for a long visit. They had a wonderful time, and when they parted they hugged each other for a long moment, vowing to keep in closer touch and to see each other again soon. And so this was the good thing that grew from the flood, that at last she had talked to her brother, and at last he had heard her.

By the next summer, the last year before the century would turn, the news stories at decade's end were of murders and suicides, accidents and crises, massacres and bombings. So when you heard about nature's wrath—the hailstorm that depleted a farmer's life savings, the tornado that roared through "like a freight train"—you saw the starkness of what was outside human purpose.

And the second flood had come as close as anything to breaking the father. One terrible night during an argument that erupted routine talk the daughter was delivering about bucking up and rebuilding their lives he had uttered unutterable words, ones he failed to grab back before they spilled out and so would remain always.

"I could kill you!" he shouted in fear and helplessness to his wife. "And you too!" he said to the daughter. "I swear I could!"

But this was the nadir of the despair, and from this point he began to move back toward the life he had lived, toward the lives of the family, with more hopeful reflection.

For they were still a family. And it became easier for them to become so anew, for the son to comfort his wife after she lost her job, for the daughter to teach and garden, for the mother to love the water once again. To build again the house that had born witness to so much in the family.

After a storm there is a soft breeze, and with shadow there is light. A caterpillar breaks its bonds with the earth but carries another life along, toward its end. Before May had become June and the Texas summer sucked away the breath of everything in its watch, the family met at a beach house they rented on the gulf coast. They watched their skin change to colors of copper and bronze; they boiled shrimp and crawfish over a fire they made from sticks in the sand. They luxuriated in the sun and gazed at the millions of stars over the ocean. They walked on the sand, where the warm gulf water rushed in to bathe their ankles and wash their footprints away. Water rushing into the shallow indentations made by six pairs of feet standing together. And then back to the line of the horizon, where the sun dipped by degrees into the sea.

LEAPING LEO

★

Pat Ellis Taylor

—when you're down and out in dallas you are down and out
—fr. de dallas blues

S
O IN DALLAS LEO IS ALWAYS WORKING ONE PLACE AND I AM
working another, I get up in the morning while he's still in bed
or after he's already gone to work, hours and days erratic working temporary jobs. I walk through the alley in back of our apartment
house in the morning to gaston avenue to catch the bus to wherever
kelly girl services say I should be going, the exhaust fumes flooding
over the curbs and crashing in rush-hour waves against the darkening
brick mix of apartments/tattoo-parlor/mex-tex-bars/and/fast-foods on
both street sides. And leo coaxes the pick-up truck to his jobs, he's registered with manpower, atlas, and peak-load, he loads gatorade and
drives a delivery route and makes electric circuit boards and sprays
paint on pipes. And he comes home telling stories, you know how the
newspaper said that street guy fell into downtown traffic and was
killed? he tells me. Well, he didn't fall he was pushed, that's what one
of the men down at atlas told me today. He was a pursesnatcher and

the cops couldn't catch him, so they finally pushed him under the wheels. And he tells me where some of the men sleep, under the free-way, and where they told him to go on the highway to ask truckers for work unloading in town, little pieces of labor pool lore, who's hiring where, and how many at a time. He works for two or three days at a time, then lays off for two or three days, sitting around in the efficiency apartment, watching teevee in his shorts, drinking beers, letting the aluminum cans pile up in grocery bags under the kitchen window, writing poems about how workers hate working and how he wishes he was alone and free and unencumbered and somewhere else.

In the evenings when I get off of work, sometimes leo and I walk down gaston avenue to tom thumb supermarket which is a grocery store like the neighborhood built in more peaceful, more affluent tree-lined times for the sweet-stay-at-home-housewives who were our mothers who abandoned these city neighborhoods for the safer cleaner north dallas suburbs. Now it is sticky-floor-broken-glass-crowded-aisles, votive candles and mountain-pass cans of chile across from wonton wrappers, strong-smelling men in salvation army suits cruising with grocery carts full of plastic-sacked beans and boxed rice, iron bars between the store doors and the parking lot to keep the carts from getting ripped off by grocery-bagged walkers. The store sits at the end of a horse-shoe mall, but the dimestores and baby-knitting-fabric shops which once must have lined the other two sides of the parking lot are long gone, windows boarded up, one corner ex-drugstore now mario's lounge, black plywood across the window glass, low-riders parked in front, young chicanos lounging against the chrome-nosed hoods at night, mario's door open and loud music coming out. One night at the supermarket check-out stand I am so happy to be off work for the day, so happy to be with leo, who is holding my hand, I say isn't this romantic, the two of us here checking out groceries, and leo looks at me like I am crazy. You've got to be kidding, he says, no romanticism left in leo anymore, he can see very clearly where he is, and it's no place good.

Because the truth is that the landscapes of leo's memory/mind are like a series of snapshots from a family album, there are rolling green lawns of suburban homes and university campuses and country lots, and there is a family standing together on the front steps of a tidy home or in front of a tidy christmas tree or lined up on the sides of a tidy turkey dinner: a small-boned beautiful angel-faced wife and two angel-boy-babies calling him leo instead of daddy in the liberal unitarian style, him pointing out nature to them in the ravines and hills of the paradise of nuclear family life they are growing up in. So leo's present reality dances across the stage in front of these green landscapes like a wino reeling his way through a montessori school, hey where *are* we? Just where the hell are we? Wife, children, house and car, all gone, university job finally taken away for all the scandal and chaos which once kicked up like chicken feathers in a whing-a-ding transformation from leo-the-professor to leo-the-man falling falling falling for a shady woman with teen-aged children (who is me) and poetry as a way of life. And somehow or another it has all come to this: leo creating the plot of his own story from labor pool lounge to tom thumb barrio-market and seeing (incredibly!) himself in the faces of the other men there too old too poorly educated too alcoholic too suicidal too lonely to be anything like him, but there they are anyway, wheeling the aisles of tom thumb together at night and in the daytime sharing the same set of folding chairs.

Now if leo didn't love me, he could be a poet and live alone in a cardboard box (like a man who lived somewhere up east leo read about in the dallas morning news) and then he wouldn't have to work very much at all, he could simply eat cheap mackerel and soda crackers and write poetry all day. Or if I were simply myself alone, then we could be gypsies together, we could ride the rails and hitchhike and explore deserts and mountains and meet south american shamen and learn universal secrets from listening to the grass sing across the canadian tundras and from kundalini-fucking in the dry bed of the rio grande. But I never seem to be myself alone, that sharp thin blade of a female-fantasy-companion fit for a gypsy-poet-man, I always seem instead to have these children always tying me to the world of work. And in dallas at first there is only one of these children, there is only morgani, who is a grown child and who works himself at a car wash bringing in one-third of the rent every month. But then there are two others, calling long-distance from el paso no longer wanting to live with their father, wanting to come for the school year to dallas and live with me. And I am a mother, born under the sign of mother, called by the name of mother and all of its variations wheeling off three children's developing tongues: the continuing chorus of all my adult years. So because of these children wanting to come, I think, well, we've got to be somewhere, we've got to have a place to sleep at least, the word *we* no longer meaning leo and me, having wider and weightier implications.

So leo thinks maybe he will get a grant of money. But he doesn't. And then he thinks maybe someone rich will give him some money for the sake of poetry, but nobody does. And then he thinks maybe if we take off in the camper for two weeks in july for the annual-naked-hippie-rainbow-family-gathering we will get a revelation and some new kind of future other than temporary labor pools and dallas apartment-semi-migrant-neighborhoods will open up. And we do go to the rainbow-family-gathering all right. But it rains, we only have wet wood and don't know how to build a fire, we get diarrhea, the wind blows toilet paper from the shitter around our tent poles, the tent falls down around our ears. So we're back in dallas and poorer than we were before, and I start looking around for a bigger place with a lease that allows children because it's already august and the school year is about to begin and my children are coming.

So one day I tell leo, there is an apartment for rent just three doors down big enough for everybody, and leo says how much a month?

I say 325.

And he says utilities?

I say we pay them.

And he says well, that's over a hundred dollars more a month than what we're paying now.

But I say I'll pay more than you need to, to cover the kids.

Who'll pay the deposit? he says.

Oh, don't worry, I'll get it together, I lie-hope-wish-dream, because there's no more than fifty dollars in the envelope underneath the rug in the closet where I keep my money, and kelly services hasn't called me for work in over four days. Leo looks at me like he knows I am lying and he is mad-as-hell but he isn't saying anything, because he's seen again that I am not alone, even though I try every night to make him forget it by making him concentrate on that singular body under the covers, but the truth is always there below the surface: *leo is working in labor pools in dallas instead of crab-fishing on the acapulco-tibetan-desert-beach because the woman he has chosen is always shadowed by children not even his own.*

So it is toward the end of the summer to beat all summers, july murdering grass and shrubs, august murdering babies, old people stroking and dying, burnt-out trees like torches outside the apartment window dead-green and still. It is too hot to wear clothes so I am hanging around the apartment with nothing on but a white half-slip pulled up to my armpits. And in the corner of the kitchen is a pile of used carpet which someone brought home from a dumpster because it is perfectly good. So I lie down on top of that and look out the window at nothing like a floundered fish pining for my kids because they're so good and I'm so bad, singing that old bad mother song. And oh these kids, I am thinking, they've been through shit with me, I quit their bankrupt ad-agency boozing dad thinking for sure I could make something better for us all than that but where am I now, baby, where am I now? My arm is over my eyes listening to leo running bathwater on the other side of the wall, and I start to cry because I'm living in a two-room efficiency apartment in an east dallas neighborhood where the winos piss in the park bushes across from the elementary school and I don't have a job and I don't even have a place for my kids to stay. And

I don't even have a place for them to stay! Oh I should have bought a
pair of hose, I should have lacquered my fingernails and put my papers
in a briefcase and finished my degree and copied my resume and
stopped pretending to be a writer, and I should have married someone
other than leo who would give me money anytime I asked for it, or
stayed married to the children's dad who has become successful-
sober-and-dull without me around, or I should have never moved to
dallas I should have stayed in the country and gone to work in wills
point for champion mobile homes or gotten a job at the local dairy
queen dishing ice cream.

The front door opens, and it is morgani coming in from the car
wash, he comes into the kitchen and opens the refrigerator but
doesn't say anything to me like I am probably sleeping with my arm
over my face. And thank god thank god, I am thinking, at least a little
money coming in from morgani thank god for a grown son, oh, and I
keep lying on that pile of carpet, not only am I not able to take care of
my own children, I am not able to take care of myself. Here I am, I am
thinking, no better than a fat-black-shawled peasant mother being
taken care of by a grown son (and I am getting lower and lower)—how
can this be when I am such a *smart* person? How can such a bright-
young-looking-kind-of-woman-for-her-age, such a—I would even
say—sometimes *sexy* woman—who at the same time writes funny
things as well as serious things, someone who is sometimes somewhat
of a female folklore scholar, how can such a charismatic person like
myself be so down and out?

The telephone rings and leo answers it. He comes into the kitchen
a few minutes later, and he looks his worst, his arms and legs look
skinny, his hair looks stringy, when he looks at me I hear him saying
you-limpbag-of-depression-and-doldrums-you-witch-bitch, and when
I look at him he can hear me saying you moneyless-no-good-bummer-
nonpoet-of-a-man . . . That was gray eagle on the telephone, he tells
me, he's going to come over and drive us to his house so we can see
some slides he took of the rainbow gathering. And I am thinking oh no

oh no, not gray eagle, not the rainbow gathering why oh why did I ever go to the naked-hippie-rainbow-family-gathering this summer in west virginia, why did I let leo talk me into spending my money on that? So I don't say anything, I just lie there with my arm on my eyes.

Leo says so do you want to go?

And I say no.

He says I think you should go, I think you should get out of this apartment.

So I take my arm down but don't look at him, I look around for my shoes, I'll go I say, reaching around for the pants I had on which are somewhere.

Just then someone knocks at the door and morgani answers it, and it is my biker-brother who came passing through el paso on his way to dallas and gave one of my kids a ride. So I hug this particular kid, who is blonde and sixteen, and I tell him that he looks good, because he does, and we walk out of the kitchen into the other room and he says, so this is it, huh? And I say yes, this is it.

And he says well, where am I going to sleep?

And I wave to the floor and say here for right now.

He says where's the other kid going to sleep when she comes?

And I say, she's going to sleep here, too.

My biker-brother sits down on the couch, red beard frazzled, face red, leo brings him a beer, this city is already freaking me out, my biker-brother says, I don't see how you can stand living in the middle of the city. I called out to your house in the country first thinking you'd be there. Some other people had your number. They said they had people calling for you all the time.

Well we haven't been out there for a long time, I say. For one thing, our truck's on its last legs, so leo has only been using it to drive to jobs.

I don't know why you don't live out there anymore, my biker-brother says.

Well, we're not living out there because we ran out of money and there wasn't any work out there, I say.

Oh you could have worked if you wanted to, leo says.

Where? I ask him.

You never even asked around.

Well at any rate it certainly seemed to me that there wasn't any way to make a living there.

Someone is knocking on the door again, and this time it is gray eagle, leo introduces gray eagle to my biker-brother and they shake hands. And on one side of the hand-shake is gray eagle whose beard is gray and whose cheeks are rosy from hippie vitality who lives by himself on bee pollen and rose hips (like leo himself might look if he were fifty and lived alone) and on the other side of the hand-shake is my biker-brother full of biker-blood-lust, his face already dark-red from homicidal city vibes. Leo asks my biker-brother if he wants to come and see slides of the rainbow gathering and my biker-brother says yes, and we leave the apartment with morgani and the other kid sharing a joint. We drive to gray eagle's ranch-style house with trimmed-up bushes in a quiet north dallas neighborhood. He sets up his carousel slide projector on a coffee table in the living room and starts projecting larger-than-lifesize photographs of two nude blonde women, one a well-preserved fortyish, the other in her teens. These are mother and daughter, he says, who came to dallas from new mexico and convoyed with me to the hippie rainbow gathering the rest of the way. I took these shots of them in the shower the night they were staying here. We were just goofing around.

Now that's quite a mother, my biker-brother says.

The older woman is lathering the younger woman's boobs for several slides in a row, then for several others the two of them change places.

I wouldn't mind some of that ass, my biker-brother says.

These are my rainbow sisters, gray eagle says like a gentle reprimand.

Jesus look at those tits, my biker-brother says.

Gray eagle picks up the pace, clicks through five or six fast glimpses of blonde pubic hair and smiles and stoops and bends. Then the blonde women are suddenly replaced with panoramas of nude women bathing in streams, hiking along forest trails holding hands, eating fruit, carrying babies, everyone looking free from the cities, from working, for the taking, for gray eagle or my biker-brother or leo, anyone who can claw through the screen. And my biker-brother is going crazy. He is drinking up gray eagle's red wine, he is talking cunt and tits, so gray eagle shuts off the slides and turns to him. If you're going to talk like that about the rainbow sisters, he says, I won't be able to show you the slides.

Leo has been sitting on the floor not saying anything drinking one long-neck lone star after another, but now he speaks up. Well you do show more photographs of nude women than you do nude men, he says, although maybe it's natural if you're a man to have that bias, and his words are thick but precise.

I want to see some more of the shower girlies, my biker-brother says.

The thing is, gray eagle says, these people let me take these photographs because they know me, they know I'd never hurt them in any way.

Oh I'd never hurt them either, my biker-brother says, oh maybe I'd want to fuck them but I wouldn't want to hurt them.

Well they know that we are like brother and sister, gray eagle says.

Or maybe I would only hurt them a little, my biker-brother says, if they hurt me or something like that.

Gray eagle turns off the slide projector. Well I guess it's time to take us back, I say. So we're back in the car, I sit in the front seat with gray eagle, leo and my biker-brother in the back seat, driving back the way we came, through the quiet winding streets of north dallas to the freeway back south toward downtown. Gray eagle tells me maybe I should write a story, maybe I should write something about women who work for the railroads and he could take the photographs and we could make some money collaborating that way, and a mercedes whizzes past

us, and my biker-brother throws the driver a finger and yells fuck you!
out the window at him. Then another car passes and he throws them
a finger, too, and yells fuck you! fuck you! Then leo starts throwing fingers out the back window at the car behind us, I see him fluttering his
fingers in and out of his ears, and gray eagle says or maybe we could
do a story together about women who work for the highway department fixing roads. Leo is yelling you rich bastard! You rich filth! And
gray eagle pulls up to the curb in front of our apartment, and my biker-
brother says—Trisha stays calm through everything, she runs the
show.

There is a pause, and then leo says yes she does run the show,
doesn't she?

Then he slams out of the back of the car and runs up the apartment
steps and disappears. My biker-brother gets out, he has a happy booze
smile on his face and is swaying back and forth holding the last of a
gallon bottle of red wine he took from gray eagle's house and one of
gray eagle's glasses. I wave to gray eagle as he pulls away from the curb,
my biker-brother puts his arm around me, I love you, he says, because
you're always running the show.

When we walk into the apartment leo is throwing clothes books
papers into a duffel bag. I am leaving here! he yells out when he hears
the door open, and I never want to see any of your faces again! He
walks out, slams the door. Morgani and the other kid are sitting on the
couch watching teevee, hardly look up when leo walks out the door.
Maybe we don't want to see him again either, morgani says.

Well he must love you, my biker-brother says. He probably left so
that he wouldn't beat you up.

So leo walks out the apartment to gaston avenue where the buses
run, but before he gets on a bus he walks down to mario's lounge and
gets *really* drunk. And then afterward he gets his suitcases stolen while
he's waiting for the bus. And he heads for austin where his ex-nurse-
wife is living with the children which at least are his own. But I don't
know any of this until he calls me the next night from the nurse-wife's

phone. Why don't you come down to austin? he says. You could work kelly services down here. But I say no.

Then two days later he calls up again and he's now in galveston as a poet-in-the-schools living in a camper truck because he happened to walk into the right office at the right time. Why don't you come down to galveston? he says. But the ocean is behind him and the sea gulls are swooping down on his shoulders and back up and down again and calling, and the beach is all sand and no rocks, and leo is already dancing with the galveston dancers and singing to the blonde sisters who are not yet mothers in the galveston bars, leo unencumbered as light itself since gaston avenue took all his papers and clothes.

from THE LIARS' CLUB

★

Mary Karr

MY DADDY HAD GROWN UP WITH THREE LOUD BROTHERS and a sister in a logging camp in the piney section of East Texas called The Big Thicket. His family lived mostly without hard currency, buying coffee and sugar with credit vouchers at the Kirby Lumber Company Store. Other than that and such luxuries as calico for dresses, they grew and shot and caught what they needed.

That world was long gone before my birth, but I remember it. In fact, my father told me so many stories about his childhood that it seems in most ways more vivid to me than my own. His stories got told and retold before an audience of drinking men he played dominoes with on days off. They met at the American Legion or in the back room of Fisher's Bait Shop at times when their wives thought they were paying bills or down at the union hall. Somebody's pissed-off wife eventually christened them the Liars' Club, and it stuck. Certainly not much of the truth in any technical sense got told there.

Except for Christmas Eve morning, when they met in the Legion parking lot at dawn to exchange identical gift bottles of Jack Daniel's from the windows of their pickups, the men had no official meeting time and place. I never saw evidence of any planning. They never called each other on the phone. No one's wife or kids ever carried a message to meet at thus-and-such a place. They all just seemed to meander together, seemingly by instinct, to a given place and hour that had magically planted itself in their collective noggins. No women ever came along. I was the only child allowed, a fact frequently held up as proof that I was hopelessly spoiled. I would ask Daddy for money for a Coke or shuffleboard or to unlock the pool table, and it was only a matter of time before somebody piped over at us that he was spoiling me and that if he kept it up, I wasn't going to be worth a shit. Comments like that always rang a little too true to me. Sometimes I'd even fake starting to give the coin back or shying away from the pool table. But Daddy would just wag his head at whoever spoke. "Leave her alone. She can do anything she's big enough to do, cain't you, Pokey?" And then I would say I guessed I could.

Of all the men in the Liars' Club, Daddy told the best stories. When he started one, the guys invariably fell quiet, studying their laps or their cards or the inner rims of their beer mugs like men in prayer. No matter how many tangents he took or how far the tale flew from its starting point before he reeled it back, he had this gift: he knew how to be believed. He mastered it the way he mastered bluffing in poker, which probably happened long before my appearance. His tough half-breed face would move between solemn blankness and sudden caricature. He kept stock expressions for stock characters. When his jaw jutted and stiffened and his eyes squinted, I expected to hear the faint brogue of his uncle Husky. A wide-eyed expression was the black man Ugh, who taught him cards and dice. His sister pursed her lips in steady disapproval. His mother wore an enormous bonnet like a big blue halo, so he'd always introduce her by fanning his hands behind his head, saying *Here comes Momma*.

My father comes into focus for me on a Liars' Club afternoon. He sits at a wobbly card table weighed down by a bottle. Even now the scene seems so real to me that I can't but write it in the present tense.

I am dangling my legs off the bar at the Legion and shelling unroasted peanuts from a burlap bag while Daddy slides the domino tiles around the table. They make a clicking sound. I haven't started going to school yet, so the day seems without beginning or end, stalled in the beer-smelling dark of the Legion.

Cooter has just asked Daddy if he had planned to run away from home. "They wasn't no planning to it," Daddy says, then lights a cigarette to stall, picking a few strands of tobacco off his tongue as if that gesture may take all the time in the world. "Poppa had give me a silver dollar and told me to get into town and buy some coffee. Had to cross the train tracks to get there. When that old train come around the turn, it had to slow up. Well, when it slowed up, I jumped, and that dollar come with me.

"Got a job threshing wheat up to Kansas. Slept at night with some other old boys in this fella's barn. Man by the name of Hamlet. Sorriest sonofabitch ever to tread shoe leather. Wouldn't bring you a drink from sunup to lunch. And married to the prettiest woman you ever seen. A butt like two bulldogs in a bag." This last makes everybody laugh.

I ask him how he got home, and he slides the story back on track. While I'm waiting for his answer, I split open a fresh peanut with my fingernail. The unroasted shell is soft as skin, the meat of the nut chewy and almost tasteless without salt. Daddy finishes his drink and moves a domino. "About didn't make it. Hopped the Double-E train from Kansas City to New Orleans. Cold?" He glares at each of us as if we might doubt the cold. "That wind come inching in those boxcar cracks like a straight razor. It'll cut your gizzard out, don't think it won't. They finally loaded some cattle on somewhere in Arkansas, and I cozied up to this old heifer. I'd of froze to death without her. Many's the time I think of that old cow. Tried milking her, but it come out froze solid. Like a Popsicle."

"It's getting high and deep in here," Shug says. He's the only black man I've ever seen in the Legion, and then only when the rest of the guys are there. He wears a forest-green porkpie hat with the joker from a deck of cards stuck on the side. He's famously intolerant of Daddy's horseshit, and so tends to up the credibility factor when around.

"I shit you not," Daddy says and sprinkles some salt in the triangular hole in his beer can. "You hop one of those bastards some January and ride her. You'll be pissing ice cubes. I guarangoddamntee you that." They shake their heads, and I can see Daddy considering his next move by pretending to study his dominoes. They're lined up like bricks in a wall, and after he chooses one, he makes a show of lining it up right on the tabletop, then marking down his score. "They unloaded one old boy stiff as a plank from down off the next car over. He was a old one. Didn't have no business riding trains that old. And when we tipped him down to haul him off—they was four or five of us lifting him—about a dozen of these round fuzzy things rolled out his pant leg. Big as your thumb, and white." He measures off the right length on his thumb.

"Those were the crown pearls, no doubt," Shug says.

Daddy stares seriously into the middle distance, as if the old man in question were standing there himself, waiting for his story to get told properly and witnessing the ignorance that Daddy had to suffer in the process. "Wasn't no such thing. If you shut up, I can tell your thickheaded self what they was."

"Let him tell it," Cooter says, then lowers his head into a cloud of cigar smoke. Cooter is bothered by the fact that Shug is colored, and takes any chance to scold him, which the other guys tend to ignore. Shug gives me Fig Newtons out of his glove compartment, and I feel evil seeing him scolded for no reason and not saying anything. But I know the rules and so lay low.

"One old boy had a big black skillet in his gear. So we built a fire on the edge of the freight yard. It was a kind of hobo camp already there, some other guys set up all around. Nobody bothered us. This old fella's stretched out behind us stiff as this bench I'm sitting on here."

"The dead one?" I ask, and the men shift around in their chairs, a signal for me to shut up, so I do.

"That's right. And you ain't never gonna guess what happens when they thaw." This is the turning point. Daddy cocks his head at everybody to savor it. The men don't even fake indifference. The domino tiles stop their endless clicking. The cigar smoke might even seem to quit winding around on itself for a minute. Nobody so much as takes a drink. "They pop like firecrackers and let off the biggest stink you ever smelled."

"They was farts?" Cooter finally screams, more high-pitched than is masculine, and at that the men start to laugh. Daddy's Adam's apple googles up and down, and Ben slaps the table, and Shug has to wipe his eyes after a minute.

When everybody settles down, Daddy passes the bottle around again and jumps back to the story of his coming home without even a stab at a segue. "Ain't nothing else to tell. I just walked up through the razor grass to Daddy's old dirt yard. And there's the old man, sitting on the porch. Just exactly like I left him the year before. And he looks up at me serious as polio and says, 'You git the coffee?'"

PLAYING COWBOY

───── ★ ─────

Larry L. King

WHEN I WAS YOUNG, I DIDN'T KNOW THAT WHEN YOU leave a place, it may not be forever. The past, I thought, had served its full uses and could bury its own dead; bridges were for burning; "good-bye" meant exactly what it said. One never looked back except to judge how far one had come.

Texas was the place I left behind. And not reluctantly. The leave-taking was so random I trusted the United States Army to relocate me satisfactorily. It did, in 1946, choosing to establish in Queens (then but a five-cent subway ride from the clamorous glamour of Manhattan) a seventeen-year-old former farm boy and small-town sapling green enough to challenge chlorophyll. The assignment would shape my life far more than I then suspected; over the years it would teach me to "play cowboy"—to become, strangely, more "Texas" than I had been.

New York offered everything to make an ambitious kid dizzy; I moved through its canyons in a hot walking dream. Looking back, I see myself starring in a bad movie I then accepted as high drama: the Kid, a.k.a. the Bumptious Innocent, discovering the theater, books, a bewildering variety of nightclubs and bars; subways and skyscrapers and respectable wines. There were glancing encounters with Famous Faces: Walter Winchell, the actor Paul Kelly, the ex-heavyweight champion Max Baer, bandleader Stan Kenton. It was easy; spotting them, I simply rushed up, stuck out my hand, sang out my name, and began asking personal questions.

Among my discoveries was that I dreaded returning to Texas; where were its excitements, celebrities, promises? As corny as it sounds, one remembers the final scene of that bad movie. Crossing the George Washington Bridge in a Greyhound bus in July 1949—Army discharge papers in my duffel bag—I looked back at Manhattan's spires and actually thought, *I'll be back, New York.* I did not know that scene had been played thousands of times by young men or young women from the provinces, nor did I know that New York cared not a whit whether we might honor the pledge. In time, I got back. On my recent forty-sixth birthday, it dawned that I had spent more than half my life—or twenty-four years—on the eastern seaboard. I guess there's no getting around the fact that this makes me an expatriate Texan.

"Expatriate" remains an exotic word. I think of it as linked to Paris or other European stations in the 1920s: of Sylvia Beach and her famous bookstore; of Hemingway, Fitzgerald, Dos Passos, Ezra Pound, and Gertrude Stein Stein Stein. There is wine in the Paris air, wine and cheese and sunshine, except on rainy days when starving young men in their attics write or paint in contempt of their gut rumbles. Spain. The brave bulls. Dublin's damp fog. Movable feasts. *That's* what "expatriate" means, so how can it apply to one middle-aged grandfather dodging Manhattan's muggers and dogshit pyramids while grunting a son through boarding school and knocking on the doors of magazine editors? True expatriates, I am certain, do not wait in dental offices, the Port Authority Bus Terminal, or limbo. Neither do they haunt their original root sources three or four times each year, while dreaming of accumulating enough money to return home in style as a gentlemanly rustic combining the best parts of J. Frank Dobie, Lyndon Johnson, Stanley Walker, and the Old Man of the Mountain. Yet that is my story, and that is my plan.

I miss the damned place. Texas is my mind's country, that place I most want to understand and record and preserve. Four generations of my people sleep in its soil; I have children there, and a grandson; the dead past and the living future tie me to it. Not that I always approve it or love it. It vexes and outrages and disappoints me—especially when I am there. It is now the third most urbanized state, behind New York and California, with all the tangles, stench, random violence, architectural rape, historical pillage, neon blight, pollution, and ecological imbalance the term implies. Money and mindless growth remain high on the list of official priorities, breeding a crass boosterism not entirely papered over by an infectious energy. The state legislature—though improving as slowly as an old man's mending bones—still harbors excessive, coon-ass, rural Tory Democrats who fail to understand that 79.7 percent of Texans have flocked to urban areas and may need fewer farm-to-market roads, hide-and-tick inspectors, or outraged orations almost comically declaiming against welfare loafers, creeping socialism, the meddling ol' feds, and sin in the aggregate.

Too much, now, the Texas landscape sings no native notes. The impersonal, standardized superhighways—bending around or by most small towns, and then blatting straightaway toward the urban sprawls—offer homogenized service stations, fast-food-chain outlets, and cluttered shopping centers one might find duplicated in Ohio, Maryland, Illinois, or Anywhere, U.S.A. Yes, there is much to make me protest, as did Mr. Faulkner's Quentin Compson, of the south—"I *don't* hate it. I don't hate it, I *don't.* . . ." For all its shrinkages of those country pleasures I once eschewed, and now covet and vainly wish might return, Texas remains in my mind's eye that place to which I shall eventually return to rake the dust for my formative tracks; that place where one hopes to grow introspective and wise as well as old.

It is a romantic foolishness, of course; the opiate dream of a nostalgia junkie. When I go back to stay—and I fancy that I will—there doubtless will be opportunities to wonder at my plan's imperfections.

For already I have created in my mind, you see, an improbable corner of paradise: the rustic, rambling ranch house with the clear-singing creek nearby, the clumps of shade trees (under which, possibly, the Sons of the Pioneers will play perpetual string-band concerts), the big cozy library where I will work and read and cogitate between issuing to the Dallas *Times-Herald* or the Houston *Post* those public pronouncements befitting an Elder Statesman of Life and Letters. I will become a late-blooming naturalist and outdoorsman: hiking and camping, and piddling in cattle; never mind that to date I have preferred the sidewalks of New York, and my beef not on the hoof but tricked up with mushroom sauces.

All this will occur about one easy hour out of Austin—my favorite Texas city—and exactly six miles from a tiny, unnamed town looking remarkably like what Walt Disney would have built for a cheery, heart-tugging Texas-based story happening about 1940. The nearest neighbor will live 3.7 miles away, have absolutely no children or dogs, but will have one beautiful young wife, who adores me; it is she who will permit me, by her periodic attentions, otherwise to live the hermit's uncluttered life. Politicians will come to my door hats in hand, and fledging Poets and young Philosophers. Basically, they will want to know exactly what is Life's Purpose. Looking out across the gently blowing grasslands, past the grazing blooded cattle, toward a perfect sunset, with even the wind in my favor, and being the physical reincarnation of Hemingway with a dash of Twain in my mood, I shall—of course—be happy to tell them.

WELL, WE ALL KNOW THAT VAST GAP BETWEEN FANTASY AND reality when True Life begins playing the scenario. Likely I will pay twice to thrice the value for a run-down old "farmhouse" where the plumbing hasn't worked since Coolidge, and shall die of a heart attack while digging a cesspool. The nearest neighbor will live directly across the road; he will own seven rambunctious children, five mad dogs, and an ugly harridan with sharp elbows, a shrill voice, and a perverse hatred for dirty old writing men. The nearest town—less than a half mile away and growing by leaps, separated from my digs only by a sub-division of mock Bavarian castles and the new smeltering plant—will be made of plastics, paved parking lots, and puppy-dog tails. The trip to Austin will require three hours if one avoids rush-hour crushes; when I arrive—to preen in Scholz Garten or The Raw Deal or other watering holes where artists congregate—people will say, "Who's that old fart?" Unfortunately I may try to tell them. My books will long have been out of print; probably my secret yearning will be to write a col-umn for the local weekly newspaper. Surrounded by strangers, memo-ries, and galloping growth, I shall sit on my porch—rocking and cackling and talking gibberish to the wind—while watching them build yet another Kwik Stop Kwality Barbecue Pit on the west edge of my crowded acreage. Occasionally I will walk the two dozen yards to the interstate highway to throw stones at passing trucks; my ammuni-tion will peter out long before traffic does. But when I die digging that cesspool, by God, I'll have died at home. That knowledge makes me realize where my heart is.

But the truth, dammit, is that I feel much more the Texan when in the East. New Yorkers, especially, encourage and expect one to per-form a social drill I think of as "playing cowboy." Even as a young sol-dier I discovered a presumption among a high percentage of New Yorkers that my family owned shares in the King Ranch and that my natural equestrian talents were unlimited; all one needed to affirm such groundless suspicions were a drawl and a grin. To this day you may spot me in Manhattan wearing boots and denim jeans with a matching vest and western-cut hat—topped by a furry cattleman's coat straight out of Marlboro Country; if you've seen Dennis Weaver play McCloud, then you've seen me, without my beard.

Never mind that I *like* such garb, grew up wearing it, or that I find it natural, practical, and inexpensive; no, to a shameful degree, I dress for my role. When I learned that Princeton University would pay good money to a working writer for teaching his craft—putting insulated students in touch with the workaday salts and sours of the literary world—do you think I went down there wrapped in an ascot and puffing a briar pipe from Dunhill's? No, good neighbors, I donned my Cowboy Outfit to greet the selection committee and aw-shucksed and consarned 'em half to death; Easterners just can't resist a John Wayne quoting Shakespeare; I've got to admit there's satisfaction in it for every good ol' boy who country-slicks the city dudes.

New Yorkers tend to think of Mississippians or Georgians or Virginians under the catchall category of "southerners," of Californians as foreigners, and of Texans as the legendary Texan. We are the only outlanders, I think, that they define within a specific state border and assign the burden of an obligatory—i.e., "cowboy"—culture. Perhaps we court such treatment; let it be admitted that Texans are a clannish people. We tend to think of ourselves as Texans no matter how long ago we strayed or how tenuous our home connections. When I enter a New York store and some clerk—alerted by my nasal twang—asks where I am from, I do not answer "East Thirty-second Street," but "Texas," yet my last permanent address there was surrendered when Eisenhower was freshly President.

More than half my close friends—and maybe 20 percent of my overall eastern seaboard acquaintances—are expatriate Texans: writers, musicians, composers, editors, lawyers, athletes, show-folk, a few businessmen, and such would-be politicians or former politicians as Bill Moyers and Ramsey Clark. Don Meredith, Liz Smith, Judy Buie, Dan Jenkins, you name 'em, and to one degree or another we play cowboy together. Many of us gather for chili suppers, tell stories with origins in Fort Worth or Odessa or Abilene; sometimes we even play dominoes or listen to country-western records.

There is, God help us, an organization called The New York Texans,

and about 2,000 of us actually belong to it. We meet each March 2—
Texas Independence Day—to drink beer, hoo-haw at each other in the
accents of home, and honor some myth that we can, at best, only ill
define. We even have our own newspaper, published quarterly by a
lady formerly of Spur, Texas, which largely specializes in stories bragging on how well we've done in the world of the Big Apple. Since people back home are too busy to remind us of our good luck and talents,
we remind ourselves.

No matter where you go, other Texans discover you. Sometimes
they are themselves expatriates, sometimes tourists, sometimes busi-
ness-bent travelers. In any case, we whoop a mutural recognition, even
though we're strangers or would be unlikely to attract each other if
meeting within our native borders. Indeed, one of the puzzling curiosi-
ties is why the Dallas banker, or the George Wallace fanatic who owns
the little dry-goods stores in Beeville, and I may drop all prior plans in
order to spend an evening together in Monterrey or Oshkosh when—
back home—we would consider each other social lepers. Many times
I have found myself buddy-buddying with people not all that likable or
interesting, sharing Aggie jokes or straight tequila shots or other peculiarities of home.

If you think that sounds pretty dreadful, it often is. Though I am
outraged when called a "professional Texan," or when I meet one, certainly I am not always purely innocent. Much of it is a big put-on, of
course. We enjoy sharing put-ons against those who expect all Texans
to eat with the wrong fork, offer coarse rebel yells, and get all vomity-
drunk at the nearest football game. There is this regional defensive-
ness—LBJ would have known what I mean—leading us to order "a
glass of clabber and a mess of chitlins" when faced by the haughty
ministrations of the finest French restaurants. (My group does, anyway, though I don't know about the stripe of Texan epitomized, say, by
Red Reed; that bunch has got so smooth you can't see behind the
sheen.) I hear my Texas friends, expatriates and otherwise, as their
accents thicken and their drawls slow down on approaching represen-

tatives of other cultures. I observe them as they attempt to come on more lordly and sophisticated than Dean Acheson or more country than Ma and Pa Kettle, depending on what they feel a need to prove.

That they (or I) need to prove anything is weird in itself. It tells you what they—yes, the omnipotent They—put in our young Texas heads. The state's history is required teaching in the public schools, and no student by law may escape the course. They teach Texas history very much fumigated—the Alamo's martyrs, the Indian-killing frontiersmen, the heroic Early Day Pioneers, the Rugged Plainsmen, the Builders and Doers; these had hearts pure where others were soiled—and they teach it and teach it and teach it. I came out of the public schools of Texas knowing naught of Disraeli, Darwin, or Darrow—though well versed in the lore of Sam Houston, Stephen F. Austin, Jim Bowie, the King Ranch, the Goodnight-Loving Trail over which thundered the last of the big herds. No school day was complete but that we sang "The Eyes of Texas," "Texas our Texas," "Beautiful Texas." I mean, try substituting "Rhode Island" or "North Dakota," and it sounds about half-silly even to a Texan. We were taught again and again that Texas was the biggest state, one of the richest, possibly the toughest, surely the most envied. Most Americans, I guess, grow up convinced that their little corners of the universe are special; Texas, however, takes care to institutionalize the preachment.

To discover a wider world, then, where others fail to hold those views—to learn that Texans are thought ignorant or rich or quite often both, though to the last in number capable of sitting a mean steed—is to begin at once a new education and feel sneaky compulsions toward promoting useless old legends. Long after I knew that the Texas of my youth dealt more with myth than reality, and long past that time when I knew that the vast majority of Texans lived in cities, I continued to play cowboy. This was a social and perhaps a professional advantage in the East; it marked one as unique, permitted one to pose as a son of yesterday, furnished a handy identity among the faceless millions. In time one has a way of becoming in one's head something

of the role one has assumed. Often I have actually felt myself the reincarnation or the extension of the old range lords or bedroll cowpokes
or buffalo hunters. Such playacting is harmless so long as one confines
it to wearing costumes or to speech patterns—"I'm a-hankerin' for a
beefsteak, y'all, and thank I'll mosey on over to P.J. Clarke's"—but
becomes counterproductive unless regulated. Nobody has been able
to coax me atop a horse since that day a dozen years ago when I proved
to be the most comic equestrian ever to visit a given riding stable on
Staten Island. Misled by my range garb, accent, and sunlamp tan, the
stable manager assigned what surely must have been his most spirited
steed. Unhorsed after much graceless grabbing and grappling, I heard
my ride described by a laughing fellow with Brooklyn in his voice:
"Cheez, at foist we thought youse was a trick rider. But just before
youse fell, we seen youse wasn't nothing but a shoemaker."

Though I wear my Texas garb in Texas, I am more the New Yorker
there; not so much in my own mind, perhaps, as in the minds of others. People hold me to account for criticisms I've written of Texas or
accuse me of having gone "New York" in my thinking or attitudes.
"Nobody's more parochial than a goddamn New Yorker," some of my
friends snort—and often they are right. I, too, feel outraged at Manhattan cocktail parties when some clinch-jawed Easterner makes it
clear he thinks that everything on the wrong side of the George Washington Bridge is quaint, hasn't sense enough to come in from the rain,
and maybe lacks toilet training. Yet my Texas friends have their own
misconceptions of my adopted home and cause me to defend it. They
warn of its violent crime, even though Houston annually vies with
Detroit for the title of "Murder Capital of the World." They deride
New York's slums and corruptions, even though in South El Paso (and
many another Texas city) may be found shameful dirt poverty and felo-
nious social neglect, and Texas erupts in its own political Water-
gates—banking, insurance, real estate scandals—at least once each
decade. So I find myself in the peculiar defense of New York, waving
my arms, and my voice growing hotter, saying things like "You god-

damn Texans gotta learn that you're not so damned special. . . ." *You goddamn Texans,* now.

My friends charge that despite my frequent visits home and my summering on Texas beaches, my view of the place is hopelessly outdated. Fletcher Boone, an Austin artist and entrepreneur—owner of The Raw Deal Cafe—was the latest to straighten out my thinking. "All you goddamn expatriates act like time froze somewhere in the nineteen-fifties or earlier," he said. "You'd think we hadn't discovered television down here, or skin flicks, or dope. Hell, we grew us a *President* down here. We've got tall buildings and long hairs and some of us know how to ski!" Mr. Boone had recently visited New York and now held me to account for its sins: "It's mental masturbation. You go to a party up there, and instead of people making real conversation, they stop the proceedings so somebody can sing opera or play the piano or do a tap dance. It's show biz, man—buncha egomaniacal people using a captive audience to stroke themselves. Whatta they talk about? 'I, I, I. Me, me, me. Mine, mine, mine.'" Well, no, I rebut; they also talk about books, politics, and even *ideas*; only the middle of these, I say, is likely to be remarked in Texas. Boone is offended; he counterattacks that Easterners do not live life so much as they attempt to dissect it or, worse, dictate how others should live it by the manipulations of fashion, art, the media. We shout gross generalities, overstatements, "facts" without support. I become the Visiting Smart-ass New Yorker, losing a bit of my drawl.

Well, bless him, there may be something to Fletcher Boone's charge as I found recently when I returned as a quasi-sociologist. It was my plan to discover some young, green blue-collar or white-collar, recently removed to the wicked city from upright rural upbringings, and record that unfortunate hick's slippages or shocks. Then I would return to the hick's small place of origin, comparing what he or she had traded for a mess of modern city pottage; family graybeards left behind would be probed for their surrogate shocks and would reveal their fears for their urbanized young. It would be a whiz of a story, hav-

ing generational gaps and cultural shocks and more disappointments
or depletions than the Nixon White House. It would be at once nos-
talgic, pitiful, and brave; one last angry shout against modernity before
Houston sinks beneath the waves, Lubbock dries up and blows away
for lack of drinking water, and Dallas-Fort Worth grows together as
firmly as Siamese twins. Yes, it would have everything but three tits
and, perhaps, originality.

Telephone calls to old friends produced no such convenient study.
Those recommended turned out to have traveled abroad, attended college in distant places, or otherwise been educated by an urban, mobile
society. A young airline hostess in Houston talked mainly of San Fran-
cisco or Hawaii; a bank clerk in Dallas sniggered that even in high
school days he had spent most of his weekends away from his native
village—in city revelry—and thought my idea of "cultural shock"
quaint; a petrochemical plant worker failed to qualify when he said,
"Shit, life's not all that much different. I live here in Pasadena"—an
industrial morass with all the charms and odors of Gary, Indiana—
"and I go to my job, watch TV, get drunk with my buddies. Hail, it's
not no different from what it was back there in Monahans. Just more
traffic and more people and a little less sand." I drove around the state
for days, depressed by the urbanization of my former old outback even
as I marveled at its energy, before returning to New York. Where I
might feel, once more, like a Texan: where I might play cowboy; dream
again the ancient dreams.

IT IS SOMEHOW EASIER TO CONJURE UP THE TEXAS I ONCE KNEW
from Manhattan. What an expatriate most remembers are not the
hardscrabble times of the 1930s, or the narrow attitudes of a people not
then a part of the American mainstream, but a way of life that was
passing without one's then realizing it. Quite without knowing it, I witnessed the last of the region's horse culture. Schoolboys tied their
mounts to mesquite trees west of the Putnam school and at noon fed

them bundled roughage; the pickup truck and the tractor had not yet clearly won out over the horse, though within the decade they would. While the last of the great cattle herds had long ago disappeared up the Chisholm or the Goodnight-Loving Trail, I would see small herds rounded up on my Uncle Raymond's Bar-T-Bar Ranch and loaded from railside corrals for shipment to the stockyards of Fort Worth—or "Cowtown," as it was then called without provoking smiles. (The rough-planked saloons of the brawling North Side of "Cowtown," near the old stockyards, are gone now save for a small stretch lacquered and refurbished in a way so as to make tourists feel they've been where they ain't.) In Abilene, only thirty-two miles to the west, I would hear the chants of cattle auctioneers while smelling feedlot dung, tobacco, saddle leather, and the sweat of men living the outdoor life. Under the watchful eye of my father, I sometimes rode a gentle horse through the shinnery and scrub oaks of the old family farm, helping him bring in the five dehorned milk cows while pretending to be a bad-assed gun-slinger herding longhorns on a rank and dangerous trail drive.

But it was all maya, illusion. Even a dreaming little tad knew the buffalo hunters were gone, along with the old frontier forts, the But-terfield stage, the first sodbusters whose barbed wire fenced in the open range and touched off wars continuing to serve Clint Eastwood or James Arness. This was painful knowledge for one succored on myths and legends, on real-life tales of his father's boyhood wander-ings in a covered wagon. Nothing of my original time and place, I felt, would be worth living through or writing about. What I did not then realize (and continue having trouble remembering) is that the past never was as good as it looks from a distance.

The expatriate, returning, thus places an unfair burden upon his native habitat: He demands it to have impossibly marked time, to have marched in place, during the decades he has absented himself. He expects it to have preserved itself as his mind recalls it; to furnish evi-dence that he did not memorize in vain its legends, folk and folklore, mountains and streams and villages. Never mind that he may have removed himself to other places because they offered rapid growth, new excitements, and cultural revolutions not then available at home.

We expatriate sons may sometimes be unfair: too critical; fail to give due credit; employ the double standard. Especially do those of us who write flay Texas in the name of our disappointments and melted snows. Perhaps it's good that we do this, the native press being so boosterish and critically timid; but there are times, I suspect, when our critical duty becomes something close to a perverse pleasure. Easterners I have known, visiting my homeplace, come away impressed by its dynamic qualities; they see a New Frontier growing in my native bogs, a continuing spirit of adventure, a bit of trombone and swashbuckle, something fresh and good. Ah, but they did not know Texas when she was young.

There is a poignant tale told by the writer John Graves of the last, tamed remnants of a formerly free and proud Indian tribe in Texas: how a small band of them approached an old rancher, begged a scrawny buffalo bull from him, and—spurring their thin ponies—clattered and whooped after it, running it ahead of them, and killed it in the old way—with lances and arrows. They were foolish, I guess, in trying to hold history still for one more hour; probably I'm foolish in the same sentimental way when I sneak off the freeways to snake across the Texas back roads in search of my own past. But there are a couple of familiar stretches making the ride worth it; I most remember one out in the lonely windblown ranch country, between San Angelo and Water Valley, with small rock-dotted hills ahead at the end of a long, flat stretch of road bordered by grasslands, random clumps of trees, wild flowers, grazing cattle, a single distant ranch house whence—one fancies—issues the perfume of baking bread, simmering beans, beef over the flames. There are no billboards, no traffic cloverleafs, no neon, no telephone poles, no Jiffy Tacos or Stuckey's stands, no oil wells, no Big Rich Bastards, no ship channels threaten-

ing to ignite because of chemical pollutions, no Howard Johnson fla-
vors. Though old Charley Goodnight lives, Lee Harvey Oswald and
Charles Whitman remain unborn.

Never have I rounded the turn leading into that peaceful valley,
with the spiny ridge of hills beyond it, that I failed to feel new surges
and exhilarations and hope. For a precious few moments I exist in a
time warp: I'm back in Old Texas, under a high sky, where all things
are again possible and the wind blows free. Invariably, I put the heavy
spurs to my trusty Hertz or Avis steed: go flying lickety-split down that
lonesome road, whooping a crazy yell and taking deep joyous breaths,
sloshing Lone Star beer on my neglected dangling safety belt, and
scattering roadside gravel like bursts of buckshot. Ride 'im, cowboy!
Ride 'im. . . .

THE BALLAD OF THE URBAN COWBOY

★

Aaron Latham

DEW WESTBROOK IS A BIG-CITY COWBOY. THE RANGE HE rides is a Houston honky-tonk saloon called Gilley's, which is as big as a ranch inside. The animal that carries him is a bucking bull. He straddles this dangerous beast right there in the saloon's south forty, where the landscape is dotted with long-necked beer bottles (in place of sagebrush) and verdant pool tables (in place of pastures). The bull is mechanized, but it bucks as hard as a real one, breaking an occasional arm, leg, or collarbone. Sometimes it crushes something worse. A honky-tonk cowboy has to risk his manhood in order to prove it.

Dew, the beer joint bull rider, is as uncertain about where his life is going as America is confused about where it wants to go. And when America is confused, it turns to its most durable myth: the cowboy. As the country grows more and more complex, it seems to need simpler and simpler values: something like the Cowboy Code. According to this code, a cowboy is independent, self-reliant, brave, strong, direct, and open. All of which he can demonstrate by dancing the cotton-eyed Joe with the cowgirls, punching the punching bag, and riding the bull at Gilley's. In these anxious days, some Americans have turned for salvation to God, others have turned to fad prophets, but more and more people are turning to the cowboy hat. Dew paid $35 for his on sale.

One way the Cowboy Code is transmitted to the new urban cowboy is through country-and-western music. How Dew sees his world is shaped by the songs he hears on the radio and the lyrics sung by the band at Gilley's. Country music is the city cowboy's Bible, his literature, his self-help book, his culture. It tells him how to live and what to expect.

Actually, the life story of Dew, the urban cowboy, sounds as if it should be set to twangy music and sung as a country-and-western ballad. Dew met Betty at Gilley's, *twang-twang*. Dew fell in love with Betty at Gilley's, *twang-twang*. They had their wedding reception at Gilley's, *twang-twang*. But they quarreled over the bull at Gilley's, *twang-twang*. And then Dew met somebody new at Gilley's, *twaaaang*.

A few months after the breakup, I made a date to go to Gilley's with Dew and his new girl friend. I knew his ex-wife would be there too. When the three of them met at the bullring, it might be like Frankie and Johnny.

BEFORE WE COULD GO TO GILLEY'S, DEW HAD TO CHANGE clothes. He had curly hair the color of the beach at Galveston, worn a little long for a cowboy. His nose had a slight hump in it like a bull's back. And he had pale blue eyes that squinted. He was a good-looking cowboy who had had a hard, uncowboy day.

"The foam glass is eating me up," Dew complained. "It'll take the hide off you real quick."

Dew, who works six days a week, had spent his Saturday sawing foam glass, a form of insulation, at Texas City Refining. All of the maze of pipes and towers at the refinery needed insulation. At twenty-two, Dew has already spent over three years insulating petrochemical plants. It is hard, boring work. All assholes and elbows, as he puts it.

After work, the big-city cowboy had come home to his covered wagon: a mobile home. He lives in a trailer park that is built in a circle, so at dusk all the mobile homes really do look a little like a wagon train circled up for the night.

"I'll just be a minute," Dew said.

He was ready to turn into an urban cowboy. He exchanged his hard hat for a black felt cowboy hat with toothpicks stuck in the band and his name spelled out in small gold letters on the back. (No country cowboy ever decorated his hat with gilt lettering.) He traded dirty bell-bottom blue jeans for clean bell-bottom blue jeans that had just been ironed. (No country cowboy ever wore anything but unironed, straight-legged jeans.) Then he swapped his work sneakers for cowboy boots with a flat, rubber heel designed for a range made up mostly of asphalt, sidewalks, and linoleum. (No country cowboy ever wore anything but high, pointed, leather heels designed to let a cowboy dig in his heels if he roped something mean.) And his workingman's T-shirt was replaced by a cowboy shirt with mother-of-pearl snaps and short sleeves. (If a country cowboy wore short sleeves, his arms would be scratched off the first time he passed a mesquite tree.) Now the urban cowboy was ready to mount his pickup truck and ride forth to Gilley's in search of adventure. He had his armor on. The cowboy has always been America's knight-errant. During the Middle Ages, dressing a knight in his armor was a solemnly important ritual. The dressing of the urban cowboy is no less so.

When a city cowboy dons his cowboy clothes, he dons more than garments: He dons cowboy values. These values evolved among people who lived fifty miles apart. While they were away from everyone else, they *had* to be independent and self-reliant. And when these people did occasionally see one another, they could not afford to waste time being anything but open and direct. And now these values, forged by people who lived too far apart, are serving people who live too close together.

When Dew puts on his cowboy hat, it temporarily drives from his head the memory of his job at the refinery. When he pulls on his cowboy boots, he can temporarily forget that he is a member of insulators union local 22, which ties him to the city that he is always saying he is going to leave. His life is divided into hard-hat days and cowboy-hat nights. It is a way of coping. It may sound crazy, but it works. Or, as the band down at Gilley's sings:

I've always been crazy,

But it's kept me from going insane.

On the way to Gilley's, Dew drove his orange-and-white pickup fast and loose. He made it buck. Beside Dew on the pickup seat sat Jan Day, twenty-four, with whom he has lived ever since he broke up with his wife, *twang-twang*. Auburn-haired Jan possessed a porcelain beauty that made men want to save her from breaking. She was so fragile, in fact, that she sometimes fainted at Gilley's, which is no place for the porcelain-hearted. She wore cowboy boots, flared jeans, and a transparent top with nothing underneath. (No country cowgirl could afford to let her breasts roam free as dogies.)

"I'd never go to the Nesadel," Dew said of a joint down the road from Gilley's. "It's a rock place. A different set goes there. Sometimes there's tension between the two groups. I'd never go in the Nesadel without twenty ol' cowboys to back me up."

From the road, Gilley's Club looks like a little old shack. But when you walk through the door, you see that it is a great deal more. It's just a honky-tonk, but it looks about as big as the MGM Grand Hotel or St. Patrick's Cathedral. It has about forty pool tables, which makes it roughly equal to forty bars under one roof. On a busy night, this capital of the urban-cowboy culture has a population greater than most state capitals had during the heyday of the Old West. When Willie Nelson played Gilley's, 4,500 people crowded inside.

On our way to the dance floor we passed a gang of downtown cowboys gathered to pay a quarter to smash the punching bag just to prove how hard they could hit. A dial measured the force of each punch. If the honky-tonk cowpokes slugged hard enough, a siren went off. And most of them did hit hard enough. That part of Gilley's sounded like a firehouse. When the saloon cowgirls are watching, the saloon cowboys often hit the bag until their hands bleed and their knuckles break. At the end of an evening, there is often blood on the bag.

Jan and Dew tried to teach me how to dance the cotton-eyed Joe. You make a line and kick a lot. And every time you kick you yell: "Bullshit! Bullshit!" It is a perfect shit kickers' dance.

Then everyone danced the Shotess, which was followed by a crow's step, which was followed by a polka, which was followed by the whip. All the cowboys danced with their hats on. When they danced slowly, the cowgirls hooked the cowboys' belt loops with the fingers of their left hands. And the cowboys held onto the cowgirls' hair with their right hands.

When the band took a break, everyone headed for the bullring. It costs two dollars to ride the bull, and you have to sign a waiver saying you won't sue no matter how bad you get hurt. A cowboy on the sidelines runs the bull by remote control, making it buck according to his whim. One cowboy got so good at running the bull that he claimed he could throw off a cowboy's hat, turn the cowboy around, and then throw him on his hat.

Dew, who hadn't ridden the bull for some time, was apprehensive. He had brought two ace bandages from home. He used one to wrap his right knee and the other to swaddle his left wrist. Then he pulled a bull-riding glove onto his left hand.

"Why do you ride left-handed?" I asked. "I thought you were right-handed."

"I am," Dew said, "but that's what I make my living with." He held up his right fist. "I'm crazy to ride, but I'm smart."

He placed his cowboy hat on a chair in front of Jan like a votive offering. Then he climbed aboard the big, bad bull.

As the bull started to buck and spin, Jan took in a deep breath and looked worried. As I scanned the bullring, I noticed another intent face It belonged to Betty, Dew's ex-wife. I knew she was still in love with the bull rider, *twang-twang*.

DEW'S REAL NAME IS DONALD EDWARD WESTBROOK. THE cowboys at Gilley's made a nickname out of his initials. Everybody at Gilley's has a nickname. There's Gator and the Hippie and Armadillo. . . . But Dew's family calls him Eddie. One night a couple of years ago, Eddie met Betty Jo Helmer at Gilley's. At the time, he was nineteen and she was eighteen. Betty and Eddie liked each other right away. It seemed like destiny. After all, their names rhymed the way the names of lovers in a good country song should. At the time, it didn't occur to them that all country songs have unhappy endings.

On that first night, Betty came to Gilley's with her girl friends. She wore pants, not having worn or even owned a dress for years. She had a turned-up nose, an adolescent pout, and long brown hair. She wasn't quite beautiful, but she was as cute as a picture on a T-shirt. Dew came up and asked her to dance. She accepted.

"Now you're stuck with him," one of her girl friends said.

But that was fine with Betty. She had been watching him dance, and she liked what she saw. An urban cowboy doesn't have to know how to brand or rope or hog-tie or bulldog . . . but he does have to know how to dance. Eddie took hold of Betty's hair, and she hooked her finger through his belt loop. They danced until closing time as the band sang good old honky-tonk lyrics like: "Help me make it through the night. . . ."

The next night, Betty and Eddie came to Gilley's together. And the next. And the next. Betty and Eddie were lovers.

One night after 2:00 A.M. closing time, Betty and Eddie went from Gilley's to Granny's all-night omelet joint. (There are more nicknames ending in "y" and "ie" in Texas than there are at an eastern girls' boarding school.) At Granny's, Eddie tickled Betty until she pinched his leg. He got mad and hit her right there in front of everybody. But Betty loved Eddie in spite of the pain, *twang-twang*.

They decided to get married. Eddie wanted to have the wedding at Gilley's. (Actually, there have been several marriages performed in the saloon. Judge West, a colorful old-time justice of the peace, comes over and joins the couples in matrimony.) But Betty refused to get married in a honky-tonk. She wanted a Baptist minister to perform the ceremony in church. So they compromised, agreeing to get married in church but to have the wedding reception at Gilley's.

The only dress Betty ever wore at Gilley's was her wedding dress. And she didn't want to wear it. She wanted to change right after the exchange of vows so she could go to her wedding reception in her Levi's. But her father insisted that he wanted pictures of his daughter dancing in her wedding dress. So another compromise was in order. Betty went to her Gilley's wedding reception in her wedding dress and danced just long enough for the photographer to snap a few pictures. Then she went into the ladies' room and took off her wedding dress. When she emerged to enjoy the rest of her wedding reception, the eighteen-year-old bride wore pants.

Betty had expected Eddie to want to stay until closing time. She was shocked when he suggested leaving early. They spent their honeymoon at the Roadway Inn, which is only about a mile from Gilley's. There was no place to stay any closer. The Roadway is built in the shape of a tower. Because the building is round, all the rooms are triangular. When they ordered breakfast on the morning after their wedding night, room service brought it up on a tray with plastic silverware.

DEW SPURRED THE BULL, EVEN THOUGH HE DIDN'T REALLY HAVE spurs on his boots. He slammed his heels again and again into the machine between his legs. The mechanical bull bucked and spun. Dew was getting bruised and dizzy. He came up off the bull's back and thought he was headed for the mattresses that surround the bull, stacked two layers thick. But somehow Dew saved himself. He crashed back onto the bull's back, his sexual organs taking a beating. Dew winced in pain.

A honky-tonk cowboy named Steve Strange was manning the bull's remote controls. He made it spin first one way and then the other. Cowboys who have ridden real bulls say that in some ways the mechanical bull is harder to ride because you can't watch its head and tell which way it is going to turn. The treachery of the bull depends upon the treachery of the man at the controls. Steve, who was once badly hurt by a real bull, is treacherous indeed. He seems to believe that everyone should get mangled as badly as he did when a real bull gored him in the chute. He told me that as a result of his injuries he had a plastic bone in his leg, a plastic plate in his head, and a plastic testicle. I was not sure whether to believe him, so he knocked on his leg. It sounded like plastic. Then he knocked on his head. It sounded like plastic too. I was afraid he was going to keep on knocking, so I stopped him. Bragging about your injuries is another important part of being an urban cowboy. The more banged up you are, the more of a he-man you are.

Dew pitched forward on the bull, which is how you can get hurt the worst. I knew what he was going through because I had tried riding the bull myself a couple of days earlier. When I asked for instructions, one of the cowboys told me: "Put your left nut in your right hand and hang on." Armed with this advice, I crawled aboard. When the bull started bucking, I desperately wished I could think of some way to do what the cowboy had told me to do. I kept crashing into the rigging, which was supposed to hold me on but had become a hammer banging between my legs. A bell tied to the bull clanged maddeningly in my ears. I was frightened. Deciding it was time to get off, I began to wonder how you let go of a tiger. I looked for a good place to land. Then I felt myself flying horizontally through the air. I hit the mattresses with my right shoulder first. Stumbling to the sidelines, I sat down to record my impressions, but my hand was shaking so much I couldn't write.

Dew pressed himself back up into a sitting position, somehow staying aboard. The bull on which he rode had the heart of a pickup truck. A piston rather than sinews made it buck. The urban cowboy was trying to tame a wild, woolly machine. Which was as it should be because the urban cowboy knows a lot more about horsepower than about horses. He lives in a world where machines have replaced every animal but himself, and he is threatened. In his boots and jeans, the urban cowboy tries to get a grip on and ride an America that, like his bull, is mechanized. He can never tame it, but he has the illusion of doing so.

A sideline cowboy yelled, "Hurts your nuts, don't it?"

As Jan watched, she was obviously afraid the cowboy might be right: Had Dew hurt himself badly? As Betty watched from a greater distance, she was worried about something else: Could her former husband ride better than she could?

BETTY AND EDDIE SPENT MUCH OF THEIR MARRIAGE AT GILLEY'S. When they weren't honky-tonking, they both worked. Betty worked in construction, putting hardware in houses. Eddie insulated petrochemical plants and moonlighted at an auto racetrack.

Betty and Eddie are both second-generation noncountry cowboys. Betty's father works in construction like his daughter. And Eddie's father is an insulator like his son. Way back, one of Betty's grandfathers did have a trading post, but it doubled as a wrecking yard.

Eddie was born in a small Texas town named Longview. But he lived there only seven years before moving to the Houston area.

"I lived in a town on top of a mountain," Dew reminisced one evening in his trailer. "That's how the town got its name. I'd like to get back to Longview someday. Have my own insulation shop."

All the urban cowboys talk about going back to the great good country. In the meantime, they keep going to Gilley's, or some other honky-tonk. "It's like Peyton Place out there," Betty said one night at Gilley's. "Everybody's been with everybody." She even told me which cowgirls had given venereal disease to which cowboys and vice versa. Gilley's is a *very* small town in the middle of one of America's biggest cities.

While the Gilley's cowboys keep saying they are going home to a real small town someday, they grow more tightly bound to the big city, the union, and the petrochemical plant every day. They are ready to move at a moment's notice, but they don't move. They live in mobile homes that aren't mobile. Dew would need a semi to move his trailer. He lives in a home on wheels that has never rolled an inch since he moved in.

Dew has two pickups and used to have even more vehicles before he smashed up several cars. The driveways of the homes in his neighborhood are overrun with cars and trucks and campers. Everyone seems to have a herd of cars in his front yard. These car pokes have stored up all this potential mobility without going anywhere. As the band at Gilley's sings:

So many times these few dreams of mine
Seemed hidden behind a mountain too high to climb. . . .

Betty was born in the Houston area. The closest she ever came to real cowboy life was gathering eggs on a relative's farm. But if she is not part of a long cowboy tradition, she is part of a long Gilley's tradition. Back in the alleged good old days, her mother used to run around with Mickey Gilley and Sherwood Cryer, the creators of Gilley's Club. Gilley, the country canary who sings "A Room Full of Roses," gave his name to the honky-tonk, but he owns only a piece of it. The principal owner and real boss is Cryer. This king of the urban-cowboy business never wears anything but mechanic's coveralls. Betty's mother knew the two partners many, many dollars ago. Which makes Betty second-generation Gilley's.

The old honky-tonk has been around under one name or another for almost exactly as long as Betty has been alive: twenty years. It was originally called Shelley's which was what Sherwood Cryer's kids called him before they learned to say Sherwood. It started out as a slab of concrete to dance on and a small shack to lock the beer in. Eventually, Cryer, who was a welder by trade, put a tin roof over the slab. And then he got around to closing it in.

Meanwhile, Mickey Gilley was over on the good side of town playing at the Bell Air Ballroom and going broke. He couldn't even pay his band. So in desperation he went to Cryer and asked for help. Cryer asked Gilley if he would come back to the bad side of town and set up shop. Cryer even offered to name his honky-tonk after Gilley. Mickey Gilley came over and looked at the place and quickly saw it was no room full of roses. In fact, a rose wouldn't have a chance in a dump like that.

"Gilley said he'd come over," Cryer remembered, "if I bulldozed it and started over."

The man in the coveralls didn't go quite that far, but he did put in air-conditioning and paint some of the old chairs and put up the world's tackiest ceiling. So Gilley came on over. That was 1970.

Both Gilley's Club and Gilley's career started doing pretty well. The honky-tonk went from a place that would hold 500 to one that would hold almost ten times that many. Cryer kept tacking on tacky additions. As Gilley became better known, he started coming to the club less often because he was touring more. Now Gilley plays Gilley's only a couple of times a year.

When George Jones was playing Gilley's, the president of his fan club was murdered after she left the saloon. She was raped and beaten to death with a tire iron. The police suspected all the Gilley's regulars. Even Cryer had to take a lie-detector test. The case was written up in *True Detective*. Eventually, the cops arrested a local auto mechanic who seemed to fancy his tire iron as a six-shooter.

When Jerry Lee Lewis was playing Gilley's, Cryer himself got hurt. A woman hit a man over the head with a bottle of V.O. When Cryer went to the man's rescue, she cut the back of his head and neck with the broken bottle. His white shirt suddenly turned red, and he was terrified. The next day, he ran into the woman in a liquor store buying another bottle of V.O.

"She looked at me like she knew me," Cryer remembered, "but couldn't place me."

There is a local Monopoly-like game with a card that says not "go directly to jail" but "go to Gilley's and get stomped."

Cryer began trying to think of ways to cut down on the violence. So he put in the punching bag to give the honky-tonk cowboys something to hit besides one another. When the cowboys started lavishing more attention on the bag than on the cowgirls, the women cut the cord. But Cryer had it fixed. And he says the number of fights has gone down.

Then Cryer heard about the mechanical practice bulls used on the rodeo circuit. He thought a bull would go over in his shit-kicking honky-tonk. The bull was installed shortly after Betty and Eddie's wedding. The merciless machine was rough on the marriage. At first, Eddie did not want Betty to ride the bull. He said she would get hurt, but perhaps he was already worried she could outbuck him. Eddie even went so far as to order the man who ran the bull not to let Betty ride.

"I don't like anyone to tell me I can't do something," Betty told me one night at Gilley's. "To me, it's them saying I can't because I'm a girl. And I've got to show them I can."

She and her husband quarreled about whether she would be allowed to ride the bull. In the end, she decided she would have to show him. She had a drink to fuel her courage and to kill the pain. But when she got on the bull's back, she felt all too sober. When she got off, she was drunk.

The bull can be adjusted to buck hard, harder, or hardest. Betty kept riding it at higher and higher and higher speeds. Eddie rode the bull too, but he had a hard time keeping up. After all, a woman has an advantage over a man when it comes to bull riding. As the cowboys around the bullring put it: "A woman has nothing to lose." As strange as it may seem, bull riding is really woman's work. Poor Eddie.

Soon Betty wasn't only riding at higher and higher speeds, she actually started trick riding on the bull. She learned to stand up on the bucking bull's back. While Eddie had to hang on just to keep his seat, Betty was riding the bull like it was a surfboard.

Eddie found himself married to a honky-tonk Annie Oakley whose theme song seemed to be: "Anything you can do, I can do better. . . ."

AFTER ABOUT EIGHT SECONDS ON THE BULL'S BACK—LONG enough to qualify in a rodeo—Dew yelled that he had had enough. Steve pressed the bull's off switch. Sliding down, Dew staggered to the sidelines. He had lived up to the Cowboy Code, proving himself brave and strong, but it made him walk funny.

"That's the longest eight seconds I've ever seen," Dew said. "I'm shaking like a fucking leaf. Stand still, leg. My insides are going everywhere."

Jan handed him his hat.

"Were you worried?" he asked her.

"Just a little bit," Jan said.

Then the women took over the bullring. Jessie LaRive, a nineteen-year-old barmaid at a pool hall, rode the bull wearing jeans and a halter top. Her breasts bucked along with the animal. Standing up on the heaving back, she taunted all the men who had gathered to watch.

"Get up here and ride," Jessie challenged. "It's tame. I done tamed it. I'll ride with you. That's bad, lettin' a girl outride you. If I can ride with no hands, you can ride with one."

When she finally jumped down, Jessie came over to the cowboy running the bull. She had a favor to ask.

"Would you put this on my ass?"

She held out a Band-Aid. He agreed to help her out, and she lowered her jeans partway. The bull had rubbed a blister.

The next rider was Rita Sharp, a twenty-six-year-old waitress at the Red Lobster. She too challenged the men. If she could ride it, why couldn't they?

"I can ride her," called out one honky-tonk cowboy.

"I'll bet you can't stay on," she called back. "If you've got $100, we'll see."

"Can I help it," said the cowboy running the bull, "if the girls are better at riding on top than we are?"

Then Debbie Welburn, a nineteen-year-old waitress at the Pizza Hut, rode the bucking bull so well it seemed she could have ridden and carried a pizza on a tray at the same time. She is something of a legend around the bullring because she rode last fall right after her feet were operated on. She came to the bullring on crutches with her feet encased in soft casts. Cowboys had to carry her out to the bull and set her on its back. If she had been thrown, she would have ripped out all her stitches or worse. She might have been crippled. No male rider ever did anything that brave or that crazy. The honky-tonk cowgirls keep putting more and more pressure on the honky-tonk cowboys.

After Debbie's impressive ride, two cowgirls got on the bull and rode it together. They faced one another, bending, swaying, bouncing, moving together in a rhythm that was almost sexual. They were the queens of the mountain.

Then a woman mounted the bull who had never ridden it before. With the speed turned down, she rode the bucking machine easily.

"Throw her," begged her boyfriend, "or I'll never hear the last of it."

But she wasn't thrown.

Several cowboys responded to the cowgirls' challenges. They paid their two dollars and took their chances playing Gilley's roulette with their sex lives. One by one, they were thrown. And one by one, they crawled off the mattresses with their hands between their legs.

"I just busted two nuts," Steve bragged after throwing one cowboy. "He won't get none tonight."

The lot of the urban cowboy becomes harder and harder. He tries to escape from the overwhelming complexities of his petrochemical days into the simplicity of his honky-tonk nights. But then Gilley's turns out to be a complicated world too. Once the bullring was the simplest of the simple entertainments at Gilley's. Either you rode the bull or you got bucked off. You beat the bull or it beat you. It was perfect for an urban cowboy who never beat anything beyond the walls of the saloon. But then Eve entered the bullring. The cowboys were no longer simply measured against the bull, they were measured against the cowgirls.

And yet the values represented by the cowboy hat prevailed. The cowboys did not try to exclude the cowgirls from the bullring, for that would have violated the code of egalitarianism. The cowboys didn't tell the cowgirls that a woman's place wasn't on the back of a bull. No, the cowboys just tried to keep up with the cowgirls as well as they could. I could tell, though, that they weren't happy with the way things were turning out.

"My favorite thing," said Betty, who had come up to talk to me, "is to watch all the guys fall off. Then I get up and ride it."

Dew decided to ride again. He got back on the bull a little stiffly. He braced himself, leaned back, and raised his right working hand. He was ready. The bullring master put the bull into a dead spin. It turned about half a dozen circles in a row. Dew did not sit the bull very prettily, but he sat it.

"I think," Betty said, "I can ride it better than he can."

BETTY AND EDDIE'S MARRIAGE TURNED OUT TO BE A ROUGH RIDE. They quarreled about the bull and many other things too. He didn't want her to ride the bull, so she rode it. He told her not to do other things, so she did them. Soon Eddie was going to Gilley's without Betty, *twang-twang*.

One Friday night, Dew met Jan. He felt her watching him on the bull. Actually, he had sensed her studying him for two months. But now he decided to do something about it. When Dew got down off the bull, he walked over to chat with the bullring master. The woman came closer. They continued to circle each other warily for a while, like beginners approaching the bull.

Then Dew spoke his first words to Jan: "When are you going to take me home and rape me?"

Reminiscing about his opening line later on, Dew explained that he was a "direct" person. He said meeting someone was like driving a car. He didn't want to "piddle around." He wanted to get where he was going. Directness is one of the cardinal cowboy virtues. Dew had his cowboy hat on so he could say what was on his mind.

Jan answered: "Whenever you get ready."

Sometime after they had agreed to sleep together, they got around to introducing themselves. But these introductions were not really necessary. After all, they both had their names clearly tooled on their belts. Everyone at Gilley's does. It is part of the Cowboy Code of openness. The belt goes with the hat.

Dew and Jan stayed until closing time. He showed off by riding the bull again for her. And then Jan took Dew home and raped him.

They stayed together all night Friday and all day Saturday. Then they went back to Gilley's Saturday night. Sunday night they went back to Gilley's again. Monday night they went bowling.

On Tuesday, Dew started work insulating an offshore drilling rig. That meant working a twelve-hour shift from noon until midnight. Jan would drive down to the dock, pick him up, and whisk him back to Gilley's. They would get there just before closing time, but they would get there.

Betty obviously must have known something was going on, but she didn't know just what or with whom until she came home and found Eddie ironing his blue jeans. She asked him why he was ironing. He said he was going riding with Jan. Which was bad enough. What made it worse was that Eddie was going riding with Jan on Betty's horse. As the band at Gilley's sings:

Honky-tonk, the same old song,

Honky-tonk, all night long,

Honky-tonk, my money is all gone,

Honky-tonk, he done me wrong.

Betty went home to live with her parents in a little house on Peach Street with a herd of cars out front. But Betty, who still loved Eddie, was so unhappy that she wanted to get out of town completely for a while. She decided to visit her sister in San Antonio for a couple of weeks.

Betty was happy to get away to San Antonio, perhaps the most beautiful city in Texas. But when the sun went down, she missed Gilley's. The later it got, the more she pined for her saloon. She missed the music and the dancing and the friends. And perhaps most of all she missed the bull. The next morning, Betty called Les Walker, one of the bull masters, and asked him to come get her. Les drove to San Antonio and picked her up. Betty lasted exactly one night away from Gilley's.

But Betty still did not know herself. A short while later, she decided she had to get away again. She went to visit a girl friend who lived in Huntsville, the home of the prison rodeo. This time she didn't even last the night. At 11:00 P.M., Betty told her girl friend that she had to get back to Gilley's. They drove to Houston together. Without even stopping by Betty's home, they went straight to the saloon. The two cowgirls arrived at Gilley's at 1:30 A.M., a half hour before closing time. The night was saved. Betty could ride the bull before she went to sleep.

Meanwhile, two months after they met, Jan agreed to move in with Dew on one condition: She wanted him to give up riding the bull at Gilley's. She didn't want the man she slept with to get hurt. They had a big fight. He would ride the bull if he damned well wanted to. Not if he wanted to sleep with her, he wouldn't. He was threatened with a kind of sexual strike unless he gave up his violent ways. It was *Lysistrata* in cowboy clothes. Dew chose loving over bull riding. And Jan moved in.

DEW KEPT HIS PROMISE. HE DIDN'T RIDE THE BULL AGAIN UNTIL I came into his life. And I brought a photographer with me. The old bull rider could not resist riding for the camera, but his bull riding days are really behind him now. At least, they are behind him as long as he stays with Jan. When a real cowboy rides a bucking animal, he is trying to break it, to tame it. But Dew could never break the mechanical bull. A motor doesn't get tired. But an urban cowboy can be broken. Jan has broken Dew.

After Eddie's ride, Betty walked up to him and said hello. But Jan was there, so Eddie did not return the greeting. This scene has been repeated at Gilley's ever since Betty and Eddie broke up. It usually ends with Betty going to the far side of the bullring and crying. The worst night was back in May, when Betty saw Eddie at Gilley's and tried to tell him that their divorce had come through that day. But Jan wouldn't let him talk to her. Betty went in the cowgirls' room and cried for a long time, *twang-twang*.

But Betty didn't cry this Saturday night. She decided to try to make Eddie jealous instead. Walking up to Steve, the head bull master, she asked him to put his hands up in the air. He looked like a badman caught by the sheriff in a western movie. With her victim now properly positioned, Betty reached out, grabbed the front of his cowboy shirt, and popped open all his mother-of-pearl snaps with one motion. Steve just stood there for a moment, more or less topless, with his shirt gaping open from his navel to his throat.

Then he counterattacked. Steve grabbed Betty and started trying to pull her knit halter off. The honky-tonk cowboy bulldogged the cowgirl to the floor and kept trying to do to her what she had done to him.

They rolled together on the bottom of the saloon with the cigarette butts and the expectorated chewing tobacco. Steve got Betty's top partway off, but then she pulled away from him.

Dew and Jan tried to ignore this whole scene. They moved off toward the dance floor. If Betty had expected her ex-husband to come to her rescue, she was disappointed.

Steve got up and resnapped his cowboy shirt, but by then the urge to unsnap had become infectious. Another cowgirl came up and popped open his shirt. This time Steve's counterattack was more fruitful. Since his new assailant wore a cowboy shirt, Steve reached out and unsnapped her from top to bottom. She had nothing on underneath.

Betty stood by calmly combing her hair. When she finished, she returned to her favorite toy. Jan had gotten Dew, but Betty had gotten the bull. She crawled up on its bucking back and played. She stood up, moved from one end to the other, sat down, turned around, and rode backward.

DEW HAD TO GET UP AT SIX-THIRTY MONDAY MORNING TO GO TO work. After getting dressed hurriedly, he drove his pickup thirty-eight miles to Texas City Refining. That is a long commute for someone who lives in a mobile home. He could move his trailer closer to the refinery, but then he would be farther from Gilley's. He would rather commute to his hard-hat days than to his cowboy-hat nights.

Pulling into the refinery's dusty parking lot, Dew got out of his truck with his tape measure strapped to his hip like a six-gun. He walked into the plant a little stiffly. He was still feeling the aftereffects of his bull ride.

Inside the refinery, Dew found himself swallowed up by one of the most denatured landscapes on the face of the earth. The petrochemical cowboy works on a giant spread crowded with metal trees (oil derricks and cracking towers), with metal underbrush (valves and pipelines), and with metal lakes (giant oil tanks). This is petrochemical pastoral.

Taking hold of his saw, Dew cut into the foam glass, which in turn dug its teeth into him. And as he worked, he remembered the band at Gilley's singing: "Take this job and shove it!"

It is one of Dew's favorite songs. After a day spent working inside the refinery, no wonder Gilley's seems like the great good place. When Dew talks about his saloon, he sounds idealistic. But when he talks about his job, he sounds sullen, complaining about Mexicans who, he says, will work so cheap they are taking away union jobs. At work, the urban cowboy is a small, threatened creature, but at the honky-tonk, he rides tall in the saddle.

A mechanized refinery can actually be a lot more dangerous to ride than a mechanized bull. An explosion recently killed seven workers at Texas City Refining. Luckily, Dew was home asleep at the time. Back in 1947, almost all of Texas City blew up. Close to 550 people were killed.

One workday at the killer refinery, a valve near Dew caught on fire. He dropped everything and ran as fast as he could in his track shoes. He doesn't wear boots on the job. He wouldn't be able to run fast enough. This time someone put the fire out before the killer refinery went up again.

Dew has had much worse falls on the job than he ever had in the bullring. He once fell off a scaffold 200 feet in the air, but he landed half on and half off a grating ten feet below. Somehow he hung on.

Right now, Dew works in the shop sawing and sawing. When all the foam glass is cut in just the right curving shapes, like pieces of a giant girdle, Dew will help fit these pieces around towers soaring hundreds of feet in the air. Some days, he will work on scaffolds high over the dead earth. Other days, he will labor suspended at the end of a rope, like a spider.

Dew makes $9.60 an hour and time and a half on Saturday—a forty-eight-hour week. But he pays 25 cents an hour to his union. Theoretically, he earns $460 a week, but he only takes home $250. He wants to save up to move to Longview, but so far he has not been able to save anything. He says he hopes his little brother stays out of the refineries.

Quitting time is 4:00 P.M. After work, the refinery parking lot is full of men in pickups taking off hard hats and putting on cowboy hats. Some of the pickups have bucking broncos painted on them.

When Dew reached his mobile home Monday evening at five o'clock, he found an unexpected note waiting for him. It had not come in the mail. It had been hand delivered and tucked under the windshield wiper of his second pickup. It was a request for money to pay for a vacuum cleaner. Eddie had given Betty the vacuum cleaner as a Christmas present, but he had never made any payments on it after the marriage broke up. Now Betty was convinced she was going to jail. So she carried the bill over to the trailer park. It was more than a bill, it was also a love letter. On the back, Betty had written in huge block letters: "I LOVE YOU."

A love letter on the back of a bill . . . it sounded like a honky-tonk song.

Dew looked up from the love bill and said, "Bein' a cowboy ain't easy."

He didn't go to Gilley's that night. He stayed home and saved his money.

At 6:00 P.M. Monday evening, Betty started getting ready, as she does almost every day of her life. She took her time. She washed her hair, and she dried it while she watched some television. In all, she spent almost four hours getting ready. At 10:00 P.M., right on time, according to her rigid internalized schedule, she walked through the door at Gilley's.

As always, Betty headed right for the bullring. On the way, she looked for Eddie, but she didn't see him. She hoped he would come later, but even if he did, he wouldn't come back to the bull. The bull was all hers now.

Entering the ring she vaulted onto the back of the beast. She stood, she sat, she jumped back and forth over the rigging. From on high, Betty surveyed the saloon again, looking for Eddie. But he still wasn't there. Oh, well. She clung to the bull, which pounded her harder than any man had ever been able to.

Wrung out, she slid off the bull and came to the sidelines. She would take a break and then ride again. She would ride over and over all night long.

"I've got people to tell me," Betty said, "that I care more about this bull than anything else."

METAMORPHOSIS NO. 5

Don Webb

MARCO PHILLIPS WAS BORN UNDER THE SIGN OF THE Second Banana or, as they say in the Texas Hemisphere, The Sidekick. So when it came to pass that W.B. Porter, the Last of the Singing Cowboys, was to be born in San Antone, Marco moseyed over to San Antone to wait. And W.B. was born and wrapped in swaddling clothes from Neiman Marcus. W.B. was too small to need a sidekick, so Marco was placed in temporal stasis at the Armadillo Self Storage.

After W.B. got his degree in Chemical Engineering from Rice University, he rode off on his Palomino to San Antone and revived Marco. There was some trouble with the bill. Who foots the bill for storage, the cowboy or the sidekick? It's not in *Cowboy Etiquette*. But finally W.B. paid. W.B. smiled and the gleam of the smile burned the smog off of the city. And as W.B. and Marco were riding out of the city, the Mayor of San Antone rode up in his Cadillac and gave the boys the key to the city on account of the smog removal. And W.B. said, "Shucks, 'tweren't nothing."

And Marco and W.B. rode out into the mesas. They camped beneath a beautiful Texas sunset. Marco began the beans and the sourdough and W.B. began to yodel. He yodeled better than the Yodeling Kid from Pine Ridge. The spirits of Tom Mix and Gene Autry drew near.

After the meal W.B. said he needed to go into the scrub alone. Now, all Texans know what it means when you go off to the bushes. But Marco felt a strange urge to follow W.B. A man's got to trust his hunches.

So Marco sneaked down the mesa through the mesquite and the soapberry and the yucca. And he came upon a strange golden glow. Marco crawled on his belly like an Injun scout. Through a cedar he saw Varuna and Vishnu and Hathor and all the other cow gods and goddesses and they was givin' W.B. a mission. Marco knew W.B. was the cowboy he'd waited for.

Marco creeped back to camp real quiet like.

THE MENDOZA GANG WAS RIDING INTO EL PASO. THEY WERE tough hombres schooled in the Fourteen Mysteries of Toltec Sorcery and besides they packed laser-targeting Uzis. Nobody knew what the Mendozas wanted. But W.B. and Marco felt the call and rode through the night.

KRISHNA WAS ALSO FAVORED BY THE COW GODS. HIS NAME MEANS "dark" or "stained." He had the divine power and it could rub off. Many demons gained salvation by Krishna's touch in combat. Many shepherds' daughters achieved salvation (not to mention prolonged orgasms) by Krishna's lovemaking. Some people hope Krishna's divinity will rub off on them if they chant his name long enough.

Laura Enfield put down the Krishna book. She decided the shepherds' daughters had the best idea. She went to her Avon products. She would be ready when W.B. rode into town.

Twenty minutes after dawn W.B. and Marco rode in. Marco's chestnut gelding's hide was black with sweat, but W.B.'s Palomino stallion seemed bright and fresh. The boys stopped at a Winchell's for doughnuts. The counterman said, "Y'all just ride in?"

Marco said, "We heard the call. We came from the badlands."

The doughnutman didn't seem to hear.

Marco said, "From the *malpaís*, the alkali flats, the poverty flats, the wasteland, the filth land, the barrens."

The doughnutman still didn't notice.

W.B. said, "Yep."

The doughnutman said, "Oh, what'll you have?"

Marco learned Second Banana Rule No. Twenty-Seven, "No one listens to the sidekick."

There's a corollary to this rule that doesn't occur in this story, so I'm passing it along for your information: "They listen to the sidekick if he's forming a rescue party for the boss." I could've created a situation for that rule to show up, but I reckoned you'd want the story just like it happened. Natural like.

The Mendoza gang ate at a Coco's. After breakfast they scanned the papers. Rico spotted it, an article on developers pouring a lot of money into houses and condos north of Houston. Rico read the article aloud. The Mendozas laughed. They would ride to Houston and hijack those big mixer trucks full of money ready for pouring. They would drive them like cattle across the Mexican border and pour the money into money-hungry Mexico. Fausto, the *jefe*, twirled his mustachios with delight. "Genaro," he said, "ride over to the Exxon station and buy us a map showing how to get to Houston."

THE BOYS ENJOYED THEIR COFFEE AND DOUGHNUTS WHILE THE doughnutman went to the back to call Laura Enfield. He said, "W.B. Porter came in this morning. He and the little guy plan to shoot it out with the Mendoza gang and after the shootout the boys will light out to the barrens."

Laura said, "The alkali flats?"

The doughnutman said, "Yeah. So you better be quick."

Laura said, "Thanks, Al, I owe you one." Laura dialed up Rosa. There were pleasantries and then Laura said, "Rosa, I need a favor. Could you warn Fausto that W.B. hit town?"

"Sí. But why?"

"I want Fausto to ride on so I can have W.B. to myself."

"Consider it done."

FAUSTO STUDIED THE MAP. HE MARKED AN X BETWEEN HOUSTON and Conroe. F.M. 1960. He called upon the first of the Fourteen Mysteries and the wind cloaked the Mendozas from human eyes and ears. Just as W.B. and Marco left the Winchell's, the wind blew off Marco's Stetson. The wind spooked the horses.

W.B. sang and calmed the horses. The boys rode to the Holiday Inn where the Mendozas were last seen. W.B. kicked open the door.

The suite was empty except for Laura and a king-size bed.

"You better wait outside. There may be trouble," W.B. told Marco.

"DO NOT HASTEN TO BID ME ADIEU," SAID LAURA.

But W.B. kept on buttoning his shirt and smiling his prairie smile.

"Remember the Red River Valley and the cowgirl that loved you so true." Laura's geography was weak but her heart was in the right place.

But W.B. wouldn't look back for he knew Laura had tipped off the Mendozas.

Marco was cooling his feet in the pool.

W.B. said, "Git your boots on. We've got to ride to Houston."

SEVERAL HOURS EARLIER, THE MENDOZA GANG ARRIVED AT F.M. 1960 and IH-45. They let their horses graze on the highway right-of-way and Genaro climbed up a ponderosa pine to spot a mixer truck.

Rico asked Fausto, "When we get the money to Mexico what will we do?"

Fausto said, "Find a pocket of poverty and let it pour—after taking fifty percent for handling."

"What will you do with your share?"

"I will get my Uzi silver-plated except for the notch."

"The notch?"

"Sí. The notch I will carve when I shoot W.B. Porter, Last of the Singing Cowboys."

From high above came a voice, "I've spotted two mixers."

The mixers were headed for the Twin Oak Heights development. Fausto called forth the second of the Fourteen Mysteries, an Invocation of Ah Puk, god of death, paperwork, and fake IDs. Small bright plastic badges appeared on the Mendozas' shirts. The Mendozas saddled up and rode across country to the Twin Oak Heights development office.

As the Mendozas rode in they fired their automatic weapons into the air and cried out, "'Riba, 'riba!" The developers took fright and fled the development in Toyotas, Datsuns, and Nissan pickups.

The Mendozas had just hidden their Uzis when the mixer trucks drove in.

The trucks stopped. One of the drivers swung out and approached Fausto.

The driver didn't like the sombrero or the mustachios or the bandoliers, but relaxed when he saw the kelly green badge. The driver said, "You're Mr. Meyer?"

"*Sí*. Why don't you have coffee with my men?"

"Don't got time. show us where to pour the stuff."

"My men will do the pouring."

"How are we supposed to get back to Houston?"

"Rico—er, eh, Bill, get these men some horses."

"I ain't gointa take—"

　　　　　　　　　　　"—You see this badge. You know what it means?"

The driver knew. The two drivers saddled up while Fausto signed the invoice for two-and-a-half tons of money-slurry.

"Jefe, we've got two trucks, let's head home before W.B. Porter and Marco catch up with us."

"Are you kidding? There's lots more where this came from. Besides, I have a plan."

Fausto dipped a ladleful of money from a mixer. He rode to a nearby Dairy Queen. Soon its marquee read, "Welcome W.B. Porter."

W.B. and Marco rode out of El Paso. Hours later Laura Enfield would follow them in a VW Microbus.

At the outskirts of Houston the boys saw two greenhorns trying to ride two beautiful Arabians. W.B., whose mind is as Clear as the Light of the Void, suspected something was wrong. He called out, "Whoa! Where you boys headed with those two fine horses?"

"Not much of anywhere, mister. Know where we can rent a horse trailer?"

"Why'd greenhorns like you come riding anyway?"

"We didn't do this on purpose. We delivered our trucks to the development and they said they'd do their own pouring and gave us these horses as loaners."

"Cement trucks?"

"No sir. Money trucks."

"And these 'developers'—did they wear sombreros?"

"Yep."

"Which way is this development?"

The greenhorns pointed. W.B. and Marco rode off.

A mile further down the road was the Dairy Queen. The boys almost passed it.

"Can't pass up a genuine Texas welcome," W.B. said. So they dismounted and Marco hitched their horses to the picnic tables.

"Look girls, it's W.B. Porter. Won't you sing for us, Mr. Porter?"

A singing cowboy can never turn down a fan. It's the Code of the West. So W.B. unslung his guitar and a stage appeared.

W.B. sang.

He sang the songs of Gene Autry and Tom Mix and Buck Jones and Roy Rogers. He sang the old ballads, the new ballads, and the ballads of middling age. A day and a night and a day passed. W.B. unslung his sitar and began to sing the hymns of the Gopastami or Cow Festival, the most sacred cowboy hymns.

Laura burst into the Dairy Queen and leapt on stage. "Still your sacred sitar!" she cried, "Look at your audience!"

W.B. looked. Except for Marco they were all wearing Walkmans. He'd been duped. W.B. and Marco ran to their horses. W.B. shot a last look of gratitude and desire Laura's way. As he looked upon her lithe form he thought of *boopis* or "cow-eyed," the adjective used by Homer to describe the divine Hera. But he said nothing, there wasn't time for mushy stuff.

During W.B.'s stay at the Dairy Queen, the Mendozas had acquired sixteen mixer trucks.

THE MENDOZAS WERE HEADED FOR LAREDO. W.B. AND MARCO set off at once. W.B. cautioned Laura not to follow. It would be too dangerous.

Laura caught a plane out of Houston Hobby. Unfortunately, Fausto had guessed that Laura would be the loyal type. Alberto and Juan nabbed her at the Laredo International Airport.

The Mendozas had parked the mixers in two rows of eight near the Rio Grande. They would cross here where there was no bridge. No one would find this spot. They would use sorcery. Fausto invoked the third of the Fourteen Mysteries. The Rio Grande left its banks and hovered like a glistening lasso in the air. It was moving north, taking the border of Mexico with it. When it touched down the sixteen trucks would be safely in Mexico.

Six shots rang out.

W.B. had shot the bottom of the floating river. There was a cloudburst. The Rio Grande splashed over the Mendozas. The water flowed back to its natural boundaries, leaving the trucks and the gang on the U.S. side. Only the *jefe* Fausto had been prepared for this contingency. He laughed from beneath his umbrella.

Fausto said "Gringo, if you come any closer your woman will die." He had his Uzi right against Laura's silken neck.

W.B. said, "I'm sure Laura understands the need for certain sacrifices."

Laura's expression showed clearly she did not understand the need. Fausto shrugged and said, "Plan Two."

Rico led a yearling out from behind a truck. Fausto pointed his gun at the cow and said, "If you don't drop your gun, amigo, it's veal-time!"

W.B. was shocked. The words of the third-century *Mahabhrata* came to mind, "All that kill, eat, or *permit* the slaughter of cows rot in hell for as many years as there are hairs on the body of the cow so slain." It looked like a pretty hairy yearling. W.B. dropped his guns. Marco dismounted and began to drop his guns.

Laura tripped Fausto. He fell forward, a rain of gunfire fortunately missing the sacred cow. Marco shot the falling bandit chief. W.B. retrieved his six-shooters. The Mendozas took aim and discovered that their Uzis wouldn't fire.

W.B. and Marco had the drop on them. The Texas Rangers arrived and carted away the Mendozas. The Houston development money was safe.

In gratitude for his works, the cow gods and goddesses transformed W.B. Porter into a giant saguaro cactus. Every day he meditates in vegetable bliss, luxuriating in sunlight. He guards the border and his brow is wreathed by flowers in the spring.

Marco and Laura married and lived happily ever after. Sometimes they picnic near W.B.

WHAT TEXAS
MEANS TO ME

——————★——————

Stephen Harrigan

L YING IN A FEATHER BED, IN THE GUEST ROOM OF A
friend's two-hundred-year-old house in western Massachusetts, I suffered a lapse of faith in Texas. I'm not sure what
brought this crisis on. Perhaps it was simply the act of waking up, looking out the window at the syrup buckets hanging from the maple
trunks, at the banked snow glistening in the sharp air, and realizing
that Texas would never be that.

I could stand to live here, I thought. I would keep my cross-coun-
try skis propped by the front door, a bowl of apples on the kitchen
table, a steady fire by which I would read during the dim winter nights.

But it was not just Massachusetts. The hard truth was that I was
getting tired of Texas and was now able to imagine myself living in all
sorts of places: on one of those minor Florida keys where a little strip
of land containing a shopping center and a few houses counted as

barely a riffle in a great sheet of translucent ocean; in an adobe house, even a fake adobe house, in the foothills of the Sangre de Cristos; or perhaps in a city like Los Angeles, which with its corrupted natural beauty seemed so much more likely a center for the development of urban chaos than Houston.

These were uneasy rumblings, and I was enough of a Texan to feel heretical in even allowing them access to my conscious mind. But my affection for Texas had gone unexamined and untested for so long that it was time to wonder just how much affection was there after all. There are certain people who are compelled to live in Texas, but I was never one of them. I am not a two-fisted free enterpriser, I have no fortune to make in the next boom, and my ancestral ties to the land itself are casual and desultory. Like a lot of other Texans, I am here because I am here, out of habit, out of inertia, out of a love of place that I want to believe is real and not just wished for.

Because I was born in Oklahoma and lived there until I was five, I missed being imprinted with native fealty for Texas. I don't recall having any particular image of the state when, on the occasion of my widowed mother's marriage to an Abilene oilman, I was told we were going to move there. But I did not much care to leave Oklahoma City, where my baby footprints were embedded in cement and where the world of permanence and order was centered. In the park behind our house was a sandstone boulder where several generations of children had scratched their initials. This boulder, whose markings seemed to me to have some ancient significance, like the markings on a rune stone, was one of my power centers, one of the things that persuaded me that I had not been placed arbitrarily on the earth but was meant to exist here, at this particular spot. In the same park was a little garden with a semicircular rock wall dominated by a bust of Shakespeare and brass plaques containing quotations from his plays. It was a place to ponder and reflect on the immortal bard, but its hushed and reverent aspect made me mistake it for a tomb. I had no real idea who Shakespeare was, only that he was one of those exalted characters like Will Rogers, and so it seemed perfectly appropriate to me that he would be buried in Oklahoma.

But all such reverberations stopped at the Red River. I filed them away, and with a child's tenacity I resisted letting Texas invade my essence. Abilene, Texas, had been named for Abilene, Kansas, and that fact was a convincing enough argument that it would be a dull and derivative place. Our house there had a dry, nappy lawn and a cinder-block fence. My brother and I attended a Catholic school that, in this West Texas stronghold of stark and bilious religions, was like a foreign mission. On feast days the nuns would show us western movies and serve us corn dogs. Nearby there was a dispiriting lake where drab water lapped at a caliche shoreline, and on the southern horizon were low hills—looking on a map now, I see they are called the Callahan Divide—that I longed to think of as mountains.

But I surprised myself by being happy there. I liked the excitement of being rousted from sleep on summer evenings and taken to a neighbor's storm cellar to wait out a tornado warning. Though I did not know what an oilman was exactly, I enjoyed visiting my new father's office, looking at the charts and drilling logs and playing with the lead dinosaurs on his desk.

"Well, they sure do grow 'em tall down there in Texas," my relatives in Oklahoma would say when we went back to visit, and I began to imagine they were right and to cultivate a little my Texan identity. In my heart I knew that I lived in Anywhere, USA, that I watched *Crusader Rabbit* after school just like the kids in Winnemucca, and that my image of my own environment came from the same sources that everyone else's did: from *Giant*, from *Davy Crockett*, from a thousand stray pieces of folklore and merchandising.

But even this stitched-together notion of Texas had its power. Everybody else seemed to believe that Texas children were out there on the raw frontier, riding horses to school and pumping oil in the back yard, so who was to blame for us believing it a little ourselves? Even the false image provided a certain pride of place and left one more open for the real but impalpable expressions of the land itself. It became easier to imagine that the trim suburban streets down which I teetered uneasily on my first bicycle had been the setting for trail drives and Comanche raids. And there were other times when the land was almost unbearably evocative. Riding home at night from one of those Oklahoma trips, with the windows open, the car smelling of spoiled fruit, and the seats strewn with comic books and cracker crumbs, I would allow myself to become hypnotized by the way the headlights illuminated the barbed wire and mesquite on the sides of the road, creating a corridor, an endless bower that led us on but seemed never to deliver us into the land's ghostly heart. And then we would hit some little nothing town and the headlights would fall on the bobbing pump jacks, whose rhythms were keyed to a languid, eternal pulse that seemed to be everywhere, in the swooping wingbeats of nocturnal birds crossing the road, in the pistons of the car, and in my own heavy blood.

"I can see Abilene," my father would say when we were still fifty miles from home. "I can see a fly sitting on the window of our house."

"Where?" I would say, peering hard through the windshield, believing it was possible to see that far, as far as Texas went.

WHEN I WAS TEN WE MOVED TO CORPUS CHRISTI AND I FOUND that the image of Texas I had been cultivating and was now at ease with did not apply to this semi-exotic coastal city with its manicured bay front. This was not cowboy land. It was a sultry, complicated place, although the agoraphobia induced by the stillness of the ocean was reminiscent at times of the West Texas plains.

For my first six months there I was virtually felled by the humidity. I moved about in a tentative, purposeless way, like the anole lizards that wandered around the yard.

It was not a seductive place, but once you had purged your mind of false expectations and your pores of the last lingering traces of dry West Texas air, you began to feel accepted and absorbed by it. And of course Corpus Christi had its traditional charms as well—beaches and such—that the people at the tourist bureau seized every opportunity to promote. They kept shoving into the public view Buccaneer queens and Miss Naval Air Stations, who posed seductively among the sailboat rigging for brochures that advertised "The Sparkling City by the Sea."

A ten-year-old boy could tell they were trying too hard, but I secretly wished the boosters luck. Corpus seemed isolated not only from the world at large but from the conventional stereotypes of Texas. It was not until the TV show *Route 66* deigned to film an episode there that I felt I had been provided with convincing evidence that the city was real.

I remember going to the courthouse one day to watch the filming of a scene. Within sight of this spot, Alonso de Piñeda had passed on his great reconnaissance cruise in 1519. On this bay shore Zachary Taylor had brought in 1845 nearly half of the United States Army and encamped while waiting to provoke a war with Mexico. On this very spot, perhaps, stood the makeshift stage on which Lieutenant Ulysses S. Grant had played Desdemona during a production in that camp of *Othello*. I was ignorant of all that, but there on the courthouse steps strode Martin Milner, and it was as if the shadow of history had passed across me.

There were not many moments like that, and the study of Texas history in the seventh grade served only to confirm my suspicion that the state seemed somewhere to have gone flat. Texas history began with Indians, conquistadores, pirates, with revolutions and wars, but by the time the student reached "Texas Today and Tomorrow" in the history book he saw only pictures of sorghum fields, refineries, and official portraits of dowdy governors.

So as time wore on and the universal ill humors of adolescence began to work their magic, I slid deeper into the down cycle of what I fear may turn out to be a lifelong mood swing about Texas. Corpus especially rankled and galled me. As a college-bound high school graduate, I had a clear shot at leaving Texas for good, but when it came down to actually making a decision about where I was going to go to school I threw in with thousands of other freshmen who chose that year to go to the University of Texas at Austin. The quality of education I might receive there never entered my mind. I liked Austin because it was an exotic place, where students rolled about on skateboards and wore surfer shirts and water buffalo sandals; and I quickly adopted the smug view that Austin, with its "cultural aspects," was not really Texas at all. The lesson I failed to grasp, of course, was that it was Texas, and that I had not really wanted out of the state as much as I wanted to believe.

THAT WAS YEARS AND YEARS AGO, AND IN ALL THE TIME SINCE, I have never made a conscious decision that Texas was where I was to be. Texas always seemed right for the moment, and the moments grew longer and longer, and here I remained.

Now I was beginning to feel that those years of dawdling and indecision amounted to a subconscious investment, that I had built up without meaning to a certain equity of place. That was one reason why the Massachusetts epiphany was so unwelcome.

I reacted to this crisis in a typically Texan way. I flew to Amarillo, rented a car, and took off driving. I had no plan really, just the raw desire to get out on the highway system and immerse myself in Texas. There were a few old haunts I wanted to see again and a few places I wanted to visit for the first time, but for the trip itself there was no excuse other than a self-prescribed saturation therapy. I was ready for the up cycle, ready to believe in Texas again, but I wasn't counting on that to happen. I had a vague apprehension that in some way I was laying it all on the line, that if Texas didn't "take" with me on this trip the clear inference would be that I really didn't belong here at all.

When my plane landed in Amarillo the man in the seat next to me nodded toward the window and said, "Pretty, isn't it?"

I'm afraid I gave him a rather blank look, because all I saw through the same window was a vast field of concrete and, far in the distance, the hazy Amarillo skyline, which at first I took to be a cluster of grain elevators.

"The weather, I mean," the man said, sheepishly. "The *weather* is pretty."

And the weather was pretty; it was a cool, spring day, and every time the sun broke free from the ragged, thin clouds it seemed to deliberately spotlight some subtle facet of that monotonous land: the geometrical pattern of the crops, the sight of black cattle against a field of frost-white native grass, the occasional swales in the landscape that were no more significant than the furrows between rows of wheat, but toward which the eye gravitated hungrily for relief from the flatness.

At a McDonald's in Amarillo I noticed a framed poster on the wall that told the story of the creation of the High Plains. God had been working on the Panhandle one day when it got dark and He had to quit. "In the morning," He said, "I'll come back and make it pretty like the rest of the world, with lakes and streams and mountains and trees."

God came back the next morning and discovered that the land had "hardened like concrete overnight." Not wanting to start all over again, He had an idea. "I know what I'll do," He said. "I'll just make some people who like it this way."

It surprised me how kindly disposed I was to this country. It was good land to drive through, though I could see what a nightmare it must have been to Coronado, day after trackless day in an unbroken field of nothingness. He and his men found some relief in Palo Duro Canyon, which to a traveler in that region is a startling rift in the plains, an opening into another dimension.

I drove through the canyon and was impressed but not overwhelmed. Texas scenery is spectacular only to Texans. Palo Duro pales beside the Grand Canyon, as the mountains of the Trans-Pecos pale beside the Rockies, as the coasts of Texas, its forests, deserts, hills, and even its cities, seem minor variations of grander and more definitive things in other parts of the country. Texas is a zone in which the stunning vistas more or less peter out, leaving us with only one great geographical distinction: size. The prudent and prideful Texan takes in the whole package while retaining an affection for the few component parts with the necessary spit and polish to be thought of as scenery. He develops an eye for breadth, along with an ability to look close and hard at the unlovely places and graciously accept them for what they are.

So I drove out of Palo Duro with a chauvinistic fondness for the place and kept heading south through the plains. Over the stripped cotton fields the dust rose almost vertically, and the wind riled the surface of the shallow, haphazard ponds that lay by the side of the road waiting to evaporate.

Soon the land gave way a little, and there was a miniature canyon where the Floydada Country Club golf course could be seen as a brilliant green strip beneath the eroded skirts of the mesas. After that, things were flat again for a while until the Cap Rock, where the ground buckled and broke all at once. Raptors suddenly appeared, patrolling the precipice. The change in the landscape was extreme and definite. Below the Cap Rock there were scraggly, alluring vistas, adorned with the supersaturated greenery of cedar and mesquite. That late in the season there were still beds of wildflowers, and soft, thick grass cushioned the banks of the minute creeks all the way to the waterline.

I drove through Matador, Glenn, Spur, Clairmont, and only then realized that I would be driving through Snyder, where my wife's parents lived. I came into town on State Highway 208 and passed through the town square with its windowless courthouse and its fiberglass replica of the white buffalo that had been killed near there in

1876. The buffalo was Snyder's totem, and though a drunken oil-field worker might occasionally knock a hole in the statue's head with a pipe wrench, most of the people I knew looked upon it with civic reverence.

It was dinner time when I arrived at my in-laws' house, and it went without saying that we would all go out to eat a big steak.

"How about if I order for you?" my father-in-law said.

"Fine."

"Bring him the Winchester. And we want an order of fried shrimp for an appetizer."

I ate three of these shrimp, each nearly the size of a potato, before the Winchester arrived. It was a big slab of beef, but I was hungry from driving and correctly calculated that I could put it away.

While we ate, my father-in-law complained with genial fervor about the state of the world. Since Reagan had been elected, he did not have quite so much to gripe about anymore. But even so, he had a few things on his mind. He was mad because the Democratic Congress wouldn't let the Republicans take a measly billion dollars from the synthetic fuel fund to stimulate the housing industry; mad because the British and the Argentineans were going to have a war over the Falkland Islands and guess who was going to have to go in there after it was all over with billions of dollars of foreign aid; mad because he had casually returned his YES token to the *Reader's Digest* sweepstakes and now he was being deluged with junk mail.

"There's something you should write an article about for your *Texas Monthly*," he said as we pulled out of the driveway of the restaurant, indicating a long-bodied motor home parked next to us. "These vans or whatever they are that block your view of the street when you're trying to pull out."

All of this good-natured grumpiness made me feel at home, and I lingered into the evening and finally ended up walking across the street to the high school with my mother-in-law to watch the production of *Ah, Wilderness!* that had recently won the state one-act-play competition. I was glad to have an excuse to see the high school where my wife had been a student, where she had edited the paper and written a column, under the name of Sonya Stifled, complaining about the Vietnam War and the lack of paper straws in the cafeteria.

The production took place in an immense auditorium that had been built with tax money from the great fifties oil boom. The play itself was minor O'Neill but showed Snyder High School's drama department to superlative advantage. One or two of the actors even managed very creditable New England accents. When the play was over and the audience was strolling out into the spring night, Snyder appeared less like a West Texas oil town than the idyllic Connecticut village that had been depicted in the play, a place with a tight matrix of tradition and community. It did not seem like the stifling place my wife had written about years ago, the place I might have glanced at contemptuously from the highway as I barreled through on my way to some hippie mecca in New Mexico. It seemed alarmingly like home.

THE NEXT DAY I GOT ON INTERSTATE 20 AND DROVE TO ABILENE, finding by dead reckoning the house we had lived in more than twenty years earlier. The owners had painted it yellow and put a ceramic burro in the yard, and the neighborhood itself was largely shaded from the searing sun I had known there by all the trees that had grown up and over it in the last two decades.

It was all so comfortable and congenial: the creeks were swollen with bright ocher water, the streets were lined with upscale shops and the great Danish modern cathedrals of the Protestant faith, and the movie theaters were showing *Deathtrap* and *Conan the Barbarian*. I wondered if I was feeling warm toward Texas again because it was more acceptable than I had thought or simply because it was familiar.

The land between Abilene and Dallas was unremarkable, but it held the attention of the practiced eye. In another month it would lose its verdant sheen; it would be dry and scruffy, and the very contours of the landscape would appear to recede and lose definition. But I had a fondness for that too, tucked away somewhere.

In this accepting mood I surged through Dallas in the shadow of the Reunion Tower, which had always looked to me like the center-piece to a bush league world's fair. But there was no city in the country that was honed to such a fine edge as Dallas, and you could sense its organic singleness of purpose, its obsession to project style and busyness. You were either on the team or not.

I was on the team that day, and I drove confidently through the streets, enjoying the familiar feel of the city. Then I headed south on I-35, going through Waco and Temple and past a wacky entrepreneurial jumble on the side of the highway that included a crumbling replica of the Matterhorn. Then on U.S. 183 to Lockhart, where I arrived in time to witness a reenactment of the Battle of Plum Creek. Bleachers were set up on the battlefield, microphones were planted into the ground. This epic, with its meager cast of dozens, required some thrifty stage management. A Texas Ranger would ride in on a horse and announce, "I been shot by one of them dad-blamed Indians," and his mount would then be led off the stage, shuttled around behind the bleachers, and ridden in from the other side by a Comanche with a beer gut.

The pageant served less to bring the past to life than to make the present seem anemic and unreal. But Plum Creek itself, several miles away, had not been milked of its drama. It was Edenic, and along with every other creek I passed that day on my meandering way south—La Parra, Agua Dulce, Papalote—it had a lush, overgrown, hummocky quality that made you understand why this part of the country had been the fertile crescent of Texas history.

Even farther south, in the brush country of Jim Wells and Duval counties, the land was surprisingly green, so much so that the dilapidated, boarded-up main streets of the less successful towns looked as if they were in danger of being reclaimed by jungle. Swallows dipped ahead of my car in relays, and turkey vultures and caracaras fed together on dead baby armadillos that had been struck down on the highway in their earliest forays.

A friend's father was being buried in San Diego that day, and I had adjusted my itinerary so that I would pass through town in time to attend the funeral. The church stood across the street from a zocalo whose gazebo and benches had been overgrown with grass and whose function as the center of town had been usurped by the highway a block away. Inside, the church was stolid and secure, its walls painted a light blue. Beside the altar was a full-color pietà, with dark red blood trickling from Christ's wounds and Mary bent down on one knee, holding her son's body in a way that suggested both sorrow and verve. It was a fine, grisly statue, with that admirable Mexican trait of being on square terms with mortal matters, a trait that was not echoed in the liturgically trendy stained glass windows bearing happy cubist depictions of doves and chalices and unsplintered crosses.

The congregation was dressed in suits and pressed ranch clothes. The service moved along in an unflinching manner, its bone-deep rituals making death seem real but not necessarily final.

I got back into my car feeling sobered and transient, a little flicker of movement on the landscape. But soon enough my attention was drawn outward again. The country was full of arresting things, from the painted bunting I saw preening its iridescent body in a mud puddle in Swinney Switch to a herd of Brahman bulls that had gathered at dusk near the gate of a fence outside Floresville. In that light the bulls' hides were the color of marble; their pendulous scrotums swayed above the rich grass, and their curious humps twitched when they shifted their weight from one hoof to another. At the gate stood a man in a red cap. He was not doing anything, just standing there with the bulls, and they in turn seemed thoughtlessly drawn to him.

It began to grow dark, in a peaceful, sodden way, as if the air were absorbing darkness rather than relinquishing light. The radio said that the widow of Pancho Villa had died, but then the station disappeared in a flurry of static before I could hear details. I tuned in an ad for Diamond Head water troughs, followed by a self-conscious country song in which Hank Williams, Jr., managed to drop the names of Willie and Waylon and Kris in lamenting the sad fact that nobody wanted to go out and get drunk with him anymore. The night deepened and the voices on the radio grew more desperate:

> You got to look that devil in the eye if you're sufferin' from satanic oppression. You got to say, "Devil, in the name of Jesus of Nazareth, take your hands offa my finances!"

And Bob?
Yessir.
I just wanted to say something about this El Salvadorian business.
Sorry. We're about out of time.
I don't see why we just can't take one of them tactical nuclear bombs . . .
Gotta go.
Now, wait a minute. Put that bomb in downtown Nicaragua or wherever . . .
Bye . . .

I COASTED HOME TO AUSTIN ON THE STRAINS OF A SONG ABOUT A honky-tonk cowboy who was doomed to a life of loneliness because he couldn't dance the cotton-eyed Joe. I went to bed feeling glum and perplexed, having expected that by now all those images and impressions of Texas would have formed themselves into a single testament. But I was still at arm's length, still mildly estranged. I just couldn't dance the cotton-eyed Joe.

IN THE MORNING MY FIVE-YEAR-OLD DAUGHTER WAS WHINY AND irritable when I took her to school, and after pacing around the house for a while in more or less the same mood I drove back to the school to pick her up.

"Where are we going?" she asked. "To the dentist?"

"No. To Enchanted Rock."

"What's that?"

"It's a special place."

"Oh. Like Disneyland."

We listened to her Little Thinker tape as we drove west through the LBJ country, where the roadside peach vendors were just putting up their stalls, and on through Fredericksburg, with its Sunday houses and German bakeries and relentless old-country quaintness.

The first we saw of Enchanted Rock was a bare salmon-colored nubbin erupting from the serene Hill Country vista ahead. The nubbin quickly loomed larger, until it was clearly a great stone mountain, so huge and abruptly *there* that all perspective dropped away and the rock had the one-dimensional clarity of a scene that has been painted on a panel of glass.

I felt an impatience to be there, to climb to the top. Enchanted Rock was perhaps my favorite Texas place, an immense granite batholith that the Indians had considered sacred. I had found it to be sacred too, and it was to Enchanted Rock that I used to come when I was in an especially powerful sulking mood.

We came quickly to the base of the rock, and above us, as we got out of the car, we could see the deep crease across its brow along which several minute figures crept upward.

"Wow," said my daughter. "Are we going to climb that?"

We were. We jumped across the half-dozen or so separate threads of water that composed Big Sandy Creek and followed the trail upward until it was lost in the expanse of solid rock. Then we walked up at a sharp angle, stopping about every fifteen yards so my daughter could rest and express disbelief at how far we had come. Near the top, where it was very steep, she got a little testy, so I picked her up and carried her to the summit.

"Boy," she said, as I staggered along with her in my arms, "mountain climbing is hard, isn't it?"

Finally I set her down next to a plaque that had been riveted into the rock.

"What does it say?"

"It says, 'Enchanted Rock. From its summit in the fall of 1841, Captain John C. Hays, while surrounded by Comanche Indians who cut him off from his ranging company, repulsed the whole band and inflicted upon them such heavy losses that they fled.'"

"What does that mean?"

"It means a guy had a fight with Indians up here."

"But Indians are nice now, aren't they? They only use their bows and arrows for practice."

Yes, Indians were nice now. Texas itself was nice, no longer a hostile country battled over by contentious spirits, but a reasonably representative American place, filled with familiar and ephemeral things: Wal-Marts, civic ballets, wind surfing, cable TV, Hare Krishnas in business suits. But Texas had not been wholly digested somehow, and in places like Enchanted Rock you could still get a buzz, you could still feel its insistent identity.

From the top the rock was as barren as the moon, and its vast surface canted forward slightly, so that there were two horizons, the rim of the mountain and, beyond it, the edge of the true world. I hoped this sight would take with my daughter; when her sisters were older I would bring them up here too so that Enchanted Rock could seep into their memories. I felt this place belonged to them, more than to me; they were native Texans, after all.

The lag, the missed beat I felt in my relationship with Texas, was something that I trusted would be corrected in future generations. And for the present, Enchanted Rock was every bit as much a power center for me as that sandstone boulder back in Oklahoma City. And there were others: a certain stretch of the Frio River, where after weeks of senseless brooding I had made up my mind to go ahead and be happy and get married; the lobby of the Menger hotel in San Antonio, where there was a plaque dedicated to the memory of Sidney Lanier and where you could find a gigantic Titianesque Nativity scene hung near a painting titled *Venting Cattle on the Frisco Range*; the Indian pictographs in Seminole Canyon; the mud flats and back bays of Laguna Madre; the old Shanghai Jimmy's Chili Rice on Lemmon Avenue in Dallas, where you were served chili by the man who claimed he had introduced that dish to China during the Boxer Rebellion; the Chinati Mountains; the Flower Gardens coral reef; the thick, suffocating Big Thicket forests, where you could find quicksand and wild orchids; any number of places that would give you all the barbecue you could eat for $7 or $8, where you could sit beneath a pressed-tin ceiling on a humid midsummer evening, give the baby a rib bone to gnaw on to help her with her teething, and pursue the illusion that life outside Texas would be bland and charmless. Texas for me was a thousand things like that, a thousand moments that in my mind had been charged with a special quality of place that I could not explain or understand. I only knew that the quality, and the place, was Texas.

A fault line ran across the back of Enchanted Rock like the stitching on a baseball. There was a sort of cave there, illuminated by the gaps between the collapsed boulders that had formed it, where we went to drink our apple juice. My daughter announced she wanted to play Indian.

"You be the daddy Indian," she said. "You can be taking a nap while I make the tea."

I closed my eyes obediently and felt the cool air of the cave on my face. I let the whole Texas question rest. "I'll just make some people who like it this way," God had said. I wasn't sure if I had been put on the earth with an inborn love for Texas, but I certainly seemed to have a high tolerance for it. Lying there in the cave, on the summit of an ancient and hallowed mountain, I still felt a mild longing to live someplace that was more exotic, or more ordinary; someplace that was not Texas. One of these days I might do that. Just not today.

WHY TEXAS IS THE WAY IT IS

★

Betty Sue Flowers

I F YOU LOOK UP "MYTH" IN THE DICTIONARY, YOU'LL SEE SEV-
eral definitions. One characterizes "myth" as a story that isn't
true, which is the usual way we use the term. Another defines
"myth" as a story told about the gods. But the third and most interesting definition of "myth" is a story that we accept uncritically—a definition that doesn't say anything about whether or not the story is true.

It's that third definition of myth that helps to explain why Texas is
the way it is. Texas is not just a state, as the cliché goes, it's a state of
mind. The mythology of Texas is known throughout the world, the
mythological landscape of Texas appears in hundreds of films, and the
stereotypical image of Texans is so familiar that all it takes is a hat,
boots, a drawl, and attitude to make a character recognizably Texan.
Myth of this type—a story we accept uncritically, which embodies our
values and expresses our identity—usually tends to err on the side of

the positive. But every myth casts a shadow—the bigger the myth, the larger the shadow side of the myth.

The Texas myth is a particularly strong myth, and arguably, you could say it's done a lot to hold together a large, disparate space. But Texas is in transition now, and it's time to think about the story we tell about who we Texans are and what our values are. How does the Texan myth contribute to our development? How does it possibly hold us back? We're more diverse than ever, and that old cotton, oil, and cattle nexus that forms the background for so many Texas stories is shifting to other places—high-tech, for example.

I was reminded of this shift a few years ago. My four-year old child and some of his friends were playing cowboys and Indians in the playscape at McDonald's. The girls had to be the Indians, of course, which means they spent most of the time in captivity while the boys got to run around pretending to shoot guns.

Suddenly, as if on cue, the boys began yelling, "The Indians are coming, the Indians are coming!" Of course, the Indians were already captured—but if you're playing cowboys and Indians, there's always a new group of Indians coming. "The Indians are coming, the Indians are coming!" Now I knew what the next lines would be: "Call out the cavalry." But they said, "The Indians are coming! Quick, dial 9-1-1!"

A characteristic of myths is that they evolve.

The facts of our lives are always changing. But our destiny as a state depends not just on these changing facts but on the story we tell about what's happening and who we are and what we want to do about these changes. In the same way, an individual's life is shaped not just by the facts, but also by the story the person tells about these facts.

You can tell the story of the facts of your life as a hero tale. You can tell the story as a victim tale. You can choose any of a number of plots on which to talk about the story of your life. And while we may or may not have much control over the facts, we do have control over the plot, and it's the plot—the myth rather than the facts—that shapes the future.

Given the power of our Texas myth, we should look very closely at the story we have traditionally told about who we are and what we aspire to be. There are four main features of the Texas myth, based on the four central myths that have shaped us in the West: the hero myth; the religious myth (remembering that a "myth" is not necessarily untrue); the enlightenment myth, in which, fortunately, our country was founded; and the economic myth, in which we now reside.

Of these four myths, the one that has shaped the Texas myth most particularly is the hero myth. Myths do not just emerge full-blown, like Athena from the head of Zeus. They're made up of bits and pieces of other myths—and the Texas myth is made up of bits and pieces of the hero myth.

Certain aspects of the hero myth are important to consider. For example, the hero myth emphasizes the individual and not the community. We praise the self-made man. The hero myth puts a premium on the will, not the heart: "A man's got to do what a man's got to do."

Every schoolchild in Texas to some extent still grows up with this myth. Many towns name their public schools after heroes of the Alamo—Travis, Bowie, Fanin, Crockett. The names of the half-dozen main heroes of the Alamo were familiar to all of us—so familiar that as a third-grade Girl Scout on a field trip to the Alamo, I was shocked to realize that there were more than six people who died there. I thought it was six people against the whole Mexican army. That was how focused we were on the individual hero myth.

We admire the rugged individualist, the wildcatter, the risk-taker, whether he's up or down. There's no end to stories about Texas heroes. They're so familiar to us that I won't dwell on this aspect of the Texas myth, but move on to the next.

Second, the Texas myth is related to the land itself. It's a distinctive version of the Promised Land myth. The German immigrants to Texas, among many others, came here in part because of the sales job that was done on what a great land it was. The idea was that you could just throw a seed on the ground, and it would grow immediately.

Texas was described as a kind of Eden so often that the first book published in English in Texas mentioned this hype. The book was written by Mary Austin Holley and was based on letters she sent back from a visit to Austin's colony. In this book, Holley criticized the extravagance with which admirers of the Texas myth talked about the land—"as if enchantment had indeed thrown its spell over their minds." This was 1831—and we were already bragging about our land.

Another example can be found in Scene Two of one of the earliest poems published in Texas—a book-length poem by Hugh Kerr published in 1838 and entitled: "A Poetical Description of Texas, and Narrative of Many Interesting Events in that Country, Embracing a Period of Several Years, Interspersed with Moral and Political Impressions: Also, an Appeal to Those Who Oppose the Union of Texas with the United States, and the Anticipation of that Event. To Which is Added the Texas Heroes, No. 1 & 2."

I shall quote four lines from that poem:

Gonzales and Victoria

Are towns upon the Guadalupe;

The first is distant from the bay,

The latter, some thirty miles up.

Lines such as these prompted a contemporary critic to say, "Oh, Kerr, Kerr, Kerr / what did you write those poems fur?"

Now, Kerr also praises the beauty of Texas extravagantly. A quote: "Few spots on earth can this excel." But even he admits:

In these remarks we do not mean

    The whole of Texas to include:

Some parts of Texas, we have seen,

    Which from this praise, we must exclude.

In any case, there's another facet to this land of milk and honey myth, or land of oil and money, as it later became, and that's valuing of the land not so much for its beauty or its history or flora and fauna particularly—just the land itself. This is not the European or East Coast custom of a second or country home. You get to a certain point in life in Texas, you get your deer lease, or if you're lucky, your ranch. This is not sightseeing. This is not relaxation. This is *possession*.

The Texas Centennial poet, Grace Noll Crowell, wrote a poem in that centennial year of 1936 called "Texas the Woman" in which these lines appear:

As if she were a woman, men have loved
Their Texas through the years:

. . . .

And men are men, and love is what it is;
Impelling each to grapple with his hands
For his beloved, possessing what is his:
Texas the woman, soft-eyed, gracious, fair,
Her head held high, a star caught in her hair.

Of course, any state can be personified as a lady, but what makes this analogy so pervasive in Texas poetry is that Texas, unlike most earlier states, was pictured as independent from its beginning—liberty as a woman with a star "caught in her hair." The 1836 struggle was seen not as a civil war with one section of Mexico rebelling against another, but as a war of liberty against tyranny, with Texas as liberty.

And that leads to the third feature of the Texas myth, which is that the Texas myth is a subset of the myth of the United States as the home of liberty. In fact, Texas founders consciously grafted what they were doing onto the U.S. myth of the Revolution—even though the story didn't exactly fit, because our relation to Mexico was not the same as the colonists' relationship to Great Britain. But we did graft our myth onto that myth, and then it simply froze into place.

The U.S. myth went on to incorporate things like the melting pot, the immigrant, and the great cities, such a Chicago and New York. Many different details were added to the U.S. myth as it developed. But Texas stayed in a kind of perpetual state of primal, rural independence of mind, and that is important for our myth.

I have been told that even our electric grid is so independent that it connects to the rest of the world in only two places. And perhaps we stayed in that formative state of the U.S. myth for so long because our economy stayed tied to cattle, oil, and other products of the land. We're a little like Jefferson's ideal of a nation of farmers and small landowners—only transposed a bit to ranchers and large landowners.

So these three features of the Texas myth—the hero, the land, and a version of liberty—are very powerful. Let me give you an example of how this works even today.

Texas recently had a very effective campaign against littering, which was called "Don't Mess with Texas." What this Texas ad company, GSD&M, did, whether consciously or not, was to take three aspects of our myth and perform a kind of Aikido movement on it. That is, they took the energy that comes from our macho "don't mess with me" ethos and the fierce possessiveness we have in relation to our land and used it to a different end. After that campaign, those of us who felt we had a constitutional right to throw beer cans on the highway out of our pickups, almost overnight, quit throwing beer cans. During the next five years, there was a 72 percent drop in litter. That's a phenomenal change, one largely attributed to this campaign. What made it so effective? It used the energy of the Texas myth and turned it to other ends.

This little story about the anti-litter campaign points to a key feature about myths—that while they can be very powerful, their power can be moved to other ends. And if any people can use the power of myth to new ends, Texans can. Why? Because of the fourth feature of the Texas myth: that we hold our myths as myths. We tell them consciously as myths. In fact, many Texans buy their first pair of boots only when they're heading off to Harvard. We may never wear boots in Texas, but we'll put them on before heading up north.

We support our myth overtly. It's not just Senator Kay Bailey Hutchison and President George Bush who were cheerleaders. We all are when it comes to Texas and we're outside of Texas. We've been known to exaggerate, to tell tall tales. We're master storytellers. And that means that we have it in our power to transform the story of who we are and what we aspire to be.

TEXAS WOMEN: TRUE GRIT AND ALL THE REST

────────── ✦ ──────────

Molly Ivins

T HEY USED TO SAY THAT TEXAS WAS HELL ON WOMEN AND horses—I don't know why they stopped. Surely not because much of the citizenry has had its consciousness raised, as they say in the jargon of the women's movement, on the issue of sexism. Just a few months ago one of our state representatives felt moved to compare women and horses—it was the similarity he wanted to emphasize. Of course some Texas legislator can be found to say any fool thing, but this guy's comments met with general agreement from his colleagues. One can always dismiss the entire Legislature as a particularly deplorable set of Texans, but as Sen. Carl Parker observes, if you took all the fools out of the Lege, it wouldn't be a representative body anymore.

I should confess that I've always been more of an observer than a participant in Texas Womanhood: The spirit was willing but I was declared ineligible on grounds of size early. You can't be six feet tall and cute, both. I think I was first named captain of the basketball team when I was four and that's what I've been ever since. I spent my girlhood as a Clydesdale among thoroughbreds. I clopped along amongst them cheerfully, admiring their grace, but the strange training rituals they went through left me secretly relieved that no one would ever expect me to step on a racetrack. I think it is quite possible to grow up in Texas as an utter failure in flirting, gentility, cheerleading, sexpottery, and manipulation and still be without any permanent scars. Except one. We'd all rather be blonde.

Please understand I'm not whining when I point out that Texas sexism is of an especially rank and noxious variety—this is more a Texas brag. It is my belief that it is virulence of Texas sexism that accounts for the strength of Texas women. It's what we have to overcome that makes us formidable survivors, say I with some complacency.

As has been noted elsewhere, there are several strains of Texan culture: They are all rotten for women. There is the Southern belle nonsense of our Confederate heritage, that little-woman-on-a-pedestal, flirtatious, "you're so cute when you're mad," Scarlett O'Hara myth that leads, quite naturally, to the equally pernicious legend of the Iron Magnolia. Then there's the machismo of our Latin heritage, which affects not only our Chicana sisters, but has been integrated into Texas culture quite as thoroughly as barbecue, rodeo, and Tex-Mex food.

Next up is the pervasive good-ol'-boyism of the *Redneckus texensis*, that remarkable tribe that has made the pickup truck with the gun rack across the back window and the beer cans flying out the window a synonym for Texans worldwide. Country music is a good place to investigate and find reflected the attitudes of kickers toward women (never ask what a kicker kicks). It's your basic, familiar virgin/whore dichotomy—either your "Good-Hearted Woman" or "Your Cheatin' Heart," with the emphasis on the honky-tonk angels. Nor is the jock idolatry that permeates the state helpful to our gender: Football is not a game here, it's a matter of blood and death. Woman's role in the state's national game is limited, significantly, to cheerleading. In this regard, I can say with great confidence that Texas changeth not—the hopelessly intense, heartbreaking longing with which most Texas girls still want to be cheerleader can be observed at every high school, every September.

Last but not least in the litany of cultures that help make the lives of Texas women so challenging is the legacy of the frontier—not the frontier that Texas women lived on, but the one John Wayne lived on. Anyone who knows the real history of the frontier knows it is a saga of the strength of women. They worked as hard as men, they fought as hard as men, they suffered as much as men. But in the cowboy movies that most contemporary Texans grew up on, the big, strong man always protects "the little lady" or "the gals" from whatever peril threatens. Such nonsense. Mary Ann Goodnight was often left alone at the JA Ranch near the Palo Duro Canyon. One day in 1877, a cowboy rode into her camp with three chickens in a sack as a present for her. He naturally expected her to cook and eat the fowl, but Goodnight kept them as pets. She wrote in her diary, "No one can ever know how much company they were." Life for farm and ranch wives didn't improve much over the next 100 years. Ruth White raised nine children on a farm near High, Texas, in the 1920s and thirties. She used to say, "Everything on this farm is either hungry or heavy."

All of these strains lead to a form of sexism so deeply ingrained in the culture that it's often difficult to distinguish the disgusting from the outrageous or the offensive from the amusing. One not infrequently sees cars or trucks sporting the bumper sticker HAVE FUN— BEAT THE HELL OUT OF SOMEONE YOU LOVE. Another is: IF YOU LOVE SOMETHING, SET IT FREE. IF IT DOESN'T COME BACK, TRACK IT DOWN AND KILL IT. I once heard a legislator order a lobbyist, "Get me two sweathogs for tonight." At a benefit "roast" for the battered women's shelter in El Paso early in 1985, a couple of the male politicians told rape jokes to amuse the crowd. Most Texas sexism is not intended to be offensive—it's entirely unconscious. A colleague of mine was touring the new death chamber in Huntsville last year with a group of other reporters. Their guide called to warn those inside they were coming through, saying, "I'm coming over with eight reporters and one woman." Stuff like that happens to you four or five times a day for long enough, it will wear you down some.

Other forms of the phenomenon are, or course, less delightsome. Women everywhere are victims of violence with depressing regularity. Texas is a more violent place than most of the rest of America, for reasons having to do with guns, machismo, frontier traditions, and the heterogeneous population. While the law theoretically applies to male and female alike, by unspoken convention, a man who offs his wife or girlfriend is seldom charged with murder one: we wind up filed under the misnomer manslaughter.

That's the bad news for Texas women—the good news is that all this adversity has certainly made us a bodacious bunch of overcomers. And rather pleasant as a group, I always think, since having a sense of humor about men is not a luxury here; it's a necessity. The feminists often carry on about the importance of role models and how little girls need positive role models. When I was a kid, my choice of Texas role models went from Ma Ferguson to the Kilgore Rangerettes. Of course I wanted to be Rangerette: Ever seen a picture of Ma? Not that we haven't got real women heroes, of course, just that we were never taught anything about them. You used to have to take Texas history two or three times in order to get a high school diploma in this state: The Yellow Rose of Texas and Belle Starr were the only women in our history books. Kaye Northcott notes that all the big cities in the state have men's last names—Houston, Austin, Dallas. All women got was some small towns called after their front names: Alice, Electra, Marfa. This is probably because, as Eleanor Brackenridge of San Antonio (1837–1924) so elegantly put it, "Foolish modesty lags behind while brazen impudence goes forth and eats the pudding." Brackenridge did her part to correct the lag by founding the Texas Woman Suffrage Association in 1913.

It is astonishing how recently Texas women have achieved equal legal rights. I guess you could say we made steady progress even before we could vote—the state did raise the age of consent for a woman from 7 to 10 in 1890—but it went a little smoother after we got some say in it. Until June 26, 1918, all Texans could vote except "idiots, imbeciles, aliens, the insane and women." The battle over woman's suffrage in Texas was long and fierce. Contempt and ridicule were the favored weapons against women. Women earned the right to vote through years of struggle; the precious victory was not something handed to us by generous men. From that struggle emerged a generation of Texas women whose political skills and leadership abilities have affected Texas politics for decades. Even so, Texas women were not permitted to serve on juries until 1954. As late as 1969, married women did not have full property rights. And until 1972, under Article 1220 of the Texas Penal Code, a man could murder his wife and her lover if he found them "in a compromising position" and get away with it as "justifiable homicide." Women, you understand, did not have equal shooting rights. Although Texas was one of the first states to ratify the Equal Rights Amendment, which has been part of the Texas Constitution since 1972, we continue to work for fairer laws concerning problems such as divorce, rape, child custody, and access to credit.

Texas women are just as divided by race, class, age, and educational level as are other varieties of human beings. There's a pat description of "what every Texas woman wants" that varies a bit from city to city, but the formula that Dallas females have been labeled with goes something like this: "Be a Pi Phi at Texas or SMU, marry a man who'll buy you a house in Highland Park, hold the wedding at Highland Park Methodist (flowers by Kendall Bailey), join the Junior League, send the kids to St. Mark's and Hockaday in the winter and Camps Longhorn and Waldemar in the summer, plus cotillion lessons at the Dallas Country Club, have an unlimited charge account at Neiman's as a birthright but buy almost all your clothes at Highland Park Village from Harold's or the Polo Shop, get your hair done at Paul Neinast's or

Lou's and drive a Jeep Wagoneer for carpooling and a Mercedes for fun." There is a kicker equivalent of this scenario that starts, "Every Texas girl's dream is a double-wide in a Lubbock trailer park. . . ." But I personally believe it is unwise ever to be funny at the expense of kicker women. I once met a kicker lady who was wearing a blouse of such a vivid pink you could close your eyes and still see the color; this confection was perked up with some big rhinestone buttons and a lot of ruffles across an impressive bosom. "My," said I, "where did you get that blouse?" She gave me a level look and drawled. "Honey, it come from mah coutouri-ay, Jay Cee Penn-ay." And if that ain't class, you *can* kiss my grits.

To my partisan eye, it seems that Texas women are more animated and friendly than those from, say, Nebraska. I suspect this comes from early training: Girls in Texas high schools are expected to walk through the halls smiling and saying "Hi" to everyone they meet. Being enthusiastic is bred into us, as is a certain amount of obligatory social hypocrisy stemming from the Southern tradition of manners, which does rather tend to emphasize pleasantness more than honesty in social situations. Many Texas women have an odd greeting call—when they haven't seen a good friend for a long time, the first glimpse will provoke the cry, "Oooooooo—honey, how good to see yew again!" It sounds sort of like the "Soooooey, pig" call.

Mostly Texas women are tough in some very fundamental ways. Not unfeminine, nor necessarily unladylike, just tough. It may be possible for a little girl to grow to womanhood in this state entirely sheltered from the rampant sexism all around her—but it's damned difficult. The result is that Texas women tend to know how to cope. We can cope with put-downs and come-ons, with preachers and hustlers, with drunks and cowboys. And when it's all over, if we stick together and work, we'll come out better than the sister who's buried in a grave near Marble Falls under a stone that says, "Rudolph Richter, 1822–1915, and Wife."

SOCIAL STUDIES

———— ★ ————

Kinky Friedman

T O THE 6.1 BILLION PEOPLE ON THIS PLANET WHO ARE NOT Texans, the very idea of Texas etiquette may seem like a contradiction. These culturally deprived souls, sometimes known as the rest of the world, go blithely through life believing implicitly in lady wrestlers, Catholic universities, and military intelligence, yet they scoff at the notion of Texas etiquette.

We Texans believe if it ain't King James, it ain't Bible. We believe in holding hands and saying grace before eating big, hairy steaks in chain restaurants. If the steak is the size of a sombrero, the meal is followed by the belching of the Lord's Prayer, which is then followed by projectile vomiting. Extreme cases may result in what some Texans commonly refer to as "squirtin' out of both ends."

The only thing that really differentiates Texas from any other place in the world, however, is the proclivity of its people to urinate out of doors and to attach a certain amount of importance to this popular pastime. Urinating outside goes much further than merely meeting the criteria of what is socially acceptable; it is the way of our people. To walk out under the Texas stars and water your lizard is considered the most sacred inalienable right of all citizens of the Lone Star State.

Though Texans are always a relatively considerate bunch, things do seem to get a little wiggy when a certain type of woman meets another woman from the same substratum whom she hasn't seen since Kennedy was croaked in Dallas (which we don't really consider to be part of Texas). The announcement of JFK's death, by the way, was rumored to have been greeted with cheering in certain boardrooms and country clubs in the state, which, of course, was a mild lapse in Texas etiquette. So, no doubt, was killing President Kennedy.

As I was saying before I heard voices in my head, there is a traditional greeting used by women in Texas who haven't seen each other in a while. In a sort of latent lesbian mating ritual, the first one's face lights up insanely, and she shrieks, "Look at *yeeew!*" The other one, her countenance locked in an equally demonic rictus, responds, "Look at *yeeew!!!*" There is little doubt that this increasingly frenetic, insectile exchange would continue indefinitely if not for the intercession of a third party. Suddenly a big cowboy walks up, strikes a match on his wranglers—he has two Mexican wranglers who work for him—and proceeds to set the women on fire.

Now the women are dancing around like vapid versions of Joan of Arc, sparks flying from their big hair, still screaming "Look at *yeeew!!!*" and they would have no doubt fallen through the trap door in tandem if not for the appearance of another party. Fortunately a man nearby just happens to be urinating out of doors and saves the day by taking the thing into his own hands and extinguishing the fire with Hose Number One.

Sometimes Texas etiquette manifests itself far beyond the boundaries of the Lone Star State. When I was working in Borneo with the Peace Corps, I decided to take a little trip to Thailand with a few other volunteers. This was the height of the Haight-Ashbury era and, of course, the Vietnam War. In a seedy little bar in Chiang Mai, these two forces came together. By forces, I mean *special* forces, as in Green Berets. A group of them, on R&R from Vietnam, had been drinking rather heavily at the bar. There were four of us Peace Corps kids, all skinny as Jesus, with long hair and native beads, and one of our party, Dylan Ferrero, happened, rather unfortunately, to be sporting a flower in his hair. In the air, the sense of impending doom was almost palpable. The Green Berets, like ourselves, had been culturally out where the buses don't run for possibly a little too long. They thought we were real hippies. And they were in no mood to let Saigons be bygones.

A wiry, dangerous-looking little Hawaiian guy from this gang wandered over with a glaze of hatred in his eyes that almost wilted Dylan's flower. I remember his words quite well because he chanted them with a soft, evil cadence: "Ain't you cool." A bar in Chiang Mai could be a godless, lawless place in 1967, almost as lawless and godless as a lonely road outside Jasper in 1998. But it was just at that moment that I thought I heard a familiar accent—a Texas accent. The deep, drawling tones were emanating from the largest man I'd ever seen. He was sitting with the Green Berets, watching the ongoing tension convention at the bar. With a sudden confidence that must have come from deep in the heart of Texas, I walked over to a table of cranked-up Special Forces. With my beads and Angela Davis Afro, it would have been the stupidest thing I'd ever done in my life if I hadn't been so sure that Goliath was from Texas. Texas saved me.

In a matter of moments, I had learned that the guy was from Dublin, Texas, and he knew my old college friend Lou Siegel, who was also from Dublin. The next thing anybody knew, the invisible bond of latent homosexual Texas manhood had transcended all the other human chemistry in the bar and the world. Years later I thanked Lou for being spiritually in the right place at the right time. I never saw Goliath the Green Beret again. Maybe he just got Starbucked into the twenty-first century like everybody else and is sipping a decaf latte somewhere and reading the *Wall Street Gerbil*.

I wish I could say that Texas etiquette really exists. Maybe it's like God or Santa Claus or brotherly love—something no one's ever seen but just might be there after all. Years ago my mother had a little sign on her desk at Echo Hill Ranch, a summer camp for boys and girls. It read: "Courtesy is owed. Respect is earned. Love is given." That may be as close to Texas etiquette as any of us will ever get.

THE LAST HISTORY EVER OF FATIGUE IN TEXAS

★

William C. Gruben

THE READER IS ADVISED TO PAY CLOSE ATTENTION TO THIS history, because no others on the subject will ever be written. While this is not the writer's decision, he agrees that it is all for the best. Nevertheless, it is a sad state of affairs when so modest a summary must be the final statement on fatigue in Texas.

Like oil, fatigue existed in Texas long before its commercial possibilities were appreciated. The Tejas Indians had seven different words for *tired*, and the Lipan Apaches had twenty-two, not counting words used only in secret ceremonies. These last will never be known. Some Indians had no actual words for *tired* but did have as many as forty-one different ways to look tired.

The early Spaniards brought to Texas a large vocabulary of words for *tired*. Later they invented new phrases to describe varieties of fatigue not experienced in the old country, such as "tired of mountain lions and bears," "tired of rattlesnakes," and "generally tired of Texas."

The Anglo-Saxon settlers also devised new phrases to describe the peculiarities of exhaustion in Texas. In addition, they worked out a series of hand gestures, signs, and finger movements that allowed them to depict fatigue at times when they were too tired to talk about it. A proficient settler could close his mouth, close his eyes, lie flat on his back, and still tell his friends that he was tired, through the judicious use of just one finger. Modern Texans have been unable to improve upon this mode of communication, although it was developed more than a hundred and fifty years ago.

The Anglo-Saxon settlers greatly increased fatigue in Texas, however, because they prevented Indians from getting a good night's sleep. The Indians responded in kind. Sometimes one of these groups would be up all night making loud noises, as revenge for what the other had done the night before. The Indians improvised percussion instruments from hollow logs and would work in shifts to keep the settlers awake. The Anglo-Saxon settlers organized all-night watches, during which they fired rifles into the air. The women would strike ladles and spoons against stewpots in order to do their part.

These mutual antagonisms sometimes erupted in violence that was later regretted by both sides. In one particularly sordid incident a group of settlers gave neighboring Indians several jars of peach preserves laced with a virus that caused sleeping sickness. The Indians retaliated by burning the bedrooms of several settlers' log cabins.

After Texas became an independent nation, a Treaty of Silence was signed with the Indians. According to this compact, everyone agreed to stop making loud noises and go home and go to bed.

On the great Texas cattle drives the invention of the swing shift resulted in many sleepless nights and led to the state's first fatigue-related commercial enterprise—the fatigue market. The market began informally. Someone who had got, say, twelve hours of sleep the night before would trade a few of his hours for a jackrabbit stew and some homemade liquor.

As the market developed, traveling "rest merchants" began to buy sleep in towns with an excess supply and sell it in towns with a short-age. An efficient rest merchant could put together enough sleep from different people to package an entire night's shut eye. He would then sell it to a cowboy who had been up all night directing a stampede. For a while everyone was happy. Someone with nothing better to do could make a good income just by sleeping late on Sunday mornings. Before long, however, unscrupulous businessmen began to smuggle in poor-quality sleep from foreign countries and even to steal sleep from drunks who had passed out. Cowboys who bought sleep from rest merchants started to complain of frequent headaches. When federal agents realized that some of the contaminated sleep was crossing state lines, they stepped in and shut down the market forever.

AT THE TURN OF THE CENTURY THE OIL BOOM BROUGHT FATIGUE to Texas in epidemic proportions. After fourteen hours on a drilling rig many oilfield roughnecks suffered from insomnia. The price of a sleeping pill jumped to ten dollars, and a glass of water to wash it down cost three dollars. Some roughnecks would pool their money, break up a pill, and just get drowsy together. Others got religion. Denominations with long sermons on biblical minutiae were popular among rough-necks who otherwise would have had to count sheep.

These measures did not work for everyone, though, and not a few roughnecks took to drinking all night and shooting each other with horse pistols. In response one town council secretly legalized the eighty-minute hour and hired Pinkerton detectives to break into homes and adjust watches and clocks to comply with the law. The idea was that if roughnecks worked fourteen eighty-minute hours, they would have to go right back to work as soon as they got off, and couldn't cause any mischief. The ruse was discovered the next morn-ing, however, when the sun came up at three A.M.

The roughnecks retaliated by hiring the same Pinkerton men to adjust the town's clocks to a forty-minute hour and a twenty-three-hour day. The Greenwich International Dateline and Hour Commission soon learned of the misdeeds, as it always does, and the guilty roughnecks were arrested.

While insomnia and insufficient sleep time were plaguing oilfield workers and cowboys, Texas farmers were suffering from too much sleep. After their first views of West Texas's unrelievedly flat terrain, newly arrived farmers would sometimes go to sleep for days, only to wake up and, seeing the same thing all over again, go right back to sleep. Realizing that cotton would never be king at this rate, the governor authorized emergency shipments of hot coffee in tank cars. Soft-drink manufacturers were ordered to include stimulants in their formulas. These efforts proved fruitless.

Soon, however, oil and cattle were discovered in West Texas, and roughnecks and cowboys moved in to drink and fight all night. Farmers woke up with a start, and the cotton crop was saved. The roughnecks were all given official pardons for their earlier shenanigans with the clocks.

An outbreak of bedding-related violence occurred in 1914 with the onset of the so-called Bandit Wars. Overtired Mexican revolutionaries often invaded Texas on foraging expeditions and were not shy about taking mattresses by force. To get a decent night's rest, many South Texas ranchers had to take their bedding to urban centers and sleep in town. Others placed mattresses on buckboards and hired teamsters to drive them around all night. This discouraged bandits from creeping up and yanking mattresses out from under unwary sleepers and then running away, but the expense was prohibitive for all except the well-to-do. In spite of these safeguards the bandit-revolutionaries were able to steal many mattresses and destroy even more. On some nights the border skies were black with the smoke of burning bedding. Many Texans were forced to sleep in hammocks. Finally U.S. National Guardsmen were called up and stationed along the border, and the ranchers went back to bed.

Today subtler influences have replaced armed conflict and bedding sabotage as major causes of exhaustion in Texas. The increasing complexity of city life has resulted in much confusion that leads to fatigue. Faced with a myriad of urban pressures, many Texans now get so mixed up that they forget to go to bed until eight or nine in the morning. Soon they lose their jobs and live in the streets as "fatigue derelicts," begging for "your old pajamas" or panhandling money for pillow rental. Others turn to crime. All too often an urban Texan will come out in the morning to his car, only to discover that it has been broken into and slept in.

The future of Texan fatigue is uncertain, but some researchers believe that much of the damage will be self-inflicted. It has long been known, even among the ancient Indian tribes of Texas, that fatigue is an altered state of consciousness. Through the improper use of history books Texas teenagers have found out about this. As a result some young people are wearing themselves out just to "get a buzz" and because it is "something different." Police officers are even beginning to see young children who refuse to go to bed or, worse, secretly stay awake under the covers, until they "get wasted." Because of this abuse of history a new state law forbids any mention of fatigue in print. The discussion you are reading is the last reference to fatigue that will ever be allowed in the state. Although it is sad that no one will ever again learn about the fatigue problems of the early settlers and Indians, it is a small price to pay to stop all this.

NOTES ON CONTRIBUTORS

ANDY ADAMS (1859–1935)
Born in Indiana, Adams lived in Texas as a young man during the trail-driving days of the 1880s. In 1903 he published his first and best book, *The Log of a Cowboy: A Narrative of the Old Trail Days*. The book was written in part to refute the romanticized portrait of the cowboy in Owen Wister's *The Virginian* (1902).

JOHN HOUGHTON ALLEN (1909–1997)
Born in Austin, Allen identified far more closely with the lonely, rugged brush country in remote Jim Hogg County in south Texas, where he lived for a time on the Jesús María Ranch. Next to it was the ranch that captured Allen's imagination, the Randado, which he wrote about in his best book, *Southwest* (1952).

DONALD BARTHELME (1931–1989)
Although born in Philadelphia, Pennsylvania, Barthelme grew up in Houston where he attended the University of Houston. In the 1960s he moved to New York and became one of the most innovative practitioners of the short story in America. His stories in *The New Yorker* were the latest in avant-garde experimentalism, and the novel *Snow*

White (1967) and collections such as *City Life* (1970) and *Amateurs* (1976) extended his influence. *Sixty Stories* appeared in 1981.

RICK BASS (1958–)
Born in Fort Worth, Bass was educated at Utah State University. His books include the novels *Where the Sea Used to Be* (1998) and *The Hermit's Story* (2002), and story collections such as *The Watch* (1988) and *In the Loyal Mountains* (1995). Bass lives in Troy, Montana.

GERTRUDE BEASLEY (1892–?)
One of the least known of Texas memoirists, Beasley is easily the most shocking and sensational. Born and raised in west Texas, she got out of the state as soon as she could. Her autobiography, *My First Thirty Years*, was published in Paris in 1925. H. L. Mencken reviewed it with gusto, but the book was so frank and outrageous that it was banned in England. To date, nothing is known of Beasley's life after 1928.

ROY BEDICHEK (1878–1959)
A native of Illinois, Bedichek grew up in Texas and acquired two degrees at the University of Texas, where he worked for many years as director of the University Interscholastic League. Bedichek wrote his first book, *Adventures with a Texas Naturalist* (1947), at the age of sixty-nine. Other books include *Karankawa Country* (1950) and *Letters of Roy Bedichek* (1985).

BETSY BERRY (1958–)
Born in Puerto Rico, Berry grew up mostly in Texas. She received her Ph.D. from the University of Texas in 1994, writing on the British modernist, Jean Rhys. Berry has published poetry, short fiction, and essays. She lives in Austin, where she teaches and writes.

BILLY LEE BRAMMER (1929–1978)
Born in Dallas, Brammer graduated from North Texas State College and worked for several years as a journalist before joining the staff of Senator Lyndon B. Johnson, 1955 to 1959. During that period he wrote his only novel, *The Gay Place*. Published in 1961, it traced the political fortunes of a Texas governor modeled closely on LBJ.

BILL BRETT (1922–2002)
Born in Daisetta, in east Texas, Brett held many jobs during his life, including postmaster, cowhand, construction worker, truck driver, deputy sheriff, and writer. His books include *Well, He Wanted To Know and I Knew So I Told Him* (1971) and *The Stolen Steers: A Tale of the Big Thicket* (1977).

JOE BOB BRIGGS (1954–)
Born in Frontage, Texas, Briggs attended college at Tarleton State University briefly before taking up his life's work as a critic of drive-in movies. His books include *Joe Bob Goes To the Drive-in* (1987) and *A Guide to Western Civilization; or, My Story* (1988). He has hosted "Joe Bob's Drive-in Theater" for the Movie Channel and appeared in such films as *Casino*. Briggs lives in New York.

ROBERT A. CARO (1935–)
A New Yorker first and last, Caro has devoted over two decades to researching and writing the life of President Lyndon B. Johnson. His books on LBJ—to date—are *The Path to Power* (1982), *Means of Ascent* (1990), and *Master of the Senate* (2002).

PAT CARR (1932–)
Born in Wyoming, Carr grew up in Houston and holds a Ph.D. from Tulane University. She has lived in El Paso and South America and now resides on a farm near Elkins, Arkansas. Her books include *The Women in the Mirror* (1977) and *Night of the Luminarias* (1986).

GARY CARTWRIGHT (1934–)
Born in Dallas, Cartwright at the outset was a sports writer in Fort Worth and Dallas. Although he has published a couple of novels, he is best known for his journalism and crime reporting, much of it appearing in *Texas Monthly* for the past thirty years. His books include *Blood Will Tell* (1979) and *Confessions of a Washed-up Sportswriter, Including Various Digressions about Sex, Crime, and Other Hobbies*. Cartwright lives in Austin.

RAFAEL CASTILLO (1950–)
Born and raised in San Antonio, Castillo was educated at St. Mary's

University and the University of Texas at San Antonio. His short stories have appeared in numerous quarterlies, and in 1991 a collection, *Distant Journeys*, was published. Castillo lives in San Antonio and teaches at Palo Alto College.

SANDRA CISNEROS (1954–)
Born in Chicago, Cisneros is a poet and fiction writer whose work includes *My Wicked, Wicked Ways* (poetry, 1987), *The House on Mango Street* (1984), *Woman Hollering Creek and Other Stories* (1991), and in 2002, the novel *Caramelo*. Cisneros has lived for a number of years in San Antonio.

JAMES CRUMLEY (1939–)
Born in Three Rivers, Crumley is the author of several highly regarded detective novels such as *The Last Good Kiss* (1978) and *Bordersnakes* (1996). A volume of short stories, *Whores*, appeared in 1988. Crumley has for some time lived in Missoula, Montana.

J. FRANK DOBIE (1888–1964)
Born into a ranching family in the brush country south of San Antonio, Dobie became the best-known Texas writer of his generation. He taught the famous course Life and Literature of the Southwest (which he invented), at the University of Texas, ramrodded the Texas Folklore Society, and wrote prolifically, including such books as *Coronado's Children* (1931), *The Longhorns* (1941), and *Cow People* (1964).

BETTY SUE FLOWERS (1947–)
Flowers was born in Waco and holds a Ph.D. from Queen Mary College, London (1973). She has published a book of verse, *Extending the Shade* (1990), and, with Bill D. Moyers, has collaborated in the publication of four television tie-in books, including *Joseph Campbell and the Power of Myth*. Flowers lives in Austin and is director of the Lyndon Baines Johnson Library and Museum at the University of Texas.

ROBERT FLYNN (1932–)
A native of Chillicothe in west Texas, Flynn for many years taught at Trinity University in San Antonio. He is the author of numerous

books, including *North to Yesterday* (1967), *Seasonal Rain and Other Stories* (1986), and *Wanderer Springs* (1987). He lives in San Antonio.

KINKY FRIEDMAN (1944–)
Born on a ranch near Kerrville, Texas, Friedman has had two careers, first as a singer/songwriter with his band, Kinky Friedman and the Texas Jewboys, and second as a prolific author of lighthearted crime novels such as *Elvis, Jesus, and Coca Cola* (1993), *The Love Song of J. Edgar Hoover* (1996), and *Meanwhile Back at the Ranch* (2002). Friedman lives in Medina, Texas, where he writes and maintains the Utopia Animal Rescue Ranch.

MARY LADD GAVELL (1919–1967)
Born in Cuero, Texas, Gavell graduated from Texas A&M University in 1940. She married Stefan Gavell in 1953, had two sons, and was managing editor of *Psychiatry* magazine in Washington, D.C. She published no fiction during her lifetime, but following her death one of her stories appeared in print, and others were collected and published in *I Cannot Tell a Lie, Exactly*, in 2001.

DAGOBERTO GILB (1950–)
Born in Los Angeles, Gilb lived for many years in El Paso. His books include *The Magic of Blood* (1993) and *Woodcuts of Women* (2001). He currently teaches creative writing at Southwest Texas State University in San Marcos.

RAY GONZALEZ (1952–)
Born in El Paso, Gonzalez is a poet and essayist who has edited numerous volumes of Latino writing. Among his publications are *Memory Fever: A Journey beyond El Paso del Norte* (essays, 1993), *The Hawk Temple at Tierra Grande: Poems* (2002); and *The Underground Heart: A Return to a Hidden Landscape* (essays, 2002). He teaches at the University of Minnesota.

JOHN GRAVES (1920–)
One of the most admired of contemporary Texas authors, Graves grew up in Houston, attended Rice University, served in the Marine Corps

in World War II, and eventually returned to live and write on a farm near Granbury, Texas. His books include the much celebrated *Goodbye to a River* (1960), *From a Limestone Ledge* (1980), and *A John Graves Reader* (1996).

A. C. GREENE (1923–2002)

Born in Abilene, Greene started out as a newspaper writer and for many years worked as a columnist for the *Dallas Times Herald* and, later, the *Dallas Morning News*. Among his numerous books are an autobiography, *A Personal Country* (1969), and a collection of short stories, *The Highland Park Woman* (1983).

WILLIAM C. GRUBEN (1943–)

Gruben, who has family roots in Spur, was educated at the University of Texas, where he wrote a dissertation in economics titled "A Regional Approach to Some Applications of Multivariate Statistical Analysis to the Assesment of Bank Performance" (1977). His recent publications include "The Mexican Economy Since the Tequila Crisis" (2002). In the 1980s he wrote humorous pieces for the *Atlantic Monthly*. Gruben lives in Dallas, where he is vice president of the Federal Reserve Bank.

J. EVETTS HALEY (1901–1995)

Born in Belton in central Texas, Haley spent most of his life in west Texas, where he worked on numerous historical projects for the Panhandle Plains Historical Society. His books include such notable works as *Charles Goodnight, Cowman & Plainsman* (1936) and *Fort Concho and the Texas Frontier* (1952), and the wildly controversial polemic, *A Texan Looks at Lyndon* (1964).

STEPHEN HARRIGAN (1948–)

Born in Oklahoma City, Harrigan has made Texas his home for much of his life. He worked as a journalist with *Texas Monthly* for many years. His first novel, *Aransas*, was published in 1980, and *The Gates of the Alamo* appeared in 2000. He has also written teleplays such as *The O. J. Simpson Story* (1995). Harrigan lives in Austin.

SHELBY HEARON (1931–)

Born in Kentucky, Hearon lived in Austin for many years. A prolific novelist, she has written numerous works dealing with Texas, including *Hannah's House* (1976), *A Prince of a Fellow* (1978), and *Ella in Bloom* (2001). She lives in Burlington, Vermont.

O. HENRY (WILLIAM SYDNEY PORTER) (1862–1910)
Porter, who took his pen name from his habit of calling to his cat, "Oh, Henry," was born in North Carolina and came to Texas in 1882. After being convicted of bank embezzlement in Austin, Texas, Porter was sent to a federal prison for five years. Behind bars, he began to write the stories that would make him a household name as an author of popular short stories. Many of his Texas-based stories appeared in *Heart of the West* (1907).

DAVE HICKEY (1940–)
Born in Ft. Worth, Hickey has spent much of his adult life in places like Nashville, where he was a songwriter, and New York, where he began to write criticism on modern painting. Today he lives in Las Vegas, where he teaches at the University of Nevada. His books include *Prior Convictions: Stories from the Sixties* (1989) and *Air Guitar: Essays on Art & Democracy* (1997).

ROLANDO HINOJOSA-SMITH (1929–)
Hinojosa-Smith comes from Mercedes, a small town in the Rio Grande Valley. A Korean War veteran, he received a Ph.D. from the University of Illinois (1969). He is the author of numerous novels set in south Texas that form part of the "Klail City Death Trip" series. Typical are *Sketches of the Valley and Other Works* (1980), *Rites and Witnesses* (1982), and *The Useless Servants* (1993). Hinojosa-Smith lives in Austin and teaches at the University of Texas.

JAMES HOGGARD (1941–)
Born in Wichita Falls, Hoggard received his education at Southern Methodist University and the University of Kansas (MA, 1965). He has published poetry, essays, fiction, nonfiction, and translations, including *Breaking an Indelicate Statue* (poetry, 1986), *Trotter Ross* (novel, 1981), and *Riding the Wind and Other Tales* (1997). Hoggard lives in Wichita Falls where he is a professor of English at Midwestern State University.

WILLIAM HUMPHREY (1924–1997)
Born in Clarksville in northeast Texas, not far from the Red River, Humphrey wrote a number of novels, including *Home from the Hill* (1958), which was made into the film of the same title in 1960, and *The Ordways* (1964). His memoir, *Farther Off from Heaven* (1977), recounts his childhood. His *Collected Stories* appeared in 1985.

MOLLY IVINS (1944–)
Ivins was born in Monterey, California, but grew up in east Texas. Educated at Smith College and Columbia University, she has worked as a reporter and columnist for several newspapers, including the *Texas Observer*. *Molly Ivins Can't Say That, Can She?* appeared in 1991 and *Nothin' But Good Times Ahead* in 1993. Ivins lives in Austin.

MARY KARR (1955–)
Born in southeast Texas on the Gulf Coast, Karr is a poet and memoirist. *Abacus*, her first volume of poetry, appeared in 1987. Two memoirs, *The Liars' Club* (1995) and *Cherry* (2000), related experiences from her childhood and adolescence. Karr teaches at Syracuse University in Syracuse, New York.

ELMER KELTON (1926–)
Kelton was born in Andrews in west Texas. Following a stint in the U.S. Army at the end of World War II, Kelton went to work as a journalist in San Angelo and for many years wrote for *Livestock Weekly*. Author of over thirty novels, he is best known for *The Time It Never Rained* (1973). *The Good Old Boys* (1978) was made into a film directed by Tommy Lee Jones. Kelton lives in San Angelo, Texas.

LARRY L. KING (1929–)
Born in Putnam in west Texas, King served in the U.S. Army and at one time worked on the staff of Senator Lyndon B. Johnson. A journalist, playwright, and novelist, King is the author of such collections as *The Old Man and Lesser Mortals* (1974) and the autobiographical *Confessions of a White Racist* (1971). He is best known for the musical *The Best Little Whorehouse in Texas* (1978), based on a piece he wrote for *Playboy*. King lives in Washington, D.C.

PETER LaSALLE (1947–)
A native of Rhode Island, LaSalle was educated at Harvard University and the University of Chicago. He moved to Texas in the 1970s and today teaches creative writing at the University of Texas. A prolific short story writer, he has published two collections of stories, *The Graves of Famous Writers, and Other Stories* (1980) and *Hockey Sur Glace* (1996), and a novel, *Strange Sunlight* (1984).

AARON LATHAM (1943–)
Latham grew up in Spur, Texas, and received a Ph.D. from Princeton University in 1970. His books include a collection of his journalism, *Perfect Pieces* (1987), and a novel, *Code of the West* (2001). He cowrote the screenplay for the film *Urban Cowboy* (1980), based on his article published in *Esquire*. He lives in New York City.

JOHN A. LOMAX (1867–1948)
Although born in Mississippi, Lomax grew up in ranching country in west Texas near a branch of the Chisholm Trail, where he heard the cowboy songs that he would eventually publish in his first book, *Cowboy Songs and Other Frontier Ballads* (1910). He became a major collector of American folk songs and blues, recalling his life in his autobiography, *Adventures of a Ballad Hunter*, in 1947.

SALLIE REYNOLDS MATTHEWS (1861–1938)
Matthews was born on a ranch in Texas, married a rancher, and had nine children. Late in life she recounted her experiences in *Interwoven: A Pioneer Chronicle*, published in 1936.

JAMES EMMIT McCAULEY (1873–1924)
McCauley grew up in east Texas and worked as a cowboy during the trail-drive era. The only education he had was on a cow ranch, he said. After he became bunged up from life in the saddle, he married and became a farmer in Baylor County, near Seymour. His lively, idiosyncratic book, *A Stove-Up Cowboy's Story*, was published posthumously in 1943.

LARRY McMURTRY (1936–)
Born in Wichita Falls, McMurtry burst on the Texas literary scene in

1961 with his first novel, *Horseman, Pass By*, filmed as *Hud* in 1963. Since that debut, he has gone on to write more than twenty books of fiction and nonfiction, including such well-known works as *The Last Picture Show* (1966), *Terms of Endearment* (1975), and the novel that everybody acknowledges as the greatest Western ever written, *Lonesome Dove* (1985), winner of the Pulitzer Prize and the basis for a successful television miniseries of the same title. Today McMurtry lives in his hometown of Archer City, where he sells rare books and continues to write fiction, memoirs, and travel books.

HARRYETTE MULLEN (1953–)
Mullen was born in Florence, Alabama, but grew up in Fort Worth. She holds a Ph.D. from the University of California at Santa Cruz, and teaches at UCLA. Primarily a poet, she has published several volumes of poetry, including *Tree Tall Woman* (1981) and *Sleeping with the Dictionary* (2002).

NAOMI SHIHAB NYE (1952–)
Born in St. Louis, Nye moved to Texas in the 1960s. She writes poetry, essays, stories, and children's books, and has published several works, including *Different Ways to Pray* (poetry, 1980), *Never in a Hurry: Essays on People and Places* (1996), and *Habibi* (young adult fiction, 1997). Nye lives in San Antonio.

CAROLYN OSBORN (1934–)
Born in Tennessee, Osborn has for many years lived in Texas. Her short stories have appeared in a number of literary quarterlies, and she has published three volumes of short fiction: *A Horse of Another Color* (1977), *The Fields of Memory* (1984), and *Warriors and Maidens* (1991). Osborn lives in Austin.

WILLIAM A. OWENS (1905–1990)
Owens grew up on a hardscrabble farm in northeastern Texas, near a tiny community called Pin Hook. After much struggle he acquired an education and eventually became dean of the Summer School at Columbia University. His books include the novel *Fever in the Earth* (1958), and two memoirs, *This Stubborn Soil: A Frontier Boyhood* (1966) and *A Season of Weathering* (1973).

AMÉRICO PAREDES (1915–1999)
A native of Brownsville, Paredes received his Ph.D. from the University of Texas, where he also taught for many years. A talented musician, he sang and recorded the Mexican ballads called corridos. His most significant book, a seminal study that helped launch the Chicano literary movement, was *"With His Pistol in His Hand": A Border Ballad and Its Hero* (1958), filmed as *The Ballad of Gregorio Cortez* (1983). In his later years he published several volumes of fiction, including the novel *George Washington Gómez* (1990).

GEORGE SESSIONS PERRY (1910–1956)
Born in the small town of Rockdale, Texas, Perry remained there most of his life. As a writer he struggled until hitting upon the right subject, the story of a tenant farmer and his family living on a cotton farm, that became *Hold Autumn in Your Hand* (1941). It was filmed by Jean Renoir in 1945 under the title *The Southerner.* Perry's nonfiction work includes *Texas, A World in Itself* (1942) and *Tale of a Foolish Farmer* (1951).

KATHERINE ANNE PORTER (1890–1980)
A native Texan, Porter left the state after her first marriage ended and spent much of the rest of her long life living variously in Mexico, Greenwich Village, Europe, and finally Georgetown, Washington, D.C. Her Texas experience formed the core of some of her best writing, including the stories published under the heading "The Old Order" in *The Leaning Tower, and Other Stories* (1944), and short novels such as *Noon Wine* (1939). Porter's *Collected Stories*, published in 1965, won both the Pulitzer Prize and the National Book Award. Her childhood home in Kyle, Texas, south of Austin, is a National Historic Landmark.

CLAY REYNOLDS (1949–)
Reynolds was born in Quanah, Texas, and received his Ph.D. from the University of Tulsa in 1979. He has published a number of novels, including *The Vigil* (1986), *Franklin's Crossing* (1997), and *The Tentmaker* (2002). He lives in Denton and is an administrator and professor at the University of Texas at Dallas.

TOMÁS RIVERA (1935–1984)
Born in Crystal City, Rivera worked as a migrant worker until he was

twenty, then attended college, acquiring a Ph.D. in Romance languages and literature at the University of Oklahoma in 1969. He eventually became chancellor of the University of California at Riverside. Rivera's most celebrated work is . . . *y no se lo tragó la tierra* (1971), translated as *And the Earth Did Not Devour Him*. In 1991 *Tomás Rivera: The Complete Works* was published.

BENJAMIN ALIRE SÁENZ (1954–)
Sáenz, a poet and fiction writer, is the author of such books as *Dark and Perfect Angels* (poetry, 1995), *Carry Me Like Water* (novel, 1995), and *Flowers for the Broken* (short stories, 1992). He lives in El Paso and teaches at the University of Texas at El Paso.

JIM SANDERSON (1953–)
Born and raised in San Antonio, Sanderson has a Ph.D. from Oklahoma State University (1982). His books include a volume of stories, *Semi-Private Rooms* (1995), and the novels *El Camino del Rio* (1998), *Safe Delivery* (2000), and *La Mordida* (2002). He lives in Beaumont and teaches creative writing at Lamar University.

DOROTHY SCARBOROUGH (1878–1935)
Born in east Texas, Scarborough earned a Ph.D. in literature at Columbia University in 1917, at that time an unusual feat for a woman. She wrote a number of novels about cotton culture, but the one that made her reputation was *The Wind* (1925), set in west Texas. In 1927 it was made into a distinguished silent film starring Lillian Gish.

EDWIN SHRAKE (1931–)
A native of Fort Worth, Shrake began his writing career as a sports writer for newspapers in Fort Worth and Dallas and the magazine *Sports Illustrated*. His novels include *But Not for Love* (1964), *Strange Peaches* (1972), and *The Borderland* (2000). Shrake lives in Austin.

HALLIE CRAWFORD STILLWELL (1897–1997)
During her long lifetime Stillwell (who lived to be just two months short of the century mark) married a rancher, helped him run his ranch, taught school, raised a family, and went into many other enterprises, from making candles to barbering and being a coroner. Her

autobiography, *I'll Gather My Geese* (1991), captured the flavor and appeal of her independent character.

PAT ELLIS TAYLOR (1941–)
Pat Ellis Taylor was born in Bryan, Texas. She holds two degrees from the University of Texas at El Paso. Her publications include *Border Healing Woman: The Story of Jewell Babb* (1981) and *Afoot in a Field of Men* (1988). She now goes by the name of Pat Littledog.

DON WEBB (1960–)
Born in Amarillo, Webb has published widely in sci-fi and fantasy magazines. His books include *Uncle Ovid's Exercise Book* (1988), *The Double: An Investigation* (1998), and *Endless Honeymoon* (2001). Webb lives in Austin and works for the Writers' League of Texas.

WALTER PRESCOTT WEBB (1888–1963)
Born in east Texas, Webb grew up in west Texas, and the experience of farming in arid country influenced his entire career as an historian. Educated at the University of Texas, Webb became the state's leading historian with the publication of *The Great Plains* in 1931. Other books include *The Texas Rangers: A Century of Frontier Defense* (1935) and *The Great Frontier* (1952).

C. C. WHITE (1885–1974)
Born and raised in the Piney Woods of east Texas, White became a preacher of the Church of God in Christ and founded a food bank called God's Storehouse. He told the story of his life to journalist Ada Morehead Holland; the result was the book *No Quittin' Sense*, published in 1969.

LAWRENCE WRIGHT (1947–)
Born in Oklahoma City, Wright grew up in Dallas and was educated at Tulane University and the American University of Cairo. A staff writer for *The New Yorker*, Wright is the author of, among other titles, *In the New World: Growing up with America, 1960–1984* (1987), the screenplay for the film *The Siege*, and the novel *God's Favorite* (2000).

CREDITS

───────★───────